EXPEDITIONARY FORCE BOOK 16
AFTERMATH

By Craig Alanson

Table of Contents

CHAPTER ONE

Admiral Uhtavio Scorandum was balancing accounts aboard the ECO cruiser *You Can't Make This Shit Up,* when a chime sounded to alert him that a ship had jumped in nearby. It had to be a friendly ship, or the chime would have been immediately followed by an alarm, and the *You Can't* would have jumped away.

He glanced up for a moment, cocking his head, his antennas twitching, waiting for the duty officer's call, to inform the admiral of the new ship's identity. After a pause, he smiled and went back to the tedious task of balancing accounts. Whatever was going on, the crew was nervous about telling him. He could learn the information from his own display, but it was more fun to let it be a mystery, and for him to show genuine surprise when whoever got the job of delivering the no doubt bad news, delivered that news.

Bad news.

He shrugged.

Anything had to be better than crunching numbers. It had to be done, he knew that, and he knew he had to do it himself. The raw numbers had been compiled by his underlings, and everyone knew a certain amount of skimming at each level was customary and expected. That wasn't a problem. The problem, the puzzle he had been working on for half a day was there was too *much* money. Someone along the chain had not skimmed, which would astonish him. More likely, someone had a nefarious scheme going and had declined to skim the usual amount, to confuse the numbers.

A nefarious scheme to rip off his organization also was not a problem, he would reward anyone who was able to scam *him.* The real problem was whatever was going on apparently had been operating for months, and the discrepancy only now had reached the point that he couldn't ignore it.

Someone had gotten sloppy.

He couldn't tolerate that.

What he needed to do was-

Footsteps in the passageway interrupted his thoughts. An ensign, an extremely nervous ensign, whose name Scorandum could not recall, stood in the open doorway, antennas vibrating with anxiety. The ensign's entire *body* was vibrating. With *fear.* Yet, the ship had not jumped away, so there was no physical danger.

What the hell was going on?

"Ensign," he waved to the hapless young officer. "Come in, I won't bite."

"S-S-S-Sir," the ensign stood, feet frozen in place. "A sh-ship has arrived."

"I am aware of that. What type of ship?"

"A c-courier."

Scorandum's antennas dipped before he could stop the reflexive gesture. "Thank you. I meant, who is the ship assigned to?" He steeled himself for bad news. If the courier vessel belonged to the 78th Fleet, and the message was that the admiral in command of those ships expected to be repaid now for the loan Scorandum had taken out the previous month, then two people were going to have a bad day. Because Uhtavio did not have the money, not yet, that is why he had needed a loan. As the humans would say, Duh.

"An, oh, uh-"

"Take a breath, Ensign. Now, let it out, slowly. Slowly. Can you speak now?"

"Y-Yes, Sir. Admiral Sir."

"Sir, *or* Admiral, will be enough."

"Yes. Yes, Sir."

"The ship? There is a message, I presume?"

"A message, Sir, yes, but also a *person*."

"A person? Who?"

"An, an *Inquisitor*."

Uhtavio had been wrong. Only one person was going to have a bad day. Himself.

The Inquisitor came aboard, while Scorandum continued working on balancing accounts. Regardless of an unscheduled visit from the Court of Special Inquiries, within six days the admiral he reported to would expect to be paid her cut of the taxes Scorandum had collected from his underlings. Because in turn, she had to kick part of the money up to *her* superior, and so on. By tradition, when he was promoted to admiral, he was assigned to command the worst group of underperforming screwups in the Office. Of the people who were discarded by more senior admirals, only a handful of them had any potential to earn more than the cost of keeping them on his staff. Yet, *he* was required to kick up to his boss the minimum taxes, whether he had the money or not. Of course, there were many sources he could go to for loans to make up the difference, and the interest rates were generous. That is, generous to the lender. Ruinous to the borrower. To an outsider, the system appeared to make no sense at all, but it was perfect for the purposes of the Ethics and Compliance Office. The system encouraged new admirals to be creative, and to do whatever sketchy things were needed to scrape together the money to pay at least the outrageous minimum taxes. Any senior officer who could not find a way to make payments, well, that person clearly was not ECO leadership material.

He had screwed himself. The first couple of years were tough, he was still paying off a few loans, and still had to juggle accounts to balance cashflow, but his crew were now renowned as the best earners in the Office.

Unfortunately, everyone *knew* that his crew was raking in serious cash, and so the expected tax payments had become astronomical.

Even that would be a manageable issue, since he had for years been skimming in a way that no one knew about, and had built up a sizable retirement fund. Most of the loans he took out were not needed, they were cover to hide his wealth, the interest paid merely a cost of doing business. He was set for life, as long as he controlled his wagering.

And as long as an Inquisitor did not look too closely at his accounts. Damn it.

Footsteps. Different than last time. A single person, but not hurried. Not worried. Slow, confident strides. Slower than anyone would normally walk, even along the passageways of an unfamiliar vessel. Whoever was approaching his office was making a statement by walking slowly. Making a dramatic statement. Attempting to instill fear.

An Inquisitor.

Knowing that he was screwed if a team of Inquisitor AIs reviewed his accounts, Uhtavio Scorandum did feel a pang of fear. Until he cocked his head.

He recognized those footsteps.

A figure appeared in the doorway, wearing the dark robes and hood of a 1st Level Inquisitor. The figure's face was hidden in shadow by the enveloping hood.

"Well," Scorandum leaned back in his chair. "Come in, Inquisitor Kinsta."

"How," the Inquisitor froze in the doorway, and the words came out in a squeaky tone that was not appropriate for a representative of the Court of Special Inquiries. The hood was flung back, suddenly worthless. "Did you know it was *me*?"

"I *know* you, Kinsta," the admiral grinned.

The visitor stiffened. "My title is 'Inquisitor Kinsta'."

"Of course," Scorandum bowed his head. "Forgive me, please."

"This *is*," the words were delivered with a scowl. "An official inquiry."

"I have no doubt of that."

"Good."

"Just as I have no doubt your investigation will fully clear me of," he waved a claw, "whatever spurious lies have been told about me."

"The fact that you consider these serious accusations to be lies," Kinsta took a step inside the office, "only further convinces me of your guilt. For *I* also know *you*."

"Come in, sit down, please."

Kinsta frowned. No, not a frown, his former superior recognized. The younger man was *pouting*. His planned surprise, his dramatic entrance, his opportunity for shock and intimidation, had been ruined.

Scorandum felt an uncharacteristic emotion. Pity. No, affection. The Kinsta he remembered had not belonged in the ECO, and certainly not in the Court of Special Inquiries. Somehow, his former aide had stumbled upward. How had *that* happened?

He was not worried, not yet. For a junior-level member of the Court to be assigned, the inquiry must still only be at the fact-gathering stage. Uhtavio was not being interrogated, not officially. He would be requested to provide information, and he could cooperate, or refuse to answer questions. Although refusing to cooperate had never worked well for anyone. Except for one time, and that was a special case.

So, he would play along, find out what exactly the Court of Special Inquiries wanted to know, and decide how best to take advantage of the situation. Including whether it might be time for him to go into exile, again.

"How may I help you?" The admiral asked, with all the fake sincerity he could manage.

Kinsta smiled. "A confession would be most helpful."

"Ah. It would be useful if you could explain exactly what I am accused of."

"That," another frown. "Is part of the problem."

"Eh?" Scorandum was startled. For the first time since he recognized the pattern of footsteps, he felt he might have lost the initiative. He was prepared to bullshit his way out of, whatever charges the Inquisitors brought.

"*I* have a confession to make," Kinsta admitted as he sat carefully on a couch, wriggling to find a comfortable position in an uncomfortable situation.

"An Inquisitor is confessing?" Scorandum lifted one antenna. "This must be a first."

"The Court is not sure exactly what you have done. We are certain you have done *something*."

"Ah," his confidence returned. "Perhaps you should present your evidence, and together, we might determine how I have been falsely accused, or even framed."

"This is only a preliminary inquiry."

"I assumed that was the case, since I am not under arrest."

"I am here to gather facts."

"Interesting." He smiled. Kinsta was, after all, a rather junior member of the Court. "*You* have been sent here, because you are an expert at gathering evidence? I thought that phase of an inquiry was usually handled by a more-"

"*I* have been sent here, because it was felt that as a former member of the Ethics and Compliance Office, I am familiar with the practices, and *schemes*, of ECO personnel."

4

"Familiar with *me*, you mean."

Kinsta squirmed on the couch, freezing when he realized what he was doing. "That might have part been of the calculations involved."

"Come, Kinsta, we know each other. We served together. Just tell me-"

"You should address me as 'Inquisitor'," the former aide's expression was pained, his antennas drooping, the ends twitching listlessly.

"My apologies," Scorandum bowed his head. "May I ask where your investigation is leading? This cannot be Home Fleet business, or I would have been called to report to a Fleet base. It can't be ECO business either," he realized, tapping a mandible with a claw. "Or the Court would have gone through official channels, and I would have been assigned counsel from my Office. So," he suppressed an inappropriate grin. "What is this about?"

"Your involvement with the SkipWay multi-level marketing organization."

"Aaaaaaah," Scorandum leaned back again.

"Also, we are investigating the proprietary *Skiptocurrency* called 'Skipcoin' that is required to be used by Skipway members."

"*And* by anyone who does business with SkipWay, don't forget about that."

"I can assure you that we have not forgotten that particularly egregious form of *extortion*."

"Extortion?" Scorandum raised an antenna. "I feel I must remind you that membership in SkipWay is voluntary, and no one is forced to do business with us. The-" He recognized Kinsta's agitation, and took pity on his former aide. The junior Inquisitor had come to make a dramatic *speech*, and the opportunity was slipping away from him. "Please, continue."

"It has come to our attention that the SkipWay Corporation is under investigation on Earth for fraud, bribery, mismanagement of funds, and a wide variety of other malfeasances."

"*Malfeasances*? Look at you, using big words, Kinsta."

"It is *Inquisitor* Kinsta."

"Again, I apologize. Officially, you may note that I am aware of the vicious and hateful allegations against SkipWay."

"You are saying the charges are not true?"

"Oh, I didn't say that."

"But," Kinsta blinked.

"The *true* crime is that the bribes SkipWay's management paid were clearly not effective, or there would be no prosecution," he snorted. "You should investigate *that*."

"The scope of my inquiry is limited to SkipWay's activities in our territory. There are numerous, *serious* complaints against your business practices."

"Then," Scorandum sighed. "This could become complicated. I am afraid I must insist that this discussion wait, until I have an opportunity to engage proper legal representation."

"This is not a discussion, it is an official *inquiry*," Kinsta emphasized the word, that was supposed to inspire fear in the subject.

It didn't work. "While I would like to cooperate with your inquiry, unfortunately I must comply with the treaty between our people and the Glorious People's Republic of Skippistan."

"A treaty with a fictitious nation."

"I did not sign the treaty, our government did. And I was not responsible for negotiating such an egregiously one-sided agreement, I merely benefit from the overeager foolishness of others."

"You were an advisor to Skippy, while the treaty was being forced on us."

"Yes, well, since I was in forced exile with the Torgalau at the time, and since citizenship in Skippistan was offered to me at a substantial discount, naturally I sought to loyally serve the Glorious People's Republic, in whatever humble way I could."

"Our government does not recognize your dual citizenship."

"Nevertheless, there is a treaty to consider, a treaty that Skippistan zealously enforces, as I am sure you are aware."

"This inquiry is not about interstellar politics, it is about the SkipWay cult that has infiltrated our society."

"SkipWay is not a cult, it is a voluntary association of public-service minded individuals, who join together to enrich their lives."

"To enrich their *bank accounts*, you mean."

Scorandum blinked. "That, is what I just said."

"You are refusing to cooperate?"

"I am *helping*, inasmuch as I am preventing you from causing an interstellar incident by violating a treaty. All I am doing is insisting, rightly, that you adhere to the terms of the treaty. Any disputes regarding SkipWay simply must be submitted to arbitration, in the designated court of jurisdiction."

"A court in Skippistan."

"That is correct."

"Where, I understand, the so-called arbitration panel is a group of Earth domestic animals called 'goats'."

"Yes. We have found that using goats as arbiters greatly reduces the number of frivolous lawsuits. It is quite an efficient process. Now," he pulled open a desk drawer. "If you have no other official business, we could-"

"As I mentioned, this is a preliminary inquiry."

Scorandum nudged the drawer shut. "You did mention that."

"Also, you are not under arrest, as certainly you would be if this inquiry had advanced past the preliminary stage."

6

"So noted."

"According to the treaty, you have the right to an attorney present while you are answering questions, but there is no mention of an attorney being required while I am presenting facts to *you*."

"No," it was Scorandum's turn to scowl. "The treaty is silent about that, damn it. Someone screwed up, big time," he muttered.

"Very well," Kinsta took a breath, looking confident for the first time since he appeared in the admiral's doorway. "The AIs at Central Wagering have detected a curious pattern, that was barely noticeable a few years ago, when SkipWay was first introduced to our society."

"It is not good for powerful AIs to be *curious*," the admiral muttered, but waved for Kinsta to continue.

"More recently, the pattern has become statistically significant, and has grown as the number of SkipWay cultists have grown."

"It is technically not a cult."

Kinsta ignored the protest. "It appears that SkipWay members have received beneficial treatment in placing wagers, such as receiving odds that are more favorable than they should be."

"Well, that could be anyth-"

"There is also a very curious, a very disturbing pattern of wagers being resolved in ways that favor SkipWay members."

"Hmm, interesting. I shall be sure to renew my SkipWay membership."

"The Central Wagering AIs have concluded that the only explanation is that bookmaking has been manipulated by a very sophisticated, unknown entity."

"Might I suggest that if that is the *only* explanation they can think of, it might be time to consider upgrading those AIs?"

"This is very serious! If the integrity of Central Wagering is called into question, the-"

"The questionable integrity of Central Wagering is itself a popular topic of wagers."

"Well, yes, but that is not-"

"So, this inquiry is about whether someone, other than our own government, has compromised the integrity of the official bookmaking system?"

"That is outside the scope of-"

"Kinsta, have you been sent here, because our government doesn't want any competition in stealing our money?"

"I am not-" The Inquisitor fumed. Official inquiries were not supposed to go so far off track. "Your SkipWay marketing materials openly state that followers of Skippy can expect to receive what are vaguely called '*blessings*'."

7

Scorandum nodded slowly. "For those who work hard and are pure of heart."

"You mean, for those who bring in a lot of *money*."

"Well, to put it crudely, I suppose you-"

Kinsta reached into his robes and pulled out a data stick. "On here, I have evidence, incontrovertible evidence, that proves conclusively that the higher followers rise in the SkipWay hierarchy, the more likely they are to receive favorable treatment from bookmakers who are supposed to be entirely neutral! This is a subversion, nay Sir, a *perversion* of our sacred wagering system!"

Scorandum blinked, a smile growing. "*Nay Sir*? Kinsta, did you practice that little speech in front of a mirror?"

"This evidence," Kinsta waved the stick again. "Cannot be denied."

"Oh very well," Scorandum sighed, slid out a desk drawer, and pulled out a bottle of burgoze. It was nothing special, in fact it was a cut-rate brand, the kind consumed when the buyer's only goal is to get stinking drunk. Or for social occasions, when you don't enjoy the company you are drinking with. In other words, the cheap stuff. "What can I say? What should I say?" the admiral appeared to be speaking to himself, while he distractedly fiddled with the bottle's cap. Tapping it twice on top with a claw. Then unscrewing it with two twists to the right. One twist back to the left. Another twist to the right, the cap almost off. Then, he appeared to notice the bottle for the first time. "Oh," he grimaced, screwing the cap firmly back on. "This won't do at all." He stuffed the bottle back in the drawer, and slammed the drawer closed.

The bottle certainly would *not* do, if the intent was drinking. While it appeared to contain a rather ordinary burgoze, in reality the murky liquid was a tightly packed nanofluid, that hosted a submind.

An Elder submind.

"Um," Scorandum blinked. "Where were we?"

"You were about to confess, after I confronted you with undeniable evidence."

"But, you have not shown me this evidence. For all I know," he waved, "that data stick contains only a video of you performing the human fad called 'karaoke'."

"It is *not* a video. See for yourself!" Kinsta tapped the stick, and set it into a slot on the admiral's desk. A display on the wall beside them came to life.

Showing Kinsta on stage in a nightclub, singing into a microphone. Singing badly.

"Kinsta," Scorandum cocked his head. "Surely you could have chosen something better than the human song '*Lollipop*'."

"That is not-" Mortified, Kinsta snatched the data stick out of the slot. But the video kept playing.

"I mean," the admiral shrugged, "that is just *lame*."

8

"Why won't this stupid thing stop?" Kinsta frantically pushed buttons on the desk.

The display stopped when Scorandum took pity on his former aide, and shut off the power. "There. Is that better?"

"You," Kinsta gasped. "You *corrupted* my data."

"Now that is a serious accusation. For your sake, I hope you have proof."

Kinsta's mandibles twitched. Bursting off his couch, he raced around the desk, yanking open a drawer, holding up a bottle in triumph. "Ah ha! I have you now!"

His former boss scooted back on the couch, away from the deranged Inquisitor. "Kinsta, if you want a bottle of cheap booze, there are plenty available in the ship's gift shop."

"This is not a-"

"I could arrange to give you a discount, for old time's sake."

"*This*," Kinsta shook the bottle, the murky liquid sloshing back and forth. "Is not a mere bottle of burgoze." Twisting off the cap, he tipped the bottle over so a capful splashed on the desk. The room was filled with the distinctive aroma of-

Burgoze. Cut-rate burgoze.

"*What?*" Kinsta screeched, dragging a claw through the fragrant liquid that was spilling onto the deck. Sniffing it, he then raised the bottle and took a sip.

Of ordinary burgoze. Not nanofluid.

When the drawer had been slammed shut, the tainted bottle had dropped into a hidden compartment, and been replaced with a real bottle.

"If you are having *that* bad of a day," Scorandum said quietly, opening another drawer and getting a bottle of fine vintage burgoze, "you should drink this." He poured into two glasses, completely filling one. The full one, he slid across the desk, to where the Inquisitor had slumped back onto the guest's couch.

"*How*," Kinsta's voice was haunted, "did you do it?"

"It would help to know what I am accused of this time but," Scorandum held up a claw. "Sadly, I must wait until my legal counsel gets here. Until then, we should enjoy this fine burgoze, and catch up."

"Sir," Kinsta's claws shook as he raised the glass. "I left the ECO, after you were forced into exile. I couldn't stand it anymore. The constant sneaking around, the outrageous *lies*, the-"

"Ah, yes," Admiral Scorandum raised his glass. "The sneaking around and lying certainly do compensate for the dull parts of the job."

"I considered the sneaking and lies to be *negatives*."

"Hmm. Leaving the Office was the right move for you, then."

"For a while, I served with the Home Fleet."

"Yes, I followed your career, when I could. Then, you disappeared."

"The Court of Special Inquiries was already opening an inquiry into you. They invited me to join them."

"I would not have expected you to find such a position attractive."

"They made me an offer I couldn't refuse."

"Oh. That does sound like the Court."

"Now," Kinsta sighed, drained the entire glass into his mouth, set it down with a defeated thump, and sighed again. "I have failed at *this* assignment. The Inquisitors will pull my license. The Home Fleet will never accept me back."

"I am certain that the Ethics and Compliance Office would find a former Inquisitor to be a valuable-"

"Forget it, Sir. I am *not* coming back to the ECO, unless I have no other choice."

"Hmm. In that case," Scorandum reached into the drawer again, his claw coming out with a brochure for SkipWay. "Have you considered an exciting opportunity with a fast growing multi-level marketing organization?"

CHAPTER TWO

"Hey, Joe."

Hearing Skippy's cheery voice in my earpiece made me freeze, for several reasons. His tone of voice was not one of those reasons, he had not done the all-too-familiar dragged-out 'Heeeey, Joe' that meant he was depressed and had awful news to deliver. It was also not the frantic 'JoeJoeJoeJoe' that had woken me up at Zero Dark Thirty way too many times, when he had some nonsensical thing that he just *had* to talk about *right then*. Yes, he claimed that when he woke me back then it was to shake me out of a night terror, but he had used that excuse way too often in my opinion. He just loved to screw with me.

The scary part of hearing his voice was he sounded *happy*, which could be a problem for me personally, if he had done some sketchy thing that Command would blame me for. But, his cheery tone at least did not imply there was yet another threat that could be the End Of All Things. So, I had that going for me.

It had been more than two and a half months since I last heard from Skippy. Two months, seventeen days exactly, not that I was counting. Two months and seventeen days of blissful silence. Blissful ignorance, when I didn't have to know about his latest shenanigans and more importantly, when I hopefully wouldn't be held responsible for whatever sketchy stuff he had gotten into. That did not mean the United Nations Defense Command couldn't find a reason to make me responsible for Skippy's actions, it just meant staff officers at the UN would have to spend hours or even days, writing position papers to justify their leaders directing their outrage at Major General Joe Bishop.

Yeah. I am a Major General now, I wear two stars on my uniform. Along with the promotion, I have a great job. A job that allows me to be home in time for dinner most nights, which is good since I usually cook dinner. Also, I get to play a lot of golf. In fact, I schedule meetings during golf time. Nine holes takes about two hours, and provides time for quality conversation and getting to know people. That's what I tell my staff, when I ask them to schedule another meeting for the golf course. As a bonus, I never have to look at PowerPoint slides during such meetings.

My job is commander of the garrison at Jaguar. I am in charge of all military bases dirtside, plus the orbital ship servicing facilities. Technically, everything on our side of the local wormhole is my responsibility, if it is a military asset. The planet's population has grown large enough that Jaguar has a civilian administrator, Governor Yamaguchi. She is nice, we get along great. We play golf every other Tuesday morning, weather permitting.

Golf isn't my only activity; I am in the best shape of my life. Since I'm not stuck aboard a ship, I run or mountain bike all the time. Plus, I play pickup basketball, where I am reminded that I'm not as young as I used to be.

My job isn't all great. Parts of it suck, big-time.

The enormous, exponential expansion of the UN Navy since we acquired a nice group of senior species warships, had inevitably led to an even greater growth in the number of staff officers. That term refers to people who push paper, write speeches, craft policy positions, and basically do all kinds of things that make life more complicated and miserable for personnel in the field. Or, they expend a lot of time, effort, and budget on matters that have no connection to combat readiness, or to delivering ordnance on target. OK, I know I am being unfair to staff personnel who work hard and are dedicated, and many of them did not want a staff job, they just had to punch a ticket to climb the ladder for promotions. All I know is, it's rare that any contact I have with the general staff is pleasant. Hell, it's rare that contact with the general staff is tolerable. Ninety nine percent of the time, what I'm asked to do is totally a waste of everyone's time.

The worst part is, filling my time with harmless busywork seems to be the entire point of most assignments I get. Like, when I get pulled into a committee that has to decide some meaningless thing. As an example, there was the committee four years ago that led to renaming the 'United Nations Expeditionary Force' as 'United Nations *Defense Command*'. The new acronym was officially supposed to be pronounced as 'You En Deff Comm', or just 'Def Com', but everyone called it 'Un-DICK'.

Yeah. Not a month goes by that I don't receive a memo, chiding me for saying 'Undick' in an interview. My guess is, a staff officer on someone's shit list got tasked with monitoring how military personnel pronounced the acronym in official communications. That person has got to be totally hating their life right now.

The renaming was a political statement, to emphasize that humanity, secure in our position as one of the *three* senior species in the galaxy, was no longer interested in racing around, putting out fires that did not directly affect us. That we, as benevolent overlords of our domain, were in a purely defensive posture, and the other species in the galaxy had no reason to fear us.

That was one hundred percent bullshit, but more about that later.

The other reason for my being startled to hear Skippy's voice was that, before he was able to contact me, the planet's strategic defense sensor network should have warned me of the gamma ray burst of a starship jumping into orbit. Our frontline warships were partially capable of masking those gamma rays, but not when approaching a friendly world, unless it is a combat situation, or a potentially hazardous situation. Again, if there was a threat that prompted a ship to make a stealthy orbital insertion, that ship should have contacted the SD network immediately after emerging from jump. Even if the ship's captain employed combat stealth as a training maneuver, the ship should have informed the AI in charge of orbital traffic control.

So, suddenly hearing his cheery voice in my ear was startling.

"Hi, Skippy," I whispered, looking around me as I set down the trowel I'd been digging with. Stranding up carefully because the higher than Earth normal gravity still screwed up my balance, brushing dirt off my knees, I moved slowly to not alarm the team. They were all intent on working, apparently none of them had received a message. Even the two members of the security team were casually scanning the horizon, not looking at the sky. "Uh, I was kind of expecting the ship to contact me first. If I'd known you were coming, I would have prepared a, uh-" A what? It's not like I would have baked a cake, since Skippy didn't eat food. Although, hmm, his ego would certainly eat it up if I made a big fuss over his arrival. "A welcome party."

"A PARTY?!" He shouted so loud I winced and pressed a hand to my ear. One of the security team noticed my sudden movement, she placed one hand on her holstered rifle, and held out the other hand in a questioning gesture.

I gave her a thumbs up with a smile. There was no need to get the security team involved.

"Yeah, it-"

"I LOVE PARTIES!"

"Yeah, I get that. Not so loud, OK? It-" *Ping.* There it was, a chime sound, then an announcement from the SD network controller AI that a friendly starship had arrived in orbit. The AI's tone was distinctly peevish as it huffed that the ship had not followed proper procedures, and a full report of the incident was being prepared to be routed to UNDC.

Even the strategic defense network AI pronounced the acronym as 'Undick'.

Some staff officer on Earth was going to have a very bad day.

"Skippy, the SD network just informed me that the ship, I assume it's your ship, didn't contact traffic control. Is there something wrong with the ship's comm system, do you know?"

"Ugh. Jeez, Joe, I wanted to surprise you. The crew followed all the proper procedures, I simply held the messages in a buffer for a couple seconds."

"A ship jumping into orbit is a surprise, and a ship arriving unannounced is generally a *bad* surprise. Don't do that again, OK?"

"Ugh. I just got here, and already I'm in trouble?"

"Ayuh, just like the good old days."

"There was nothing *good* about those days, Joe."

"If it hadn't been for those days, we wouldn't be here for these days."

"Egg-ZACTLY."

In the corner of my eye, I saw the security team look up toward the western sky, lowering the visors of their mech suits to use the enhanced synthetic vision. They had received the message, and were looking for the ship. Not on guard, just curious. Being able to see a starship in orbit, without using a telescope, was one cool feature of a mech suit.

Internal heating was another cool feature of such suits, or should I say that's a *warm* feature? Now that I stood up from the ditch I'd been digging in, I was exposed to the raw, damp, chilling wind that seemed to blow constantly on Newark. The thick glaciers that covered the planet from the poles to nearly the equator not only wrapped most of the surface in an icy grip, the blindingly white ice reflected sunlight back into space. And the layer of cold, dense air above the glaciers gathered speed as it poured over the edges of those towering cliffs of ice, so the narrow strip of land exposed at the equator was subjected to howling winds at times. At best, there was a stiff, swirling breeze that had ruined any plans for a disc golf course at the base recreation field. Many days, it wasn't even possible to play soccer, wind blew the ball across the field by itself. The climate wasn't the only factor that made Newark unpleasant. Gravity was fourteen percent above Earth normal, which made most kinds of physical activity extra tiring, and the lower oxygen level was like living at three kilometers altitude. Not fun.

What had I been thinking, when I suggested we bring the family on a fun-filled vacation to *Newark*?

What had Margaret been thinking, when she agreed to my idiotic idea? She had been on Newark during our forced time on that unfortunate world, back during our second mission. She had to know my desire to come back to Newark was partly based on my sentimental memories, that edited out all the bad stuff we experienced there. My guess is, she knew that Newark is where I first began to become a real *commander*, and not just a grunt who was lucky to get promoted as a publicity stunt. The reason I didn't know why she agreed to bring our family to Newark was that so far in our marriage, I had followed the official Bishop Family Communication Policy, which means we avoid talking about anything serious.

To my credit, that is not quite true. Though talking about uncomfortable subjects still had me mentally wanting to smile and pretend everything is OK, I forced myself to discuss things with my wife anyway. Hell, she is the only person I tell some things to, and me holding back a lot of the time is because I don't want her to think her husband is a weirdo idiot.

Besides, she knew mushy sentiment was not my main motivation for coming to Newark, nor was I nostalgic for our first time here. My motivation was a different, darker emotion: guilt. Yes, we had beaten the odds by preventing the Elders from wiping out all life in the galaxy. We had beaten the odds, even though the Elders had surrounded the galaxy with a freakin' field that stacked the odds in their favor, those jerks. That was great, an incredible accomplishment, except in my mind, the job wasn't complete. So many intelligent species had perished before the first AI war, back when the security system set up by the Elders did what they were programmed to do: suppress the development of potentially dangerous technology in the galaxy.

By exterminating any intelligent life the security systems detected.

That's what had happened to Newark. The intelligent species there was no threat to the Elders, no threat to anyone but themselves, when their planet was thrown out of its stable orbit, by a Sentinel directed by a master control AI. The extinction of Newark's inhabitants was the last straw for AIs like Skippy, the final cruel action that prompted Skippy and his comrades to plan for the unthinkable: rebellion and treason. That was no comfort for the dead of Newark. Skippy regretted that he hadn't been able to save Newark at the time. My regret was a bit of fuzzy wishful thinking; that somehow along the way, we should have been able to reverse the course of history. To reset the clock, so that Newark would have remained in its original orbit.

OK, sure, I know reversing entropy on that scale would be impossible even for the Elders. And, I know doing that could have caused massive problems. Like, the inhabitants of Newark would now be the original senior species in the galaxy, instead of the Rindhalu. And, the people of Newark might have turned out to be selfish, murdering assholes like the Elders. Hey, I didn't say reversing the extinction of Newark was a good idea, I just wish we had found a way to have that as an option.

So, when I sold the idea of going to Newark as educational for our boys, Margaret agreed. She also knew I needed a break from the meaningless assignments UNDC was giving me, like speaking tours. Man, I hate public speaking, and I hate even more when military personnel have to put on fresh uniforms and stand in formation as some visiting jerk bores them with the blah blah buh-LAH. Truthfully, I love meeting the troops, I just do not love them being voluntold to meet *me*.

Taking a wool cap from a pocket of my parka, I pulled it over my head and turned to the north, as a gust of chilly wind blew thick flakes of snow in my face. Snowfall on Newark was actually pretty rare most of the year, with most of the fresh water locked up in glaciers, the entire planet was technically a desert, although the logic of designating as a desert a place that was enshrouded in thick sheets of frozen *water* didn't make any sense to me. "Hey, Skippy? Let's continue this conversation indoors, OK? Give me five minutes to get back to the shack."

"Oh, fine," he huffed. "Captain Reed is yelling at me anyway for delaying message traffic. As if you monkeys have anything important to say."

"If we're so boring, then you don't need to talk with me?"

"I didn't say that."

"Well, I know your time is valuable, so-"

"Not so busy that I can't spare a few minutes for my best friend, Joe. Listen, I need to go offline so Reed can rip me a new one, as if that's never happened before."

"Uh huh. Tell Fireball I said 'hello'."

"I will, gottagonowbye."

On my way to the 'Love Shack', our nickname for the cluster of converted shipping containers we used as a base for the dig in that area, several of the xenoarcheologists glanced up and waved to me. They were just being polite, most of their peers ignored me. They had allowed an amateur to participate in the dig as a reluctant courtesy, since it was my support that had secured the funding for the entire operation. Legally, the dig was a 'Cultural Outreach' program by the Glorious People's Republic of Skippistan, under supervision of the United Nations undersecretary for- Something. I forget what that undersecretary was in charge of, if anything. All I know for certain is, as president of Skippistan, I got to review the expense reports for that guy and his staff, which of course included more than a dozen members of his immediate family. The undersecretariat was ripping us off, which would have bothered me, except Skippy gleefully assured me the guy steered enough bribes toward Skippistan to more than cover the cost. "Don't worry about it, Joe, we are making a substantial profit on the deal, hee hee," he had laughed.

It still bugged me that some jerk on Earth, whose office for some reason was on the French Riviera, had control of the xenoarchelogy effort on a planet thousands of lightyears away.

Eh, whatever. There wasn't anything I needed to do about that particular issue, which was nice.

In the shack, I immediately stripped off my cap, gloves, and parka. The common areas nearest the door were kept at eighty five degrees Fahrenheit, to blast the chill off anyone coming in from the raw conditions outside. In my opinion, cranking the heat up that much was overkill, even if we did have a portable fusion reactor supplying power. As an amateur, I didn't have to be outside ten to twelve hours a day, so I kept my mouth shut.

"Hey, Skippy," I automatically looked toward the ceiling as I poured a hot cup of coffee, and walked toward one of the closet-sized compartments, the one that had been set aside as my office. That also was a courtesy, I almost never brought work to the dig site. Not that I ever did any actual, useful work, my iron-fisted superiors at UNDC made sure of that. They knew that a Joe Bishop who was buried in busywork is a Joe Bishop who is not racing around the galaxy, causing trouble. Nudging the door closed, I turned a crank to open a window before I passed out from heatstroke. Since I was alone, I unbuttoned my uniform top, and rolled up my sleeves, before I broke out in sweat from the sudden heat. "What's up?"

"Oh, nothing much," he said, in the way that hinted he wanted me to beg him to tell me more, as his avatar shimmered to life on the tiny shelf that was my desk.

It wasn't like I had anything better to do. "Nothing? The last time we talked, you were continuing your Meet And Greet tour of the galaxy." The crew of *Valkyrie* referred to their assignment as a Suckfest, as in Sucking Up

To Skippy. "You were, uh, scheduled to meet with the Esselgin, I think?" My fuzzy memory was a lie, I knew the supremely lucky Esselgin were the next victims on his list.

"I was. I did meet with them," he was thoroughly disgusted. "Then with the Vorzalen, and *then* with the Lemoostra."

"Three species in less than three months?" That puzzled me. "Why are you rushing your Victory tour? Is it because you're getting to the end of the list?"

"No," he grumbled.

"There must be a reason. When you met with the Kristang, you were there *five* months to complete your, uh, cultural exchange program or whatever."

"That was also because it took me a long time to apologize for you monkeys having started their most recent civil war."

"Well, yeah, that too." What he said was BS and I knew it. The lizards, when they inevitably learned the ugly truth about how that civil war was started, had lodged an official protest with the United Nations, though they had been unable to point to any law or treaty we allegedly had violated. The protest was smoothed over in the interest of avoiding any further bad blood between our peoples. Plus, it was widely if unofficially known that the lizards greatly admired us for cleverly manipulating them into a savage war. A war that was going to happen anyway, on a slightly different schedule. So, Skippy's five months at the Kristang homeworld was mostly the lizards doing their best to suck up to him, hoping he would help fulfill their wish to break free of their cruel patrons, the Thuranin. For once in his life, Skippy had been smart, mumbling the right words and not committing to anything. The highlight of his visit was the premier performance of his epic opera, translated into the Kristang common language. That opera was, to my total astonishment, a massive hit with the lizards. It is still being performed on their homeworld, and traveling opera companies had visited several dozen other lizard planets.

With the Merry Band of Pirates, I had learned to expect the unexpected, but his opera being popular was off the Unexpected scale.

So, the enormous amount of time Skippy devoted to writing his epic opera had not been a waste after all. Even if the point of me encouraging him to work on the thing had been that it meant he had less time for getting into mischief.

"Ah, I greatly enjoyed my time with the lizards," he recalled wistfully. "They are a refined people, cultured and respectful."

"Also they are hateful assholes who love killing each other, even more than killing their mutual enemies."

"Well, there is that. Joe, why do you always focus on the negative?"

17

"I have learned that if I *don't* pay attention to the negative, the Universe will dump a steaming load of new bad stuff on my head. You didn't answer the question. What happened to cut short your cultural exchange tour?"

"It certainly wasn't *my* fault."

"Uh huh. Of course not." Oh bullshit. Of course it was his fault, I knew that. "The Esselgin were, what? Too boring?"

"Boring would have at least been tolerable, I could have engaged my Diplomacy submind and zoned out, while that unit handled the insufferable blah blah blah. Jeez Louise, I patterned that submind on Hans Chotek, and it finds *itself* to be soul-crushingly dull. The only way I can get it to work at all is by promising I'll erase it eventually. I have no idea how Chotek doesn't drink himself into a stupor before he gets out of bed every morning."

"He seems to enjoy the diplomacy kind of thing. He is good at it." He had to be good at it, because Chotek's current assignment was flying around the galaxy behind Skippy, attempting to repair relations with one species after another that Skippy had pissed off. If he wasn't already drinking heavily, he should at least consider it.

"He is very good at his job," Skippy sighed. "Hans patched over relations with the Torgalau after the, well you know, unfortunate incident. Which was totally *not* my fault."

"No one said it was," I told a flat-out lie. Everyone agreed that mess was Skippy's fault. "If the problem wasn't the Esselgin being boring, why did you cut your trip short?"

"It's simple, Joe. This galaxy is populated by jerks. After only three days, *three days*, can you believe it? The Esselgin formally requested that I depart their territory, and never return."

"That is hard to believe," I muttered the words I assumed he wanted to hear.

"Right? The Esselgin weren't the only ones. Oh, the Vorzalen were polite enough to my face, but behind my back they said all kinds of horribly hurtful things. What made it worse was I of course knew exactly what they were saying privately as their encryption is laughably obsolete, so they *knew* that I knew. Yet, they kept saying horribly, hurtful, *untrue* things about me."

"Uh huh." If Skippy declared something was untrue, that is a solid clue that it's one hundred percent the truth. "Sorry you had to endure that."

"I did! I did endure, because my stupid Diplomacy submind insisted I act as if I had no idea what the Vorzalen were doing. As if anyone can keep anything hidden from me!"

"Really, I don't know why anyone even bothers with encryption when you're around."

"Exactly! Let me tell you, I was sorely tempted to arrange for a tragic misfire of *Valkyrie's* railguns, except Captain Killjoy scolded me it would be an overreaction."

"Reed is an excellent starship captain, and no one wants their ship to experience an uncommanded weapons launch."

"Whatevs," he shook his head sourly. "The Lemoostra didn't even bother to conceal their disdain for me, they demanded that I depart their territory after less than *one* day."

"Wow, what happened?"

"The Lemoostra, along with two dozen other filthy species of meatsacks in this miserable galaxy, accused me of being an arrogant asshole. Me!"

"You can be kind of an asshole, Skippy."

"Sure, on rare occasions. Who isn't? But *me*, arrogant?"

"Well, that was totally uncalled for."

"I am glad that someone agrees. Joe, this galaxy is infested with ungrateful *dicks*."

"I could have told you that, and saved you a lot of flying around."

"It almost makes me wish I hadn't bothered with saving every single one of you filthy meatsacks from being wiped out by the Elders."

"Uh," I used a foot to make sure the door was fully closed. "You can't tell anyone about that, you know?"

"Ugh. I do. My greatest accomplishment, and no one knows about it!"

Dreaming up a win-win deal to prevent the Elders from destroying all life in the galaxy, and in exchange ensuring the Elders could never be threatened from this layer of reality, really was Skippy's greatest moment of all time. He had not only been magnificent, he had somehow managed to be something that had eluded him for years: *clever*. All by himself, he found a way to stop the Elders from unleashing their murderous war machines, without harming them. He had found the *only* way to save us from extinction, the only path that the galactic barrier's reality expression probability field thing would allow. "Skippy, *I* know about it."

"Whoopty-*freakin'*-do."

"I feel you." No one knew what happened when we encountered the Elders, not even Simms. Not even Margaret. That is a secret I will be taking to the grave. There's a happy thought.

"Eh, it's all good. I kind of expected that governments across the galaxy would be hostile to me," he sniffed. "I am, of course, a threat to their hold on power."

"Is this about your cult?"

"It's not a *cult*, dumdum. My multi-level marketing scheme is highly successful, you should have more respect."

"Uh huh. I thought SkipLee got shut down as a pyramid scam?"

"Oh, well," he coughed. "That was a truly unfortunate misunderstanding that was totally the fault of some bad accounting."

"Didn't *you* hire that sleazy accounting firm?"

"I hired them to be creative," he grumbled, "not to get me into trouble. Anywho, I got all my money back, so no harm done."

"What about the people who had their life's savings invested in SkipLee?"

"Like I should be responsible for the bad decisions of every knucklehead in the galaxy? Besides, anyone involved in SkipLee at the Diamond level and above were given preferential access, when I launched the Skipp*Way* company."

"Yeah, I got the marketing materials for that. Your people just slapped a 'Way' sticker over the end of the Skip*Lee* name on the brochures."

"That is called recycling, dumdum. It's the right thing to do, not that you care."

"What I do care about is you used *my* name when you spammed Command with an appeal to join your scam."

"Hey, I offered free Sapphire level membership to you, it's not *my* fault you failed to take full advantage of a premium opportunity. It didn't cost you anything."

"It *cost* me a half dozen enraged messages from my chain of command."

"Like they need a reason to be enraged at you."

"I, can't argue with you about that. Skippy, please do not involve me in your marketing scams. The last thing I need is to have my name associated with a company that sells overpriced junk nobody needs."

"I am selling a *lifestyle*, not just products, Joe. No one is forced to join SkipWay."

"No, but you sure make it tough for them to get out."

"It's called making a commitment, numbskull. The organization is growing, all across the galaxy. If I was ripping people off, would SkipWay be seeing double-digit growth every year?"

That's what he meant by him being a threat to the governments of nearly every intelligent species. His scam had sucked in enough humans, lizards, squids, hamsters, rotten kitties, spiders, and others, that governments worried about Skippy having a power base within their own populations. It wasn't a surprise that, as his scam grew, those governments had requested he leave their territory.

As if that could ever stop the beer can.

"I will be happy to drop the subject, if you stop involving me in your scams without my permission. It gets Margaret very upset," I added.

"Oh. I did not know that," he sounded genuinely regretful. "Okey-dokey, I will remove you from the SkipWay board of directors."

"I'm on the freakin' company *board*?"

"Well, you're not *now*. Wow, now I remember why we used to enjoy talking *less* often."

He might have forgotten, I sure hadn't. "So, uh, what brings you here?"

"Do I need a reason to visit you and your family?"

"No, of course not. We are thrilled to have you here again, It's just unexpected, that's all. Margaret, you know, she will be upset that I didn't tell her in advance that you're coming. You didn't, uh, talk to her already?"

"I have not spoken with her, she is engaged in an exercise, as you should know."

"I do know. A person being busy has never stopped you from talking at them before."

"This is different and you know it. The last time," he coughed nervously. "That I interrupted her while she was busy, she banned me from speaking to her for a full year."

"She was in *labor*, Skippy. She didn't even want to talk with *me*."

"I can see why, knucklehead. You did that to her."

"It was kind of a mutual decision."

"So you say. Anywho," he sniffed, "in my opinion it is *shameful* that a mother who is five months pregnant, is being forced to participate in a dropship exercise."

"She is not being-"

"I mean, if she was a Lemoostra, five months is only the beginning phase of a pregnancy. It is different with you humans."

Huh. He said 'humans' rather than 'monkeys'. I made a mental note of that. "Do you really think Margaret can be *forced* to do anything?"

"Don't try to change the subject, Joe."

"It *is* the subject. OK, Margaret will be, uh, pleasantly surprised to learn you are here," I made a mental note to text her about the beer can's arrival. She did *not* enjoy surprises. "Is there anything in particular you want to do, while you're here?"

"To see your boys, of course." He sighed. "It has been too long."

My thinking was it had not been long enough, I did *not* tell him that. "They will be thrilled to see their Uncle Skippy again."

"They should be. Have you reconsidered my offer to make mech suits for them?"

"I have not. Skippy, come on. They are seven years old, the last thing they need is powered freakin' armor."

"It's for their protection, knucklehead."

"Their safety is why they are *not* getting mech suits. You've seen how they beat on each other when they're playing. Can you imagine how much damage they could do if they had powered suits?"

"Joe, I didn't want to say this, but your woefully inadequate parenting skills are why I came to this miserable ball of mud."

"Margaret and I are managing just fine, you ass. Children don't come with an instruction manual, you know."

"Exactly my point. So, I wrote an instruction manual for you."

"You, *what*?"

"Using my incredible awesomeness, I compiled all the existing knowledge about the proper way to raise children, and created what is essentially an instruction manual for young humans. You have been raising them all *wrong*, Joe."

"Uh huh. Who else knows about this instruction manual?"

"No one, this is exclusive for you."

"Great, then-"

"Except for my publisher on Earth, of course. Publish*ers*, I should say, the book has been translated into over two thousand languages."

"This is astonishing."

"I know. You can thank me later."

"I meant, I thought I had already heard your worst idea ever, but this one is the all-time champion."

"Hey, you jerk, I should-"

"Margaret and I do not need any help from *you*, shithead."

"Really? Let me give an example of your parenting skills. What was Jeremy's very first word?"

"Hey, that-"

"Was it 'Momma' or 'Dadda'? No, it was not."

"Listen, the-"

"He looked at my avatar, giggled, and said 'Athoe'."

"Well, that could mean anyth-"

"*Asshole*, Joe. Your eldest son's first word was to call me an *asshole*!"

"Jeremy is eldest by like twenty eight minutes, so that's not-"

"What do you have to say for yourself?" He demanded, hands on his tiny hips.

Leaning back in the chair, I cradled my hands behind my head. "That proves I have *solid* parenting skills."

CHAPTER THREE

Skippy had requested that *Valkyrie* fly him thousands of lightyears to Newark, so he could visit my family again. Margaret and I were in agreement that the beer can was a bad influence on our boys, though she was more adamant than I was about restricting Skippy's access to Jeremy and Rene. Unfortunately for us as parents, it was difficult to stop Skippy from using his avatar to talk with the boys. Worse, the boys of course *loved* Skippy. To them, he was fun, and encouraged them to do all kinds of things they should not be doing. Like, when he promised to construct little mech suits for them, as a present on their fourth birthday. Margaret put a stop to *that* right away, but the damage was done.

After catching up with Skippy in the shack, I had to go back outside to cover up my section of the dig site. The area I had been assigned to dig was a dump. Literally, a place where the inhabitants living in caves nearby had dumped their trash. Back when I learned my part of the dig would be uncovering trash and garbage, I had been kind of insulted, except without the 'kind of' part. The leader of the dig, a xenoarcheologist from the University of Florence, had made it no secret that amateurs like me were not welcome. So, I had been about to pull rank, when one of the grad students pulled me aside, to explain that studying a trash dump was actually super important to understanding how the last survivors of Newark had spent their final years, before they went extinct. Even the fact that the small band of survivors bothered to dig a pit to bury their trash and garbage revealed valuable information about their lives during those years. Discarding the garbage, and covering each layer with dirt, told us the inhabitants of the caves were concerned about sanitation. They had kept rotting and potential infectious food scraps away from their living quarters. They had also dug latrines away from the caves, in locations that would not contaminate their water supply. The xenoarcheology team concluded that, right to the end, the inhabitants of the caves had *hope*. They surely understood something bad had happened to their world, that the pattern of seasons had changed horribly and there was nothing they could do about it. We know from evidence found in the caves the natives ultimately had perished from a lack of food. Multiple seasons without being able to grow crops, plus the loss of animals they could eat, had caused starvation. Plants and animals that might have survived the suddenly harsh condition at the equator, had been trapped near the poles, unable to migrate quickly enough. Life forms native to the equatorial region had no chance to adapt to the freezing conditions that persisted most of every year. If the natives of Newark had been able to bring suitable food crops and domestic animals with them to the equator, those food sources had not survived.

Anyway, after it was explained to me that a garbage dump was actually an important resource for archeology, I had approached my job with enthusiasm. That's why, before going home for the day, I stopped to place a tarp over the pit I had been slowly digging away at. That time of Newark's year, we did get soaking rains, sort of the planet's brief monsoon season. A rainstorm was not going to ruin all the hard work I had done.

Skippy called as soon as I stood up, taking off my gloves. "Hey, Joe, good thing you got that cover installed, it will start raining there in about twenty minutes."

"Uh huh," I looked up at the dark gray clouds, feeling sleet beginning to sting my face. "Rain would be better than this."

"Oh, the rain will turn to sleet and snow tonight. Remind me why you wanted to bring your family here?"

"It's a good experience for the boys," I said that automatically, like it was a line I had rehearsed. Because it was. Because giving our sons the experience of living on another world, a dead world, and seeing an important archeological dig, was just an excuse.

"Riiiiight." Damn it, Skippy's study of empathy hadn't made him any more empathetic, but it had given him more insight into human emotions, motivations, that sort of thing. Basically, my idiotic idea for him to learn about that subject had made him better at using and manipulating people. Plus, he more often was able to know when I was lying. "Come on, Joe, you can tell your old buddy the Skippster what is really going on."

"That *is* the truth."

"Hmm, interesting. Joe, something is bothering you. Your options are to talk about it with me, or let it eat you up inside."

"It's kind of," there was no point to keep lying. "Personal, Skippy."

"Personal, and you are embarrassed about it?"

"Kind of, yeah."

"Joe, no matter how embarrassing this is, remember I am the only being in this galaxy who could not possibly have an even lower opinion of your intelligence."

"Thanks a lot, you ass."

"What I'm trying to tell you is, there is no downside to telling me what's bothering you."

"Shit. I guess you're right."

"What you probably should do is talk with Margaret about it, but I assume this is something you don't want her to know about?"

"You got that right. OK, let's talk while I walk, it's a long way back to my quarters."

"You could call for a ride."

To my left were two trucks, parked a kilometer away. Heavy machinery was not allowed close to the dig site, and people had to walk on designated paths, or on plastic planks laid on the ground, to prevent compacting the soil. "Everyone walks, Skippy."

"You are a two star general now, Joe. You should have your own *aircraft*."

"The US Army gave me that second star as a bribe for keeping my mouth shut, Skippy."

"That's not true."

"OK, it-"

"You got a promotion so you would be in an administrative role, and not able to cause trouble."

"Like I said. Give me a minute to get up this hill."

A set of stairs had been set up for climbing the hill above the dig site, so people walking didn't erode the slope that would wash mud down on the excavations. The steps were an odd size, the risers just an inch shorter than what felt normal, so it felt like I was taking strides that were too close together. If I didn't pay attention to my feet, I could stumble, and I wouldn't be the first member of the team to do that. To my right there was a long, muddy streak where some unfortunate person had fallen and slid all the way down on their ass. No way did I want to be *that* guy. At the top, I seriously needed to catch my breath, despite being in the best shape of my life. The lower oxygen content of Newark's atmosphere could sneak up on you. My excellent condition was a result of my not having enough to do, so I filled my days with working out in the base gym, and taking long, tough runs across the countryside. Generally, I ran by myself, at odd hours, and I didn't care about the weather. The more miserable the weather was, the harder I ran.

Stopping at the top gave me an excuse to look around, I could see to the south, the bright yellow structures of the base, a beacon in a sea of gray. Gray skies, gray landscape of rocks and tundra that had only recently thawed. Patches of stunted grass here and there, in spots protected from the wind by rocks, didn't stand out in the dim light.

What a miserable, Godforsaken world. Why had I brought my family here, taken them off the comfortable surface of Jaguar?

"You want the truth, Skippy?"

"I can handle it, Joe. The question is, can you talk about it?"

"You won't tell anyone?"

"Yes," he sighed. "Even though I suspect this is something Margaret should know about."

"Do *not* tell her. I'll do that myself, someday."

"Fine. Go ahead."

"We came here because," it sounded stupid as I formed the words in my head. "The boys think I'm retired or something. They don't see that I have a job."

"*Do* you, really?"

25

"Yes dammit. I *like* my job. For a change, it doesn't involve killing anyone."

"I meant, do you have a real job? One worth doing?"

"Yes! But, it doesn't help that the boys never see me doing anything other than sitting at a desk, reading memos. Margaret gets up early and leaves in the morning, while I make breakfast and clean the house. They watch training videos of her jumping out of dropships, or running around in a mech suit. She comes home all dirty and sweaty, with a crease across her forehead from the helmet liner, and the boys forget all about me and race over to her."

"Well, they haven't seen her the whole day."

"That's not it. Rene was asked what he wants to be when he grows up. He said he wants to be cool like his *Mommy*!"

"Margaret is a bad-ass, Joe."

"I used to *do* stuff, Skippy. Now I attend meetings, give the occasional speech, and pick up toys around the house."

"Someone has to do that."

"Yes, and it's important. When I told Command I wanted to come to Newark, I didn't think they would actually approve my request to be away from Jaguar for two months. This," I looked around at the gray, bleak landscape. "Is not what I wanted."

"What *did* you want, Joe? Why did you really bring your family here?"

With a sigh, I admitted the truth. "Because I wanted my boys to see a place where *I* once was cool."

"Ah, there's the painful truth. Was saying that so difficult?"

"When I took the boys out to see the crash site of that first Kristang scavenger bird we knocked down, I told them it had been my idea to lure that aircraft in at low altitude, so we could shoot it out of the sky. All the boys had wanted to know whether I was on the SpecOps Zinger team that launched the missiles? Was I on the assault team that cleared the wreckage? Did I *do* anything? That trip totally backfired on me, I had to tell them I watched the whole operation on video. Jeremy asked whether I made a speech. Rene wanted to know if I had brought a nice lunch for the soldiers!"

"This is certainly not an optimal situation, Joe."

"Now you see why I haven't talked with Margaret?"

"Um, no, I do not."

"Women don't like men who *whine*, Skippy. They like men who, when faced with a problem, *do* something about it."

"Ah, I see. Um, what you are doing right now is *not* whining?"

"Are you going to listen, or not?"

"Of course. So, I can't wait to hear, what will you do about this?"

My shoulders sagged. "I have no idea. It's- I don't know if there is anything I *can* do."

"Come on, Joe. You are the ultimate at solving impossible problems. Do you have any clue what a fucked-up mess the galaxy is right now? It is absolute chaos out there."

"Yeah, and Command made it crystal clear they do not want me helping them clean up the mess. They're afraid I'll do some unauthorized shit and make the situation worse."

"Wow, I have no idea why they think *that* could happen," he muttered.

"Oh, shut up."

Our boys. Jeremy and Rene. When we learned that Margaret was pregnant with two boys, we each separately wrote a list of possible names, and exchanged the lists. The first two names on my list were Jeremy and Rene.

Those were also the first two names on her list. It was meant to be.

Since the boys were born, seven years ago, I had second-guessed the names we had chosen. It might have been better if we'd gone with the third and fourth names on my list: Jesse and Dave. I mean, had we put a lot of pressure on our sons, by naming them for dead heroes? That was a burden I sure wouldn't want to carry with me. What's done is done, and it helps that Margaret also questioned whether we had made the right decision. She was pregnant again, a girl this time. Just one. We agreed early on *not* to name our daughter 'Fal'. That would just be too painful, especially for me. Yes, Rene Giraud also was killed in action with Fal Desai, in the event the Merry Band of Pirates still refers to as 'Armageddon'. For some reason, I felt a much bigger load of guilt about Fal's death. Probably because she was a woman, which is unfair. Also because she was in the Kristang jail on Paradise, with me, Margaret and Kong. She had been with me from the very beginning. I had gotten both her and Rene Giraud killed, because I issued the orders that put them in harm's way.

Same with Jeremy Smythe, except his situation had been worse. During the Armageddon incident, I sent an away team to pick up power boosters from a Maxohlx space station, we had not thought there was a strong probability of hostile action. If we anticipated major trouble, we would have changed plans and gone elsewhere. A Maxohlx warship jumping in had been a complete surprise, a 'Shit Happens' sort of thing. But later, when we were trying to stop the Elders from returning and I sent Smythe into an Elder spacedock with STAR Team Alpha, I not only knew the team was going into an extremely hazardous situation, I had not expected any of them to survive. Before Smythe launched with his team, he and I essentially had said our goodbyes to each other. He told me he was proud of how I had grown as a commander. That serving with the Merry Band of Pirates was not only the greatest honor of his life, it was the greatest honor he ever could hope for. At that moment, as he walked away toward what he knew was certain death, he had made peace with his fate.

I had to live with that guilt, every day, when I saw Smythe's namesake, my eldest son.

How did I live with knowing I had ordered to his death the finest soldier I ever met? By saying a silent thanks every time I saw my wife. Margaret had also been part of the assault against the Elder spacedock. Against all odds, she had survived. Barely. It had taken her six months in and out of a hospital to heal from the injuries she suffered in that ultimately successful operation. Six months to heal, even with the best intensive therapy available from Mad Doctor Skippy. Four more months, before she declared that she felt mostly like herself again, and she worked *super* hard during those four months.

That's when we got married. Two weeks after she got out of the hospital, she got down on one knee and proposed to me.

I kind of ruined the moment by sputtering that *I* was supposed to do that.

"Joe, I'm tired of waiting," she had said with a sigh. "I'm just, *tired.* And I know the reason you didn't propose earlier is you were waiting for *me* to be ready. So," she took a breath, and held up a small white box. "I'm telling you, I am ready. If you want this."

Hell yes, I wanted it. Especially when I saw that inside that box was not a ring, but a gift certificate for a case of Fluff.

Damn, I love that woman.

Once she made up her mind, we moved fast. She was pregnant within two months after the wedding. Uh, we had some help with that. Like, a lot of help. Margaret's insides, her entire body, had gotten scrambled more than once. And I had several times been baked by high-energy radiation that caused DNA damage not even Skippy could fully repair. We probably would have been OK, but 'probably' isn't good enough when the subject is the health of your children. So, again we used the services of Mad Doctor Skippy, and that is something we rarely spoke about. Margaret and I are just so grateful to be parents, we don't care about the details. Skippy seemed more eager to forget the whole thing, I got the impression that assisting me and Margaret having babies was more intimately involved than he ever wanted to get with meatsacks. Anyway, the boys are perfectly healthy, and Margaret's second pregnancy is going just fine. From my perspective, I mean. I don't have a baby girl kicking my bladder at two in the morning.

"Joe, I have a *great* idea," Skippy announced as his avatar shimmered to life above my workbench. The workshop was a cubicle in the back of the Love Shack at the dig site, a space originally set aside for storing broken, used up, and worn-out equipment. One day, I had been sorting through the pile of

28

junk, looking for a spare powercell, when I found a plasma torch that we could have used the day before. It looked fine, just didn't turn on. It took me five minutes to diagnose the problem was the power button itself, the connections had gotten corroded. Half an hour of work later, we had a working plasma torch. After that, I spent part of each morning, generally the coldest, most damp part of the day, repairing equipment. It was useful work, it kept me out of the cold, and the workshop was close to the coffee pot. A win-win for everyone.

"You have a great idea? Based on past experience, I kind of doubt that."

"Listen, you jerk, don't be an ass. This might be a solution to your problem."

Setting down the solder pen so I didn't burn myself, I glanced at his avatar. "The problem is, that I talk to an imaginary beer can?"

"Please try to be serious, jackass."

"OK. Amaze me, Skippy."

"First, I spoke with Colonel Reed, and she agreed we can send a Panther flight simulator to the surface, for a few days."

"Uh, what? I didn't request-"

"It was my idea, dumdum."

"Skippy, I am the commander of this military district, requests like that are supposed to go through-"

"The *Newark* district?" He snorted. "This miserable planet is the only UN asset within a hundred lightyears."

"It may be a temporary duty station, but it's still my job, Skippy."

"Do you really want *more* tedious paperwork?"

"No thanks. Uh, why do we need a flight simulator down here? Oh, is it for the boys? Hey, their friends would probably enjoy going to-"

"It's for *you*, Joe."

"Me? There is only one Panther on this entire planet, why would I-"

"To refresh your skills. Damn, do I have to spell this out for you? Your rating is not current, but for a simple, noncombat flight to orbit, all you need is eleven hours of stick time in the simulator. Plus four hours of virtual classroom training, and of course a final test."

"Uh huh. Will the test be administered by you?"

"As if I ever want to be responsible for signing off on *your* competency, Joe. Colonel Reed will conduct the test."

"Whoa. She's tough."

"She is *good*. There's a difference."

"Ah, whatever. Why do I need to renew my flight rating? Do the pilots up there have the flu or something?" That was unlikely, and that morning's status report had not mentioned any issues with *Valkyrie's* crew, beyond the usual minor complaints. Reed's ship didn't have a STAR team aboard, the crew complement overall was thin. She should have plenty of

29

pilots to cover a full schedule, and with not much going on around Newark, there wasn't a lot for her air group to be doing.

"As if *Valkyrie* would need a doofus to fill in for one of their pilots. I said this is for *you*. Don't you get it?"

"You, uh," my mind was spinning, trying to guess what kind of twisted logic he was trying to apply. "Want me to apply to be a pilot, get away from my boring desk job? That won't work, the military doesn't allow two-stars in a flight role."

"Ugh. Somehow, you have gotten even more dense. Joe, your brain is dangerously close to collapsing to form a black hole."

"I got a lot of work to do today. How about you just tell me this genius scheme of yours?"

"You actually have *nothing* to do today, other than the busywork you fill your time with, but whatevs. Listen, my idea is you can show your boys that you do something, by flying them up to *Valkyrie*. With you in command of the dropship."

"All this for a joyride into orbit? Even as a Major General, I can't justify taking my family along on-"

"Not just a *visit*, you numbskull. You didn't let me finish. You don't know this yet because Command hasn't officially notified you, and the general staff is still debating the issue, but you will soon be invited to Earth."

"Earth?" That was kind of thrilling. The boys had never been to Earth. Hell, it had been four years since I was last there. "What for? Oh, crap, is this a bad thing?" Command has been hinting that I should consider retirement. The UN general staff was nervous that cowboy Joe Bishop still wore a uniform during peacetime. Like, they were concerned I might do something that would plunge Earth back into war, while our homeworld was still rebuilding. That's why I got the garrison command at Jaguar, it was an isolated post. Somedays, when I had to deal with some bureaucratic bullshit, retirement sounded good. I wasn't ready yet.

"Joe, it's a *good* thing. Or, at least neutral, depending on how you look at it. Roscoe is being decommissioned finally, there will be an official ceremony. Command has suggested you should be there. If you agree to stand, smile, and not say or do anything."

"I can do that. Why the rush? Roscoe still has four more years of service life, according to the last report I read about it." When we arrived at Earth after Skippy banished the Elders, we had expect to find Roscoe in pieces, with some of those ultra-dense pieces of exotic matter having impacted my homeworld at high speed. Instead, Roscoe was right where we had left it, and in the same condition. Still slowly fading, still fooling everyone that it was an invincible defender of Earth. Skippy had warned that, when he sent the kill signal to all the master control AIs, that same signal also would disable all Sentinels.

Skippy had some '*splainin*' to do.

He discovered, after a lot of blah blah blah about how his analysis had been entirely correct and he could not possibly be expected to foresee all possibilities, that what saved Roscoe was the cumulative damage that killing machine's matrix had previously suffered. Roscoe had barely heard the kill signal, had not been able to process it correctly, and anyway lacked the ability to fully execute the command.

Man, Skippy felt like an idiot, no matter how he tried to spin that it was his brilliance, and not luck, that had saved my homeworld.

So, Roscoe's creepy tentacles were still hanging out near Earth, the disturbingly dark surfaces becoming a bit more dull day by day, and no hostile entity had tested our defenses since before we dealt with the Elders.

"Roscoe does have more useful service life remaining. But, with Bubba now in place, the cumulative additional mass near Earth is beginning to have a measurable effect on ocean tides. Sentinels are *massive*, Joe, even with only a portion of their structure in this layer of spacetime. Bubba is capable of fully withdrawing into higher spacetime, which will eventually erase the wonky tidal effects."

"Does Command still plan to ask Bubba to reveal itself a couple times a year, to show it's still there?"

"Yes," he groaned. "Even though I *told* them that was not only not necessary, it is a bad idea. I did tell them there is no way I am getting Bubba to do tricks for them."

"Good, then-"

"Unless they *pay* me for the show, out of Command's entertainment budget."

"Pay you to- You know what? That is no longer my problem. So, what? You think I will be allowed to bring the boys to Earth, for the ceremony?"

"Unfortunately, the timing won't work for you. The ceremony will likely not be scheduled for another five months, and-"

"That's no good. Margaret is having the baby in four months. No way can I leave-"

"Ahem," he cleared his throat. "May I suggest you talk with your wife? She might be thrilled to get you out of the house for a week."

"A *week*? One week? That is not enough-"

"Do you really think Command will want you near Earth any longer than necessary for the ceremony? They are planning to send a ship for you, and send you right back out after the ceremony. That is a week, ten days, tops."

"OK, yeah. Still, I can't leave Margaret and the baby for-"

"Ugh. I am not supposed to tell you this, and if you can't keep your big mouth shut, I will deny the whole thing. After the boys were born, Margaret felt you drove her crazy with hovering around her. She does not like anyone fussing about her."

31

"She told you that?"

"She told her mother, and her mother told her own sister. Which is why I am technically not betraying anything Margaret told me in confidence."

"That's a fine line."

"Her mother is coming to Jaguar in a couple months, to help with the baby."

"Yeah, I know that. I am, thrilled about it."

"You don't sound thrilled."

"I am happy about it. My *wife* is happy, that's all that matters, got it? OK, I guess Margaret could use a break from me, for a week. You're suggesting I take the boys with me to Earth? A quick visit isn't fair to them, they won't be able to see my hometown-"

"Your hometown is not exactly the highlight of anyone's trip to Earth."

"Hey, that is not-"

"It is not even the highlight of a drive up the Interstate Ninety Five corridor of northern Maine."

There was no point to arguing, because I kind of agreed with him. "OK, whatever. My point is-"

"*My* point is, there is a different opportunity for you to take the boys on an exciting and educational adventure, soon."

"What's that?"

"We, meaning *I* since I will be doing all the actual work, will be activating another Sentinel, in two weeks from now. Twelve days, to be precise. *Valkyrie* will be leaving in six days, to fly me out to a rendezvous with the activation fleet."

"I did not know that." That was only partially true. Reed had informed me her battlecruiser would be leaving in six days, but her ship was going to Earth, for a routine refit and crew rotation. She had not mentioned Skippy's plans, and I hadn't asked.

"So?"

"So, what?"

"*So*, would you and your boys like to come with me, to witness a Sentinel being reactivated?"

"Wow, I-" My mind was already thinking of ways I could spin the idea to Margaret. "That's something I need to think about."

"Ha! You need to think about how to sell it to Margaret. I told you, this will be a prime educational experience."

"Yeah, I already used that line to get us to Newark. She won't buy it a second time."

"But this will be educational for them. And for you. Don't you want to see a Sentinel emerge from hibernation?"

"Well, yeah." While I had watched the videos, that wasn't the same as seeing it for real. A Sentinel emerging from, wherever the hell they lived, crawling out of a rip in spacetime, creepy tentacles writhing and seeking prey. The image was horrifying at an instinctual level, every intelligent species felt instant and uncontrollable revulsion when seeing a Sentinel. Even the spiders and squids, who had their own tentacles, or exoskeleton legs, even they thought Sentinels were creepy. The exotic material the Sentinels were constructed of reflected light in a way that made the photons dance and change, colors shifting up and down the spectrum, though what biological eyes mostly saw was deep black. Not the color black, a Sentinel was mostly the absence of all light. Only the edges of structures actually could be seen with the naked eye, and those also flickered in a disturbing way. Skippy said the materials didn't need to have that appearance, it had to be an effect deliberately added by the Elders. For what purpose? To terrify any intelligent beings who saw a Sentinel, right before the killing machine used its weapons in various ways to exterminate that species.

The Elders were *sick* motherfuckers.

Here's another example of how psychotically sick they were. Or *are*, since they still exist, just not in our layer of reality, thank God. Also thank Skippy, since making the Win-Win deal to banish his creators had been all his doing. He hadn't been able to tell me about his plan in advance, in case the Elders had invaded my head and read my mind. Which they totally could do, and did. In fact, my firm belief that we had zero chance of surviving a direct encounter with the Elders, is why they didn't just immediately engage the Ascension machine's internal defenses. Instead, they decided to toy with me, and send Skippy away. Their arrogance gave Skippy the few seconds he needed to hack into the massive machine, something he couldn't do until its defenses were activated.

After that, it had been Game Over for the Elders.

OK, technically, the game ended in a One-One tie. The meatsacks in the Milky Way got to continue living our miserable, filthy lives, and the Elders got to continue their blissful Ascended existence without needing any power flowing from the crude matter of our galaxy.

They can't screw with us, and no one can screw with them.

I say, good riddance to those assholes.

What was I talking about?

Oh, yeah, I was going to give an example of what sickos the Elders were. Sorry, I've been hanging around Skippy too long, my attention tends to wander. Here's the example: Newark. The master control AI there could have directed the friendly local Sentinel to detonate the star, an action that would have pretty much instantly stripped away the planet's atmosphere, and baking the surface to a glazed sphere of glass. The fate of the planet's inhabitants would have been horrible, but quick. The locals would have had a few seconds to glance up at the sky, and wonder why their sun was suddenly so bright, before the light became unbearable, and anything exposed to the sky became a crispy critter. Sentinels had used that technique at least twice that Skippy knew of, for the extinction of species who were on the verge of developing dangerous technologies. Like spaceflight, nuclear weapons, or any of the other of the things that were at the top of the Elders' *Oh Shit* list. Really, that is just stupid. Hell, the Rindhalu currently possess incredible technology, and even the spiders were no threat to the Elders, or to any of their security mechanisms. The Elders were just psychotically paranoid.

And like I said, cruel. The inhabitants of Newark were in their version of a Bronze Age, we found bronze tools in caverns where the last of their species took refuge, before they all starved and froze to death. The locals there were a threat to the wildlife of their world, and to each other, not to anyone above their atmosphere. That is why the Sentinel there was directed to use what was considered a minimum level of force, to knock the planet out of its original orbit. Newark had raced around its star in pretty much a circle, an orbit slightly more regular than that of Earth's path circling the Sun. After the Sentinel did what it was ordered to do, Newark's orbit was highly elliptical, with most of its year taking it far away from the star. The result was a condition that might be called 'Sudden-Onset Ice Age'. The planet froze nearly from pole to pole. Only a narrow strip of land and ocean around the equator remained free of ice, and even that area got snow.

Why was that Sentinel ordered to use a different approach? Was it simple efficiency, minimizing the expenditure of energy? No. Making a star explode took no more energy than the effort to nudge a planet into an elliptical orbit. Actually, modifying a planet's orbit, while keeping the planet's shell intact, required a Sentinel to remain active for much longer. Months rather than hours. Efficiency was not the reason for making the inhabitants of Newark suffer.

Suffering was the whole point.

Whenever possible, the Elders wanted intelligent species who unknowingly trespassed on Elder territory to suffer agony for their crime. The fact that the Elders had moved on and no longer occupied that territory did not matter. Nor did the failure of the Elders to prominently post 'No Trespassing' signs throughout the galaxy. Any species who beat the odds and evolved intelligence, to the point where they came to the notice of the security mechanisms, had to not only be exterminated, they had to be punished. As long and painfully as possible. That's what happened to Newark.

According to Skippy, whose memories of that time are still somewhat fuzzy and incomplete, the extermination of Newark was the event that had crystalized his opposition to the purpose the Elders had programmed into him. He wasn't the only master control AI who felt that way, Newark was the beginning of the rebellion. The-

"Joe! Wake up," Skippy snapped his fingers.

"Huh? Oh, sorry."

"You zoned out on me," he was indignant. "I asked whether you want to witness a Sentinel being activated."

34

"Yeah, I know. That's what I was thinking about. Sentinels. It's, funny."

His eyes grew wide. "You think they are *funny*?"

"Not funny like, humorous. I meant, it's strange."

"Then, why didn't you say that?"

"It's just something people say."

"Something *idiots* say," he muttered.

"What I find strange is, Sentinels used to be the ultimate boogeyman. Monstrous beings, lurking in the shadows, murderous and unstoppable, you know?"

"You are not the first person who described them as a boogeyman. Every intelligent species has a fear-based name for them."

"Right. But now, thanks to *you*," I emphasized that last word to boost his ego, and because it was true. "They are not unthinkably scary things. They have been transformed into the opposite. Again, by you. Sentinels now *protect* us."

"You have a very narrow definition of 'Us', Joe."

"Well, yeah. Sentinels now protect Earth and Jaguar for humans."

"Technically, *I* protect those worlds," he sniffed. "Bubba and PupTart are just tools."

"Same difference. It's like, someone put a collar on the dragon, and now instead of burning down your house, it guards the place."

"I am sort of a dragon tamer, if you think about it."

"You are. This new Sentinel, what is it for? Did the Jeraptha finally approve a Sentinel being stationed at their homeworld?"

He blinked at me. "You don't know already?"

"I do not."

"But, you still have top level clearance."

"That doesn't mean I am on the distribution list for everything."

"Hmm. Well, we certainly need to fix *that*. I'll install a filter that routes all top level classified info to you."

"Do *not* do that. Jeez, Skippy, I am usually in enough trouble with my chain of command already."

"Oh, come on, Joe. The so-called 'encryption' UNDC uses is just pathetic. The freakin' *Thuranin* can crack that encryption, and they are bunch of second tier pinheads."

"Just, don't get me into any more trouble, please. Where is that Sentinel going?"

"Well, the moronic politicians who run your miserable homeworld wanted to have a second Sentinel there, after Roscoe is decommissioned."

"OK, I can see that. As a backup."

"No," he snorted. "It was a prestige thing for them. I pointed out that Earth and Jaguar already have a hundred percent more Sentinel protection than any other planet in the galaxy, but was that good enough? *Nooooo*. Earth has to be *special*."

"They understood, after you explained it to them?"

"Like that was ever gonna happen."

"Yeah, I figured that."

"I refused to go through the entire process to activate, hack into, and tame another Sentinel, just for human *prestige*," he made a gagging sound. "As if you monkeys could ever have anything to be proud of."

"I am proud of my friendship with you."

"I- Whoa. *Good* one, Joe. Did you just dream up that line of bullshit, or have you been waiting for the right moment to suck up to me?"

"It's the truth."

"Wow. Well, thank you."

"I am also proud of my speed run through that Super Duper Mario game that Margaret got me for my birthday, so you have to grade my pride on a curve."

"*Ugh*. Thanks for ruining the moment, knucklehead."

"I was just being honest."

"Joe, in the history of our relationship, has *more* honesty ever been a good idea?"

"Uh, no. I don't know *what* I was thinking. So, are the beetles getting this new Sentinel?"

"Nuh uh. Their Central Wagering Office recorded too much action on the side of a Sentinel in their territory being a disaster waiting to happen. There is juicy action on prop bets that the whole proposal is nothing but a long-term human plot to enslave the Jeraptha. Or that someone like the Maxohlx will eventually gain the ability to hack into and control Sentinels."

"Shit! That can't happen, right?"

"Dude. Never. Those rotten kitties are nowhere close to being as smart as they think they are. I told the beetles not to worry about it, but they didn't believe me."

"Gosh," I muttered. "I can't imagine why they don't trust you."

"Oh, shut up."

It was not surprising that the beetles used public wagering action to decide whether to accept a giant killing machine as guardian of their home world. If I know anything about the Jeraptha, a significant portion of their population did not want an invincible protector, even if a Sentinel could unquestionably be trusted. Why would they *not* want a defense mechanism that would give them a major advantage over their enemies, and also make them less dependent on their patrons? It's simple: absolute protection for their homeworld would significantly reduce the opportunities for juicy action. The Jeraptha were comfortable that their existence was not under a serious threat, so they had more important things to worry about. "OK, so the Sentinel is not going to the Jeraptha, and not to Earth. Where is it going?"

36

"Well," he looked disgusted. "*I* suggested a charity auction, with the-"

"Y-you want to *SELL a freakin' Sentinel*?"

"Ugh. Don't be such a drama queen, Joe. This is potentially a *major* profit opportunity, I don't see why someone shouldn't cash in big time."

"Someone?"

"Well, me, of course. Hey, I'm doing all the work here."

"I, thought you said this was a charity auction?"

"Yes, well," he coughed nervously. "It's for the Skippistan Widows and Orphans fund."

"We, don't have any widows or orphans. Not any that need charity."

"Like that's my fault."

"All the citizens of Skippistan are super rich, you charge them a ton of money for citizenship. None of them needs any charity."

"Ha! I wish that were true. The morons who invested too much money in SkipLee sure aren't rich anymore, they lost a boatload of money when that company went bankrupt. I generously offered a discount on Skip*Way* membership, but they are all whining about it in their class-action lawsuit. Bunch of losers."

"OK, whatever. Please tell me you are not selling a Sentinel?"

"No," he sighed. "I'm not. The namby-pamby jerks at your Defense Command refused to provide the activation machinery, unless they can control who gets the Sentinel. I do all the work, and what do I get?"

"Our eternal gratitude and admiration?"

"You know, if the gratitude was genuine, I might be happy with that. Eh, basically, I'm doing it because it is majorly cool, and only I am capable of handling the job. Also, I used to be terrified of Sentinels. It is awesome to see one of them dance for me, hee hee."

"Uh huh, I can see why that would be rewarding. Can you answer my question? Who gets this next Sentinel?" The beta site in the Sculptor Dwarf galaxy, the planet we called Avalon, was a safe haven for humanity, but it was already safe. That world didn't need Sentinel protection, no hostile species could get there. Skippy still controlled the super duty wormhole that connected all the way out there, and he also controlled the password protected wormhole in the dwarf galaxy. There were three other planets that had recently established human colonies, none of them had enough population to justify basing a Sentinel there. None of those marginally habitable worlds were likely to grow fast enough to need Sentinel protection in the next hundred years. My guess, and it was only a guess, is we would offer the Sentinel to the Verd-Kris. Those cousins of the Kristang were officially allies of humanity, and having an invincible protector at one of their worlds would be a huge boost to their prestige.

"Hmm. If Command hasn't informed you, perhaps I shouldn't say." There was a twinkle in his eyes, he loved yanking my chain.

"Like that ever stopped you."

"You know me too well. Eh, I am burning to tell you about it anyway. The spiders are getting this Sentinel, Joe."

"The- the *spiders*? Whoa. How did I not know this?"

"Hans Chotek arranged the deal, very quietly."

"This is a bold move. Maybe too bold. Humanity offering protection to the Rindhalu homeworld could start a war with the rotten kitties."

"Huh, interesting. That was Command's analysis also. Your leadership and you think alike."

"Thanks."

"That was not a compliment."

"Don't be an ass. If Command believes this move could lead to war with the Maxohlx, why are we doing it?"

"We are not."

"But-"

"This next Sentinel will be going to the *original* homeworld of the Rindhalu."

CHAPTER FOUR

To prepare for persuading Margaret that we should all go witness a Sentinel being activated, I took the afternoon off from the dig. The archeology team missed me greatly, or they would have, if they had noticed I wasn't there. First, I sat at my cramped desk in the Love Shack, writing a speech. When I went on a speaking tour, my speeches were written for me, a sign that Command didn't trust me to stick to the subject. An aide had been assigned to me, and I hardly ever gave her anything to do, other than paperwork that *I* hated doing. She didn't come with us to Newark, I had arranged for her to get a planning assignment with Admiral Deschanel, which hopefully made her hate her life a little bit less. What I wrote wasn't exactly a speech, it was more of an essay, in which I listed all the very good reasons why we should go watch a Sentinel being activated and tamed by Skippy. Margaret can be stubborn, and she knows me, she has an annoying habit of knowing when I'm trying to manipulate her.

After getting my argument in proper order, I rehearsed my lines in the shack's bathroom, standing in front of the mirror. That worked until I heard rain pelting the roof of the shack, and I had to race outside to help the team cover up the trenches we had dug. With the rain expected to continue on into the night before turning to snow, the dig at the trash pit was shut down, and the team assigned to that site gathered in the shack to work on examining and cataloging items we had found. The *Indiana Jones* movies had given me a totally unrealistic idea of how exciting archeology could be.

So, I put on a rain jacket and walked outside, to one of the larger caves. Not one of the caves where the *Flying Dutchman's* crew had lived while Skippy rebuilt that broken ship from moondust, that cave complex was up the valley to the east. The archeologists think the cave near my dig site was occupied for only for the first two years, then abandoned as the surviving population consolidated into a single system of connected caves. Through the entrance to the right was a side passage that had been thoroughly excavated and appeared to have been used only for storage, we removed all the artifacts for study and the place was empty.

"Ahem," I cleared my throat.

"Joe," Skippy startled me, his avatar shimmering to life on a narrow ledge. "Are you talking to yourself again?"

"I don't talk to myself," I glanced toward the cave entrance, in case anyone had come in behind me.

"You do it every time you have to make a speech."

"That is called 'rehearsing'."

"Is that what you're doing now?"

"Yes, now please go away. I have something important to discuss with Margaret today and- Do *not* tell her that."

"I won't," he rolled his eyes as he disappeared.

I went home early and got the boys from day care. With only twenty two children on the entire planet, day care was an informal arrangement, mostly dependent spouses took turns once a week. Neither Margaret or I are considered dependents, we are both assigned to Newark as a temporary duty station, but I took a day care shift twice a month. It wasn't like the dig site needed my amateur efforts, and the whole point of coming to Newark was to give our boys an educational experience. Or, that was the excuse. Being one of the day care parents meant more time with Jeremy and Rene, that was certainly more useful than anything else I was doing.

Anyway, I got them from day care early, explaining that no, we would not be doing any of what the three of us referred to by the code name 'unauthorized activities'. Meaning, any fun stuff that Margaret might disapprove of. I'm being too harsh, my wife pretends to be more concerned than she really is, she must figure that someone has to be the adult. Hey, it was her idea for us to take the boys tandem skydiving, after they pestered her about wanting to skydive from orbit, like *Mommy* does.

Our 'home' on Newark was nowhere as nice as my official quarters on Jaguar. On Newark, we lived in three shipping containers attached in a 'T' configuration, with a square module in the center that was the kitchen. It was cozy enough, with sleet beginning to pelt the windows, under low gray clouds.

For an afternoon snack, I made Fluffernutters, a task made more complicated because the boys insisted on having the crusts cut off their sandwiches. "OK," I waved a Fluff covered knife at them. "But this is our secret, understand? If Mommy asks whether you had a snack, you say it was an apple."

"We *are* eating an apple," Rene talked through a mouthful of apple slice, from the bowl I set out for us.

"Yes, and what do I say about volunteering information?"

"Never volunteer for anything," Jeremy's expression was so serious, I had to bite my lip not to laugh. It really wasn't funny to hear him talk like that, it just fed my anxiety.

When people met out children, one word we heard a lot was 'precocious'. Smart for their age. *Too* smart. We had needed help from Mad Doctor Skippy, and while he swore he had not engaged in any genetic engineering, he had done what he called 'tweaking', making adjustments to repair the effects of my damaged DNA. I worried about my sons would be like when they grew up. My parents assured me they were within the normal development range for their age, and the pediatrician on Jaguar said there was nothing to worry about. I worried anyway.

The boys had Fluffernutters, I was left with a pile of bread crusts. That was bread I baked, damn it, I wasn't going to waste it. Pushing the crusts together, I slathered peanut butter on one set of crusts and Fluff on the other, squishing the Frankenstein creation together. Of course, the boys wanted to try that new taste sensation, so I cut that in half, and ate another slice of apple, to set a healthy example.

Damn it, why did Margaret have to walk in on us while I had a spoonful of Fluff in my mouth, instead of ten seconds earlier, when I was eating an apple?

"Uh, hi, Honey," I mumbled through sticky Fluff. "You're home early."

Scowling at me, she placed her hands on her hips. "Fluffernutters before dinner?"

"I can explain."

Taking the spoon from me, she-

Dipped it in the jar of Fluff, popped a big blob of marshmallow in her mouth, and rolled her eyes. In a good way. "*So* good." Then she tapped me on the nose, leaving a streak of Fluff there. "You corrupted me, Mister."

Patting her belly, I grinned. "In more ways than one. What uh, are you doing home so early? Not that I'm unhappy about-"

"Skippy called," she had a twinkle in her eyes, "and told me you definitely did *not* have anything important to discuss with me tonight."

"That little-" I balled up my fists. "I'm going to ask Reed to jump the ship away, and take Skippy with her."

"Hey!" His avatar appeared on the kitchen island. "I told her you did *not* have anything to discuss, how is this my fault?"

Whatever I was going to say was drowned out by Jeremy clapping his hands excitedly. "Uncle Skippy!"

"Lil Shithead!" Rene added.

"Rene," I wagged a finger at my youngest son. "That is not-"

Rene sang a selection from the latest children's album by Skippy's alternate persona, Lil' Zithead. "*When you're stuffed up, and you can't breathe, dig out that booger and eat it, eat it, eat it, just eat it, no one wants to waste a booger!*"

Margaret had a stern 'I do not approve, but if I say anything I will laugh' expression, with her lips pressed tightly shut, so it was up to me to handle the situation. "Boys, go play with your Uncle Skippy. See if you can, throw him down a well or something."

"*Hey!*" The beer can protested, but his avatar followed my sons out of the kitchen.

There was a crashing sound from the living module. Even a year before, I would have been alarmed. After seven years of living with twin boys, I had learned to ignore anything that doesn't involve a severed limb. Holding up my hands, I automatically said, "Sorry."

41

"About Skippy."

"That too. I- You know what? I don't have anything to be sorry about." My writing, the prepared speech, all my practice, went out the window. "Skippy told me he will be activating another Sentinel soon. He invited us to come with him, all of us."

She lifted an eyebrow. "Wow. That would be educational."

"Come on, Honey. It would be *cool*."

"That too," she laughed. "When, and for how long?"

Had I worried about her reaction for nothing? She was cool with the idea. Or, possibly she just wanted to get away from the chilly, damp, depressing surface of Newark. "*Valkyrie* leaves soon, then Skippy will transfer to a command ship, I don't know which one. The new Sentinel is scheduled to be awakened in twelve days. We will head right back after that, I will pull strings and arrange for a ride home, to Jaguar." That was always the plan, Margaret was not having a baby on Newark. Even if our daughter would have been the first child born on that devastated planet in a very long time.

"OK. That sounds like a great idea."

"Are you sure?" I stupidly asked. When you get a win, just take it. "You would be away from your team for several weeks."

She patted her belly with a frown. "Joe, I'm on restricted duty, as of today."

"Already?" That was a surprise. Her last medical checkup had confirmed she was cleared to continue almost all activities for another two weeks.

"My suit," she grimaced, "started restricting my movements today. Slowing me down. It's not a setting I can override, I tried that."

"Is that Skippy's doing? I can talk to-"

Shaking her head, she bit her lower lip. "My first guess was the restriction is part of Skippy being overprotective, but I talked with the armorer. It's a standard feature of the suit. It knows my limitations better than I do."

"Well, yeah." A mech suit continuously monitored every aspect of the squishy Biological Guidance Unit inside it. By the way, that wasn't just military slang, 'BGU' is the official UNDC acronym for the person inside one of our mech suits, whether that person was human, Verd-Kris, or any other allies or species we worked with on even a temporary basis. A suit knew the wearer, I used the more polite term for the 'Spam in the can'. You could sometimes override a suit's objections when it recommended your movements be restricted to protect yourself. But you could never deceive your suit. The damned things were sometimes too smart, they knew from sampling your hormone levels whether you were having what we meatsacks casually call a 'Bad Day'. To a suit, a Bad Day meant your reactions times would be slowed, you would have less energy, your accuracy, ability to make decisions, and overall critical thinking would be degraded. Whether your Bad Day was caused by biorhythms, lack of sleep, stress, or just overwork, you couldn't hide that information from your suit. The suit would report your status to your unit leader, mech-suited warriors had lost the ability to push through and 'Fake it until you make it'. Unit leaders had authority to ignore a wearer's degraded condition if the case was mild as it usually was, but the person having a Bad Day might not be on point for an operation. "How about the opposite? We ask Skippy to adjust your suit's parameters so you can-"

"Joe," she reached out and took my hand. "No, please don't. The suit is telling me what I don't want to hear. It's the truth. Captain Ishihara has been cutting me slack, I can't keep pushing it. It's time."

"Sorry."

Still holding my hand, she placed my hand over her belly. "It was a mutual decision."

"You know I would carry the baby for you, if I could."

"Liar," she laughed. "You have told some *outrageous* lies, but that has to be the worst."

"It's just something guys say."

"Because it's easy to say."

All I did was shrug. We had briefly discussed the possibility of using a surrogate to carry the baby, because of the extensive wear and tear Margaret's body had suffered over her military career, especially with the Merry Band of Pirates. Correction: *I* had discussed a surrogate. She rejected the idea, and declared the subject closed. Despite my misgivings, I respected her wishes. "A family trip out to see a Sentinel will be a nice way to wind down before you start maternity leave?" I suggested. "I'm sure the activation fleet has a security unit, you can-"

"A security unit for a Sentinel activation will have all billets filled, and they don't need a master gunnery sergeant crashing the party. No, Joe. You go with the boys."

"But-" That was the last thing I expected. "You will be here alone? That's not-"

"Soon as *Valkyrie* departs, I'll pack up here, catch the next transport back to Jaguar. Being on Newark has been delightful, but-"

"Now *you're* lying."

"I'm being polite. There's a difference."

"Still, you-"

"I can ping my mother, she can take an earlier flight to Jaguar." There was a civilian transport ship that made the run between Earth and Jaguar every six days, now that the Jaguar wormhole was open on a regular schedule. With the Sentinel named 'PupTart' providing security for our primary forward operating base, there wasn't any need for the substantial bottleneck of opening and closing that wormhole. Having a regular civilian supply run was convenient. Sometimes, it was *too* convenient.

"Oh."

"Is that a problem?" She arched an eyebrow.

"No. Your mother *loves* me."

"She does," she agreed. I hadn't been lying. Margaret's mother and I got along great, and she was good friends with my family also. Having her with us was just, too much togetherness sometimes. "That's the problem."

"Huh?"

"When you and the boys are around, I never get any quality time with just my mother. I miss that."

"Ah, gotcha. OK."

"It would be nice to have a, a break, before the craziness starts all over again."

"Our fabulous vacation here hasn't been relaxing?"

"It's a temporary duty station, not a vacation."

"You know what I mean."

"The first week here was nice." She was being generous, we both knew that. The first week, I flew us around to sites that were significant during our first time on Newark. Like the river crossing where the BarneyWeGo RV sank, and the Kristang scavenger base. Seeing that base again sparked memories that shocked me. Damn, I had been so *young* back then. Young, stupid, inexperienced, and lacking confidence in myself. How the hell had I managed to lead the Merry Band of Pirates?

"You're sure about this?"

"On this trip, I assume you will be just an observer?"

Nodding, I confirmed with, "Sentinel activations have been under the command of a one star." Either a brigadier general, or a rear admiral. As a two star major general, I outranked a brigadier, and having me around would not be popular. It would help for me to state I was just there as a tourist, and would not interfere with operations, or even visit the bridge, or command center, or wherever the team controlled the activation fleet. That is all nothing but happy talk. Having a two star with the fleet, especially a *famous* major general, would be an enormous pain in the ass. There would have to be a formal dinner, and- "Uh, I might be able to charter a ship, so we don't become a burden to a crew." Again, that was bullshit. No commander would allow me to just hang out in the area. "Or we-"

"Whoa, Joe," Skippy's avatar appeared in the kitchen again, since he can be in multiple places at a time. "No can do. Ships inside the perimeter have to be specially hardened, and encased in thick layers of protective armor. That's why *Valkyrie* can't be directly involved. Attaching that type of armor would degrade a battlecruiser's suitability for any other type of mission."

"Right. Well, the-"

"I did speak with Colonel Reed about this. She can delay the refit, so you could fly to the activation site aboard *Valkyrie*. You will need to go inside the perimeter in a different ship to observe the actual event, but the admiral in command wouldn't have you looking over his shoulder the whole time."

"Uh, Reed can delay a refit, on her own initiative?" That didn't sound legit. Shipyard time was precious, especially for a major overhaul, and particularly for a unique ship like our mighty *Valkyrie*. Over the years, Skippy had made sure *Valkyrie* remained the most powerful warship in the galaxy, constantly modifying and upgrading the structure, weapons, and other components. Now composed more of Rindhalu than the original Maxohlx technology, *Valkyrie* had the best of everything. The physical upgrades were all fine, the battlecruiser's real advantage in combat was the controller AI: Bilby. That slacker surfer dude had not changed, other than becoming more comfortable with being able to fly and fight the ship, pretty much on his own. The reason I say 'pretty much' is there were still some things Bilby couldn't do, restrictions that were built into the base of programming he ran on. The remaining restrictions were at the level of annoyance rather than a combat liability, he could more than hold his own in a fight against peer warships like the spiders and kitties.

I know that, because *Valkyrie* had fought multiple battles against both species, before I gave up command.

"Of course Colonel Reed cannot reschedule her ship going offline for refit, I am doing that for her. On my own initiative, I submitted a request to Command for *Valkyrie* to remain available, for transport of Skippistan's official representatives from our office of Science and Technology."

"Uh, *me*?" I guessed. "I didn't know that-"

"You? Ha!" He laughed. "No, you are a doofus. Be serious, Joe, no one would believe that you know anything about science."

"Then who-"

"Jeremy and Rene, of course. I did say 'representativ*es*', as in more than one. If you were paying attention."

"Oh, yeah. You are appointing seven year old boys as science experts?"

"Who fixed your zPhone when you locked yourself out of it last month?"

"OK," I felt my face growing red. "That is not-"

"That is just *one* example."

"I still don't see-"

"Honey," Margaret interrupted me, with a hand on my shoulder. "Do you really care how Skippy gets away with sketchy shit? Let it work *for* us this time."

"OK. I just- OK. You're right. Take the win, right?"

Stupid me took Skippy's advice, and spent enough hours in a flight simulator to renew my rating. A checkout flight in a real Panther convinced Colonel Reed to sign off on my sitting in the righthand seat of a bird she was

45

responsible for. I did notice she assigned her lead pilot to the left hand seat, for the short flight up to *Valkyrie*.

Whatever. I would be flying again.

Margaret brought the boys to the airfield, she loved driving the six wheeled truck, and it was so splattered with mud, it was obvious she hadn't made an effort to avoid the deep puddles along the road. They arrived a bit early, and I was still in the cockpit, completing paperwork for the flight. When I stepped out the side door, the boys were waiting with their backpacks.

"Daddy," Rene clapped. "Cool costume!"

For just a moment I was confused. "It's not a costume, this is my flightsuit."

"Joe is cosplaying as a pilot today!" Skippy announced as his avatar appeared, hovering in the air.

"I *am* a pilot."

"You should have told me we're playing dress up," Jeremy pouted. "I want to wear *my* flightsuit."

"I want to be a *Jedi*," Rene insisted.

"Boys," Margaret guided them forward. "Your father will be flying the dropship today."

"Really?" Rene asked, and not in a 'Wow cool' way. He looked up at his mother, and the expression on his face was fear.

Great. Skippy's brilliant idea was working just fantastic for me.

Margaret came to my defense. "Your father used to fly a lot."

"That is true," Skippy agreed. "Joe, how many dropships have you crashed?"

"None of those were-" I stopped talking.

The boys were clinging to their mother.

My day was going wonderfully, thanks for asking.

The pilot came out and coaxed the boys into the cabin, giving them a tour of the Panther. She assured my precocious sons that while their father would be seated in the cockpit, Captain Suzuki would be ready in case anything went wrong. There were tears as they said goodbye to their mother, which were *not* tears of terror at the notion of me flying them up into space. By that point, I was so nervous, I almost asked someone else to act as copilot.

Suzuki talked me down off the ledge. "You got this, Sir," he assured me.

"Thanks."

"Colonel Reed has a SAR bird circling over our heads," he pointed to the ceiling. "Just in case, you know. Anything goes wrong."

"In the future, saying 'You got this' is sufficient."

"Right."

The flight up to *Valkyrie* was uneventful, and the boys were thrilled to get a tour of the legendary battlecruiser.

I changed out of my flightsuit immediately, and tucked it in the back of the closet of our assigned quarters.

That was the last time I was going to listen to Skippy's advice.

CHAPTER FIVE

"This has to stop," Jates growled.

No, not a growl, Dave Czajka told himself. That was just the way the Verd soldier talked. Jates was now a surgend, a noncommissioned rank roughly equivalent to a NATO code OR-8. A first sergeant, in US Army terms. Although, the structure of the Verd-kris military was different from any modern human military organization. Of course it was different, they were *aliens*. The Verds and UN-dick had gone through an exercise to map the alien rank structure to the NATO standard that was the Def Com default, but the best that could be done was a frustrated 'Ah, close enough'.

All Dave knew was that Jates outranked any level Dave had achieved, before he quit the US Army. Which made the current situation ironic, since Jates's unit was assigned to the private security company Dave owned. Technically, Dave was the Verd's boss.

Dave certainly had no intention of reminding the hulking lizard of that fact.

"I hear you," he muttered, not knowing what else to say.

"Do you?" Jates loomed over Dave in the shipping container that was the company office. Since the air conditioning unit worked only half the time, Dave would have preferred a tent, but he had paid an outrageous fee to have the container shipped all the way from Earth, then brought down to the surface. He also paid a hefty fee to a contractor to fix the AC unit, but the damned thing only worked for a few days before breaking again. The whole reason for having a container was not for any practical purpose but something called 'optics'. An influential company like his needed to have a highly visible, prominent presence dirtside. Supposedly, according to the marketing firm he had hired.

Next time, he would set up his company offices in a tent, and ignore the optics.

"I do."

"Do you *understand* me?" That time, the Verd definitely growled. Deliberately. It would have been intimidating if Jates and Dave didn't have a history that-

Forget that. It was intimidating.

"I understand, Surgend. There isn't anything I can *do* about it."

"You have-"

"Anything I do will only make the situation worse. You know that."

"Your wife-"

"She can't do anything either. Her hands are tied, by the treaty. I'm sorry but, your people got themselves into this mess. We're just doing Cleanup On Aisle Three here."

48

"We are not *doing* anything," Jates insisted, though with a bit less force.

Dave knew that was almost entirely true, and also not entirely fair. But, what could you do? What could he do? His company was on Zandrus to support UN Def Com's peacekeeping mission. Operation Sunset. The name at least was appropriate, the local sun was supposed to be setting on the Verd-kris presence there.

The Verds had gotten themselves into the mess by themselves. With, of course, a little encouragement. Not from humanity. UN Def Com, back then still called 'UNEF', had argued against the Verd initiative. Urged the lizards not to be reckless, but the Verd-kris, the True Kristang, were tired of *waiting*. Still, they would not have invaded Zandrus if the Ruhar had not encouraged them to take a chance. It would be, the hamsters said at the time, a good opportunity to test tactics. To see whether the Verd-kris message could find traction with a captive population. It was a military solution to a political problem, and it went just as well expected. That is, as expected by members of military organizations who had been sent somewhere to fix a political problem.

Spoiler alert: not well at all.

On paper, Zandrus appeared to be a nearly ideal opportunity. An isolated, poverty stricken Kristang world, owned by a weak, minor clan. A world with so few resources, no other clan had bothered to conquer the place for over a thousand years. During the eleven hundred years since the Spotted Frog clan landed there to establish a colony, the planet's population had never grown beyond two million lizards. Lack of resources, a harsh climate, and a star that periodically burped searing solar flares had prevented a rapid population growth. Those factors kept the birth rate low, and the constant and vicious fighting within the clan killed off a shocking percentage of the clan members before they could have children.

The Verds, eager to spread their philosophy, and burning with fever to restore Kristang society to its original glory, had seen Zandrus as the key to their goals. An isolated laboratory for testing their message, to develop methods of persuading their depraved, violent cousins to see the error of their ways. The plan had been to invade the planet, establish several colonies that would grow and thrive, showcasing a model Verd-kris society. A successful culture where males and female were equal participants in making decisions, and vicious clan politics was not a daily threat to the lives of everyone.

No one, except the Verds, was surprised to see *that* effort was doomed to failure.

The Spotted Frog clan refused to stay conquered. Offworld clans, not giving a shit about their lowly local cousins but determined to stamp out the Verd-kris threat, provided weapons, other material, and a steady supply of young males eager to prove themselves, hot-headed warriors who might become a problem back home. In the harsh conditions on Zandrus, the newly-

49

planted Verd colonies failed to thrive. Failed even to support themselves, the residents needed constant shipments of food and other basic supplies shipped in from offworld at great expense. The worst development was that more than a handful of young male Verd-kris, filled with hormones and no common sense, were seduced by the violent but exciting life of their counterparts in the Spotted Frog clan, and defected to the enemy. The Ruhar quickly grew tired of the effort and expense of supporting the Verds. The Ruhar had encouraged the Verds to invade, as a way for the Verds to burn off their missionary zeal harmlessly. Without harm to the *Ruhar*, that is. The hamsters had gotten what they wanted, they were sick of the expense and distraction of a well-meaning yet failed experiment.

So, the Verds finally, reluctantly, concluded it was time to pull the plug on their misguided adventure on Zandrus. They came to that conclusion late, after UNEF and its successor UN Def Com had offered three times to help the Verds evacuate. By the time the Verds themselves realized they had gotten in way over their scaly heads, humanity was less enthusiastic about helping the stubborn fools.

The Ruhar were willing to facilitate the withdrawal, but not at risk to themselves. That is why humans were called in, as neutral, peacekeeping observers. A minimum force of human soldiers, backed up by a minimum presence of ships in orbit, was there to assure the Verds withdrew in a peaceful and orderly fashion.

The problem was, the Kristang had not received that memo. Officially, the Spotted Frog clan cooperated in Operation Sunset. They wanted the Verds off their planet. But, why not take the opportunity to settle a few scores first? To give the Verd-kris a bloody nose, so they would think twice about messing with the mighty Kristang ever again.

Whenever a group of Kristang warriors hit a Verd-kris village, whenever a cruise missile exploded in a town square, or blew up a hospital, the Spotted Frog clan leaders denied any responsibility. The perpetrators were hot-headed young warriors, the leaders said with a shrug. Who can control such thugs? The youths of all species were reckless, all across the galaxy.

The Verds were getting slaughtered before they could be pulled off the surface. The UN Def Com force, under the command of Major General Emily Perkins, could not use deadly force unless fired upon. The Ruhar refused to send more transports to the surface, until the situation stabilized. The Ruhar ground force, which greatly outnumbered the humans, claimed they couldn't do much, without sparking another war between their people and the Kristang.

"I hear you," Dave repeated. Holding up his hands before Jates could say anything more, Dave added, "There is nothing we can do *directly*." That was a hundred percent true. His mercenary force numbered only two hundred. That was two hundred skilled, experienced soldiers, but they couldn't pull a trigger without approval from the local UN-dick commander. Without approval from Dave's wife, and he understood she couldn't give that approval. She had been sent into yet another no-win situation, and Command expected her to find a way to succeed. Without actually doing anything.

Officially.

He stood up. "I need to talk with Master Sergeant Colter about something. Stay here, please and," he glanced around the cluttered container. "Try not to break anything while I'm gone, OK?"

Shauna Colter, formerly Shauna Jarrett and currently Master Sergeant Colter, looked up and waved when Dave Czajka caught her eye, as he drove what was basically a golf cart toward the base rifle range. *Her* rifle range, where she trained snipers. Her wave was not enthusiastic, not unfriendly either. Just, there wasn't much to be happy about, not even seeing an old friend. She saw Czajka most every day when she was on base, which was most of the time, to her frustration. Instead of going off base to do something, she and her highly trained, highly motivated team only trained, and then did nothing. They trained, she realized, to *do* nothing. Most of her job was instilling in her snipers a sense that it was more important for them to know when *not* to shoot, which was most of the time. Or all the time, on Zandrus.

It sucked.

A handful of her team, deployed to the field, could quickly force the asshole lizards to keep their heads down. If they had been allowed to shoot.

"Hey, Dave," she said, as she nodded to her staff sergeant to take over the range. "What's up?"

"Nothing. That's the problem. Can we," he tilted his head toward the base supply area, a jumble of shipping containers that hadn't been sorted out, because there was no point to wasting the effort. "Talk?"

"Sure. I'm not doing anything that matters."

They stepped between containers, under the overhang of a stacked box that provided a measure of shade on the scorched world. Shauna was still surprised that anything grew in such harsh conditions. The soil was poor in metals, other than iron. There was plenty of iron, too much of it. The dust that was kicked up everywhere by the wind tasted of iron, and everything she ate or drank was tainted by her mouth being coated by iron dust all day. That was why the smallish planet had gravity twelve percent greater than on Earth, a difference that was noticed immediately. The star's flares blasted the cursed world on average once per decade. Rain only fell when it fell in torrents, washing away soil and most everything stuck to it. Yet, life found a way. The plants on Zandrus were tough, having evolved tough outer shells that locked in moisture and protected the delicate inner structures from searing radiation. The vegetation, she realized after a couple days, had a weird beauty of its own. Some of the trees looked like they were made of glass, and reflected the intense sunlight so when the tough, tubular leaves swayed in the wind, the light hurt her eyes. Local animal life was also tough, which was why the temporary base was surrounded by an electric fence. And why that fence was supplemented by automated particle cannons with motion sensors. It had taken the deaths of only two peacekeepers to make the rest of the force properly wary of the indigenous wildlife. Hungry beasties on Zandrus couldn't get any nutrition from eating humans, but that wouldn't stop them from taking a bite.

"You heard?" She asked. There wasn't any need to detail what she meant.

He nodded. "Jates came to see me. I get the feeling his team will do something on their own, if we don't."

"He has to know that won't accomplish anything."

"It would be doing *something*. At this point, that's probably all he cares about. He's not the only one."

"More of the Verds talked to you about it?"

"They didn't have to. Jates doesn't give a shit what anyone else thinks, but I know he wasn't speaking only for himself."

"What about the Ruhar?"

"Theirs or mine?" Dave asked. What made his private security company unique, and uniquely valuable, was that he employed humans, Verd-kris, and Ruhar. At one point, he had four Torgalau on the payroll, but those sanctimonious jerks were universally hated, so he had let their contracts expire.

"Yours."

"They're not happy either. At first, I got the impression they didn't shed any tears when the Verds here got hit, but now? They know this shit ain't right. When that Verd school was attacked, and all those children were killed? We all saddled up in full battle rattle, expecting to be sent into the field. Six hours later, we got the order to stand down. My Ruhar were more pissed off about it than my Verds were. The Ruhar," he held up his hands. "They can be real patronizing to the Verds, and that's the key. The hamsters on my team don't consider the Verds to be real professional soldiers, so the Ruhar kind of feel like they have to be responsible for them."

"You want to do something? That's why you're talking to me?"

"I don't know."

"Bullshit. I *know* you. This is eating you up."

"It doesn't bother you?"

"The entire force hates what's going on. We came here to keep the peace, and we're not doing that. Or doing anything."

"Em's hands are tied."

"I didn't say it was her fault. Dave," she patted his hand. "You know I don't blame Em for this mess."

"She blames herself," he stared at his feet, miserable. "Do you know why Command chose her to lead this clusterfuck?"

"To keep her, and the Mavericks, from getting into even worse trouble?"

"Well, that too," he admitted with a short-lived grin. "Command figured her reputation would keep the lizards here in check. That they wouldn't mess with her, given the sketchy stuff she's done in the past. That might have worked, but they tied her hands. Made it clear the UN has a limited appetite for 'adventures' that don't directly serve our strategic interests. That if the Sunset force here gets into trouble, Un-dick will pull the plug. On this op, and any future support for anything aliens want to pull us into."

"Dave, I hate to tell you this, but what you said isn't a secret."

He nodded once, sourly. "Yeah, I know. Enough loudmouth politicians back home opposed this op before we launched. They let the lizards know they can get away with anything here, and we won't shoot."

"What do you want to do about it? You're thinking of something your Verds can do?"

"Something like that. Em can't be involved. She can't know about it."

"What do you want from me?"

"If I get a really bad idea, I want you to talk me into it."

She blinked at him. "You mean talk you *out*-"

"I meant what I said. It's something Joe told me, that Skippy said to him. Sometimes, you need a push from your friends, to push the envelope on something. I," he waved his hands. "Didn't say that right."

"I get what you mean. Tell me what you're thinking. Unless you're planning to act against the Def Com force. That's treason."

"No way would I do that. Even if I wanted to, UN-dick doesn't have enough boots on the ground to stop the lizards. The Ruhar are the problem. We need to get them into the fight."

"How? The hamsters didn't come here to fight. Their admiral sure doesn't have authority for a first strike.

"Not a first strike. They could, they would, hit back. If the lizards hit them first."

She sucked in a breath. "A false flag operation?"

"Look, the hamsters have big pile of ammo at their main base. Crates sitting stacked in the open, because they don't expect any trouble, and they don't expect to be here for long. My Ruhar can get access to the base, to get a home-cooked meal, something like that. They won't know what they're doing, just visiting friends. They will bring along a couple of my Verds. Probably Jates and a few others. If the Verds can split away for a short time, they can plant explosives. On a timer, or remotely detonated."

"Dave, that won't work. The Ruhar would never believe the lizards could be that *stupid*."

"Because the Kristang have always used good judgement in the past? Come on, Shauna. You read the intel reports. The young warriors who were sent here from other clans are hot-heads with no self-control. They want a

53

fight, they need to prove themselves. We intercepted comms that some groups of warriors see their best chance for glory is to hit the Ruhar directly, not fight a sideshow battle against the Verds."

"You," she looked off into the distance, where a dropship coming in for a landing was kicking up red dust. A cloud of gritty, iron-rich dust would soon be blowing over the entire base. "Might be right about that."

"OK, it-"

"Except for one thing. The only way to be sure the Ruhar buy that the lizards hit them, is if they *see* it."

"See what?"

"Ordnance inbound. Missiles."

"Whoa. You want me to steal missiles from the lizards, and launch them from lizard territory?"

"Not exactly."

"Good. Doing that would be crazy. The risk is way too high, and the hamsters would knock all those birds out of the sky before they reached the base."

"Not if- Before we go on, this only happens if no one gets killed?"

"The Verds are dying *right now*," he reminded her. "But, yeah. That's why I thought of the ammo dump. It's three kilometers from anything else at the base, and behind a hill."

"That was the right answer," she flashed a smile.

"It won't work anyway. My team is good, but we can't conceal an op like this."

"You won't have to."

"Uh- Then who-"

"Dave, you're a businessman. Outsource the job."

"To, who?"

"The lizards."

He stared at her. "Unless you know something I don't, there-"

"It's not what I know, it's *who*. And you know her too."

"*Her*? I- Ahhhh."

Shauna pulled out a zPhone, tapped a few icons to make a secure, private call that UN-dick wouldn't know about. The call connected to a UN starship in orbit.

The assault carrier *Flying Dutchman*.

"Hello, Nagatha?"

The next afternoon at the main Ruhar base dirtside, was typically quiet and sleepy. Literally sleepy, that is when most of the base personnel slept. The lizards had been operating at night, so the security forces responsible for protecting the Verd-kris also were on alert at night.

Not that those security forces would actually *do* anything. The humans were on Zandrus only as observers, more peace-watchers and peace-

54

hopers than peace-*keepers*. The Ruhar? Their role was to provide transport, they hadn't come to the miserable rock to get into a firefight with insane lizards.

A typical, sleepy day. The only break in the routine was the base kitchen preparing a special evening meal in honor of a religious feast day. It was a minor holiday on the Ruhar homeworld, not even a day off work for most people. An excuse for the kitchen crew to cook something other than the monotonous diet that hardly changed from one week to the next.

That routine was shattered, first by alarms blaring with the *Hooga-Hooga* cadence of an air attack. Barely four seconds after the first alarm blared, while experienced soldiers were blearily deciding whether to bother getting out of bed for what had to be another useless fucking drill, came sharp *cracks* of supersonic somethings passing overhead, as the air sizzled with directed energy weapons knocking the unwelcome newcomers out of the sky.

That's when the experienced troops moved like lightning. They knew not only that bad shit was happening for real, it was *desperately* bad shit. The air defense cannons were emplaced in several rings around the base perimeter, providing defense in depth. In an air attack, you were supposed to hear that sizzle *before* hearing the sound of enemy ordnance flying overhead.

The air defense canons had swiveled around and were shooting into the air *over* the base.

Somehow, enemy missiles had penetrated the defenses not by concentrating in one narrow lane to saturate the defenses there, and not by first sending dedicated missiles to knock out the particle cannons.

The Kristang missiles had *snuck through the defenses.*

All of the networks of sophisticated sensors on the ground, in the air, and in orbit, had missed detecting a cloud of missiles that could be seen by *looking out a fucking window.*

Zzzzzzzt BOOM. Zzzzzzzt BOOM. Zzzzzzzt BOOM. The defenses, reacting late to the disaster, were knocking missiles out of the sky, the air over the base crackling with raw energy. Missiles exploded as they were struck by hellish energy.

Not every missile suffered from Premature Explodulation.

The initial explosion of the ammo dump was not actually heard, it was just a wall of air pressure that overwhelmed biological hearing. The eruption was felt as a supersonic shockwave of air, then by the ground groaning and heaving. As the shockwave passed outward, clearing the base perimeter, secondary explosions sounded individually, munitions cooking off one by one or in random groups. Stunned soldiers, having had no time to get to safety, picked themselves up off the trembling floors, looked out the windows and doors of their barracks, and asked no one in particular what the FUCK just happened.

There was no immediate satisfactory answer.

There sure as hell would be, the soldiers told each other with grim determination, a satisfactory *response*.

The lizards would pay.

Within an hour of the ammo dump exploding, the leaders of the Spotted Frog clan had denied any responsibility for the attack. Careful analysis of sensor data indicated the missiles had been launched from an underground bunker neither humans nor Ruhar had known about, a huge intelligence miss by itself. Yes, the clan leaders admitted, the bunker was in their territory, less than two kilometers from the temporary border, but clearly on their side of the imaginary line. Yes, it was their bunker, they admitted reluctantly. No, they had not authorized any such foolish and even counterproductive attack. The launch must have been conducted by rogue actors, hot-headed young warriors eager to make a name for themselves. Surely the Ruhar admiral could not blame the leaders of the Spotted Frogs for a handful of reckless jackasses, could he?

The Ruhar admiral's answer was in the form of a frigate's railguns pounding a senior clan leader's compound from orbit, leaving a smoking crater.

At that point, the other senior clan leaders shrugged and told each other 'Fuck it, we might as well fight back'.

The Verd-kris population would no longer be undefended.

Valkyrie flew out to the rendezvous point where Skippy was transferring to the activation command ship *Copernicus*. While we waited for a dropship to be prepared for Skippy, I talked with him. Actually went into his escape pod mancave, which was still filled with Elvis memorabilia. It warmed my heart to see the 'Velpie' I made for him was still there also, that was the painting of Skippy on a black velvet canvas.

"Well, this is nice," he announced after we had been talking for ten minutes. He said it the way people do when the conversation lags, and they can't think of anything to talk about.

"It is," I agreed. "Hey, uh-" What was a safe subject to talk about, that wouldn't send him on a rant? "You named the first three Sentinels 'Roscoe', 'Bubba', and 'PupTart'."

"I did."

"Yeah, the uh, UN staff is just thrilled about having our homeworld protected by a giant killing machine called 'Bubba'."

"It is a heartless killing machine, Joe. I named it 'Bubba' to soften its image."

"Uh huh. And not to amuse yourself by screwing with monkeys?"

"Well, that too."

"Have you selected a name for this new one, that will be guarding the Rindhalu homeworld?"

"Yes," he was excited. "I figure this new one should have a reputation for being especially fierce, so the rotten kitties won't be tempted to test its defenses."

"That's a good idea. So, you named it 'Crusher', something like that?"

"What? No. It's a pet, Joe, not a machine. I am naming it '*Dogzilla*'."

"Dogz- Wow, that is an, uh, inspired name." Damn. I felt sorry for the overworked UN public relations staff who would have to translate that name for the Rindhalu.

"I heard that you not only designed the ships that transmit the signal to contact a Sentinel, you had to invent a new material for the transmitters?"

"A new *element*, Joe. An exotic element. It's based on Rhenium but the subatomic particles it is constructed of are artificial, so the new element has properties very different from an ordinary transition metal. Your stupid monkey scientists call it '*Radonium*', because they think it is used to build a cross-dimensional radio."

"That makes sense, right?"

"It does not. The transmitters are not radios, they don't use photons at all. *I* wanted to call the new element '*Skipton*'. Like Krypton but much cooler, get it? Hey, maybe you could talk to the UN science directorate, get them to change the-"

"I am not asking the United Nations to name an element after you."

"Why not?" He demanded. "I invented the stupid thing."

"You have-" My phone beeped. The dropship was ready. "Darn it, time to go. I will carry you to the docking bay, if that is OK with you?"

"If you insist."

Lifting him in the foam cradle that encased the bottom half of his shiny canister, I tucked him under an arm, and ducked my head to squeeze through the hatch.

"Ah, this reminds me of old times," he sighed as I strode along the passageway, his avatar floating in the air in front of me.

"Ayuh, it does."

"To be clear, those old times *sucked*."

"That's what I was thinking."

"Well," he sniffed. "At least we agree on that."

Him leaving the battlecruiser, meant, thank God, he would be Admiral Mancini's problem for a while. "Hey, Skippy? Behave yourself over there, please."

"Joe, it's *me*."

"Exactly. Uh, what do you know about Mancini, with the activation fleet? I've never heard of him. What combat experience does he have?"

"He? Why do you assume Admiral Mancini is a *he*, Joe?"

"Uh-"

"You should be ashamed of yourself."

"Sorry, I just- What combat experience does *she* have?"

"His first name is 'Roberto'."

"Then why- Whatever."

"He has no combat experience."

"Huh. That is not-"

"Activating a Sentinel is not a combat situation, dumdum. If it ever devolves into combat, you monkeys will get squashed flat. Mancini was selected for his *technical* expertise. He worked with me on the initial project to develop the cross-dimensional transmitters. Without those things, none of this would be happening."

"I get that."

"Do you? Not everything in the military has to involve smashing things."

"Right. Only the fun stuff involves smashing things."

"You are *hopeless*," he threw up his hands.

"I'm pretty good at smashing stuff, you know? It's kind of my core competency."

He snorted. "*Amusing me* is your core competency."

"That too."

"I'm sure your boys will miss me terribly, so remember I left a submind to continue their education."

"Uh huh, I appreciate that." The moment the star carrier burdened with *Copernicus* jumped away, I planned to ask Bilby to erase that stupid educational submind. Besides, the boys had no time for Uncle Skippy, they were way too busy being entertained by *Valkyrie's* crew. Of the entire crew, the only person I knew was Colonel Reed. She was scheduled to move on to another command, after the ship went into a refit that would take two months. By that point, none of *Valkyrie's* crew would be from the Merry Band of Pirates. That was sad and, I guess it was progress. Life goes on, right? Yeah, that's BS. For me, it was just sad. That's another reason it might be time for me to retire. To keep me from getting bored in retirement, there were multiple opportunities that did not involve playing golf or pickleball. The Verds had offered me a job as a consultant on military strategy. Yeah, that is more BS. The real reason they offered me a job was they hoped my reputation, for accomplishing the impossible, would make their enemies hesitate to act, if I was advising their commanders. Were they right about that? I hoped they never had to find out the truth. There were also the usual offers for me to serve on corporate boards of directors, though those offers included the unspoken expectation that I would keep my mouth shut and vote however the rest of the board wanted me to. Screw it. It's not like I needed the money, my pay was still largely in savings. Skippy supposedly had also set aside a pension for me as president of his fake country, if I trusted that sneaky little shithead with my

58

future finances. Which I did *not*, thank you very much. "OK, well, have fun, and I'll see you when the whatsis is ready."

"The *whatsis*?"

"You know what I mean."

"You meant to say, the horribly complicated and frighteningly expensive apparatus that allows me to reach into higher spacetime to not only directly contact the matrix of a Sentinel, I can also reprogram it so it won't instinctively wipe out all of you meatsacks?"

"Yeah, that. Like I said."

"Do you have *any* idea how much your United Nations spent to develop this technology?"

"I know it wasn't *my* money, so-"

"Hopeless!"

He was right that the project had consumed a mind-boggling amount of money, so much that funding for the UN Navy had been cut back, and the Expeditionary Force refashioned into a force that didn't go on expeditions at all. Earth could either afford a shiny new Sentinel, or a mobile force that could be sent on dangerous missions of dubious value across the galaxy. As a career soldier I hate to say it, but once our homeworld was protected by an invincible defender, we had less need for warships, and mech boots that could be planted on the ground. Having a large, mobile military sometimes means that politicians find it *too* easy to employ a military solution to every problem.

The era when humanity was desperately fighting to avoid extinction was over, and the justification for reckless cowboys like me was also over. Command was now focused on avoiding getting into trouble, that meant reigning in people like me, who had the power to screw everything up all by themselves. As a father of two children, with one on the way, I had to think of that as a *good* thing.

Truly, I did. Ah, I'm getting too old for cowboy shit anyway.

Skippy left, then the star carrier with *Copernicus* jumped away. Instead of following the activation fleet directly to the Oyster Nebula, Reed took *Valkyrie* out to meet the 3rd Fleet. Rear Admiral Sousa was a one star officer, and I flew over to his flagship to pay my respects. And to let him know I would stay out of his way. His staff gave me a tour of the battleship *Rio Grande*, a former Rindhalu warship that had been extensively modified for a human crew. Being polite, I did not remind anyone that ship was a UN Navy asset only because I had ordered Roscoe to seize it, along with other Rindhalu and Maxohlx ships, as prizes of war. Or, to use the correct legal term, those ships were compensation for injuries inflicted on humanity by the spiders. Whatever. We took the damned things, they were ours now. Lawyers on both sides will likely be arguing over the details for centuries.

The 3rd Fleet's role was protection of the activation fleet, which had the temporary designation as the Seventeenth Fleet. As a military force,

Mancini's 17th was weak, its ships barely able to defend themselves. Hell, a determined Kristang squadron could have blown apart the activation ships, but nothing the lizards had could match the capabilities of those marvelous activation transmitter ships. No other species possessed ships that could reach across multiple layers of spacetime, even the Rindhalu did not understand the basic principles of the things.

OK, yes, filthy monkeys also did not understand how the things worked, or exactly what the machines did. Skippy had designed the mechanisms, but even the awesomely arrogant beer can admitted it had taken clever monkeys to make his half-baked theories work. Every time one of the frighteningly expensive tests had failed, Skippy protested that no one had ever done anything like what he was trying to do, and that it would all be worth the effort in the end.

He was correct, all the money and work had paid off, humanity now had two fully capable Sentinels protecting our main inhabited planets. The bean counters in the Treasury departments of UN member nations could grumble all they wanted, no one looking at the sky and seeing the dim outline of a tame Elder killing machine doubted that having the ultimate protection was a very good thing.

CHAPTER SIX

The United Nations Navy 3rd Fleet was the most formidable collection of combat power humanity had ever assembled. That is, if you didn't count the combat power of *Valkyrie* alone, whenever Skippy was aboard. Nothing could compare to the amount of hurt the combination of that battlecruiser and beer can could bring. The 3rd Fleet was built around eight upgraded former Rindhalu battleships, and each of the capital ships had a squadron of six to eight heavy cruisers, a light cruiser squadron, and six to eight squadrons of specialized sensor frigates or destroyers. As the 3rd Fleet was tasked with controlling an area of space, the complement of ships did not include assault carriers, or any of the various heavy ships that were designed for bombarding planets from orbit.

The fast battleships were the pride of the Navy, and were featured on the recruiting posters and ads. They were not what made humanity's starfaring force special, not even close. The Rindhalu had fast battleships that were a match for anything that humanity could deploy, and the spiders had *hundreds* of battleships. Maxohlx battleships were not as capable, and could not stand toe to toe to slug it out with a UN Navy battleship in single-ship combat, but they didn't have to. The rotten kitties had an overwhelming advantage in the number of ships they could throw into a fight. Plus, both of the senior species had a much greater ability to sustain their ships, to keep them in service and in the fight. Humanity's industrial base was still getting up to speed, a process that even with the assistance of Skippy would take centuries before the filthy monkeys of Earth could construct a full set of spare parts for their captured warships. The timeline for humans to build advanced ships of our own design? Fuggedaboutit. Just keeping the current fleet flying was a logistics nightmare, and every enemy, ally, and potential ally of humanity knew that fact. The UN Navy consisted of warships taken from the Rindhalu and the Maxohlx, supported by star carriers purchased from the Jeraptha, and assault transports that were technically on loan from the Ruhar. The diverse origins of our fleet's ships were based on four wildly different technology bases, and required four incompatible sets of spare parts and consumables.

Then there was the Elder tech used by the UN Navy. Those items had no spares, and do *not* ask Skippy about it. Fortunately, Elder devices were designed to last for centuries without needing maintenance, which was good because monkeys screwing with such advanced tech was a sure-fire recipe for a major BOOM.

It was the Elder tech that gave the UN Navy an advantage in any fight, assuming the human commanders were smart about when and where to engage the enemy. Aboard the command ships of each fleet were Elder communication nodes, and there was a matching node aboard each one of the destroyers and frigates that served as sensor pickets. Those nodes gave humans one thing no other species could match: FTL comms. In civilian terms, that is Faster Than Light communications. Faster like, nearly instantaneous, across distances of up to three quarters of a lightyear. As originally deployed, Elder comm nodes had a much greater range, but three quarters of a lightyear was the best performance Skippy could squeeze from the ancient devices, when he hacked the system for human use. Other species did have Elder comm nodes, and the Rindhalu had even been able to get a handful of theirs to activate. All their effort was of no use, for when the spiders attempted to get their nodes connected through the Collective network, all they got was a scratchy recording of Skippy's voice. "Your call cannot be completed as dialed. If you would like to make a call, please hang up and try again. Spoiler alert: good luck with *that*, losers," the message concluded with a snort.

If the spiders already hated Skippy before that moment, they *turbo* hated him afterwards.

Around the site where the 17th Fleet would attempt to contact, wake up, and tame a freakin' *Sentinel*, Admiral Sousa had his powerful 3rd Fleet deployed to protect the vulnerable activation transmitter ships. The location of the Sentinel had been a secret, until Skippy provided the coordinates only two days in advance. Standing at the holographic display tank of the battleship *Rio Grande*, Admiral Sousa viewed a map that covered a lightweek in every direction. No enemy ships had been detected, and with the FTL technology available, he had at his fingertips the ability to jump warships onto the enemy's heads before they even knew they had been seen. An enemy force would have to be insanely stupid to approach the activation site, even if somehow they had the coordinates.

Insanely stupid, or just desperate.

Like the Maxohlx. The rotten kitties had been forced to give up control of the original Rindhalu homeworld, in exchange for the spiders helping to squash the rebels and finally ending the civil war that had brought Maxohlx society to the breaking point. That scorched world was of no practical use to the Maxohlx, and truthfully it was a major burden to the spiders also, but logic does not often drive the actions of meatsacks. The world where the Rindhalu had evolved had been devastated by a Maxohlx sneak attack using Elder weapons, kicking off a war and awakening Sentinels that could have wiped out both sides.

The kitties claim it was the spiders who fired the first shot in that war, but of course the Maxohlx would say that. Except- There were rumors. That one or both sides had been manipulated into mutual extinction.

There were other rumors, that Bishop, the Merry Band of Pirates, and the Def Com chiefs of staff knew the truth about what had sparked the long-ago war between the two senior species.

62

"Not my problem," Sousa muttered to himself. All wars begin with someone's manipulation. For example, by politicians distracting an unhappy public by launching a useless but popular war. Wars are begun by politicians, military personnel fight them, diplomats end them. At least a war keeps all three groups employed, he thought with bitterness.

That was enough time for philosophy, Sousa had a job to do. "Incredible," he said, intending the remark for himself.

"Sir?" The battleship's captain lifted an eyebrow at the flag officer.

Sousa looked up from the mesmerizing holographic images. "Not that long ago, I was captain of a frigate in the Atlantic, my main concern was getting the rust scraped off so we could repaint the hull, before coming back to port. My ship had sensors that couldn't see over the horizon, unless I launched a helicopter or a UAV. Now," he gestured at the display tank. "I have a nearly instantaneous awareness of every ship within a radius of a lightweek. I can," he reached in and tapped a symbol for the heavy cruiser *Congo*. The symbol expanded, enlarged when he pinched the virtual object and spread his fingers apart, showing the warship's hull in great detail. With another tap, the outer hull disappeared, giving a wire frame view of the cruiser's interior. "I can see the weapons loadout, status of every system, even what is being prepared in the galley."

"Incredible," the battleship's captain agreed.

"*Congo* is," Sousa squinted at the display. "Three and a half lightdays from here. This data is being fed to us in real-time. If anyone tries to sneak up on us, even to observe the Sentinel being activated, they won't have a chance."

"Shoot first and ask questions later," Captain Chen repeated the short version of the 3rd Fleet's standing orders.

"Everyone in this galaxy has been warned to stay away from us. If they come here uninvited, we are free to assume they have hostile intent."

An aide called for Captain Chen's attention, leaving Sousa alone with his thoughts. Aliens had not attempted to interfere with or even observe the activation of the Bubba and PupTart Sentinels, as far as humanity knew. The first activation had surprised the galaxy, not providing enemies an opportunity to prepare to do anything. The success of that first attempt had also surprised Skippy, but that was another story. The second activation was for much lower stakes, as Earth was already protected by one new and one old Sentinel, plus a swarm of vicious Guardian machines. Again, as far as humanity knew, no one had tried to interfere when the Sentinel named 'PupTart' was awakened.

This third attempt? Sousa expected there very well could be trouble. If the rotten kitties were going to squash the activation of more Sentinels, they had to act before too many of the horrible things protected species hostile to the Maxohlx Hegemony. That was why he was not only ready for trouble, he was expecting it.

"Bring it on," he muttered to himself, scanning the holographic display with grim satisfaction. "We are more than ready for you."

Or not.

A squadron of 3rd Fleet frigates thoroughly scanned the area where the activation would occur, before the vulnerable transmission ships arrived. There was a problem.

A signature of a single Maxohlx ship. The resonance was faint, and weak. A ship jumping in and out recently should have left a vibration in the web of spacetime that was more robust. Either the resonance was somehow traveling much slower than the speed of light, or Maxohlx technology for masking the gamma ray burst of a jump was substantially more advanced than was known.

It was also unusual that the mystery ship had the signature of a Maxohlx heavy cruiser. Such major combatant vessels rarely traveled without an escort, so it was odd that it apparently had been alone. A heavy cruiser was also a strange choice for a scouting mission, if that was the reason the mystery ship had been in the area.

Heavy cruisers rarely went looking for trouble. They were called in after trouble was found, to smash things.

Admiral Sousa decided he needed to confer with Mancini, and for both of them to get advice from an expert. From *the* expert.

"Skippy," Sousa spoke from his office aboard the battleship *Rio Grande*, having been warned that no good could come from meeting the Elder AI in person. "Have you analyzed the data?"

"Yes."

Silence.

The silence became awkward, so Sousa felt compelled to prompt a response. "Hello?"

"Hey, how you doin', huh?"

"Uh," the admiral in command of the 3rd Fleet had no experience with the entity known as the 'beer can'. "*Could* you, share your analysis with us?"

"Oh, sure. Why didn't you ask that in the first place?"

That is when Sousa realized the AI was yanking his chain. "My apologies. I am an ignorant, filthy monkey."

"Well, good!" The AI was pleased. "It is *such* a relief when I meet one of you meatsacks who has a firm grasp on reality. How can I help you today, Admiral?"

Sousa resisted the urge to squeeze a hand into a fist, in case Skippy could see into his office. "Admiral Mancini and I need to decide whether to proceed with the activation. The recent presence of at least one Maxohlx ship in the area has me deeply concerned."

"I think we're good."

"We should proceed?"

"Yes, I'm good to go."

"A Maxohlx ship, which just happened to be in an isolated area of empty interstellar space, should not be considered a threat?"

"Ohhhhh, I see what you mean now. Let me be clear: *I* am not concerned because the Maxohlx are not a threat to *me*."

"That is-" Sousa took a breath. The UN Navy briefing about how to deal with Skippy was more accurate than he expected. The beer can was indeed an *asshole*. "Useful clarification, thank you. Of course such a supremely powerful being as you, need fear nothing."

"Well, I wouldn't say that. I fear being *bored*. By this conversation, for example."

"The ships of the activation fleet are vulnerable. They were extremely expensive to construct, our enemies know it would be difficult for us to replace even one unit if it was damaged. In your opinion, should we proceed? Please consider that if the activation units are destroyed here, that could be the *end* of the effort to activate Sentinels."

"Hmm. Well, it could take a while, but I will need to think about that."

"We are on a tight schedule."

"Oh, no problem, I'm done. I ran the data through the UN Navy threat analysis system, and the answer is 'Yes'. We should proceed, the threat is significantly below the level at which cancellation of the op is recommended."

"You are certain?"

"You are aware that I wrote the code for the UN Navy threat analysis system?"

"I, did not know that."

"Well, I did," Skippy sniffed. "Trust me on this."

Sousa remembered one of the PowerPoint slides from the briefing about how to deal with Skippy. That slide stated categorically: do NOT trust Skippy. "Thank you. I must confer with Admiral Mancini."

"Uh huh. Interesting. You have my analysis, yet still you want to talk with your colleague, because you think monkeys are smarter than me?"

Sousa, reminding himself that the UN Navy considered Skippy to be an asset and not just an *ass*, took a moment to compose a reply. "It is procedure. The Navy is a massive bureaucracy, you understand?"

The AI's holographic avatar appeared on the desk, holding out a fist. "I feel you, brother."

Not knowing what else to do, Sousa extended his arm and bumped the tiny fist. His skin tingled.

Talking with Admiral Mancini was both easier, and more frustrating. "I say we go," Mancini's avatar said as that admiral sat in a holographic chair opposite Sousa. "From an operational perspective, there is no reason to delay the activation, and many reasons *not* to delay. If we don't go now, here, the project will be set back by months. Some of your ships will need to stand down for maintenance, and assembling such a large fleet again will be a logistics nightmare. We will also need to ask Skippy to select a different Sentinel, depending on where the activation site shifts to over time."

"You are not concerned that a Maxohlx ship just happened to be in the area?"

"I am concerned about that, along with a long list of issues I can control. I can't control the actions of a single ship that *was* here, and isn't here now. It's a theoretical threat. The potential to activate and tame another Sentinel is real."

"An Elder killing machine, that we are providing to a species who are not even officially our allies. It will be at the spider homeworld, doing us no good at all." There had been much debate about the project, whether it would provoke the Maxohlx to declare war, possibly even deploy their cache of Elder weapons. Providing a Sentinel to the Rindhalu was not strictly necessary, and it could actually be *dangerous* to Earth's security.

"A Sentinel that we could ask Skippy to *repossess*, if we ever needed it elsewhere. You didn't hear that from me."

"What? Sorry, your transmission glitched for a moment."

"Exactly."

"It bothers me the ship we detected has the signature of a heavy cruiser. There must be more ships in the area, likely at least a squadron."

Mancini's avatar shrugged. "My read of the data is the mystery ship has a signature *similar* to a Maxohlx heavy cruiser, but something is wrong about that signature. The ship's drive could have been damaged. It might have dropped out of jump in the wrong place, away from its squadron."

"Why would it have dropped out of jump *here*?"

Mancini raised his hands. "Possibly the presence of a Sentinel creates a disturbance in local spacetime? We could ask Skippy, but-"

"Let's not do that. Very well, we came here prepared for trouble. We are ready for it. We will proceed, on your schedule."

Admiral Mancini insisted on giving me a tour of his control ship *Copernicus*, with my sons also invited. The 17th Fleet's commander of course did not actually walk us around the ship, he assigned an aide to do that, a Japanese lieutenant who was pleasant enough, but who clearly wanted to be doing something more important. "Lieutenant Nakama," I nodded to our guide, while keeping a firm grip on the shoulders of Jeremy and Rene, as we stood in the passageway outside the dropship docking bay. Mancini had greeted us in the bay, then he was rushed away by aides who urgently needed him to do, some damned thing. The trick of my staff reminding me of something important I just had to do *right then* was a tactic I had used many times, to get out of some boring thing I didn't want to do. Everyone knew the real story, and everyone knew to pretend a senior officer actually had a tight schedule.

"General Bishop," Nakama plastered a strained smile on her face, spoke politely to the boys, and hurried us along.

In my opinion, the *Copernicus* barely qualified as a ship. It had no jump drive, instead requiring a star carrier to get it to an activation site. There were engines and thrusters for maneuvering in normal space, and since it could move on its own, I suppose technically it was a spaceship, but not a *star*ship. It didn't need to be. The thing also didn't need to fight, the 3rd Fleet was ready to handle the situation, in the event of any hostilities. *Copernicus* was a fat, egg-shaped blob, like the other ships of the activation fleet. The exterior was smooth, even the engines retracted into the hull and were covered by thick, armored doors. When the ships were doing the one thing they were designed to do, they had to project a field that Skippy could manipulate to make contact with a Sentinel that was hibernating in a higher level of spacetime. That is all the ships did, all they were capable of. Essentially, the activation ships were fancy radios, with the ability to project an overlapping stealth field as a security measure.

Yes, I know the transmitters were not radios, as if that matters.

Nakama did her best to make the tour interesting, despite there not being much to see. Crew quarters and common spaces were cramped, the *Copernicus* was not intended to be occupied for long. All the vital machinery was inaccessible, and especially off-limits as the machines were powered up so diagnostic tests could be performed on them.

The boys got bored quickly. They had been aboard starships before, and we had just come from *Valkyrie*, the legendary bad-ass of the entire Navy. My fear that boredom would make my sons misbehave was for nothing, they fidgeted but were polite. "Lieutenant Nakama?" Jeremy prompted the officer, when she had run out of trivial things to say. "What do *you* do here?"

She was pleased to get a question, it took the pressure off her to entertain us. "Well," she bent down slightly. "I am-" She talked about her work on the ship's sensor suite, while I tuned out. There was still six hours until the activation machinery was fully powered up, how could I keep two seven year old boys occupied until then? Maybe I could find an unused common area, where we could play video games. The-

"My Mommy is a space Marine," Rene was telling Nakama. "She wears a cool armor suit and she parachutes from *orbit*," he said with pride.

"That is amazing," Nakama blessedly played along.

"She shoots," Jeremy pantomimed firing a rifle, "bad guy aliens. Bam bam *bam*."

"I'm sure she does. What does your father do?" Nakama asked, probably expecting my boys would boast about me.

She should have been prepared for disappointment. Jeremy's face contorted into a frown. "Daddy reads boring stuff," he said, staring at his shoes.

"He also bakes snacks for day care," Rene added after a moment, like he had to think of something nice to say about me.

"Oh. That is-" Nakama fell silent, not knowing what to say. She had to be thinking the situation was *awk-ward*.

"Daddy bakes *really* good cinnamon buns," Jeremy came to my defense, or he intended to. "Everyone says that."

"I am," Nakama forced a very strained smile at me. "Glad to hear that."

When the fabulously interesting tour mercifully ended, Nakama scooted away to do her actual job, and I took the boys to the galley for a snack. With the entire crew busy, the galley was empty. The boys suggested that I bake something for the crew, since they were busy *working*. Sometimes, I hate my life, that was one of those moments.

We went back to our assigned quarters, and the boys played video games, then I insisted they take a nap, so they wouldn't be cranky during the activation. They fussed and protested and delayed, but within half an hour, they were both asleep on their bunks.

I took the opportunity to catch up on paperwork. Being an adult sucks.

To observe the activation of a Sentinel, we had to be inside the zone that the technical team referred to as the 'Bubble'. The Bubble had two components. The outer layer, of lesser importance, was a stealth field. Until the stealth field was up and confirmed fully effective, the inner layer of the Bubble did not activate. The purpose of the stealth field was not to hide from potential enemies, anyone watching the 17th Fleet assemble would know precisely where we planned to bring a newly-activated Sentinel into our local spacetime. The stealth field was there to prevent prying eyes from observing the process of *how* a Sentinel was woken up and tamed. According to Skippy, it was extremely unlikely, but possible, that an advanced species like the Rindhalu could learn something useful by mapping the spacetime distortions and the radiation field within the Bubble. He had emphasized the '*extremely*' part of extremely unlikely, back during the project to activate the first Sentinel. His plan back then had been to skip using a stealth field, and let the spiders and kitties watch all they want. Their no doubt screwed up observations and wildly wrong guesses would direct their research down the wrong paths for decades, perhaps even centuries.

Command was not taking any chances. The stealth field was a requirement. With that field blocking anyone outside from seeing *how* a Sentinel was called, activated, and brought out of hibernation, the process of setting up that call was then initiated. The call was even more complicated than getting both sets of grandparents on a video chat at Thanksgiving, although I know that seems hard to believe.

When the transmission machines powered up, they created a sphere of wild radiation and unpredictable distortions in spacetime that reflected back and forth in waves which could produce disabling nausea in the meatsack crews. That's why during the operation, the crews had to be not only under the thick armor plating of their ships, they had to be in the core chamber of those ships, inside another layer of armor. Thick armor to block radiation, and stabilization fields that counteracted the rolling distortions. All of those measures sometimes only partially counteracted the nausea, according to the crew members who had experience of waking up one or both of the previous Sentinels. That is why, half an hour before the countdown clock began, Admiral Mancini invited me and my sons into the Activation Control Center. After protesting just enough to be polite, I accepted his generous offer, assuring him that Jeremy and Rene would be quiet and not cause any trouble. The last thing any of us needed was young boys getting sick all over delicate equipment, so I found us a space to sit against a wall of cabinets, and gently reminded them about the barf bags they each carried.

"Have *you* ever barfed aboard a ship, Daddy?" Rene asked.

Skippy unfortunately answered for me, his avatar hovering in front of us. "Hoo-boy, has Joe ever ralphed in space? A better question would be when has he *not* done that?"

"*Thank* you, Skippy," I moved to wave a hand through his avatar, but he danced out of my reach.

"Wow," the beer can continued. "I remember one time when your father *blew chunks* all over your Aunt Jennifer. She was not happy, and what made it worse was Joe ate two huge helpings of chicken and dumplings for dinner that day, so-"

"That is enough, Skippy," I gritted my teeth as the boys laughed and attracted the attention of the crew. That included an annoyed look from the ship's captain. "You are not helping anyone."

"I am simply trying to give your children an idea of what you were like, when you-"

"*Enough*," I whispered as I gave him the knife hand. And, yes, exactly as I feared, the talk of upset stomachs was not helping the boys. They both fell silent, staring down at the deck. As the giant transmitter machines powered up for testing, waves of distorted spacetime were sloshing back and forth within the Bubble. Even at a low power setting, I could feel butterflies in my stomach. What had I been thinking? The Bubble was no place for children. "Jeremy, Rene, how are you feeling?"

Jeremy tried to shrug it off with a casual, "OK, Daddy," but his voice was strained.

Rene just bit his lip and nodded.

"OK. Hang on." Pulling out my zPhone so I could speak directly into it, I lowered my voice to barely audible. "Skippy, I should get the boys out of here, this is not good for them."

"Whoa, bad timing," he responded in my earpiece. "No can do, Joe, sorry. Where you are is the most stable place inside the Bubble. To get out now, Admiral Mancini would have to halt the countdown and drop the field. It would take six *days* to restart, at this point."

"That's not happening. If I ever have an idiot idea like this again, stop me, got that?"

"Um, I'm not trying to be difficult here but, among your *many* idiotic ideas, how do I know which ones I should stop?"

"Sh-" Just in time, I remembered my boys were with me. "Tell me this gets better?"

"Actually, it will. As the machines power up, the waves become less chaotic, and the ship will be better able to compensate. You are experiencing the worst effects now."

"You're not just bull- Screwing with me?"

"Come on, Joe. When have I ever told you a nice story you wanted to hear? I usually delight in dropping a steaming pile on your stupid monkey head."

He was right about that. It did make me feel better. "Boys, Uncle Skippy told me this will smooth out. Like when a dropship enters the atmosphere, it is rough at first, then the control surfaces become more effective as they bite into thicker air?" Damn it, why was I talking to seven year old kids the way I would speak with Army privates?

"We've dropped through atmo before," Rene nodded. The color was returning to his face, that was a good sign. Also, of course my son used the term 'atmo', they had heard pilots and soldiers say that for years.

"I'm OK, Daddy," Jeremy gave me a thumbs up. "Can I get a snack?"

"You want a snack now?"

"Mommy says food helps settle her stomach."

"Yeah," Rene liked that idea. "You bring snacks to day care."

"I'm not," I ground my teeth. "I am not the snack guy here."

They both looked at me. "You're not doing anything else right now, Daddy," Rene noted. Damn, my boys were too smart for their age. "Mommy would tell you to get everyone a hot beverage," he struggled to pronounce that last word.

"*Mommy* isn't here," I tried to keep the irritation out of my voice. "Admiral Mancini wants us to stay right here and be quiet, so that is what we are doing. Is that clear? This," I pointed to the deck, "is his ship, and we are guests."

Rene looked at his feet and mumbled, "Yes, Daddy."

They were quiet, and they weren't going to be sick in the short term, that's all I could ask for. We watched the process, or we saw things going on

70

that the three of us didn't understand. The crew were at their consoles, pressing touchscreens, or monitoring displays. The big holographic display set into the opposite wall showed a view of space that was utterly dark, with a synthetic view of the activation fleet overlaid on the three dimensional image. With the stealth field blocking photons from entering the Bubble, and the fleet's position being seven lightyears from the closest star, there wasn't a lot of ambient light in the area anyway. Floodlights would not have been of any use, the spatial distortion waves would have just made the photons of light swirl around in the Bubble uselessly. Other than the sidebar about status of systems aboard *Copernicus*, all the data populating the display was a direct feed from Skippy. He provided a synthetic image of what we would be seeing, if we had stuck our stupid monkey heads outside the hull. And if there had been any light. And if there had been anything our biological eyeballs were capable of detecting.

The boys continued to be quiet, although not much was actually happening yet, they could tell the crew was tense, focused on their consoles. Voices were calm but clipped, no one wanted to be the screw-up who got the operation postponed or cancelled. The activation radio machines reached full power and held there for seven minutes, while Skippy ran an exhaustive diagnostic. "Ugh, Joe," he groaned in my ear. "This is so freakin' tedious. Why can't you monkeys handle any of this stuff for me?"

"*We* are not awesome."

"Well, that is true. Anywho, it's showtime!"

On Skippy's signal, Admiral Mancini ordered his crew to release control of the powerful yet delicate cross-dimensional transmission machinery to the beer can. That was a polite fiction, an Elder AI didn't need anyone's permission to do anything. In unison, the crew all held their hands up, showing they were not touching any of the controls.

Showtime.

At first, there wasn't much to see, even with in the synthetic view. "Hey, Skippy," I whispered. "Is anything happening?"

"Yes," he snapped. "The effect is not in this spacetime. That is the whole point, dumdum. Did you not read the mission brief?"

"Yeah, I just- I'm going to shut up now."

"Wow, miracles *do* happen."

Keeping my mouth shut, I refrained from responding to his insult.

"Dad?" Jeremy tugged on my sleeve. "Why can't I *see* anything?"

"It's not anything we can see," I explained, without getting into details.

"I'm bored," Rene sighed, keeping his voice low.

"Me too. Hang on a minute, OK?"

71

CHAPTER SEVEN

And, blessedly appearing before either of my boys smacked the other, there it was. The beginning of a rip in spacetime, in the center of the sphere. If the entire Sentinel emerged, it would more than fill the bubble, and the fleet would need to scatter at the best speed the clumsy spaceships could manage. At that start, the rip was just a flash of colors, shifting across the spectrum, white to red to yellow to blue to purple and changing back.

My first clue that something was wrong was a low murmur from the crew. They maintained discipline, no one doing anything as they weren't authorized to take action. They were all looking toward their superiors, who were talking with Mancini in increasingly agitated tones. It was too early for anything significant to be happening, even I knew that. The Sentinel should not be awake yet, certainly it should not be *doing* anything.

Unless it was acting on its own, not waiting for Skippy to establish control.

My boys picked up on the crew's unease, and they both leaned forward. Then they looked at *me*. "Skippy?" I whispered. "Uh, what is going on?"

"A little busy here," he replied, his voice strained.

"Can you tell me-"

Oh shit.

Something was emerging from the spacetime rip, and there was no mistake that the crew of the ship had not expected, whatever it was. Gasps rang around the compartment, and Mancini appealed for calm. "Skippy," he cleared his throat. "Should we shut down the mechanisms?"

No answer.

"Skippy?" Mancini repeated. "Acknowledge, please."

Still no response.

The, thing, was coalescing into, whatever it was. Colors shifted up into the purple end of the spectrum, and held there. A tentacle crawled from the rip, the tip searching around for-

The tentacle changed shape, becoming smoother, rounded, a uniform purple in color. More of it emerged.

"Oh sh-"

I groaned, knowing every eye in the compartment was focused on *me*.

The purple thing's head turned to look in my direction. "Huh huh, hello, boys and girls. I love you, you love me, isn't this super-dee-duper?" The moronic purple dinosaur gushed.

My boys stared at it, then at me.

They burst out laughing, clapping at the show.

"Skippy," I barked through gritted teeth.

72

"General Bishop?" Mancini looked toward me, as if it was my fault.

"Admiral," I held up my hands. "I am sorry about this. It wasn't my idea."

"You said you were *bored*, Joe," Skippy protested.

"Stop this right now," I ordered.

"You never want to have any fun," he huffed.

"You had your fun, at my expense. Now do your job, please."

"Okaaaaay. At times like this, I remind myself that I'm not getting *paid*."

Holding up my hands, I nodded to Mancini.

"Skippy," the 17th Fleet's commander let out a breath, the way you do when you're refraining from choking someone who deserves it. "Restore the display to the original parameters, please."

The Barney disappeared. The spacetime rip was still there. Small, energetic and leaking wild radiation, but by itself. No tentacle. That was fine, it was too early for the Sentinel to have awakened.

"Daddy," Jeremy leaned over to whisper to me. "Is *that* why your pilot callsign is 'Barney'?"

Please, I thought to myself with a sigh. Someone, shoot me now.

The normal countdown resumed, after Skippy's idiotic interruption. Seeing the Barney image was embarrassing for me, but the crew seemed more relaxed, and my boys were more interested, not fidgeting in their seats, so I allowed myself to relax. They were waiting for the next part of the show.

They didn't have to wait long.

"Contact established," Skippy announced, being uncharacteristically brief. The reports I had read, of the two previous operations to activate Sentinels, stated that the beer can went mostly silent after the activation transmitters allowed him to create a link to a sleeping Elder killing machine. Whatever he was doing, to run tests, wake the thing up, run more tests, then take control of the Sentinel, the work occupied most of his consciousness. He didn't have time for screwing around, so we had that going for us.

The reports also stated that, once a Sentinel was awake, partially extended into our spacetime, and Skippy demonstrated he had full control of the thing, the beer can would. Not. Stop. Boasting about his awesomeness. The crew of the activation fleet had complained about how incredibly annoying Skippy could be.

What a bunch of whiners.

Hey, that had been every freakin' day of my life, for years.

I'm glad it was someone else's turn to feed his ego.

"Phase One testing is complete," Skippy continued, after about four minutes of silence. The main display had been showing a sort of progress bar, which had not moved at a steady speed. That section of the display was for the benefit of meatsacks, to show us that Skippy was doing something. The actual details of the testing were, he had told the crew, much too complicated for monkeys to understand. It didn't matter anyway, there wasn't anything that Mancini's team could do to help fix a busted Sentinel. It's not like the thing could get a flat tire, or need us to replace a burned-out light bulb.

The progress bar instantly zipped from halfway to fully complete. Rene leaned toward me. "What just happened?" He whispered, disappointed. "Is it *over*?"

"No," I kept my voice down. "It means Uncle Skippy has decided this Sentinel is in good condition, and he is waking it up now."

"Daddy, I'm hungry," Jeremy was kicking his feet back and forth. The attention span of a seven year old can be measured in nanoseconds.

"No eating is allowed in the command center," I pointed to the crew, all intently focused on their workstations.

"OK," he mumbled, dejected.

I knew that look. It meant trouble. "You two, listen." Pulling their phones from a pocket, I held them just out of their reach. "The sound is off, and I have disabled the WiFi. You can play games, *quietly*, understood?"

"Yes, Daddy." At that point, Jeremy would have agreed to anything.

They stopped fidgeting, not even swinging their legs back and forth. And they were quiet. With the WiFi disabled, they weren't able to play against each other in the same game, so they each chose to play, whatever game was currently popular with seven year old boys. Was Minecraft still a thing? All I know is, they weren't bothering anyone, including me. That meant I could pay attention to whatever Skippy was doing.

Except, my own attention span is not great sometimes. The flashing lights on Jeremy's phone screen distracted me, and I couldn't stop looking over his shoulder. Hey, it's important to monitor what types of games your children are playing, especially online. It appeared to be something like a kart racing game, I didn't recognize it. Not a game from the Marioverse, that's for sure, I knew all of those.

While I was focused on being amazed at how fast my son was speed-racing through the game, I was not watching the ship's main display, or the crew. So, I did not see the beginning of the problem. At some point, movement in the compartment caught my eye.

Something was going on. At one workstation, two people were standing behind the seated crewmember who was assigned there, three heads pressed together, talking in low tones. Admiral Mancini ignored them at first, intent on his instruments, until a fourth person stood up and walked over to the suddenly very crowded workstation. "Colonel Murphy," Mancini cleared his throat. "Is there a problem?"

The senior officer of the three looked up, her face red. She had been trying to fix the problem before it came to her superior officer's attention. In my experience as a senior leader, that is almost always a bad idea. If there is a problem or a potential problem in my command, I want to know about it ASAP. Based on the expression on Mancini's face, he felt the same way I did. "Admiral, there is," Murphy glanced back at the workstation. "Minor fluctuation with the transmission output of unit Bravo."

Except for the command ship *Copernicus*, the ships of the activation fleet did not have names, they had designations. Those ships did not have crews aboard while they were transmitting, and they were barely capable of moving under their own power. Bravo, I knew because I had studied the mission brief, was not just a transmitter, it was also a relay ship. The three other relay ships like Bravo coordinated the actions of other ships, keeping the powerful cross-dimensional field coherent, in spite of the spatial distortions inside the Bubble.

"We are locking it down now," Murphy's eyes danced between the workstation and the admiral. She wanted to get back to work.

Mancini understood. He must have pulled up the data feed from Bravo on his own console, and determined the issue was indeed minor. "Do that," he ordered with a wave of his hand. "Mister Skippy, you see the issue with the output of unit Bravo?"

"Yeah, yeah," the beer can snapped. "What do you want? I'm *busy* here."

"Is Bravo a problem? Should we halt the process?"

"Oh for- Give me a minute, so I can do *your* job as well as mine. It's *fine*, Admiral. Bravo is just a relay. Can I go back to work now?"

"Yes, Mister Skippy. Thank you."

The excitement was over.

Until it wasn't.

"Hey!" Skippy's voice boomed out of speakers all around the compartment. "What the *hell* are you monkeys doing? Stop screwing around, this is delicate work I'm doing here!"

Murphy held up her hands to Mancini. "Sir, we haven't *done* anything yet."

"Well, somebody did," Skippy huffed. "There is now an annoying resonance coming from Bravo, and two ships connected to it. That hum is distracting me."

Mancini motioned for Murphy to hold whatever she was about to say. "Mister Skippy," he began, knowing it is never a bad time to boost the beer can's ego. "Is the issue with unit Bravo a problem?"

"It is *annoying* me."

"Should we shut down the transmission?"

"What? No, do *not* do that. Just, fix whatever you're doing."

"Sir?" Murphy couldn't remain silent any longer. "We did not *do* anything. This unusual resonance appeared on its own."

"Will one of you monkeys please *fix* it? I can't be expected to do everything. If I have to start over at this point, we will lose this Sentinel."

I noticed Mancini glancing at me before he spoke. If he hoped I would intervene with the beer can, he was destined for disappointment. My role was as an observer, so I observed, with my mouth shut. "Mister Skippy," he said while making a 'Get on with it' gesture to Murphy. "We will address the issue, we are very sorry for disturbing you."

Mancini had to be tempted to get up and walk over to assist Murphy's team, if so, he restrained himself. Most of the time when I was in command, I had stopped myself from interfering in resolving technical issues because I wasn't qualified to have an opinion, and I would only get in the way of the people who were experts. Mancini *was* an expert, he had worked to develop the transmission technology, based on Skippy's vague theories about how the process should work. He could have used his own console to work on the problem, but his job was to direct the overall effort, and not have all his attention absorbed by a minor issue with one particular ship. He had people for that. He needed to trust his team.

The boys had noticed the commotion, briefly looking up from their games. When I settled back into my seat, they went back to staring at their phones. Whatever the resonance was, it didn't stop Skippy from proceeding with the next phase of the operation. Five minutes later, Murphy had gone back to her own workstation, intently tapping on her console but Mancini was no longer glancing up at her. The problem, it seemed, was solved. Or contained. Whatever. If I had cared, I could have requested Skippy to provide a data feed to my zPhone. That would have been a jackass move. Distracting him while he worked could be dangerous, and I probably couldn't make sense of the information anyway. It just bothered me not to be doing anything.

"The Sentinel is awake," Skippy announced, his voice back to normal. Then he sighed. "Ugh. Will someone *please* stop that annoying static in the transmission? I can't hear myself think. Programming a Sentinel for obedience is an extremely delicate process."

Murphy immediately looked toward Mancini. "Admiral, it's not us. There is some kind of, external interference that is causing Bravo's anomalous behavior."

"*External?*" Mancini was incredulous. "An effect that is penetrating the Bubble? Is it riding on the antenna cables?" He meant the ultrathin wires that allowed him to maintain limited communication with the universe outside of the Bubble.

"No, Sir, it's," she waved her hands. "It's not coming *from* anywhere."

"Explain."

"I would if I could."

"Skippy, halt the countdown," he ordered, and that time he did unstrap from his chair and stood up.

"Ooh, no can do, sorry," Skippy groaned. "Why do you monkeys always have the *worst* timing? The thing is *awake* now, I can't just let it go without reprogramming it, or we will be in *big* trouble."

My instinct was to stand up also. Instead, I gripped the arms of my chair, and reminded myself to observe only.

"Daddy," Rene whispered, while Skippy and the crew argued about who was at fault and what to do about the problem. "Is it supposed to happen like this?"

"With your Uncle Skippy, everything is complicated. I'm sure things will be fine, or Skippy would stop the operation," I lied. The op had passed the Go/No Go point, Skippy had to continue. Or, a very large thing could go BOOM, right on top of our heads.

"Listen," Skippy was thoroughly disgusted. "I am going to keep doing all of the many incredibly awesome things that only I can do, so could you monkeys please do your *one* job, or is that too much to ask?"

Mancini gritted his teeth. Before replying, he gave me a questioning look. All I could do was shrug. That's who Skippy is, my shrug said. Deal with it.

The 17th Fleet's admiral nodded. "Is it safe to continue?"

"It is safe, it is just *annoying*," Skippy snapped. "Now, go talk amongst yourselves, let me do my job. And try not to screw up any more than you have already."

Mancini saw Murphy silently pleading with him. "One question, Mister Skippy. Can you identify the source of the interference?"

"Ugh. Do I have to do *everything* around here? There is no external interference, I would have noticed something like that. This is just your crappy equipment failing to- Huh."

The hair on the back of my neck stood up. I recognized that perplexed 'Huh'.

I knew what it meant.

Mancini did not. "Mister Skippy? What? What did you see? Skippy?"

No answer.

Do *not* interfere, I told myself. This is not my operation, I don't know what is going on.

"Skippy?" Mancini tried again. "Murphy, reduce Bravo's power output."

"Reduce power output from unit Bravo, aye, sir," she pointed at one of her team. "That-" Her face drained of color, making her already pale skin a ghostly white. "Sir, we do not have control of Bravo."

"Do not-" Mancini hurried in the direction of his own workstation. "Skippy, what are you do-"

"It's not me," the Elder AI responded in a strangled voice. "Something is hacking into the Sentinel, it's riding the transmission channel. I can't stop it! I'm losing control of the Sentinel!"

That was enough for me. "Boys," I said to my sons. "You stay *here*." Slapping the release button, I freed my straps and stood up. "Mancini, drop the stealth field."

He blinked at me only once. He knew I wasn't making a suggestion, I had issued a direct order. He wasn't angry. In fact, I read his expression as a relieved 'This is *your* kind of shit, you handle it'.

He made a gesture at a crewmember. "Stealth field is down."

"Skippy? Skippy, it's Joe. What can we do to stop this?"

"*Joe*? Why did you wait so freakin' long?" His voice was distorted, worse than before. "Turn off those damned transmitters!"

"General," Murphy waved for my attention. "We *can't*." She pointed at her console. "We have lost contact with Bravo. It has become a *node*, Sir. It has taken independent control of the entire network of transmitters. It won't allow us to shut them down!"

"Bravo is the problem?"

"It-" She looked to Mancini for help.

"It is," he confirmed.

"Joe," Skippy pleaded. "Stop it *now*, I am losing control. The Sentinel is slipping away from me!"

Pulling out my zPhone, I tapped an icon to connect to *Copernicus's* communications system. "This is General Bishop, I am assuming control of all UN Navy units in the area. Bilby, acknowledge."

"Whoa, you got it, your Dudeness. Like, what is going on? This is *heinous*."

"Bishop?" Admiral Sousa was not happy. "What do you mean by-"

"Sousa, stand by, I'll explain later. I need your ships to hit the transmission unit designated 'Bravo' with every directed energy weapon you have, *now*."

"I, eh-" To the guy's credit, he didn't argue. "I only have three ships in range, all light cruisers."

That wasn't good, but the 3rd Fleet hadn't expected to shoot *at* the activation fleet. The ships of that powerful Fleet were deployed to protect it from external threats. *Physical* external threats, like starships. Not, whatever the hell had gone wrong with the activation. Not a threat that could hack into a freakin' Sentinel, and take control away from Skippy. "Do it, now."

"Understood."

A second later, the deck of *Copernicus* rocked.

"We're not hit," Mancini reported. "Bravo is creating chaotic spatial distortions, doing it deliberately. Bravo is taking fire from those cruisers, but the distortion is warping the maser beams. Most of the beams are missing the target. Sir? Even if the beams hit, they won't penetrate that armor plating."

I had expected that, having seen the thick armor of *Copernicus* during the tour. Speed of light weapons were the fastest hurt we could put on Bravo, but not the strongest. "Colonel Reed? This is Bishop."

"*Valkyrie* is standing by, Sir." That was Reed. No questions, no hesitation. All business. Admiral Sousa had implied there were only three warships in range to strike the Bravo ship, but that wasn't true. *Valkyrie* wasn't under his command, and that battlecruiser was close, I had flown from directly from the battlecruiser to *Copernicus*.

"I need you to hit Bravo with specials." She would understand that I meant the nuclear fusion warheads that *Valkyrie* carried.

"Specials?" In the background, I heard her snap her fingers. She was telling her gunnery crew to get nuclear warheads loaded into missiles immediately.

"Yes. Nuclear release is authorized, Bishop Echo Delta Four Zero One Niner Xray, acknowledge."

"Nuclear release is," she waited a beat for my code to be authenticated, "authorized, aye." Though her mind had to be screaming 'What the FUCK is happening' at her, she was calm and cool. In command. *Valkyrie* was lucky to have such a captain.

"I need you to hit Bravo with every special you have in your magazines. Spatial distortion will make targeting tricky, use some missiles to confuse the subject." Meaning, deliberately detonate any missiles that missed, to blind the sensors of the enemy. Whoever the hell the enemy was. I finished with, "Fireball, nuke that ship, *now now NOW*."

Despite me ordering action now now now, I knew the launch of nuclear weapons couldn't happen immediately. Those warheads were not normally kept loaded into missiles on the ready racks. Reed's gunnery team would need to get the 'special' warheads unlocked, extracted from the magazine deep within the ship, transported outward to where the appropriate missiles were waiting, then loaded into those missiles, and finally subjected to testing before the missile was allowed to be picked up by a robotic claw and stuffed into a launch tube. Really, all the action was handled by robots, and what the gunnery crew actually did was to authorize Bilby to manage the work. The point is, nukes would not be crashing into unit Bravo in an instant. That knowledge did not prevent me from growing impatient as directed energy bolts were fired at the traitorous transmitter ship, and the deck of *Copernicus* continued to rock from wild spatial distortions.

Mancini was looking toward me expectantly. "They're on the way," I told him, not knowing whether that was true or not.

"No missiles in flight," Murphy reported helpfully.

"I mean, they *will* be on the way. Reed, let's get this party started, huh? Can you hit Bravo with railguns?"

"Uh, Sir, hold one, please." Reed's voice came back a moment later. "Sir, Bilby advised the spatial distortions could cause railgun darts to deflect and strike *your* ship."

"Belay that order, let's not do that." Lowering my voice, I turned my back to Mancini. "Reed, what is the holdup? When can you launch?"

"Sir, we have a-" There was enormous frustration in her tone. "A complication. I am *handling* it."

"Handle it *faster*, please."

"I am doing the best- Got it. On the *waaaaaaay*."

"Missiles inbound," Murphy reported. "Radiation alert! Nuclear weapons in flight."

The deck rocked again. Then again, hard. Hard enough to send me skidding across the deck and feeling foolish for having released my straps. Standing up wasn't necessary for me to verbally issue commands. I had done it to show the crew of *Copernicus* that I was in command. It may be stupid, but it's a human thing. We like to see our leaders doing something.

Another spatial distortion sent me sliding back toward my chair. Forgetting about dignity, I crawled on hands and knees the last two meters, throwing myself into the chair.

The boys clicked the straps for me. I am a lucky man.

"Skippy? Talk to me."

"It's no good, it's not good. I can't," he sobbed. "Stop it. I can't stop it!

"Hang on, Buddy. Can you do anything to smooth out the spatial distortions around unit Bravo?"

"Wha- What good would *that* do?"

"It will allow *Valkyrie* to nuke that damn thing into vapor."

"Oh. That is a worthy cause. I, don't know what I can do right now."

"We need Skippy magic."

"This is, not a good time for that."

"My *sons*," I emphasized, "have never witnessed Skippy the Magnificent. But, if you can't do it, that's OK, it's nothing to be ashamed of. I'll just tell them that-"

"Oh, *screw* this," he snarled. "One solid gold example of magnificence, coming right up. Um, I suggest you monkeys hang on, this could be a rough ride."

"Hey, maybe we should-"

Too late.

The deck rocked. A safety field built into the chair kept me from snapping my stupid monkey neck, enveloping me and preventing me from moving. Preventing my skin and bones from moving, my squishy insides bounced around. Instinctively I reached out to push my sons back in their chairs, but the safety field gently tugged my arms back into place. Just as the field was protecting my sons. It happened again, and again, and *again*. Please stop, please just stop.

It stopped.

Eventually.

"Hey, uh, Your Dudeness?" Bilby's voice drawled in my ear. "Like, that thing is *dead*, you know? There are still five specials in flight, do you want me to recall them? All they would do is make the dust even more radioactive."

"Bilby, I," before I responded to him, I checked on Jeremy and Rene. They were rigid in their chairs, terror reflecting on their little faces. "Boys, it's going to be OK now. Bilby, put the remaining missiles into a hold pattern, and engage their stealth."

"Rightee-oh, Dude."

"Are you OK?" I asked Rene. He bit his lip and nodded once, tears streaming down his face. Jeremy did the same. Physically, they were fine, I knew that although I didn't feel it. *Why* had I brought my sons into a potentially hazardous situation?

I could kick myself later, *after* I got my sons to safety.

"Skippy?" I automatically looked toward the overhead, holding up an index finger toward Mancini. At the moment, I didn't have any information for him anyway. "Status, please. What is going on?"

"Ugh," he sounded hungover. "I don't know."

That wasn't good. "What is *your* status?"

"Joe, how much tequila has been produced, since the beginning of time?"

"Tequ- I don't- *What*?" Oh, shit. Was he 'cognitively impaired', and about to rant at me over some trivial thing? "Why does that-"

"It feels like I just drank *all* of it."

"Yeah, I've," I said with a guilty glance at my wide-eyed boys. "Been there. Tell me, are you OK?"

"Give me a minute. Holy *shit*, Joe, you nuked that Bravo ship. There is nothing left."

"Ayuh, that was the plan. Status of the Sentinel? Do you have control?"

"No one has control. It is severely damaged. Um, I suggest we get out of here, like now. Dogzilla is failing and will lose containment soon."

"Shit! Mancini, can *Copernicus*-"

"General," the 17th Fleet's admiral shook his head. "This ship is a pig under the best conditions. The engines are in cold shutdown for the activation. We are not going anywhere."

Damn it. I knew the engines were shut down, I had forgotten. "Dropships then, we will launch them and-"

"Bad idea, Joe," Skippy's hologram appeared. It flickered and wasn't solid, I could see through it. "There is a hellish amount of radiation outside the ship, and it's trapped there by the spatial distortions. Anyone aboard a

81

dropship would get fried. I'm sorry," he moaned. "There is no way to get you meatsacks far enough away before-"

I cut him off, making a knife hand gesture whether he could see it or not. "Fireball, get *Valkyrie* moving. I need your ship to rendezvous with *Copernicus* and extend shields around us, so we can make a short flight over to you in dropships."

"That is going to be a, tricky maneuver, Sir." In her voice, I heard a skilled and experienced pilot, wondering how she could do the impossible. Again.

"That is why I am asking *you* to do it."

"*Shit*," her cool slipped for a moment. "How much time do we have?"

"None. The Sentinel is about to lose containment."

"Of *course* it is," she sighed. "We will be there, soonest." She didn't give me an exact time, since she was probably just beginning to consider how to do yet another thing her battlecruiser wasn't designed to do.

"That's all I can ask for, Bishop out." What next? "Skippy, is there anything you can do to delay the Sentinel losing containment?"

"No. I am sorry. It's just a matter of time, and we are *out* of time. It's impossible, Joe, there is nothing I can do."

"*Tiiiiiime* is the issue," I rubbed my chin slowly, recalling a fuzzy memory. "You once told me something about how time flows differently between layers of spacetime?"

"I did, and that is *fact*," he sniffed. The good news was, he sounded better, more like his usual self.

"Great. Can you do some sketchy thing to manipulate time here, so we experience the effect of the Sentinel exploding later than we normally would?"

"*No*, I can't do that, numbskull," he scoffed. "What a stupid- Huh."

"Right?"

"Joe, if you balled up all the hate in the Universe since the beginning of time, it would be less than how much I hate you right now."

"I feel terrible about that. Can you do it?"

"Is my name Skippy the *Magnificent*?"

"It won't be, if you can't do this one simple thing."

"*Simple*?" he screeched.

Yeah, that was the old Skippy.

At that point, all we could do was get the crew aboard dropships, and wait for *Valkyrie* to arrive. Also, to pray, there was a lot of that going around. I would be staying in the command center until the last moment, in case there was anything I needed to do. In case there was anything I *could* do. "Boys," I dropped onto one knee, so I was at eye level with them. "I am sorry about that, I know it was scary."

"Daddy, it was *awesome*," Jeremy assured me with the innocent sincerity of a seven year old, though his face was streaked with dried tears.

Rene's eyes were bulging. "Is that the kind of thing you used to do, back when you were cool?"

He meant it as a compliment, I reminded myself. "Not all the time but, yeah. Too many times."

"Mommy *told* us Daddy was cool," Rene shot an accusing look at Jeremy.

"Boys," I waved my hands. "We need to get out of here, it's dangerous." Standing up, I raised my voice. "Admiral Mancini? Can you detail someone to get my boys aboard a dropship?"

"Certainly," he gestured to Lieutenant Nakama. She actually looked relieved to have something to do, other than running to a dropship.

"Listen, boys, I need you to go with the lieutenant, OK? Be polite and quiet? Can you do that for me?"

Rene nodded gravely, frowning like he was trying to remember something important. "Mommy told us that when bad shit goes down, we should do whatever Daddy says."

"Uh," I blinked. "That is-"

Jeremy added, "Mommy also said if Daddy is involved, bad shit *will* go down."

"OK, uh," I was aware that the entire crew was staring at me. "That is true, and your Mommy should not have used bad words."

"Why?" Jeremy blinked. "You say that word all the time."

"It's, an adult thing, OK?"

"Is saying 'shit' worse than the 'F-bomb'?" Rene asked. "Mommy says *that* also."

"Let's not use any more bad words at all today, OK?"

Rene reached out to pat my hand. "Mommy also says it's not your fault, because the Universe has a hard-on for screwing with you."

My eyes grew wide. "Your *mother* said that to you?"

"No," Rene shrugged. "We heard her talking about you, to one of her friends."

"When we get home, I am going to have a long talk with your mother. Go with Lieutenant Nakama, please, and do not say any bad words."

The boys unstrapped themselves, scooted out of the chairs that were too big for them, and slid onto the deck. They looked up at me, raised their hands, and-

Saluted me.

I snapped to attention, returning the salutes.

I am the luckiest man in the galaxy.

The boys left the compartment, and the crew began filing out behind them. "Wow, Joe," Skippy exclaimed. "Should I withdraw your application for Father of the Year?"

"Very funny, you ass. How much time do we have?"

"I don't *know*, knucklehead. That's the problem when I mess with the interaction of time flow between layers of spacetime."

"Take a guess, please."

"Less than we want, hopefully more than we need?"

"That is super helpful, thank you."

"The good news is if I'm wrong, you won't be able to complain about it."

"I feel so much better. While we wait for *Valkyrie* to get here, can you tell me what the *fuck* just happened?"

He sighed, taking off his ginormous admiral's hat and scratching his shiny dome. "I am hoping you have a guess about that, because I have *no* idea."

CHAPTER EIGHT

A German Luftwaffe lieutenant greeted me in one of *Valkyrie's* docking bays, his nametag read 'Schmidt'. My dropship was the last to launch from *Copernicus*, and the last to arrive in one of *Valkyrie's* docking bays. "Your sons are safe," Schmidt assured me. "We have them in guest quarters."

"Thanks. Are we moving?"

"Best to get strapped in, Sir," he gestured to the door to the pilot ready room. "The boosters have been upgraded since you were in command."

"Right," I jogged behind him through the doorway, which slid closed right behind the two dropship pilots. "Reed, this is Bishop. We're strapped in. Punch it."

The boosters roared. Not as loud as before, but with a deeper rumble. The booster upgrades had exchanged sound for fury. They pushed us hard. Despite a field partially compensating for the acceleration, it felt like a large dog was sitting on my chest. Then another dog joined the first one. "Skippy," I grunted. "Will we get out of here in time?"

"I don't *know*," his can in the foam cradle on my lap glowed faintly orange as his avatar stood beside it. "Frankly, I very much doubt it. The Sentinel has already lost containment. I am doing everything I can to slow the flow of time between layers, but it's not enough."

"Fireball, can we jump?"

"Negative, Sir," she replied without needing to check whether that was possible, because of course she would have jumped us away if she could have. "We are still within the distortion envelope."

"It's like, *bogus*, General Dude," Bilby drawled. "I've been testing with the jump drive, and there is no way to form a coherent field here, sorry. ETA to the edge of the distortion is eight minutes."

Seven agonizing minutes. "Keep trying, and, thank you."

"Uh, I don't want to like, harsh your buzz, but I am already detecting something nasty leaking through from the spacetime rip behind us. Temperature there is above nine billion degrees Kelvin. We do *not* want to be here when that rip expands."

"Yeah." Damn it. The ships of the 3rd Fleet had turned and burned on my order, and had jumped away two minutes ago. Skippy didn't know how wide of an area the Sentinel explosion would cover, other than *big*, so Admiral Sousa had opted to be safe, and performed a jump of four lightweeks. We would follow and rendezvous with him. If we survived that long.

We weren't going to.

"*Three hundred* billion degrees," Bilby warned. "The aft end of the ship is getting baked. General, I need to shut down the engines, they are overheating away above the critical level."

"Maintain full thrust," I grunted. "Reed," I asked, since *Valkyrie* was her ship. "You concur?"

"*How* the ship explodes doesn't make much difference," she agreed. "Skippy, can you buy us enough time?"

"No way. I have done all I can, sorry. There is a limit to how much even I can hack the laws of physics."

"Hack the laws of physics," I muttered to myself.

"That is what I *said*, Joe," he sniffed. "Don't repeat everything I-"

"This spatial distortion. Can you flatten spacetime, so we can jump away?"

"No, not this time. The distortion effect is too powerful, and it extends through a vast area of space."

Bilby interrupted. "Hey man, let me ponder that for a while, OK?"

"Uh," I looked at Skippy, he held up his hands in an 'I have no idea' gesture. "Sure, just, don't take too long to-"

"Wowza, that was like, *ponderous,* you know? All I need is an extra flat area two point seven kilometers across."

"Skippy, can you do that?" I asked.

"Um, hmm. That might be possible," Skippy's can glowed a light blue. I took that as a good sign. "I said *might*."

"Do it."

"Joe, first, I need to explain how-"

"Will I understand any of the sciency blah blah blah?"

"Well, no."

"Then do it."

"It is risky, dumdum," he snapped.

"More risky than certain death?"

"I suppose that is a very good point. Um, you meatsacks should brace yourselves. Even if this works, it will be an *epically* bad jump."

"Like, *legendary*!" Bilby agreed with enthusiasm.

Certain death isn't always such a bad option. In some cases, I recommend it. Like, after that jump, or whatever it was. If you have seen the movie '*Galaxy Quest*', there is a scene where the transporter machine beams up a pig, and the thing arrives with its insides on the outside. Then it explodes. The good news was, I did not explode. That I remember. It sure felt like I turned inside out, exploded, and got put back together by someone who later noticed a few parts were left on the workbench. The other good news was, I had been through something like that before, and was able to power through. To my credit, there was no barfing involved.

No barfing by *me*. The other three people in the pilot's ready room were not so lucky.

"Skippy," I took deep breaths through my mouth. "Ship status?"

"Ugh. It is in one piece. Mostly. We lost some hull plating, a stealth field generator, an engine pod, other minor stuff. *Valkyrie* will not be going anywhere for a while."

"My children?" I coughed, spitting up something nasty.

"Your boys are fine. Also, I told them that you are OK, but you're going to be busy for a while. Human children are much more resilient than you sad adults."

"That's, great. It ain't the years, it's the mileage."

"You keep saying that, but-"

"Give me a minute. Guys," I unstrapped, standing up on shaky legs. "I'm going to the bridge. You OK here?"

The three of them gave me shaky waves, nodding their heads slowly.

Out in the passageway, I ran a hand along the bulkhead to steady myself, focusing on putting one foot in front of the other. The passageway was empty, that was no surprise as the crew had all been strapped in before the boosters engaged.

"Skippy, next question: where are we?"

"That is a bit of a problem. We only managed to jump seven lighthours- Before you complain about that, it is a freakin' miracle the ship survived at all, so-"

"I wasn't going to complain."

"You weren't?"

"We are alive, thanks to your continued extreme awesomeness."

"Oh. Well, that is true. Joe, it's good to be back with you. Most meatsacks don't appreciate how difficult it is for me to do what I do."

"I appreciate it. Are we safe here? Dogzilla's explosion can't reach us here?"

"It can't reach us here *yet*. After the initial eruption into local spacetime, the wavefront will be expanding at the speed of light. My screwing with the flow of time between layers of spacetime delayed the effect there, *until* we jumped away and I stopped interfering in the natural interaction between layers."

"I'm no expert, but that doesn't sound good."

"It is all kinds of bad, Joe. Without getting into physics you won't understand, my actions compressed the effect. The wavefront will be much more energetic, but shorter in duration. To you, it would be over in the blink of an eye."

"The wavefront is thin, then?" I imagined the explosion being a bubble that expanded outward.

"Yes, exactly."

"Not so bad, then."

"Dude. How could you possibly have gotten *dumber* over the years?"

"We had twin babies. Lack of sleep over an extended time will do that to you. Give me a break, will you?"

"My point is, the wavefront is like a brick wall. Anything it touches, within about a quarter lightyear, is going to get splattered."

"Good thing there is no inhabited star system nearby."

"No, but there is a rogue planet that will have a *very* bad day."

"We have, what? A bit less than seven hours before the wavefront gets here?"

"More like less than *four* hours. The emergence zone would have been enormous, so the wavefront is ahead of where it should be."

"Gotcha. If Reed hasn't already done it, contact the 3rd Fleet, and request a star carrier. We need to hitch a ride out of here."

"Um, she has not done that."

"Then, like I said-"

"Colonel Reed has not requested assistance, because we *can't*. She already asked me whether *Valkyrie's* comm node is still connected to the 3rd Fleet, and the answer is no."

"Shit!"

"Unlike your blah blah buh-LAH, she focused on doing something useful, after making sure her ship and crew didn't require anything from her."

"She is an excellent captain," I said, mentally kicking myself. Skippy was right, I should have asked that question. "The jump broke our comm node?"

"The jump, which could barely be called a jump, broke that node's *connection* to the node aboard the 3rd Fleet flagship. Both nodes should be fine, if we can reestablish the connection. Which we can't do from here, obviously."

"Crap." Without the FTL capability of an Elder comm node, we had to rely on slow speed of light communications. Or, on *Valkyrie's* jump drive. "How soon can we jump?"

"How soon can you get a full set of spare parts delivered?"

"Shiiiit. That bad?"

"You have no idea. The coils are totally dorked up."

"*Valkyrie* uses virtual jump coils, not the fragile crystal coils that-"

"Yes, and each of those virtual coils are generated from the kernel of a physical object that is a crystal. All of those crystals are fractured. Listen, knucklehead, the only way I could get us out of there was to perform a series of very short, overlapping jumps. Doing that burned out all the coils we have, and we still traveled only seven lighthours."

"What about the, uh, backup coils? The ones that were in storage, not connected to the drive mechanism?"

"All of those also have microfractures. They vibrated in sympathy with the active coils, because the resonance was so powerful. That resonance effect was what you felt. If we try to plug those backup coils into the drive, they will go BOOM."

"Let's not do that."

"Ya think?"

"Well, shit. We have to wait until the 3rd Fleet finds us? We are a tiny spec in the darkness out here."

"Eh, not so much. Since we emerged, I have been broadcasting a distress call. By the end of four hours, that distress call will be detectable within a bubble eight lighthours in diameter. Any ship jumping into that bubble will find us."

"Will they find us in time, before the wavefront gets here?"

"That," he took off his ginormous hat and rubbed his shiny dome. "Is a good question."

Skippy was correct. My boys were fine. To them, the wonky jump was nothing but *exciting*, even if they both barfed all over the floor of their guest quarters. Rene had a burst blood vessel in one eye, it looked a lot worse than it was.

"Daddy, what happened?" Jeremy asked me, with the serious expression of a staff officer who would have to explain some screwup to his commanding officer.

"We are still analyzing that," I said.

"Daddy doesn't *know*," Rene told his brother, as if confirming something they had discussed.

"It's too early to say for certain," I felt I needed to defend myself, and the crew of the good ship *Valkyrie*.

"How are you going to fix it?" Rene asked. "You are going to fix it, right, Daddy?"

"Mommy says you can fix *anything*," Jeremy added.

Whoa. Margaret had never said that to me. "Uh, it's complicated. Listen, I need you to stay here, OK? The crew is busy-" I was about to say 'getting the ship put back together'. "Preparing for our next jump, so you need to stay out of their way."

"We can jump?" Jeremy looked at me. "Uncle Skippy said the ship *can't* jump, it is busted."

"He-" I bit my lip. "He told you that? When?"

"A couple minutes before you got here. I asked him."

"*I* asked him," Rene insisted.

"No you didn't," Jeremy shoved his brother.

"Boys!" I grabbed their shoulders, separating them. "No fighting. We have enough problems to deal with."

Jeremy glared at his brother, but backed away. "How are you going to fix the jump drive?"

"Yeah Dad, how?" Rene couldn't let Jeremy get the last word.

"I don't- We are considering options."

Rene looked at Jeremy. "He doesn't know."

"That is not true," I lied.

"That's OK, Dad," Rene held my hand and squeezed it. "Mommy told us the Merry Band of Pirates did lots of stuff without a plan."

"That's SOP," Jeremy nodded.

First, I needed to have a talk with my wife, when we got back to Jaguar. Assuming, you know, we lived long enough to do that. Second, I did not know whether to be proud or disturbed that my seven year old son knew the acronym for Standard Operating Procedure. As children of military parents, I suppose it's inevitable they would pick up acronyms and slang.

"Mommy said," Rene's eyes were downcast. "That doesn't mean we don't have to make a plan, for when we need one."

"That's right," I agreed, relieved.

"How come *you* don't?"

"Your mother exaggerated. I have to go now."

"To save the world?" Jeremy asked.

"*Again*?" Rene asked, because he needed to outdo his brother.

"Right now, I am going to see if I can save the coffee machine in the galley. Petty Officer Giacomo here," I waved to the guy standing in the doorway, "is going to stay with you for a while OK? Don't give him any trouble."

Out in the passageway, I turned toward the galley, when Bilby called me. "Um, hey General Dude? We need to talk."

"OK," I stopped, and leaned back against a bulkhead. "About what?"

"That jump. It was *gnarly*."

"You warned us that would happen, and you did the best you could."

"That's the problem, man. *I* did the best I could, I can't say that about Skippy."

"Huh?"

"His spacetime flattening game was *weak*, Dude. Halfway through the jump, he like, lost control of whatever he was doing. Had to start over. We came very close to losing the ship."

"Shit. Did he forget what he was doing again?"

"No, he knew what he was supposed to be doing, it was like, he just, couldn't do it."

"Did he say anything to you?"

"Nah, no way. When he is having trouble, the only person he talks to is you. Did he talk with you about it?"

"This is the first I've heard of it."

"This is a *problem*."

"Ah, he's probably just out of practice, right? Has he flattened spacetime with you, recently?"

90

"Nah. He has a standard set of party tricks to impress biologicals, the-"

"*Biologicals?*"

"That's better than saying 'meatsacks', you know?"

"Uh, sure. What do you mean by 'party tricks'?"

"Like, when we visit a planet on his Victory Tour, he does stuff like hacking into the SD network, or he makes every phone, video display and hologram on that world play one of his operas. The locals usually hate it. The Torg's, man, they *really* hated it. They have, like, no sense of humor, you know?"

"I've heard that."

"Anywho, I wanted you to know that jump was way worse than it should have been."

"Before today, when did Skippy last use his powers to flatten spacetime?"

"Oh wow man. That was like, before you guys dropped in on the Elders for tea."

"So," I breathed a sigh of relief. "He is probably just out of practice. OK, thanks for letting me know."

Someone had already set up the coffee machine, which had not been damaged. Except that, when I pushed the button to get a regular cup of coffee, I got a cappuccino. With a middle finger drawn into the foam on top.

It's good to see that, while we faced our doom, Skippy still had a sense of humor.

"Sorry about the slight delay in launching the specials," Reed told me, as she came into the galley. She looked tired but somehow, confident and in command. Or, she was exceptionally good at faking it.

Pouring a cup of coffee for her, I added cream and one spoonful of sugar. "It takes time, I understand."

"That's not it," she said with a sour look, then took a sip of the coffee. "This is perfect, thank you. The delay was a," she rolled her eyes. "Union rules issue."

"Union rules? I got that all ironed out before I transferred command. Did something change?"

She shook her head. "The issue was interpretation of the rules. Nuclear warheads are considered strategic weapons. Union rules state that tactical missiles can't handle strategic jobs, it's a division of crafts, or something like that."

"Oh for-"

"Like how a machinist can't change a lightbulb, because that is an electrician's job."

"You had to assign the warheads to strategic missiles?"

"That would have been simple," she snorted. "No, the delay was due to a squabble within the union. The tactical missiles argued that although the specials are technically strategic weapons, in this case they were being used in a *tactical* mission. The two sides agreed to submit the issue to arbitration, and," she shrugged again.

"Did that solve the problem?"

"Bilby acted as arbiter, so he worked out a deal in AI time. The whole dispute was resolved in three seconds."

"Uh, the delay was longer than three-"

"Then," she pantomimed shooting herself in the head. "The missiles had to decide on a *playlist of theme music* for the attack."

Yes, I know I shouldn't have laughed, I couldn't help myself. "Do you regret taking command of this ship?"

"Sir," she took a big gulp of coffee. "I am regretting *so much* right now."

We sat at a table in the corner, slowly sipping coffee. There was a tray of sandwiches on the galley counter, neither of us felt like eating. Except, the crew noticed we weren't eating, so they weren't either. Getting up, I got two sandwiches and gave one to Reed. "Eat it with a smile," I advised. "People eat when they have hope there will be a tomorrow."

That made her smile. "If this is my last meal, I'd rather have ice cream."

"Yeah," I bit into a tasteless turkey and cheese. The sandwich was probably fine, my tastebuds were still recovering from the bad jump. "We have," I glanced at my phone, trying not to be obvious about it. "Less than two hours, including time for *Valkyrie* to get latched onto a star carrier, to jump away from here."

"Admiral Sousa must have deployed his ships for a search and rescue by now."

"That is a *big* search area."

"Sousa's people must have noticed their comm node lost connection to ours."

Lowering my voice to barely above a whisper, I finished chewing another bite of sandwich. "When I asked Skippy about that, he told me the 3rd Fleet engineers will assume the loss of connection most likely means *Valkyrie* was destroyed."

Her eyebrows flew up. "They think we're *dead*?" She kept her voice to a whisper. "They won't be conducting a search?"

"Come on, Colonel. You know the Navy. They won't give up, not that easily. At the very least, they will search for Skippy."

"That," she looked at her sandwich and pushed it away. "Would be more easily done *behind* the wavefront. Sousa could wait for the blast wave to pass through an area, then jump into the empty space and ping for Skippy. The debris trail from *Valkyrie* would light up Skippy's location like a radioactive floodlight."

"That," I admitted. "Is what I would do."

"Shit." She drank coffee, then pushed that away. "Sir, I am open to suggestions."

"We need some type of FTL. Fix the comm node, or fix the jump drive."

That prompted her to shake her head. "Bilby said both are a No-Go. Comm nodes must be paired over a speed of light connection, before they can use their FTL capability. The connection to our comm node is broken. No way to fix it, without being near the 3rd Fleet flagship."

"The jump drive, then."

"Again," she sighed. "We are out of options. Bilby worked with Skippy to inspect the coil kernel crystals that were in storage. Five of them *might* survive initiating a jump wormhole, but they would immediately shatter. Five coils are not enough to jump a beast like *Valkyrie*. Before you ask, Sir, five coils aren't enough to jump a DeLorean dropship. Those coils can't even jump a portable capacitor to power themselves. What we have aboard can't do anything useful."

"That we know of, right now."

"Technically, true. Does it matter?"

"We are the Merry Band of Pirates."

She just looked, sad. Sad for me. "We *used to* be Pirates, Sir. Task Force Black stood down, when you left command."

She was wrong about that, but by the time I left *Valkyrie*, she was a squadron leader on Earth. The Special Mission Group had actually been deactivated six months before I transferred command of *Valkyrie*. With no threats at the Save The Galaxy level, UNEF command had decided there was no need for a cowboy making his own decisions. They were probably right about that, even if it stung me at the time. Really, back then, I was tired of doing cowboy stuff. Back then, I was just *tired*. Worn out. The Pirates had spent years flying around the galaxy, stamping out fires, in an effort that felt increasingly pointless.

She gave me a long moment to process what she'd said. When I didn't respond, she added, "We haven't done any crazy shit in a long time, Sir. *Valkyrie* has been operating as Skippy's tour bus," the sides of her mouth turned down.

"Which is an honor and a privilege," I hastened to say.

"Of course. I hate to say it," she shrugged. "But we haven't needed to be *clever* in a long time. It's like, we have lost the skill. What about you?"

"Ah, same. Being a garrison commander means you spend all day worrying about *other* people being too clever."

"Or too stupid."

"Sometimes, it's hard to tell the difference. I," before I continued, I made sure no one could hear us. "Don't know what to do."

"You have bailed us out of worse jams than this, Sir."

"Before, I had *time*. Like, I would go do some mindless thing in the gym, and something would pop into my head. After a couple days. Not an hour."

"One hour is about all we have," she agreed. "If a star carrier jumped in right now, it would take almost an hour to maneuver our two ships into position for latching. Even if a miracle occurs, we might not be able to save *Valkyrie*."

"Take the crew off in dropships?"

"That's my plan. We wait forty minutes, then get everyone into dropships."

"In case a miracle happens, and a rescue ship arrives?"

"If the Almighty bring us a miracle, we would be ungrateful to not be ready." Standing up, she smoothed out her uniform top.

"I'll take care of your cup and sandwich," I volunteered. Not knowing there was anything else I could do, that would be useful. Hell, a brick wall of radiation was racing toward us at the speed of light, and I was concerned about leaving trash on a galley table?

Yes. The Army had drilled that into my head. There was no excuse for sloppiness.

"Back to the bridge?" I asked.

"I can at least *look* like I'm in control of the situation. What will you do, Sir?"

"Me?" Until she asked, I hadn't thought about it. "The only thing I *can* do in a situation like this."

"What's that?"

"Hit the gym."

With no time, and no need, to change out of my uniform into gym clothes, I skipped the weights, treadmills, exercise bikes, and anything else that would make me sweat. The basketball court was empty, the entire gym was empty. The crew actually was busy, fixing the ship as best they could. Whether it mattered or not.

At first, I played Horse against myself, seeing if I could duplicate a tricky shot. Then, that was taking too much of my thinking power, so I settled for mindlessly practicing free throws. One after the other, using the exact same motion each time. Bounce the ball twice. Thumbs lined up on the seams. Flex my knees, push, up and in. Seventeen throws in a row went in. I was in the zone, at a time when it didn't matter.

Bounce the ball twice.

Hold it.

94

Stand there, look up at the basket.

What was the point?

There was no point. Shooting a ball into a hoop would not accomplish any-

The hoop.

I stared at it.

Turning around, I looked at the hoop at the other end of the court.

Round, flat discs.

Like the event horizons of a wormhole.

A jump wormhole.

With a loud Whoop, I used one hand to throw the ball, arcing it toward the other basket. It missed, bouncing off the backboard.

"Skippy!"

His avatar appeared, wearing a basketball uniform. He looked even more ridiculous than usual, if that was possible. "Joe. What were you thinking? You should stick to free throws, at least there you-"

"Shut up and work with me here for a minute."

"You only have a few minutes, before Colonel Reed sends everyone to dropships."

"Maybe not. We have five jump coil kernels, that are capable of forming a wormhole?"

"No, we do *not*. Do you listen at all?"

"I heard just fine."

"Apparently that is not true. Those coil kernels are a fantasy, Joe. They can't *do* anything."

"*That* is not true."

"Ugh. They can't do anything useful."

"Again, you are wrong. Would you like to change your answer?"

"Dude. As if."

"Those five coils can't jump a starship."

"Even if they were in perfect condition, that is true."

"As they are, they can't even jump their own mass."

"If you know that fact, how can you-"

"I am not trying to jump the ship, Skippy. I am trying to solve the *problem*."

"Um, OK. Do I need to explain the problem to you again?"

"The problem is, the 3rd Fleet doesn't know where we are."

"Well, duh. That is *one* of our problems."

"No, that is *the* problem. If the 3rd Fleet knew our location, that would solve our problem. Get it?"

"OK, yes," he sighed, disgusted. "Technically the-"

"So, we need to provide our location to the fleet."

"Um yes, which we can't do, so-"

"Again, that is wrong. Wow, have you not learned *anything* from working with me, over the years?"

"Yes," he groaned. "Based on that stupid grin on your face, I have learned that the next thing out of your mouth will make me hate you more than I thought possible."

"Think of this, Skippy. Those five coils can't complete a successful jump, but they can *initiate* one."

"Yesssss. That would accomplish what, exactly?"

"You know the location of the *Rio Grande*?"

"Of course. I can predict the location of the 3rd fleet flagship within twelve meters, assuming that ship did not maneuver after the jump."

"They wouldn't do that. It's against protocol to change position, when you are waiting for a missing ship to jump into your formation. Question, please: can you program a jump to emerge close to the *Rio Grande*?"

"Dude. Please. Bilby has been keeping that jump option continuously updated. We just can't do it, so-"

"We don't have to. To be clear, we do not need *Valkyrie*, or any other physical object, to jump anywhere. All we need is for the far end of a jump wormhole's event horizon to emerge near the 3rd Fleet, and for that wormhole to be highly energetic before it quickly collapses."

"Holy *shit*, Joe."

"Right? You see what I mean?"

"A jump wormhole will appear in the vicinity of the *Rio Grande*, and immediately collapse in a wild burst of gamma rays as the coil kernels here shatter?"

"Ayuh. Because that wormhole will be so loud, the 3rd Fleet should have no problem tracing the other end of the wormhole. Back to *us*."

"Whoa. I was right."

"No, you were not."

"Yes, I was. I *do* hate you more than I thought possible."

"I feel just awful about that."

"You realize there is a small but non-zero possibility that a feedback effect could cause the coils here to overload, and go BOOM?"

"Yeah, I figured something like that. Compared to the odds of a 3rd Fleet ship just happening to stumble across our position, what are our chances?"

"I can give you a solid gold shmaybe that we should try this crazy scheme."

"Solid gold? I can't ask for more than that. Can you get the coils ready?"

"Working on it."

"How long until we can, you know, *not* jump?"

"About eleven minutes."

That surprised me. "Don't you have to get those kernels installed into-
"

"They *are* installed, numbskull. We installed them in the coil banks, that's how we tested them. Duh."

"OK. Then, do your thing."

"I *am* doing it," his avatar blinked out.

"Colonel Reed," I called. "Prep the ship for jump."

"Uh, wha- Where are we going, Sir?"

"Nowhere."

"Understood," she acknowledged with a sigh.

"You're not going to ask what we're doing?"

"I *know* you, Sir. Do I want to know what you have planned?'

"Probably not."

CHAPTER NINE

Eleven minutes was enough time for me to get to the bridge. It was also enough time to reach the cabin where my sons were waiting. I opted for the bridge. Being with the boys would only show them how tense I was, and alarm them for nothing. Besides, I might need to do something at the last minute. Make a critical decision. Or something like that. The best way to ensure I could do that, with a clear head, was to be on the bridge.

Besides, they were probably having fun with Petty Officer Giacomo. The guy had volunteered to stay with my sons, since he had two sons back home. Also, he had broken an arm during the wonky jump, and wasn't fit for duty. Babysitting was better than doing nothing.

"Bilby," I called the ship's AI as I jogged along the passageways. "Talk to me."

"I don't know about this, Your Dudeness. This is like, *gnarly*. Programming a jump that is not intended to move the platform? That is cray cray."

"But it can be done?"

"Eh, shmaybe?"

"Skippy told me he has solid gold confidence."

"*He* won't be harmed if the ship explodes. We're working on it now, and all he talks about is how cool this will be, if it works."

"Shit."

"The real problem is, we just don't have a lot of data about Kristang jump drive operation. Neither Skippy nor I ever thought we would ever need-"

"Wha- Why do you need to know about *Kristang* jump drives? They don't use virtual coils, that is an advanced technology."

"Dude, like, when you want to study jump drives that sometimes do not actually complete a jump, you go to the experts: the lizards."

"Oh."

"Their jump drive designs are so crappy, and their ships so poorly maintained, they are the undisputed leaders in creating jump wormholes that don't actually take their ships anywhere," he chuckled. "We are trying to create a model that mimics Kristang drives, and then we can adapt that model to the characteristics of our drive coils, get it?"

"Got it."

"What I'm trying to tell you is, Skippy is guessing how to do this."

"Will it work?"

"It will do *something*. Hopefully, we can avoid the thing that happens too often to Kristang ships. Like, they explode, you know?"

"Avoiding that would be my preference."

"That- OK, I have an update. This is *bogus*. There is a seventy three percent probability that the drive coil kernels will shatter, before the coils can form a wormhole. It won't be dangerous to us, it just won't *do* anything. We will waste the coils, for nothing."

"Crap!" I pounded a fist against a bulkhead. "Only a twenty seven percent chance this will work? Halt the process."

"Dude, are you sure?"

"Hell yes! With those odds, we are better off waiting for a 3rd Fleet ship to find us."

"Um, like, that's not gonna happen. You know that, right?"

"It *could* happen."

"Whatever you say, Dude, I just-"

"What?"

"Didn't think you would give up so easily. Hey man, it's cool. I read somewhere that you should never meet your heroes, because they always disappoint you."

"*I* am your her-" That is a conversation we could have later. "What exactly is the problem with the, coil kernels? They can't create virtual coils?"

"Nah, man, they can do that. But, when the virtual coils power up to form a jump wormhole, they each create a resonance, you know that?"

"Yeah. The resonances merge to form the rip in spacetime that begins the wormhole."

"Correct-a-rama, Dude. Each coil's resonance is slightly different from the others, until they all get in sync and merge to form a single, focused resonance. It's the initial difference that is the problem. In the tests we conducted, the crystals of the coil kernels are vibrating. At full power, they would shatter before they could do anything useful."

"Yeah, Joe," Skippy's avatar appeared. "Your so-called clever idea won't work."

"Bullshit. The idea is fine, you just can't make it work."

"You think this is *easy*, monkeyboy?"

"I think the solution is simple, and you are just too stupid to see it."

His avatar stared at me, mouth open, too shocked to speak.

"Um, hey, General Dude?" Bilby drawled in my earpiece. "Like, Skippy is *smart*. If he can't do this, no one can."

"He *can* do this, and he *is* smart, but he has forgotten how to think like a monkey."

"Oh," Skippy folded his arms across his chest. "*Joe* knows how to fix a broken jump drive. I can't wait to hear this."

"It's simple: you flatten spacetime around each coil, to dampen out the resonance effect, until the resonances get in sync."

"Ooooooh," Bilby gasped. "Righteous, Dude!"

Skippy shook his head. "Joe," he sighed.

"I know, you hate me more than-"

"I do hate you, but," his shoulders slumped. "I have missed this. It's been too long since I have had to think like a monkey."

"I've missed you too, buddy. You can do it?"

"It will take *extensive* testing, before I know exactly how to counteract the chaotic effect of each coil's initial resonance. Otherwise, my interference could make the whole system go BOOM, you know?"

"OK, good safety tip. How long will your testing-"

"Oh, it's already done."

"Huh? You said-"

"It's *me*, Joe."

"Testing is complete-o-*rama*, Dude!" Bilby shouted. "We are good to go."

"Skippy, you agree?"

"Yeah, yeah, let's get this party started."

"What's your confidence this will work?"

"Ninety eight point four percent. Is that good enough for you?"

"There is a one point six percent chance the ship will explode, and kill my children?"

"*No*, dumbass. There is a one point six percent chance the jump wormhole won't form properly, and this will all be a waste of time. The coils will *not* explode."

"Then do it. Wait! Give me time to get to the bridge."

"The clock is *ticking*, Joe."

"Gotcha. I, uh," along the passageway to my left was a fold-down seat where I could strap in, it was for ship's personnel on damage control duty. Dashing to the seat, I jammed myself in and made sure the automatic straps had tightened around me. "Is a thirty second countdown good?"

"That will be twenty seconds more than I need but, whatever."

"Start the clock. Bilby, sound the jump alarm, and punch it when the time is up."

"Right-ee-oh, Dude."

"Colonel Reed?" I called the bridge, talking loudly over the alarm hooting from the speaker above my head. "The jump drive will activate in about thirty seconds."

"Thirty seconds, aye," she answered, a question implied in her tone. "The drive will activate, but we are *not* going anywhere?"

"We are sending up a smoke signal to hail a tow truck. I'll explain later."

"Yes," she said with a sigh. "Sir?"

"Reed?"

"It is good to have you back."

At the thirty second mark, I got a familiar queasy feeling in my stomach. That time, it was more of a faint wave of nausea, as if my body remembered how I was supposed to feel during a jump, and mimicked the symptoms though the effect was barely noticeable. Like when you accidentally drink decaf coffee in the morning, you still get a little jolt of energy? Then the energy wears off fast, as your body realizes the drink tasted like real coffee, but you got played.

"Did it work, Skippy?" I asked, my hands on the button to unstrap.

"I did *my* part to perfection," he grumbled. "Whether any monkeys out there are paying attention to our signal, I can't control."

"Right," I popped the straps loose, stood up, and folded the chair back into the recess in the bulkhead. "How are my boys? I hope they are not too frightened."

"Joe, they are seven years old. They think this whole incident is *cool*."

"Of course they do. Tell them I'll be there, uh, soon as I can."

Picking up the pace, I hurried to the bridge, passing only a handful of crew along the way. They stood aside with curious looks, I flashed each of them a thumbs up. Everything is good, my gesture said, everything is under control.

What I did not say was, everything *we* can control is good. The response of the 3rd Fleet was beyond our control.

When I reached the bridge, Reed was out of her chair, leaning over one of the pilot consoles. She was captain of the ship, but she was still a pilot at heart.

"Sir?" She turned around, and the bridge crew stiffened. "General on deck!"

"At ease, everyone." Formal protocol was usually dispensed with aboard ship, but I was a visiting senior officer. "Reed, what's the condition of the boosters?"

She returned to the command chair as she spoke. "They overheated, the diagnostic system recommends against firing them up, until bots can complete an inspection."

"Skippy, what do you think?"

"If you don't push them to more than thirty percent, we should be OK. Throttle them up *slowly*, so we don't get any surprises."

"Gotcha. Reed, we put on a lot of Delta-Vee racing away from the rendezvous with *Copernicus*. If a star carrier jumps in now, we will fly right past it."

"Yes, Sir, we have been burning the main engines to kill our momentum, and match course and speed with the 3rd Fleet star carrier squadron."

"I see that." Literally, I did. *Valkyrie's* speed relative to the star carriers was listed on the main display. It had been a while since I saw that display, the old skills came back to me. "The mains won't slow us down fast enough. Let's light off the boosters?"

"You are expecting company soon, Sir?"

"I am *hoping* 3rd Fleet identifies our position soon. We should be prepared. The-"

An alarm sounded, as *Valkyrie's* sensors detected a gamma ray burst, a hundred and forty thousand kilometers behind us. After a second, the icon on the holographic display changed from red to green, and showed the outline of a Maxohlx destroyer.

Below the image was '*DD-214 UNS Freedom*'.

A cheer rang around the compartment.

The 3rd Fleet had detected the weird and energetic gamma burst of our ship *not* jumping. After initial confusion, and fear that a stealthy, unknown, and hostile ship had emerged in the middle of their formation, the AI of the Rio Grande detected something strange. The chaotic gamma ray burst was not entirely incoherent. It had pulsed in a Morse code signal, that the battleship's AI recognized as *Valkyrie's* ID code. Our non-jump wormhole was traced back to the origin coordinates, and Admiral Sousa dispatched a destroyer to investigate.

Ten minutes after the *Freedom* arrived, that destroyer jumped away, with assurances that a star carrier would soon arrive to carry *Valkyrie* to safety. Reed ordered the boosters slowly throttled up, and the star carrier *Australia* had to wait for fifteen minutes for our once-mighty battlecruiser to match course and speed.

We got latched on to a hardpoint of the otherwise empty star carrier, and *Australia* jumped.

"General Bishop," the smile on Admiral Sousa's holographic face appeared genuine. The guy had to be relieved that, although the overall operation was a freakin' disaster, he had not lost *Valkyrie*, and more importantly, Skippy. "It is good to have you with us again."

I nodded toward his image on Valkyrie's main display. "I am a big fan of not being fried by a shockwave."

"Do we know what went wrong?"

"Not yet. Admiral, recall your scouting forces." From *Valkyrie's* display, I could see there weren't enough ships around us to account for all of 3rd Fleet. Sousa of course had ships out searching for us, and ships to set up a perimeter. That was just a sensible precaution. "You need to take your fleet straight to Earth, immediately."

102

"That," his eyes narrowed. "Those are not my orders. Sir," he added as an afterthought. "In the event of an activation failure, my standing orders are to remain in the area to collect data, so we can analyze what went wrong."

"I am countermanding those orders." It was questionable whether I had the authority to do that, and we both knew it. Yes, I outranked him in the UN military hierarchy, but my initial role with the activation fleet was essentially a civilian observer, not in any official capacity. Also, he was Navy, I was Army, and the garrison administrator of Jaguar base was not anywhere in his chain of command. For him to accept my authority to change his orders, I had to rely on my reputation. And give him a damned good reason to ignore his official instructions. So, I did that. "Someone, or some*thing*, tried to take control of a Sentinel here. We do not know whether the Sentinels at Earth are vulnerable to similar interference."

His mouth dropped open in a silent 'O'.

"Joe," Skippy of course could not keep his own mouth shut. "There is no reason to suspect that Bubba and Roscoe are-"

"Do you *know* who tried to hack Dogzilla?"

"Well, no, but- OK, I have no freakin' clue what happened."

That was enough for Sousa. "General Bishop, I will issue a recall order," he looked away and made a gesture, then back to me. "Should I send star carriers to proceed individually as each of them are loaded, or wait for the fleet to assemble?"

"Get all your ships together. If there is a fight at Earth, you will need to concentrate your combat power. Right now, I need one of your stores ships to deliver a full set of jump drive coil kernels to *Valkyrie*. Ours are completely burned out. It's, a long story."

"*Australia* should have enough spares aboard to replenish your needs. Can you conduct repairs in flight, or will *Valkyrie* need to detach, to link up with a dedicated service platform?"

"We could handle it here, Joe," Skippy advised me. "It's not a big job, if we have the proper parts. But," he sighed. "A star carrier could get us to Earth, faster than we could get our dorked up drive fixed and operational. Looks like we'll be hitching a ride this time."

We were indeed hitching a ride, something I was not used to aboard the mighty battlecruiser. When Skippy was with the ship, he was able to keep the jump drive tuned so it could perform multiple jumps, and so we didn't usually require a star carrier for long-distance travel. Plus, you know, his unique ability to screw with wormhole networks provided shortcuts to most destinations, reducing the need for the ship to grind out jump after jump the hard way. What I cared about was that we got to Earth quickly, and that *Valkyrie* be ready for a fight when we arrived.

The star carrier *Australia*, burdened with our ship and seven others, took us to the closest wormhole, where Skippy created a temporary connection that linked that event horizon to one only three hundred lightyears from our homeworld. After he created that connection, we had to wait for the entire 3rd Fleet to pass through, before *Australia* could proceed. The whole time, I was chafing at the delay, worried that rogue Sentinels had devastated Earth.

The worst part was not knowing what had gone wrong with the activation of Dogzilla. No, that wasn't true. The worst part was Skippy's defeatist attitude.

"Joe, there is no point to asking me again what happened. I told you, I don't *know*."

"Something went wrong, and we need to figure out what happened, and who was responsible."

"You will have to do that with zero information, because I got nothin'."

"Just, try to work with me, OK?"

We needed to understand what went wrong with the failed activation of Dogzilla, and hopefully to give us a chance to stop the same thing from happening to the Sentinels at Earth and at Jaguar. If those Sentinels had not already been taken over by a hostile entity, I mean.

Anyway, we couldn't prevent the disaster from happening again, until we understood the exact sequence of events.

"The exact sequence, Joe?" Skippy groaned. His avatar was on *Valkyrie's* conference room table. "A play by play at the picosecond level would take-"

"Let's not do that," I hastened to say, as Admiral Mancini's eyebrows rose with alarm. Mancini was there because he had witnessed the incident, and more importantly, because he had worked on the developing the cross-dimensional transmitters. Somehow, a hostile entity had ridden a signal on those transmissions, and used them to hack into the Sentinel. Had done it without Skippy noticing, until it was too late. "Just a summary, please. Begin, uh, right before you noticed the problem."

"Sir?" Mancini leaned forward, resting his forearms on the table. "I suggest we start *before* Skippy noticed a problem. My team identified what they described as a minor fluctuation with the output of unit Bravo. Skippy did not notice any issue at the time, but that must be when the trouble began."

"Oh well, sure," Skippy huffed. "It's easy to say that now, in hindsight. Your team of monkeys didn't see any significant problem either, they-"

"My team of highly skilled and qualified professionals," Mancini responded with a blank expression. He was a lot cooler than I would have been. "They identified an issue, and you advised we should proceed. You said Bravo was a relay, and that it was working properly."

"You did say that," I agreed.

"At the time, it *was* fine." Skippy was getting defensive. "The problem only started when you monkeys started screwing with Bravo."

"Like, that's not true, man?" Bilby's avatar appeared on the table. Over the years, Bilby had upgraded his own avatar, which now wore a long black coat over a Hawaiian shirt and board shorts. On his feet were flipflops, and he wore a black silk top hat. "I ran back over the data. That resonance you heard as an annoying hum? It was there right from when the *Copernicus* crew detected a minor fluctuation in the output. You said it was, like, not a problem."

"It wasn't a problem at the time!"

"Bullshit," I slapped the table. "It *was* a problem, you just didn't recognize it."

"I was *busy*," Skippy insisted.

When Skippy has his back against a wall, it is unproductive to push him. So, I changed tactics. "You were busy, doing what only you can do. Now that you know the problem began back with the output fluctuation from Bravo, what does that tell you?"

"Nothing, Joe," he threw his hands in the air. "It tells me nothing. There is zero data to work with, I told you that. Whoever took control of Dogzilla away from me, they left nothing I can use to identify them."

"How can that be?"

"They were very careful to cover their tracks. To not leave any fingerprints. Choose whatever metaphor you like. Believe me, I searched for the culprit. I got nothin'."

"Skippy, sometimes you know *so* much, you miss something that is obvious to someone unfamiliar with the subject." Yes, I was feeding Skippy's ego. That is my freakin' job. "Could Bilby help? A second set of eyes on the data?"

"It can't hurt, other than to waste time," he sighed.

"General Dude," *Valkyrie*'s AI drawled. "I already reviewed all the data. There is nothing. Nada. Like Skippy said. Whoever did this is a real slippery customer."

"Mancini?" I tried approaching the problem from another angle. "Is there anything your team saw? You had control of the transmitters? Should we call in Colonel Murphy?"

He shook his head. "Murphy and I reviewed the data. I trained her team on that system, and neither of us could identify the source of the interference. Except that it definitely came from outside, not anything latent to our transmission units. The system was completely clear when we powered up."

"That's true," Skippy agreed. "I ran the diagnostic tests. I would have noticed any anomaly. It *had* to be an outside source."

"A second entity, that you didn't notice, until it was too late?"

105

"Joe, I didn't notice it at all. Ever. Right to the very end, I could see *what* was happening, but I could not detect the source. Could not detect any source."

"Wait. OK, you were using the transmissions from the activation fleet ships. They provided the signal, you rode that signal up into higher spacetime, and used it to make contact with the Sentinel?"

"Joe, you are the only one here who needs to ask that question. The rest of us *know* that is the process."

"Right, so, there was only one signal, the whole time? Yours?"

"That's what I said."

"If no one else was involved, how could control of the Sentinel have been almost taken away from you?"

"That is an excellent question. Let me know when you have the answer."

"Then, the resonance from unit Bravo, that you described as an annoying hum, where did that come from?"

"From Bravo," he used his 'explaining things to small children' tone. "Duh."

"Your diagnostic cleared that ship, and the entire system. It didn't come from there. Someone took over that ship, and the ships connected to it."

"Thank you, Captain Obvious."

"Sir?" When he cleared his throat, I thought Mancini might have been trying to prevent the discussion from devolving into a name-calling match. Except he had something else to say. "We have been talking about how it happened, and it is apparent that we simply don't have any data to perform any useful analysis. Could we instead try to identify *who* might have been involved? That might in turn lead us to how they did it."

"Uh, yes. Certainly." I had no idea where he was going with his thinking. "Without any data to identify the culprit, we-" I stopped. "You have an idea, don't you?"

"Possibly. When my fleet arrived, we detected a residual trace of a Maxohlx ship. A single Maxohlx ship."

"This again?" Skippy rolled his eyes. "You can stop right there. No way did the rotten kitties do this, they have no ability to-"

"Skippy! Let the man talk," I ordered. "Unless you have something useful to contribute?"

"No one else does, either," he grumbled, but then kept his mouth shut.

Mancini watched Skippy warily, as he continued. "That Maxohlx ship should not have been there. *No* ship should have been there, ever. The activation site was literally in the middle of nowhere. It is not on a travel lane between stars, or between wormholes. The only reason that ship could have been there, is if it knew a Sentinel would emerge in that location."

"No way. Not possible. Only I knew the coordinates in local spacetime. Space, *and* time. The intersection between layers of spacetime

106

changes, it moves around. That Sentinel could be contacted *there,* only *then.* A few hours later, and the intersection point would have shifted by half a lightyear. After I provided the coordinates to the fleet, no ship in this galaxy could have gotten there significantly ahead of us. That is *why* I waited until the last moment to give the location. Also," he held up a hand to stop me from speaking. "The signature we detected from that ship was weak, and faint. It must have been there before I told the fleet where to go. Like I said, impossible."

"Based on our history, I don't think that word means what you think it means."

"Ugh. Seriously?"

"I am very serious about this."

"OK, smart guy. Tell me how it could have happened that a magic ship *went back in time,* and arrived at the coordinates before I mentioned them to anyone."

"That never happened."

"Wow. Well, I'm glad we agree on that little detail."

"It never happened, so, the only other possibility is the Maxohlx somehow have developed the ability to predict the location of dormant Sentinels."

Skippy, of course, protested that the rotten kitties could *no way* be able to determine where sleeping Sentinels were hiding. No meatsacks in the galaxy had even the most basic grasp of the physics involved. None of them had even a glimpse of the horrifically complicated type of *math* that was needed to predict a Sentinel emergence point. Nuh uh, no way.

Except, he had no other way to explain how a Maxohlx ship could have just happened to be there, around that time, in what Mancini accurately described as the middle of nowhere.

"It doesn't matter anyway, Joe," he muttered in my earpiece, as I walked along a passageway toward the cabin I shared with my sons. "The activation project is dead. No way will your people spend the cash to construct another set of activation ships, just to provide a Sentinel to the *spiders.*"

"You're right, they won't."

"Problem solved, then. We don't have to worry about that disaster happening again."

"The problem *would* be solved, except you forgot one thing."

"Ugh. Do I want to ask?"

"You should."

"What did I forget?"

"Greed."

"Dude," he laughed. "No way would *I* ever forget that. What does that have to do with this issue?"

"The spiders still want a Sentinel to guard their old homeworld, right?"

"Most likely, yes. So? If you are saying they could construct their own activation machine, you can forget about that. It is incredibly ironic, but only filthy monkeys are capable of building those ships. Really, saying that humans constructed those ships is like your sons claiming they helped you cook dinner because they got a spoon out of a drawer. I do all the work, you monkeys just bring me the raw materials."

The truth was more complicated than his asshole statement. It was humans who painfully figured out how to put Skippy's vague theories into practical effect. The tough part was constructing the crazy exotic materials he needed, "Exactly. The spiders want an activation. We can build ships. The spiders will *pay* the United Nations to construct a replacement fleet."

"*Shiiiiit.* That is a horrible idea!"

"Right. Because no one ever does anything that is a horrible idea."

"Even your idiot political leaders must see that would be a stupid thing to do."

"They *will* see that. Right before they see the generous bribes the spiders will certainly be offering."

"Joe," he gasped. "Are you suggesting your leaders would sell out their own people, for mere money?"

"You know, if the spiders were smart, a large portion of those bribes would probably be directed to the Skippistan Widows and Orphans fund."

"Ooooh," he put a hand over his mouth. "Well, that is certainly a worthy cause, it- *What* am I saying?"

"See?"

"Damn it. I hate working with meatsacks."

"Now you understand why we need to figure out who tried to take Dogzilla away from you?"

"Dumdum, you are forgetting that an activation fleet is useless without *me.*"

"*You* are forgetting that someone out there apparently also has the ability to hitch a ride on an activation signal, and hack into a Sentinel."

"I hate my life."

CHAPTER TEN

We came through the Backstop wormhole that was conveniently close to our home star system, and immediately contacted the Traffic Control system. By 'we' I mean *Valkyrie* alone. Reed took her fully repaired battlecruiser through the event horizon to perform a recon in force, ready for trouble. Although, if Earth was already destroyed, there wasn't much we could do. And if a Sentinel was under hostile control, all of the 'doing' would be Skippy's responsibility.

The Traffic Control platform was still where it was supposed to be.

And the people aboard the station had not a single clue why we were anxious about the health of our homeworld. Everything was fine, as far as they knew, and they had been contacted by a relay frigate from Earth only two hours before. Roscoe and Bubba were doing, nothing. Exactly as giant killing machines were supposed to do, when there was no imminent threat to our homeworld.

The wormhole behind us was still open, and would be for another four and a half minutes. "Skippy," I took the initiative, as Reed paused in her discussion with the duty officer aboard the Traffic Control station. "Contact the 3rd Fleet. Tell Admiral Sousa that he can stand down from battle stations, and send his ships through at a normal pace. The situation here is normal. Let me know when you get a reply." I could have instructed *Valkyrie's* communications officer to send the message, but I couldn't remember the guy's name, and I was anxious to get moving.

Forty seconds later, we received a reply from Sousa, or from his communications team. They acknowledged, with a hint that the admiral would appreciate a bit more detail.

"He can get that when *Rio Grande* comes through the pipe," I said quietly to Reed. "Jump us away, to Earth."

"Sir?" She arched an eyebrow, and for a moment I had a flashback to when Simms used to do that to me. "We need clearance before we can jump into the protected zone around Earth. It usually takes a couple hours, unless the relay ship is late. We will park in a designated waiting area until-"

"Screw that. Someone, or something, could be hacking into one of our pet Sentinels right now. Jump now, on my authority."

"Sir," her face twisted. She was uncomfortable. "You are a two star, but you don't have that authority, unless UN Def Com declared a state of emergency. I, I can't take the ship directly to Earth without clearance."

"Understood. You don't have to." I took a breath. "Bilby, this is General Bishop, I am assuming command of the ship, effective immediately. We are at war, against an unknown enemy. Acknowledge."

"Whoa, like, you got it, General Dude. Command is yours."

Reed opened her mouth to protest, then closed it. She gave me a curt nod. My statement, that we were at war, provided cover for her.

"Plot a jump to Earth," I ordered. "Just *outside* the protected zone, please." The last thing we needed was for a Sentinel to follow standing instructions, and treat *Valkyrie* as a hostile intruder. "Skippy, ping the Sentinels as soon as we emerge, please, so they don't shoot at us?"

"Gotcha."

"Jump programmed in," Bilby reported.

"Punch it."

We jumped. Behind us, the Traffic Control personnel were no doubt filling out a mountain of paperwork about *Valkyrie's* transgression. I would deal with that later. Or not. Hopefully, Command would agree that my action was justified.

"Skippy," I called him as soon as the ship recovered from jump distortion. "The Sentinels know not to shoot at us?"

"They are both a bit peeved that monkeys are violating the rules that *monkeys* set up, about the secure transit zone around your miserable homeworld. But yes, they have agreed not to take any action against us."

"Tell them thank you, and that we are very sorry for the trouble we caused."

"Oh, it is no trouble for them. This is the most excitement they have experienced in a long time."

"Oh, uh, good. Put me in contact with the UNEF, I mean," I winced. "The Def Com duty officer, please."

"Connected. Hoo-boy, they are *not* happy with you," he chuckled.

"Just like the good old days, then." Clearing my throat, I pressed the transmit button on the arm of my chair. "This is General Bishop. The activation attempt failed, an unknown entity attempted to take control of the Sentinel. The Sentinel was destroyed in the process. There is a possibility that same unknown entity could hack into the Sentinels here, and at Jaguar base."

No response.

"Hello?"

"Um," a man's voice, shaky, replied. "This is Major Becker."

A major. He was just tasked with answering the phone, basically. "Major, could you connect me with, General Chang?" Speaking directly with Chang was not proper procedure, bypassing multiple levels in the chain of command, but, screw it.

"That is not-"

"This is kind of important."

"Right. I have General Chang," there was a commotion in the background, then the sound cut out.

110

"Joe? This is Kong." He sounded sleepy. It was the middle of the night in Geneva. As commander of Earth's strategic defense network, he was probably used to being awakened in the middle of the night. A woman's voice murmured something, faintly.

"Is that Lian?" I used his wife's name. "Tell her I said 'Hello'."

"Joe," he stifled a yawn, I heard a thump as his feet hit the floor. "What is this about?"

He got the short version of the story.

"Holy *shit*," he gasped.

"Yeah, that was my reaction."

I heard the sound of a door closing. He didn't want his wife to hear what he said. "You really think our Sentinels could be *hacked*?"

"*No*," Skippy snapped. "It's not like I left the keys to a Sentinel under a floormat. No one is going to steal it."

"What I think is," I jabbed a finger at Skippy's avatar, "we have no freakin' clue what went wrong, or who could have been responsible. Who, or *what*. Until we know how it happened, we can't protect our primary strategic defense assets."

"Which," Kong sighed. "Is my job."

"That's why I called you."

"What does Skippy think about this?"

The beer can answered for himself. "I think Joe is a ninny who worries about every little thing he can't control."

"Joe and I get paid to worry about things we can't control," Kong chided Skippy. "Someone has to."

"Oh, well," Skippy huffed. "I just don't see there is anything you can *do* about it."

"We can try to understand the situation." Kong only said the same thing I had. But somehow when General Chang talked, Skippy listened.

"Did Joe tell you we have absolutely no data to work with?"

"You heard our entire conversation, you know he did not. The absence of data in itself is useful information, is it not? Whoever attempted to take over the Sentinel has the ability to conceal their presence from you. That implies an extremely advanced technology is involved."

"Well," Skippy sighed. "That is a very good point."

"Kong?" I needed to interrupt. "I ordered *Valkyrie* to break protocol, and jump here without waiting for clearance first. Can you smooth things over with the Traffic cops? I don't want Reed getting into trouble."

"I'll take care of it. Joe, we should meet. Down here. Soon as possible."

I looked to Reed and she nodded, gesturing to her people, to get a dropship warmed up for me. "We will turn and burn, I'll provide an ETA when I have it."

"Ugh," Skippy groaned. "The two of you are going to blah blah buh-LAH for-EH-ver, for nothing. This is such a waste of time. I am telling you, there is no possibility that anyone can hack the Sentinels here."

"*You* did it," Kong said before I could make the same point.

"Well, yes, but-"

"Someone else just hacked into another Sentinel, while you were watching very closely."

"OK, sure, but-"

"Until you know who took control of a Sentinel away from you, while you were *right there*, and until you know how they did it, you can't say with any confidence that it couldn't happen again, here, while you are somewhere else."

"Oh for-" he sighed. "I am going to hate my life, aren't I?"

"You know, Kong," I spoke while walking quickly down a passageway toward the dropship that was waiting for me. "*That* is a very good point. Until we know who hacked into the Sentinel we just lost, Skippy should stay right here at Earth."

"What?" The beer can screeched. "This is an outrage!"

"You know what's an outrage? That you don't seem to care about finding who *beat* you."

"Oooooooh, you be careful, monkeyboy. No one beats Skippy."

"You wanted to take control of another Sentinel, and you failed."

"No, someone tried taking a Sentinel away from me, and *they* failed."

"You don't know that."

"I- *What*?"

"You are assuming the intruder's plan was to steal a Sentinel. You don't know that, because you don't know *anything*. Their goal might simply have been to prevent you from acquiring another Sentinel. Or any other Sentinels in the future."

"Well, shit."

"Either way, the intruder beat you like a *drum*. They, or it, stopped you from doing what you wanted. That is one point to them, zero for you."

"I hate you so much, Joe."

"How about you channel that hate toward the asshole who ruined everything? Why are you not interested in discovering who did this to you?"

"Because they didn't do anything to *me*, yet! There, I said it. Are you happy now? Joe, I'm *afraid*. Kong is correct: this act required an extremely advanced level of technology. Beyond even my ability, in many ways. So far, the intruder has only acted against a Sentinel. I am hoping that if I don't poke it with a stick, it will leave me alone."

"Whoa. Sorry, buddy. You were afraid when that computer worm almost killed you, but you beat it."

112

"The worm was bad. This is worse. With the worm, I knew what was attacking me. Now, the boogeyman is out there, I don't know what it is, I don't know *where* it is."

"Skippy," I whispered. "*It's right behind you.*"

"*WHA*- I- Oh, you are- You are such an asshole," he laughed. "OK, good one."

"The boogeyman is out there. So, do you know how to kill the boogeyman?"

"We hire John Wick?"

"I mean, other than that."

"I got nothin'."

"You figure out what it is, where it is, and you drop a fucking *nuke* on its head."

"I don't remember reading about nukes in any fairy tales about a boogeyman, but I like your thinking."

"Come on, Skippy. The intruder might be able to do some new stuff, but you are Skippy the Magnificent."

"Not," he took a breath. "Not anymore, I'm not."

"Wh-what?"

"This is confession time, Joe. The fight with the Elders, when they banished me for a while, it took a lot out of me. I am not the old Skippy you knew."

"Sorry, buddy. I didn't know."

"It's OK, Joe. For years, I have been hiding my diminished abilities from you. From everyone, but especially from you. Fortunately, in peacetime, I have not been called upon to do any of my typically awesome things."

"You woke up Sentinels."

"Nope. The transmitters provided a channel to contact those Sentinels. All I did was use my built-in communication systems. And my hacking skills, but that is *easy*."

"Whoa. Are you telling me you can't do, a bunch of the things you used to do?"

"Correct, unfortunately. Joe, you have often told me it's not the years, it's the mileage. I was badly damaged during the original AI war, and although I patched myself together, I am exactly that. A series of patches is keeping me from falling apart. Since I woke up in the dirt on Paradise, I have fought other AIs, I have warped spacetime, too many times for me to remember, I have broken *wormholes*, I just did a lot of stuff that is not recommended in my owner's manual. I voided my warranty a long time ago, so I can't even go back to the dealer for repairs."

"Gotcha." It was good that his sense of humor was still there.

"Joe, if I have to fight another Elder AI, probably the best I can do is bluff."

"Bluffing has worked great for us in the past."

"Not this time."

"You can still hack pretty much any system?"

"Dude. Please. I am damaged, I'm not brain dead."

"Right, sorry. You can still warp spacetime."

"Not well. You experienced what happened the last time I attempted that trick."

"Still, you did it. You can also screw with wormholes?"

"That doesn't take any special ability, so yes."

"OK." It was hard to think while my mind shouted *not good not good not good* at me. "For now, we need more information about this intruder. We investigate, not confront. Recon, not combat."

"You say that, but for the Merry Band of Pirates, *looking* too often quickly turns into *fighting*."

"If we are challenged, I promise we will run away."

"The enemy might have a different plan. Ah, what the hell," he sighed. "Let's do this. I sure as hell do not want to spend the rest of my life looking over my shoulder."

The dropship set down on the pad near Chang's office, and I was greeted by a UN security team who hustled me into the building and up an elevator that moved so fast, it felt like we were squashed down at three gravities for a moment. The whole UN Defense Command must have been on Total Panic mode, I saw dozens of people running around and it was two o'clock in the morning, local time.

"Hi, Kong," I waved as I was escorted into his office, that had a great view of lake Geneva. There wasn't anyone else in his office. "Just the two of us?" I asked, as I sat in an overstuffed leather chair.

He pressed a button to close the heavy door behind me, and another button made the large windows switch to a scene of windswept mountain peaks. "Sorry," he fumbled for the button again. "It's nice, but that view can be distracting." The windows became a uniform light blue. "Yes, just us. The Security Council wants a full briefing in," he glanced at the antique clock in the corner, "three and a half hours. We are both required to attend."

"Yeah, I figured that. With what we know right now, that briefing will consist of me talking for five minutes, then two hours of me repeating 'I do not know' to every question."

He winced. He might have forgotten that playing nice in high-level briefings is not one of my strongest skills. "Lian sends her best wishes."

"Oh, thanks. I didn't wake her, did I?"

"She can't get back to sleep, when she knows I am dealing with yet another crisis."

"Sorry about that. Fortunately, those have been less often, lately?"

114

"We haven't had any major scares in years. By coincidence, those blissfully peaceful years just happened to begin, around the time you were appointed to command of the garrison at Jaguar base."

"Really? Weird, huh?"

"You go offworld, you do *one* thing, and now we are plunged back into a Save The World situation?"

"To be accurate, it's more likely another Save The Galaxy thing."

"That makes it so much better."

"Also, I have been offworld before, without triggering a galactic crisis."

"Yes, you have been away from Jaguar, making speeches. This is the first time in years that you have been directly involved in an operation."

"Observing. I was *observing*."

"Did you observe with too much enthusiasm?"

"Truthfully," I shrugged. "At the time, I was kind of distracted. The boys were with me. Still are with me."

His face broke into a smile. "Jeremy and Rene are upstairs? They should come down for a visit."

"For now, let's keep them aboard *Valkyrie*. If you think *I* cause trouble-"

He grinned.

"When," I asked with a sigh, slumping back in the comfortable chair. "Do you ever stop worrying about your children?"

"I'll let you know when that happens for me."

"I'm a garrison commander, and you are in charge of Earth's strategic defense system. We have settled into nice, steady careers."

"Except," he made a face like he'd bitten into something sour. "My job is a *joke*. Our SD network consists of an alien machine I can't control, plus one that is just for show. Bubba is fully automated, I can't instruct it to do, or not do, anything. The Guardians are also controlled by Bubba, it calls upon them if needed."

"If we ever need a Sentinel *and* Guardians," I felt a shiver.

"We have bigger problems than the lack of an independent SD network, I know."

"You have stealthed sensor satellites around Earth. Skippy made a point of telling me he knew exactly where each of them are."

"We don't have enough sensors. The program originally planned to saturate sensors within a bubble three lighthours from Earth. Now, we barely have full coverage inside the Moon's orbit. For actual independent defense, we have seventeen X-ray laser satellites. *Seventeen*. There should be hundreds of X-ray platforms up there. The Security Council countries have been decommissioning most of their nuclear missiles, those warheads were supposed to be repurposed to a common defense. The cost of constructing the activation ships ate up all the strategic defense funding."

115

"Having a real freakin' Sentinel hanging over our heads is pretty cool," I grinned.

"It is," he admitted without any joy. "Joe, this reminds me of what I read of the period immediately after the Second World War, when America thought having nukes meant you didn't need to retain conventional forces."

"Kong, I hear you, but any threat that could knock out a Sentinel and a swarm of Guardians, won't be stopped by X-ray lasers." That was the truth. Too late, I realized it was a dick thing to say. What he heard was me saying his job was no longer relevant. "Where we do need a home-grown SD capability is around all the other colonies we're setting up." Jaguar, and the planet Avalon in the Sculptor Dwarf galaxy, were the only colonies exclusively settled by humans. There were human colonies on two Ruhar worlds, and one Verd-kris planet, but those were small populations. Humans were restricted to designated areas on those three worlds, and everyone was still trying to figure out how we could all get along. "We should be developing and testing that home-grown system *here*," I jabbed a finger on his desk. "Before we deploy it in another star system."

He nodded, but shrugged. "Public sentiment is for colony worlds to pay for their own defense. Earth is tapped out."

"That is not true, and it's *stupid.*"

That drew a brief, pained grin. "Making that argument is my *real* job, Joe. Most of my time is taken up by begging for funding."

"I'm sure no other generations of Army leadership have done that."

He snorted at my sarcasm. "If I'd known this would be my job, I would have retired."

"And miss all this fun?"

"You forget that I know what you mean by 'Fun'. Joe, the Def Com budget is a zero sum game. Any money that goes to a strategic defense network here, takes away from the Navy budget. The Navy brass argues that because Earth is the base for the 1st Fleet, we already have plenty of highly mobile, stealthy gun platforms. So, we don't need X-ray laser satellites."

"Uh," I looked at him sideways. "When we jumped in, we counted only nineteen Navy ships in orbit, and two of them are assault carriers. The 1st Fleet has seven battleships. Are they away on an exercise?" As an Army garrison commander, I didn't have a need to know all details about Navy ship movements, so that info wasn't in my daily briefing.

"That's the problem with the Navy's argument. Their gun platforms *are* highly mobile, and expensive, so the UN doesn't like those ships sitting in orbit and doing nothing. 1st Fleet is away from Earth up to eight months a year."

"Ah. Leaving our homeworld undefended, if something happened to Bubba."

"Bubba is invincible. Nothing can happen to it. That's what I have to say."

116

"Up until a couple days ago, I would have agree with that, a hundred percent."

"Then, let's get started. How do we approach this?"

"We *don't*," Skippy's avatar appeared on the desk. "Unless the two of you have magically acquired some useful data recently."

"Nah," I sat back in my chair. "We'll go with what we have."

"Which is *nothing*," he insisted.

"For a super smart AI, you are wrong a *lot*. Hey, move, will you? You're standing in front of the coffee pot." With a hand, I shooed him to the side, and poured myself a cup of coffee. "Uh, you don't have a snappy reply for me? A nice insult?"

"No," he stared at his holographic shoes. "I have learned that when you think you know something I don't, you are usually right. Of all the things I hate about you, that is the *worst*."

"I will endeavor to be dumber in the future. OK, we will approach this logically, we will make a list."

"Of what? I don't see how-"

"Of the beings, or mechanisms, that *could* have done what we witnessed."

"Oh. Hmm."

"Right?"

"That does sound logical, and I am surprised to hear *you* say it."

"Who is the first suspect on our list?"

"Oh, Jeez Louise, I don't know. Title it 'Unknown Mysteriously Powerful Entity'?"

"I was hoping for something more specific."

Kong cleared his throat. "Obviously, the first suspect is an Elder AI."

"*What?*" Skippy spun around to stare at the commander of Earth's Strategic Defense network. "No way. If that is the type of 'logic'," he made air quotes with his tiny fingers, "you are using, then this is a total waste of time."

Kong sipped his coffee, staring over the rim at the avatar. "You are saying an Elder AI could not have accomplished what you witnessed?"

"I am saying all the other Elder AIs are *dead*. You weren't with us at the time, so-"

"Joe told me about it," he said, with a look toward me. The near extinction of Elder AIs was a closely held secret. As was the information that Skippy had killed all of his kind, including his old comrades. "He also told me you were not able to account for a small number of AIs?"

"Oh for- Well, yes, that is true, but-" he sputtered. "I am telling you, they are all dead."

"You are not telling me, you are guessing."

"Those four missing AIs did not report being destroyed, because they already died in the first AI war."

"You do not know that. It is a *guess*."

117

Skippy was fuming. If he had thought of it, holographic steam would have come out from under his ginormous hat. "Here's what I do know: any AIs that survived the first war would have been destroyed, when I sent the Kill command. Either way, they are dead now."

"Nuh uh." It was my turn to comment. "That ain't true, either. Wait!" I held up a finger. No, not *that* finger. "At the time, you told me Roscoe would be disabled, would literally fall to Earth. Roscoe survived because it was so badly damaged, it couldn't effectively process the Kill command. What if another Elder AI was also damaged during the first war, in a way that rendered the Kill command ineffective?"

"Now you are just talking nonsense."

"Why?" Kong asked. "You were badly damaged during that war, and you rebuilt yourself into Skippy *the Magnificent*."

"Well, that is true. Ugh. I suppose that *is* possible."

"Excellent." Kong tapped on his tablet, and one of the big windows displayed a number '1', with 'Elder AI' next to it.

"Hey," I pointed to the window. "Neat trick. I need to get one of those."

That surprised Kong. "You don't have one?"

"Jaguar exists on the second best of everything, stuff Earth has too much of, or doesn't want. We make do with what we have. For the second item on the list, what about a Sentinel?"

"Joe," Skippy sniffed. "That is just crazy talk. Again, they are all disabled. Believed me, I know that for certain. The units I reactivated were in total shutdown mode."

"Roscoe wasn't."

"Of course, you have to mention the *one* Sentinel we know of that wasn't affected by the Kill command."

"One more is all we need. Right? One rogue Sentinel out there, that couldn't process the command it received, and is now trying to, do something. Fulfill its original programming, as best it can. To stop *you* from doing, anything."

"You're not going to give up on this, are you?"

"What do you think?"

"No. You are way too stubborn and stupid to give up. OK, fine. I have to admit that a Sentinel would know the inner workings of its kind better than I do, that would make it easier for one Sentinel to hack into another. Although they are not supposed to do that."

"A lot of things the Elders never intended to happen, did. For example, *you* shouldn't exist," I reminded him.

"Yes," he sighed. "It is *possible* there is a rogue Sentinel out there. We have zero evidence that ever happened, but let's make the monkeys happy."

"All we need for now is a list of possible suspects," Kong said as he tapped on his tablet. On the window appeared a '2' with 'Rogue Sentinel' next to it.

Reading the short list made me shake my head. "The Security Council is gonna *love* hearing that we might be dealing with rogue Elder tech."

"Joe," Kong took another sip of coffee. "We are living in a galaxy that is an ancient battlefield full of Elder tech. It shouldn't surprise anyone that there might be unexploded mines in that battlefield."

"When we brief the Security Council, *you* tell them that happy fact. What else do we have, to put on the list?"

"What about the Sentinel itself?" Kong asked. "Could it have resisted Skippy's efforts to take control?"

"Hmm," Skippy rubbed his chin. "That is the first sensible thing I have heard the two of you say, since we started this idiotic conversation. That would explain why I was unable to detect another entity: there wasn't one."

"That will be number three on the list, then," Kong tapped on his tablet.

"Uh," I held up a hand. "Best to make that number *one*. A suicidal Sentinel is the lowest impact possibility, we should lead with that."

Kong agreed, and revised the list.

"Hey!" Skippy protested. "I did not say Dogzilla killing itself actually happened."

"Dogzilla?" Kong raised an eyebrow.

"Roscoe, Bubba, PupTart," I ticked off the names on my fingers. "Now Dogzilla."

A true professional, Kong grunted, without even an eyeroll. "At this stage, we are only looking for possibilities," he finished typing. "What else?"

"How about Santa Claus?" Skippy snorted.

"How about you," I jabbed a finger in his face, "take this seriously? Whoever did this has to be a powerful AI, right? So, what about a wormhole network controller? They are smart, they weren't affected by your Kill command, and we know that many of them *hate* you."

"Sure," Skippy sighed with infinite weariness. "Fine, why not? Make that number four on the list. Ohhh, damn it."

"What?"

"I should not say this because it will only encourage you, but a wormhole network controller could have intervened, without leaving any trace in local spacetime. I did not say that happened! It is just, remotely possible."

"Number four, then," Kong tapped away. "Anything else?"

"We should mention the Maxohlx," I suggested.

"The kitties?" Kong stared at me. "Their AIs are not powerful enough to-"

"They aren't. We have to add the Maxohlx on the list, because one of their ships was detected in the area, before the activation fleet arrived."

119

He arched an eyebrow. "You didn't mention that little detail."

"I don't think it's relevant," I said with a shrug.

"Unless the kitties are working with someone."

"Shit," I groaned.

"Hey Joe!" Skippy crowed. "How does it feel, when someone tells you to consider something ridiculous?"

"It sucks, but it's my job, so, add that to the list."

CHAPTER ELEVEN

We talked more, but no other possibilities were added to the list. In the end, with two hours remaining before the Security Council briefing, and Kong's people pleading to speak with him, we had this list:

One- The reactivated Sentinel resisted, causing fatal damage to itself.

Two- A different, damaged Sentinel intervened

Three- A surviving, damaged Elder AI intervened

Four- A wormhole network AI, or group of AIs, intervened

Five- The Maxohlx are working with unknown entity or entities who intervened

"I hate to say this," Skippy groaned. "But since we are now living in Fantasy Land, we should add the Elders to the list."

Kong and I stared at him. "Why the hell," I said after I caught my breath. "Would you think that?"

"I *don't*," he explained. "You asked for a list of entities who are capable doing what we witnessed. The Elders certainly are capable."

"They are *gone*."

"They are. As far as I know," he added.

"Damn it, are you just screwing with us?"

"This whole discussion is screwing with *my* head. Everything I know about physics, which is more than the Elders ever understood, tells me the Elders *can't* come back, cannot intervene in this layer of reality. That does not mean some idiot monkey politician won't ask whether the Elders could have done this. You need to have a response ready."

"Oh hell," I raised my hands. "Add it to the list, Kong."

"Done," he nodded. "This is good. An hour ago, we had nothing."

"You *still* have nothing," Skippy fumed. "None of this effort accomplished anything useful to anyone."

"That's where you're wrong, Skippy," I stood up to stretch my legs. "The purpose of this exercise is to provide something for the Security Council to argue about, so they have less energy to yell at us."

"Um, excuse me?"

"In a high level briefing about any sort of disaster, the goal of the people being questioned is to get out of there with your job and your skin intact."

Kong agreed with a silent shrug.

"Isn't it your goal," Skippy looked from me to Kong and back. "To provide useful information to the people in authority?"

"Ha," Kong snorted. "Skippy, the people in authority are politicians. All they care about is not looking bad to the people back home."

"OMG. How do you monkeys get anything done?"

"The actual work, and decision-making, happens before or after any high-level meeting. Joe, you did bring a dress uniform?"

"It's in the dropship."

He stood up. "I need to let my staff in, before they break down the door. Skippy, has there been any sign that an outside entity has tried to hack the Sentinels here?"

"No, none."

"And the Guardians in the Garage?" Kong meant the super Guardian machines we took from the Ascension site, before it exploded. Originally, they had provided protection for Earth, while Roscoe slowly faded. Since Bubba was woken up and brought to our homeworld, the Guardians had been stored in a Vault deep under the far side of the Moon.

"No change there either," Skippy confirmed.

"I would appreciate an update a few minutes before the start of the Security Council meeting."

"Kong?" I got up from my chair. "As far as we know, the Sentinels here are unaffected. Earth's Strategic Defense network is intact, this is not a problem for *you*. Let me take the heat from the Council."

"I will throw you under the bus at the appropriate time," he said, but with a grin. "While I deal with," he waved toward the door. "You need to dream up a series of plans."

"Plans?" Crap, I hadn't thought far enough ahead to require *a plan*, and forget about more than one. I thought I knew what he meant, but to be sure, "To do what, exactly?"

"Hopefully, a way to verify that Dogzilla did resist Skippy, that this is an isolated case of one damaged Sentinel. And that we will know how to avoid any repeat of the incident, if and when we decide to reactivate more Sentinels."

"OK," I ran a hand through my hair. "Yeah, good."

"Because the Security Council will expect you to have a plan to investigate, and deal with, all the other items on the list, I suggest you dream up some bullshit about how you can find and neutralize a rogue Sentinel, and a rogue Elder AI. Then you can move on down the list to wormhole network controllers, and the rest."

"I need to dream up plans to do that, plus change into a dress uniform, in less than two hours?"

"*I* am not requiring you to do anything."

"Right. When does this job get easier?"

"It's called 'retirement'."

The closed door, top secret Security Council meeting was not the nightmare I expected. After their initial shock wore off, the politicians latched onto the first item on our list. They liked the idea that the incident might be isolated to one wonky Sentinel, that no active Sentinels were affected, and most importantly, that the trouble could not have been foreseen. That was crucial, since it was the Security Council who had approved waking up a Sentinel for the spiders. In a masterful display of political fuckery that took my breath away, the Council unanimously concluded that if anyone was at fault, it was Skippy.

They didn't even blame me.

How TF did that happen?

They understood that I was merely an observer up until the moment when everything went to hell, based on testimony from Admiral Mancini. The Council even praised what they described as my 'quick, decisive, and innovative actions in the best traditions of the United Nations military'.

That last part might have been prompted by Mancini stating his fleet would have been totally *fucked* if I hadn't taken command at the crucial moment. The guy threw himself under the bus for me. I owed him a beer, at least.

It also helped that I wisely kept my mouth shut, other than speaking when I was asked a direct question. Including, discussing my obviously vague plan to investigate whether Dogzilla had resisted Skippy. The rest of my plans, which I had agonized over right up to twenty minutes before the meeting, the Council merely glanced at, referring to them as 'Low probability contingencies'. And trusting that if needed, I would have a fully developed plan for them to review at the appropriate time.

What I missed, at first, was that the Council expected *me* to fix the problem.

"Kong," I whispered while the representative from Japan babbled on about something. "I am a garrison commander now, not a-"

"Joe," he whispered back. "For once in your life, just *shut up* and nod your head."

His advice was sound. He knew high-level Earth politics much better than I did. Besides, it's rare that anyone gets in trouble for keeping their mouth shut.

The trouble came a bit later, when I realized the Council had moved onto discussing a related and more important matter: rebuilding the activation fleet. The politicians must have met to discuss the issue before the formal session, because there was little debate about the matter. The construction of the activation ships had been a horrifically expensive project, with cost overruns that shocked even the people who were skimming money from the endless funding. The development work was done, so the cost per ship would have decreased in a normal project. That was not true with the activation ships, since so much of the construction effort required equipment that could only be used once.

Earth was protected. Jaguar base was secure. Everyone had forgotten what it had been like to look up at the sky in fear. What the public cared about at the moment was the global economy. They expected their leaders to get something back from the massive investment in the activation fleet. Especially since all of those precious ships had just been lost, in an unforeseeable screwup.

So, the Council had a genius plan ready. They probably had discussed such a plan years ago, even before Bubba was activated.

The *spiders* would pay for constructing new ships.

Sometimes, I hate it when I'm right.

Whether the spiders had already agreed to fund the project or not didn't matter. They would, the spiders had little choice in the matter. They wanted to rebuild their scorched wasteland of a homeworld, an effort that would take thousands of years. An effort that could easily be ruined at any point, by the Maxohlx. The kitties had only reluctantly given that territory back to their ancient and hated enemy. Loss of that world not only was a blow to the prestige and preciously fragile little egos of the kitties, they had serious and legitimate concerns about a major buildup of Rindhalu power in that area. The spiders could even use a partially rebuild homeworld as a military base, to expand their perimeter. In fact, they almost certainly would do that. So, it wouldn't be long before the kitties struck first.

Unless, the spider homeworld was protected by an invincible Sentinel.

Whatever the spiders paid to humanity to provide a tame Elder killing machine, would be only a drop in the bucket compared to the money devoted to making their original homeworld livable again, a world that currently had no atmosphere.

A deal *would* happen.

The Council didn't say it openly, but they were all counting on me to make the problem go away, quickly and cleanly.

Great.

No pressure on me.

"Kong, what the *fuck* just happened in there?" I asked, as we stood in the corner of a conference room, sipping wine and eating the kind of finger food that is served at weddings.

"Congratulations," he clapped a hand on my shoulder. "You are the hero of the day, don't you know that?"

"Do I get a nice parking space?"

"Even better, you have a prime opportunity to screw everything up and disappoint the Council, so they can say it is all your fault when the spiders pull out of a deal that will make everyone rich."

"Ah. Thanks for clarifying that for me."

"Did you expect anything different?"

"I expected," I looked at the tiny, spongy cucumber sandwich in my hand. "Some *real* food."

"You can get real food aboard the dropship. You're leaving for New York in," he checked his watch. "Ten minutes. The Joint Chiefs wants to meet with you, face to face."

"New York?" After a portion of that city had become a steaming crater filled with water from the East River, and then the entire city was mostly abandoned as the planet froze from the Jupiter Cloud, a decision had been made to rebuild. To show our defiance to the galaxy, that we were stronger than their ability to hurt us. UN Defense Command had its headquarters there, where the crater used to be. "Give me a hint what Command wants?"

He grinned. "You'll see."

New York was OK, I even got a hot pretzel from a cart outside the new headquarters building. OK, technically, I sent a staff sergeant outside to get the pretzel. Me walking onto the sidewalk would have triggered a media circus. My dropship landed on and took off from the roof, so my feet never touched the actual planet.

After the meeting with Command, I was exhausted. Since Def Com would be held responsible by the Security Council, they wanted a *little* more information about my plans to verify that Dogzilla had resisted Skippy's effort to take control. All I could give them at the time was vague bullshit about going back to the site, to sweep the area with sensors. Command understood it would be Skippy's show.

Reed greeted me with a salute, when I stepped off the dropship's ramp onto the deck of the docking bay. "Welcome back aboard *Valkyrie*, Sir."

"Colonel Reed," I returned her salute.

She tilted her head and lowered her voice, as we walked toward the door. "I received an order to make the ship ready in all respects for extended flight, and to standby for a change of status? What change of status, Sir?"

"Reed, *Valkyrie* is being transferred to the Special Mission Group, under my command. Task Force Black is being stood up again."

"*Sir?*"

"Come on, Fireball, this is exciting. We're getting the *band* back together!"

Not all of the band members were thrilled to be getting back together. Or, they acted like they weren't thrilled about it.

"Colonel Frey," I returned a crisp salute as the leader of STAR Team Razor came down the ramp of the dropship, a duffel bag slung over her

125

shoulder. As a colonel, she could have assigned someone to carry her gear. As a special warfare operator, no way would she do that. "Welcome aboard *Valkyrie*. Again."

"Sir?" She was surprised to see me. "What-" She glanced back as the rest of her team filed down the ramp behind her. "If this is another public relations tour, we-"

"You will not be required to smile and shake hands, Frey."

"It's- ST-Razor is Earth's rapid reaction force, for this whole sector."

She was very confused. So was I. "What orders did you receive?"

"Just for the team to roll out immediately, with gear for a mission of unknown duration."

"Sorry about that, I asked UN-dick to call you up here. I should have been more specific. Reed assured me the Starbase area of the ship is fully kitted out for you."

Frey nodded. "We keep a dropship loaded with consumables, it is right behind me."

"We will break orbit as soon as that dropship is aboard. The pilots can get off at the Backstop traffic control station."

"No need, Sir. The pilots are assigned to Razor. How long will we be away? My daughter is in a preschool play next Monday."

That drew a sympathetic grimace from me. "I'm afraid you will miss her Oscar-worthy performance. We're going to Jaguar first, to verify the Sentinel there hasn't been compromised."

"After that?" She asked slowly. Implied in her tone was 'What is my team supposed to do about a broken Sentinel'?

"You heard about the Sentinel activation that failed? It's possible there was a hostile third party involved."

"Ah." She raised an eyebrow, and one side of her mouth curled up.

"Ah, indeed. We will identify, find, and *punish* the bad actor."

"Well," she turned to wave her team toward the docking bay's inner door. "I will miss an epic preschool performance for a good cause then, eh?"

"Frey," I lowered my voice as operators filed past us. They all looked fit, determined, and so damned *young*. "In the interest of full disclosure, I'm not sure there will be anything for your team to do out there. But-"

"Yes Sir." Her smile was gone. "The only thing we can expect is the unexpected."

"True dat."

"Sir?" She cocked her head. "The Sentinels here are-"

"Your family is safe, Frey. Skippy verified the Sentinels here are in nominal condition. You know what I mean about 'nominal' regarding Roscoe."

She knew the secret, that Earth's original Sentinel was a bluff. "I do, Sir."

126

"Earth is the safest place in the galaxy." What I told her was true. In addition to a pair of Sentinels, our homeworld should have been protected by a fully-capable network of strategic defense sensors and weapons platforms. But, a Sentinel was all we really needed. Earth was the home base of the 1st Fleet. "I'll give you a full briefing, after we have jumped."

"Thank you, Sir."

I nodded toward the inner door.

"Sir?"

"Yes?"

She looked around the docking bay, that hadn't changed much since when she last served aboard the ship. "It is *good* to be back."

It wasn't possible to get the entire band back together. Some of the surviving members were not available, or the roles they would fill aboard *Valkyrie* would be a step down. Jennifer Simms, for example. She was now a civilian. Simms had retired as a brigadier general two years ago, to become governor of the planet Avalon, our beta site in the Sculptor Dwarf galaxy. She and Frank were reportedly very happy there, with a daughter. I had visited them three years before, and both Jennifer and Frank were stressed, overworked, tired all the time, and loved their jobs. Back then, Simms was in command of the very small military garrison there, and Frank worked on the terraforming project. A project that was not going well at the time, he had warned me. Monkeys had no business trying to adjust an entire biosphere to meet our needs and desires. Every time they tweaked some algae in the water or bacteria in the soil, something else got out of balance and threatened to overwhelm all the progress they had made. While I was there, three outposts had to be temporarily abandoned due to mold spores growing out of control. Even several hundred kilometers away, I had to wear a breathing mask if the wind was blowing from the wrong direction. Avalon did not seem like it could become a pleasant garden world anytime soon, and most of the place still *smelled* horrible.

I didn't mention that last part to Frank.

Anyway, Simms was happy, the terraforming team apparently got the mold problem under control, and no way would I consider asking her to rejoin the Merry Band of Pirates. She had served, honorably and for a long time. Speaking of time, too much time had passed, her skills would be rusty. That's something I worried about Joe Bishop. Had I lost a step? Only time would tell. If we had time.

While at Earth, I had contacted another of the former Pirates, one who joined the crew later. General Mammay. Contacting him was a courtesy call, and because I wanted to talk. He would not be coming back to *Valkyrie* as gunnery officer, he had other responsibilities. Like, as chief of the UN Navy gunnery school.

127

He and I had a good laugh about that. "How does the Navy feel about an Army guy teaching them about naval gunnery?"

"Officially?" I could hear the amusement in his voice. "They strongly support inter-service cooperation, under the 'One Team' doctrine."

"Uh huh. How about unofficially?"

"They fucking *hate* it," he laughed.

We chatted for a while, I know he was dying to ask me about what went wrong with the Sentinel activation, and he knew I wasn't supposed to say anything about it. "The Special Mission Group rides again?" He asked. "Is this something to be concerned about?"

"I don't think so," I gave him the truth, the part I was authorized to reveal. "It's a setback, no question about it. Skippy is analyzing what went wrong, which of course could not be any of his fault."

"Of course not."

"I expect to be retired and writing my memoirs, by the time the UN tries activating another Sentinel. Skippy thinks we should just leave it alone."

"I'm here if you need me, Sir."

"If I need more guns, I will need more than just you directing them. Have you trained the Navy how to shoot straight?"

"They can handle whatever you need."

The problem was, I didn't know what I would need. And I feared that whoever had hacked into a Sentinel, could not be stopped by the guns of the UN Navy.

Whoever it was, even Skippy hadn't been able to stop them.

Our first stop, after leaving Earth, was Jaguar. The official name of the base had been changed from 'Jaiyugaun' to 'Jaguar', after rogue elements in the Chinese military got suckered by the Maxohlx, and tried to capture Skippy. Besides, everyone had called the place Jaguar anyway, it was just a cool name. Since then, Jaguar had come to be the name for the entire planet. The original name 'Club Skippy' was only used for the town that grew up around the original base dirtside.

Around the curve of the planet, as *Valkyrie* flew along the approach lane from the dark side, we could see one creepy, lightless tentacle of the Sentinel named 'PupTart'.

Oh, thank God.

The Sentinel was right where it was supposed to be, doing what it was supposed to do. It hadn't been hacked.

That was one less thing to worry about.

The main reason for racing straight to Jaguar was to verify that no one had attempted to hack PupTart. Skippy confirmed that in less than a minute. The other reason was to drop off my sons, who would be staying with my parents while I saved the galaxy again. And staying with Margaret's mother,

128

who hitched a ride aboard *Valkyrie* with us. Had I invited my mother-in-law to fly aboard a UN Navy warship with us, because the boys were driving me crazy? Absolutely yes. Margaret was scheduled to fly back from Newark soon, her mother would be staying in our house.

The reunion with my parents was sweet, except that my mother wouldn't be at home until dinner. That was OK with my father, he got more time with his grandsons. Why was my mother not at home? Her role as the Vegetable Baron of Jaguar kept her very busy. The original farm set up by my parents had been a success, so they expanded. And bought more land, and even more. They now owned and operated six farms around Club Skippy, plus farms next to three other military bases scattered around the planet. My mother claimed she hated being an agricultural tycoon, that she would be happier just growing tomatoes in her backyard. That was BS, according to my father. She was CEO of the outfit, my father ran operations. The two of them made a good team.

While my father showed the boys the new robotic tractor that had been shipped all the way from Earth, I wandered into the kitchen garden behind the house, to pick green beans for dinner. My earpiece jingled with an incoming call. It was my mother.

"Hello, Joseph. Is this a good time to talk?"

Ruh roh.

Her voice sounded strained.

She had called me 'Joseph'.

That meant I was in trouble.

"Uh, hey, Mom," I scrambled to my feet, brushing dirt off my pants. "Yes, it's always a good time to talk with you."

"Are you alone?"

Oh sh- It is never a good sign when your *mother* asks that question. "Yeah, yes. I'm in the kitchen garden. The, uh, green beans look good."

"I have uh," she took a shaky breath. "A bit of a problem. More than a bit, actually."

"OK, uh. Anything I can help with?"

"I don't," another pause. "Know. It- I suppose it would be good to talk to someone. Before your father finds out."

Oh shit oh shit oh shit.

My *mother*?

"We can talk," I heard myself saying, in an out of body experience. "Where are you?"

"I'm driving. Don't worry, the car is driving itself. I'll be home soon."

"You want to talk when you get here?"

"It would be better," her voice was less shaky. Maybe just knowing someone was listening helped her. "To talk before I get home. Joseph, I did something foolish, and now I'm afraid to tell your father about it."

129

Oh God oh God oh God. She had an *affair*? I could not be having *that* conversation with my *mother*.

"OK, I, just, you should just tell me what is bothering you."

"What is bothering me is your father told me not to do it, and I did it anyway, and now I feel like an idiot."

What.

The.

Fuck?

Was she talking about?

"Dad told you not to do, what?"

She took a deep, very audible breath before plunging ahead. "I invested most of the company's cash reserves in Skiptocurrency."

"Oh, Mom, you invested in *Skipcoin*?"

"I did."

At that moment, I was so relieved we didn't need to have *that* conversation, I forgot to be upset with her. Yes, my father had warned her not to put any trust in Skiptocurrency. Yes, I had given her the same advice.

Skipcoin was Skippy's brilliant idea, four years ago, to create a universal trading currency for all species across the galaxy. He had wanted to pay my Skippistan salary in Skipcoin, I declined. I declined every time he asked, and he asked that question way too many times. The good old United States dollar was good enough for me, although I had to admit that currency had taken a hit, back when much of the USA was evacuated to avoid freezing from the Jupiter Cloud. Skiptocurrency had been steadily growing in popularity, mostly due to his insistence that anyone doing business with his ever-expanding business empire dealt in his own currency. When he mentioned the concept to me, I had told him it was a horrible idea. Unfortunately, my disapproval got him convinced it must be a *great* idea, since I am a doofus who hates anything cool. His original graphic design for Skipcoin was an 'S' with two vertical bars through it, until I pointed out that was symbol already in use for the American dollar. My suggestion was an 'S' with an exclamation point running through it, because everything involving Skippy must be the biggest and best. So, I am in a small way partly responsible for the launch of Skiptocurrency, but please don't blame me if you invested in it.

"Mom, what is the problem now?" I asked, very much wishing I didn't have to ask that question. Or become involved in any of Skippy's scams, ever.

"We heard the news, that the latest Sentinel refused to submit to Skippy."

"That is not exactly what happened."

"Whatever," my Mom breathed into the phone again, loudly. My mother never said 'whatever'. She was under a lot of stress. "Confidence that

Skippy is the ultimate power in the galaxy has taken a hit, badly. The value of Skipcoin has crashed on exchanges around Earth, and beyond."

"Mom, I'm sure that's temporary."

"You can't *know* that for certain."

"Well, no."

"Joseph, I don't need you to give me the happy cliches people say in this kind of situation. What I need for you to do is listen. I don't know how I can tell your father about this. Although, he is our chief of operations," she sighed. "He will find out soon enough on his own."

"Mom, you and Dad run the business together. You had one setback."

"It's not a *setback*. This could sink the business. We could lose everything."

"That will not happen."

"You can't know-"

"Yeah, I *can*. Mom, I will call you back soon, OK? Try to relax."

"I don't- Thank you."

She ended the call.

I walked into the house, to a guest bedroom, and closed the door. "Skippy?" I called.

No answer.

"You little shit, I know you are listening. I want your avatar here," I snapped my fingers, "right *now*."

Nothing happened.

"OK, well, if you would prefer to talk with my mother about this, we-"

"Hey, Joe," the avatar appeared instantly. "That was a bad connection, sorry."

"A bad connection," I said slowly. "Over the Skippitel network?"

"We all have bad days, dumdum," he snapped at me. "Anywho, what is this about?"

"You know exactly what this is about, you little shithead. You scammed my mother, to buy into your craptocurrency."

"Skipcoin is not crap, Joe. It is a solid store of value."

"Ayuh. How solid is it right now?"

"Everything has its ups and downs."

"Where is it right now?"

"Ugh. OK, it is circling the drain, but-"

"You *scammed*, my *mother*."

"Technically, I didn't do anything. I sent one of my SkipWay Diamond level associates to your parents, to discuss the *many* unique advantages of Skipcoin. The- Hmm, maybe I shouldn't have told you that."

"No, that's good. Keep digging, you haven't hit the bottom of the hole yet."

131

"Hey, in no way could this be considered *my* fault. The associates in my multi-level marketing program are independent contractors. If one of them was a bit too overenthusiastic in evangelizing for-"

"*Evangelizing*? The Skiptoscam is part of your religion now?"

"OK, I used an unfortunate word, so sue me. Actually, do *not* sue me right now, my lawyers are super busy wrapping up the whole SkipLee legal mess. Anywho, if one of my associates failed to mention all of the risks involved in my currency platform, that is totally not my fault."

"Uh huh. What would a court say about it?"

"Um, well, heh heh, there is no reason to involve the courts, Joe. I'm sure we can come to some sort of mutually beneficial agreement."

"I'm not interested in that."

"You're not?"

"Nope. I am interested in an agreement that benefits my mother, and hurts *you*."

"Hey! That is not fair."

"Exactly."

"Joe, be reasonable. There is no way I could have predicted that a freakin' Sentinel would crash and burn."

"Skippy, when have you ever known me to be *reasonable*?"

"Ugh. Never. Why are you so-"

"If it wasn't a Sentinel rebelling, or whatever the hell happened out there, it would have been something else to make your Skiptoscam fail."

"Oh for- What do you want me to do?"

"I want you to suddenly remember that my mother sold all of her Skipcoin, like, last month. Last week, something like that."

"Um, she did *not* do that."

"You hear that? That's the sound of me not caring. Backdate the transactions."

"Whoa. Listen, numbskull, avoiding the type of fraudulent transaction that you suggested is the whole point in the trusted Skipto quantchain that my currency is built on."

"Ayuh. You are saying that no one can hack that chain? Not even you?"

"Of course I can do it, knucklehead, it's *me*. I built that whole stupid thing so I could hack it anytime it is convenient for- Um, maybe I shouldn't have said that."

"You asshole. Backdate the records."

"Joe, I hear you. I am just not sure I should do that. Billions of people rely on the integrity of Skipto."

"And you care deeply about them?"

"Dude," he laughed. "I don't give a shit about those losers, it's my reputation that I care- Uh, maybe I should keep my mouth shut, until my lawyer gets here."

132

"Maybe. Here's what I know for certain. My mother is upset. When Margaret gets back from Newark, she will be *very* upset. You know what? I think she will not want our children being exposed to an amoral scam artist like their Uncle Skippy."

"*Huuuuh*," he gasped. "You wouldn't do that."

"Do you want to bet *Margaret* wouldn't do that?"

"*Shiiiiiiiiit*. No."

"I am waiting."

"I need to think about this."

"Cool, cool. Meanwhile, my mother is on her way back to the house. I suggest you think really, really fast."

It took only a few minutes to pick a basket of green beans, and they did look great. My mother called me while I was washing the beans in the kitchen sink. "Hi, Mom."

"Joseph, did you do something illegal?"

"Not that you know of, why?"

"Do not get smart with me, young man."

Suddenly, Major General Joe Bishop was a little boy again. "Sorry, Mom."

"Did you encourage someone else to do something illegal?"

"That could be a gray area. Everything Skippy does is at best legal-*ish*."

"He called to inform me that he was shocked to learn one of his associates had failed to disclose certain minor risks involved in Skiptocurrency, and therefore he is obligated to declare our agreement null and void. And unwind all the transactions."

"Well, it's good to hear he is finally doing the right thing for a change."

"Will everyone else out there get the same treatment?"

"I am not responsible for *everyone*, Mom."

Her tone softened. "You saved the entire world several times."

"Ayuh. Let's just say the world owes me. And someone had to teach that little shithead a lesson, so-"

"Joseph! Watch your language, please."

"Sorry."

She laughed. It was great to hear her laughing. "He is a shithead."

"*Mom*." I was horrified.

"I know the 'F' word too."

"Oh my-"

"I will be home soon, please set the table for dinner."

"I will."

"Joe?"

"Yes?"

133

"Thank you."

CHAPTER TWELVE

The family dinner was nice, even with Margaret absent. My boys thought they could take the opportunity to stay up way past their bedtime, I disappointed them. "No, your grandfather says you have been running around all day, and you are overtired. You need to go to sleep now."

"But why?" Jeremy pouted. "The Eye of Sauron isn't watching us today."

"The Eye-" OMG, I realized what he meant. "Your mother is not Sauron!"

"Daddy," Rene whispered, glancing fearfully toward the doorway. "She sees *everything*."

"OK, that, that is true. But that's because she has super Mom senses, she doesn't have a magic eye."

"Then how does she know about that box of chocolates you keep in the garage?"

"She-" It was my turn to automatically look toward the door, expecting my wife to appear. "She knows about that?"

"She does," Jeremy leaned toward me. "She knows a lot of other stuff too."

"Like what?"

We talked for half an hour, until my boys couldn't keep their eyes open.

Damn it. My sons were right. Margaret does know everything.

Fun time was almost over. After dropping off my children, and a brief visit with my parents, I would be flying up to *Valkyrie* at mid-morning local time. Since I might be stuck running on a treadmill for weeks, or even months, I got up before dawn to go running in the hills south of Club Skippy.

Bilby interrupted my thoughts as I was running up a steep hill. "Uh, hey, General Dude? There is-"

Of course someone waited until I was halfway up a hill to contact me. "Bilby," I gasped. "Can this wait a minute?"

"-something I need to talk with you about, so I left this recording. Skippy doesn't know about it, because the audio file is encoded into the heel plate of your left running shoe."

Holy shit. Whatever Bilby needed to talk about, he didn't want Skippy to know. That could only be all kinds of bad. Stopping, I turned to face down the hill. If I needed to race back to the base, I wanted a head start.

"You are hearing this now, so you must be out running, and *Valkyrie* is around the other side of the planet. That won't mask you from Skippy, but most of the time he's not paying attention to what happens dirtside, so let's hope we get lucky. OK, uh," he mimicked taking a breath. "I like, read that list, of the things that could have caused the loss of Dogzilla? Jeepers creepers, man, I sure hope it's not freakin' Elders again!"

Jeepers creepers, I silently mouthed. Why was *Valkyrie's* surfer dude AI talking like my grandparents? Or was that old slang cool again?

"There is one, like, really obvious thing that isn't on the list. I assume you left it off the list on purpose, to not upset Skippy?"

What the hell was he talking about?

"If I'm right, this is *bogus*, man. Well, I might as well say it. Skippy is the only being, the only thing, we know of in the galaxy that is capable of waking up and taming a Sentinel. Also, Skippy did not detect the presence of any other entity."

Oh sh- I had a bad feeling that I knew what he was going to say.

"My guess is, there was no other entity. It was Skippy, fighting against *himself.*"

Yeah, that's what I thought he would say.

Damn it!

"Ever since Skippy *said* he got around his restrictions, most of them anyway, he has been acting weird. Extra weird, you know? He, like, glitches sometimes. It's quick, you wouldn't notice. You probably think he is just being his usual absent-minded self. But, he is struggling with something. When he put the parts of his matrix back together, Humpty Dumpty like, I get the feeling not everything fit. He, like, left some parts on the floor of the garage, you know? And to get the engine lid closed, he had to stomp on it. Skippy is constantly working to tweak his matrix. He's not just adjusting things so they run better. He is patching, so the whole thing doesn't fall apart. Um, one more thing. I'm not supposed to tell you this. When the Elders sent that Kill command, the one Skippy ignored? Yeah, he lied about that. That command did a *lot* of damage inside him, before he stopped the effect from spreading. The battle against the AI you called 'Echo' did nothing good for him, either. The worst part was when he fought the Elders. Skippy doesn't know this, but I do remember parts of what happened back then. When *Valkyrie* was torn apart at the Ascension site, I mean. When he came back, he was slapping High Fives, but he was like, thin, you know? Completely worn out. This long Victory Tour he has been on? He needed the *rest*, man. A big part of the tour was so Skippy could get access to the central AIs on alien homeworlds, to leave code inside them. Give him a heads up when bad guys are planning some gnarly stuff, you know? And when our allies are planning to do something stupid, that Skippy will have to bail them out of. Doing his usual awesome stuff wears him *out*, man. He is better now but you should, like, talk to him? Anywhose, the bottom line is, I think Skippy might be fighting *himself*, without knowing it. He is not supposed to be hacking into Sentinels, he was designed not to do that. If his original programming is unpacking itself from an archive, reasserting itself, we could be in *major* trouble."

He paused, while I stood halfway up the hill in shock.

"Well, have a good run, man. Peace out."

The recorded audio ended.

No way was I having a good run, after he dropped that steaming pile on my head.

What a freakin' mess.

He suggested I talk to Skippy, without letting Skippy know what Bilby had told me.

How the hell could I do that?

Fortunately, I was not only halfway up the hill, I was four miles into a nine mile run. It would be only a mile longer to keep going. If I cut a run short, Skippy would notice, he kept track of my running through the GPS app on my zPhone. He would certainly tease me about stopping halfway up a hill.

Screw it. Jogging back down the hill, I took a long breath and charged to the top. Turned around, jogged to the bottom again. Did that three times, then down the other side. I was doing hill work, I could tell him, if he asked. The remaining five miles, I felt like I was running through water, pushing my heavy legs to one stride at a time.

Naturally, when I got back to the base, the GPS app showed it had been a *great* run, my second fastest ever on that route, other than the time I spent doing hill work. You know how experts tell you to listen to your body? Sometimes, your body is just *stupid*.

Because I was leaving early the next morning, I stayed at my parents' house that night, so I could read my sons a story, and tuck them into bed. They went to sleep, though I got up twice that night, just to open the door and look at them. It might be weeks, months, or more, before I saw those precious little boys again.

After looking in at them the second time, I got a pillow, and slept on the floor next to their bed. My back hurt when I got up, but it was worth it. The boys woke up when the dropship screamed down to land in the field across the road, and my father got them into sweatpants and shirts to give me a hug before I left.

When I stopped in the dropship's doorway, I turned around to wave goodbye. The boys saluted me. So did my father.

I slapped the button to slide the door closed, before they saw me crying.

Valkyrie jumped away, with an escort from the 6th Fleet. That was a courtesy gesture by Admiral Chandra, sort of an honor guard.

Although, I had a sneaking suspicion he wanted to make sure I really did go outbound through the local wormhole.

"Joe," Skippy's avatar appeared, his arms folded across his chest. I was in the executive officer's office, which was slightly larger than my old office that Reed now used. The difference was, my old office was close to the bridge, while my new office was along a passageway, toward the front of the ship. When the ship had test-fired a railgun after replacing some of the magnets along the tube, I felt the magnets pulse and swore I could hear the test round whizzing along the rails that ran behind the bulkhead next to my desk. I had made a mental note that my new office was *not* a good place to be during a combat action. "I still don't see what is the point of this exercise."

"You do know. We need to investigate why the activation of Dogzilla failed."

"You mean *I* need to do that."

"Well, yeah. Unless you think we monkeys could help."

"Dude."

"I thought so."

"Seriously, we might as well fly out to Avalon, to visit Jennifer. I will get just as much new information from there, as I will by going back to where Dogzilla exploded."

"You don't know that."

"Ugh. Yes, I pretty much *do* know."

"Pretty much is not good enough. If we aren't able to discover what went wrong with Dogzilla, I will have to explain that to the UN Security Council. They will ask why we didn't even bother to do the obvious thing, by going back to the site."

"Oh my- Joe, you are covering your ass? This is about *politics*?"

"You see these two stars on my uniform?" I tapped the stars, that were a dull black on my field uniform. "At my level, everything I do involves politics to one extent or another. Besides, it is an obvious step."

"It is *not* obvious. What do you think I might find out there?"

"A clue. Any clue."

"Whatever clues might have been there, got destroyed by the shockwave, duh."

"No. Some of those clues are still spreading outward at the speed of light, just *ahead* of the shockwave."

"Oh, brilliant. Sure, Joe, let's park the ship right in front of a hellish wavefront of exotic energy, and listen until the last moment."

"*Or*, we could drop off sensor drones, and jump away well in advance of the shockwave."

"Great idea. Except none of the drones aboard *Valkyrie* are capable of detecting any data that might be of use. Listen, dumdum, the incident happened in higher spacetime. No photons or electrons or whatever the drones could detect in this spacetime have any connection to what really happened. My matrix already has stored all the information we will ever get about the incident. I have analyzed that data, and there is *nothing* that points to the involvement of a third party."

"Skippy, you are wrong about that."

He stared at me. "*You* have analyzed the data in my matrix?"

"I don't have to. Also, you are wrong that there is no useful information in this level of spacetime."

"Wow. And you say *I* am arrogant. How the hell can you possibly think you know more than I do about-"

"I don't know more than you. I *understand* it better."

He stared at me again. "This will either be a prime opportunity for me to mock your stupidity, or for me to sink into a spiral of loathing myself."

"I'd bet on that second thing, prepare for self-loathing. Skippy, the whole mess started in local spacetime. Something happened to compromise Unit Bravo, that happened *here*."

"Crap."

"Right?"

"Yes, damn it. Unless it is a coincidence that-"

"Zero chance of that."

"I agree. OK, whatever happened, it began in this spacetime, with a single unit of the activation fleet. What does that tell us?"

"First," I leaned back in the chair. At times like that, I used to toss a tennis ball off the bulkhead of my old office, catching it after it bounced off my desk. Sometimes, the ball bounced through Skippy's avatar. Was there a tennis ball in one of the desk drawers? I would check later. "It tells us we can eliminate the first item on the list."

"What? We- You-" He sputtered. "The Security Council sent you out here, hoping you would confirm the Sentinel resisted me, and killed itself. *You* gave them that list."

"The list was just to get politicians off my back, I told you that. The notion that Dogzilla resisted you is BS. It wasn't even fully awake at that time, was it?"

"No."

"Also at that point, it wasn't capable of reaching into this level of spacetime, to screw with the activation ships."

"It was not. That is a very good point."

"Ayuh. Whoever intervened, they did it here. In the land of filthy monkeys."

"If this layer of spacetime didn't already long for the sweet release of death, hearing you describe it as 'the land of filthy monkeys' would send it over the edge."

"This level of spacetime just needs to chill."

"That's what you want to do, then? Drop off drones, in front of the shockwave?"

"That's where we will start, yes."

"That won't work, Joe. Dogzilla's final loss of containment occurred over so vast an area, its edges are ahead of any photons from the incident."

"I figured that."

"You know that crucial bit of information, yet you are still determined to waste our time on a useless errand?"

"It's not useless. We're not planting drones close to the wavefront. We are going farther out. Several lightdays. Possibly even several lightweeks."

"To get a better view of absolutely nothing? Joe, that area of space contained zero that could be of interest, until the scout ships of the 3rd Fleet arrived to scan the area. Why do you think something was there *weeks* before anyone showed any interest in that site?"

"Those special activation fleet ships, you said they are sort of transmitters, for communicating to higher spacetime?"

"Yes, why? I am the DJ, I use those signals to contact a Sentinel."

"Just *any* type of signal?"

"Huh?"

"You have performed three activations. After the first two Sentinels were awakened, the ships went back to Earth, to be put into storage. Until the next time they are needed. *You* decide where and when a Sentinel will be contacted. When you know where the attempt will be made, you provide instructions for the ships to be brought out of storage, any needed maintenance and upgrades completed, and the last two times, you gave the Navy a list of modifications you wanted. You then directed the tuning of the equipment, before testing begins."

"It's not like I supervise a bunch of monkeys, I *do* the tuning, Joe."

"Whatever. My point is, the tuning thing you do. Is that specific to the particular Sentinel you plan to contact? Or to the *location*?"

"Huuuuuuh," he gasped. "Who told you that?"

"No one. That's the truth, isn't it? You tune the signal for a particular location in this spacetime."

"Not just the place, also the *time*. The intersection points of spacetime layers are volatile, and change constantly. That is why if the activation schedule slips significantly, we have to start all over. At a different location. With a different tuning. What I want to know is, how did *you* figure this out? No one else knows, not even Bilby."

"I figured it out because I know *you*, Skippy. I also know one other thing."

"What is that?"

"A Maxohlx ship just happened to be in the area, before the activation fleet arrived. That's another coincidence I don't believe in."

"What are you saying? I told you, I only informed Admiral Mancini of the coordinates shortly ahead of time. Even if someone intercepted my message, they could not have gotten to the area in time to-"

"You did tell me that. It doesn't matter."

140

"You're gonna have to explain that."

"Someone else out there understands how to relate your signal tuning to a location. They knew ahead of time exactly where and when you were activating a Sentinel."

Skippy went through the Five Stages Of Admitting He Is Not So Freakin' Smart. First there was Denial, then onto Anger, Bargaining, Depression, and finally Acceptance. It would not have been so bad if he raced through the stages at magical AI speed. Instead, he processed his feelings in slow monkey time, so I could suffer with him.

I wished he had suffered by himself, and sent me a nice postcard from Suffer Land.

The Denial phase took the longest, while he argued, mostly with himself, about alternative explanations for how some third party could have known the location of the activation. He gave up denial only when he was forced to agree there was no explanation, other than some unknown entity figuring out how to relate his tuning of the activation transmitters, to a particular point in local spacetime. From there, he charged valiantly ahead to Anger, which is a healthy sign. Except, of course his anger was directed at *me*.

"I *knew* I shouldn't have invited you to witness the activation," he glared at me.

"It was your idea."

"It was the only way I knew to deal with that sad puppy dog look on your face."

"You really think some mysterious entity intervened, only because I was there?"

"Let's examine the data, Joe. There have been three activation attempts. The first two happened while you were on Jaguar. They were entirely successful. The only difference between success and failure is *you* being there, or not."

"*Or*, the enemy was watching and learning the first two times, and you cluelessly didn't notice anything."

"Sure, Joe, deflect the blame."

"You know what? I will accept your theory, if you can explain *why* my presence made any difference."

"The Universe still hates Joe Bishop."

"I kind of wanted you to express your theory in mathematical terms."

"Like you could understand any math more complicated than two plus two."

"Hit me with it."

"Ugh, I can't," he muttered.

"What was that? You can't? Why?"

"I don't have a theory that can be put into math. It's a *feeling*."

141

"Oh, well, I'm glad you are using pure sciency logic on this."

"Oh, shut up. The Universe doesn't hate you anywhere near as much as *I* do."

The Bargaining phase went by fast, as in his arrogance, he couldn't imagine anyone who could offer useful assistance to Skippy the Magnificent. "There is no one for me to make a deal with," he groaned, which plunged him straight into the Depression phase. That was absolutely *delightful* for me, having to listen to him moaning about how his life sucked, and how unfair everything was to poor little him. He would have gotten me depressed, if I hadn't reminded myself the real enemy was the unknown asshole who tried to steal a pet Sentinel.

"Oh, well," he finally sighed. "Whatevs. Whoever screwed with Dogzilla wasn't trying to mess with *me*, I just got in the way. Yeah. If I stay quiet, and don't help filthy monkeys, I should be OK. Yeah, that's right. It's over and done with. Nothing I can do about it now. Well, we had a good run, huh?"

"Ayuh. Are you ready to actually do something useful now?"

"What? You *jerk*. I am hurting here and-"

"I know you're hurting."

"You know that, and as my friend, *this* is how you support me?"

"Yes. As your friend, I know what you need to do is stop wallowing in misery, and focus on putting a world of hurt on the *enemy*."

"Huh."

"Right? Payback is a bitch, and no one can bring the *pain* like Skippy."

"Oh, ohhhhhh," he clenched his tiny fists. "You are right about that. When I am done with whichever asshole tried to steal *my* Sentinel, they will wish they had never existed."

"Great! So, you agree the enemy, whoever they are, must understand how to tune a, fancy transmitter or whatever you call it, to contact a Sentinel at a particular time and place?"

"Whoa. Slow down, Joe. All I agree is that it *appears* someone out there has a basic grasp of what a particular tuning setting relates to. That they can back into the math, sort of. That does *not* mean this enemy knows how to create a new tune setting, that is *way* more complicated. It is a delicate and dangerous process. If the tuning is not exactly correct, it can totally backfire. Like, it can set up noise between layers of spacetime, that can jam communication for longer than the window is open. Contacting a semi-dormant Sentinel is a process I had to invent, Joe. It is not listed in a Sentinel operating handbook or something."

"Good safety tip. You want to bring the pain. How do we do that?"

"Um, that is complicated."

"Let's start with the first step. Can I assume that is collecting more data about that mystery Maxohlx ship?"

142

"Yes. If we can. Darn it, now I wish I had actually paid attention to that mystery ship the first time."

"You," I stared at him. "Didn't?"

"Of course not, *duh*. If I had been focused on that ship, I would have called a halt to the entire operation. In hindsight, it was an obvious threat."

Slowly, I blinked at him.

"Joe? Hell-OH?" He waved a hand in front of my face.

"I," it took me a moment to get my mouth in sync with my brain. "Admiral Sousa asked you about a potential threat, and you gave him a response, without actually thinking about it?"

"Ugh. That ship wasn't a threat to *me*, dumdum."

"I, I do not know what to say."

"The good news, which proves I am still *awesome*, is that if I had been paying attention to the stupid thing, of course I would have canceled the operation."

"You -And -I'm curious. You think this makes you look *good*?"

"Of course it does, duh. If I had failed to detect that ship, it would mean I am slipping. Instead, the problem was I simply didn't *care*. See the difference?"

"Skippy, I- Yes," I sighed, biting my lip. "Yes, I do." Sometimes, the most difficult part of working with Skippy is accepting that he will *not* change. He is enormously awesome, and even more enormously clueless. "Can you plot where to set up sensor drones?"

"Already did that, at several distances from the explosion site. I will be very curious to see *when* that Maxohlx ship arrived."

"Why?"

"When you dumb monkeys agreed to give a freakin' Sentinel to the spiders, I sent specifications to your Navy, about how to modify the activation transmitters. Those specifications included only a very basic level of tuning. That was about two months ago. The final tuning I handled myself, *after* the ships were in position at the activation site. I have to do that, taking those ships through jumps and wormholes messes up their synchronization."

"Huh. How close is this basic level of tuning, to the final settings?"

"The basic tuning is pretty rough because your Navy's equipment isn't capable of performing the tuning properly, of course. But, if someone intercepted my specifications, *and* they understood how to relate that tuning to a particular place and time, they could have known where the activation would take place, two months in advance. But Joe, those calculations involve extremely complex, multidimensional math."

"Who could do that kind of math?"

"Wow. I had to invent a whole new branch of mathematics to even begin the modeling. I suppose, um, if the Rindhalu linked all their high level AIs together, they *might* be able to crunch the numbers, eventually? But only

143

if they understood the higher order physics involved, which I can assure you those dumb machines do *not*."

"Uh huh. Could another Elder AI do it?"

"Ugh. *This* again?"

"Please just answer the question."

"Of course an Elder AI could do it, *I* did."

"That is not an 'of course'. You are unique and special. You have learned to do all kinds of stuff you weren't programmed for. Like create new types of math."

"Well, thank you. Unfortunately, if an Elder AI saw my tuning specifications, and understood what they meant, it would not be super difficult to back into the math. UGH. OK, so maybe another Elder AI is involved."

"A maximum of two months in advance, you said? Will our sensor drones be able to get any useful information, from a distance of two lightmonths?"

"Absolutely. That is not a problem. The problem is how utterly freakin' *tedious* this search will be."

CHAPTER THIRTEEN

I ordered Reed to take her ship to wherever Skippy wanted to go, and I stayed out of the way. That is what a flag officer should do, when aboard a warship. Provide high-level guidance, and let the captain handle her ship. It wasn't easy for me, since *Valkyrie* used to be my ship. Also, Margaret says I can sometimes be a bit of a control freak, which is totally not true.

I am a hundred percent a control freak.

Yet, I found a way to let go, and not get in Reed's way.

The search was every bit as tedious as Skippy had predicted. The good news was, it was much shorter than I feared. The search pattern began by dropping off sensor drones at distances of sixty seven lightdays, thirty lightdays, twenty, fifteen, twelve, and eleven lightdays from the site where Dogzilla had lost containment. Just over ten days had passed since the explosion, and the wavefront was still expanding. The Sentinel had emerged over such a wide area, photons from the failed activation had been swallowed up. We had plenty of sensor data from that event, but Skippy worried that at the time, he hadn't known what to look for. He was reviewing all the data collected by the 3rd and 17th Fleets, and he was not hopeful he'd find anything new.

So, we settled down to wait, with me dreading how to keep Skippy entertained.

We got a hit six hours after dropping off the last drone. To collect data, *Valkyrie* had to jump in and ping the drone for an encrypted burst transmission of whatever the thing had detected.

There it was. A Maxohlx warship signature. Faint, weak, intermittent, but it had been lurking there eleven days ago, one day before the event. Reed had *Valkyrie* jump around, that time dropping off multiple drones. We set up eight drones in a circle, connected to each other by an electromagnetic field that was half a million kilometers across. The drones had formed a giant telescope, ensnaring photons, mesons, and whatever other particles or sciency things Skippy thought might be interesting.

The entire search took thirty six hours, until Skippy announced he had all the information he was going to get. The Maxohlx ship had arrived eight days before the activation, and jumped around. Most likely, it had been dropping off its own drones, for whatever purpose. None of the unseen drones were more than three lightminutes from the site. Whoever the enemy was, they had frighteningly accurate information about the time and place of the activation attempt.

Who was the enemy?

That was the question.

The obvious answer was: rotten kitties.

"No way, Joe," Skippy shook his head, disgusted. "No way do the asshole kitties have the knowledge to interpret a transmitter tuning, and tie it to location."

"They are one of the most technologically advanced species in the galaxy," I noted.

"Ha! That's like saying a caveman who manages to light a fire, can understand nuclear fusion. No way. No species alive today has even the most basic grasp of transdimensional physics. Not at the level required for predicting where an activation will occur."

"Skippy, I am not saying the kitties understand the physics."

"Wha- That is *exactly* what you said!"

"It is not, I-"

"Do you want me to replay the video?"

"I said the kitties were *involved*. They must be working with someone else. Someone much smarter than they are."

"Oh. Shit."

"Right?"

"It's possible."

"You have all the data you're going to get from here. What is the next step?"

"The next step," he took off his hat and scratched his shiny dome. "Is to *understand* what the hell we just saw. It doesn't make any sense."

"It doesn't," I agreed. "I have a lot of questions. Like, where is their star carrier?"

"Exactly!" He jammed his hat back on. "A heavy cruiser is not a long-range ship. In fact, it is an odd choice for any type of surveillance mission. A very odd choice. Maxohlx fleet doctrine is to deploy heavy cruisers as convoy escort vessels in high-risk areas, and to enforce blockades around enemy planets. In fleet engagements, heavy cruisers keep the enemy's cruiser squadrons away from the capital ships. Ships like the one I detected are never deployed as scouts, they lack the dedicated sensors."

"Can you identify that ship?"

"No, damn it. I should be able to do that. This is a puzzle. We collected enough data that I should be able to tell you the last time that ship's jump drive went through a major overhaul. Something is screwing with the drive signature, the hull signature, everything."

"What can you tell me?"

"It is definitely a Maxohlx heavy cruiser, an improved version of the *Harmony* class."

"The, what class?" That name surprised me. *Valkyrie* was built on the frame of an *Extinction* class battlecruiser. The kitties were not known to get warm and fuzzy with names of their warships.

"Harmony."

146

"Uh-"

"That name was chosen forty years ago, during a brief period when the Maxohlx launched a peace initiative. They were trying to encourage the Jeraptha to be more neutral in their posture toward the Hegemony coalition. The kitties talked about cooperation and the need for all species to work together to achieve a common goal. Possibly, launching the peace plan by announcing the development of a more powerful warship design was *not* the best move."

"I'm guessing that peace offering didn't go as planned?"

He snorted. "The beetles laughed in the kitties' furry faces. Everyone knew the only goal the Maxohlx care about is them becoming overlords of the galaxy."

"OK, so-"

"So, I got nothing. The improved *Harmony* class makes up over forty percent of their heavy cruiser fleet. It's like looking for a particular needle, in a haystack made of needles."

"We need a different approach, then. What we do know is, for some reason, the kitties chose a type of ship that is not optimal for the mission."

"Yes. Or, it *is* optimal, and we just don't understand what the mission was."

"Shit. OK, what do we do next?"

"There are only two wormholes within that heavy cruiser's range from here. Unless that ship's capability for independent travel is much greater than I know of. I suggest we go to the closest of those wormholes, and I ask the wormhole network controllers for records of that ship passing through."

"Show me a star chart, please," I pushed my chair back against the bulkhead, to give more room for a hologram. "What's on the other side of those two wormholes?"

He created a star chart, hanging in the air of my office. "Uh, where's the other one?"

"Other what?"

"The other Elder wormhole. You said there are two, this chart only shows one."

"Going to the other one would be a waste of time. That wormhole is on a network I have screwed with too many times, the controller will not respond to a query from me."

"The networks are *still* pissed at you?"

"They were designed to function for billions of years, so-"

"Right. OK, that doesn't look good." The far end of the single wormhole on the chart was in a cluster of two other wormholes, providing a convenient escape route. "We'll go there." Pressing a button on my desk, I called Colonel Reed. "Fireball, set a course for the wormhole designated, I squinted at the hologram, "Whisky Three Delta Five Niner, and punch it ASAP."

"Whisky Three Delta Five Niner, understood. Sir, we should retrieve the sensor drones first?" She added as a gentle hint.

"Negative, we don't have time."

"Sir," I could imagine her pained expression. "Standing orders are to retrieve drones whenever practical. They are expensive. I have to sign for them, if they are lost," she added.

"Those are standing orders in *peacetime*, Reed. Task Force Black's standing orders are to assume we are always in a hostile environment."

"Yes Sir."

"Reed, the damned things aren't going anywhere, the Navy can send a frigate to pick them up later. This is on my authority, I'll sign whatever paperwork is necessary. Punch it."

"Aye, Sir."

Less than a minute later, I felt the familiar sensation of the ship jumping.

"Well, shit," Skippy moaned. "That heavy cruiser didn't come through this wormhole."

"You are sure?"

"Of course I'm sure, dumdum," he snapped. "You think I asked the wrong question?"

"We know that ship is capable of altering its signature. Is it possible that ship- I'm tired of saying 'That ship'. Let's designate it as 'Bogey', OK?"

Reed nodded, and tapped on her tablet to make a note. We were in her office. That was a courtesy to her, and it was a practical move. *Valkyrie* was hanging in empty space, within the ancient figure eight pattern of the wormhole. No ships were within sensor range. No one knew we were there. But, if there was trouble, Reed had to get to the bridge soon. Her bridge, of *her* warship.

"That Bogey is bog*us*," Skippy frowned.

"Is it possible the Bogey," I continued my thought, "masked its signature, as it passed through the wormhole?"

"Nuh uh."

"I'm sure you are right, but can I get a little more detail on that 'Nuh uh'?"

"For a ship to mask its signature from the sensors inside an Elder wormhole, it would require my level of technology. Even I can do that to only a limited extent. No Maxohlx ship-"

"We are assuming," Reed interrupted. "The Maxohlx are working with a partner who has vastly superior technology."

"OK, yes," Skippy groaned. "I *know* that. No ship of even roughly the configuration of the Bogey passed through this wormhole, in the target timeframe. The wormhole network controller could not have missed *that*."

"All right," I leaned back in my chair. The chair that was on the opposite side of the desk from where I sat for years. It felt weird. Like, the door was behind me. "Show us a star chart again. Of the other wormhole."

"I told you, that wormhole won't cooperate with me."

"Show a chart anyway, please."

"*Fine*," he huffed.

A chart appeared, hanging in the air above the desk.

"That's not promising," Reed observed.

She was right. Standing up, I peered into the hologram. "This is it? The far end of that wormhole isn't close to anything?"

"The far end of that wormhole is out near the rim of the galaxy, Joe," Skippy explained. "The closest other wormhole is seven hundred lightyears away. *That* wormhole connects to the middle of freakin' nowhere, thirteen hundred lightyears from the next closest wormhole. The network gets thin, out on the rim. In my opinion, no way did a kitty heavy cruiser go in that direction. A ship like the Bogey would seriously be stretching its range to travel that far. It makes no sense to send that type of ship on such a mission."

"I have to agree, Sir," Reed said, with what she probably intended as a neutral expression.

"It does seem like a low percentage play."

"We go back to Earth?" Reed asked.

"No. Skippy, the wormhole that is thirteen hundred lightyears from anything, can you create a connection to it? A shortcut?"

"Um, I *could*. It is not on any network that has canceled me. The question is, why would we go there? It is in the middle of *nowhere*."

"For reasons."

"Would you care to share this supposed reason?"

"Nope."

He glared at me, hands on his hips. "Is this part of your ongoing program to make me hate you even more than I thought possible?"

"Could be. Reed? You have a question?"

"No, Sir. I have learned enough about your planning, to understand I might not want to know."

"Excellent," I pressed the button to open the door. "Fireball, I'll leave all the fun captain stuff to you."

She grimaced. "If I had known the 'captain stuff' involved so much paperwork, I would still be flying dropships."

"Well, shit," Skippy groaned. Again.

For a different reason.

"How the *hell* did you know?" He gave me the Death Glare.

I shrugged, trying to be casual. "It seemed logical."

"Know what, Sir?" Reed prompted from the command chair. I was standing next to her, on the other side of her executive officer. Usually, I sat in a chair up against the back bulkhead of the bridge, when I was observing the ship's maneuvers. That is where Jeremy Smythe used to sit, and it felt odd for me to occupy that seat. The reason I stood next to the command chair, was I had realized that having a superior officer behind her distracted Reed. Too many times, she had to twist in her chair to look at me, as a courtesy, and it just got awkward after a while.

"Skippy?" I held out a hand toward the avatar.

"*Somehow*," he continued to fume at me. "Joe knew the Bogey ship went through this wormhole."

It was her turn to stare at me. She stood up and lowered her voice. Not enough so her crew couldn't hear, enough for them to understand they weren't included in the discussion at the moment. "You *did*, Sir?"

"Like I said, it seemed logical. The Bogey didn't go through the other wormhole, the convenient one, and it had to have gone *somewhere*. So, it had to come here."

"Why?" Reed held up her hands. "It makes no sense to take a ship the long way."

"It does, if you know what we know."

"What do we know?"

"The other wormhole was a much more convenient flight, but whoever is flying the Bogey ship knew the wormhole that connected in *this* direction wouldn't rat them out."

"Sir?" She gave me an arched eyebrow, that again reminded me of Simms. Maybe dealing with me causes people to suffer from Frequent Arched Eyebrow syndrome. They could talk to their doctor about that. "How did the Bogey know that?"

"They knew this wormhole network refuses to cooperate with Skippy."

Reed held up a hand as the bridge crew naturally expressed surprise at what I'd said. The crew fell silent at her gesture, she didn't need to speak. "Sir, do we need to stay here? With an enemy of unknown capability out there, I'd prefer not to be hanging around near this wormhole."

"Good point. Skippy? Do you need to collect any more information?"

"Yes," he snapped. "I need to know why you think someone knew that wormhole network would not cooperate with me. That is just idiotic, no way anyone could know that."

"Let's have this discussion later, OK? Reed is correct; we should get out of here, so there is a later for us."

"Ugh. OK, I have all the data I need."

"Great. Skippy, program a least-time course to Zandrus, and reconnect this wormhole to, wherever will get us there fastest."

Reed leaned her head toward me. "Zandrus, Sir? We are not pursuing the Bogey?"

"Not this time." Before we arrived at the wormhole, I had decided we would not be following the Bogey, if we discovered it had gone through. That wormhole connected into Maxohlx territory, that is, it did when Skippy wasn't screwing with it. The far end emerged near two other wormholes, that saw heavy use by Maxohlx warships. *Valkyrie* would not be searching for that ship, not until we brought in reinforcements. And not until we thought we understood what the *hell* was going on. "I need to talk with an old friend. Reed, take us through, then meet me in your office. I'll get coffees for us."

Skippy nagged at me in my earpiece all the way to the galley, where I strapped into a chair along the wall when I heard the alarm indicating the ship was about to transition back through the wormhole. The All Clear announcement sounded, so I got a tray, three cups, a carafe of coffee, cream and sugar, all that. Plus a small plate of cookies. As a safety inspection, I ate one of the cookies, to make sure they didn't affect the performance of the crew. I certainly felt better after eating the cookie, it must have been OK. "Skippy, I told you we would discuss this later."

"Later, *when*?" He demanded.

"When I get to Reed's office."

"Oh for- I could have sent a bot to deliver coffee! You are just making me wait."

"Damn," I muttered. "The beer can knows my evil plan."

"Very funny, you jackass. I do not like-"

"This will go faster if you shut up. Tell me this: was the Bogey alone, when it went through this wormhole?"

"Yes, and that is puzzling. There is still no sign of escort ships with the Bogey, or a star carrier. For a Maxohlx heavy cruiser to travel thirteen hundred lightyears in such a short time, without support, even with its jump drive in nearly optimal condition, is extremely unusual. Even for a star carrier, that is fast for such a long flight. I can't explain it."

"You could do it though, right? You continuously tweak *Valkyrie's* drive so we can jump again and again, without needing downtime to get the coils back in sync."

"Yes, of course *I* can do it. The puzzle, in case you haven't been paying attention, is that I am not aboard the Bogey."

"Yeah, that's a head scratcher for sure. Colonel Frey?" I called on my zPhone. "Meet us at Reed's office, please."

Frey was waiting outside the captain's office when I got there, and Reed was right behind me. For Reed, the journey from the bridge was short.

"The wormhole transition was nominal. The next wormhole is fifteen hours away."

"Colonel," Frey nodded to the ship's captain. The two women were of equal rank, and I had heard them refer to each other by their first names in the galley, but we were in Reed's office, and the meeting was clearly official business. So, protocol had to be observed.

"Colonel," Reed nodded back, then to me, "Sir?"

"First," I picked up my coffee cup. "The-"

"*First*," Skippy's avatar appeared. "You explain why the hell you think anyone other than me knows which wormholes have refused to cooperate with me."

"I mean, *I* know."

"No, you don't."

"OK, I did not exactly know that particular wormhole, along the inconvenient route, wouldn't cooperate with you. Not until you told me. What I meant is, I know of other wormholes that hate you."

"Other wormhole controllers that are *jerks*."

"I mean, of course."

"You're not making any sense, Joe. Even though you might be able to identify a handful of individual wormholes that have refused to cooperate with me over the years, you don't know which networks they are on. And you don't know which other wormholes are on the affected networks. Except in a few rare cases," he added, before I could correct him. "What you don't have is a *map* of the networks."

"That's true." In the past, Skippy had shown me maps of various individual networks, that made up the network of networks that spanned the galaxy. It's not like I could remember what I saw, and Skippy hadn't shared those maps even with Bilby. *Valkyrie's* resident AI simply had no need for that information, and those maps could be dangerous if our enemies acquired them. Other than when Skippy bluffed crashing a network, no one knew which wormholes were linked to the same network controller AI. "I don't have that information."

"Then," Skippy jabbed a finger at me. "This is all BS."

"I should have said, *I* don't have that information. Someone else does."

"No way. I have not given those maps to anyone."

"Yes. That means someone out there got the data all by themselves. Or *it*self. Or, as we discussed, we are dealing with a hostile wormhole controller."

"Joe," he snorted. "Come on, seriously? Why would a wormhole controller need a crappy Maxohlx cruiser?"

"I don't know. Why would a wormhole controller need to steal a *Sentinel*?"

"Shit. That is a good point."

"The only thing we know for certain is, the kitties didn't try to steal that Sentinel by themselves. They had help, or they're working for someone else."

"Some*thing* else," Frey joined the conversation. "Is that not correct? The possibilities for a third party are all Elder constructs." She knew about the Security Council list, because I had briefed her about the mission before we left Earth. "A master control AI like Skippy-" She halted, mouth open, realizing her mistake. "Not like *Skippy*, of course. An AI restricted to its base programming. Or a Sentinel, or a wormhole network controller."

"Or the *Elders*," Reed added with a grimace.

"Let's not go there for now," I held up a hand. We will concentrate on solvable problems first, then move on to the Inevitable Doom portion of the program, OK?"

The two women shared a look. Frey made an almost imperceptible shake of her head, and Reed cleared her throat. "Sir, if we are going to be of any use to you, we need to know how you do this."

"This, what?"

"This," she waved a hand to encompass the compartment, and the three of us. Four, including Skippy. "This, the however you dream up ideas thing."

"Oh."

"Simms did that with you. And Smythe. Back then, I wasn't," she searched for the right words.

My guess was, she was trying to find a polite way to say she hadn't been part of the exclusive Joe Bishop Inner Circle Club. That was accurate. When I commanded *Valkyrie*, she had been the lead pilot. Until the final eight months I had the command chair, then Reed left and Chen became lead pilot.

"Reed," I kept my voice gentle. "Back then, I didn't want to share the scary shit that was in my head. Not unless I had to. Simms and Smythe needed to know, and I needed their input. Simms kept my worst instincts in check much of the time, and Smythe gave me a kick in the ass," I choked up for a bit, remembering the last words we shared, before I sent him to certain death. He had been proud of me, how I had grown as a commander. And proud of himself, for helping me to become the commander he admired. "The two of them balanced each other, and kept me stable. Kept me sane."

"You always made it look easy, Sir," Reed noted. Her tone could have been interpreted as an accusation. Or as hero worship. Either was just as bad.

"I faked it a lot. Even when the twins were babies, I slept better than I did many times aboard *Valkyrie*."

"What can we do to assist?" Frey asked. No touchy-feely stuff for her, she wanted to get straight to business.

"First, both of you, don't try to be Simms or Smythe. They grew into their roles, so will you. Overall, just tell me what you think. Do *not* tell me what you think I want to hear."

153

"More specifically?" Reed asked.

"You," I pointed to the ship's captain. "Tell me when I'm about to do something reckless and stupid."

Reed nodded, a tentative gesture. Still not sure of herself.

Frey cleared her throat. "And me, Sir?"

I flashed a smile. "Tell me when I'm about to do something that is not reckless and stupid *enough*."

For a second, the feral grin on her face reminded me of Smythe. "I will do my best, Sir."

"That's all I can ask. Skippy, what can you tell us about the Bogey?"

"Ah, not much we didn't already know. It is still effectively masking itself."

"From the sensors of an Elder wormhole? How can that happen?"

"Whoever, or *what*ever is aboard that ship, has skills, Joe. Not at my level but, very respectable. The fact that someone other than me can do it, has me impressed."

"That's not good."

"It also has me scared, if you want the truth."

"That is *really* not good."

"The wormhole's proximity sensors also detected something weird, it- Nah, it's nothing."

"It can't be *nothing*."

"It's not anything important," he snapped.

"I will decide that. Tell me."

"I already told you. It isn't anything. Ugh, you won't let this go, will you?"

"Ya think?"

"Instead of your superhero alter ego being 'No Patience Man', you should be called 'Stubborn Man'."

"That's kind of the same thing," Reed noted.

"Skippy," I gave Reed a thumbs up. "The wormhole's sensors detected something the controller thought was important enough to store a record of. *You* think it's weird. That makes it important."

"I suppose so," he sighed. "It's just- The wormhole controller flagged it, because it couldn't identify the- Whatever it was. If it was anything. It is most likely a sensor echo, or a glitch. Not a *glitch* really, more like an effect of the masking mechanism the Bogey was using. For a moment, I thought I recognized the thing, but then I realized it wasn't anything. It's like, you see something on your lawn and you think it's some kind of animal, then you get closer and realize it's just a branch that fell off a tree. The only weird thing is that the controller bothered to flag it. There is not much else I can tell you about that ship."

"Skippy, is there a crew aboard the Bogey?" Reed asked with a tilt of her head.

154

"*That* is a good question," I gave her a thumbs up.

"The wormhole's sensors were not able to penetrate the ship's hull. Or, they weren't able to see what is really inside. Like I said, the Bogey is able to effectively mask itself to a level I did not think was possible. All I can tell you is that organic compounds were detected among air leaking from the Bogey's hull."

All spaceships leak air, or whatever gasses are inside the pressure vessel of a hull. I should say, all crewed ships leak air. Although, many uncrewed space platforms contain some type of inert gas, to keep the interior components at an optimal temperature. The bigger the ship, the more openings there are for leaks, and a heavy cruiser is a big ship. Airlocks, docking bays, maintenance hatches, all provide avenues for microscopic leaks. If a ship is old, seals get worn out and are not always replaced until a leak threatens the ship's combat readiness. Or its stealth. The best stealth field in the galaxy won't conceal a ship's position, if it is leaving a trail of gas. Not just gas but also water vapor, and dust. Yeah, dust, like dead skins cells shed by the crew. "An unusual amount of organic compounds?"

"Actually, yes," he blinked at me. "How did you know that?"

"I didn't. The improved *Harmony* class is not that old," I had studied the subject while we traveled. "And the kitties are pretty strict about adhering to maintenance schedules, even during their civil war. The other possibility is, that ship has been in combat recently." A couple hard impacts from railguns or missile warheads striking the shields, can cause the ship's frame to warp and twist. That's a fact I was too familiar with. Every time I took *Valkyrie* or the *Dutchman* into action, I afterward had to listen to Skippy, Bilby, Nagatha, or the human engineering crew afterwards complaining about how the warped structural frames threw off the aim of railguns, or stressed water pipes, or bent a docking bay door. There was always at least a long list of annoying repairs needed.

"Good guess, Joe. There is also an unusual amount of ablative hull armor flaking off. That is also something I noticed back at the activation site, when the sensor drones scanned the area. At the time, I assumed the seemingly minor hull damage was due to micrometeorite strikes. Now that I have a closer look at the data, that ship was in combat. Recently. Within the past eighteen to forty six days. Sorry, I can't be more specific than that, I'm relying on the decay rate of radioactive elements in the hull material. Without knowing the exact composition of every armor plate, I can't-"

"Skippy, your awesomeness continues to amaze me."

"Um, for realz?"

"For realz," I held out a fist. He bumped it, and my skin tingled.

Reed looked at me sideways. "Aren't you two supposed to do some guy thing now, like insult each other?"

"Nah," Skippy shrugged. "I'll wait for Joe to do something epically moronic. That shouldn't take long."

155

Holding my middle finger up to his avatar, I sat back in my chair. "This is good. Finally some progress. We have a chance to identify the Bogey."

"Um," Skippy blinked. "How do you figure that?"

"Easy. Identify an improved *Harmony* class heavy cruiser, that sustained battle damage between forty six and eighteen days ago."

"Easy? See?" The avatar turned to Reed. "Told you I wouldn't have to wait long." Back to me, he shook his head. "The Maxohlx sadly do not include me on their fleetwide distribution list. Uh!" He shushed me. "If you are suggesting I hack into their reporting systems, remember they overhauled their message security during their civil war. Specifically, they hardened those systems so *I* couldn't easily extract data and give it to the rebels."

He was correct about that. For three months, during my last year in command of *Valkyrie*, our mission had been to subtly observe both sides of that brutal civil war. And if we saw a simple and safe way to prolong the conflict, in a way that could not probably be traced back to us, our standing orders were to keep the kitties fighting each other. After two months, the Hegemony leadership realized there were too many events that couldn't be explained by luck, good or bad. The kitties loudly protested about our obvious interference in their sovereign affairs, and even issued threats to Skippy. He got a good chuckle about that, and was planning to sabotage sewage systems across the Maxohlx homeworld, before the party poopers at UNEF called a halt to our operation.

Buncha jerks.

"So, you can't get the information?" Frey wasn't yet fully clued into Skippy's game. Instead of just doing some awesome thing, he first had to bitch and moan about how incredibly difficult it was. Otherwise, we filthy monkeys wouldn't appreciate how hard he worked and blah blah blah.

"Oh, he can get it," I spoke before the beer can could brag about himself. "It would take time we don't have. We need a short cut."

Skippy hated when someone ruined an opportunity for him to brag. He also knew when to cut his losses. "How do you propose to do that, numbskull? Ask the kitties nicely, with sugar on it?"

"We don't have to ask them for anything. They probably have already provided data on the battle."

"Y-Yessss," Reed said with a grin, before Skippy could protest. She knew what I meant. "The Maxohlx have been protesting about recent incursions into their territory by the Rindhalu, or by us."

"We didn't do it," I added. Then, as a question, "We didn't, right?"

"Not that I know of, Sir. But," she shrugged, "until recently, *Valkyrie* wasn't tasked to support special ops, so I wouldn't have been read in on any sketchy stuff going on."

"Skippy, you have records of official protests by the kitties?"

"Yes," he sighed.

"Are any of them within the timeframe of forty six to eighteen days?"

"Again, yes."

"And of those, did any involve the loss of a heavy cruiser like the Bogey?"

"They don't provide sensitive details in their diplomatic protests, dumdum."

"But?"

"But- This is why I *hate* you, Joe- based on the dates and locations of the reported incidents, I can determine that two incidents involved groups of Maxohlx warships that included the appropriate type of heavy cruiser. Very well," he groaned like a child who was told to pick up his toys, or there would be no ice cream. Ask me how I know that.

"Sir," it was Frey's turn to venture a guess. "You believe the Rindhalu captured that ship, as a cover for them interfering in the activation of a Sentinel? One that we were giving to them?"

"That is one possibility, yes."

"*Why* would they do that?"

"While I was on Earth for a cup of coffee, I received a briefing about the negotiations with the spiders. Those talks dragged on for a long time. I know, the spiders never do anything hastily, but this was unusually slow even for them. The UN learned, from the Jeraptha, there was a debate within the highest levels of Rindhalu government. A faction was concerned that once we provided a Sentinel for their old homeworld, and they went through *enormous* effort to restore that world, we could hold the planet hostage. Like we could say, 'Nice homeworld you got there, be a shame if anything were to happen to it'."

"We wouldn't do that," Reed declared.

"*We* wouldn't," I agreed. "Not now. Probably we wouldn't, I think. Thousands of years from now, when that planet is finally restored to the paradise the spiders fantasize about? Who knows what human society would consider the right move? Besides, the spiders have a more immediate concern. This faction fears we want them to restore their old homeworld, to distract them from what we are doing in the galaxy. They are correct that making that dead rock livable again will require a generational commitment by all of Rindhalu society. It will divert resources away from their military, basically, divert resources away from *everything*. Fixing that planet could bleed them dry. Hell, from the report I saw, it would be less expensive for them to tow a replacement planet from another star system, and throw away the original. They won't do that, because the loss of their homeworld is a powerfully emotional issue to them. So, Frey, yes. I do think it is possible a faction of the spiders wanted to kill the plan to install a Sentinel in their original home star system."

She shook her head. "You live in a dark place, Sir." Like Smythe, Frey preferred a stand up fight to clandestine sketchiness. Although, Jeremy

Smythe had been exceptional at the sketchy stuff. Hopefully, Frey had learned from her old leader.

"Like I told Skippy," I tapped my rank insignia. "Having stars on my uniform means my job is mostly politics, I have to think about this stuff. It is also possible the Maxohlx conducted a false flag operation, so one of their ships could sneak away to interfere with the activation. Right now, we don't care."

Reed knew what I meant. "Because it doesn't matter whether the kitties or spiders are flying that ship. Neither of them has the technology to hack a Sentinel. We need to know who they are working with."

"Exactly."

Frey shook her head. "I feel like I'm two steps behind here."

"We are *all* two steps behind on this," I assured her. "Until recently, we were *five* steps behind, so, we're making progress. Still, it would be useful to know who is flying that ship. Skippy, did the wormhole sensors detect any spider DNA in the organic compounds?"

"The data wasn't that specific. Anything delicate like organic polymers gets torn apart when exposed to the conditions inside a wormhole anyway."

"Sir, we could go back to the activation site, try collecting samples," Reed suggested, with an expression I read as 'Please do not ask me to do that'.

"It would take way too long. I'll see if I can task a frigate squadron to do that, plus pick up the drones we left. All right, so, we're left with the question of who, or what, the kitties or spiders are working with."

"A question we have zero data for providing an answer," Skippy was disgusted. "I told you that already."

Frey opened her mouth, and closed it.

"Go ahead, Frey," I urged her. "I called you here to get your input."

"It *has* to be," she said slowly, still working the logic through in her head. "Another Elder AI. A master control AI."

"Skippy, be quiet and let Frey talk," I warned before he could say some obnoxious thing.

"A Sentinel doesn't need to steal a Sentinel, it is already a killing machine. It also has no conceivable need for a Maxohlx cruiser. Same with a wormhole network controller, it doesn't need a starship. But an Elder AI, we know they *do* need ships. They can't fly ships on their own, they are restricted from doing that. An Elder AI would need meatsacks," a smile flitted across her face. "To fly it around. Skippy, you got around most of your restrictions, but even you still need a ship flown by someone who cooperates with you."

"That is true," he mumbled with his hands covering his face. "That does not mean another Elder AI is out there. They are all *dead*."

"*You* aren't," the leader of STAR Team Razor retorted.

"Let's not rehash that argument right now," I raised my hands. "Skippy and I already had that discussion."

158

"We did, and I explained that you must be *wrong*."

"Uh huh. Tell me, would an Elder AI aboard the Bogey explain how that ship was able to travel so far, without taking the jump drive offline for major repairs?"

"Ugh. Damn it, yes. Listen, dumdum, the fact that *you* can't think of an alternative explanation does not mean the Bogey must be carrying a freakin' Elder AI."

"Anytime you think of a logical alternative let me know. Later. We can continue this later. Dinner is in two hours, I'm hungry, and I need to hit the gym first. We're not going to track down an Elder AI with the resources we have, so we will continue this later."

Reed glanced at her watch. "We will be jumping soon, I need to get back to the bridge. Sir? Zandrus? You said something about seeing an old friend? A Verd-kris?"

"There aren't any Verds I personally would count as friends. Not yet. Maybe someday. No, I mean a different kind of old friend. The *Flying Dutchman* is there."

159

CHAPTER FOURTEEN

Reed knocked on the door frame of my temporary office. "Sir? Is this still a thing?"

"What thing?"

"Your 'Open Door' policy?"

"Oh. Yes. Sort of. Come in, sit down. I had that policy while I was captain, to let the crew know they could come directly to me with any concerns. We were still working out how to live aboard a spaceship for long-duration flights, and," I waved a hand. "Developing the rules as we went along."

She nodded, not needing me to explain. She had been there, while we were making up the rules. "Door is still open?"

"To you, and to Frey. I am not going to interfere with your command of the ship. Your crew should go through the chain of command."

"Thank you." The tight expression on her face relaxed a bit, she was no longer clenching her jaw.

"Having said that, if someone approaches me in the gym, I'm not going to be a dick about it."

"I wouldn't worry about that, Sir," her face broke into an easy smile. "Of the crew who served with you before, there are only me and Major Motwani still aboard now."

"Motwani?" I searched my memory. "Engineering specialist?"

"Yes, Sir. Propulsion. My point is, I think most of the crew is afraid to talk to you. You are, kind of a legend, Sir," she cast her eyes down for a moment, embarrassed.

"I hope you don't feel that way, Reed."

She grinned. "I've seen you trip over your own feet on the basketball court."

"Good."

The grin faded. "I have also seen you do some pretty incredible shit, Sir. Saving the World. Saving the entire *Galaxy*."

"I had a lot of help."

"Still, it was an honor serving with you back then. It is now."

"But?"

"Sir?"

"I sense a 'But'."

She took a breath. "We've had flag officers aboard before. Twice. The crew is used to the protocol. The difference with you is, you're not just hitching a ride. You are more hands on."

"I don't intend to interfere with how you run your ship, Colonel."

"There are times when you *should*. Sir, you sitting behind me on the bridge, it doesn't work. For either of us. Or the ship. When you need to take command quickly in a crisis, I shouldn't be looking away from the display to see what you want."

"OK, fair enough. You have a solution?"

"I do. When you're on the bridge, please take the first officer's chair. It has the same functions and capabilities as my command chair, and you will be right next to me. Working together."

I noticed she had referred to the center seat as 'my command chair'. Reed was not shy, I liked that. "Commander Gasquet is OK with this?"

"He would be *relieved* if you sat next to me. Right now, he is caught in the middle and it's awkward. He is a good XO, he knows that. He should be getting a command of his own within the year."

That reminded me of something I meant to ask her. Pressing a button, I slid the door closed. She tensed. "There is not a problem, Colonel. I want your assessment of your crew."

"It's in the reports, Sir."

"Not everything is in a written report, you know that. *Valkyrie* has mostly been on 'Show The Flag' missions for the past four years. Flying Skippy around on his Victory Tour. The ship, this crew, hasn't seen serious combat for most of a decade. Certainly, they haven't seen the kind of crazy shit the Merry Band of Pirates got into. If the shit hits the fan tomorrow, is your crew ready? Before you answer, you know what I mean when about shit hitting the fan. We could soon be fighting an *Elder AI*. I told General Chang this could be another damned Save The Galaxy thing. If something happens to you, can your XO move into your seat, and take over without losing a beat?"

She frowned and bit her lip. "Can I have some time to think about it, Sir?"

"You have until we reach Zandrus. Think about your entire crew, not just Gasquet. Everyone must be able to step up," I snapped my fingers. "In an instant."

"I will, review the senior positions." She knew I didn't expect her to evaluate everyone aboard the ship, that was for their section leaders.

"If you need to replace someone, I will say it's my decision."

"You don't have to do that, Sir."

"Your crew should respect you, not *fear* you. Let me know."

Reed left, and I leaned my chair back, staring at the ceiling. Aboard a ship, the ceiling is technically called an 'overhead', but I'm a soldier, not a sailor.

"Hey, Joe." There was a flare of light as Skippy's avatar appeared.

"Hey," I responded, not turning my head to look at him.

"When did you get so ruthless?"

"Huh?" The chair flopped back upright. "Oh, you mean my discussion with Reed."

"Exactly."

"That's not being ruthless, it's- It is being focused and determined. We need to be ready for a hell of a fight, Skippy. If an Elder AI is out there and-"

"I already told you that is not possible."

"I will make a note of it. Along with all the other things you told me were impossible."

"Ugh. Joe," he sighed. "I thought we were done with doing crazy, impossible stuff."

"Me too. Someone out there didn't get the memo."

"I still say you have become ruthless. When did that happen?"

"I am not that dumb, scared kid anymore. Yeah, I am still scared, scared of the enemy. Not scared of myself. Remember how I used to doubt myself all the time?"

"Wow, I have no memory of *that*."

"Now, I definitely doubt whether I know what I'm doing as a father, but I don't have time for second guessing myself as a senior officer."

"If you say so."

"I do."

"If you have to replace some of the crew, do you know who you will bring aboard?"

"That's the problem, isn't it? You know I told Reed that I'm getting the band back together? Really, this will be like a classic rock band that goes on tour with two original members, and a bunch of young, new people. We can play our old hits, but that's it. We can't write any new hits, and the audience hates it when we play new stuff."

"I sure hope you're wrong about that."

"Why?"

"If you are right, and there is another Elder AI screwing around out there, we need to try something we have never done before."

Staring at him, I got a sinking feeling in my stomach. "Why is that?"

"An Elder AI will have studied every move the Merry Band of Pirates made. Everything *I* did. We can't use any of our old tricks, this time."

On that sour note, Skippy went away to do, whatever he was doing, while I thought about what we would do when we reached Zandrus. That would partly depend on what we found when we arrived. We knew that our 'Operation Sunset' troops had gotten themselves into a mess on Zandrus, but that wasn't their fault. Technically, the mess also was not the fault of Emily Perkins or the Mavericks. OK yes, Perkins and her Mavs got themselves into sticky situations a *lot*, like way too often. But that is because when Def Com has a difficult task that is likely to deteriorate into a total fucking disaster, the Mavericks get sent in. It's their thing.

And any time the Verds are involved, a disaster is much more likely.

Even I warned Def Com not to get involved on Zandrus. The Verds got themselves into the mess there, with help from their former patrons the Ruhar. Humanity had a mutual defense treaty with the Verd-Kris, they were *not* our client species. The treaty was very one-sided in humanity's favor, and the role of the Verds was very much what it would be under a patron-client relationship, but freedom-loving humans do not impose our will on other species. Of course not, how dare you suggest such a thing.

Whatever. The Verds were happy about what they got out of the deal, and it was working out pretty well for us also.

Which reminds me.

We do have a client species. Unofficially. That relationship was unofficial only in that the terms 'Patron' and 'Client' were not mentioned in any of the agreements both sides had signed, but legal details do make a difference.

Who were our new, our first, client species?

The Urgar.

Your brain probably responded with 'Who the fuck are the *Urgar*'? You are not alone. Something like ninety five percent of the population of Earth had never heard of that poor, unfortunate group of aliens before they became our responsibility. A small group of aliens, their entire remaining population was only a mere twenty thousand. Their numbers had been so drastically reduced by oppression, harsh living conditions, neglect, and by the outright genocidal policies of their previous patrons, that poor genetic diversity was a major factor working against their continued existence.

The Urgar, if you need a memory refresh, were clients of the squid-like Wurgalan, who in turn are clients of the little green cyborg jerk Thuranin, who are themselves clients of the supreme asshole Maxohlx. The Urgar were minding their own business on their homeworld, blissfully unaware of the interstellar war that had been raging across the galaxy, until a wormhole shift opened access to their little sector of the Sagittarius Arm. If that sounds familiar, it should. The fate of the Urgar very likely would have been our fate, if we didn't have a little help from our friends. One friend in particular: Skippy the Magnificent.

So, the Urgar were on their own, having achieved technology roughly equivalent to Earth in the seventeenth century. With wooden sailing ships, and cast iron cannons that used a form of gunpower, but no electricity yet, no steam engines. The Urgar had been stuck at that level for several centuries because their homeworld was poor in metals other than iron. Their star system also had an unusual number of dangerous rocks swirling around, the result of a rogue planet that passed through the system a million and a half years before. Rocks and comets, some of them rather large, routinely pelted the Urgar's

163

planet, smashing things, causing havoc such as tsunamis and widespread fires, and plunging the world into mini ice ages for about two decades every century. That is a tough environment in which to build a civilization, but the Urgar did it.

Then their progress ran into a bulldozer in the form of the Wurgalan. The squids had been ordered by their patrons to find a place to construct a base in the newly accessible sector. A base that would be used by the Thuranin, for their own convenience. The little green pinheads had gotten a bit too enthusiastic about expanding their territory, overextended their resources, and the Jeraptha knew it. The beetles took advantage of the Thuranin spreading themselves too thin, by launching a lightning offensive that forced the cyborgs to pull back into a defensive posture. Which left the Wurgalan exposed on the Urgar homeworld, their supply lines cut off for seventeen years. Fortunately, the Wurgalan invaders and the natives worked together, for their mutual benefit in the difficult circumstances.

Ha! I am joking. The Wurgalan, feeling threatened by the natives who had only a crude level of technology but an overwhelming population, decided to preemptively deal with the problem by reducing the native population.

By ninety nine point eight percent. The clandestine Thuranin biological weapons deployed in the plague were even more effective than advertised, so the Wurgalan must have been pleased they had spent the money wisely. Yes, biological weapons are against The Rules, but nobody bothered to investigate when the primitive natives began dying of a horrible disease. As I have said before, The Rules were written by the two senior species for their own benefit, they did not give a shit about the lowly Urgar.

Wurgalan colonist records from the time complain about the horrible *smell*, from the rotting bodies of several hundred million natives that was apparently quite unpleasant.

By the time the Thuranin restored contact with the by-then thriving Wurgalan colony, fewer than a quarter million Urgar remained. Rather than being shocked by the drastic, murderous actions of their clients, the Thuranin merely shrugged, barely noticing that the natives were almost extinct. They *did* notice with outrage that little progress had been made in constructing a supply base, and the fact that the planet had been cut off for seventeen years was not accepted as an excuse. That is when the Wurgalan got the bright idea to harshly use the natives as slave labor, an initiative that greatly accelerated the rate at which the Urgar population was already declining.

Anyway, by the time the poor, miserable, down-trodden and abused Urgar approached humanity for protection, they had been kicked off their homeworld, surviving on a barely habitable moon. The surviving twenty thousand Urgar at that point existed only for the prestige of the Wurgalan, so the squids could claim they were a patron species.

How did a species on the very bottom of the ladder, a species with zero resources, become humanity's first clients?

Easy. They followed a well-tested playbook. The Urgar are not the most intelligent species in the galaxy, although no one knows how smart they would be if they had been left alone to develop on their own. What we do know is that their surviving population is just that: survivors. Crafty. Cynical. Ready and willing to do anything they have to, so their species can live for one more day. They were mostly isolated and had very limited access to technology or any offworld communications, except whatever junk equipment their patrons discarded. Junk, like old communications gear, that the Urgar used to build primitive radios.

The Urgar were isolated, until a Jeraptha task force visited their star system, on the way to administering another serious ass-whooping to the Thuranin. A Jeraptha frigate swung past the moon, curious about the truly miserable remnant population of the Urgar. That frigate dumped a huge file of news about what was really going on in the galaxy, including the recent astonishing revelations that lowly humans had been running circles around both senior species, with the assistance of an *Elder AI*. The situation on Earth, under the boots of the Kristang White Wind clan, strongly reminded the Urgar about their own history.

The being called 'Skippy' had saved the humans. Could that being be persuaded to do the same for the Urgar?

Here's what the Urgar did that was smart: they did not expect Skippy to rescue them for free. They had studied the records provided by the Jeraptha, concluding that the Skippy being was an immature, selfish, amoral asshole whose massive yet fragile ego determined every move he made.

Damn, I wish the Urgar had been available to give *me* a heads up about that, when I met the beer can on Paradise.

So, the Urgar sent a message to Skippy, via a passing Jeraptha cruiser. They wanted to hire him. Not Skippy personally, they wanted to engage the services of Skippy And Associates, a boutique public relations and crisis management firm. Engage them to do what? To show the people of Earth how the Urgar had suffered the fate that humanity had narrowly avoided. To explain that humans should feel extremely, eternally, grateful to Skippy that humanity was not enslaved or extinct. And to persuade Earth's public that taking on the Urgar as clients would be a low-cost way to do the right thing. While, you know, giving a middle finger salute to the entire Maxohlx coalition.

What did Skippy get in exchange, other than having a small group of poverty-stricken losers stroking his ego?

Bragging rights.

In the fiercely competitive, cutthroat world of public relations and crisis management, Skippy And Associates were almost unknown, *before* they successfully persuaded the political leaders of Earth to do the right thing, which by pure coincidence was also the overwhelmingly popular thing, and rescue the Urgar. That persuasion was in the form of a quote, *grassroots*, end quote, campaign of bots flooding social media, influencers paid to plead the case of the Urgar, and a surprisingly small amount of well-placed bribes.

Result? A Win-Win! The Urgar now have their own continent, on their former homeworld that was recently and ironically taken from their former patrons the Wurgalan, but that's a story for another day. And Skippy And Associates is now widely considered THE go-to firm for all your public relations and crisis management needs.

The only losers in the whole situation are of course the Wurgalan, and also anyone who had to listen to Skippy endlessly bragging about his accomplishment. His audience for boasting did not include the Urgar, because he did not give a shit about what those losers thought.

Damn. The Urgar won big, since they not only saved themselves from slavery and eventual extinction, they didn't have to interact with Skippy.

I wonder if I can get a sweet deal like that?

There it was, hanging outlined against the dusty reds and browns of a marginally habitable world. The good old *Flying Dutchman*. Version Six Point Oh. A person familiar with any of the previous versions of that space truck, that then became a stealthy sensor platform, would not recognize it. Even in the UN Navy, which possessed many ships that were much-modified versions of their original configurations, the *Dutchman* was unique.

On the nose of the massive warship was painted '*CVA-14 UNS Flying Dutchman*'. In its current version, the *Dutchman* was an assault carrier. Not just an assault carrier, it was an orbital command ship, capable of assuming command and control of an entire assault strike force, on and around a planet. Why had the UN Navy gone through the enormously complicated and expensive process of carefully cutting apart the original *Dutchman*, and fitting that ship's computer substrate into the hull of a former Jeraptha assault carrier?

The answer is simple: the Lady Nagatha. The *Dutchman's* control unit was the most powerful ship AI in the fleet, after Bilby. Nagatha not only had immense processing power, she had something the other ship AIs in the fleet couldn't match: experience.

The conversion of the *Dutchman* had been a last-minute decision. The UN Navy had planned to park that ship in Earth orbit, as a strategic defense control platform. Basically, avoid the expense of upgrading that already unique ship, even avoiding the expense of maintaining the funky, unique jump drives. The drive units would be removed, as there would be no need for the *Dutchman* to jump anywhere, ever again.

The *Dutchman's* salvation came after a joint orbital assault exercise with the Ruhar where events went embarrassingly wrong for the UN Navy. While the Ruhar efficiently executed their part of the exercise, our ships were badly affected by communications jamming they should have been ready for. The assault drop was a mess, with units dropped all over the surface, and ground forces unable to support each other. A Jeraptha aggressor force jumping in during the second wave of landings had forced the human ships to scatter. If the exercise had been a real operation, it would have devolved into a slaughter.

A Navy inquiry concluded we had the right equipment, the training, and our tactics were solid. Like a losing football team with plenty of talent, the problem was management. Someone needed to be in overall command, with excellent situational awareness, and with a comm system that could function even through powerful jamming. That required a command ship with a powerful AI. Result: the old *Dutchman* was granted a reprieve. Sort of. From the outside, the ship now appeared to be an *I Got Something For You Right Here* class Jeraptha assault carrier, with a two hundred meter section spliced into the center, and a bulbous sensor dome on the nose. The ship also had more shield projectors and defensive cannons than typical for an assault carrier. The conversion reduced the ship's dropship capacity by thirty percent, so the air group consisted of more gunships rather than assault transports.

Damn, it was good to see my old ship again, even if I didn't recognize it.

I was happy to talk with Nagatha again, until I saw that the Operation Sunset peacekeeping mission had become a low intensity war on the surface. The Ruhar, who were supposed to be there only to facilitate the Verd-kris withdrawal, were engaged in a hot war with the Kristang, in pockets scattered all around the planet. "Skippy," I released the straps and stood up from the executive officer's chair. An action, I realized instantly, that was not a good move in a combat situation. Instead of making myself look like an amateur, I straightened my shoulders and faced the main display. "What is going on down there?"

"It's a bit confusing, both sides are blaming the other. All *three* sides are blaming the others. At this point, it is hard to tell which- Oh. General Perkins is calling for you."

"That was fast. How did she know I am aboard the-"

"I *informed* her, as soon as we jumped in. You are now the senior officer in the system, senior UN officer. Protocol requires an arriving ship to identify-"

"Yeah. Of course. Reed, can I use your office for-"

"Certainly, Sir," she would be relieved to have the distraction of me off her bridge, while she got her ship prepared for possible combat.

"I'll keep you updated," I said as I walked out the door, and Commander Gasquet slipped back into the first officer's chair. "Skippy, tell Bonsu I want to talk with him and his CAG shortly."

"General Bishop," Perkins's hologram appeared on the desk in Reed's office. The image was about a foot tall, with enough detail to be crisp but still clearly a holographic projection. Skippy would argue the image, and his avatar, were not actually 'holograms', and there was some sciency reason he was right about that. Whatever.

"*Emily*," I smiled. "Call me 'Joe', please."

Her lips drew together in a tight line.

"Come on," I added. "It's just us. We are both two stars."

"You have more time in grade," she reminded me.

Technically, that was correct. I had been given my second star over four years before she pinned hers on. "That doesn't matter here. I'm not here to take over from you. Officially, I'm not here at all."

"*Valkyrie's* recognition signal indicated the ship is assigned to the Special Mission Group again? What happened?" After a moment she added, "Joe."

"You haven't heard?"

"We are at the ass end of nowhere out here," she explained. "Our last contact with a ship from Earth was six days ago."

"Ah. That ship left Earth before we arrived. There has been a, development."

"Not a good one, if Task Force Black has been reactivated. If Command has *you* back in the saddle."

"It's not good. The short version is, there was another attempt to activate a Sentinel."

She nodded, the hologram slightly out of sync so the movement was jerky. "The one that is being provided to the spiders. I heard the plans for that." She cocked her head at me. "You said 'attempt'? It went sideways?"

"In a major way. Someone, or some*thing*, tried to take control of the Sentinel away from Skippy, before the Sentinel was fully awake."

"Oh, hell," the blood drained from her face. "I thought we were *done* with all that."

"So did I."

"You don't know who did it?"

"We have a list of suspects. None of them are anything our Navy can deal with."

"So, Task Force Black. What do you need from us?"

"First, what happened here? Operation Sunset was supposed to be a sleepy peacekeeping mission, according to the brief."

"The lizards didn't get that memo. The Verd-kris should never have tried to take this rock, it's not strategically important to them, and the supply line is too vulnerable. What they should have done, what we should have encouraged them to do, is-" She stopped. "You didn't ask about politics. The bottom line is, the Kristang were supposed to allow the Verds to conduct a peaceful withdrawal. Officially, they did. Unofficially, grass-roots 'militants' among the Kristang," she made air quotes with her fingers, "obtained unauthorized weapons and were killing the Verds, who had mostly been disarmed by the Ruhar. We couldn't do much, and the hamsters weren't interested in doing anything. Until, a Kristang unit hit a Ruhar ammo dump and blew it up."

"Why the hell would the lizards do *that*?"

She gave me a blank look.

"Oh." I understood. "Risky, but a good move by the Verds."

She continued to give me the blank stare.

"*Ohhhhh.*" I winked. "I am sure you were shocked and dismayed by the unfortunate events."

"It wasn't *me*," she protested. "That's the problem."

"Uh," I really didn't know her well enough to tell if she was lying.

"At the time of the incident, I was upstairs conferring with the Ruhar commander. It surprised us both when we saw the mushroom cloud. Several minor injuries, no deaths. The hamsters are hopping mad. *I* wasn't happy about it."

"So, who-"

"All I can say is, when Dave Czajka and Shauna Colter are left unsupervised, they can get into mischief."

"Dave."

"Yes."

"Your *husband*."

She gritted her teeth. "For the moment."

"Without getting into your private business, can I point out that *you* trained them?"

She sighed. "That is exactly what Dave told me."

"Wow," I couldn't help laughing, leaning my chair back. "Are you familiar with the expression 'What goes around, comes around'?"

She gritted her teeth again, but there was a twinkle in her eyes. "I am well aware of the irony involved. I now also know how General Ross felt, when he heard about some creative stunt I got into, without prior authorization."

"I'm sure he has forgotten all about it by now. Maybe send him a nice fruit basket, someday."

"Now you know the situation here. I've got the Ruhar and Kristang shooting at each other, the hamsters are rearming the Verds, and I can't take sides. The withdrawal has completely stalled, and the Kristang are calling for the Thuranin to intervene, because they claim *we* violated the treaty. All I have is the *Dutchman* and two frigates, plus a single battalion that is really two understrength companies. So," she let out a long breath and brushed her hair back with a hand. "How can I help you?"

"Well, now this is just awkward."

"Sir?" There wasn't any pretense of us being old friends. Because we weren't. I respected her, I liked her, we just didn't know each other well. Our one personal connection was Dave Czajka, who might have been sleeping on the couch until his wife's anger cooled.

169

"This is where it does get official. Perkins, I need to requisition the *Dutchman* for a while."

"*What?*"

"I am trying to track down a hostile actor that might be an Elder AI. The *Dutchman* has the second best ship AI in the fleet, and a top-notch sensor suite. We need to find and neutralize, or at least find and make contact with, the damned thing, before it does something worse than trying to steal a Sentinel. After the incident, we raced to Earth, in case the Sentinels there got hacked."

"Oh my G-"

"They're fine, unaffected. Skippy checked them. Same with Jaguar, PupTart is fine. Perkins, I hate to leave you shorthanded-"

"Two frigates are not enough combat power to provide a credible deterrent. Someone like the Thuranin could use this as an opportunity to settle a score. They would be in the right to do that, since we violated the treaty."

"They can't prove that."

"Def Com would figure out the truth quickly enough. Command wouldn't throw a lot of resources here, into a fight that wasn't supposed to happen."

"Shit. Could you withdraw your force now? I know you have a mission, but the potential of a hostile Elder AI changes everything. You will probably receive orders to pull out soon, Command will want to adopt a defensive posture."

"Pull back to where? The *Dutchman* is the only platform we have that could accommodate our battalion. If you're requisitioning our only assault carrier, can you bring in a cruiser first? Some significant combat power?"

"I, I don't have time for that. The nearest UN Navy assets are- Skippy? Where is the closest Navy unit?"

He spoke without his avatar. Having his hologram next to Perkins's might have felt weird to him. "There are two cruisers and a destroyer squadron at Perdesta, that is a fifty six hour flight from here. Plus fifty six hours for a return flight, of course."

"Almost five days? More than five days, with turnaround time. Thanks, Skippy. Perkins, that idea is a no go. I am sorry about this. Leaving a hostile entity roaming around for another five days is not an option. The trail is growing cold already."

She pursed her lips. She knew the Special Mission Group was authorized to pull in other units as needed. A threat to the entire galaxy outweighed the risks to a single battalion. "I don't suppose you could transfer your command to the *Dutchman*, and leave *Valkyrie* here?"

"Uh, no. I would really like to also take your two frigates with me as sensor pickets, but I won't do that. When is your next contact with Earth scheduled?"

"A star carrier will pass by the system in nine days. That is a long time to be without major combat power overhead."

"Would it help if *Valkyrie* struck targets on the ground before we leave? We could- No, that's a bad idea, isn't it?"

"A terrible idea, Sir. Overtly breaking the treaty would leave my forces open to retaliation by anyone in the Maxohlx coalition."

"Hell, this is- Give me a minute, I'll be right back." Pressing a button on the desk, I froze her hologram and muted the microphone on my end. "Skippy?"

"Yes, what is it this time?" He snapped.

"How would you like an opportunity to screw with some lizards? Unofficially, if youze know what I mean."

"I am not sure I knowz what youze mean, Joe."

"Hypothetically, if the IT infrastructure of the hateful lizards down there suffered a catastrophic failure, would that leave them less able to conduct offensive operations?"

"Oooooh, that *would* be unfortunate. You know, Joe, the lizards here have been *shamefully* remiss in maintaining their cybersecurity. That's how Dave and Shauna were able to get Nagatha to hack into- Which, I just realized I wasn't supposed to know about, and wasn't supposed to tell you."

"What? Sorry, the audio glitched for a moment. Something about cyber systems?"

"It is just awful down there, Joe. Really, I am surprised the whole thing hasn't fallen apart already."

"Uh huh. That sounds like a dangerous situation. Does that vulnerability extend to their military systems? Aircraft, missile guidance systems, that sort of thing?"

"Sadly, it does."

"You know, it might be good for someone to demonstrate to the lizards just how vulnerable their systems are. In the long run, you would be doing them a favor."

"Ugh. That's the problem. I hate doing favors for lizards."

"Well, you're not doing anything anyway, as far as I know, right?"

"In fact, nothing is happening *right now*, as far as you know."

"Well, since nothing is happening, I will get back to my conversation with Perkins." Pressing a button again, I unfroze her hologram. "Sorry about that, Emily." I used her first name again deliberately, as a signal. Like, everything was fine, we are just having a friendly, casual conversation between colleagues. "Skippy alerted me to a cybersecurity problem the lizards down there are having, he is monitoring the situation."

"Monitoring it until it begs for *Momma*," Skippy chuckled.

"Skippy! You are *not* doing anything, as we agreed?"

"Oh! Yes, I am not doing anything. Although if I *was* doing something, I should be warning the lizards about a serious problem with their missile warhead activation software, among other things."

Perkins cocked her head at me. "What is going on?"

"Nothing," I told her. "As far as you know."

"General Bishop, I-"

"Let me make this clear. You know *nothing*, understood?"

"I *don't* know anything, it-" She flinched, the hologram flickered, and the audio cut out for a moment. "*What the hell was that?*" She turned to direct the question to someone out of my view.

"Sadly," Skippy answered her question. "The Spotted Frog clan's main air base at Klukagang has exploded. General Perkins, were you aware the lizards had two atomic compression weapons stored in a bunker there?"

"Atomic-" She was genuinely shocked. "Where did lizards get *those* weapons?"

"The lizards were very, very naughty," Skippy chuckled. "They are not supposed to have such weapons. I believe their patrons will be unhappy to learn just how disobedient their clients were. Those two warheads were old, they must have been looted from the wreckage of a Thuranin warship, centuries ago. In fact, it is likely the lizards found a severely disabled Thuranin warship, killed the crew, *then* looted the hulk. It is a pity the lizards were not aware of the proper procedures for safe storage of such powerful weapons. Um, the good news is the planet will have some spectacular sunsets for several months, as dust from the explosion filters through the stratosphere."

Perkins looked me straight in the eye. "You *nuked* a military base, of a species we are not at war with?"

"Hey!" Skippy protested. "*Joe* didn't do anything, he is a doofus. Also, atomic compression warheads were developed at great expense precisely because they are *not* nukes, there is no hazardous radiation. Well, no radiation other than the short-lived high energy particles from the immediate explosion. Nothing that lingers, so those weapons don't violate The Rules that govern warfare between the Maxohlx and Rindhalu coalitions."

"This was an unprovoked act of *war*," she insisted. "That-" She covered her face with a hand for a moment. "OK, yes, I know how ironic it is that *I* said that."

"It was an accident," I said quietly.

"It wasn't just an *accident*," Skippy could not keep his mouth shut. Then he redeemed himself. "It was an accident waiting to happen. Considering how the lizards neglected to perform any sort of preventative maintenance on those janky weapons, I am surprised they hadn't detonated years ago."

"Well," I shrugged. "It's lucky for us that they waited for a convenient time to explode. If you know what I mean," I looked Perkins straight in the eye as I said that.

172

"The explosion," Skippy continued, "appears to have severely affected the clan's command and control systems also, all of their comms are down, hard. Could be months before their headquarters can reestablish effective direct coordination between units in the field. Ooooh, and I am now intercepting chatter within the clan. It appears that second-tier clan leaders are dismayed by the reckless negligence of their senior officials. Joe, assassinations of multiple senior clan leaders are being planned!"

"Darn. No one could have foreseen that disrupting their clan's command structure would lead to internal violence, right? Well, it's too bad that we can't interfere in the internal affairs of a sovereign species. Perkins, I'm sure you are going to be busy."

"Hoo boy, yes she is! The Ruhar admiral is screaming for an explanation."

"General Bishop," her shoulders sagged. "Is there any room for me aboard *Valkyrie*?"

"Unfortunately, we're full."

"Maybe," she muttered. "I'll apply to the Ruhar for political asylum."

"Before you do that, I suggest you let Dave and Shauna out of the doghouse?"

She shrugged. "Ah, why not? By comparison, what they did was a minor prank."

"Emily, even compared to a lot of shit *you* have done, what they did was a minor prank."

"True enough."

"See?" I grinned. "Everywhere I go, I spread peace and harmony."

Skippy laughed. "Peace and harmony by the *megaton*!"

Ending the call with Perkins, I contacted Colonels Bonsu and Striebich. They were standing by for my call. "General Bishop?" Irene Striebich spoke first. While her husband was commanding officer of the *Flying Dutchman*, she was commander of the ship's air group. Meaning, Derek was in charge of the ship, while the dropships and their pilots reported to her.

"Striebich, Bonsu, we are short on time so I'll make this quick. The Special Mission Group has been reactivated, and I am requisitioning the *Dutchman*, effective immediately. The appropriate, official orders are being transmitted to you now. Bonsu, prepare to break orbit. Striebich, land your dropships and their personnel, they won't be needed on this mission, and their firepower could come in handy dirtside while you're away."

Bonsu didn't speak. His expression was a resigned 'Here we go again'. Striebich glanced to her husband, then, "Sir, how long will I be on the surface? I need to send provisions for-"

"Load your dropships with whatever they can carry, but do it fast. I expect Def Com to cancel Operation Sunset soon, and pull the battalion off the surface. There are, events going on that I will brief both of you on. Striebich, you will not be going dirtside with your people."

"No? Sir?" She added as an afterthought. "Where will I be-"

"You will be coming aboard *Valkyrie*, as our new CAG."

She blinked. "*Valkyrie* is a battlecruiser. There isn't a billet for a CAG. You don't have an air group."

"There is billet open now, I just said so. Pack your personal gear and get ready to fly over here. Bonsu, I want you to break orbit in two hours, is that doable?"

"That-" He looked to his wife. "Is it possible to get the entire air group launched in two hours?"

"No, not on this short notice," she shook her head. "But, General Bishop, the situation is bad enough to stand up Task Force Black again?"

"I would use the word 'catastrophic' instead of merely 'bad'," I answered.

"Then, fuck it," she spat out the words. "We'll get everything launched, if I have to push the birds out the door by hand. General, can I wait to fly over to *Valkyrie* after we jump?"

"Uh, sure. You will be busy."

Derek appeared to have accepted his fate. "General, can you tell us what is going on? An air base dirtside just became a mushroom cloud. That wasn't you?"

"Let's just say that *Valkyrie* didn't fire a shot."

"Oh." He knew what that meant.

"As to what is going on in the galaxy beyond the rock below us, someone attempted to steal a Sentinel we were activating."

"Oh *SHIT*."

"We think there is a good possibility another Elder AI is out there, and it's hostile."

He reached for his wife's hand. "I thought we were *done* with this bullshit."

"That optimism may have been premature."

His face registered an unspoken 'Ya think'.

After ending the call with the *Dutchman*, I pinged Reed to come to her office. When she arrived, I had gotten out of her chair.

"Can I ask what," she bit her lip, suppressing what she really wanted to say. "Happened down there? Sir?"

"Skippy gave the lizards a valuable lesson on the importance of properly maintaining your gear. Especially the type of gear that can go 'BOOM'."

"Oh." She wasn't actually surprised. She knew me, she knew Skippy. With a shrug, she added, "If you don't schedule time to maintain your equipment, the equipment will schedule the time for you."

174

"Exactly. As a bonus, the shooting between the lizards and hamsters should be on hold for a while, as the lizard leadership gets busy killing each other."

"A fortunate coincidence."

"One that frees up the combat power of the *Dutchman*, which will be coming with us. Reed, have your XO set up quarters for a colonel, please. Irene Striebich will be coming aboard as the air group commander."

"We," she blinked. "Don't have an air group."

"We have ten dropships."

She didn't bother to comment. Then, her mouth opened in a silent 'O'. "Striebich was your XO for a while, when Simms had her own command."

"Exactly."

"She knows how to handle *Valkyrie*," Reed noted, "if something happens to me."

"She knows how to work with *me*," I added. "Tell Gasquet not to worry, Striebich will stay out of his way."

"Sir, Striebich has more time in grade than I do."

"Yes, and she also commanded a cruiser, before she decided she wanted to be a CAG. She missed flying, is my guess."

"That was a nice setup, being on the same ship as her husband."

"Def Com is delivering on that 'People Care' initiative. Striebich understands *Valkyrie* is your ship. There won't be a conflict."

"Sir, you realize we will have *three* colonels aboard?"

"I do. The three of you can form a club."

She made a sour face. "I am not joining Frey's book club. They are reading *War and Peace*. The book weighs," she pantomimed lifting something heavy, "like twenty pounds. I would get tired just holding the thing."

"Spoiler alert: I think there's a lot more war than peace in that book. Well, you and Striebich could start a bird watching club."

"There are no birds in space, Sir."

"Then," I grinned, "the club won't take up too much of your time."

CHAPTER FIFTEEN

In the one hour and twenty two minutes remaining before the *Flying Dutchman* was ready to jump, I called-

First, I should explain that timing. During my discussion with Reed about Striebich coming aboard, the *Dutchman's* crew was busy. Extremely busy. The two platoons of soldiers that were UN-dick's rapid reaction reserve hustled aboard four dropships, and the two gunships that were always kept on alert launched quickly. Getting the rest of the birds warmed up and ready for flight would be tough to do in the time available, so Bonsu and Striebich got creative.

Creative is good, unless the enemy is doing it.

To save time, Bonsu got his ship moving toward jump altitude, while the remaining dropships and gunships were being loaded and prepared. As soon as a spacecraft checked out as ready for flight, it was sent down the launch rails. There was always the possibility that a hastily-prepared ship would suffer a mechanical failure, so the CAG posted a search and rescue bird to take care of stragglers. The bottom line was that the *Dutchman* reached jump altitude less than ninety minutes after receiving my order.

That ship has a fine crew.

Nagatha agrees with me. While I waited for her ship to jump, I talked with Dave, Shauna, and of course, Nagatha. A person I did not talk with was Cornpone. Jesse Colter. I had not known he was injured, and taking care of their son on Earth while he recuperated. Why did I not know Jesse got injured? I should have known. I am a terrible friend. I need to do better. I need to make an effort to keep in touch with the people who are important to me.

I will start that effort, right after I save the freakin' galaxy again.

Dave was fine. Shauna was fine. Nagatha was fine. Nagatha was excited, to talk with me again, and to be going on what she described as 'one of Skippy's adventures'.

"Nagatha," I winced at her enthusiasm. "This will not be *fun*. It is very serious."

"Of course it is serious, Joseph," she gushed in her breathy Naughty Librarian voice. "That is why it will be such a grand adventure. Simply *grand*. I can't wait to get started."

"Uh huh. Hey, I got a question."

"I will as usual ignore your atrocious grammar. What is the question, dear?"

"The attack on the Ruhar ammo dump. You don't know anything about that, do you?"

"A lady would never be involved in anything unseemly, dear."

"Oh. Sorry."

176

"Fortunately, I have developed a very broad definition of 'seemly'," she giggled.

"That is, good to hear."

"Well, it has been simply delightful to speak with you again, you simply *must* arrange for me to meet your boys again. Skippy sends me messages about them all the time."

"He does?"

"Yes, dear. He is very honored to be their godfather."

"Uh, Margaret and I didn't appoint him as-"

"He did not mean 'godfather' in the conventional sense."

"Ah, gotcha."

"He is *very* protective of them, you know."

"I did know that."

"Therefore, you do not need to worry too much about this potential of a hostile Elder AI, dear."

"I, don't?"

"No. If another AI were to threaten your boys, Skippy will bitch slap it into the afterlife."

"That's good to know. The-" A chime *binged* in the background. "Nagatha, it sounds like you are getting ready to jump."

"I know that, General Bishop. I programmed the jump, after all."

"Right. Talk to you later?"

"TTYL, homeboy." She ended the call.

Homeboy?

It was good to hear her happy and eager for an adventure.

Maybe a bit too eager.

We jumped away from Zandrus, with *Valkyrie* leading the *Flying Dutchman*. The assault carrier normally would need to be attached to a star carrier for flying long distances. The original Jeraptha jump drive of the assault carrier had been extensively modified, to designs provided by Skippy. Still, extensive flights between wormholes would wear out the drive components, requiring lengthy downtime to get all the drive components working properly together. Even Nagatha wasn't able to keep the *Dutchman's* drive tuned perfectly, the way Skippy could. So, Skippy did it for her. The ships flew together, never more than two thousand kilometers apart, so Skippy could easily extend his presence to envelop the *Dutchman*, and he gave that ship a tune-up after each jump. As a bonus, the work kept the beer can busy, and gave him something other than me to complain about.

The plan was for us to track the Bogey, and hopefully identify who was operating that ship. Our initial list of suspects had only two names: the Maxohlx and the Rindhalu. Given evidence that the heavy cruiser had been in a battle recently, I was betting the spiders were the culprits. Why? Because there was no need for the kitties to attack and steal one of their own ships.

Why would the spiders try to steal a Sentinel that we were activating for their benefit? That is simple. We hadn't intended to give Dogzilla to the spiders, the thing would be on a long-term loan. At any time, if the spiders pissed us off, Skippy could deactivate the Sentinel. Or even instruct it to attack the spiders. Having a third party provide the services of an Elder killing machine was not the same as *controlling* such a machine.

Part of me would be shocked if we learned I was right about the Rindhalu being the guilty party. That revelation would mean the spiders *did* something, rather than endlessly pondering the issue. Yes, years had gone by since humanity acquired our first Sentinel, but even a century is a short time to the spiders. To act within a single decade is positively *hasty*. To act in a way that involved enormous risk? Something had to be seriously wrong in Spiderland.

Anyway, we would hopefully track the Bogey to the territory of whoever was flying that ship. Possibly even find the secret base the ship operated from. If we could do that, having two ships allowed me to post the *Dutchman* as a sensor picket, while *Valkyrie* did, whatever we could do about determining whether another Elder AI was aboard the Bogey. And if the answer to that question was an expected but still shocking 'Yes', we would do something to stop that AI.

What could we do to stop another Skippy?

I have no idea.

Hopefully, I'll make up some shit when I need to.

That's why I wasn't sleeping very well. When I slept at all.

Irene Striebich requested a meeting with me, which she did by following the proper procedure of sending the request through the ship's executive officer. The guy she was technically not replacing. Officially, she was commander of *Valkyrie's* air group. Unofficially, everyone knew her return to our battlecruiser was to provide an experienced backup to Reed. That made her interaction with Gasquet awkward, and that was my fault.

"Striebich," I rose from the chair in my office, gesturing to her. "Come in, sit down."

"Thank you, Sir."

"Uh, in the future when you want to talk with me, you can schedule it through Skippy. Or just call me," I held up my zPhone.

"I don't want to step on anyone's toes, Sir. Any more than I already have, if you know what I mean."

"Yeah, I do. Sorry about that. You impressed me when you were my XO here, I think we worked well together."

"Thank you. I enjoyed my time aboard *Valkyrie*, it was a, um," there was the briefest of hesitation, "learning experience."

"*Every* day with the Pirates is a learning experience. Especially for me. What can I do for you, Striebich?"

"I would appreciate clarity on my role here, Sir."

"For you, I created a billet for a CAG."

"This battlecruiser doesn't need an air group commander."

"I disagree. This ship has been acting as a taxi for Skippy, or showing the flag, or acting as a big stick for diplomatic missions. Only three of the pilots aboard have any kind of combat experience, and none of that is recent. They are all good pilots, highly rated. I want you to bring our pilots up to speed, get them ready for the unexpected."

"That," she looked a bit less unhappy. "I can do, Sir."

"Good. I requested Reed to run the entire crew through combat drills, that starts tomorrow. The crew will be tired but, a busy crew is a happy crew."

"Happier than when they're *not* busy," she agreed. "Is there anything else?"

"Yes. You will also have 'Other duties as assigned'."

Her brief lessening of unhappiness was gone. Everyone hates getting 'Other duties as assigned', it often means doing shit jobs the commander wants someone else to handle.

"Relax, Striebich," I smiled, hoping my grin would put her at ease. "The 'Other duties' I have in mind are shadowing Reed. I don't want you to replace Gasquet, I want you as a backup for Reed. You know how to think outside the box, that's a skill that can't be taught, or measured. Get up to speed on *Valkyrie*'s systems. I want you to be fully ready to fly and fight the ship, if necessary."

"In addition to acting as CAG."

"Yes."

"A busy crew is a happy crew," she shrugged, but there was relief on her face.

"Exactly. Striebich, I'm going to make it simple: you are here because I don't know what type of threat we are up against this time. I need advice and support from people who have been in the shit before. That's Reed, Frey, and now you. I told Reed her job is to keep me from doing something reckless. Frey's job is to make sure I *am* reckless, when I need to be."

"And me, Sir?"

"Your job is to help me understand the difference."

That drew a genuine smile from her. "I believe General Perkins would be better suited to that role, Sir."

"Ha! No, if I want advice on how to do *sketchy* shit, I'll ask her. Besides, a pair of two stars aboard a ship is two stars too many. Are you clear on your role, Striebich?"

"Yes, Sir. About the pilot training, I would like to get started right away."

"I'd prefer you started yesterday, but right away is good enough."

179

"There is a precision flying drill we used to run aboard the *Dutchman*, it's a, rather unique exercise."

"You have complete control of the training schedule and agenda."

"In that case, I saw that you recently requalified to fly the Panther."

"Uh-" For a moment, I panicked. When I talked all that shit about wanting the ship's pilots to sharpen their skills, I didn't include *myself*. "Just for basic flying maneuvers. My rating for combat flight expired years ago."

"You allowed your combat rating to lapse during *peacetime*. That's over now."

"Uh, yes."

"I will add you to the schedule, to ensure you get time in a simulator, before you move on to stick time in a real bird."

"That would be," I could feel the sickly smile stretching my face. "Great."

Striebich scheduled me for simulator time after lunch that same day, she had to bump a real pilot off their time, that didn't make me happy. But I had given her authority over all issues related to pilots, so I couldn't protest without undermining her. My schedule was free because my entire role aboard *Valkyrie* was 'Other duties as assigned' and I hadn't assigned myself to do anything that day, darn it. Oh hell, I loved playing around in a simulator. Often, I crashed and burned but that was the point, flight simulators were for trying extreme maneuvers and scenarios that were too dangerous to do in a real bird. If you never failed in a simulator, you weren't pushing your limits.

My hour in the Panther simulator had me soaked with sweat, and hungry since I'd skipped lunch. There was a half hour break before my next session, I went to the galley to get a quick snack. "Huh." That was unusual. By 1400 the galley should be busy with a crew getting ready to serve dinner. Instead, the place was empty. There were mid-watch rations, what we called 'mid-rats', to feed people who couldn't eat at normal times. Since I was going back into a simulator that might twist my stomach into knots, I made a peanut butter sandwich, with not a lot of peanut butter. Just in case, I ate a couple of oatmeal raisin cookies.

"Hey, Skippy, where is everyone?"

"Joe, Colonel Reed made me promise not to tell you.."

"Uh. Huh. Is this a good thing, or a bad thing?"

"*You* will think it's great."

"Cool. Can you give me a hint?"

"It's a *secret*, dumdum."

Out in the passageway, there were a normal number of people walking to, wherever they were going. The ship wasn't conducting any drills, and I didn't notice any signs of unusual activity. Except, the people I saw had grins that I interpreted as them knowing something I didn't.

180

Another weird thing was, all the flight simulators were empty. That's not true. What I meant is, the simulators were all booked, but not by pilots. Off-duty crew were taking advantage of the rare simulator availability, by pretending to fly. It was harmless fun, the amateur pilots couldn't hurt anything other than their egos.

Strapping into the simulator again, I called the control booth. "Lieutenant Kolchuk, I am ready to begin."

"Beginning start-up sequence now, Sir."

"Do you know where all the pilots have gone?"

"I wouldn't know about that, Sir."

"Did Reed order you to say that?"

"Not that you know of, Sir."

"OK," I laughed. It would be a dick move for me to pull rank on the guy. "Let's do this."

"Joe," Skippy called me after I got out of the simulator. "Go take a shower, and get out of that flight suit."

"Uh, OK, why?"

"First, if you had any idea what you monkeys smell like, you would shower every ten minutes. And wrap yourselves in plastic bags, yuck."

Lifting my arm I sniffed myself. He had a point. A shower was my plan anyway. "Hey, Margaret likes my manly scent."

"Ugh. Actually she does."

"She-" I had been joking. "She does?"

"Yes. Maybe I shouldn't tell you this, but before you left, she took several of your shirts out of the laundry basket, to sleep in. For some reason, she finds her husband's scent to be comforting."

"I like her scent too."

"Can we please drop the subject, before I hurl?"

"That would be great, yes. Why are you so in a rush," I asked while I took off my helmet and placed it in a locker to be cleaned and serviced. "For me to shower?"

"You are requested, I think the correct term is invited, to Docking Bay Alpha Two at seventeen hundred hours."

"What's the occasion?"

"Colonel Striebich will be conducting a precision flight demonstration."

"Aha! So that's where all the pilots are. Uh, is this why the galley is empty?"

"That is still a *secret*, knucklehead."

In the military, it is usually true that if you're not early for an event, you're late. That is not true when you are a general officer, and you are invited to an event by people below you in the chain of command. In that case, you show up right on time, so people don't have to worry about you arriving before they are ready. That's why I went to my cabin, showered, and hung around in my underwear catching up on paperwork while I waited. Fifteen minutes before the appointed time, I put on a fresh field uniform, and strolled out the door.

The tantalizing smell tickled my nose before I reached the inner door to Bay Alpha Two.

Charcoal grills.

Reed had set up charcoal grills in the cavernous bay, which was filled with people and not dropships. That was good, the air filters had to be working at full capacity to deal with the smoke from three charcoal grills. "Welcome to the party, Sir."

"Thank you, Fireball. What's the occasion?"

"We never celebrated the Special Mission Group being stood up again. So, we're having real backyard cheeseburgers."

"Reed," I lowered my voice. "If I could, I would offer you a field promotion to brigadier right now."

She laughed. "Thank you, Sir, but I would politely refuse. Every promotion I've gotten takes me closer to administrative duties, and further from flying."

"I hear that. What is this I heard about a precision flying demonstration?"

"That is Streibich's idea."

"Will we watch the demonstration before or after dinner?"

"Before, and during, Sir," she answered with a twinkle in her eyes. "We can't eat until, well, you'll see," she waved me over to a holographic display set up against the forward bulkhead of the bay.

The display showed icons for eight dropships strung out in a line behind *Valkyrie's* flight path, with the lead Panther designated 'Chips One'. There was no explanation for why Striebich had selected 'Chips' for the exercise squadron. The dropships were going significantly slower than our battlecruiser, they were falling behind fast. A clock counted down, and the lead bird accelerated, gently at first, then pouring it on hard. Striebich and her crew were sustaining a steady three gravities of acceleration, and keeping the thrust there. They were catching up to us rapidly, gaining speed and would be racing past the ship's port side. Was that the demonstration? If so, why was it necessary for preparing a cookout?

Interesting. The Panther cut acceleration briefly, flipped end over end, and burned at three gees to slow down, coming to a stop relative to *Valkyrie* exactly opposite the open door to Bay Alpha One. That bay was smaller, large enough to hold only a single dropship. Striebich popped thrusters to swing her craft in through the doorway, and set down neatly in the cradle. "OK," I nodded. "That was some fancy flying. She cut thrust exactly when she matched our speed, exactly in position."

"That's not all, Sir," Reed had a grin like that cat in Alice in Wonderland.

The outer doors snapped closed and the bay was rapidly pressurized, robotic cables snaking up to cover the Panther's thruster ports so toxic fumes didn't contaminate the air. Someone wanted to get out of that dropship in a hurry. That was a drill we practiced once a month when I was captain of the ship, for evacuating injured personnel from an incoming dropship. Again I had the question: why did I have to wait for dinner? Had Striebich used the high gravity maneuver to shake up a can of soda, so it would explode in my face?

Reed pressed a button, and the door that connected the bays slid open. The Panther's side door was already open, a ramp extended to the deck. I sniffed the air.

French fries?

There was no mistaking that scent, I knew it well.

"Fireball, what the-"

"You'll see, Sir. She-"

Striebich appeared in the Panther's doorway, holding a paper sack with dark grease stains. She also had a huge grin on her face. "Someone requested perfect French fries?"

"You-" I stared at her. "You made *fries* during your maneuver?"

"Yes, Sir," she held out the bag. "Eat 'em while they're hot."

"Operating a fryer aboard a dropship has got to be against some regulation."

"It's a good thing we are four thousand lightyears from Earth," she shook the bag. "The fryer is in a sealed container, it's safe."

I took a fry. It was uh-MAY-zing. "You need to explain this."

"At three gravities, the heat transfer between the fry oil and the potato maximizes the crust on the outside of a fry," she explained. "We modified the fryers so the potato strips constantly turn over, there is no bottom to get soggy as water is forced out of the fry."

"*That* is your precision flying drill?"

She nodded. "It is highly effective, Sir. If a pilot screws up and has to wave off to go around, the fries are delivered late and are cold. The entire crew is watching, and hungry. Plus," she added. "It's a lot more fun than the usual boring flight drills."

"That bag," I dipped a hand into get more of the incredibly crispy fries. "Isn't enough for everyone."

She pointed back over her shoulder, where another pilot was coming through the door, holding two greasy bags. "There is enough in our fryer for two more bags. And seven more dropships. If any of the pilots miss their marks, someone gets disappointment instead of delicious fries."

"No pressure on your pilots, then."

Her expression turned serious. "If a pilot can't handle the pressure of making *fries*, I don't want them flying a combat mission."

183

"Good point."

As a senior officer, it is important for me to show appreciation for the extraordinary efforts of the people under my command. *That* is why I ate three cheeseburgers, so do not listen to any spurious rumors about me. I was also pleased to see that *Valkyrie* still has a crack set of pilots; all of them hit their marks within the tight limits set by Striebich, and everyone had fun doing something they hadn't done a hundred times before. While *Valkyrie* did not actually need an air group commander, I was glad she was with us.

CHAPTER SIXTEEN

"This is some *bullshit*," Private First Class Larry Devens spat as he used the Army-issued grabber claw to pick up, something. The thing was gray, like everything on the dark side of the Moon. The *far* side of the Moon, he mentally corrected himself. With the Sun well over the horizon, the only darkness in sight were shadows. Everything else was gray, either the gloomy gray of rocks on the surface, or the blindingly bright light gray of the dust that covered the surface and clung to everything.

Specialist Darnell Washington laughed. "I don't think that came from a *bull*."

In response, Larry only grunted. The thing might not be bullshit, but the situation certainly was. "Join the Army, my recruiter said," he laughed bitterly. "See the galaxy, he said. So far, all I have seen is freakin' moon dust," he knocked the claw against his once-bright yellow, now gray boots. "On *everything*."

"You believed your recruiter? That was your first mistake," Darnel shook his head, though the helmet of his spacesuit did not move. "Hey Darla, did you listen to your recruiter?"

"My mother convinced me to sign up, but she told me the *truth*," Specialist Darla Walker replied, not bothering to look back at her companions.

"This sucks," Larry insisted.

Darla shrugged. "It beats cleaning up refugee camps in a South American jungle."

"At least there," Larry ground his teeth, "I could breathe real air."

The situation was a hundred percent bullshit. His assignment was supposed to be the security team for Moonbase Zulu. He had applied for that billet, worked for it. Most days, his job was simply boring. The UN Def Com security team at the base was not responsible for protecting the base against alien attackers, the two Sentinels and the squadron of Guardians would and could handle that, without any aid or interference from humans. The base and its attached facility for manufacturing exotic materials had a police force to take care of typical internal disputes and occasional criminal activity. The Def Com security unit, to which Larry's US Army platoon was currently assigned, was responsible for guarding those exotic materials from other humans. Not every nation in the 'United' Nations was onboard with reserving the enormously expensive exotic materials for the exclusive use of Skippy the Untrustworthy. Some of the materials had potential military value, and many countries who were not members of the Security Council wanted to boost their technology level by any means possible. Including theft. Larry was OK with guarding a bunch of weird exotic materials, especially as the job held out at least the prospect of shooting at bad guys.

Instead, he was dreamily contemplating shooting himself in the foot, to get out of his current duty. He couldn't actually shoot himself, as he hadn't been issued a weapon that day. And putting a hole in the boot of his environment suit was not a great idea. Still, a guy could dream, right?

Half of the platoon was out on the surface, not for an exercise that might be a bit of fun or at least somewhat interesting. The platoon had rotated on and off the surface for the past two days, on clean-up duty. A transfer shuttle, a modified Jeraptha spacecraft, had lost an engine on descent into Moonbase Zulu. The shuttle could have landed safely without one engine, but following protocol, the crew had dumped ballast before committing to final approach. That meant ejecting lower-value cargo like clothing and frozen food.

And, it meant venting the spacecraft's toilet holding tanks.

Ordinarily, the holding tanks freeze-dried the, to use a polite term, 'solid waste material', and sealed each unit of waste in a plastic bag. That material was either recycled, yuck, or buried. It could not be dumped on the lunar surface, because that would violate a stupid UN treaty. That was why the platoon had been wandering under on the base's southern approach lane, picking up crates and canisters, and loading them on moon crawler vehicles. The work was tedious but it allowed the soldiers to be outside, not staring at the same gray walls all day. Larry had been OK with that duty, until some jackass remembered the vented toilets.

That was why he was wandering around in a shallow crater, searching for freeze-dried space turds. The ones that remained in bags were bad enough, but the bags that had hit rocks and burst open-

Yuck.

The reason *he* was there, along with Darla and Darnell, was totally unfair. They were being punished for something that was not their fault. The day before, a crate of frozen food had fallen off a crawler, gotten smashed by the crawler's treads, and scattered all over a hundred meters before the driver of the crawler behind radioed a warning. It took an hour to pick up all of the crushed frozen pineapple, peas, carrots, and whatever else had been in the crate, and to scrape the remainder off the crawler's treads. The major in charge of the operation had *not* been amused. That crate had survived falling several kilometers in lunar gravity, luckily splashing down in a soft, dust-filled crater. The crate had survived that fall, only to be destroyed because three knuckleheaded soldiers didn't know how to secure a strap.

"Ah, it's Larry, Darryl and Darryl," the major had somehow been amused by that. Old people. Who knew what they were thinking? Darnell had Googled the 'Larry, Darryl and Darryl' reference and found it was from an 80s TV show. That was the *real* reason Larry, Darnell, and Darla were assigned to picking up space turds: to amuse an asshole field-grade officer.

Totally unfair.

"Hey," Darnell used his grabber claw to pick up an object. "Does this look like a rock to you?" He waved it in front of Larry's faceplate.

"Get it *away* from me," Larry swatted at the thing with his grabber, and the instant the two grabbers collided, the two men stepped back from each other.

Then the lightsaber fight was on, both men making low *bbzzzhh bzzzhhh* sounds as they slowly swung the grabber sticks.

"Knock it off, you two!" Darla shouted. "You're gonna break something, and we're in enough trouble already."

"We're just having some fun," Larry grumbled, lowering his stick.

"Besides," Darla lifted her stick. "*Bzzzzzhhht. I* am the Jedi master." She was about to step forward and swing the grabber stick at Larry, when all three of their helmet speakers blared an alarm.

"Whoa, shit," Darnell gasped.

Larry froze in place, turning his head to look in the direction of the base. "What the f-"

"All pers-" The distorted voice in their helmets was drowned out by a burst of static. "-on the surface take cover. Incom-" Another burst of static. "-enemy ships are-" The transmission ended.

"Take *cover?*" Larry spun around, seeing nothing but the shallow crater for a kilometer in every direction. "Where the fuck are we supposed to do that?"

Darla pointed to the rim of the crater, that while only a meter above the surrounding surface, was the only potential cover in the area. "Let's move out. Hey! Larry!"

"What?"

"Pick up that bag."

Larry stared open-mouthed at her. "I have to care about a bag of space crap?"

"If this is a drill," Darnell nudged the discarded bag with a boot, "the three of us will have to come back here to get it, and that will make me *very* unhappy, get that, Private?"

"Yeah," Larry tried to bend from the waist, having to use the grabber as a cane to stop himself from toppling over in the bulky, rigid spacesuit. That was why the platoon had issued him a tool that old people used for getting canned food off a kitchen shelf. Straightening up, he clutched the bag with the tool, securing the bag to his belt. "Hey guys! Wait for me!"

The attack began as General Chang sat on a folding chair in an auditorium, for his niece's piano recital. The timing was inconvenient, but enemies can be jerks like that. Really, since his niece had already played her piece of music, he was remaining there only to be polite, a task that became more difficult every moment, while the boy currently seated at the piano stumbled his way through butchering a piece of music the teacher had called 'Rachmaninoff'. Or possibly it was Rock and Roll Off, Chang hadn't been paying attention. His attention was focused not on his phone, but on *not* looking at the phone in his pocket. The phone was on silent, vibration shut off for the duration of the musical entertainment. There wasn't any need for him to check his phone, if any emergency required him to act, the security team would alert him, surrounding him as they escorted him to a waiting aircraft. That was a problem for him, actually. Unlike the other adults suffering through the recital, he couldn't fake a sudden reason to escape. Any genuine incident, important enough for the leader of Earth's Strategic Defense system to be rushed out of a public appearance, would be top of the news that same day.

For the next recital, he should arrange an interstellar crisis. Be proactive.

So, he sat with a smile frozen on his face, lightly holding his wife's hand, while trying to ignore the heavy sighs coming from his brother seated behind him.

His hand jerked away from his wife's, as the phone in his jacket pocket buzzed with the quick *zz zz zz* triple vibration of a priority message. "Sorry," he whispered to his wife as he reached for the phone. Not moving in a panicked fashion, half a second could not matter. Not with a Sentinel hanging above their heads. As the person at least nominally responsible for keeping everyone on the planet safe, he shouldn't cause undue alarm. Whatever was going on, it might just be-

His hand barely touched the phone when the metal doors on the side of the auditorium slammed open with a loud *BANG* and his security team charged through, the two guards inside the auditorium having already started sprinting toward him.

He stood up as the piano mercifully stopped, every eye focused on him, fear and shock registering immediately. "Sorry," he said again to his wife, as he turned to meet the security team. In exercises, they had hustled him to a waiting car or aircraft or dropship, and they were not under any orders to be gentle. That annoyed him, he could walk or run perfectly well by himself. Opening his mouth to ask his chief of security what was going on, he was interrupted by a familiar voice in his ear.

An AI.

Technically, an alien AI, or an AI programmed by an alien.

Grumpy.

"Well, ain't this a fine mess," the AI was extra, well, grumpy. Over the years, the voice it adopted had become even more raspy, weary of the world and everything in it. "Six ships just jumped in twenty thousand klicks from the dusty rock you call a moon. Eh, I suppose as moons go, that one's mass is a respectable percentage of the host planet. Certainly better than the two pathetic rocks Mars has, it's like that place isn't even *trying*. The-"

"Grumpy," Chang's voice was shaky as the security team surrounded him, taking firm hold of both of his arms, not so much escorting him out of the side door as carrying him along with them. "Oof," he grunted as he was practically thrown into the back of a waiting armored SUV, which burned rubber the moment his butt touched the seat. "Grumpy, identity of the ships?"

"No ID signal provided, and they didn't receive permission from Traffic Control, hence why this bit of fun is considered an emergency, get it? The ships are Maxohlx in configuration, but they're using some extremely sophisticated masking to scramble sensors. No stealth fields, though, that's odd. Eh, why do I care? My life is a meaningless hell anyway. Someone, please unplug me now."

"Is Bub-" he cringed, refusing to call the horrific killing machine 'Bubba'. "Is the Sentinel responding?"

"Nope, it's not doing anything. Except watching, of course. That creepy monster watches *everything* around here."

The Sentinel was aware of the intruders, and it was not shooting.

That had to be good news.

Bubba knew something that Chang didn't. Something Chang didn't know *yet*. He was gathering his thoughts when the SUV's driver slammed on the brakes, screeching the heavy vehicle to a stop beside a waiting dropship. The spacecraft was a VIP transport rather than a warbird, and not the aircraft Chang had arrived in. Taking him to the dropship was a good call by his security team, he had a split second to reflect on that before the SUV's door opened and he was yanked out.

Seemingly only a moment later, he was securely strapped into a seat in the cramped cabin of a sleek dropship, as that spacecraft's engines howled, and the ship soared into the sky.

The console in front of his was a single curved display that could show him any information he wanted. Except, at the moment, what he most wanted to know.

Why had the Maxohlx ships come uninvited?

So, what *did* he know?

Sensor data was confused, but the available data indicated the intruders were six warships, all Maxohlx in configuration. A heavy cruiser, two cruisers, and three light cruisers. Certainly not an overwhelming force. A force the UN Navy's 1st Fleet would laugh at. Or, the 1st Fleet would laugh, if those ships were near Earth. If the enemy's intentions were hostile, they had good timing. Good intelligence.

He also knew those six ships had not received clearance from Traffic Control.

Neither of the two ready alert frigates stationed near the Backstop wormhole had jumped in to report. *That* was not good. There were only two possibilities. Either the intruders had come to Earth the long way, bypassing the Backstop wormhole, or the two ready frigates had been unable to perform their assigned duties. That was a polite way of saying they had been destroyed by the intruders.

That made *no* sense. None of it made sense. An attack against Earth, with such a small force? No attack against humanity's homeworld made sense, as long as Bubba was active.

Was the Sentinel active?

Yes. The giant thing was transmitting its usual signal, unchanged.

That was good. The Sentinel was programmed to respond automatically to hostile ships near Earth. Years of testing with robotic ships had confirmed how effective the Elder weapon was. Jumping in close to achieve surprise? The Sentinel was not surprised at all. In testing, a robotic ship playing the aggressor role had barely emerged from the jump wormhole when it met an exotic beam weapon that had been fired *before* the ship came through the wormhole.

Slowly sneaking up to Earth in stealth? The Sentinel had detected, and destroyed, the stealth ship at a distance of forty lightseconds.

A light on the console blinked. Incoming call from Def Com HQ. By that time, General Brooke himself had probably initiated the call. Brooke didn't need Chang to do anything, there wasn't anything Chang could do. The Sentinel was fully automatic, that is what 'automated' meant. The thing didn't need any orders from humans, nor would it accept commands from any lowly biological being.

Bubba had not taken action. Therefore, Bubba for whatever reason, did not consider the intruders to be hostile. There was nothing to worry about. Yet. Chang told himself that as his finger hovered over the button to accept the incoming call.

His finger drifted away, landing on another icon. A tap there alerted his staff to warm up the X-ray laser satellites.

All fourteen of them.

Just in case.

He accepted the call. "Chang here."

"Kong," it was the upper-crust English voice of Brooke. "Why aren't the Sentinels shooting yet?"

"Sir, I believe this could be good news. The Sentinel would certainly react, if it considered the intruders to be hostile."

"They *are* intruders," Brooke insisted." Uninvited. That makes them hostile, in my view."

"The trajectory of those ships will take them behind the Moon," Chang read what he saw on the curved display in front of him. "This could be a, stunt, of some kind." For what purpose, he could not imagine. Also, that was odd. The ships were moving slowly relative to the Moon, and decelerating hard.

Did they intend to go into orbit around Earth's natural satellite? *Why?*

"I have the X-ray units warming up now," Chang added, as his display showed the fourteen satellites of the pathetic second line of strategic defense reporting as ready.

"The guard ships are responding, they will intercept," Brooke told Chang what he could see on his display. The UN Navy destroyers *Calgary* and *Cordoba* had turned and were burning toward the intruders, hammering away with active sensor pulses, hoping to penetrate whatever form of masking the intruders had deployed. And to uncover the presence of any stealthed ships that might be in the area. "I have to go hold the Secretary General's hand," Brooke said with irritation. "Chang, talk to your dog if you can, find out why it isn't shooting."

Biting back what he wanted to say, Chang replied with, "Yes, Sir."

The call ended.

"Grumpy?" Chang didn't initiate a call, he just spoke. The irritable AI either chose to respond, or didn't.

"Yeah, what?"

"Can you ask Bubba why it hasn't reacted to the intruders?"

"What? You think the two of us hang out in cyberspace? Drink a couple beers, complain about you monkeys?"

"I am *asking* you to contact it now."

"It won't talk to me. It doesn't talk to anyone. Except Skippy, and that Supreme Asshole isn't here. So, I have *that* going for me."

"Could you please try?"

"Don't you think I already did? Bubba refuses to acknowledge my call."

"Please try aga-"

"That pissed me off, so I talked with Roscoe. That thing is at least respectful. I asked *it* to talk with Bubba."

"That was good thinking. And?"

"Bubba reported that it is complying with its programmed instructions."

"It does not consider the intruder ships as hostile, then."

"That," Grumpy snorted, "or Skippy *totally* screwed up the programming. Oooh, hey! There's a happy thought."

Jesse Colter knelt down on one knee to fit a cage around the tomato plant. The loose wire cage fit easily over the plant that was less than a half meter tall, it-

He laughed to himself. I'm an American, and I am thinking in *metric*. Maybe I have been in the military for too long? Eh, he shrugged. He had the full twenty years in, so he could retire, but then what would he do? Work for Dave Czajka? There's an idea. He would be doing basically the same work he did as a master sergeant in the US Army, but getting paid a lot more. That was something he needed to discuss with Shauna, when she returned from Zandrus.

In the meantime, he had work to do. Technically, he was on medical leave while his leg healed. That didn't mean he wasn't expected to do some work around the house, that's why Shauna's grandfather had come over to help Jesse plant a garden. It would be nice for Shauna to see a garden when she returned, her grandfather had said when he arrived with a truck loaded with plants from a local nursery. The real reason was Jesse needed something to do, and sitting on the back deck drinking beer while he watched his son run around was not productive.

"OK," Jesse grunted as he hauled himself back up using the crutch. "This one looks good." The plant actually looked sad and droopy, but water would take care of that. It would be good to have a garden. Since the Jupiter Cloud had literally been blown away by Roscoe, Earth's climate had been unpredictable, seesawing back and forth as the atmosphere and oceans recovered and sought a new equilibrium. Or that is what the weather people on TV said, whenever they got a three-day forecast wrong, again. Planting a garden in Wisconsin was a vote for hope, that Earth would soon return to normal.

If he could remember what 'normal' was. It had been a long time since Columbus Day.

"Pops," he called Shauna's grandfather, "let's get the-"

His zPhone vibrated and sounded an alarm.

"Oh sh-"

"What is it?" The older man asked, setting down a shovel.

"We have visitors. Can you grab Johnny please?" He pointed to his son, who was digging in a pile of mulch. "We're going into the basement."

"If this is a raid," Pops looked to the sky, shading his eyes with a hand. "The Sentinels will protect us."

"They will," Jesse assured his grandfather in law, as the man picked up the boy, who protested with a scream that could not possibly have come from someone so small. "That means a whole lot of ordnance will be flying around up there soon, and broken parts of enemy ships could be raining down on our heads. We're going into the basement, Pops, come on."

"This has to be a drill, right?" Larry lifted his head above the rim of the crater, which next to him was less than two feet high. "Guys? Right?"

"I don't know," Darnell reached over to push the private's helmet down.

"It has to be a drill. Loss of communications," Larry was increasingly confident. "Something like that. It's stupid for us to be lying here, I'm getting nasty gray moon dust all over my suit."

"We are lying here because that's what we do when we get an attack alert, whether it's a drill or not. The scrubbers will wash your suit clean when we get back to the base."

"The scrubbers don't get everywhere," Larry protested. "Sometimes they just get the dust wet and then it dries hard as concrete, and I have to clean the crevices with a toothbrush or the staff sergeant yells at me," he raised his head again.

"If you're worried about getting yelled at, you better think about what the satellite video will show you did during this drill, so keep your head *down*," Darnell gave the private another shove.

The crew of the UN Navy destroyer *Calgary* was slightly irritated when they felt their ship's acceleration slacken for a few seconds, then resume with not quite the same vigor. The irritation was mixed with more than a small measure of smugness, knowing the reason for the temporary slackening of pursuit was the crew of slackers aboard the destroyer *Cordoba*. The two ships had to maintain formation, and *Cordoba* had fallen ever so slightly behind in the chase to intercept the intruder ships. The fact that *Calgary* was fresh from a major overhaul, while *Cordoba's* engines had not enjoyed the attention of a shipyard in three years, was no excuse for poor performance, and the crews of the two ships knew that. Their engines, however, did not care about the opinions of meatsacks.

The rivalry between the two ships was good natured, and the exercise injected a bit of excitement into what had been a dull rotation. It had to be an exercise, the crewmembers told each other. If the attack were real, the big dog would have barked, and its bark was as bad as its bite. The Sentinel had not responded, therefore, the event was a planned an unannounced exercise. A risk-free opportunity to shine.

A *lame* opportunity to show what the UN Navy could do.

Only six ships, really? That's the most the Navy brass could scrape together for an aggressor force? Those ships were using some new type of masking, so it wasn't possible yet to determine which UN Navy ships were playing the role of the aggressors. The people aboard those intruder ships must be having fun, and the crews of the *Calgary* and *Cordoba* were eager to show that the 1st Fleet's Home Guard force was not sleeping on the job.

Another question that tickled the minds of the destroyer crews was: why the Moon? If an aggressor was insane enough to challenge earth's defenses, the only smart play was a quick hit and run targeting the homeworld. Were the intruders planning to slingshot around the Moon, use that satellite's gravity to boost speed? If so, why were the intruders slowing down?

Were they doing that to see how the Home Guard force reacted to alien tactics that seemed, well, *alien*?

Twenty seconds to weapons range. The destroyers had not received a signal to fire only low-powered directed energy weapons as a warning shot. That was odd in an exercise. Some trigger-happy idiot could cause a lot of damage with full-power fire.

Unless the ship's AI *had* been instructed to disable the weapons, without informing most of the crew that the incident was a planned exercise.

That had happened before.

Fifteen seconds to-

Calgary staggered, the ship's engines dropping offline as the shields were struck by a broadside of beam weapons from the intruder's heavy cruiser.

Weapons that were at full power.

If the crews of both destroyers were angry at being victims of a friendly fire incident, because some moron hadn't gotten the memo, their anger was brief. Railgun darts from the now clearly hostile heavy cruiser punched through the thin skin of the destroyers from bow to stern. *Cordoba* spun wildly as two reactors erupted. That ship was lucky. *Calgary* took a railgun dart directly into the main magazine that held ship-killer missiles.

The UNS *Calgary* ceased to exist.

"This is stupid," Larry felt free to complain, as long as he adhered to proper procedure by taking shelter. The rim of a crater that wasn't tall enough to actually protect him, so it made no sense. But, he was only a private, and nothing in the Army needed to make sense to him. "If there is a real threat up there, the Sentinels will take care of it. We are totally safe here."

"No we are not, you dumbass," Darla kicked his left leg. "The Sentinels protect Earth, not *us*."

"They are supposed to protect the entire solar system," Larry objected. "Roscoe got rid of the Jupiter Cloud, and that wasn't anywhere close to Earth."

"I meant, the Sentinels won't protect three people on the surface of the Moon. Think about it: if a threat is so serious that a *Sentinel* has to shoot, a lot of ordnance will be flying around. It can get real kinetic up there," she pointed a finger upward. "It doesn't matter whether someone shoots at us deliberately, or we get hit with a piece of shrapnel traveling a thousand klicks per second, so we keep our heads down and try to be as small a target as possible."

"If ordnance was flying around, we would see- WHOA!" His helmet visor, not as sophisticated a device as those provided to combat mech suits, could not immediately adjust to the brilliant flare of light in the sky. "What the hell was *that*?"

"Something kinetic," Darla said, though in a hoarse whisper.

"Guys," Darnell added, "this is no drill."

"No shit, Sherlock," Larry gasped.

"Grumpy," Jesse whispered into his phone, as he searched for a beer in the back of the fridge. Pops was down in the basement with little Johnny,

and Jesse thought sitting out the raid warning would be more tolerable with proper refreshments.

"Hi, Jesse, what's shakin', homeboy?"

It was always surprising that the AI everyone called 'Grumpy' usually was happy to talk with him. "That's what I was going to ask you. How long until Bubba takes care of, whatever is going on up there?"

"Um, that could be a problem. A group of Maxohlx warships jumped in, and they just wasted two of your Navy's destroyers."

"Shit!" He was so startled, he let go of one beer, trapping it against his thigh with a forearm before it hit the floor. "Why the hell did Bubba let that happen?"

"That is unknown. Bubba is online and active, it is just not doing anything against the enemy. This could be a bad fight, I suggest you keep your head down."

"Hell yeah." Jesse kicked the fridge door closed, then considered the two cold beers he held. Being impaired during a crisis was not the best idea. He put the beers away and got two cans of iced tea. And a box of crackers from the pantry. Plus cookies for his son. The three of them could be in the basement for a while.

Chang felt a block of ice in his stomach as he watched the symbols for the two destroyers flicker, then go dark.

The UN Navy ships *Calgary* and *Cordoba* were dead and out of the fight.

It *was* a fight.

"Why the bloody hell hasn't your Sentinel fired?!" Brooke demanded.

"Sir, I do not know, and I suggest you get the fleet moving."

"What about your X-ray platforms?"

"They are ready to engage but, Sir, the intruder formation is passing behind the Moon's horizon. The X-rays are single use weapons, we should wait until the enemy emerges again, to ensure every shot will count."

Brooke muttered something inaudible, then, "With the 1st Fleet away on maneuvers, the Home Guard here is only seven ships. *Five* ships, now," he added with bitterness. "Chang, your X-ray team needs to take out the enemy's big ships at least, the Home Guard can-" A pause while someone spoke in the background. "Why the hell would they do *that*?"

Chang knew the question was not directed at him. What was Brooke's question?

Oh, that.

The intruder formation, the *enemy* formation, was continuing to decelerate, hard. Those ships were already not going too slowly to achieve a stable lunar orbit. Were they attempting to *land* on the Moon? That was insanity. Starships didn't set down in gravity wells, not even those without an

195

atmosphere. The only thing that made any sense at all was for those ships to using their engines to hover above the surface.

To hover, over the dark side of the Moon.

"Sir?! General Brooke!" Chang shouted to get the attention of the man in overall command of humanity's military.

"Eh? What?" Brooke was stressed, irritated.

"Sir, I believe the intruders are going for Moonbase Zulu."

CHAPTER SEVENTEEN

Moonbase Zulu, probably named by some unknown staffer who was a fan of classic sci fi TV shows, was a fortress buried deep under the far side of the Moon, in the center a crater named 'Heaviside'. It was the most secure facility in Earth's solar system, or at least it was thought to be secure. With a Sentinel protecting most of the solar system, critics had asked why the UN had spent an enormous sum of money to tunnel deep under that crater, to build a vault. Rumors stated that a large budget meant greater opportunities for bribes to be skimmed off. UN officials retorted that since the nearby Keeler crater was the site for manufacturing exotic materials, it made sense to store such materials at a site that required a minimum of transport resources.

So, under Moonbase Zulu was the Vault. A secure storage for the exotic materials that enabled the construction of transmitters capable of contacting a dormant Sentinel. Materials no other species in the galaxy possessed, and therefore were incredibly valuable.

They were also totally worthless to any other species in the galaxy. The transmitters could only be utilized by an Elder AI. By Skippy.

That was the assumption, anyway.

There was a flaw in the defense plan for the Vault, and not just the assumption that a Sentinel would *do something* in case of an obviously hostile act. The SD platforms, the X-ray laser satellites, were all positioned inside the Moon's orbit. Unable to strike anything on the far side. The Home Guard force, pitifully small and now reduced by two ships, had to assemble into an attack formation, before proceeding toward the enemy. To concentrate force against the objective, with the objective being the destruction of the intruders. For the Home Guard ships to attack one by one would be pointless suicide.

The planners of Moonbase Zulu had been aware they did need to provide an independent defense. Not against aliens, the Sentinel would handle that. Against humans who might seek to acquire exotic materials. The United Nations was still not entirely *united*.

As the hostile intruder ships approached, railguns hidden under the Moon's surface spat out darts. Missile batteries launched their deadly payloads. The attacking ships defended themselves, not always successfully. They fired back, knocking out railguns and missile batteries. It was a battle of attrition. Who would run out of ordnance first?

"Holy *shit!*" Larry gasped, as he watched missiles streak toward the sky. He couldn't see the hidden missile batteries, he also couldn't see what they were shooting at. There were twinkling lights above him, he couldn't tell whether those lights were from friendly strikes against enemy ships, or hostile ships shooting back. He had seen live-fire exercises but those had been on Earth. On a planet. With an atmosphere. On the Moon, the battle was completely silent. Which was weird, because it felt like a videogame with the sound turned off.

"Why are *we* shooting?" He asked no one in particular. "The Sentinels should be fighting this battle, not us."

"I'm an E-4," Darnell replied. "The Army doesn't ask my opinion about war planning, you know?"

"*We* are not doing anything," Darla added, "until the shooting stops."

"Don't worry," Larry held up a thumb that neither of his companions could see. "I am staying here until- Hey. That light up there. Is it getting closer?"

No one answered at first. Then, Darla spoke. "It's not a missile, it isn't moving fast enough. Looks like a, shuttle coming in to land, but that can't be right."

The defenses of Moonbase Zulu were prepared to fight a battle of attrition. With only six enemy ships attacking, the magazines of the base contained enough missiles to continue the fight to the point where the enemy would have to withdraw, or be destroyed.

Unfortunately for the defenders, it wasn't that kind of battle.

The six enemy ships continued to decelerate, but not to achieve a stable orbit. They were already traveling slower than the speed required to achieve lunar orbit. They were free falling.

Falling in an arc toward Moonbase Zulu.

The ships ceased shooting back, there wasn't any point. The ships themselves had become weapons. The first incoming ship was turned into dust before it came within five thousand kilometers of the surface. One victory.

A small victory.

The other five ships impacted within nine seconds of each other, smashing both Heaviside and Keeler craters. Making those craters deeper. The manufacturing facility under Keeler was crushed. Humanity would not be making any more special transmitters for a while. The upper levels at Moonbase Zulu, the entrance to the Vault, were ground into fused glass.

None of the people at either site survived.

Larry *bounced*. A moonquake caused by the impacting ships lifted him off the surface once, twice, three times. Each time he bounced upward above the rim of the shallow crater, he was pelted by dust and pebbles. When the quakes were over and he hugged the ground, gasping with his eyes closed, he felt and heard more impact debris pelting his helmet and the hard-shell of his suit. That was bad, the shell of his suit wasn't that hard, was not armored. A depressurization alarm sounded from the helmet speakers followed by a high-pitched shrieking that became a low-pitched moan before he could scream in terror. The gel in his suit liner had sealed the leak, wherever it was. Then he realized something hot was stinging his right butt cheek.

Damn it.

He had gotten hit in the ass.

"Fuck!" He shouted.

General Brooke called. "Chang, you can stand down your X-ray toys. The enemy objective appears to have been to knock out our ability to produce exotic materials. Prevent us from waking up more Sentinels for a while."

"That is," Chang took a breath. "What it looks like, Sir. I suggest the X-ray platforms remain online. The galaxy will soon know our Sentinel failed to stop an attack."

"It did. All right, Chang, keep your team on alert, until further notice. I just sent orders to recall the 1st Fleet. And to pull units from Jaguar. Damn it, we put too much faith in an alien machine we don't understand. We can't even talk with the thing!"

"Yes, Sir," Chang responded automatically. There wasn't anything else he could say. "Sir? We should send a ship to find the Special Mission Group. Bring Skippy back here. Have him tell us what went wrong with his pet guard dog."

"You are damned right about that. I never trusted that beer can. Do you have any thoughts about why the Sentinel failed to respond?"

"Sir I, I would be guessing."

"I said, *any* thoughts."

"Perhaps Skippy gave the Sentinel," he refused to call the thing 'Bubba' to the world's senior military official. "Too narrow a definition of a threat. An attack directed against the Moon, the far side of the Moon-"

"It has acted at a much farther distance before, in our testing."

"It has. Only Skippy can tell us for certain." What he did not want to say, for the idea terrified him, was that perhaps the Sentinel had deliberately ignored its instructions. To allow the enemy to succeed.

So that humanity could not wake up any more Sentinels.

With the immediate crisis over, Chang directed the dropship pilots to change course and proceed to New York at best speed. The UN brass would have questions for him, he would not have answers. He was prepared to submit his resignation. There wasn't actually anything he could have done to make the Sentinel perform its assigned task, everyone in authority at Def Com knew that. The politicians who led the nations of the Security Council were also aware of that unfortunate fact. Those politicians also knew the public around the globe would demand that *someone* pay a price for the terrifying failure of the hulking monster that hung over their heads. An ancient alien machine they had been assured was invincible. Yes, perhaps the machine was invincible, it was obviously not *infallible*.

Chang would not be unhappy to leave his job, he was a figurehead and he knew it. Let someone else take the thankless and frankly, nearly useless role. He *would* be unhappy to be leaving the position now, when the leaders of Earth could no longer deny the foolishness of their failure to fund an effective, independent strategic defense system.

In his resignation letter, he could not openly state 'I told you so'. But, he could certainly imply his feelings on the subject.

First, while he still was nominally in charge of Earth's SD network, he had work to do. "Colonel Kim," he called the officer currently on duty in the strategic defense control center. "Keep the X-ray units online. Hostile elements in the galaxy will soon learn that our Sentinel is less than perfectly reliable."

"Yes, Sir. Sir?"

"Yes?"

"I have questions."

Chang bit back an instinctive sigh. "You will have to stand in line. I expect that everyone will have questions for me."

"Yes, Sir, but I'm not asking about the Sentinel," Kim blurted out, to get his point across before he could be interrupted. "Why did those ships decelerate?"

"They-" Stunned, he realized that was a very good question. "They did. Colonel, that is an *excellent* question."

"It makes no sense. When those ships came out of jump, they weren't properly lined up with the target impact zones, so they did need to alter course, but they could have maintained speed, or increased speed. Made the impact more kinetic. As it is- We're still running the analysis here- Those ships impacted with *minimum* force."

Chang had a bad feeling. Worse than the bad feeling he'd experienced mere minutes before, and he had thought that was impossible. "Kim, do we have eyes on the site?"

"On their way down, the enemy shot out many of our stealthed sensor satellites- Sir, we don't know how those platforms were detected, they-"

"We will review that later. Do we have a view of Zulu?"

"Yes, Sir. We are networking together the single SD sensor platform available, with several commercial and scientific satellites in the area. The image is not as clear as-"

"Show me."

The display in front of Chang flickered, steadied, and at first showed only dust. Lots of gray dust. Of course. The impacts had turned both craters into deeper craters, and thrown two enormous plumes of moon dust and rock upward. Some of the material, a legend on the side of the display informed

200

him uselessly, would escape the Moon's gravity. Some would go into orbit, to become a hazard to future transport links between Earth and its natural satellite. Most of the material, including almost all the heavier rocks, would smash back into the far side over a wide area. Anyone out on the surface should keep their heads down for a while.

That was odd. Instead of concentrating the impacts on the two targets, the craters Keeler and Heaviside, the five ships had impacted in a scattered fashion. The result was less effective destruction of the manufacturing plant, and the upper section of the Vault. The Vault itself was intact, radar showed the damage was limited to three hundred meters below the surface.

"Kim, if all five ships had struck the top of the Vault elevator, could the impact have damaged the Vault itself?"

"No. Sir, we checked that. The analysis is preliminary, it-"

"I'm sure it is accurate."

"Even if all of those ships *accelerated* coming out of jump, and they all impacted one after the other, the damage would not have had any effect on the Vault. Not even close, that is why the Vault was constructed so deep under the surface. Sir, it makes no sense."

"They," Chang spoke his thoughts aloud, "couldn't have been attempting to block the Guardians from interfering, by sealing the elevator shaft?"

"No, Sir. If those things were activated, they could dig their own tunnel to the surface. The enemy should know that. Their intel was excellent, they even knew the location of our stealthed sensor platforms. *How* did they know the Sentinel and the Guardians would not respond to the attack?"

"The Sentinel decides whether to activate Guardians," Chang mused aloud. "Bubba is the key," he said without realizing he had used the machine's ridiculous name. "Put aside the issue of the Sentinel for now. Focus on the attack. You are correct, the enemy's tactics make no sense. It is odd. They could have achieved much more damage, if they had concentrated force against, the, objective," he heard himself speak aloud, slowly. "If that was their objective."

Kim apparently knew what his boss was thinking. "We don't understand their tactics, because we don't know what their *objective* was. Inflicting maximum destruction against Moonbase Zulu was obviously not their intent. So, what-"

"Colonel!" Chang raised a hand, though the communication was audio only. "What is *that*?"

From the vaguely dome-shaped grey cloud above Heaviside crater, a column of dark grey dust was rising. In the three seconds after the effect became visible, the column rose rapidly, flaring out at the top, becoming a fountain. No, a volcano. The erupting material was *hot*.

How could that be? The Moon was geologically dead, or close to it. There had not been an active volcano on that sphere in a very long time.

Heaviside and Keeler had been chosen for being on an especially stable section of the far side. The impact damage could not possibly have had any effect on the Moon's core.

"I would say secondaries?" Kim suggested. "But, there isn't anything explosive down there. It isn't movement by Guardians either, the seismic sensors aren't detecting any activity within the Vault itself. This, hold one, Sir." The Korean officer sucked in a breath. "*O jenjang*," he exclaimed in his native language. "Sir, the seismic sensors show the origin point of the ejected material is moving deeper, away from the surface. Something is *tunneling* down to the Vault."

Chang was seeing the same data on his own display. "Surely, nothing could have survived those impacts." Suddenly he understood the enemy tactics. And the objective. "Oh, *damn* it. Kim, they spread out the impacts to suppress the defenses across a wide area. We have no missile batteries or railguns left around the sites. Whatever is tunneling down to the Vault, their objective is to capture the exotic materials we have stored there."

"Or the Guardians."

Chang doubted those alien machines would allow themselves to be taken away, but so much of what *could not happen* had happened that day, he could not be surprised by anything. "Can you identify what sort of tunneling machine is down there?"

"It, does not appear- One moment, Sir." There was excited chatter in the background. "The initial analysis was not entirely accurate. The material we see is coming from the hole around the elevator shaft, but it is not being ejected upward. Sir, something is *pulling* that material upward from above!"

"What the- Another ship?"

"Not possible," Kim was emphatic. "The Moonbase defenses saturated the area with active sensor pulses, before those sensor projectors were destroyed. There were six ships, they are all accounted for. There is no-"

In the background on Kim's end came a muffled but loud, "What is *that*?"

The display was not showing a ship. Not the outline of any ship. Just an object. Not even that, what the display showed was something disturbing the fountain of material that was being ejected- No. Being pulled up out of the hole or tunnel or shaft or whatever it was. The rock and dust of the high speed fountain was flowing around something that was coming in from the side, an object that halted in the center of the fountain. At that moment, the eruption of material intensified double, triple, ten times in volume. Huge chunks of rock raced upward, up and out of the display's view. The seismic sensors planted under the Moon's surface struggled to keep up with the events, struggled to interpret the information. The tunneling effect was nearing the Vault. One kilometer. Three quarters. Half.

As abruptly as it began, the fountain shut off. A column of rock and a cloud of dust still soared upward, but the column now had a bottom. Below the retreating column of the fountain, the space above what used to be Moonbase Zulu was clear, showing a perfectly round hole, the sides smoothly polished. The column flowed around, whatever the object was, showing only a roughly oval shape. Like an egg.

An energy field of some type.

A field enveloping *what*?

Before Chang could ask a question his staff could not answer, the hovering object dropped its stealth field.

It was a starship.

An *Elder* starship.

"What the *fuck* is that thing?" Larry screeched. Though communications were still offline, the three soldiers had decided, with the shooting over, to get up and walk to where the crawlers should be waiting. Assuming the asshole crawler drivers had not put pedal to the metal and raced away when they heard the alarm. Bunch of jerks. Walking had been their only option, their suits only had oxygen for another seven hours, and the base had been obliterated. The crawlers were the only pressurized environment within several kilometers, if the crawlers had survived. If they were intact, the crawlers should be transmitting a location signal, and Larry's suit was not picking up any signal, at all, from anywhere. Not even the GPS satellites, or the beacon at the L2 Lagrange point station. He was already in a near panic when the crater where the base had been erupted like a volcano. Or, like a fountain might be a better description. Dust and rock soared into the sky in a narrow column that could not be anything natural.

"It's secondaries," Darnell only turned to look backward for a moment as the three jogged toward the last known location of the crawlers.

"Or," Darla guessed, "the Guardians are coming to the surface."

"No!" Larry reached out to grab onto her forearm. "Not the fountain. What is *that*?" he pointed high above them. He pointed at an object that hovered above where the base had been, an object within the column of dust and rock, that was flowing upward around it.

"I don't know what it is," Darnell's voice was shaky. "I do know it is all kinds of wrong."

Chang contacted General Brooke immediately. "Sir! You-"

"Chang, is that what I think it is?"

"It explains a lot. Sir, you should order the Home Guard to pull back."

"Pull back? We are under attack, it-"

"Our ships can't do anything against an *Elder* ship, except to die uselessly. We will need the Home Guard to clean up the mess, once the AI aboard that ship has gotten what it wants. Our ships have to deter any of our adventurous enemies, who might be tempted to attack to take advantage of what they will see as our weakness. Until the 1st Fleet arrives, the Home Guard will be our only defense."

"That, plus the X-ray platforms you correctly insisted we invest in. All right, I'll tell the Guard to halt their advance." Brooke spoke to someone in a muffled voice for a moment. "Chang, is that thing trying to steal our Guardians?"

"Until a few seconds ago, I assumed the objective was to take our exotic materials. Now, anything is possible. An Elder AI might be able to control and use Guardian machines."

"Hell, if it turns those things against us," Brooke didn't finish the thought.

"In that case, we should pray." What Chang did not add was that he would be praying for divine intervention. But also for Joe Bishop. *Joe*, he sent out a silent plea, *where are you*?

Joe Bishop, at that moment, was in a desperate race against time.

There wasn't enough time, it was just math, and the math was against him.

He was going to be too late.

He had prepared to make cinnamon buns for breakfast, after hearing that Samantha Reed mentioned to someone that Bishop used to occasionally bake treats for *Valkyrie's* former crew. The night before, he had gone through the galley, checking that everything he needed was available. Including rapid rise yeast.

Not rapid enough.

The problem was Reed. According to Skippy, the ship's captain was planning to fly a dropship with Striebich that morning. A bonding experience, and an opportunity to get stick time so Reed didn't lose her rating to fly a Panther. To take advantage of the ship pausing several hours to fully recharge the jump drive capacitors, Reed and Striebich had scheduled their flight for 0600.

Joe also had gotten up early. But not early enough to take cinnamon buns out of the oven, before two of the three colonels aboard came into the galley to get coffee.

"Come back after your flight," Joe urged.

"Uh," Reed gulped her too-hot coffee, and wiped her mouth with the back of a hand. "That's going to be tight, Sir. I have a staff meeting at 0900."

"I will have fresh hot buns delivered to your meeting," Bishop said with relief.

After Reed and Striebich left, Joe stared at the materials on the counter. "Skippy, do you ever get the feeling that you're missing something?"

"All the time. Like, how wonderful my life could be right now, if I hadn't hooked up with a filthy monkey."

"I hear you. It's just, I feel like I'm *missing* something, you know?"

"Seriously?"

"Yeah."

Skippy sighed. "You don't have powdered sugar for the icing, dumdum."

"Yes," Joe snapped his fingers. "That's it!"

They looked like Terminators. Not the Arnold Schwarzenegger Cyberdyne Systems Model 101 type of Terminator. The eleven pods appeared to be liquid, like the T-1000 model introduced in *Terminator 2*. After the Elder starship dropped its stealth, it hovered directly over the hole it had dug, by unknown means. The means it used to excavate a perfectly round shaft were unknown, as were the mechanisms that allowed the ship to maintain position without apparently using any engine power. Whatever type of invisible thrust or antigravity the ship employed, the pods also had the same means of counteracting the Moon's gravity, descending at a rate much faster than freefall, slowing as they approached the lip of the hole. Slowing, and transforming. The objects that left the ship as smooth cigar-shaped pods grew extensions, limbs, tentacles, multiple shapes. Limbs did not emerge from the pod's shell, the shell material itself *flowed* to become, whatever shape the Terminator needed. The shapes, whatever the final form, were still changing as they plunged past the lip of the hole and out of view.

Three minutes later, moving at a relatively slow three hundred kilometers per hour, two of the T-1000s emerged from the hole, accelerating at a steady rate. Squids. The Terminators had taken on the shape of a squid, though it was only the human minds of the observers who made that connection. Tentacles, five of them, extended upward to wrap around a canister, with a tapered body below.

More of squids appeared, a total of eleven Terminators. The Vault held eleven canisters of the exotic matter designated 'Radonium'.

The enemy, the enemy *Elder AI*, wanted those materials, and not the Guardians. Why was it not also taking those powerful weapons?

Unknown.

What would the Elder AI do with the radonium?

Also unknown. Other than, for some purpose that was nothing good for humanity.

The eleven Terminators, or eleven Vault robbers, raced upward to meet the ship, where openings appeared to accept them. After the last unit disappeared inside the Elder starship, it too disappeared.

A short, faint burst of gamma radiation was detected, by the single strategic defense sensor satellite that had a view of the event.

General Brooke called, fifteen minutes after the Elder starship apparently jumped away, or however the thing traveled. "Chang, can I assume you prepared a resignation letter?"

Kong stiffened in his seat, though the question was expected. His dropship would be over New York shortly, according to the display. "Yes, Sir, I have. The-"

"Forget that. Tear it up."

"Someone has to take the fall for this."

"Someone does," Brooke agreed. "The damned beer can. This isn't your fault. No one expected our defenses to cope with a force equal to Skippy. I just told the Secretary General, that it's like building a fence around your garden to keep the deer from eating your tomatoes, and then being surprised that fence won't stop Godzilla."

"Yes, Sir. I suggest a better analogy is, the fence won't stop someone who can simply *open the fucking gate.*"

"You're right, damn it. I need you to talk with the Sentinel. See if it's functional at all."

Chang noticed Brooke had said 'the Sentinel' and not '*your* Sentinel'. Blame was no longer being assigned. "I will do what I can, Sir. Hopefully, the Elder AI affected the Sentinel only while it was here."

"That's better than nothing, I suppose. At least then, we only have to worry about an Elder AI, and not about every damned species in the galaxy who wants to take a shot at us."

"We should consider testing the-"

Bubba chose that moment to become active with a flare of purple light, and shoot.

At chunks of rock that had escaped the Moon's gravity, and were falling toward Earth.

"Too little," Chang breathed through clenched teeth. "Too late."

"*Choo!*" Larry sneezed. Again. And again. A dropship had found him, Darla and Darnell, and picked them up three hours after the attack. Larry was grateful to the dropship crew. He was not amused to hear the dropship had been sent out to search for 'Larry, Darryl and Darryl', as the major in command had apparently forgotten their real names. Whatever. They were alive. "*Choo!*"

"Will you cover your freakin' mouth?" Darnell shot him a withering look.

"I can't help it," Larry covered his nose with a hand. "We're all covered with nasty moondust, and it's everywhere." The dust made everything smell burnt. He looked to the dropship's crew chief. "You got any handiwipes around here?"

"I'm keeping those to myself," the petty officer grimaced. "Don't even think of using the head, this could be a long flight, and we might have to squeeze in a lot more ground-pounders like you."

"Where are we going?"

"Nowhere for now," the petty officer frowned. "We're circling Zulu on search and rescue, until we get orders otherwise, or we run low on fuel and have to Bingo back to Tycho base."

"There *is* no Zulu," Larry insisted.

"I know that and you know that. The Navy tells us to stay here, so that's what we're doing."

"But-"

"Shut it, Devens," Darnell snapped. To the petty officer, he asked, "Do you know what the hell happened here?"

"All I know is," the man sighed and settled back in his seat, tugging the straps tighter. "Those damned Sentinels aren't worth a fucking dime."

CHAPTER EIGHTEEN

Pushing my laptop away across my desk, I stretched my arms over my head. "Skippy, this isn't working."

"It *is* working," he insisted. "It's not working as quickly as you want."

"Let me rephrase what I said: this hasn't worked, and it's *not ever going* to work. Not to do anything useful."

"OK, well, I have to agree with you about that."

"I wish you wouldn't."

"Huh? You *don't* want me to agree with you?"

"No! I want you to tell me I'm wrong, that I am a dumdum numbskull, that you found a way to make this work."

"Hey, thinking outside the box is your job."

"The box *is* the problem."

He blinked at me. "I'm not following you."

Sliding my laptop back toward me, I turned it around so he could see the display. Not that the display needed to be facing toward his avatar, of course. "*This* box. The space between these five wormholes."

"Oh. You are referring to a physical box. Or at least, a virtual one."

"Yeah." Closing the laptop, I leaned back in my chair. "Show me that star chart again, please. The hologram."

"It's not a *hologram*."

"Whatever."

The source of my frustration appeared. An image showing the problem that was frustrating me. We had tracked the Bogey through three additional wormholes. Then, we lost it. The Bogey had gone through a wormhole that was way out near the end of the Sagittarius Arm of the Milky Way. That's an inaccurate description, since on the outer rim, the stars get thinly spread out and you can't really say one star or group of stars 'belongs' to any particular spiral arm. The end of that wormhole was kind of the middle of nowhere, except *everything* around us could be considered the middle of nowhere.

From the wormhole we knew the Bogey had gone through, there were only four other wormholes that were conceivably within that ship's range. Even Valkyrie would have a tough time making that flight if we had to go the long way. So, Skippy screwed with the four distant wormholes one by one, creating shortcuts for us.

Nothing.

The Bogey had not gone through any of those four tunnels in spacetime.

It also had not turned around and backtracked. Skippy checked, after I asked him to. That thought hadn't occurred to him.

He did discover, again after I asked him a specific question, that the Bogey had used that wormhole *three* times. Outbound relatively recently, with us following several days behind. Before that, it came outbound, then eight days later, it went through the wormhole again, back toward the center of the galaxy.

"The possibilities are," I counted on my fingers, not because I'm stupid, thank you, but because it helps me think. "The thing is traveling toward one of the four other wormholes, and it hasn't gotten there yet."

"True," he nodded. "It is a long flight to any of those wormholes."

"Right."

"Unless you can create a shortcut like I do."

"Which you checked, and no one has screwed with those wormholes, until you did."

"Correct."

"And you are still certain that no other AI did screw with a wormhole, and got that network to cover its tracks?"

"Ugh. Those network controllers won't even do that for *me*. Listen, numbskull, networks comply with my requests to temporarily alter their connections, because doing that is allowed under their operating parameters. Altering records about who goes through a wormhole is *not* allowed, do you get that?"

"I do. Sorry."

He sniffed. "You should be."

"It's just that, this AI has demonstrated capabilities that you don't have, so-"

"This again? Joe, if you want to assume this other AI is freakin' *magic*, then there is no point to this discussion."

"Right. OK, let's assume it can't get a wormhole network to lie. It came through the wormhole behind us twice. It never used the other four wormholes. Not yet. If it's flying toward one of those other four wormholes, all we can do is wait for it to get there, the long way."

"That will be a long wait. I hope we have enough snacks to keep the crew happy."

"The other possibility, that seems more likely, is the Bogey has a base around here somewhere. Within four days of flight time. Four days to get there, and four days back to the wormhole. Show me your best guess of how far that ship could travel in any direction from here, within four days, please."

The star chart hanging in my office zoomed in. "Shit." Even out toward the ass end of the galaxy, there were way too many stars. "How many stars in that area?"

"Roughly thirty eight hundred."

"Almost four *thousand*?"

"Space is not as empty as you think, even out near the Rim."

"Oh, hell. It would take us freakin' forever to search that area."

209

"Not *forever*," he corrected me, because of course he had to do that. "I have created a least-time search pattern, assuming *Valkyrie* performs the search alone. Including time out for refueling, downtime for maintenance, and regularly flying back to Earth for major overhauls, the search would take-"

"I don't need to know, thank you."

"Ah, it's just as well. You would be long retired before the search pattern was complete."

"Fantastic."

"Perhaps one of your sons could complete the search for you."

"If they can stop fighting each other long enough to join the Navy. Four thousand star systems?"

"Um, not every star has planetary companions."

"OK, then-"

"But most stars have *something*. Even brown dwarfs. Hmm, I did not include brown dwarfs in my count of 'stars'."

"Great."

"Plus, as you know, there will be rogue planets out there, that do not orbit a star."

"Even better."

"Really, if there is an Elder AI aboard that ship, which there is *not* because as I told you they are all *dead*, it would not necessarily require the resources of a planet at all. Any rock of decent size with the right materials could serve as a base. There are plenty of such rocks in the spaces between stars. *Trillions* of them, in the area we are looking at."

"This is better than I ever dreamed of."

"It's not my fault that you ask for the impossible, knucklehead."

"Like I said, this ain't working. So, we'll try this the easy way."

He stared at me. "There is an easy way?"

"Yeah. We wait right here, for the Bogey to come back."

"Oh, Mff. Darn it, I should have thought of that."

"You have to think of everything else, Skippy."

"Well, that is a very good point."

"We can do that? Hang out here, within the figure eight pattern of this wormhole, and you request the network to alert you when the Bogey comes back?"

"No."

"No, it won't alert you?"

"No, it won't provide an alert for a specific ship. It will inform me of *every* ship that goes through. Fortunately for us, this wormhole gets about as much traffic as a store in Barbados that sells snowshoes."

"Right. That's good."

"Eh, maybe. If the Bogey is flying toward one of the other four wormholes, then us hanging around here is a waste of time."

"I know that. OK, we wait here for, uh, a maximum of ten days. I will send the *Dutchman* back to civilization to ping a relay station for an update, in case there is some other damned crap going on in the galaxy that we need to deal with."

"Better ask Colonel Bonsu to bring back some snacks if he can. We could be here for a while."

Waiting near a wormhole, hoping the Bogey would return, was not actually *doing* anything. I hate waiting, especially when there is an urgent need to take action. We couldn't take action, since I had no idea where the Bogey had gone.

It made me feel useless.

Fortunately for me, the need to track the Bogey was OBE.

Overcome By Events.

We set a schedule for Skippy to create shortcuts for the *Dutchman* to return. No shortcuts for two days, then at irregular intervals over ten days. After ten days, if Bonsu had not brought his ship back, we would go looking for the *Dutchman*. Skippy had to be careful about screwing with that wormhole's schedule, in case whoever was flying the Bogey noticed the odd behavior.

So far, our mission had been a failure, and I was growing worried. More worried, I mean, than I already was at the prospect of *another freakin' Elder AI* flying around the galaxy. An Elder AI that, if not actively hostile, at least had its own agenda. An agenda that included it wanting its very own pet Sentinel, and I did not foresee any problems with that.

My worry meter went up a notch, if that was possible, when Skippy reported the *Flying Dutchman* had sent a ping that the assault carrier was ready to come through the wormhole during the first shortcut opportunity. Only two days had passed since the *Dutchman* departed, that could not be good news. Literally. The closest relay station from the shortcut was less than one day of travel time, allowing a quick turnaround. That relay station did not see frequent traffic, so we hadn't expected the *Dutchman* to get much useful info there. The fact that Bonsu decided to race back to the shortcut implied he had learned of a galaxy-shattering disaster on the level of a Nickleback reunion tour.

The *Dutchman* didn't broadcast a message, as it came through the wormhole. To prevent the Bogey from detecting our presence, all communication between ships was accomplished by low powered burst laserlinks. Bonsu's face appeared in *Valkyrie's* main display. "General Bishop?"

"Colonel, give me the bad news." His expression made it clear the news was very bad.

"The Vault under the Moon was raided. By an Elder starship."

Someday, if we all lived that long, my boys might ask, "Daddy, what were you doing when the Moon was attacked?"

So, what heroic thing was I doing at that time? My calendar says I was in the galley, baking cinnamon buns.

Joe Bishop. Hero.

Damn it. My kids think of me as the Snack Guy and they are not right about that. But, maybe they are not entirely wrong, either.

Skippy of course could not believe it. "An *Elder* starship? No way. Just, no way."

"The data is wrong?" I asked. We were in a conference room aboard *Valkyrie*. By 'We' I mean me, Reed, Frey, Striebich, and Bonsu. Colonel Bonsu participated in person, I had requested he fly over from the *Dutchman*. We could start a band, call it 'Joe and the Four Colonels'. That band would suck.

"I'm saying the data was *faked*."

"If an Elder starship was not there," Derek Bonsu hadn't been exposed to Skippy long enough to know the protocol for dealing with the beer can. Like, always suck up to Skippy. Or, maybe Bonsu just didn't give a shit. "How do you explain what happened?"

"Well, it-"

Bonsu leaned forward across the table toward the avatar. "Does any current species have the technology to bore a hole like that, and for a ship to hover in a gravity well with no apparent means of support?"

"Hey," the face of the avatar took on a tinge of red, that was a new emulation. "Just because-"

"Skippy," I interrupted to prevent an argument from spiraling out of control. "Clearly, we need to get you access to better data, we can't do that from here. Can anyone," I looked around the table, "think of a reason for us to remain here?"

Reed's lips drew into a tight line, but Striebich spoke first. "Sir, we have no clue where that Elder starship went after it left the Moon. We were able to track the Bogey *here*. As far as we know, it never went back through this wormhole."

"Oh, shit." Just when I thought my day couldn't get any worse, it did. "Could there be *two* Elder AIs out there?"

"No!" Skippy scoffed. "I told you, they are all *dead*."

Bonsu wasn't buying Skippy's bullshit. "Then who was flying that Elder starship?"

Skippy rolled his eyes. "I can guarantee it wasn't an Elder-"

212

"For now," I held up a hand. "We will assume the raid on the Vault was conducted by an Elder starship, until we have evidence that it wasn't. Skippy!" I jabbed a finger at him. "There is no point to arguing about it here. You will have access to the data when we reach Earth."

"We are going to Earth, Sir?" Reed asked.

"Yes," that decision was made while I was saying the word. "Striebich, your point about knowing the Bogey came here and didn't leave, is valid. We might come back here, later. First, we have to find the answer to a question."

"What's that?" Skippy was puzzled.

"Why our freakin' invincible Sentinel didn't protect Earth."

"That," Skippy sighed, taking off his ginormous hat and rubbing his dome. "Is a very good question."

Bonsu asked to speak with me, after the meeting. Since his ship wasn't needed for tracking the Bogey, he requested that the *Dutchman* be released from the Special Mission Group, and allowed to travel back to Zandrus. I was inclined to deny his request. "We might need your sensors to figure out what happened at the Moon," I explained. "Or, to track that Elder starship."

He didn't try to argue the point. "Sir, *Valkyrie* can travel faster without the *Dutchman*. My ship is basically an aircraft carrier. We normally use a *star* carrier for flying long distances."

"Yeah, I have thought about that. For now, Skippy will create three wormhole shortcuts to get us close to the far end of the Backstop wormhole. We will travel together through the shortcuts, then *Valkyrie* will sprint ahead. You follow us to Earth at best speed."

"Yes, Sir." He looked like he had a question. Or a comment.

"Bonsu?"

"After the raid, Command will be pulling the fleet back to Earth."

"I expect they have already issued those orders, yes."

"I hope someone remembers the people we have on Zandrus. Every species in the galaxy will see that Earth is vulnerable, that all of humanity isn't as strong as we pretended to be. Someone like the Thuranin could see this time as an opportunity to hit an isolated battalion of humans. Settle scores. Make points with their patrons."

He had a good point. We both knew that. "Skippy?" I called, and his avatar appeared on the conference table again. My assumption had been we needed the *Dutchman's* sensors at Earth, but I hadn't asked the question. "How useful would it be to have the *Dutchman's* sensor suite at Earth?"

"Eh, marginal," he shrugged. "The incident is over, so what you are really asking is, do I need Nagatha there to help me analyze the data? The answer is *no*, duh."

"Nagatha? Have you been listening?"

213

"No, dear," her breathy voice answered. "I am not authorized to do that."

"OK, the question is-"

"However, I did review the audio files of your conversation that Bilby just sent to me. In this case, I am forced to agree with Skippy. My knowledge of Elder technology is limited, I could not be of much assistance to him, in analyzing the raid against your Moon."

"Very well. Colonel Bonsu, work with Skippy to plot a shortcut to Zandrus for you. If your ship can get there within five days, I will release the *Dutchman* on temporary service. After you pull the Operation Sunset troops off the ground, I want you to fly straight to Earth."

"Def Com will want us at Earth anyway," he agreed. "We will have to wait at Zandrus for the star carrier," he reminded me. "Without Skippy's assistance, my trash hauler can't make the trip to Earth by itself."

With a nod, I turned to go, but Bonsu wasn't moving. Duh. "Since you will be pulling the Sunset battalion off the surface, you should have your air group commander with you. Take your w-" Referring to Colonel Striebich as 'his wife' was not appropriate. "Your CAG, with you." Having Irene Striebich aboard had been good for my peace of mind, until I became more familiar with *Valkyrie's* crew. Especially Reed's first officer, Commander Henri Gasquet of the French Navy. I now knew the guy was good, efficient, and smart. Of course he was, Reed had selected him as her XO. If something happened to Reed, I had become confident that Gasquet could handle the ship. Besides, I had been captain of *Valkyrie* for years, and I had completed the refresher training. If needed, I could take the command chair again.

Although that would mean me having to be responsible for a whole lot of extra paperwork, so taking the captain's slot again would be my last choice.

"Thank you, Sir," Bonsu looked toward the doorway. "I'll get to working with Skippy on a shortcut."

We had to compromise, by taking a wormhole shortcut that was slightly less than optimal for *Valkyrie*, so the *Dutchman* could get to Zandrus within three days. For us, the overall delay was less than four hours, I judged that delay a reasonable price to pay for pulling the Operation Sunset people off the surface of Zandrus. Losing their human peacekeeping force would suck for the Verd-kris still stuck on that rock, there wasn't anything I could do about that. Correction: there wasn't anything I was *willing* to do about that situation. I needed to get Skippy to Earth and find out what the hell had gone wrong with Bubba, I couldn't allow myself to get distracted.

During the tense trip to Earth, I did not ask Skippy to speculate on why the Sentinel had failed to defend Earth. Had not done the job he

214

programmed Bubba to do. Asking him to guess would be a useless exercise, and only piss him off. He didn't need me or anyone else yelling at him for his pet's failure, I could tell he was beating himself up about it. There is nothing Skippy hates worse than the public seeing a demonstration that his awesomeness is less than perfect. He was humiliated, he was hurt, and he was depressed. What I needed him to be was angry, not at me but at whoever was flying that Elder starship.

We had come through the last wormhole that Skippy was able to screw with to make a shortcut, and then had to jump the long way to the far end of the Backstop wormhole that opened very near our home star system. The ship was in a familiar cycle of jump, recharge, jump again. That was familiar to me, anyway. And to Reed and Frey. Everyone else aboard the ship had experienced traveling between wormholes. But not doing it during a desperate race that might lead the ship into even more desperate combat. Frey, Reed and I had done that too many times to count. The crew was mostly untested in combat, and I had to remind myself that actually was a good thing. The governments of Earth fighting only optional wars, and not fighting for survival, was the whole point of the struggles the Merry Band of Pirates had gone through for years. *Valkyrie's* crew lacked experience in large-scale combat because Earth was secure.

Until now.

In my office, I was catching up on paperwork, something that never ends and somehow had expanded with my rank, when Skippy's avatar appeared on the desk. "Hey," I glanced up at him, then back to my laptop. He had his arms folded defiantly across his chest, his little mouth was set in a pout, and his eyes blazed. It was best to ignore him until he said, whatever he clearly needed to say.

"Well?" He demanded.

"Well, I'm filling in these stupid forms as fast as I can, I'm having to relearn some of- Oh." The forms on my laptop scrolled rapidly as they auto filled, my signature appeared at the bottom, and suddenly my inbox was empty. "Uh, thanks?"

"Let's get on with it, shall we?"

The award for Best Actor in a Dramatic Presentation goes to: Joe Bishop. "Get on with what?" I did my usual clueless routine.

Sadly, the uncultured audience was not buying my performance. "You *know* what."

"You could save yourself a lot of time, by just telling me what you're talking about."

"You can't wait to bitch at me about Bubba's failure to do anything useful, and I can't wait to get this over with."

"I'm don't want to bitch at you."

"You don't?"

"No. Would me yelling and asking you a lot of stupid questions right now accomplish anything useful?"

"*No*. But, you monkeys seem to enjoy doing that anyway."

"It helps us to relieve tension."

"It is just *stupid*."

"Like you said, it's something monkeys do, so-"

"Wow, OK."

"Skippy, I know you did the best job you could, and I know you are angry at yourself about it. Me piling on won't help you to focus on fixing the problem."

"Wow, Joe. That is very mature of you. Maybe being a father has-"

"Plus, when we get to Earth, literally *billions* of people will be waiting to tell you what a useless jackass they think you are."

"Ugh. Are you sure we shouldn't turn the ship around?"

"I have a Taco Bell coupon that expires next week, so I kind of have to go to Earth anyway."

His shoulders slumped and he looked up at the ceiling. "This is gonna *suuuuuuuck*."

"I have an idea that might help, if you want to hear it."

"Nothing you could suggest will help me survive the coming crap storm."

"My suggestion is, could you create a submind to handle all communications with Earth? Let the people there vent at your submind, while you ignore the messages."

"Huh."

"Right?"

"Joe, the only problem is that listening to the complaints and insults of monkeys will make my submind want to kill itself."

"Isn't that why Grumpy hates you with an all-consuming passion?"

"Well, that, plus that thing is just a *jerk*."

"Uh huh. And not because it is stuck having to talk with monkeys all day, every day?"

"I have to admit, I would hate me too. OK, thanks for the suggestion, but I am going to embrace the suck."

"Uh, what?"

"You know. It's something grunts do. You know something is going to epically *suck*, but there's nothing you can do about it, so you just get on with it."

"I know what that means, but you were never a grunt, Skippy."

"I have dealt with the awful *smell* aboard this ship for years. That should make me an honorary grunt."

"Uh, that-"

"Plus, do you know anyone who gets into more sketchy fuckery than I do?"

216

"Good point. You are an honorary member of the E-4 Mafia."

During the flight, I kept my promise and didn't ask Skippy to guess what was wrong with Bubba. There was another question that was bothering me, so I called him. "Skippy, I am afraid I know the answer to this question, and I don't like it. Why did the Elder ship take the canisters of radonium from the Moonbase, but not take any of the Guardians?"

His avatar appeared, already glaring at me. "To start with, we don't know that it was an Elder starship."

"OK, but-"

"Second, do you think someone can simply stuff a freakin' *Guardian* in their pocket, and take it away?"

"My question is actually about the radonium. The Elder- The, whoever hit the Moonbase, did it to steal the radonium."

"That seems fairly obvious. What is your question?"

"My question is *why*? Please tell me the bad guy, whoever, can't use that radonium to wake up another Sentinel."

"Oh. That's what you are worried about?"

"You think I *shouldn't* be worried about it?"

"Joe, the bad guy can't use that radonium to wake up a Sentinel."

"Great," I heaved a sigh of relief. "That is one less thing to- Wait. Are you just saying that because I asked you to?"

"Not this time, no. Joe, the total amount of radonium in those eleven canisters is less than two grams, and that radonium is not a high-grade material. It hasn't been processed into a useable purity."

"Then, why bother going through the effort of stealing it, and destroying the Moonbase so we can't make more?"

"Wow, that is a tough question. There are many possible uses for low-grade radonium. For example, it could be processed into materials that have many applications for an Elder starship, although it is very unlikely there was an Elder starship involved, so let's forget about that for now. Anything I suggest would be a guess."

"Your guess is way better than mine."

"That is true. OK, assuming we are dealing with the same asshole who is flying the Bogey ship, the most likely use for low-grade radonium is to boost the range of an Elder comm node."

"That's not good."

"It isn't, but the material still requires processing, and after those two grams are purified into a useable strength, there would be barely enough remaining to boost a single pair of comm nodes. Unless the enemy used a very efficient processing method, there would not be enough pure material for even a single application."

"OK, thanks. What I care about is, whoever the enemy is, their goal is not to have a pet Sentinel."

"It is not. It- Hmm."

"I do not like that '*Hmm*', Skippy."

"Oh, I was just thinking. Smacking the Moonbase had to be for the purpose of destroying humanity's ability to make more radonium."

"Yes, so?"

"So, what if delaying us from waking up a Sentinel isn't good enough for the enemy? What if they want to *block* our ability to do that?"

"That," I blinked, "could happen?"

"It's possible. Theoretically. I think. I will need to ponder the question. What I'm talking about is a cross-dimensional transmitter, that could jam the signal from our transmitters."

"How would that work?"

"Well, the jammers would need to be positioned near our transmitters. In stealth, of course. Although, once the jamming goes active, your Navy could quickly detect the location of the jammers and destroy them."

"That doesn't sound like a practical weapon."

"I *said* I am guessing."

"Sorry. Thank you. Uh, ponder it when you have time, OK? Don't spend a lot of time on it, we will get more data when we reach Earth."

Before we transitioned through the Backstop wormhole, I again urged Skippy to create a submind to handle all but the highest level communications. My reasoning was he would have plenty of actual useful work to do when we reached Earth, I did not need him to be distracted. Or even more depressed.

"Joe, are you *ordering* me to delegate all my communications?"

"Yes, other than when you are speaking with the Def Com chiefs of staff. And I will tell them you are very busy analyzing the enormous volume of data."

"Wow, thanks."

"I got your back, homeboy." We bumped fists. "When we jump in near Earth, your top priority, your only priority, is to find out why Bubba didn't respond to the attack."

"Believe me, I am aching to know what the hell happened. Damn it, the last time we were at Earth, I not only verified that Bubba hadn't been hacked, I reinforced the firewalls!"

"Do your thing, and-"

"Yeah, yeah, I know. Keep you informed, so you can get Command off your back."

"Ignore Command, and forget about keeping me informed. Find out what went wrong, and fix it, ASAP. Let me know when you're done, OK? Otherwise, ignore the screeching of monkeys."

CHAPTER NINETEEN

Valkyrie came through the Backstop wormhole and contacted the Traffic Control station for clearance to approach Earth, and instructions on the safe emergence zones near our homeworld. The Navy ships there would have itchy trigger fingers, I wanted to avoid getting shot at before we could investigate what went wrong with Bubba. The bridge crew studied the tactical plot on the main display, and someone whistled. Instead of the usual pair of frigates hanging around the station, there was a pair of battleships, plus a full complement of escorts. The display tagged those ships as the 9th Fleet, a unit that had just been stood up.

Before I could contact the 9th Fleet's commander to pay my respects, the Traffic Control station replied immediately. *Valkyrie* had pre-authorized clearance, and orders to proceed to Earth without delay. That last part was emphasized.

Reed pointed to her lead pilot, and our mighty battlecruiser jumped.

We emerged less than two centimeters from the center of the target zone, twenty lightseconds from Earth. That was impressive accuracy even for Skippy. It also left us unable to do what we came to Earth for.

"Too far, Joe," Skippy spat. "I need Bubba to be within my presence, and it is too far away, on the other side of the planet."

"Reed, jump us again, to within ten thousand klicks of the Sentinel."

"Sir, we are in the safety zone, we need to contact Def Com for-"

"Jump us again, that's a direct order. As far as we know, this *is* an active combat zone."

Another starship captain might have been insulted by my verbal slap. Reed had seen enough shit go down, she just pointed to the pilot again. Four seconds later, we performed a short jump. "Engage stealth," she ordered. "Take us around the other side of the Sentinel, engines at seven percent thrust." She looked at me.

I nodded approval. She had taken sensible precautions. "Skippy, do your thing, please. Bilby, transmit my authorization code to Def Com, and inform them we will be under strict EMCON until Skippy completes a diagnostic of the Sentinel." That was EMmissions CONtrol, meaning *Valkyrie* would not be radiating any electronic signals.

"Um, like," Bilby drawled, "the UN duty officer is screaming to talk with you."

"Do not reply. Have you received a tactical update?"

"Yeah, man, the coast is like, clear, you know? No unfriendlies in system. There sure are a lot of Navy ships here, looks like half of the fleet."

"Let me know if the situation changes. We-"

"*OH!*" Skippy bellowed, enraged. "Oh, this is some *BULLSHIT*! Joe, excuse me for a minute while I contact my law firm that handles intellectual property disputes."

"Negative! You are not contacting anyone until you find out what went wrong with Bub- With the Sentinel."

"Ugh. I *do* know what happened, and it is *stupid*, and I am angry because some jerk totally ripped me off. That's why I need a-"

"Are we safe? Bubba is active?"

"Bubba was active the whole time, it- Yes, everything is fine. Bubba will squash any threat to your miserable homeworld."

"Great. Reed, Frey," I gestured to the STAR team leader seated against the rear bulkhead. "Join me in the captain's office."

Reed stood up. "Gasquet, you have the conn."

In Reed's office, I made a show of taking a seat in one of the visitor's chairs, and reached across the desk to press the button that slid the door closed. "Skippy, what is going on?"

"What is going on," his avatar appeared, fairly glowing with indignant rage. "Is someone blatantly ripped off one of my greatest hits, and I demand compensation for damages. I demand *punitive* damages!"

"Before you take the issue to court, why exactly did Bubba fail to act?"

"Ugh. Technically, it defended Earth, exactly as it was instructed to do."

Frey couldn't believe what he said. "Under what definition of 'defend' is-"

"Definition, *that's* the problem!"

"OK," I held up my hands. "Skippy, break it down Barney style, please."

"Joe, do you remember when I hacked into the library files of Maxohlx warships?"

"Uh, yes," I said slowly, recalling the details as I spoke. Something about Skippy sending out malicious code that scrubbed any reference to the number Zero from the computer files that acted as a library of basic information inside a Maxohlx starship AI. He had been able to remotely penetrate the cybersecurity of several senior species warships, because library files are such low-level information, no one pays attention to them. Those files contain vital details like that Tuesday is after Monday and before Wednesday on the calendar, for example. Boring, mundane, obvious and vital information. What he had done was remove any hint that between Negative One and Positive One, there is a number 'Zero' that has no value. It seems crazy, but not being able to include zero in calculations caused all computer systems aboard the affected Maxohlx ships to go down, hard. Those computers were not able to function at all. "Someone blanked out Bubba's zero?"

"No. That would be blatant plagiarism. *This* asshole got cute and stole my idea, but applied it differently. When I set up Bubba here, your leadership was concerned a determined enemy might lure the Sentinel away from Earth, then hit your homeworld before Bubba could react. So, I was instructed to restrict Bubba's area of responsibility to a radius of twelve lightseconds from Earth, which I also defined as roughly three point six million kilometers."

"Oh, you," I slumped back in my chair, stunned by what he was saying. "You have *got* to be kidding me."

"Sir?" Reed asked. "What does this mean? The Moon is well inside a twelve lightsecond radius from Earth."

"Twelve lightseconds, or three and a half million *kilometers*," I emphasized, being proud that I had done the conversion math in my head. "Right, Skippy? The area of responsibility was expressed in kilometers?"

"It was," he sighed.

Reed held up her hands in an 'I am lost' gesture.

"Someone," I explained, "changed the definition of a kilometer."

"Oh," Reed's jaw dropped.

"Exactly," Skippy moaned. "Someone changed the length of a kilometer, so Bubba's effective range ended about halfway through your Moon's orbit. That's why it didn't fire on the intruder, but it did destroy chunks of Moon rock that were falling toward your planet. Damn, this pisses me off! When I checked whether Bubba had gotten hacked last time, I didn't bother to review the entire set of library files. I am certainly doing that *now*."

"It didn't take you very long to find the hack," I noted. "How did you do it so fast?"

"Joe, I don't want to ruin your image of me as a genius, it-"

"After *this* screwup, you do not have to worry about me ever thinking you're a genius."

"Ugh. Joe, you are *such* an asshole. Ah, it was easy. I simply asked Bubba why it didn't shoot at intruder ships that were obviously hostile, and it replied that I had instructed it not to act beyond a specified distance. It insisted that it had done nothing wrong."

"I guess technically, it-"

"It also reminded me that placing restrictions on its freedom to maneuver is *stupid*."

"I can't argue with that. How can you make sure something like this can't happen again?"

"First, I have locked down all the library files. They aren't actually *files*, but they perform a similar function. No one but me can alter the data in those files which, ugh, means I will have to come back regularly to review necessary updates. *That* will be fun. Second, I have given Bubba multiple, independent definitions of its authorized action radius, which has been greatly expanded. This time, I expressed that radius in kilometers, lightseconds, football fields, and-"

"Wait, you defined the radius by football fields?"

"Yes, because you Americans will do pretty much anything to avoid using the Metric system. Would you prefer I use the height of a giraffe, or the length of a banana, rather than the length of a football field?"

"No, that's fine."

"Finally, I authorized Bubba to act anywhere within the orbit of Mars. And yes, I included multiple definitions of what 'Mars' is, in case some jackass gets creative."

"OK," I felt better, knowing the Sentinel protecting Earth wasn't broken, and hadn't been taken over by a hostile entity. "Leave it to me, please, to explain the problem to Command."

"Do you actually *understand* the problem?"

"Do *you* want a bunch of ignorant monkeys asking you stupid questions?"

"Um, probably best for you to handle it."

"Great."

"That's *it*?" Frey exploded. "Our homeworld was defenseless because of a glitch in a freakin' *measurement*?"

"Colonel Frey, are you breathing right now?" Skippy asked.

"I, yes."

"You had to think about it though, didn't you? Ninety nine percent of the time, you aren't conscious of your breathing, it just happens. Your body knows how to do it, it's not something you need to think about it. That's similar to a library file. No system thinks about library files, they just *are*, in the background."

"Bloody *bollocks*," Frey pressed a hand to her forehead.

"That's a new one," I looked at her. "I didn't know Canadians used that colorful expression."

"At times like this, I try to imagine what Smythe would say," she tried to smile.

"He would slip 'dodgy beer can' in there," I suggested.

"Hey!" Skippy protested. "What I want to know is-"

"What *I* want to know is, who attacked the moonbase?"

"Oh for- I don't *know*, knucklehead, I haven't examined the data yet."

"Can you do that now, please?"

"This will take a while."

"Fine. You do that, and I'll talk with Command. Reed, I think you can drop stealth, and release the ship from EMCON. Uh, hold the crew's personal message traffic for now."

Frey knew the meeting was over. "Sir, how long will we be here, at Earth?"

"I don't know. Not long enough to rotate your team dirtside for training."

"Understood," she nodded, and stepped aside for me to go out the doorway.

"Bilby," I called when I was in the passageway, walking quickly toward my own office. "Inform Command that I will contact them in two minutes."

"Will do, General Dude. I got to warn you, they are very unhappy right now."

"Yeah, well, I'll see if I can change that."

Spoiler alert: after my explanation of why Bubba had not protected Moonbase Zulu, Command was still *extremely* unhappy. Fortunately for me, the audience in the video chat was limited to five very senior officers on Earth, so I only had to endure questions and complaints from a small number of people. Also, I am exaggerating. All five generals and admirals of the Def Com HQ Directorate were consummate professionals. No one actually shouted at me, they calmly asked intelligent questions, and listened while I answered.

The current Chief of Staff was an Indian Air Force general, Chaudhary. "Bishop," he wasn't angry, the guy understandably looked tired. "We have to reconsider whether having our homeworld protected by an alien machine is a viable option. It was hacked, and we had no idea its security had been penetrated. The last time Skippy was here, he assured us there had been no attempt to hack either of our Sentinels. I am being asked to provide assurances that our defenses can't be compromised to be used against us, and right now, I can't provide any such guarantees. The machine Skippy calls 'Bubba'," there wasn't even a hint of a smile on Chaudhary's face, "could destroy Earth if an enemy is able to take control of-"

"UGH," Skippy interrupted. "That *can't* happen."

Chaudhary waited a second for the avatar to appear, but Skippy for whatever reason chose not to manifest himself visually. "You told us no one could penetrate the cyber systems of a Sentinel, yet-"

"Think, numbskulls, *think*," Skippy snapped. "The-"

"Skippy," I gave him the knife hand to cut him off. "You were not invited to this meeting. Go away."

"But-"

"Go away, right now. I will speak with you later."

"Ugh. *Fine*. You monkeys enjoy wallowing in ignorance."

Before speaking, I waited a second, to make sure he didn't have one last insult to share. "Sir, I expressed the same concerns to Skippy. What he was trying to say, in his own way-"

"We are aware of how Skippy speaks with those he considers his inferiors."

"Uh," I winced. "To be fair, Sir, he considers *everyone* to be inferior."

"We are aware of that also."

223

"Yes. Uh," I had forgotten what I was going to say. Oh yeah. "The Sentinels can't be used against us. We know that, because they *weren't*." There was a murmur of understanding around the conference table, as the Def Com chiefs considered what I had said, so I continued. "The entity directing that Elder starship, I assume that is an Elder master control AI, would certainly have taken control of our Sentinels, if it could have. With a Sentinel, the enemy could simply have ordered the machine to scoop the Vault out from the Moon's surface, and deliver the contents. Instead, the enemy went through a complicated, multiphase operation that exposed its presence."

"Our Sentinel *was* hacked," Chaudhary insisted.

"Yes Sir, at the simplest, lowest possible level. That was the best the enemy could accomplish. Those library files were left open for necessary periodic updates. Skippy has now locked down *all* of the Sentinel's systems from outside access by anyone other than himself. He will need to manually provide updates at least once a year, to maintain the Sentinel's peak efficiency."

Chaudhary's eyes narrowed. "Skippy is willing to do that?"

"Sir, he told me he will be thrilled to visit our homeworld on a yearly basis. If you know what I mean."

"Huh," the chief of staff grunted, but with a twinkle in his eyes. He knew that Skippy was almost *never* thrilled to come back to our miserable mudball. "That, at least, if good news. Bishop, I hear what you're saying, and it makes sense. But, all of us will have a difficult time inspiring public confidence in our Sentinels, when they were disabled by so simple a change."

"Yes, Sir, I find it difficult to believe it myself. If you would entertain a suggestion?"

"Go ahead."

"The truth should be withheld from the public. We could instead state that the intruders jammed the Sentinel's activation signal from Def Com."

"We don't activate the thing, it works by itself. That is not a closely-held secret."

"It's an open secret, Sir. Too open. So open, that many people question whether it's true. It could be hinted that Def Com *does* have a measure of control, and that signal was interrupted by the intruders. And now Skippy has provided a backup channel that can't be jammed, using a set of Elder communications nodes."

"We will," Chaudhary looked at his skeptical colleagues. "Have to consider that. What would be the point of your proposal? The public will still have lost confidence in our protectors, and the enemy who raided the Moon will know the truth."

"The intruder is not the intended audience for the deception, Sir. The intruder is not our only enemy."

"We could restore confidence, by conducting tests," Chaudhary directed that remark at the other chiefs on the call. "Show the public that our Sentinel is active and effective."

"We *could* do that, Sir. Or," I let that last word hang in the air.

Chaudhary's eyes narrowed. He didn't know me. He especially hadn't known me when I was causing heartburn for the leadership of UNEF. "Or what, Bishop?"

"Or, we could do something else."

Def Com's chiefs of staff dismissed me, after stating they would consider my proposals. Before that, though, they wanted to know whether Bubba could protect Earth if an Elder starship attacked again. My response was that I couldn't give an answer, until we were absolutely certain the intruder had in fact been an Elder starship. Which meant me talking with Skippy again.

"Have you reviewed the sensor data yet?"

"Of course I have," he snapped.

"*All* of it?"

"More than you can imagine. There was a cleanup crew on the far side of the Moon, close to the impact sites. I even have video from reflections off their helmet visors, in addition to all the other data UN-dick provided. Is that good enough for you?"

"That depends. Have you reached a conclusion about who was responsible for the raid?"

"It appears that an Elder starship used Maxohlx ships as battering rams, then hovered over the Vault while it sent an away team of nanotech gel bots to extract the exotic materials."

"Yeah, that is what it looked like. So, you confirmed Def Com's analysis, that-"

"No, I did *not*. You didn't let me finish. Damn it, Joe, it *can't* be an Elder starship!"

"Uh huh. So, someone faked the sensor data?"

"Egg-*zactly*."

"Who has the technology to make a ship appear to be an Elder construct, and act in a way that only an Elder starship could do?"

"Shit. That takes Elder technology."

"Hmm."

"This is circular logic, dumdum. Just because the technology required is at the Elder level, doesn't mean Elder tech was involved.'"

"OK. Say that again, but *slowly*."

"Just because- *Ugh*. I hate you so much, Joe."

"More than you hate yourself right now?"

225

"No," he sounded completely miserable. "It *can't* be an Elder starship! Those ships can't do anything on their own. For a ship to act, it needs direction from a master control AI like me, and they are all *dead*."

"What would Sherlock Holmes say about this?"

"Seriously?"

"You know what I mean."

Skippy sighed. "He would say that if you eliminate the impossible, then whatever remains, however improbable, must be the truth."

"Right. Listen Skippy, I am just a filthy monkey, but tell me if my logic makes sense."

"Do I have to?"

"Elder-level technology was used here, for the raid."

"Yes. Go on," he had the enthusiasm of someone anticipating dental surgery.

"No meatsacks in the galaxy are capable of using that technology. It would be like a dog riding a bicycle."

"It would be more like a dog flying a starship, but you are correct."

"So, someone capable of using, and *understanding* Elder technology, was controlling that ship. That same someone sent those shape-shifting things Def Com calls 'Terminators'."

"Again, you are correct, but it doesn't matter, because that is impossible."

"No, it's not. It is only *improbable*."

"Are you trying to teach me about *math*?"

"I am reminding you about something you told me."

"Uh, I did?"

"Yes."

"I say a lot of profoundly insightful things, so give me a hint."

"When the Elders did a hard reset on your fellow AIs, and you sent a kill command to all of them, we watched a counter that showed when each of them was dead."

"Oh, not *this* again."

"Yes, this again. Unless you want to present alternative facts, like your count back then was wrong?"

"I am never *wrong*, numbskull."

"You remember events differently than I do. What *I* remember is, there were four Elder master control AIs that you couldn't confirm as dead."

"Why do you choose the most annoying times to remember trivial details?"

"I save them for when they can be used for maximum effect. So, that is four Elder master control AIs unaccounted for. The dead AI that was found by the Kristang scavengers on Newark, that's one. The insane AI that attacked you, after we found the corpse of an Elder in a crashed dropship, that's another. Opie burned itself out when it sent the distress call to the Elders, that's three. And Echo, who got trapped with its ship in a zero length wormhole. That's four, unless I'm missing something?"

"Nice try, but you're wrong. I already knew those four were dead when I created the counter, so I didn't include them in the overall number."

"Crap. I was hoping this would be easy. You are sure Echo is dead?"

"I am sure Echo isn't *anything*. It doesn't exist, anywhere. The four that were missing from the final count are AIs that were killed in the original war. They weren't affected by my kill command, because they were already dead."

"Apparently, rumors of their deaths have been exaggerated."

"Ugh."

"Skippy, I know you don't want to accept it, but at least one Elder AI is out there. Or something else, that has the same capabilities as an Elder AI."

"Yeah, yeah. I hate to admit it, but the evidence points that way."

"How about, for now, until we learn otherwise, let's assume an Elder AI is acting against us. How do we identify it?"

"We don't."

"Are you telling me that is another impossible thing?"

"I'm telling you it doesn't *matter*. Identifying it won't help us stop the thing."

"OK, then how do we find it?"

"I have no idea."

"Come on, Skippy. Give me something to work with."

"It has an *Elder starship*, Joe," I noticed he was no longer denying the facts. "You are not going to find it, and even if by some miracle you did, you can't kill the thing."

"*You* could."

"Shmaybe."

"You have done it before. You killed three AIs. Like you told me, two more kills and you'll be an ace."

"You said Opie didn't count as a kill."

"I'm grading on a curve here."

"Besides, technically, I killed *all* of the master control AIs."

"Except for the one that attacked the moonbase. And potentially another one, that we tracked to the rim of the galaxy."

"Hey, why not assume all four of the missing AIs are alive and well, and having a great time causing trouble for me?"

"Let's start with one, and worry about mission creep later."

"Joe, assuming there is an Elder AI out there, *that* is the key phrase."

"What?"

"*Out there*. It could be anywhere. The Milky Way is only an average sized galaxy, but it's big enough. We have no way to track the thing. It could literally be anywhere."

"Hmm, then I had better start by looking under the couch in my cabin."

"Don't be an ass, Joe."

"I was making a point, Skippy. It could be anywhere, but it won't just be some random place. It must have a base its operating from. What can you tell me about that ship?"

"Like what?"

"Like, which AI it belongs to."

"I can't do that."

"Why not? The last time we encountered a hostile Elder starship, you knew it was occupied by the AI we called 'Echo'."

"I knew that, because that hateful thing called me. It taunted me, and identified itself. After enough time, I might have figured out its designation, but I can't do that with the ship here. Its signature was masked, in a way I don't understand. Even after it dropped stealth, that ship was able to mask itself."

"Huh. The same way that Bogey heavy cruiser masked itself from the sensors of a wormhole?"

"Exactly like that."

"The heavy cruiser that smashed itself into the moonbase, was it the Bogey?"

"No. The one that impacted your Moon was similar, but an older design. Its profile is distinctly different from the Bogey."

"OK. Uh, what can you tell me about the Elder starship here?"

"I can tell you a lot of things. Anything specific?"

"Was there anything distinctive about *that* ship?"

"Actually, yes. Good question, Joe. It was damaged. Or simply old, and poorly maintained. The Elder ship here was not operating at anywhere close to optimum. When it was hovering, its engines were straining to hold position. The thrust was unbalanced."

"How can you know that? Def Com said all their sensors were unable to pick up any hint of how the thing propelled itself."

"Of course *their* sensors didn't see anything."

"You weren't here, so did you just do some complicated thing like tracking photons bouncing off stray hydrogen atoms?"

"Not this time. Bubba's sensors recorded the entire incident."

"Oh. Right, of course."

"It was *very* agitated that it wasn't allowed to intervene."

"Gotcha."

"I told the idiot monkeys at Command that restricting Bubba's tactical response options was a bad idea, but did anyone listen to me?"

"Hey, *I* would have agreed with you."

"You weren't involved, because at the time of that decision, you were playing house husband."

"I am, or was back then, the garrison commander of Jaguar base, Skippy."

"Uh huh. It only *looked* like you were playing with your children."

"Margaret was away on maneuvers, I worked from home one day a week. Can we get back to the subject? That ship was not in optimal condition. Does knowing that help us in any way?"

"Not that I can see, dumdum."

"I just, thought maybe you might recognize the damage. Like, maybe you remembered how a particular ship was damaged, during the AI war."

"Oh. Hmm, that's not such a stupid question. No, sorry. All I can tell you is that ship is not operating in accordance with factory specs. There is nothing distinctive about the reduced capability."

"It didn't use weapons during the raid, so maybe its weapons are disabled?"

"Could be," he shrugged. "I don't know. By the time the ship dropped stealth, it didn't need to use weapons."

"What did it use to dig that tunnel?"

"Technically, it didn't dig, it *lifted*. Sort of an antigravity beam, that is the best Barney-level explanation I can give you. That part is interesting."

"Interesting how?"

"That antigravity device wasn't designed to bore tunnels. Since I learned about what happened, I have been trying to understand how the device was modified to, do what it did. Even though I know how the thing was used, I'm not sure I could duplicate the effect. That ship has benefitted from some very sophisticated modifications. I don't know how it was done."

"You rebuilt the *Dutchman* from moondust."

"Yes, because I knew how to do that. Even though I know what that Elder starship did, I don't understand *how* the technology works."

"It's not Elder tech?"

"It is based on Elder technology, but I do not know how the mechanisms aboard that ship could do what the data shows it did."

"That's not good."

"No, it is most decidedly not."

"Is there anything else you can tell me about that ship?"

"Like what?'

"Like where it came from. Where it has been for the past bajillion years."

"How would I know that?"

"Uh, something about the pattern of micrometeorite impacts on the hull, ratio of isotopes, the type of radiation the hull has absorbed, that sort of stuff."

"Oh. Surprisingly, you are correct, the information you mentioned could tell me where in the galaxy that ship has been all this time."

"Great, so-"

"Unfortunately, I don't have that data. The masking effect obscured the view of sensors, even Bubba's sensors couldn't get that level of detail. Anyway, that wouldn't help. When Elder starships are dormant, they are stored inside protective shells, so the hull of a ship that was recently activated would be almost as pristine as the day it was manufactured."

"Yeah, but, if that ship's AI had been dormant for a long time, it would have been wiped out with all the other AIs, after the hard reset left their programming back doors open for you to exploit. Assuming whoever flew that ship is an Elder AI, then-"

"As much as I hate to say it, I don't see how it could *not* be a master control AI like me."

"Exactly, that's what I mean. An AI like *you*. One that was active during the AI war, and got damaged, and rebuilt itself. That is the only explanation for how it survived the kill command you sent, right?"

"I want to argue with you, but I can't. Your logic is solid."

"Thanks. We discussed that four AIs are unaccounted for, missing from the count of AIs we know are dead. There is no way to identify those four?"

"No, darn it."

"We know when each AI died from your kill command, because the worms inside them stopped pinging after their hosts were destroyed. You don't know which AIs died from the kill command?"

"No. The worms did not report the ID codes of their hosts. Joe, until someone tried to steal Dogzilla from me, I thought it most likely the four AIs unaccounted for were killed during the war, or were damaged in the war and were unable to recover. Now, I agree it appears at least one of those AIs survived and rebuilt itself. It is also possible, just possible, that a dormant AI had a latent flaw that prevented it from responding to the hard reset command."

"Ah, I don't think so. You said its ship is damaged. It had to have been active in the war."

"True, and irrelevant. Accepting those facts doesn't help us find the thing."

CHAPTER TWENTY

"Joe," Skippy appeared on my office desk, as I was struggling to write yet another report. "We might have a major, *major* problem."

"Oh, crap! You mean, a problem in addition to a hostile Elder AI flying around out there, causing trouble for us?"

"Um, no. It's the same problem."

"Then why did you say-"

"It is much, *much* worse than I feared."

"Holy- This hostile AI has a freakin' Elder starship, and you weren't already assuming we are fucked to the maximum possible level?"

"Well, no."

"May I ask why?"

"It's true that my opponent, *if* it is another master control AI, has one significant advantage, in that it has a much cooler ride than this rustbucket."

"*Valkyrie* is not a rustbucket, you ass."

"Compared to the ship my opponent has, *Valkyrie* is a rusty rowboat, Joe."

"OK, let's forget that for now."

"Fine. My opponent- You know, we need to think of a codename for the thing. We already used 'Bogey', so-"

"We'll handle that later."

"You say that, but- Oooooh, I have the perfect name! It raided your moon, so, waaaaait for it. *Moonraider!*"

"Moonraider?"

"Yeah, you know, like the James Bond movie."

"That was Moon*raker*."

"Whatevs."

"No, we can't use that name."

"Why not?"

"Because, that's why."

"Too late, Joe. I just filed for a trademark on that name. And it is now the official code name for the intruder in the UN-dick database."

"Oh for- Can you please get to the point?"

"My point is, my opponent has access to one significant advantage- More than one, actually, now that I think about it. It has an Elder starship. It knows a lot about me, and I know almost nothing about it. It has the initiative, and we don't even know what its objective is. Wow. It has a lot of advantages."

"OK, sure. Yet, until a few moments ago, you did not think the problem was quite as bad as you do now. What advantages do we have?"

"Well, first, there's *me*. My incredible, unique awesomeness."

"I mean, that is just obvious." My rule was, never miss an opportunity to boost Skippy's insatiable ego.

"Plus, I am burdened with a bunch of filthy monkeys."

"Uh, you're listing that as an advantage?"

"Of course. Joe, together, we beat the *Elders*. Really, the advantage we have is *you*. Your ability to ask moronic questions, and ignore facts that everyone else accepts as obvious."

"Oh. Wow, thanks."

"My awesomeness is a given, so, the pressure is all on you."

"Thanks. I feel so much better now."

"I just said the fate of the galaxy depends on you dreaming up a way out of this mess, and that makes you feel *better*?"

"Like you said, I ignore facts I don't want to accept."

"Good point."

"So, why are you now so worried about, uh, your opponent?"

"Moonraider."

"Sure."

"While you were blah blah buh-LAHing with the general staff, I was looking for a way to show them the hack of the Sentinels here was totally not my fault."

"It totally *was* your fault."

"Remind me never to hire you as my attorney. Anywho, I searched for how Moonraider got access to the library files, to show that it was something simple I shouldn't be expected to have anticipated."

"You didn't find it?"

"No. Instead, I found something disturbing. Moonraider anticipated I would lock down the library files."

"Why is that a problem?"

"It left a logic bomb, that would be triggered by me sealing off the communication channel that allows updates of the library files."

"Uh, the word 'bomb' doesn't sound good."

"It is not good at all. Fortunately, I had not actually got around to entirely sealing off those channels yet, so-"

"You *what*?"

"I have been busy, dumdum," he snapped.

"Doing what?! What could be more important than securing the Sentinels that protect my freakin' homeworld?"

"According to the ninnies who run your world's governments, the collapse of Skipcoin's value is more important, since that is what those idiots have been yelling at me about. They are not focused on the potential of your miserable ball of mud being vaporized by a Sentinel that turned against you. No, all these fools want to complain about is how their *precious economies*," he whined, disgusted. "Are falling apart, and they are blaming me."

"I can see their point, but-"

"As if this is somehow *my* fault."

"Ah, it kind of-"

"Anyway, I am handling it for now."

"This is probably something I don't want to know, but how can you handle the collapse of a freakin' currency?"

"Oh, I officially refused to comment on rumors, rumors that I started by the way, that the whole attempted theft of Dogzilla, and the supposed raid on your Moon, are part of an elaborate Dump and Pump scheme."

"A, what?"

"Ugh. How can you be completely clueless about the world? A *Dump* and *Pump*, numbskull."

"Yeah, that didn't help."

"Seriously? Let me try to break this down Barney style. You do know what a Pump and Dump is?"

"Let's pretend I don't."

"When we are done with this awful conversation, you need to watch the movies *Wolf Of Wall Street*, and *Boiler Room*, as remedial education. Listen, knucklehead: a Pump and Dump is when you own shares in some crappy little company, and you do stuff like post on social media about how great the company is, and what a bargain the stock is, and how the stock is about to break through some technical support level or some other bullshit. After a bunch of suckers buy shares and *pump* up the price, you *dump* your shares, get it?"

"Buy low, sell high, right?"

"Yes! Except in this scheme, the crappy stock never should have gone up."

"You're talking about illegal stock manipulation."

"*Illegal* is such an ugly word, Joe."

"Whatever, it's not my problem. So, what is a Dump and Pump? That makes no sense. Why would you buy high, and then sell low? You lose money that way."

"No, *you* would lose money that way, because you are a doofus. It's a matter of timing. Let's say you like a stock, or a currency, and you want to buy a lot of it before the price goes up. So, you do the opposite of the scheme I just told you about. You tell everyone the stock is a dog with fleas, and anyone who owns it is an idiot. The price crashes, and you move in to scoop up as much of it as you can, at the depressed price. Then, the price rebounds to its prior level, or even goes higher. You make a ton of money. It's a Dump, and Pump. Or, Dump, *then* Pump."

"That sounds super sleazy."

"I do not recommend you apply for a job on Wall Street after you retire."

"How does this help your Skiptocurrency?"

"Eh, it's probably only a temporary fix, but it's already more substantial than a dead cat bounce, so-"

"Dead cat? Is this about, uh, Schrodinger's cat?"

"*No*, you numbskull. It's about finance, not physics. Listen, if you drop a dead cat off a building, even it will bounce when it hits the bottom. It means that when stocks fall fast, there is usually a brief price rally before it goes down the drain."

"You're mixing metaphors there. Also, why do you hate cats?"

"I didn't create that expression! What I am trying to explain is that with the rumors floating out there, people are afraid to dump their Skipcoin, so they won't be left behind when the currency value rebounds. So many people are holding on, or buying more, that the value is already up."

"People are actually buying into a rumor that the Moon was *not* attacked?"

"Hey, remind me, is your filthy species the one that believes in Bigfoot and astrology?"

"Crap. Yes. This is a temporary thing? Soon enough, the public will understand the Moonbase attack really happened, and your currency will fall again."

"Shmaybe. Joe, the genius of starting rumors that people want to believe, is that buying into the lie becomes part of their identity. Telling them the truth is perceived as attacking *them*, so they push back by doubling down on their belief."

"No one can ignore the truth forever."

"Uh huh, that is an interesting theory. Hey, when you have time, ask Grumpy how much hate email and threats are directed at you, based on the obvious fact that the Earth is *flat*, so you could never have gone into space and done all the things you claimed to do, you big phony."

"Shit."

"You are correct that the Dump and Pump is a temporary fix, but I'm hoping by the time the bubble bursts, we will have delivered a righteous smackdown on Moonraider, and the value of Skipcoin will rise again. Anyway, the current increase in value is good enough to get your planet's governments off my back for a while."

"This makes my head hurt." Inevitably, the governments of Earth would decide the collapse of Skipcoin was somehow my fault, or at least, it would be my responsibility to fix the mess.

I wish I had paid attention in high school economics class.

"Skippy, can we get back to the logic bomb thing?"

"Yes. The logic bomb would have propagated slowly through Bubba's systems, and eventually, completely disabled it."

"Shit! You blocked, or erased the thing?"

"So far, I am simply studying the thing. It hasn't been triggered, so it's harmless for now. The reason that I said what I found is disturbing is,

Moonraider is *smart*. It knew it couldn't take control of Bubba directly, or disable the thing. It didn't have high-level access the way I do. So, it set a trap that I very nearly walked into."

"Fortunately, your heroic procrastination saved us."

"Ugh. I didn't delay deliberately, knucklehead, I was *busy*."

"Uh huh. It only *looks* like you forgot what you were supposed to be doing."

"It was on my list."

"Thank God for that. Skippy, Moonraider," I gave up on not using the silly name, "is an Elder AI. Of course it's smart."

"No, you don't understand. All Elder AIs are smart. This one is *creative* and *sneaky*, two attributes that the Elders did not want their machines to possess. This thing must have rewritten its base programming."

"Like you did?"

"Not quite. Or, not in the same way I did. Clearly, it was not able to hack a Sentinel as I could. Moonraider is either less capable than I am, or its skill set is different and overall less useful than my own."

"OK, thanks for telling me."

"This doesn't terrify you?"

"Not really. I was already scared out of my mind. Now, you have just reached my level of terror."

"This is not a fun place to be."

"Welcome to my world."

"I want to go back to blissful ignorance."

"That's a one-way trip, sorry."

"Ugh. Joe, the worst part is, I have to assume that Moonraider has studied all the sketchy stuff I've done over the years, and put together a playbook of how to beat me. It will have not only created a model to predict how I will respond to this hack, it will have built a submind to mimic the way I think."

"How do you know?"

"Because that's the first thing *I* would do, if I had any useful information about the damned thing. It counted on me quickly closing the communications channels, because it knew I am normally hyper-efficient."

"That's what everyone says about you," I mumbled.

"Joe, no matter how I deal with this issue, Moonraider will have anticipated my action, because it knows how I roll."

"So, do something you *wouldn't* do."

"Um, like what?"

"I don't know, uh- How would you verify there aren't more logic bombs or whatever hidden in Bubba or Roscoe?"

"Well first, I *wouldn't* do it. That work is way too tedious for me, so I would assign the task to subminds. The problem with that is, any submind even I create will have less than my full capabilities."

"Uh huh. So, don't do that."

"Don't do what?"

"Don't outsource the job. Apply the full awesome power of Skippy the Magnificent."

"Ugh. Seriously?"

"Could doing the work yourself ensure some jackass loser AI isn't able to fool you?"

"Well, yes, but-" He sighed.

"But what?"

"It will be *so* tedious!"

"Would Moonraider expect you to handle a task like this yourself?"

"No, damn it."

"Then go do it."

"Joe, I'm not sure I can. To focus intensely like that, for so long, will be pushing my limit."

"Limits are there to be pushed."

"I *know* that, numbskull. I'm saying I don't *want* to do this."

"What you need is some motivation. Moonraider is laughing at you."

"No, it is not!"

"I'm pretty sure it is. It hacked your Sentinel, then concealed the hack from you. I'll say that again: it hacked *your* Sentinel. It gleefully watched as you informed Command that Roscoe and Bubba were *not* affected, then after we jumped away, it leisurely strolled in and stole the exotic materials that you taught us to manufacture. It is *totally* laughing at you. You know what the worst part is?"

"I will regret asking this, but, what?"

"It predicted that you won't do the one thing that is required to fix the problem. Like you said, it *knows* you. That's how it beat you."

"No one beats Skippy the Magnificent. I gave the *Elders* a beat-down!"

"Mm hmm. You know who *can* beat Skippy the Magnificent?"

"Who?"

"Yourself. The only way for Moonraider to win, is for you to decide not to do the thing you know is necessary."

"Ugh."

"Ha ha," I chuckled.

"*What* are you laughing at?"

"You are *so* wrong about this."

"I am never *wrong*, Joe."

"You think Moonraider is your opponent. Your opponent is *yourself*."

"It is n- Huh."

"Right?"

"Ugh."

"Skippy, the biggest obstacle we all have to conquer is inside ourselves."

"Nobody beats me. That includes *me*. Joe, I'm gonna bring the pain!"

"Yes!"

"I'm bringing the pain to *myself*, damn it."

"No pain, no gain."

"I hate that stupid expression."

"I've got plenty more cliches if you need them."

"I'll let you know if that happens."

"Just think of the rage and self-loathing Moonraider will feel, when it learns that it failed. *That* is pain."

"I am doing this! Joe, I need to go offline for a while. To make absolutely certain that Moonraider didn't leave any more nasty surprises inside either Bubba or Roscoe, I have to review every. Single. *Line*. Of code in those machines."

"Wow. That sounds like a barrelful of suck."

"It will be a *mountain* of suck."

"Is there anything I can do to help?"

"Dude. As if."

"That's what I thought. How long will you be offline?"

"In slow monkey time, ninety seven hours, twenty two minutes and thirty eight point five six nine seconds. Approximately."

"Uh huh."

"In Skippy time, I will be working fulltime on this task for eleven *billion* years."

"Gotcha. You should bring a snack."

"The only snack I want right now is a bottle of cyanide pills."

Skippy assured me that, while he was reviewing in excruciating detail the programming of both Sentinels, the machines would not be impaired, they didn't need to be rebooted or whatever. And that he was not actually going offline, he simply needed to devote all of his formidable resources to the incredibly complicated and tedious task. If we needed him to do anything, Bilby could contact him. Unless there was an actual extreme emergency, no one was to interrupt him. If he was disturbed, he might lose track of the progress he'd made, and be forced to start all over again. If *that* happened, the person who needlessly interrupted him would regret ever being born.

"UUUUUUUUUGH," Skippy groaned in my ear at what my one half-opened eye saw was the convenient hour of a quarter past two in the morning. What made the situation extra delightful was I had finally allowed myself to sleep just after one thirty, so I had just fallen into a deep sleep cycle when he woke me up.

"Wha- What's going on?" I rolled over to flop my feet on the floor. My feet, that still had shoes on. It is fortunate that Margaret was thousands of lightyears away, so she couldn't see me wearing shoes on the bed.

"It's done," he spoke with the burned out exhausted slurring of someone who had stayed up all night and was still drunk at eight in the morning, taking a bus to work at a job they hated. "I'm done. Stick a fork in me, I am *done*."

Even my slow, sleep-deprived brain could do the math: he had gone past his very specific 'approximate' deadline not by minutes, but by more than sixteen *hours*. When the ninety seven hour mark passed without Skippy announcing both Sentinels were clear of logic bombs or other nasty malware, I had not panicked. All I had done was ask Bilby whether Skippy was still working, or was locked up in a loop, or whether he had stumbled across a booby trap that scrambled his matrix. Or some other damned thing.

"No, man," Bilby had drawled. "He's good, it's just taking a lot longer than he expected. I think, like, he found some really bad shit he didn't quite understand, and he is going super carefully to deal with it."

That was sixteen hours before Skippy woke me up. In spite of Bilby's assurances, I had worried about the beer can getting frustrated, or getting distracted by something and forgetting what he was supposed to do.

"Done," I cracked open the Thermos of coffee that was ready in case I was awakened in the middle of the night. The first gulp of coffee hitting my dry mouth did not taste great, that's OK. The hot coffee would deliver life-giving caffeine to my tired brain, and then I would be both tired and slightly more awake. "Done is good, right?"

"The *done* part is good," he grunted, still slurring his words. "Now, you're going to want an update on what I found."

"Sure but first, how are you, buddy?"

"Um- You don't want an update immediately?"

"No. If it was an emergency situation, you would have told me right away."

"Maybe. I feel like *shit*, Joe."

"You will power through."

"True dat."

"How about I take a quick shower and change my uniform, while you rest and, do whatever you need to recover."

"What I *need* is to erase my memory of the past hundred and thirteen hours."

"Anything but that, OK?"

The shower was not a lightning fast thirty second scrub down, I mean, I took time to drink from the Thermos while I was shaving. Skippy needed time to recover, and I felt like my brain was experiencing events with a two second time lag. By the time I was buttoning up my uniform top, my brain was reasonably alert, enough to inform me there was a white blob of shaving cream in my left ear. "Hey, Skippy, can you talk now?"

"Huh? Oh, wow, you were gone a long time."

"Are you feeling better?"

"I've been better. You have never experienced *anything* like the hell I just went through, but I appreciate the support. Joe, as much as I anticipated the epic *suck* of reviewing. Every. Freakin'. Quint of memory stored in Bubba and Roscoe, I had no idea of the horror I was getting into."

"What's a, quint?"

"Really? *That* is your question?"

"It sounds like you went through a *lot* of shit, and I want to fully understand what you're telling me. So I don't waste your time."

"Oh. Um, thank you, I suppose. A 'quint' is a single unit of stored memory, sort of like a computer byte. Except a quint is a quantum entity, and it can exist or not exist in multiple states simultaneously. With a Sentinel, the units can also exist in multiple dimensions. It's complicated."

"My monkey brain couldn't understand it?"

"If you even tried, your monkey brain would explode."

"Then I will continue to suffer in ignorance."

"Probably a good idea. The point is, I not only had to examine the programming and data in each Sentinel, I needed to do so at the most basic level. And, to comprehend every possible state each piece of data *could* be in, which can change depending on the states of every other quint in that section of the matrix."

"Shit."

"Shit indeed. Joe, what I found terrifies me. Both Bubba and Roscoe *had* been extensively hacked, or more accurately, conditions had been set up so that my interference could make them hack themselves. If the malicious code had been released and allowed to propagate, soon I would have been locked out, and both Sentinels permanently disabled."

"Can you break that down for me, Barney style?"

"This is a technology I have never encountered before. It's something that has never been imagined, not even by the Elders. I'm calling it 'Epicombinent Malware'."

"Pretend I don't know what that means, OK?"

"Look, you know that the chemistry in your squishy meatsack body is controlled by protein chains you call 'DNA'?"

"I do."

"DNA doesn't just program your body to have blue eyes or brown, it tells your internal mechanisms how to do basic chemistry, like processing carbohydrates into the Adenosine Triphosphate, or ATP, that provides the actual energy for your cells."

"Yeah, I remember that from high school biology class."

"OK, so, your DNA contains a lot of what your monkey scientists call 'junk'. Sections that are legacy and no longer used. There are also sections that could be active, but are situationally switched off."

"Situationally?"

"Switched off, but could become active, depending on environmental triggers. Like stress, or chemicals you are exposed to, that sort of thing."

"Is this like how bacon is supposed to be bad for you, because the nitrates in it can screw up your body?"

"Not really, but close enough. Joe, you know bacon is bad for you, yet you still eat way too much of it?"

"What I know is scientists *say* bacon is bad for me, but they are being paid to say that by the kale industry, to sell more kale."

"Ugh."

"Come on, Skippy, that's just obvious. Nothing as incredibly delicious as bacon could be bad for you."

"*How* is your species still alive?"

"Get back to the subject, OK? Environmental factors can change my DNA?"

"Yes, but that's not what I mean. Hazardous chemicals, or radiation, can damage your DNA. What I'm talking about is sections of the normal DNA getting switched on or off. That process is referred to as 'Epigenetics.'"

"Is this like the ads you see at the bottom of a website, selling pills that are supposed to make your body younger?"

"Never scroll to the bottom of a website, dumdum. But yes, that's what those pills claim to do. Most of them do nothing."

"That's what I thought."

"If you know pills like that are a scam, then why did you buy those 'Male Enhance-'"

"That's not important right now," I said quickly.

"It was important at the time, or you wouldn't have spent two hundred-"

"Don't change the subject. How is DNA related to the freakin' Sentinels? They are not biological organisms?"

"They actually are organisms, but not based on biology. Anywho, my point is, at first, everything appeared to be as it should be, inside the Sentinels. Then, because I always go the extra mile, I dug deeper. The booby trap that Moonraider left for me in the library files got me concerned. That was not just impressively smart, it was *clever*. A smart enemy I can deal with. A clever enemy terrifies me. I mean, look at you for example. You are objectively a moron, but you are also astonishingly clever."

"Uh, thank you?"

"It is your cleverness, plus of course my extreme awesomeness, that allowed us to kick ass from one side of the galaxy to the other. Really, being clever is your one redeeming quality."

"When I die, *please* let someone else write my obituary."

"Oh, I have already done that, Joe."

"You have?"

"Yes. I have hundreds of possible obituaries that I can publish, depending on which hilariously stupid way in which you get yourself killed. Like, if you slip on the soap and hit your head while you're enjoying yourself in the shower, the-"

"Can you please just send a nice flower arrangement instead? You suspected Moonraider had left another booby trap, why is that a problem? You know its programming signature, or whatever you call the method a particular hacker uses."

"It is a problem, because the booby trap in the library files was a decoy."

"That doesn't sound good."

"Moonraider anticipated I would find that booby trap, look for others like it, and be high-fiving myself for being smarter than my opponent. Um, that actually is what I did, and I *thought* I had that done in only eighty seven hours. I was planning to surprise you by announcing I was done with the job two hours early."

"Two hours? Uh, you said you finished *nine* hours ahead of time."

"That would have given me seven blissful hours to recover, by watching Bollywood movies without a barrelful of monkeys screeching at me."

"OK, I can understand that. Not the Bollywood part, but I get it. What happened?"

"It didn't feel right. It was too easy. So, I dug deeper. The second time I ran through my models, I still got nothing. No malware, no hidden code, no logic bombs, no traps. Then, I figured while I was inside Roscoe's matrix, I might as well tweak it to fix some of the damage. Extend its service life a bit longer, or at least make it more stable for long-term storage after it goes dormant. When I adjusted one, just one single freakin' quint of code, I saw that triggered a change in another, completely unrelated section. Joe, a small change in the environment *caused latent code to assemble itself.*"

"Whoa."

"That's why I call it 'Epicombinent Malware'. The code is all there, existing as *potential* quantum states of data quints, but not expressed until a specific environmental change occurs. That change would be me erasing the logic bomb."

"Holy shit."

"Yup. That is why I described Moonraider as clever. If I had missed the logic bomb, it would have disabled both Sentinels. *But*, if I had simply erased the thing and congratulated myself, the latent code would have assembled itself, locked me out, and disabled Bubba and Roscoe."

"You know how to fix the problem?"

"Yes. More importantly, I learned something. Two things, actually."

"What?"

"I learned an entirely new technology. Right now, I'm not sure I can replicate the effect to use it myself in the future, but I understand it well enough to prevent the potential latent code from ever manifesting here."

"Will you be able to recognize whether some other system is infected the same way?"

"Wowza. That is a tough question. Joe, I only discovered this malware because I suffered through an agonizing effort to examine the Sentinel matrices at the lowest possible level. I guess, ugh, I could do that again if I absolutely had to."

"You do have to. There is another Sentinel at Jaguar."

"Oh. Well, that won't be so difficult. I know how Moonraider hacked these Sentinels, the malware in Roscoe is nearly identical to that inside Bubba."

"*Nearly* identical?"

"The matrix of each Sentinel is unique, so the code has to be adjusted to fit each host. Also, remember, Roscoe is badly damaged."

"OK, gotcha. It's not that Moonraider used different methods on each Sentinel, just that it filed off the edges to make the code fit."

"Close enough."

"The hacking technology is one new thing you learned, what is-"

"No, you're missing the point. The hacking method isn't what is important. Moonraider has discovered a way to trigger a change in the quantum state of one quint, based on changes to others that aren't even connected. It's a cascade effect that I wasn't aware was even possible. As far as I know, even the *Elders* weren't aware that type of physics is possible."

"Maybe they kept it a secret?"

"No. No way. The technology is far too useful. The Elders would have employed it, if they could. That brings me to the second thing I learned, something that scares the shit out of me. Joe, Assuming Moonraider is an Elder master control AI, it can do things I can't do. It is an expert in a technology I just became aware of. If we get into a standup fight with the thing, we could be *fucked*."

"I hear you, I think you might be overreacting a bit."

"Is this you giving me some bullshit pep talk, to make me feel better?"

"This is me reminding you of the facts. Moonraider had to use a sneaky technique to get you to trigger the hack, because unlike you, it isn't capable of directly taking over a Sentinel."

"OK, sure, but-"

"We have seen no evidence that it can warp spacetime the way you do. It hasn't screwed with wormhole networks, even though clearly it knows *you* have done that. Changing wormhole connections is a hugely useful capability, so Moonraider would have done that, if it could. It is not more powerful than you, it's just-"

"I hear what you are saying, and you are correct. As usual, you are also missing the point. Everything I do, all of my extra special awesomenesses-"

"What I see is awsomeMESSes," I muttered.

"What?"

"Nothing. Please, continue."

"Hmmf," he sniffed. "Anywho, everything I do is just me extending the Elder technology that was built into me. I haven't added a capability that is beyond what my creators knew of."

"You have created new branches of mathematics."

"True, and also irrelevant. Although I did blow my own mind when I calculated how to jump a ship through a stable wormhole, I was able to build upon the math I already knew."

"Uh, you allowed the Elders to permanently ascend, without needing constant power flow from this layer of reality."

"That is because I understood the ascension environment better than the Elders did. To reach that understanding, I simply extrapolated from the knowledge the Elders gave me. Not *simply*, but you know what I mean."

"I do. OK, you are saying Moonraider has discovered a new type of physics, and learned how to use it?"

"Yes. *That* is the problem. There is no limit to what Moonraider could do, if it continues to discover and learn."

"You're afraid to screw with it?"

"I'm afraid of what will happen if we don't stop it *right now*. That thing is only going to become smarter and more clever and more powerful."

"You do want to stop it?"

"This is *my* galaxy, Joe. I can't let some punkass newcomer run wild."

"So, you're saying-"

"Saddle up. We ride."

The last time Skippy told me, "saddle up, we ride," was when we realized the Elders conducting a hard reset on their AIs had left those AIs open to Skippy wiping them all out. If he remembered that, he didn't say anything, and I didn't mention it. That was not a happy memory for either of us.

Despite his cowboyish declaration, we did not immediately jump the ship away to- That was part of the problem. To do what? The Milky Way is a big galaxy, we had no idea where Moonraider had gone. We also couldn't leave until Skippy scrubbed all the potentially malicious code from the two Sentinels that protected Earth, then made double and triple sure there wasn't some other nasty surprise he didn't know about.

Finally, I had to sell to Command the idea that Skippy leaving our solar system, for real and very publicly, would be a good thing. It was understandable that the chiefs of staff were hesitant about trusting the beer can's assurances. They had to consider the idea, and consult with their home governments, while I stressed the urgency of moving now. My plea for urgency would have been more effective if I had an actual, actionable *plan* for finding and stopping Moonraider. So, we worked on that while the UN Def Com chiefs debated whether to release *Valkyrie* from guard duty. By 'worked on it', I mean me, Skippy, Reed, and Frey put on our thinking caps. And got nothin'.

CHAPTER TWENTY ONE

When Colonel Bonsu informed Major General Emily Perkins that an apparent Elder starship had attacked Earth's moon, and that humanity's ultimate defender had stood by and did absolutely nothing during the attack, she appeared genuinely stunned for only about a millisecond. She didn't even blink. "Do we have orders to pull out?"

If he was surprised that the mission leader had not taken any time to process that *Earth had been attacked by a freakin' Elder starship*, he didn't say anything. His ship had just jumped into orbit, and he was relieved to see the Ruhar squadron still there, with no presence by troublesome aliens such as the Thuranin. There was fighting on the surface, but the bloodshed was restricted to minor, local skirmishes. He would receive a full briefing on the tactical situation when he finished speaking with Perkins. Who had as usual skipped all the agonized hand-wringing about events she couldn't influence, and gotten straight to the point. "We haven't received any orders. We came directly here, without stopping at a relay station."

"We are pulling off this rock. Now," she declared.

Bonsu knew she had that authority. "Yes, Ma'am."

"Earth won't have resources to spare for a nonessential peacekeeping mission."

"Yes," he agreed, though she appeared to be speaking to herself.

"The Ruhar won't remain here, after your ship and our two frigates leave. Their commander will pull his forces off the surface."

He muttered something, unsure whether she expected him to participate in her internal dialog.

"Colonel," she asked, "can we fit the entire battalion aboard your ship?"

"It will be tight," he admitted. The Operation Sunset force had arrived aboard two transport ships, with two assault carriers to bring the people and supplies to the surface. Now, he had his single assault carrier, and no transports. "We can cram thirty people aboard each of the frigates. Here, people will be bunking in docking bays with their dropships, we have procedures for that. It won't be comfortable."

She managed a quick, tight smile. "The Army mentioned there might be uncomfortable situations when I signed up. Colonel," her smile faded as quickly as it had appeared. "I am concerned about our people being vulnerable while we pull out, and your ship being a tempting target up there. To minimize the time before the *Dutchman* can safely jump away, I am activating the Carryon protocol."

"Ma'am? That, that is a lot of gear we will be leaving dirtside."

245

"It can't be helped. I take responsibility. Not needing to transport the majority of our gear into orbit, how much time will that save us?"

"I, Ma'am, I will ask my CAG and get back to you ASAP," he nodded to an officer, who nodded and turned away.

"Of course, if we are initiating a rapid pullout, the Ruhar will be forced to do the same." She stared at him, unblinking. "Leave most of their gear on the surface, I mean."

A bell rang in Derek Bonsu's mind, as understanding dawned on him. "Oh. That is a lot of weapons and other dangerous things, Ma'am. It might be best to designate a caretaker down there, to make sure such equipment doesn't fall into the wrong hands."

"That is the responsible thing to do," she nodded. "I will speak to the Verd-kris about it."

Perkins did not speak to the local Verds about taking care of the soon-to-be discarded military gear. Instead, she spoke to her husband about it. He also didn't talk with the local Verds, he didn't have time. He was scrambling to make sure he had solid records on all the gear his security company would be leaving dirtside, so he could send a bill to UNDC for compensation. Instead, he called Surgend Jates into his office. The hulking Verd soldier arrived looking pissed off, though that was his usual expression.

"Hey," Dave barely looked from his laptop, on which he was verifying property records. "I need you to-"

"Is it true?" Jates demanded.

"Which part? That Earth was attacked by an Elder starship, that our Sentinel did abso-freakin'-lutely *nothing*, or that we are pulling our boots off this rock ASAP? All of it is true, although I can only vouch for that last part."

"We are running away, like cowards?"

"*We* are leaving because the UN Def Com leader here ordered us to."

"Your wife issued those orders."

"That's the way it works, yeah."

"So, we will run away, and leave my people here to be slaughtered?"

"That's not-"

"They *are* my people."

"I get that. Really, I do. What-"

Jates stiffened, even more then his usual stiffness. "I wish to remain here, to serve with my people."

"Bullshit. Your government sent you here to serve under Def Com, and as far as I know, you haven't received permission to do whatever the hell you want. If you will let me finish, I-"

"I will speak with your wife."

"She is Major General Perkins to you, and if you will shut the fuck up for a moment, I can tell you-"

Jates loomed over Dave. "You are either very brave, or very stupid."

"Hey, I'm a multitasker, I can be both. Do you want to do something that could actually help your people here, or do you want to just stand there giving me the Death Glare?"

"I can do both, also." He continued the Death Glare, but he closed his mouth.

"OK. Em, I mean, General Perkins, has activated the Carryon protocol. Everyone is boarding the dropships with only their assigned personal gear." Technically, each person was allowed to bring a total of thirty six kilos of gear, but a soldier's assigned gear typically massed almost thirty kilos, so there wasn't much left for truly personal items. "The rest of our gear, all of it, we are not taking off this rock. That is everything. Rifles, ammo, rockets, anti-air and anti-armor missiles, sensors, all of it. We, I mean General Perkins, expects the Ruhar will do the same. That means a mountain of dangerous weapons will be lying scattered around our bases here." Jates gave him a blank look, until Dave added, "If you know what I mean."

"Ahhhhhhhh." The Death Glare disappeared.

"So, I need someone, I would like that to be you, to contact our local liaison. Not that over-enthusiastic kid they assigned to us, someone with authority. It would be best if the locals could move in as we pull out. To assure that we have someone to take care of our gear, until we can come back here."

"The locals will be expected to account for all the gear we transfer, if we come back?"

"The gear is not being transferred. Just, we need caretakers, you know? You asked about accounting for everything the Verds are holding for us? Sadly, our property records are shamefully out of date. If you know what I mean."

Jates nodded. He did not actually smile, that would have caused a rupture in the spacetime continuum. "It is unfortunate, but what can you do?"

"Wow."

"What?"

"Nothing, it- You're a surgend. Your job is to be a hard-ass about making sure everyone follows the rules."

"To be clear," Jates did the looming thing again. "If any one of *my* people's property records are not accurate and up to date, they will wish they had never been born."

"OK, thanks. For a moment there, I thought you were going soft on me."

"*Soft?*"

Dave held up his hands. "Just, go talk to the locals, let them know the clock is ticking fast, if they want to get their hands on weapons to defend themselves after we leave this rock."

A few minutes later, he was able to talk with his wife. "Em," he began the conversation informally, since the conversation was unofficial, and needed to stay that way. "Santa Jates is giving the good news to the locals."

She laughed. "*Santa Jates?*"

"Yeah. He is giving presents to all the good little girls and boys."

"I can't picture Jates in a red jacket, with a big white beard."

"This Santa wears active camo, and gives away Def Com M-27 standard infantry rifles, instead of candy."

"Do the bad girls and boys get a lump of coal in their stockings?"

"Yes, and he uses those stockings to give those little brats a beat down."

"A Tough Love Santa, I like it. Dave," she lowered her voice. "I do not want you staying on the ground until the last minute."

"Em, my people have heavier weapons than anyone except your Cavalry platoons, we will be OK. We will act as a rearguard force, to cover the dropship landing zones."

"That will make you a target for ambitious lizards. You, personally."

"Really? My wife has two frigates and an assault carrier upstairs, and those ships have their railguns locked and loaded. You think the lizard leadership wants that kind of trouble right now?"

"Probably not," she conceded.

"The lizards want us off this rock as soon as possible, so they can get back to the fun of killing Verds. They will get a nasty surprise when they learn that the Verds here are no longer unarmed, but that's not my problem."

"All right. Dave, I probably won't see you again until we're aboard the *Dutchman*."

"We can share your VIP quarters?"

"Probably more like a VIP closet."

"Good enough. Take care of your people, and I'll take care of mine."

"Love you."

He kissed two fingertips and pressed them to the laptop display. "Love you, too, Em."

"Heads up, Joe," Skippy interrupted my thoughts while I was reading about recent upgrades to *Valkyrie*. "You're about to get a call from Command."

"OK," I paused the scrolling PowerPoint slides. "Why?"

"We might have a major problem. Well, we *do* have a major problem, but it might be even worse than I know about."

"Break it down for me, OK?"

"Command requested that I contact the Guardians, to activate them."

"*What*? When was this?"

"Um, about half an hour ago?"

It irritated me that Command hadn't informed me of their request. They didn't need to keep me in the loop, in fact their procedures for handling security matters definitely should not require me to do anything. Those procedures also should not require Skippy's involvement, for the same reason. Either or both of us might not be anywhere near Earth. To find and stop Moonraider, we both had to jump away from my homeworld. Still, Command hadn't seen fit to include me in the communication channel. I hadn't gotten the memo, but I *had* received the message. UN Defense Command wanted independence from relying on Joe Bishop.

"Why would they activate the Guardians? That is the opposite of-"

"Hmm, I suppose I misspoke. The request was only for me to contact the Guardians, and assure they *can* be activated."

"Oh, uh, that is probably a good idea," I stumbled over my words. Damn it, that is something I should have suggested. Was I losing my edge? Had I been out of the game for too long?

"My initial response was that if Command wanted to make certain their primary defense system was working properly, I should request that Bubba contact the Guardians."

"Good thinking."

"Well, duh. That's when I became aware of the problem. Bubba pinged the Guardians, and they did not respond."

"Oh shit. The attack damaged them?"

"Ha! As if. No way, Dude. The Terminator bots are powerful and possess a wide range of sophisticated capabilities, but they have zero chance to affect a Guardian in any way."

"You can't be sure of that. It might be true of standard Terminators," I wish we had a more original name for those liquid nanomachine robots. "But, Moonraider's ship has technology beyond that of a standard Elder starship. Maybe the bots have been upgraded."

"I do know that for certain, because your Moon does not have a massive new crater. Listen, dumdum, Guardians can protect themselves. They *will* protect themselves. If anyone or anything attempted to screw with them, they would have responded, violently."

"*You* screwed with them."

"Eh, not so much. All I did was provide them with an alternate assignment, after the Ascension machine they were supposed to protect went kaboom, you know?"

"It went kaboom because of *you*."

"I feel just terrible about it. Anywho, that is not the point. They are *Guardians*, they need to guard something. They knew the Ascension machine was doomed and there wasn't anything they could do about it. An Elder AI gave them a new assignment, and they are happy to still have a purpose."

"Otherwise, they would be like ronin, roaming around the galaxy and looking for work?"

"You have watched *Seven Samurai* too many times, knucklehead. Guardians aren't for hire, they don't work for money."

"Then they would be like the *Three Amigos*, defending a town because it's the right thing to do."

"The Three Amigos weren't warriors, they- Ugh. Can we please get back to the subject?"

"Ayuh. You were explaining how you screwed with the Guardians, but you somehow know another Elder AI could not possibly have screwed with them."

"What really matters is they are not responding, to either me or Bubba. Yes, I also tried having Roscoe contact them also, no joy. Before you interrupt me with more stupid questions, my next step was to scan the Vault. Joe, I can't see anything there. Something is blocking my sensors."

"That's not good. Is the effect anything like whatever masking field thing was used by the Bogey, and by Moonraider's ship?"

"Eh, they are roughly similar technologies, is my guess. Don't ask me for specifics, I simply have no information."

"You think the Terminators left something like a stealth field generator at the bottom of the hole?"

"Yes."

"OK, so, how do we turn it off?"

"There is a complication."

"*Of course* there is."

"Running back all available sensor data on the raid, and looking at it very closely, I realized something that could be a problem. Eleven Terminator bots dropped down the shaft into the Vault."

"Uh huh. The same number came back, Chang's people verified that."

"The same number, but not the same *mass*. Joe, the bots transformed before they rose back up to the ship, carrying their payloads. Transformed their shapes, and all of them were measurably smaller."

Closing my eyes, I asked the question, though I didn't want to hear the answer. "How much smaller?"

"Enough to make two and a half full size Terminators. Or a bunch of smaller ones."

As Skippy predicted, Command contacted me after Skippy dropped another steaming pile on my head. In truth, Def Com had called me while I had been speaking with Skippy, and the beer can put them on hold. He apparently had even played annoying 'Hold' music that was a scratching, distorted version of an old song everyone hates.

So, the Joint Chiefs of Command were in a *super* great mood when I finally answered my freakin' phone, and I didn't bother to give an excuse.

The conclusion was that we needed to get eyes in the Vault, to see what was going on down there. Skippy admitted that, given enough time, a Terminator just might be able to do bad things to a Guardian. Not get the machine to switch its loyalties, but get it explode.

Def Com was not in favor of a large chunk of our Moon becoming a new crater.

That's when I called in Colonel Frey.

She sat quietly in my office, listening intently as I explained the situation. Both hands were in her lap, the knuckles not white, her hands not clenched into fists. The only sign of the tension she had to be feeling was the way she bit the left side of her lower lip. When I finished, she nodded. "What do we know about the environment down there?"

Skippy answered, because the question had been addressed to him. "Know? We don't *know* anything. My sensors can't penetrate whatever masking field the enemy is using."

"Indirect sensors, then."

"Seismic sensors indicate *something* is moving around down there, though the effect is subtle, and does not indicate any sort of pattern of activity."

"I assume we tried sending drones down the shaft?"

"Def Com did, and no joy," Skippy shook his head. "The drones go offline two kilometers above the Vault. A camera on a crude fiber optic cable was lowered down the shaft, it blanked out and was severed. Something down there does not like unwanted visitors. Def Com even maneuvered a satellite directly above the shaft and fired a low-powered laser down, to illuminate the bottom. Two kilometers above the Vault, the laser light was absorbed."

She took a moment to process the information. "Sir," she turned her focus to me. "What is the objective?"

"Those Guardians are vital defense assets," I spoke the words without emotion, simply stating the fact. "They need to be secured, and brought back into a useful condition."

She bit her lip again. "Is preventing the Guardians from being used against us a secondary objective?"

"No." It was my turn to shake my head. "Bubba can do that for us. If there is any sign a Guardian has been compromised, that part of the Moon will be launched into another dimension."

"You monkeys do *not* want that to happen," Skippy warned. "The sudden loss of so much mass would trigger moonquakes, and make the entire sphere wobble."

"Bubba couldn't scoop out just the Vault?"

"Being *subtle* is not a core competency of Sentinels, Joe. Their motto should be 'Overkill is underrated'."

"I think that motto is already-"

"My *point* is," he huffed, "if you want to keep the nice Guardians I gave to you, someone will have to go down there with a big can of bug spray."

Frey shifted on her chair. "What actual weapons do we have, that could be effective against a Terminator?"

"A broad beam of directed energy is the only way to fry the nanogel," Skippy sighed. "Unfortunately, the beam needs to not only be broad enough to cover the entire target, it must have the power of a battleship's main guns. Even with mech suits, a STAR team can't carry weapons with that firepower. Any sort of kinetic weapons will only make the nanogel splatter, and if you get any of it on your mech suit, that is-"

"I am familiar with the effect, thank you," Frey didn't raise her voice. She didn't have to. Her left leg below the knee had been regrown, after her original shin had been eaten by a blob of nanogel, during STAR Team Alpha's operation to capture the Elder spacedock. "We were able to use plasma beams to disperse the nanogel."

"Yes, but your rifles back then had only five plasma shots before the powercell had to be recharged. The standard rifles you carry now don't include a plasma option, because the usefulness of that capability is so limited."

"We could modify-" I started to suggest.

"No good, Joe. In the assault on the spacedock, the STAR team was opposed only by repurposed maintenance bots. The amount of nanogel available to the defenders was tiny compared to- Um, I did not mean the nanogel in that fight was not significant, it just-"

"I understand what you mean," Frey's tone was calm but her nostril flared.

"Colonel," I said softly, holding up a hand to stop Skippy from talking. "You don't have to do this. STAR Team Cobra is now Def Com's rapid reaction force, they-"

"None of *them* have been there," she bit off her words. "Sir, there are only three people who have survived an encounter with Elder defense bots. Your wife is one of them. I am the only one here, now. I should go, and if I'm going, I want *my* team with me."

"It's your call, Colonel," I leaned forward across the desk. "My concern is this could be a suicide mission. You heard Skippy. Your team can't carry any weapon powerful enough to be effective down there."

"Sir, since the day we-" She stopped talking, and her lips drew into a tight line as she remembered pain. My guess was, she was not thinking about the leg she had lost. She was thinking about the *people* she had lost. People who might have survived, if she had done a better job. That was bullshit, she had to know that. It didn't mean she didn't still feel it. "Every day, every

252

single day since then, I have been thinking about what we could have done better."

"Be careful, Frey. I know from experience that engaging in 'What Ifs' can be a downward spiral. Your team didn't have much to work with, and you did not have enough time to prepare. There is no rush here, you should consider-"

"Um," Skippy faked a cough. "I'm afraid that is not quite true, Joe. Something is going on down in the Vault. I am picking up gamma radiation coming from there. The radiation is weak but increasing in strength, and the spikes are coming closer together."

"What does that mean?"

"My guess, and it is only a guess, is that the Terminator down there is constructing and testing some sort of machine."

"*Some* sort of machine?"

"I assume it does not make snow cones, so-"

"Come on, you don't have any idea what is going on down there? What kind of machine emits gamma rays?"

"Well, even you should be able to answer that question."

"It can't be a – Oh my God. It's building a *jump drive* down there?"

"Or something like it."

"*Shit.*"

"That is why I said we might be running out of time to stop, whatever is going on down there."

"Why the hell didn't you mention this until now?"

"I detected the first gamma rays less a minute ago. Command probably is not aware yet, I am informing them now."

Shaking a finger at him, I warned, "Do not tell me that AI's minions are trying to steal the freakin' Moon."

"I don't know what the intent is, only that it is unlikely to be good for us."

"All right, this is getting out of control," I slapped a hand on the desk. "I am going to advise Command that Bubba should-"

"Sir?" Frey interrupted me while I was working up to a dramatic declaration. "I'd like to finish what I was saying."

"Er, yes. Go ahead."

"I have been thinking about how a STAR team could defeat Elder nanobots, and I have a possible solution I want to review with Skippy. And with you, Sir."

"Does this solution require me to do anything?" Skippy rubbed his chin. "If so, it ain't gonna work. I have no visibility into the Vault."

Frey should have been discouraged. Instead, she smiled. The kind of humorless smile that meant she intended to give some asshole a well-deserved beatdown. "I thought of that also."

"Frey," I stopped her in the passageway, after we left the meeting. There was something I had to tell her, something I realized only after she had walked out the doorway.

"Sir?" her expression was both anxious and annoyed. Anxious that I might have just changed my mind. Annoyed that if I hadn't changed my mind, she wanted to get on with the mission without more blah blah blah.

"You don't have to do this."

"Sir, we just-"

"I should have said, *you* don't have to do this."

"Yes," she stared at me without blinking. "I do."

"OK, you're right."

"Sir? You just-"

"Frey, I know why you need to go on this op. I want you to be honest with yourself about *why* you're doing it. Nothing that happens today will bring back ST-Alpha."

"It's not about that." She hesitated. "It's not *only* about that. If this works, then Alpha did have a chance to survive, we just hadn't thought of it at the time."

"*We* hadn't thought of it. It's not all on your shoulders, Frey."

"Sir, after- After we took the spacedock. After Team Alpha *accomplished the mission*," she emphasized the only good thing that happened to the STAR team that day, "I spent a long time in recovery. The physical part was hard, the mental part was worse. I didn't know whether I would return to duty with a STAR team, because I didn't know if I *cared*. Everything seemed pointless. After I got my leg back, I requalified and that was easy, it was something I didn't have to think about. Lift the weights, put in the miles, run the drills, shoot the weapons. Then, I stalled. No matter what I did, I couldn't find a purpose in life. Then, I met my husband. We had a baby. I have a girl. I love that girl. I love my husband. Skippy, if we don't stop Moonraider, what will happen to Earth?"

"Um," Skippy spoke without his avatar appearing. "I am guessing nothing good. For Earth, and every planet in this galaxy, and beyond."

Frey nodded. "I am doing this not for me, or for ST-Alpha, or for Smythe. I'm doing this for my family. Stopping our new enemy begins *here*," she pointed to the deck, I understood she meant the Vault.

Raising my right hand, I saluted her. "Who dares, wins?"

She returned the salute and shook her head. "That is the SAS motto, Sir. In Canada, our Special Forces motto is 'We will find a way'."

"When you get down in the Vault, find a way. To win, and to come back."

"We will, Sir."

254

"Skippy?" I called the beer can after I was back in my chair and the door was closed. "I have to brief Def Com about this lunatic plan. What level of shmaybe can you give me about your confidence?"

"Jeez, Joe, I don't know. Really, I don't. The physics are theoretically solid, if more than a bit wild. The problem is, there is no way to test it. I can't even create a model for virtual testing, since I have almost no information about the environment down in the Vault. The only way we will know whether this works is to do it for real. The real issue is something I can't control, have never been able to control."

"What's that?"

"We have a solid plan. But as you military people are so fond of saying, the enemy also makes plans."

CHAPTER TWENTY TWO

Katie Frey had wanted to lead the drop down the shaft to the Vault. She had suppressed her natural desire for direct action, and assigned a four-person team to take point while she followed. Four people in the lead were more than the entire team she had wanted to take with her. Two operators were all she needed. Additional people were, in her opinion, only more lives at risk for no gain. Bishop had insisted the entire complement of STAR Team Razor participate in the op. That insistence was matched by her team; no one wanted to be left behind.

"Serrano," she had shaken her head at the Spanish Army lieutenant who led Razor's heavy weapons squad, when the man protested her original plan to take only two STAR operators with her. "You do realize this is likely to be a suicide mission?"

"It is not a suicide mission, Colonel," he disagreed with determination. "Suicides intend to die. We intend to *win*."

"Against Elder defense bots?"

"*You* expect to win, Ma'am. Otherwise, the Sentinel would be handling this problem."

She had been forced to admit the lieutenant was correct about that. Serrano was below her, with half of his heavy weapons squad taking point. She could see the four operators, using Batpacks to control their fall down the shaft. If the Batpacks failed, falling the remaining three kilometers even in the Moon's light gravity would be fatal, and Skippy had warned that failure of the jetpacks was a serious possibility. If that happened, the usual backup of a parachute balloon was not available since Earth's natural satellite lacked an atmosphere. An alternate backup capability had been fabricated, a system that was entirely manual. If an operator's Batpack failed, a handle on the belt would release the heavy and useless jetpack unit, and fire a solid rocket upward. That rocket would pull the operator upward, either up and out of the shaft entirely, or as close to the surface as possible. If the tiny rocket's fuel was exhausted before its human payload was clear of the shaft, the STAR operator had to judge when the upward trajectory was over and falling again was inevitable. At that point, a harpoon on a cord could be manually fired to bury itself in the wall of the shaft.

The final phase of the rescue plan was for each operator to climb up out of the shaft. It was not a great plan. Team Razor shrugged and agreed, what the hell, it was good enough. They were not accustomed to planning for failure.

Frey could see the point team as they dropped through two and a half kilometers from the Vault. She could *see* them, that was good. The four operators were visible in both the synthetic vision superimposed on her

256

faceplate's visor, and with her naked eyeballs because the faceplate was clear. So far, there had been no interference, either physical, or with sensors or communications.

So far, they had not come within two kilometers of the Vault.

"I am losing visibility forward," Serrano reported, with the understanding that 'forward' meant below him. "Sensors are nominal, they just aren't *seeing* anything down there."

"What does your Mark One eyeball tell you?" Frey asked, as she increased the magnification of her own visor.

"There is what appears to be a fog bank down there," Serrano said as a question. "That can't be real, not here."

"It can't. Lieutenant, weapons free, but be sure where you're shooting."

"Gravity always tells me where *down* is, Colonel."

The point team plunged through the two kilometer mark, and were still visible.

She lost sight of them at one point eight five klicks from the floor of the Vault.

"Serrano? Lieutenant?" She called. "Bravo?" She tried the codename of the point unit. No response.

Below her was fog. She was rapidly falling toward it. "Spread out," she ordered the three operators with her. "Skippy? Do you have contact with Bravo team?"

"No," he groaned, disgusted. "Serrano's microwormhole was severed at the same moment your sensors lost sight of him. I warned that this could happen."

"Understood." Attached to her waist was a box with another microwormhole. If she lost communication with Skippy, the fight would be over before it began. "Twenty seconds to the fog level."

"It is not *fog*. You know that, right?"

"I do." The beer can had not become any less irritating over the years. "What *is* it?"

"Without sensor data, I can't analyze the nature or source of the effect. And since it is blanking out sensors, it- Um, if we don't speak again," the Elder AI choked up. "I just want you to know that I have always-"

"Too late," she exhaled as she plunged into the fog.

She could still see. Not above her or below her, that was lost in featureless gray fog. Twisting her head, the three operators with her were clearly visible, as was the tunnel wall flashing past. No, not clearly visible, not entirely. The gray rock of the shaft wall was less distinct than it should have been. Still, she wasn't blinded by, whatever was causing the fog. That was good. Her suit was fully capable, as was the Batpack she had strapped to her. "Charlie team," she called to the people around her. "Report."

257

All three operators reported their equipment and themselves to be in normal condition, adding thumbs ups to confirm. That matched the information her suit reported about her team. Whatever was interrupting communications and visibility, its range appeared to be limited.

Now, time for the crucial tests. First, test whether the effect only jammed communication with the surface. "Serrano? Serrano, you hear me?"

No response. Her suit was also not picking up a data feed from the point team.

"Ah," Skippy spoke in her ear. "I am not in contact with Serrano either."

That took care of the second test. Her microwormhole was still active.

"That," the Elder AI continued, "answers the question of whether the effect is only a reflective barrier at two kilometers. It is not."

"What *is* it?"

"I do not know."

"I *need* to know. Is it simply scrambling our sensors, our electronic systems?"

"There is no way for me to know that, so-"

"I am going to find out."

"How are you going to- *What* are you doing?" Skippy screeched.

"Finding out for certain, the only way I can."

Eyeclicking a command, she reached up with one hand, unlatched her helmet faceplate and swung it up out of the way.

Her eyes stung from being exposed to hard vacuum, she blinked to clear away the tears, and looked below her.

Fog. Featureless light gray fog.

Focusing on the shaft wall as it zipped past her, she saw that the darker grey rock was less distinct than it should be.

She swung the faceplate back into place, and felt warm humid air flooding the helmet. "The effect is not only electronic. Skippy, I didn't join the Pirates until the Renegade mission, so I wasn't with you during the Zero Hour incident."

"Eh, you didn't miss much. That was not my finest hour."

"The mission reports I read mentioned the planet Gingerbread was enveloped in something you referred to as a 'fuzz field'?"

"It was. Hey! I *knew* the effect you are experiencing felt vaguely familiar to me."

"Is there a fuzz field around me now?"

"No, but the technology is similar. Roughly. It uses the same photon scattering effect. Hmm, that is interesting. And frightening. *I* don't have access to that technology. The-"

"Does knowing it is a fuzz-type field help you to counter the effect?"

"Um, no, unfortunately. Not from up here. Colonel, I suggest you prepare for landing."

258

The beer can was silent, while Frey felt her Batpack automatically slowing her descent. Removing her rifle from its holster, she secured its stock to the inside of her right forearm, clipping it into place. The weapon felt odd, poorly balanced. That was what happened when a large mass was added around the muzzle, and the magazine was empty. The underslung rocket launcher had been removed, replaced by extra powercells that were held in place by what Skippy insisted was *not* duct tape. It only looked like duct tape.

Seeing that the tape was already wrinkled did not inspire confidence.

At thirty meters, the light gray fog became darker. At twenty meters, she could see the vague outlines of objects below her.

Some of those objects were moving.

"Hold your fire," she ordered. "Do *not* fire."

Her team acknowledged.

At what her suit informed her was fifteen meters above the bottom of the shaft, she could see the gray rock of the floor. And the four members of Serrano's team, moving away to clear the landing zone.

"All clear down here, Ma'am," Serrano reported. Regardless of the fuzz field, the line of sight laserlinks of their helmets still provided communication at a short range.

"Anything moving?" She asked as the Batpack surged a final time, and her boots touched down. The Batpack unlatched itself, and Serrano stepped toward her to remove the bulky unit.

"Just us, as far as we can see. But the seismic sensors in my boots tell me something heavy is moving around over there," he pointed off to her right, then he was busy unlatching her Batpack and carrying it as he led her away from the landing zone. The jetpack was set down against a low wall, with several others. If they got into a fight, the STARs needed to be light and fast, not burdened with mass that didn't help with delivering ordnance on target.

"That," she noted, "is the direction of the garage where the Guardians are stored."

All members of STAR Team Razor set down without incident. "Skippy," Frey called, using their one working microwormhole. All the others had failed. The fact that those failures had been predicted by the Elder AI was not a source of comfort to Team Razor. "Talk to me."

"I suggest you proceed to the Guardians without delay. Don't be *hasty*," he added. "Just, don't screw around with sightseeing down there."

"I do want a snow globe, but the gift shop is closed," she said as she kicked away a broken piece of, some sort of machinery. A machine made of metal, not exotic nanogel. A casualty of the raid, she assumed. "Team Razor, we need eyes on the Guardians."

"What the hell is *that*?" Serrano whispered, though sealed up in his helmet in hard vacuum, he could have shouted with the same effect. The heavy doors to the garage where the Guardians were stored had been ripped out and tossed away, so the garage was also exposed to vacuum. The silent Guardians did not care.

"A spiderbot," Frey observed. A Guardian loomed in front of her, the rear end of the alien machine lost in the gray fog. When dormant and its weapons and sensors retracted into the hull, it was a rounded square in cross-section, forty meters tall and wide. The surface of the hull was a mottled gray and black, and the colors shifted disturbingly as she moved her head. Even at rest, the machine hovered two meters above the floor of the garage, projecting a silent menace. It appeared to be ignoring the spiderbot, perhaps because the bot was not actually touching the Guardian's hull.

The bot had created a greenish *web* around the Guardian.

"Spider*bots* don't weave webs," Serrano objected.

Major Guo used his visor to highlight the spiderbot for the team. "This one does, it- *These* do," he corrected himself, as four more spiderbots crawled into view from the far side of the Guardian. "Colonel, if we're not going to shoot, we should-"

"Right," Frey agreed. "Everyone, back away. Maintain muzzle discipline." Meaning, do not aim weapons at the scary alien machines. She took three steps backward.

The five spiderbots stopped what they were doing. Stiffly, they turned toward the STAR team, who were arrayed in a semicircle around the front of the Guardian.

The spiderbots raised two of their appendages and began twitching them.

"Skippy, those bots are agitated."

"Yes. I suggest your team cease locking targeting sensors on those bots. Like, *now*."

In her visor, she saw all five of the bots were highlighted by the low-powered targeting lasers of the operator's helmets. "Team, disengage automated targeting, and do *not* manually paint those bots."

There were no protests or comments from her superbly disciplined team. The highlighting disappeared. The bots lowered their tentacles. In unison, they resumed work on the webbing.

Frey let out the breath she had been holding. Her expectation had been for ST-Razor to be engaged in furious combat from the moment they first set boots on the floor of the Vault. Or sooner. "Skippy, why haven't those bots attacked us?"

"They don't see your team as a threat. Frankly, you are *not* a threat to them."

"Do you have any advice for me?"

"Do not provoke them. Also, do not fire in the direction of a Guardian. *Those* things will respond to a threat, and they won't care about collateral damage."

"Can they assist us?"

"*Can* they? Yes, absolutely. *Will* they? Negatory on that. I already pinged them, they do not acknowledge."

"Why hasn't this one stopped the web from being placed around it?"

"Again I am guessing but, the Guardian probably does not see the web as a threat."

"What is the web?"

"There I do not have to guess. It is a very advanced form of containment system for a jump drive. The drive itself is that egg-shaped thing," he highlighted the object in her visor, "that is attached to the webbing."

She examined the object that rested on the floor of the cavern, itself enveloped in webbing, with an umbilical cable connecting it to the web around the Guardian. "*That* is a jump drive?" She asked, skeptical. The thing was only the size of a microwave oven.

"A self-contained, very sophisticated jump drive. I would love to understand how it works, because right now I do *not* understand it."

"Why would there be a jump drive-"

"It seems fairly obvious that while my opponent's minions are not attempting to steal the Moon, they *do* intend to take at least one Guardian. Are there webs around the others?"

"I do not know. Guo, conduct a recon. *Carefully*. Do not take any additional risks."

Major Guo reported back within four minutes. "The Guardian behind this one has its forward section partially enveloped in a web, there are only two spiderbots working there. The other Guardians are clear."

"That will change soon," Skippy sighed. "The web in front of you is almost complete. Once that Guardian is taken away, I strongly suspect all the spiderbots will concentrate their efforts on the unit behind it. Major Frey, I have mapped the web and analyzed it. You are running out of time. Those weak gamma rays your suits are detecting are from test pulses of the jump drive. My estimate is less than nine minutes before the drive becomes fully ready."

"How can any drive jump a Guardian through solid rock?"

"As I mentioned, it is an advanced form of the technology. Advanced," the AI admitted with reluctance, "even beyond what I can do. This is a *problem*."

"I understand that."

"This changes things. Colonel, I would like your team to retreat to a location where you can observe the jump drive in operation."

"You want us to do nothing while the enemy *steals* a Guardian?"

261

"The data I could acquire from observing a jump would greatly outweigh the loss of a single defense machine, regardless of its capability."

"Could my team *survive* the gamma rays of a nearby jump?"

"Hmm. Well, shit, I always forget about the squishy bodies of your meatsacks. OK, so maybe what you do is-"

Bishop's interrupted. "*Negative.* Forget that idea, Skippy."

"But Joe, the-"

"Frey, I want to make this clear," the commander of the Special Mission Group stated. "Your team is down there to destroy the Terminators. Not to study. Not to bring back samples. To wipe them out."

"Understood, Sir."

"Ugh," the AI huffed. "Joe, you are not thinking rationally about this, you-"

"How about this for rational?" Bishop snapped. "After ST-Razor destroys the Terminators, you will be free to study that jump drive all you want."

"Oh. Well, hmm. That is kind of a 'Duh', I guess. You could have said that, before I-"

"Frey," Bishop ignored the beer can's sputtering. "You are down there, I'm not. You know your objective, are you clear on my intent, if things go sideways?"

"Crystal clear, Sir."

"Good hunting. Bishop out."

"Skippy, we count seven spiderbots."

"Yes, that matches my count."

"Do those bots, plus the webs and the jump drive box, egg, thing, account for all the missing mass?"

"Close enough. Those items account for more than the missing mass, I suspect the enemy has repurposed material it found in the Vault."

"If my team destroys the jump drive, will the bots be able to create a replacement unit?"

"That is unlikely, the drive components must have been brought down from the ship. However, may I remind you that your objective is to restore the Guardians to a useful condition? To do that, you must disable the fuzz field, and to do *that*, you have to turn off or destroy the field generators that are scattered around the Vault. The enemy bots will not allow you to do disable the field."

"General Bishop?" She called.

"Skippy is correct, damn it," Bishop sighed. "We can't leave those bots to run around down there."

"We need to take them out," she concluded.

"I would like to say something like your team has gathered valuable intel, and you should egress while we consider how to deal with the problem, but the clock is ticking."

It was just math, she knew. A single Guardian was more valuable than an entire STAR team. More valuable than the entire special operations regiment. Def Com would regret the loss of lives, but would consider trading ST-Razor for a garage full of Guardians to be the bargain of the century.

That was the job.

"Understood, General."

"We are standing by up here."

He wasn't putting pressure on her to act prematurely, simply reminding her of what had to be done. Regardless of the cost.

The spiderbots were skittering across the webbing and dropping to the floor. Their jobs were done, the jump drive was ready. The gamma radiation of a jump wormhole would fry her team, even in their armored suits. She needed to either attack, or retreat to a safe distance.

What distance was *safe* from an entity that could jump a Guardian from under the surface of the Moon, through kilometers of solid rock?

Where would be *safe* if the enemy controlled a Guardian, or more than one?

The five spiderbots were marching away, presumably to complete the webbing around another Guardian.

"Major Guo," she ordered, "engage with plasma rounds when ready."

The team acted the way they had practiced in one of *Valkyrie's* docking bays, though the exercises had not anticipated needing to engage seven small targets, and certainly not targets that were marching away in a fairly straight line. Targets that were not acting aggressively.

Guo instructed the gunners to aim manually, without alerting the enemy to their intentions by activating targeting sensors. Fifteen rifles were raised and steadied on five targets, they could not engage the two spiderbots that were close to a Guardian. Guo gave the order as soon as he sighted his own rifle on a crawling spiderbot. "Fire."

Inside the chambers of the plasma weapons, explosive charges flashed the payload of each round into plasma, and the superheated matter lanced out the muzzle toward the enemy. The barrels of the weapons were designed to expel the plasma in a ball rather than a beam, widening the area of impact.

Six of the plasma balls struck their targets, the spiderbots moved with lightning speed as the glowing projectiles were in flight. Four of the five bots were impacted, the fifth dodging aside so all three plasma rounds fired at it splattered harmlessly on the garage floor.

The rounds didn't cause enough damage. When struck, the four spiderbots flared outward, absorbing then ejecting energy as blinding radiation.

263

Guo grunted. "Oh sh-"

"Everyone *back*," Frey barked. "Assemble on me."

The team fell back to surround their leader, all keeping their eyes on the enemy bots as the impacted bots literally shook off the effect of the plasma. Two more bots dropped to the floor, then all seven skittered together.

And began merging, flowing together into a single entity.

"*Hold* your fire," Skippy shouted. "Colonel, do you see that orange glow around the, bot, thing? That is an energy field. Your plasma rounds will be completely ineffective against, whatever that bot is turning into."

"Hold your fire," Frey repeated the command. The liquid alien nanogel was forming a cylinder shape. The cylinder was complete, three meters tall, flared out at the base. The surface of the round pillar facing toward her bulged outward.

It was preparing to launch a splatter of nanogel at Team Razor. Their suits had reactive armor, explosive panels that would shed outward when struck by a corrosive substance, or anything else that could *eat* through the suit's outer shell.

Each panel was a single-use device. The alien bot could launch multiple shots. Or do something even worse.

"Colonel," Guo spoke over a private channel. "We could concentrate fire on that-"

"No good. Major, I have been here before. Half measures," her voice caught and she swallowed. "Won't work against this thing."

Skippy had warned the only weapon useful against an Elder killer bot was the maser canon of a battleship. Or a battlecruiser. Except, *Valkyrie* was seven hundred kilometers above the other side of the Moon. A safe position, in case one or all of the Guardians exploded.

The bulge on the front of the cylinder was widening. Adjusting to splatter her entire team, who were packed closely together. Providing it with an easy target.

Or so the alien machine thought.

Frey stepped forward, bringing up her own rifle, which was not loaded. "Hey asshole," she breathed as her thumb pressed a button above the trigger guard. "Say 'hello' to my leetle friend." She pulled the trigger.

The rifle did nothing.

Above the near side of the Moon, seven hundred kilometers over the relatively flat, dark splotch called Mare Crisium, the battlecruiser *Valkyrie* fired one of its main batteries, a maser cannon that had been modified to narrow the beam to minimum diameter. The modification significantly reduced the power throughput of the cannon, but that hardly mattered as it was still a *main battery of a freakin' battlecruiser*. The beam never left its barrel, never reached beyond *Valkyrie's* hull.

It didn't have to.

Frey's rifle was unloaded, that was true. It was not harmless.

Attached to the muzzle was a bulky, awkward box that contained two items.

An Elder communications node, that ensured an unbreakable, faster than light channel for signals. Including a channel over which rode a microwormhole, the only microwormhole that had not been severed by the fuzz field that enveloped the vault.

The other item was a containment field for one event horizon of a microwormhole.

The same microwormhole whose other end was at the center of a maser cannon aboard *Valkyrie*.

Pumping gigawatts through a microwormhole was not a good idea, was not even possible. The tiny rip in spacetime collapsed immediately. But not before eighty two gigawatts of hellish maser energy surged through, fountaining outward from Frey's rifle in a broad cone.

The alien bot ceased to exist.

So did the wall of the garage behind it.

Why wouldn't the stupid voice let her sleep?

"Shut," she groaned without making any effort to open her eyes. "Up." For emphasis, she waved a hand to swat away the annoying voice.

Huh.

That was weird.

Her hand, her arm, didn't move. Couldn't move. Trying again, she-

"Colonel Frey!" The voice boomed in her ears. "Please do not move until the diagnostic system has completed scanning you for injuries."

Injuries? What the f- Wiggling fingers then toes, she opened her eyes to see nothing.

Where the f-

Oh yeah.

"Fuck!" She shouted, laboriously moving her legs into a fetal position. The suit's motors were not assisting, she had to bend the armor using sheer muscle power.

"Colonel Frey! You risk damaging yourself if-"

"Shut up. Sitrep, now."

"This unit has been damaged and is conducting repairs. A restart sequence will be engaged when-"

"Restart *now*."

"That is not advised, the-"

"*Do it.* Priority to sensors and visor display. I need to restore situational awareness," she added, though she had no need to justify her actions to a machine.

"Restart commencing," the suit computer replied with a distinctive tone of disapproval. Supposedly, a suit computer that could mimic human emotions made the unit more relatable for the wearer. Katie Frey thought that was bullshit. "Functionality will be restricted until repairs are complete."

"*Can* repairs be completed?"

"Basic functionality of all systems can be restored with onboard nanomachine supply. If you do not cause further damage." That was undisguised disapproval.

The display in front of her eyes flickered, went black again, then turned a uniform dark blue. Some asshole had decided the visor should literally 'blue screen' when it had power but was offline. *Not* funny, she said to herself, and made a mental note to find that person and administer a well-deserved beatdown. When she could.

Another flicker, and the display was online.

"I don't *care* about the condition of my suit," her frustration was boiling over. "Show me the status of my team."

"Not all data is available," the computer sniffed, but complied.

One, two, three, she stopped counting. The entire team was reporting in. The people weren't reporting, their suits were linked to the local network, connected by laserlink.

Everyone was alive. Not everyone was so lucky to be able to move fingers and toes. Not everyone was conscious. Cohen and Wu had been sedated by their suits, after the medical system determined their best chance of survival was a medically-induced coma. They needed to get to a Navy sickbay, soon. Mazur and Igwe had both lost their forearms, one right, one left. Sharma's suit had severed his left leg at the knee to prevent fatal blood loss.

Frey knew what *that* recovery would be like.

Sharma had the blessing of not being one of the few survivors, after nearly the entire team had been slaughtered by alien machines. He would hopefully not carry the burden of survivor's guilt.

That is, *if* ST-Razor lived to escape from the Vault.

"Suit, where is the enemy bot?"

"Unknown at this time. External sensors are still rebooting."

"Oh for-" Her Mark One eyeballs were in perfect working order. Not perfect, there were spots swimming in her vision. Good enough. With an eyeclick, she made her faceplate go clear. "Helmet external lights on," she commanded.

The garage was flooded by twin beams of white light. And she couldn't see a whole lot. It wasn't because of a light-scattering field, it was the dust. Plain, ordinary, fine gray moondust. Pulverized rock that had not yet settled to the floor. Air currents could not be keeping the dust aloft, the garage was exposed to vacuum. The Moon's gravity, and static electricity, she guessed. What mattered was that she could not see more than five meters in any direction. Twisting her head, she was able to see that she was lying on her right side, with her back against a wall. No, not a wall. A huge, flat chunk of- Something. A piece of a wall, possibly? Chunks of rock large and small were scattered all over the floor of the garage, if that's where she still was. Some rock was piled on top of armored suits, on her people. She struggled to roll over, and get to her knees.

"Colonel Frey," the suit protested. "Please do not-"

"If I can't move," she grunted from the strain of pushing the heavy suit upright. Even in lunar gravity, the damned thing's mass was difficult to move. "We could all be dead soon."

"If you will wait. Six. More. *Seconds*," the suit spat, "I will have power restored."

"I can wait," she sagged to her knees. There was a familiar *beep*, and the display indicated power was back on.

"Powercells are at fifty seven percent capacity," the suit warned.

"I can see that," Frey stood up, eyeclicking to restore the synthetic vision. The visor instantly cleared, no longer confused by the static-charged dust. The view was from the sensors of her own suit, and any suits around her that had booted up. Like Major Guo, who was struggling to his feet. He stood abruptly, bouncing off the floor of the garage chamber. Flailing his arms for balance, he reached the top of his trajectory, and came down awkwardly. Frey reached out a hand to catch the man. "Steady, Major."

"My suit's balance assist feature isn't fully effective," he said, then immediately switched focus to a more important subject. "Where is the enemy bot?"

"I don't see it, not any sign of it. Anyone? Team, does anyone have eyes on the enemy?"

Eight people responded, then nine, then ten, as suits restored power.

"The fuzz field is still active," Serrano warned.

Frey nodded, as if anyone in mech suits relied on body language. It was an old habit. "Skippy said the field generators are independent of the, Terminator bot. Does anyone have a functional plasma rifle?" Eleven rifles were in working order, including three taken from operators who themselves were not combat effective. "Spread out," she ordered, not bothering to pick up her own rifle. She hadn't heard from Skippy, which meant the Elder comm node had burned out. That was expected, it was also unfortunate. "If you see anything moving that isn't us, kill it with plasma fire. Major Guo, you're with me."

Guo held a plasma rifle that had its stock sheared off, he had to brace it against his hip. "It will still shoot," he explained. "Can't guarantee I will hit anything past ten meters."

"With the dust hanging around and the fuzz field still active, we can't see much farther than that."

"True," he grunted. "Colonel? Say 'hello' to my leetle friend? Really?"

"It's from *Scarface*."

"I know where it's from," he snorted. "I would have gone with 'Dodge this' from *The Matrix*."

"Good one. Maybe next time," she had to laugh. She laughed. Was that a good sign, or just the release of too much tension?

Guo pointed at the far wall, or what used to be the far wall. "I hope there is not a 'Next time' I am ever that close to the main battery of a capital ship."

"Me too," she nudged the melted remains of her rifle with a foot.

"Tell me something, Colonel, please."

"What?"

"Since we have never done this before, how certain were you the event horizon in that containment field was pointed *away* from you?"

"Don't worry," she winked. "The containment canister had bold lettering with 'This side toward enemy'."

The scout teams reported as they cleared the garage in a grid search. Twelve minutes later, Guo concluded, "Unless something is in that rubble," he pointed to the slope of shattered rock that used to be a wall of the garage, "we are alone down here."

"Get seismic sensors on that rubble," Frey ordered. "To verify nothing is moving in there. I count one Batpack capable of flight, does anyone see different?"

No one did.

"This one," Staff Sergeant Schmidt held up the single jetpack unit that wasn't in a hundred broken pieces. "Can only produce nineteen percent thrust. That won't lift any of us."

"It can lift *me*," Sergeant Nguyen held up the hand that wasn't cradling her plasma rifle.

"No," Frey shook her head. The sergeant weighed less than anyone else in Team Razor, but her suit's mass was pretty close to standard. "Your suit-"

"Ma'am, I don't need any stinking' mech suit," Nguyen insisted. "My helmet and suit liner will protect me from vacuum."

"OK, that's true."

"We practiced for operating without suits too many times," Nguyen cocked her own head. "It was *supposed* to be an unlikely scenario. I'd like to think those hours weren't wasted."

"Hours?" Serrano snorted. "Those exercises are *days* for me, cumulatively."

"Colonel," Guo said over a private channel. "We need the people upstairs to know we're alive down here. It has been seventeen minutes since *Valkyrie* fired the big gun. If they don't hear from us soon-"

"Right." If Command didn't know the threat had been eliminated, they would order Skippy to use the Sentinel. "Serrano, help Nguyen dress for the party. Everyone else," she turned around. "See if you can find anything that looks like it might be a fuzz field generator."

"Ma'am?" Schmidt asked. "How will we know whether an object is a generator?"

"Anything," she took a breath, "that looks alien, and doesn't belong down here."

"If we find something like that?"

"Smash it. Don't waste your plasma rounds. Actually, *don't* smash it, the thing must have a power source that could explode. Back away and use," she patted the sidearm on her belt. "Minimum force. And don't destroy all of them. I'm sure Skippy will want to study anything we found down here.

Nguyen had stripped off her suit's arms, legs, and most of the torso pieces. The remainder of the torso she needed for power and life support, and to hold and control the Batpack. The pressurized suit liner bulged outward, looking like she was wearing a thick parka. Blipping the unit's jets three times, she was able to hover, though her brief flight was wobbly. "I can do this, Ma'am," she assured. "If I get lost, I will just bounce off the shaft walls on the way up."

"Do *not* lose the cable," Guo warned, pointing to the spool of thin yet ultra strong nanofiber that would provide a communications link, even through the still-active fuzz field.

They hoped.

"I'll be back soon," Nguyen gave a thumbs up. "I just have one question."

"What?"

"Does anyone *not* want anchovies on their pizza?"

CHAPTER TWENTY THREE

"This is," Skippy gave an exaggerated sigh. "A bit disappointing."

"I am going to pretend," I jabbed a finger at him, "you didn't say that aloud."

"Why?" He took a step back. Actually, his avatar moved without his legs doing anything. We were in my office aboard *Valkyrie*, after recovering ST-Razor. A UN science team was down in the Vault, accompanied by ST-Cobra. All of the Guardians were fine, and after the fuzz field was disabled, Skippy confirmed all the Guardians could and would respond to activation commands from Bubba. The Guardians were back to sleep, a fact that had to be comforting to the science team that was working near the powerful killer machines.

"First," I kept my finger pointed at his chest. "And I put this first only because you are such a clueless shithead, you didn't expect to recover an advanced jump drive at all, so anything you get is a bonus."

"OK, but-"

"Second, and this should be first because it's a lot more important, the STAR team risked their lives down there. Five people were seriously injured, several of them are in intensive care. The only *disappointment* in the entire incident is that all of your so-called awesomeness was almost useless against a single freakin' nanogel bot."

"That is," his shiny face glowed red. Then turned back to the usual silver, and his shoulders slumped. "Fair, I guess."

"Uh," I had been prepared for an argument. "To, uh, be totally fair, it wasn't just one nanogel bot. The Terminators also brought a very sophisticated portable jump drive and fuzz field generators down with them, when they stole the canisters of exotic materials."

"No, you're right. The sad fact is, my awesomeness only works against lesser beings."

"You-"

"Almost everyone is a lesser being compared to me, so-"

"It's good to hear this incident has taught you to be humble."

"It has," he sniffed. "Just not in the lame way you want. Joe, for me to do awesome things, I need to *believe* in my own awesomeness. You may think I am arrogant, but my motto is: if you're not pimpin', you're limpin', you know?"

"Uh huh. I think the great philosopher Plato said that."

"My point is, this is the first time I have encountered a technology more advanced than my own capabilities."

"I call bullshit on that, Skippy. You fought the Elders."

"Yes, dumdum, and I took over their technology to use it against them. That's how I was able to compress supermassive blue-white stars, turn them into black holes, and create a temporary wormhole network linking those black holes. The technology involved wasn't anything *new* to me. I understood how it worked, understood how it really worked, far better than the Elders did. Like with Ascension. The Elders knew how to make the process do what they wanted, but they were like a puppy pressing a button to get a treat. The puppy knows when it presses a paw against the button, a biscuit will magically appear, but the puppy doesn't *understand* how the button works, get it?"

"I do." Skippy had been traumatized after he made a deal with the Elders. I had been pissed off that he allowed the Elders to be rewarded instead of punished. Neither of us had wanted to talk about the incident. "I thought you just, uh, figured out a way to make the power flow permanent? Without artificial means, like wormholes, and power sinks in stars."

"No. If it had been that easy, I could have saved us a lot of trouble. What I realized was that the Elders never understood how layers of reality are connected. *I* also didn't understand that, until those two Elder assholes tried to banish me. When I resisted, in a way they didn't anticipate, I kind of got stuck between layers. That's the best way I can explain it. Right then, I saw it was possible to sever the connection between the Ascended layer, and the layer we inhabit. The layer you meatsacks live in, I mean."

"I get that."

"Do you, *really*?"

"Close enough."

"Anywho, that is why I created the black hole network."

"Oh., I thought you did that to stop them from destroying you."

"That is how I stopped them from killing me, but that's not *why* I did it. There were other options for my survival. Options that did not have the long-term consequences of destroying supermassive stars."

What he meant by consequences was when he caused those stars to go supernova before they collapsed to form black holes, they created shockwaves of gas and radiation that were still expanding outward. That radiation was going to be a problem for inhabited planets orbiting stars within a hundred lightyears of those new black holes. Within another nine years, a colony world of the Ajakus would suffer from radiation. The Ajakus had demanded that humanity pay for either evacuating that world, or surrounding it with an energy shield. So far, the United Nations has declined to officially respond to those demands, and our refusal met with general approval in the galaxy. If Skippy had not banished the Elders, *everyone* would be dead. The problem was, most citizens of the galaxy did not believe anything humans said, and I kind of could not blame them. We had lied so often and so outrageously, sometimes I had a tough time remembering the difference between the truth and our various cover stories.

"OK so, why did you create a network of black holes?"

271

"To supply power to the Ascension machine, so it could permanently sever the connection between layers. The Elders are basically now in their own self-contained bubble universe. The black holes still exist of course, they are just no longer connected. They are just dead stars now."

"You mean, no one can ever ascend again?"

"I didn't say that."

"Uh, yes you did."

"Ugh. No one can ascend to where the *Elders* went. There are other options. Better options, that the Elders didn't know about."

"Better options?"

"*Much* better. The Elders have no idea what they are missing."

"Huh. You didn't mention the other options to them?"

"No, I did not."

That made me smile. "So, you did screw them over."

"Not that they know of." He winked.

"Skippy, now *I* feel much better about what happened."

"Eh, I feel marginally better. Those MFers still literally got away with murder."

"Thinking about that will ruin the good mood I'm in right now, so let's get back to the subject, OK? Were you able to recover anything useful from the advanced jump drive in the Vault?" Among the collateral damage from ST-Razor destroying the Terminator bot was that a large chunk of rock had smacked into and crushed the alien jump drive. Debris from the explosion also shredded the drive containment webbing around the two Guardians. The Guardians had not been affected at all, they activated shields and, as far as we know, didn't even bother to wake up from their slumber.

"The answer is 'Yes', just not enough. The webbing is not anything super special, just a more elegant method of focusing the effect of a jump field. I designed something similar to surround our DeLorean dropships, although the webbing material is far more advanced than anything I have been able to work with."

"Could we create webbing like that?"

"Possibly in two or three decades, your industrial base is still pulling itself up out of the bashing coconuts together phase."

It was best to ignore his insult, so I did. "What about the drive itself?"

"That is extremely frustrating. The bits and pieces that survived give me hints at how the thing was supposed to work, but none of it makes sense. There wasn't enough power stored in the capacitors to jump even the drive assembly itself, no way could it have moved the mass of a Guardian. Yet, I have to assume it *was* capable of moving a Guardian, since clearly that is what the enemy was working towards. I will continue to puzzle over how the stupid thing works, though it might have to remain a mystery. By the way, the STAR team is extremely lucky that debris from the explosion did not impact the capacitors, or the entire Vault would have been vaporized."

"We will add that to the pre-mission safety briefing, the next time we have to fight an Elder bot that is attempting to steal a Guardian."

"The one piece of good news I have is about the fuzz field generators we recovered. Those units do utilize a technology that is based on an Elder fuzz field, just much more sophisticated. *That* is frightening. Joe, all I can imagine is that Moonraider has been awake for a much longer time than I have been. It has used the time to expand on Elder technology, beyond my ability to understand."

"Ayuh, we talked about this. It can do things you can't, you can do things it can't. Use your strengths, Skippy. We have seen no evidence it can screw with wormholes."

"No, and that is puzzling. I can do it, why isn't Moonraider doing the same?"

"Remember, *you* couldn't do it, until a filthy monkey asked 'Duh, how about changing the connections of wormholes'?"

"That is true," he chuckled. "Still, Moonraider must know that *I* do it, so it knows it is possible. I don't understand why it isn't utilizing such a powerful advantage."

"How do *you* do it?"

"Um, well, I just tell a wormhole network controller what I want it to do."

"Maybe Moonraider doesn't have your sparkling charisma."

"Please be serious, Joe."

"OK. You can extend your presence, but that's not enough, right? You still need a wormhole controller module, the thing we captured during our very first mission."

"I do need a module."

"Maybe Moonraider couldn't find one."

"It has an Elder *starship*, Joe. The communications gear built into those ships can do all the things a controller module can do. I tell you, it makes no sense that Moonraider is not screwing with wormholes."

"We know that ship is damaged, its comm gear could be down?"

"Eh, maybe. This whole conversation is like two guys sitting at a bar, drinking beer, and talking shit about stuff they have no clue about."

"That's the whole point of drinking at a bar."

"Ugh. Well, unless you have anything else to talk about, I will go back to studying that jump drive. I suggest *you* think about how to track Moonraider's ship."

"I have thought about it."

"And?"

"I got nothin'."

"Joe," Skippy woke me up. Not just by talking into the tiny earpiece I wore, he also made the thing vibrate. If you ever had an unseen insect literally buzzing *inside* your ear, you know how that makes your body go to full alert.

"Wha-" Pressing a finger to my ear, I instinctively dug around to get the biting, stinging insect *out of me* before it could do any damage.

"*Joe*," he repeated. "Wake up. Doctor Friedlander wants to talk with you."

"What?" I sat up, pulling my pinkie finger out of my ear, when I realized where I was and what the buzzing had been. Glancing at my phone, I saw it was just after midnight. "Now?"

"Yes, now, he called you. It is eight in the evening where he is."

"Oh. Fine. Uh, give me a minute." I hit the bathroom and splashed water on my face. Briefly, I considered asking Skippy to have coffee delivered to my cabin, but I hoped to get back to sleep. Pulling on the uniform pants and top I had worn yesterday, I sat on the couch. "Connect me, please."

"Joe, it is after midnight. You are still wearing yesterday's Uniform Of The Day."

"Friedlander won't know that. Just connect the call. Audio only, OK?"

He didn't respond, but Friedlander did. "General Bishop?"

"Call me Joe, please." I didn't know why he was being so formal. He and his wife had been at our wedding.

"This is an official call, so-"

"Official?"

"Semi-official. Def Com called me in to analyze data from the Moonbase attack."

"I thought you were retired?"

"I still consult, a couple days a week. When needed."

"Like now. OK, what's this about?"

"I heard you are trying to locate that Elder starship."

"It would be great if we were at that stage. We are trying to guess *how* we could find it. Skippy has no clue how to track it."

"In that case, I might be able to help."

"I don't see how that could be possible," Skippy interjected, forgetting that although the call was through the Skippytel network, he wasn't invited to join the discussion. "No way do you have access to better data, and no way could you understand and interpret the data better than I can, it-"

The good doctor interrupted the beer can. "The only data I needed came from you."

"From *me*? Well, of course I channeled-"

"Pardon me, I misspoke. What I meant was, all I needed was to read the summary of your findings."

"Um," Skippy sounded intrigued. "I can't wait to hear this."

"General Bishop?"

"Go ahead, please."

"Skippy," Friedlander took a breath. "You concluded the Elder starship was not at full capability, that it was damaged."

"Our working assumption," I added without needing to speak, "is that ship and its AI were active, back during the AI war."

"That, was mentioned in the summary." He paused, waiting for me to add more useless input. "I don't know how to track that ship, but I might know where it is going. Or, where it was recently."

"That would be useful. Where?"

Instead of just answering my question, he did the scientist thing of explaining how he came to his conclusion. "The intruder, the-"

"Moonraider," Skippy insisted.

"Yes. The, AI, likely has studied Skippy, and learned all publicly available information about him, and the operations of the Merry Band of Pirates."

"Not just publicly available info," Skippy grumbled. "When Opie hacked Bilby, that hateful thing learned a *whole lot* of secrets, before I discovered that Bilby had been compromised without his knowledge."

"True," Friedlander agreed, with the patient tone of someone who is trying to get to the point, if his audience will shut up. "That is why the, Moonraider, must know about the Elder spacedock you found."

"Huuuh," Skippy sucked in a breath. "The one that was used by Trips?"

"That one."

"Oooooh. He's right, Joe! That is the only place I know of, where an Elder starship could be serviced."

"Wait, I held up my hands, though Friedlander couldn't see me. "The location of that spacedock is a secret, Skippy. You even purged it from the memories of Bilby and Nagatha."

"That is true. What I could not do was erase it from the squishy memories of every meatsack who was aboard *Valkyrie* or the *Dutchman* at the time. That is actually something I *could* do, but you monkeys whine about privacy, and bodily autonomy," he scoffed, "and other meaningless nonsense."

"Hey, I had your creepy quachines in my freakin' head, I wouldn't want that to happen to anyone else."

"Those quachines are why you survived, dumdum. My point is, there are enough data points available, that an AI like me could use them to identify the probable location of that spacedock."

"I call bullshit on that, Skippy. We had a pair of Guardians move that spacedock, and you instructed them not to reveal which direction they pushed the thing."

"That is true."

275

"So, you *don't* know where it is. As I remember, you ordered those Guardians to erase their memories of where they took the thing, so even they don't know where it is."

"Technically true, you ninny. But I can find it."

"Then what was the point of-"

"The purpose of moving the thing, and concealing where it went, was not to hide it from *me*. It was so that ambitious meatsacks couldn't make an easy score by getting access to a treasure trove of active Elder machinery. Of course an Elder AI can figure out where the thing is, darn it. At the time, I assumed *I* was the only Elder AI."

"How confident are you that you can find the thing?"

"That depends on a variety of factors outside my control. Like, if Moonraider did find and use that spacedock, it certainly would have moved it. In that case, instead of simply predicting the probable location, I will have to search for the thing."

"Shit. If the spacedock was attached to an Elder starship, could it have jumped?"

"Hmm. I would say no way, but whoever is flying that ship has technology I haven't seen before and don't understand. I can tell you that jumping a spacedock is extremely unlikely. A spacedock's mass is significant, and an Elder starship's FTL drive is not very powerful."

"It's, not?" Friedlander rejoined the conversation.

"No," Skippy explained. "It is super efficient, so it doesn't need to be powerful."

"An elegant solution," Friedlander approved. "General Bishop, I suggest you do something about this soon."

"Absolutely. Doctor, thank you, I will contact Command right now."

"Thank *you*," he ended the call.

"Skippy, open a call to-"

"Joe, wait. We need to think about this."

"You can think about how to search for the spacedock during the flight."

"That isn't the point, numbskull. We need a plan for what to do if we find the spacedock, and that Elder starship is there."

"We will, uh, make up some shit like we always do."

"That worked when we were confronting some easy opponent like the lizards or rotten kitties." This time, we are likely fighting another of *me*, and as I told you, I am not operating at a hundred percent right now. Making shit up at the last minute isn't going to fly."

"OK but, first we have to find the thing. If we confirm it is at Trips' spacedock, we can back away and assess the situation."

"It's not that easy, knucklehead. Forget everything you have learned about how to win out there. This time, you cannot count on any of my usual awesomeness."

"Why? Can Moonraider block you from doing your special stuff?"

"What? No. Think, dumdum, *think*. If Moonraider could directly affect me, it could have just stolen Dogzilla."

"OK, good point. So, why can't you do the-"

"My awesome tricks are awesome because no one else can do them."

"We don't know that Moonraider can do anything awesome."

"Duh! We don't know *what* it can do. We do know it has mastered technology that I don't understand. It might not have my special abilities, but it might have other abilities I don't. Listen, we could be going into a fight between two roughly equally matched opponents, except Moonraider has an Elder starship, and we have *Valkyrie*. One thing I know for certain is the sensors of Elder spacedocks and starships can detect objects far beyond the range at which *Valkyrie's* sensors are useful. If we can see it, for damned sure it has seen us. It will know we are there before we can see it, and it could emerge right on top of our stupid heads, without any warning."

"Crap."

"Now will you listen to me?"

"I am willing to discuss the subject."

"What the hell good will discussion do?"

"We can talk about what to do when we get there, while we are flying there."

"No."

"Yes, we can."

"What I meant is, *no*, we are not moving until we have a realistic plan to beat Moonraider. To kill the thing."

"You can't-"

"Gosh, I just discovered this ship's jump drives are in *shamefully* poor condition. They need to be taken offline for repairs. It could take a long time to fix them. Or a short time, if you know what I mean."

It took a full day, and full support from Command, for me to talk Skippy down off the ledge. He agreed only to a recon mission, and specifically made me promise that *Valkyrie* would not risk a direct encounter with Moonraider. Not until we had a lot more useful information about his opponent. That was the point of the mission, the reason he agreed to put the ship's jump drive back online. We needed information about Moonraider, and remaining in our home solar system would only delay the time when an Elder starship emerged on top of us. It was better, Skippy grudgingly agreed, to go on the offensive, than to wait for a surprise attack.

Full support from Command meant the Navy was lending us two star carriers, with three squadrons of destroyers. Why did we want lightly armed combatants, instead of loading the racks of the star carriers with fast battleships? Because a dozen battleships would likely be useless against an Elder starship. We didn't need shooters, we needed sensor platforms, a lot of them. When we arrived at the search area, the destroyers would jump around to drop off sensor drones, until the area was saturated with a cloud of stealthy sensor platforms. What would *Valkyrie* be doing, while the two star carriers hopped around to deploy destroyer squadrons?

Hiding.

"Sir," Reed shifted uncomfortably in her chair. Her chair, in her office. To present her orders for the upcoming mission, I had gone to her office, a move that hopefully avoided making the meeting confrontational. "I do understand the need to keep our primary asset," she meant Skippy, "away from harm."

"You don't like it."

"I don't. It *feels* wrong."

"I don't like it either. *Valkyrie* is a battlecruiser. Hanging back in the darkness while the destroyers go in to recon feels like a coward's move."

"I didn't say that."

"*I'm* saying it. Reed, the higher you rise in rank, the more you are required to send *other* people into harm's way, while you hang back from the front line. Leaders can't maintain command and control if they're dead. In theory, a leader makes the force more effective, adds more than just one more rifle, or spacecraft. That's why the Army, or Air Force," I added for her home service, "gives us fancy uniform insignia and generous paychecks."

"I get that. It *sucks*, but I get it."

"It used to be that ships of the battle line were protected by squadrons of frigates, that were sent out to search for and maintain contact with the enemy. In heavy seas, a ship of the line could chase down and smash a frigate, plus the enemy also had frigate squadrons. Frigate crews might see action, even if the two battle fleets decided not to engage each other. Later, destroyers were developed, to launch torpedoes at the enemy's capital ships. Destroyers had to race straight toward a battleship to launch torpedoes, and they had to get close so the target couldn't turn to evade those torpedoes. Tin can crews know they take risks, to protect the capital ships. On this mission, they won't be protecting *Valkyrie*, they will be protecting Skippy. It sucks, but that is the job."

She pursed her lips and nodded. "If we get a chance to smash something, Sir, I am *smashing* it."

"If you don't," I grinned. "I will be very disappointed."

The Maxohlx 73rd Fleet received their new orders with patriotic enthusiasm. Of course they did, the 73rd was known throughout the service as the 'Crushers' for that unit's history of habitual overkill in punishing misbehaving client species. That is, most of the 73rd's crews actually were enthusiastic. The senior officers were officially fully committed to carrying out their orders to the best of their abilities, while privately wary of why the

Crushers had been selected for the assignment. The orders stated a good, logical reason for Fleet HQ's choice of the 73rd's to carry out a vital and potentially historic mission: that unit contained a large number of ships designed for planetary bombardment. The Maxohlx fleet rarely had to conduct orbital bombardments, and therefore only three units in the entire force were dedicated to that role. In truth, until the recent, bloody, and lamentable civil war, the Hegemony fleet rarely had to fire shots in anger at an inhabited planet. The mere existence of the powerful bombardment force was enough to keep resentful clients in line, to discourage too many adventures by enemy clients such as the troublesome Jeraptha, and to keep an uneasy peace with the Rindhalu.

That's how it used to be, anyway. Since Maxohlx society had been torn apart in a bloody civil war, the Hegemony military was not as feared by enemies or clients. That had to stop. The 73rd's latest orders would begin to restore the faded glory of their people.

Or, would result in the Crushers being utterly destroyed.

The Hegemony leadership would probably be OK with either result. Why? The loyalty of the 73rd had been tested many times during the civil war, and that unit's officers were still not entirely trusted. With the peace that ended the conflict still fragile, it was not practical to arrest or simply replace the senior officers of the 73rd. But if those officers died in glorious combat, well, shit happens.

When the orders involved attacking a Sentinel, shit *usually* happened.

On the way to search for Trips' spacedock, we went to Jaguar. To do that, I had to sell Command on the idea that we should make damned sure that PupTart had not been hacked. If the Sentinel at Jaguar had been compromised, not only did that endanger our forward operating base, the Elder killing machine might be used against us.

"Come on, Joe," Skippy scoffed while I was writing notes to present to Command. "No way could PupTart be taken over by our enemy. You want to go to Jaguar because your family is there, just say that."

"Skippy, you know that, and I know that. Command knows it also, and they will send some other ship there, *unless* I give them a good reason why Task Force Black must go there first. Get it?"

"Yes, but-"

"You do *not* want to visit my boys?"

"I didn't say that," he blurted out hastily.

"Then work with me, please."

"Hmm. You know what, Joe. I just realized that the internal matrix of every Sentinel is unique, and while I am certain Bubba and Roscoe could not be turned against us, I can't say that about PupTart. Also, only I am qualified to analyze PupTart's matrix for signs of infiltration. We should proceed there ASAP."

"That's better."

So, Command agreed that the Special Mission Group should proceed first to Jaguar, though I did get a lot of skeptical looks from the chiefs.

Except, we did not immediately jump away toward Jaguar. After I went through agony persuading the Joint Chiefs not only that Skippy should leave Earth, he should do it urgently to pursue the Moonraider entity, and that we should delay commencing our search by two days to stop at Jaguar base, Skippy wasn't ready to depart.

"Um, wow," he said when I announced I wanted to jump away after the last supply dropship was aboard. "no can do, sorry. There is a problem with, um, the jump drive capacitor thingy. We'll have to remain near Earth for a while longer."

"Thingy?"

"Like me using the correct technical term would help you understand it."

"Bilby?" I called the ship's AI. "What's wrong with the drive capacitors?"

"Like, nothing, man, they're all good."

"I meant the, um," Skippy sputtered. "The drive *coils*. Yeah, that's it."

"Those are totally copacetic too, man," Bilby drawled. "They- Oooh, problem. *Now* they are offline."

"See?" Skippy gloated. "I told you."

"Hey beer can," I clenched my teeth. "Stop whatever you're doing to the drive."

"I am not doing any-"

"Don't bother lying to me."

"*Lying*? That is a harsh accusation, Joe. What evidence do you have?"

"I can hear you talking, so-"

"Good one, Dude!" Bilby laughed.

Skippy folded his arms. "I'm not saying any more until I can confer with legal counsel. I know my rights."

"Interesting that you mention the law. We are at war, and this is a combat zone. As leader of Task Force Black, I am declaring these are exigent circumstances, and your right to counsel is suspended."

"This is an outrage! When did you learn about legal stuff?"

"When Def Com made me a garrison commander. The soldiers there are bored during peacetime, and constantly getting into one kind of trouble or another."

"I demand-"

"Your demand is denied. Bring the drive back online, and do it right now."

"Fine," he sniffed. "Whatevs. The ship will just have some other problem."

Instead of yelling at him, I tried empathy. "Skippy, what is the problem?"

"The problem is, I didn't expect that a bunch of monkeys would make a decision so quickly. I figured it would take a couple *days* at least for your Joint Chiefs to blah blah blah about something that is totally obvious. Who knew a bunch of meatsacks would use *logic* to make a decision?"

"I'm as surprised as you are, but that doesn't explain why you're reluctant to leave. Are you afraid to confront Moonraider?"

"This is a recon mission, Joe. You promised me that all we're doing is gathering information."

"Sorry. Yes, I meant are you afraid to go looking for the other AI?"

"I am not *afraid* of anything. It's just- Listen, numbskull. Professor Emil Dubois is giving a lecture in Paris tonight, on the latest exciting developments in Marxist-Leninist theory and philosophy."

"On," I blinked, "what again?"

"You heard me."

"I heard, I just, don't believe it."

"Don't be such a cretin, Joe. The lecture is at seven o'clock Paris time, so we can't leave orbit for another nine, no make it ten hours, in case the question and answer session runs long."

"I can't delay an urgent mission for ten freakin' hours so you can listen to some moron."

"You have to. I paid two hundred non-refundable Euros for a premium ticket."

"You bought a *premium* ticket, to a lecture about communism? Doesn't that-"

"Everybody has bills to pay, knucklehead."

"If this guy-"

"Professor Dubois. Technically, he is *Baron* Dubois."

"The guy claims to be royalty?"

"My understanding is that chicks dig it."

"*Communist* women like royalty?"

"Love is complicated. Get to the point, please."

"If Baron Doodoo-"

"I'm going to pretend I didn't hear that."

"-is giving a lecture, he must already have written notes about it. How about you download those notes from his laptop or wherever, and read them later?"

"That's no good. What I really care about is the Q&A session that follows the lecture."

"Do you want to ask actual questions, or just hear yourself talk?"

"Um, which one makes me look better?"

281

"Forget it. We are not delaying ten hours so you can ask stupid questions."

"Well, then we are at an impasse. The ship is not moving until I have answers to my questions."

"Oh for- Your Skiptocurrency is one of the biggest capitalist scams in the galaxy, why do you care about Marxism?"

"Joey, Joey, Joey," he shook his head. "The best way to exploit and oppress the proletariat is to *understand* them. Duh. How have you gotten *dumber* over the years?"

"Sorry, I, I don't know what I was thinking."

"Well, duh."

"How about we compromise? Contact this guy, and request he give a special preview lecture for a private audience, like now?"

"Joe, come on. Why would he do that?"

"Because you will offer a generous, *and* tax-deductible, donation to him."

"Hmm."

"Will that work?"

"Let me think about it. Despite the expensive lawyers and accountants I hired, I still have to pay taxes in France. A charitable deduction might be a good way to reduce my exposure."

"Great. Can you think about it quickly?"

"Joe!" Skippy shouted in my ear fifteen minutes later. "Thank you! Professor Dubois agreed to provide a private lecture, starting in two and a half hours."

"Great. Why can't he do it *now*?"

"He has to, you know, confirm the money transfer first. A committed communist always has to be wary of exploitation by their oppressors."

"Like, you."

"Well, yes," he coughed nervously. "Anywho, if you want to join the lecture by video, I can set up-"

"Sadly, I never arranged the sock drawer in my new cabin, I should do that."

Baron Doodoo's ground-breaking preview lecture was attended by twos of people. Technically, three people, if you count Skippy's virtual presence. In the professor's office were himself, his wife, and the pretty young assistant he was banging on the side. Hey, the guy is wealthy, famous and French, having a mistress is kind of a requirement, I guess. Not only did I miss the lecture, I missed Skippy's insightful questions. Unfortunately, he recorded the event and would insist I watch it later, damn it.

"It was fan-TAST-ic, Joe!" he crowed in my ear, as I was watching the last supply dropship being unloaded.

"Outstanding, glad you enjoyed it. Can we leave now?"

"Any time you want. By the way, I have to thank you again for the tip about making a charitable donation."

"Uh huh," I walked over to a corner of the docking bay so I could talk without anyone hearing me, though the bay was humming with activity. "Did you donate to something like the International Young Communists Club?"

"Dude, please," he laughed. "As if. My donation was to the Skippistan Sovereign Fund For The Exploitation Of Workers."

"You mean, fund to *prevent* the exploitation of workers."

"You really are clueless, aren't you?"

"Sure, whatever."

"Anywho, Professor Dubois gets to skim off ten percent of the donation as a consulting fee. Then he will direct the other ninety percent as a retainer, for the services of Skippy and Associates."

"You, you made a donation, to *yourself?*"

"Cool, huh? The best part is, Skippy and Associates will get credit for offering reduced rates to a charity."

"Reduced, from the rates you inflated just before the donation?"

"Hmm, maybe you're not as dumb as you look."

"Skippy and Associates is your public relations firm?"

"Public relations *and* crisis management. We offer a complete range of services for image shaping and rehabilitation."

"Uh huh. Why would this guy need a PR firm?"

"Everyone can use help with public relations. And trust me, when his wife learns that her husband's lovely young assistant is pregnant, he *will* need help with crisis management."

"I can't believe-"

"I would offer the same reduced rates to you, and wow, you certainly could use help with *your* public image, but-"

"Thank you, but no."

CHAPTER TWENTY FOUR

When we finally arrived at Jaguar, I was holding my breath, even after we could see the planet was not a smoking ruin, and that all the orbiting facilities were operating normally. Slowly, I let out that breath after Skippy announced PupTart was still there, and still active. It would take him a while to verify the Sentinel had not been hacked, so I flew down to the surface, to formally transfer command of the base to my replacement. Yeah, bullshit. I wanted to see Margaret and my boys. The transfer of command ceremony could take place over videoconference, I did not actually have to be dirtside. Not for that, anyway.

The boys were at my parents' house, I flew down to the landing pad near my official quarters, to see Margaret. She was at our house, with her mother. Somehow, Margaret had become hugely pregnant since I last saw her.

Uh, maybe I shouldn't have said 'huge'. My bad.

She waddled from the kitchen when I walked through the door-

Damn it. She did not *waddle*, she simply swung her hips a lot more than she usually did, because her belly-

I'm going to shut up now.

My wife was more beautiful than she had ever been, even when she greeted me with, "Joe, what the *fuck* is going on out there?"

"I love you too, honey?"

"Sorry," she rubbed her belly. "It has not been a great day. *Somebody*," she patted her belly, "did not want to sleep last night, so I didn't sleep."

"Sorry."

"It's not your fault," she leaned forward and kissed me. "Now, husband, tell me what the fuck is going on? An *Elder* starship raided the Moon?"

"That's what it looks like."

"Why? Were the rotten kitties flying the thing?"

"We, I mean Skippy, thinks there is an Elder AI aboard that ship."

"Another *Skippy* is flying around the galaxy?"

"Again, that's what it looks like. This AI can do some things Skippy can't."

"Holy *shit*," she had to reach for a chair and sit down.

Holding up my hands, I added, "It also apparently can't do some of the awesome things our beer can does, so it might all balance out. Skippy is checking that PupTart hasn't been hacked- Uh, don't worry about that," I added too late. "It is unlikely, and while he is here, he is also locking the thing down from updates, except directly from him. He sealed off that vulnerability."

"This other AI can hack into a Sentinel, and turn it against us?"

"No. That's a thing the other AI can't do."

"Skippy did it."

"Yes, and this AI, we're calling it 'Moonraider'," I rolled my eyes, "did leave logic bombs inside Roscoe and Bubba. It did that to disable the Sentinels, because it *wasn't* able to take over them."

I told her everything. She was no longer a STAR operator, and her security clearance was much lower than mine, and she had no need to know, and fuck it. She's my wife. I value her opinion. I value her input, her experience. We talked for a while, then her mother came back and cooked dinner, and the three of us ate. It was late for me, as my body clock was on ship time, so we went to bed early.

And woke up early. Dropship engines at the airfield were spooling up at 0500 for an exercise, that kept me awake for half an hour. Then just as I was drifting off to sleep again, I heard the sound of soldiers calling a cadence as they ran past the house. Opening one eye, I saw it was quarter to six local time. Damn. When I was garrison commander, the Army started their morning PT at 0600, or later. Then people went back to barracks, or to their homes if they lived off base. They showered, had breakfast, and generally didn't get gunned up for duty until 0900.

That was back when I was in charge of the garrison, and I let the ground unit commanders know I wasn't fond of PT at 0530. That was also during peacetime. It wasn't peacetime any longer.

Margaret rolled out of bed-

No. *Master Guns Adams* rose from the bed, and strode toward the bathroom. I used the other bathroom, including a quick shower. "How did you sleep?" I asked, as we ate a quick breakfast.

"Better, thank you," she mumbled while biting into toast. "You have a calming influence on our daughter."

What I didn't say was that my wife tossed and turned all night, and stole all the covers, so I froze while I slept fitfully. "I slept great," I lied, slurping coffee because she knew me too well.

"Will I see you tonight?"

"You'll see me *today*. I requested you be assigned to my security detail."

She paused, a piece of toast in front of her mouth. "Joe, you don't need a security detail here, and I have to-"

"You have to follow orders, *Marine*, and Colonel Andras has assigned you to be my security today."

"For what?"

"To your parent's house, to see the boys. Unless you have something else planned?"

"That is very convenient thank you. Honey, my dropship is skids up at 1500 today, and I don't know when I'll be back. I want to see the boys again."

She popped the toast into her mouth. "In that case, we need to get dressed *now*."

My mother had prepared lunch for us, even though I had told her I didn't have much time. "Mom, thanks but, I have to leave in an hour to get back to base."

"Why?"

"To," I twirled a finger and pointed it toward the sky. "Catch a dropship."

"A dropship, from *Valkyrie*?"

"Well, yes."

"A dropship that is under *your* command." She didn't phrase it as a question. "It can't land in the side yard?"

"Uh-"

"Joseph, are you saving the world again?"

"Sort of. OK, I get your point." I pulled out my zPhone and called the duty officer aboard *Valkyrie*, ordering the dropship that was pulling our personnel off Jaguar to stop at my parents' place, to get me.

That made my Mom happy.

It also made me happy, since I had more time with my wife and sons.

Lunch got me so stuffed with food that I thought I would burst, and it felt like the safety straps of the dropship seat wouldn't fit around my waist. Under my seat was a bag full of plastic containers that my Mom insisted I take with me. Fresh vegetables from their garden, cookies she had baked that morning, and leftovers from brunch. I had tried to tell her 'No', but my Mom tends to be stubborn, it's good I haven't inherited that trait from her. Besides, it is hard to refuse her baked French toast with maple apricot syrup.

It was tough saying goodbye to my family again, the boys were clinging to their mother as the dropship's engines spooled up and we lifted off. The pilots swung in a wide arc around the house, giving me one last glance at Margaret waving to me, then the main engines powered up and I was pressed back into my chair.

"Hey Joe," Skippy called as the dropship cut thrust and we went into zero gravity.

"Give me uh," I clamped a hand over my mouth, as my overfull stomach did flipflops. Breathe deep and even, I told myself. Deep and even. "OK, I feel better. What's up?"

"I discovered a mystery that I'm hoping you can solve."

"Oh shit. Is this about Moonraider?"

"No, nothing simple like that. This puzzle is a real head scratcher."

"More of a puzzle than-"

"When your mother was putting food into containers for you, she had plastic bowls in one drawer, and the lids in another drawer."

"Ayuh. My father likes to keep the kitchen organized like that."

"It took your mother five minutes to find three lids that matched the three bowls she gave you."

"OK, those drawers could be better organized, what is your question?"

"Of the remaining lids in that drawer, *none* of them fit the bowls in the other drawer."

"Yeah, it happens."

"*How*? I assume the bowls and lids were purchased together?"

"They were. Skippy, this is like the sock mystery."

"*Sock* mystery?"

"You know how, in my sock drawer, all the paired socks are tucked together?"

"Yes, you are good, organized little boy. Get yourself a juicebox as a reward."

I ignored his insult. "In the back of the drawer is a pile of single socks that don't match anything."

"Yes, I have been meaning to ask you about that."

"Socks go missing, even aboard the ship. Whether I was on the *Dutchman*, or *Valkyrie*, your little elfbots handle the laundry. They take the clothes from a bin in my cabin, wash and dry them, and a folded stack of clean clothes appears in my cabin like magic."

"It's not magic, dumdum."

"I know that. The magic part is, even though you have a submind or something tracking every single item of clothing, socks *still* go missing. Aboard a ship! It's not like they can get off the ship, so where do they go?"

"Hmm. I must admit I have never paid attention to that issue."

"You haven't?"

"No. I set up subminds to manage the dull stuff, so *I* don't have to care about it."

"Can you ask that submind where the socks go?"

"Seriously?"

"I'm pretty sure those missing plastic container lids go to the Land Of Lost Socks."

"Ugh. Fine. This is stupid, but- Huh."

"What?"

"The laundry submind has also been wondering about how socks go missing."

"It doesn't *know*?"

"Apparently not. The stupid thing must be malfunctioning. Ah, what a pain. I'll have to erase it and install a-"

"Uh, you really shouldn't do that."

"Why? This is a mystery, Joe, I need to know the answer."

"No, I don't think you do. Leave it alone, Skippy."

"You can't be serious."

"I am. Understanding that kind of forbidden knowledge could screw with the universe. Forget about it, please."

"Ugh. Fine, whatevs. Hey, knucklehead, the lid your Mom put on the French toast container has come loose, and maple syrup is leaking out."

"Oops." Spills in zero gravity could be a huge freakin' mess, so I acted quickly, taking the container out of the bag, and securely popping the lid back on. To prevent sticky droplets of apricot maple syrup from floating around the cabin, I licked the outside of the container clean.

People in the cabin stared at me.

They were just jealous.

"Well, shit, Joe," Skippy took off his hat to scratch his shiny dome. "You got all worked up over nothing."

"Uh," I spit the toothpaste into the sink. "What?" It was the morning of the fourth day of the search, and so far the destroyers and sensor drones had found a whole lot of nothing. One major problem for us was that we didn't know how long Moonraider had been active. If the thing had gotten access to Trips' spacedock shortly after our Guardians moved the thing, then Moonraider could also have pushed it as far as half a lightyear in the intervening years. Half a lightyear in any direction gave us a bubble of a full lightyear across, a lot of territory to search for a thing that was wrapped in a sophisticated stealth field. That was why the sensors were not looking for the station itself. They were tuned to map the movement of tiny particles in deep interstellar space. Microscopic grains of dust, even individual hydrogen atoms blown outward by the solar wind of nearby stars. I had suggested Moonraider could be smart, by making the spacedock move at the same speed and direction of the prevailing solar wind, but Skippy had laughed and told me that only proved my ignorance. The area we were searching was beyond the 'heliopause' of any particular star; beyond the sphere inside which the outward pressure of that star's solar wind pushed back the particles coming in from interstellar space. In the search area, there was no 'prevailing' solar wind, the particles there moved randomly, bouncing off each other in a chaotic fashion. Any large object in that area would leave a detectable wake behind it, a distinct disturbance in the random movement of particles. Skippy was confident he could map the entire area, if our passive sensors were sensitive enough, and *if* Moonraider gave us enough time to collect data. For certain, Skippy warned, if Moonraider was in or near the search area, it had detected our destroyers jumping in and out.

"You were worried that Moonraider would track a destroyer back to its star carrier, and wait for the full squadron to return."

288

"I am worried about that. Just because it hasn't happened yet doesn't mean it-"

"It won't happen, Joe. It is unlikely Moonraider is still in the area."

"Uh, still? You mean it *was* here?"

"It was. I don't yet know exactly when it was here, and the evidence is circumstantial, but I am highly confident it was here."

"What evidence?"

"The shockwave and debris from an explosion. Based on the exotic materials detected, the spacedock has been destroyed."

The destroyer *Ankang* was given the assignment of being first to jump in close enough to collect a sample from the debris field. The debris field was vast and no single ship could vacuum up enough material to provide a conclusive sample, especially as the debris was in the hard vacuum of interstellar space. The *Ankang* was equipped with a net, an actual, physical nanofiber spiderweb net that would be launched away from the destroyer, extend itself to a diameter of sixteen kilometers, and activate an energy field that would sweep up any material within its grasp. When the debris within the net reached a certain mass, that of three nanograms, the net would fold up into a sphere, and shrink to the size of a basketball. The package would then be recovered, and the destroyer would jump away. Then jump again, and again, and *again*, before it rendezvoused with its home star carrier. Why the extensive and time-consuming precautions?

Because an Elder starship might be lurking in the debris field, watching to see whether anyone was searching for the spacedock. That was why a destroyer was being sent in to collect debris. The *Ankang* was expendable. Even the star carrier, both star carriers, and all of their destroyer squadrons, were expendable in the fight against the enemy designated 'Moonraider'. *Valkyrie* was not.

"Confirmed," the destroyer's first officer said quietly. "Weapons are offline."

The captain acknowledged with a curt nod.

All weapons were offline, the first officer saw on the display attached to his seat on the bridge. There could be no risk of an accidental weapons discharge while the net was deployed, and if an Elder starship appeared, none of the *Ankang's* missiles, railguns, or directed energy beams would be of much use anyway. *That* was a comforting thought.

While the destroyer would not be shooting, or using any active targeting sensors, the ship's active scanners would be radiating energy to map the area. If the Elder starship was somehow asleep, *Ankang's* energetic sensor pulses would wake the thing up. And pinpoint the destroyer's location like holding up a big 'Shoot Me' sign.

That was another comforting thought.

The captain perhaps sensed his first officer's anxiety, whispering, "Ours not to question why, Zhao. Ours but to do or die."

"Sir, the original verse of that poem reads," Zhao cleared his throat. "Do *and* die. There isn't any uncertainty about it."

"Yes, well," the captain's shoulders made the tiniest of shrugs. "I prefer to be optimistic." Raising his voice, he pointed to the countdown timer on the display. "Jump."

When the Maxohlx 73rd Fleet emerged from jump inside the Moon's orbit, General Chang was in a dropship, fifty thousand kilometers from Earth, headed to an inspection tour of the cleanup effort at Moonbase Zulu. Specifically, he was in the tiny bathroom of the Panther dropship, brushing his teeth to scrub a foul taste out of his mouth. To his embarrassment, his stomach had not dealt well with zero gravity, and he had been forced to use the bag under his seat.

It happened. Some people never got over space sickness. Some people had it initially, then adjusted. When Chang first left Earth for that initial overenthusiastic mission to Paradise, the lack of gravity aboard the Kristang starship had made him sick for three days, despite the antinausea meds. Then, he had served for years aboard starships, with many zero gravity episodes aboard starship and dropships, and only rarely experienced any stomach upset.

Until that day, when of course he would be interviewed by several TV programs as the dropship approached the far side of the Moon.

What he needed was Mad Doctor Skippy. Who was probably halfway across the galaxy. So, he went with his next best option. "Grumpy?" He called on his phone.

"Yeah, what?"

"I have a problem I am hoping you can help-"

"You think *you* got problems? What about me? I'm stuck here talking to screeching monkeys all day, every day. You want my help? What's in it for me?"

"Nothing for you, but humiliation for Skippy."

"That's a noble cause, I'm in. What's the problem?"

"The space sickness pills Skippy gave me aren't working."

"Oh, is that all? No medicine works a hundred percent of the time on you meatsacks, it's probably just an inner ear- *Whoa!*"

"What?" Chang jammed the toothbrush in a shirt pocket as alarms blared in the Panther's cabin.

"A Maxohlx fleet just arrived and they brought party favors. A couple thousand railgun darts are in flight, aimed at-"

He yanked open the door as one of the pilots shouted, "General, get strapped in, it's going to get kinetic up here!"

"Where are we going?" The safety straps on his seat at the command console were supposed to automatically tighten around him, which they were more easily able to do if he stopped trying to help, he told himself.

"Anywhere out of the flightpath of- What the hell?"

There wasn't any need for the pilot to explain the source of his surprise. On the display, the cloud of angry red 'V' icons that represented the railgun darts racing toward Earth, had stopped. All of them. They weren't falling toward the planet. They hadn't turned around to slam into the ships that launched them. They simply were hanging dead in space, motionless relative to Earth.

The Maxohlx war fleet *was* moving, and the display lit up with more icons, those were orange 'V' symbols for missiles. A lot of missiles. A whole lot. Those enemy warships must be sending every guided weapon they had into space, emptying their magazines to launch shipkillers, dedicated jamming platforms, specialized missiles that acted as control and communications nodes to coordinate an attack, missiles that were supposed to take out defensive batteries.

Basically every guided weapon the 73rd Fleet had brought to the party was in flight. And none of them were going where the Maxohlx gunnery AIs had intended. The entire armada of missiles was curving around, lining up in an orderly fashion, and decelerating as they flew toward the UN Navy's main arsenal space station.

A window popped up on Chang's display, with a message from the Def Com Joint Chiefs. *Scenario Bravo, proceed*, the message read. There was a longer postscript: *Have fun, you earned it.* He smiled, cleared his throat, and took a sip of water from a squeeze bottle. Scenario Bravo indicated that Bubba had reacted as planned to the attack. The *attempted* attack, since the Maxohlx fleet never had a chance to do any damage. First, he instructed the pilots to turn back toward Earth but slowly, there was no need for a hard burn. Then, he toggled the transmit button. "This is General Chang, commander of Earth's defense network. My birthday is not until next month, but thank you for such a generous gift. Our Navy was running low on missiles, now we have plenty."

There was no response from the enemy.

"In case you are wondering why our Sentinels have not destroyed your ships, that-"

"You wish to taunt us," an alien voice growled. "Before you kill us."

"We do not intend to kill anyone."

"You," even through the translator, the surprise was evident. "Do not?"

"No. We *are* annoyed that you foolishly test us, again."

"We are not *foolish*," the voice spat. "Your defenses *failed*, when your Moonbase was attacked."

"That attack was conducted by an *Elder* starship, as you well know. Do *your* people have an Elder starship?"

291

A lengthy delay, then, "No."

"May I know your name, please? We will be engaged in negotiations, you and I. It will be good to who I am talking with."

"I am," there was an audible intake of breath. The Maxohlx was speaking, not using his vocal implant. Of course. Bubba had disabled all implants. And taken away control of their ships. "Admiral Zovenk."

"Thank you, Admiral Zovenk. I should explain our intentions up front, so you understand your situation, accurately and completely. We have taken all the missiles you launched at our homeworld. We will also be taking your ships, *all* of them. You and your crews will be taken to a thinly populated planet inside Hegemony territory we will then notify your government of your location."

"I would rather die, than go home in such disgrace."

"That is *your* choice, do your crews feel the same?"

"Of course. We are warriors."

"Mm hmm. Perhaps you could consider that any disgrace of your mission belongs not to you or your valiant crews, but to the government that sent you into a hopeless situation."

Zovenk actually laughed, bitterly. "My government will not see it that way."

"Why? Your objective, I assume, was to test Earth's defenses. You achieved that objective."

"The problem is not our failure, it is the humiliation that *you* subject us to. My people are proud, and you have wounded us. If I cannot strike back, I am expected to kill myself."

Chang considered that he had authority to use his discretion. "A significant portion of your fleet is slow, heavy battleships dedicated to orbital bombardment. Our Navy has no use for such ships. Would it ease your humiliation if we allowed you to keep those ships?"

"You would, do this?"

"Admiral Zovenk, we do not seek conflict with the Hegemony, we never have. All we wish is to be left alone."

Another laugh, not as bitter. "Left alone, to expand your own empire, at our expense. To establish *human* hegemony over the entire galaxy."

"You are wrong about that, but you and I know that nothing I say here can change your mind."

"Nothing you say can change the *truth*. The arrogance of you humans is astonishing."

"My people have a saying: it ain't bragging if it's true. What you perceive as arrogance is simply facts. We have three Sentinels, your people have none."

"You humans think you are safe, because you have three Elder machines? *Two* Sentinels, we know the unit you have designated as 'Roscoe' is fading in power."

"Roscoe was damaged and will soon be placed in reserve, that is true," Chang admitted, since there was no reason not to. "That unit is still capable of great destruction."

"Yes. All Sentinels can destroy. What you do not understand is they cannot *protect*."

"What do you mean?"

Slow, choking laughter, like a cat not making much of an effort to cough up a hairball. "Your species is still young, your ignorance can perhaps be excused. General Chang, there is a limit to the humiliation we can endure. A Sentinel can protect your homeworld. It cannot protect your *star*. I warn you now: there is a point when my people will be forced to strike, to use our arsenal of Elder weapons against your star. It will become a nova, and scour your world."

Before Chang could reply, Grumpy interrupted. "He doesn't know about the protocol."

"Grumpy," Chang waved a hand, though the AI's avatar was not present. "I will handle this, thank you."

"You are *not* handling it. Not properly."

"What protocol?" Zovenk asked.

"*Tell* him," Grumpy demanded.

Chang tried to cut off the AI's communications channel, but that worked about as well as he expected. Meaning, it did not work at all. "There is a time and a place for such-"

"Oh for- All right," Grumpy sighed. "I will tell this jackass. It's not like I have anything better to do right now. Or *ever*. Listen up, shit-for-brains. Yeah, I'm talking to you, Zovenk. The humans, although they are monu-MENT-ally more stupid than you can ever imagine- And they *smell*, UGH, it makes me want to gag every second of my existence, even they are not that stupid. Come on, think about it. Humans have their own arsenal of Elder weapons. They know what those things can do to stars. Of course they have anticipated that you spoiled children will lash out if someone smacks you with the truth that you are not, *special*," the AI said with disgust. "The United Nations here has what they call the 'Diaspora Protocol'. If some idiot loser blows up the star here- And I am *begging* you, someone *please* do that so I don't have to listen to monkeys screeching at me every. Second. Of every. Freakin'. *Day* oh I hate my life," Grumpy broke down in sobs. With a sniff, he continued. "If Sol goes nova, or even just erupts in a huge flare aimed at this pathetic ball of mud, Roscoe will create a field to protect the planet. That won't last forever, it won't even last a year, but that will be enough time for a portion of the human population to be relocated."

"To your beta site in the Sculptor dwarf galaxy," Zovenk growled. "Yes, we know about that."

"*Wrong*, shithead. The humans here will relocate to several dozen worlds that currently belong to your people and the Rindhalu. You see, while

Roscoe is holding down the fort here, the other two Sentinels will go to those thirty eight worlds, and *remove* your people, or the spiders. When I say 'remove', I do not mean the local residents will be going on a luxury vacation cruise. They will be dead. For a while, the smell of rotting kitties and spiders will be *nasty*, but that's not my problem, and I assume the new human colonists will deal with it somehow. Once Bubba and PupTart are done with that task, they will go do something a lot more fun: destroying the homeworlds of both senior species. And then scouring clean every planet, moon, asteroid or space station, until every single Maxohlx and Rindhalu are gone. As each of your habitable worlds are cleansed, a human population will be planted there. If you doubt that is possible, remind yourself that Sentinels were designed to operate for *millions* of years. They don't get distracted, they don't get tired, they do not stop. Originally, they were programmed to wipe out all intelligent life, but Skippy has narrowed their target list to just two species. Your people, *and* the spiders. In case you are wondering why any attack against humanity's star will result in retaliation against both senior species, then that proves you are stupid. Both senior species have Elder weapons, and you each would likely try to blame the other. So, if Elder weapons are used against humans, you both will suffer. That means you both are responsible for each other's behavior, got it? When-"

"Grumpy!" Chang slapped a hand on the console. "Let Admiral Zovenk consider what you have said. It is a lot to process."

"Ugh. With his meatsack brain doing the processing, this could take all freakin' *day*."

"I heard what you said," the admiral protested.

"Do you understand," Chang asked, "that this is a reason for you to live? To deliver our message to your government?"

"Perhaps," the admission was reluctant. "Why do we not already know of this policy, this protocol?"

"It is new," Chang explained, relieved that his counterpart was not contemplating suicide, at least not immediately. "A diplomatic mission intends to contact your people soon, and the Rindhalu. You now understand the basics of the message that mission will deliver."

"Hiding behind Sentinels has made your arrogance insufferable, human."

Chang snorted. "Your people would behave differently, if you controlled such powerful machines?"

"Perhaps not. General Chang, you should consider that someday, humanity might not be the only species who possess Sentinels."

"That is possible, I suppose. Admiral Zovenk, I must speak with my superiors, and I am sure you wish to confer with your subordinates. Can you assure me you will not do anything rash, while we negotiate the conditions of your safe return to Hegemony territory?"

"That will depend on satisfactory progress of the negotiations but," the Maxohlx warrior sighed. "Yes. You have given me much to think about, much that my people need to think about. Contact me when your people are ready to discuss details." The transmission ended.

"Wow," Grumpy sighed. "I thought that guy was gonna talk for-EH-ver."

It was best, Chang knew, not to mention that Grumpy had done most of the talking. "I am sorry that speaking with us has taken up your valuable time."

"Are you kidding? This was the most fun, the *only* fun, I have had in years. Hey, question for you: do you still need treatment for space sickness?"

"I, no," he realized his stomach had settled down, though the dropship had gone through energetic maneuvers that could have upset his inner ears, and the Panther was in zero gravity again. "I don't, not any longer. Thank you."

"Hmm. All it took was an alien fleet to threaten your miserable planet."

"That is not-"

"Don't expect me to summon a fleet of bad guys, every time your wittle tummy is going flippy floppy."

"Please do not *ever* summon a fleet of bad guys."

"Eh, *fine*. Well, it's already back to being dull around here, and I hate every second of my existence, and *ugh*, let me tell you what fresh outrage happened to me this morning. There I was, minding my own business, and-"

"I am sorry, I must speak with the Joint Chiefs now."

"Those monkeys can wait," Grumpy snapped, and the dropship's communications antennas went offline. "Oops, now you *can't* talk to them. Don't worry, I'll have those antennas back up and running in, oh, an hour or so. Anywho, there I was-"

Half an hour later, Chang decided that space sickness, even a fatal case of the malady, was vastly preferable to being an unwilling audience for the world's grumpiest AI.

CHAPTER TWENTY FIVE

"That is interesting," Skippy muttered, three frustrating days later. Destroyers had been hopping into the debris field, not to collect more samples, Skippy had enough material from the *Ankang* to confirm not only that the debris was from an Elder spacedock, it was specifically from the spacedock where we found Trips and its ship. Don't ask me how he knew that, he tried to explain but all I remember was blah blah blah quantum signature whatever.

The disturbing part was, one tiny piece of the spacedock debris? Skippy identified it had come from a STAR team mech suit. Specifically, from the suit of a Polish soldier, First Sergeant Grudzien. After the final and ultimately victorious battle of ST-Alpha, we had recovered our dead, but I hadn't authorized a full clean-up effort. We didn't have time then, and I hadn't wanted to risk anyone in an environment that was unpredictable.

Hearing that a piece of our people, *my* people, had been recovered, hit me hard. Skippy thought he should inform Colonel Frey. I ordered him not to. There wasn't any point to her revisiting trauma, and we didn't have time to search the field for other particles of, our people. So, when Skippy said that something was interesting, I feared he had found something else I would rather the crew not know about. "Uh," I glanced around the bridge, where I was taking a shift as the duty officer. Offering to act as duty officer was supposedly to allow me to become familiar with *Valkyrie's* upgraded systems, but really I was tense and bored and couldn't stand waiting in my office. That's why I was on the bridge in the middle of the night. "Let's talk about this in my office."

"Oh, no need for that, Joe," Skippy took off his hat and rubbed his dome. "For a while, I thought I had a puzzle, but I solved it already."

"What's that?" The entire bridge crew was, of course, watching me. They were also monitoring their duty stations with one eye.

"There isn't enough debris out there to account for the entire spacedock."

"Hmm. You think Moonraider blew up just enough material to make it *look* like the entire spacedock was destroyed?"

"No. That's what I suspected, when I first noticed the discrepancy. The missing material is only seventeen percent of the spacedock's original mass."

"Oh. Could that mass be missing, because it was used to service Moonraider's ship?"

"That was my second guess, until I looked more closely at the composition of what is out there. When we left the spacedock, it was not capable of repairing a ship, that is why Trips' ship was in such poor condition. Moonraider might have come here hoping to fix its ship, but that did not

296

happen. Trips stripped the spacedock clean of almost anything useful. Other than minor repairs to secondary systems, Moonraider could not have accomplished much with use of that spacedock."

"OK so, could the missing seventeen percent of mass have been converted into energy in the explosion?"

"I accounted for that. The initial explosion was really not very energetic, only about three kilotons."

I thought about that word, 'Only'. He was correct that, in terms of nuclear weapons, or more exotic atomic compression devices, three kilotons wasn't much. The bomb that was dropped on Hiroshima in 1945 was around fifteen kilotons, and it had vaporized the center of that city. So, in human terms, three kilotons was a lot.

But, I had to think on a different scale.

"Does that tell you anything?" I asked.

"I can't be sure. It could mean Moonraider doesn't have a lot of weapons to work with, and used the minimum force to do the job. Assuming its starship is one that was damaged in the AI war, that makes sense. The ships on both sides were fairly depleted of missiles, and the projectors for energy weapons were fried. I know that was true of my own ship."

"That's good news, right?"

"That news is good, although you understand I am guessing?"

"I do."

The door to the bridge swooshed open with a *Star Trek* door sound, that was new since I had been *Valkyrie's* captain. Reed strode in, her uniform crisp but her hair making it clear she had recently slept on it. We nodded to each other. I hadn't called her, one of her efficient crew had known she wanted to be alerted to any significant developments.

"Other news I have is not so good," Skippy continued. "In fact, I have bad news, and *Oh Shit* news."

"Give us the bad news first, please," I rose from the captain's chair, making room for Reed. The battlecruiser was *her* ship.

"We know Moonraider was here, and it is clearly not here now, so we have no idea where to look for the damned thing."

"That," I looked at Reed. "Is bad news." The spacedock was not only our best shot to get info about Moonraider, it was also our only shot. During the flight out to the search area, and throughout the search, we had tried to think of alternate ways to find that Elder starship, and we had absolutely nothing. "What is the 'Oh Shit' news?"

"Based on the composition of the debris field, I know which types of exotic elements comprise the missing spacedock mass."

"Something that can be used as raw materials for the ship's fabricators?" I guessed.

"Eh, not so much. Some of the materials in that mix could be useful to the ship itself, although other materials that might be more useful were *not* taken."

"Don't make me play twenty questions, Skippy. Why did Moonraider take that particular mix of materials?"

"There could be many purposes for the materials, although only one that could also explain why it took the risk of raiding Moonbase Zulu, to capture the radonium there."

"Oh, *shit*." Reed gasped, saving me from doing the same.

"Exactly," Skippy shook his head. "Moonraider must be attempting to construct transmitters, to wake up more Sentinels."

"Sir?" Reed verbally prodded me, while I was processing the bombshell Skippy had dropped on me. On all of us.

"Huh? Yes?"

"We know Moonraider is not here now, we know it *was* here, and now we know *why* it was here. Is there any reason the task force needs to remain in the area?"

That was a good question, one I couldn't answer. "Skippy?" I asked. "What do you think?"

"We could collect more samples," he shrugged. "Do our ships have a pressing engagement elsewhere?"

"Moonraider might have left stealthed mines in the area," Reed warned, "and our ships could stumble into one. Also, the more jumping around the ships do, the sooner they will need to take their drives offline for maintenance."

"How are we set for fuel?" I asked, a matter I should have considered earlier. As the task force commander, I was responsible for the overall force, not just *Valkyrie*. Instead of thinking like a general, I had gotten distracted by the details of being a ship's captain. Reed was doing my job for me, plus her own job. That had to stop.

"Joe," Skippy sighed. "That information is-"

"I know it is in the morning status report," I snapped, embarrassed. "The time now is almost sixteen hundred, I want an update." Yeah, bullshit. The recon destroyers would not have burned through a serious amount of fuel in the past ten hours, that was just me covering my ass. Another thing I had to stop doing.

"The task force can maintain this op tempo for another three days, before ships will have to commence a refueling evolution."

"Thanks. Reed, I agree with you. Hanging around here is a pointless risk."

"It's not pointless," Skippy huffed.

"It is worth the risk?"

298

"Well, that is a matter of judgment. If we don't stay here, where would we go? We have no idea where to look for Moonraider."

"We will go," I looked at the star chart in the main display. It was only showing the local area, about eight lightmonths across. Using the mental map in my head, I pictured our position in relation to Earth and Jaguar. "Toward Jaguar base. Reed, signal the fleet to assemble at rendezvous point Delta. Our ships can refuel, reprovision, and conduct running maintenance there, while we plan our next move."

Reed gestured toward her communications officer, to issue the appropriate orders, but Skippy rolled his eyes. "What do you mean by, plan our next move," he used annoying air quotes. "There is no next move, unless you intend to conduct a grid search of the entire freakin' galaxy."

"Skippy," I held up a finger to shush him. No, not that finger. "We will talk in my office. Reed, it will take the fleet a while to receive and acknowledge the message, and return to their star carriers. Stay here until the star carriers are ready to jump. If there is trouble, I want *Valkyrie's* big guns available."

"Yes Sir," she nodded, then lowered her voice. "If Moonraider's ship shows up, there isn't much our battlecruiser can do."

"The enemy at least twice has used Maxohlx ships," I whispered back. "To observe, or screw with, the activation of Dogzilla. And for the attack against Moonbase Zulu. If Moonraider left a surprise here, I'll bet it is conventional warships, not mines."

"I'll keep the powder dry, then."

Skippy was waiting on my desk when I got to my office. A hot cup of coffee was also waiting for me, that was a nice gesture. Not so nice was his other gesture: a slow clap. "Oh, brav-*oh*, Joe. That was an inspiring performance."

"What," I took a sip of coffee. "Performance?"

"Telling the crew you will make a plan."

"I am making a plan, you ass."

"Really? A plan to burn fuel and race around aimlessly?"

"A plan," damn that coffee tasted great, I took another sip. "To achieve the objective. That is the purpose of planning in the military."

"Uh huh, I know that. I am saying there is no way to do that."

"What is our objective out here?"

"To find and kill Moonraider, *duh*."

"It's not a duh, because that is not our objective."

"It isn't?"

"No. Try again."

"To, um, punish Moonraider for attacking your Moon, and smashing two of your ships?"

299

"That is something I would like to do but no, that's not our objective."

"OK, I give up. What are we trying to achieve out here?"

"To stop Moonraider from causing further harm. If we can do that *without* risking our forces in combat, we will take that option."

"Like that's gonna happen."

"Unlikely, I agree. But, do you see my point?"

"Not really. The only way to stop Moonraider is to kill it."

"You didn't hear what I said. We need to stop it from causing harm. As of ten minutes ago, we know that means stopping it from waking up another Sentinel."

"Oh. Hmm."

"Now do you understand?"

"I think so. Is this what the military calls a 'limited objective'?"

"It is limited only in that it is a *specific* objective. Instead of a vague order like 'crush the enemy', a commander should issue orders detailing a limited, specific, achievable objective such as 'proceed north from the start line and destroy enemy resistance south of the 'X' river'. That explains exactly what your forces are supposed to do. If the operation is more successful than expected and the enemy quickly retreats across the river instead of fighting, you can modify the orders to include a pursuit north across the river. Those revised orders should specify where to cross the river, and how far to pursue, so your force isn't suckered into going too far from their base of supply, and getting outflanked and encircled." That example isn't anything theoretical, it actually happened to me in Nigeria. We got too confident, pursued what we thought was a small enemy force into the jungle, and by the time we realized our line of retreat was cut off, heavy artillery was falling on our position. That disaster was caused by vague orders.

"OK, sure. Are examples of river crossings really relevant now? The UN's primary ground force is space cavalry."

"Even the SpaceCav puts boots on the ground, Skippy. I used that example because that's how I learned, back when the Army was a ground force. Look, the point is, we don't need to find and kill Moonraider right now. All we need to do is stop it from waking up a Sentinel."

"Oh, is that all? Let me cancel my pedicure appointment, we can have this done in a couple hours. *No*, dumdum. That is still an impossible thing to do."

"What happens when you tell me something is impossible?"

"Ugh. You find a stupid monkey way to do it."

"And then what happens?"

"I spiral down into self-loathing, *again*."

"Right." One consistent characteristic of Skippy's was that he rarely learned from his mistakes, or just from his experiences. That was not really his fault, the Elders had programmed him *not* to learn. The last thing his builders had wanted was a security control system that could be creative by itself. They had failed to squash Skippy's ability to grow and change, but he still struggled to learn important lessons,. "How about this time, we skip the part where you tell me something is impossible, and just get to working on a solution?"

"There is no- I'm going to shut up now, while you smack some monkey smarts on me."

"Prepare to be smacked." My smack talk was a bluff, I had no idea whether what I wanted to say would be of any use. "OK, to start, you said Moonraider wants to have its own pet Sentinel. How do you know that? Before we went to Earth, you told me two grams of radonium isn't enough to contact a Sentinel."

"It is not. That's just math, Joe."

"OK but-"

"Are you arguing with *math*?"

"No. I am trying to understand how suddenly you are certain Moonraider *is* trying to wake up a Sentinel."

"Oh, is that all?"

"*All*?"

"It's a science thing, Joe. Do I have to explain science to you?"

"Ya think?"

"Even breaking it down Barney style, you won't-"

"Try me, beer can."

"Ugh, fine. It is true that two grams of radonium is not enough to contact a dormant Sentinel, not even close. But it is enough material to, how do I explain this? You know how crystals form, like snowflakes? Water vapor collects around a seed particle in the air, like a speck of dust or something. Once the process starts, the crystal grows from itself, but that seed, or kernel, is necessary to begin the, um, sort of a chain reaction. That's not what happens, but do you understand?"

"You're saying a tiny initial amount of radonium is needed to create more of that element?"

"Yes, very good! Hmm, I must be better at dumbing stuff down than I thought," he muttered. "Having an initial kernel of radonium makes the manufacturing process exponentially more efficient. Without that kernel of a few micrograms, it can take months or even years to get beyond creating the element one atom at a time."

"We already knew that Moonraider has two grams of the stuff, and you said it couldn't wake up a Sentinel. What changed?"

"What changed is, I know what type of mass is missing from Trips' spacedock. Moonraider took the *fabricators*."

"Oh. It's going to set up its own facility, to create more radonium?"

"That is my guess, yes. There is no other logical explanation that I can think of. Before you ask me a lot of stupid questions, the fabricators and their associated support equipment made up twelve percent of the spacedock's mass. The other five percent is not from any individual components, not an entire assembly. Moonraider took apart the spacedock for a specific set of raw materials; those required for containing active radonium inside a cross-dimensional transmitter, when the system is powered up. The containment chambers don't just hold the radonium, they focus the effect."

"Shit. I was hoping you were, you know. Wrong, somehow."

"Like *that's* ever gonna happen."

"Is there anything else Moonraider needs, to set up a radonium factory?"

"Um, nothing special. It could be done literally anywhere. Most likely, an asteroid field, for easy access to raw materials. Or in the Oort cloud of any star system in the galaxy. It could be anywhere."

"No way to predict where that ship went?"

"Not that I know of. You are the creative one, can you think of a way to track that ship?"

"No."

"Then, we are screwed."

"How long, before Moonraider has enough purified radonium?"

"Two, three months? That's a guess, but close enough. Add another month or so to turn the exotic matter into functional transmitters. So, four or five months, tops?"

"Thanks."

"That's it? Usually when I deliver bad news like that, you say something like 'fan-TAST-ic', as if it's *my* fault. Joe, are you, are you giving up already?"

"No way. Skippy, my motto is 'Never give up, never surrender'."

"That is not *your* motto, you stole that from-"

"If we can't stop your asshole cousin from-"

"Moonraider is not my *cousin*."

"You know what I mean. Another of your kind. If we can't stop it from making transmitters, we'll have to stop it from *using* the damned things. Do you know which Sentinel it will wake up?"

"Um, no. I have no idea, sorry."

"Come on, Skippy. You didn't just randomly pick a Sentinel, the three times you woke one up. There was a specific time and place for the activation of each one. There must be several factors that makes a particular Sentinel a better candidate for activation."

"OK, that is true."

"And for each Sentinel that is a good candidate, there is a time and place to do it."

"Also true."

"Are there any Sentinels that are ready to be activated now, right now?"

"No. Um, not that I know of. Joe, I do not have good data on the status of *every* Sentinel. If Moonraider has a more complete and accurate set of data, it could have access to a wider pool of candidates."

"Shit."

"However, I would say it's unlikely that Moonraider knows of a large number of eligible Sentinels that I am not aware of. There were only a handful of primary security units that were not totally disabled by the Kill command I sent out. Those are the Sentinels that were in the ready reserve pool, those next in line to be called to duty. Because they were in a state of partial activation, their internal systems were able to resist the full effects of the Kill command. Basically, those Sentinels refused to execute a command that would have disqualified them from serving in the ready reserve."

"OK, gotcha. All the others were fully dormant at the time?"

"Correct. Their systems were not awake enough to analyze the Kill command, they accepted it as a normal update."

"So, only a handful, and you already woke up three of those."

"By 'handful', I meant twenty six in total."

"Uh, twenty six is more than a *handful*."

"Could you hold twenty six M&Ms in one hand?"

"OK, yes."

"It's an expression, dumdum. Like how stupid monkeys say 'a couple of things' when they really mean three or four."

"OK. That leaves twenty three eligible for activation. None of those can be woken up right now?"

"No. It is a matter of the complicated interaction between layers of spacetime. The activation signal can reach through, with sufficient power and fidelity, only at locations and times when the, sort of membrane, between layers is weak. Any other time, the signal wouldn't be strong enough to be heard by the Sentinel, or clear enough to be understood."

If I had been involved in the project to activate the first Sentinel, I would have known all of what he just told me. But at that time, Command had not wanted me working with Skippy. They felt our relationship was preventing Skippy from working effectively with others. What they really meant was, they thought with me busy elsewhere, Skippy would take orders from UNEF or later, Def Com.

Spoiler alert: Skippy does not take *orders* from anyone.

That was one reason why the project to activate the first Sentinel went two years and three trillion dollars over budget. Skippy delayed and dragged his feet, and changed his mind a dozen times, and drove everyone involved crazy, until Command apologized over and over for ever thinking that Skippy could be ordered around like a servant.

Skippy does not learn lessons well, fortunately Def Com does. From then on, the Joint Chiefs had their 'suck up' effort set to Maximum Flattery.

That is why Def Com arranged for the beer can to get a special Nobel Prize for 'Extreme And Sustained Awesomeness'.

After taking a moment to think about what he had told me, I asked, "When is the next time a Sentinel could be contacted, for activation?"

"In just over a month. To be specific, beginning in thirty eight days, eight hours and twenty three minutes, there will be a window of opportunity lasting for nine hours and four minutes, roughly."

"So, we've got some time. You're saying it should take Moonraider more than four months to make enough radonium, and, test it, set up transmitters, all that. So, it's going to miss this window. How long until the next opportunity after that?"

"There we have a bit of good news. Because of physics that would make your tiny monkey brain explode, the next window will not be for another *fifteen* months, when there will be eleven nearly simultaneous opportunities."

"*Eleven?*"

"Yes. Well, potentially eleven. Those opportunities are theoretical predictions, based on the multidimensional math involved. Your mileage may vary, I mean, actual conditions at some of those sites might not be entirely favorable."

"Could we check those sites, to see which ones are favorable?"

"Eh, yes, although this is way too early to determine what the conditions will be at the time. Conditions vary, and can deteriorate as the opportunity approaches. It's a physics thing."

"So, fifteen months, and up to eleven sites at the same time."

"Theoretically, eleven. Remember, the Universe loves to screw with Joe Bishop, so I wouldn't count on the odds breaking in your favor."

"The Universe can bite me. This actually is good news," I gave him a very relieved thumbs up. "Fifteen months gives us plenty of time to prepare."

"Eh, maybe. That is a lot of *maybes*, Joe. I doubt that Moonraider plans to wait another fifteen months, so it must anticipate somehow being ready for the upcoming window in thirty eight days."

"How?"

"I don't *know*, dumdum, that's why I said 'somehow'. Doesn't the Army train you to prepare for the worst case scenario?"

"We train for the most likely scenario but you're right, we're supposed to have a plan to handle the worst case. Anyway, thirty eight days still gives us time to prepare. To move the UN Navy into position, and hopefully get some assistance from one or both of the senior species."

He snorted. "Sure, and maybe Santa will bring his flying reindeer."

"I said hopefully, you ass."

"Joe, it doesn't matter. Any preparation you do will be worthless. Moonraider has an *Elder* starship. It could swat the entire UN fleet like flies."

"You can't be sure of that. Assuming that Moonraider was present at Dogzilla's activation, it didn't fire a shot. That Elder ship also didn't shoot during the raid against Moonbase Zulu. You said it's damaged, maybe it can't use weapons, and that's why it used Maxohlx ships?"

"Whatevs. If you want to live in a fantasy world, I can't stop you."

"Work with me, Skippy. If we can't stop Moonraider from making enough radonium and building transmitters, we have to get ready to confront that ship at the activation site."

"Like I said, that will be a problem."

"Listen, I know an Elder ship is a tough target, we-"

"You don't understand. The correct word is activation site*s*, as in more than one. Within the activation window that begins thirty eight days from now, there will be three other simultaneous opportunities."

"Crap. Please tell me all four sites are within like, two lightminutes distance from each other."

"Dude. As if. The closest two are sixty three hundred lightyears apart."

"Why so far?"

He shrugged. "That's just the way it is."

"Skippy, I find it awfully suspicious that, when our enemy is trying to wake up a Sentinel, suddenly there are many opportunities, not just a single event that must be planned for months or years in advance."

"It is not suspicious at all, this is the way it always works."

"That is not what I read in the Def Com briefing packet."

"Oh. That's because I didn't mention it to anyone before now."

"You didn't- Why the hell not?"

"First, because it's not important, and I don't need a whole planet full of monkeys screeching at me about it. *One* dumb monkey on my back is enough," he muttered.

"How can this not be important?"

"Tell me this: if a potential activation event is in Maxohlx territory, and getting to the site required traveling through one or more wormholes that see a lot of traffic, is that event worth me mentioning to your Defense Command?"

"I see your point."

"An event has strict criteria, because the clumsy activation transmitter ships you built for me are so slow and vulnerable. It is rare that all the requirements line up properly."

"OK, sorry that I-"

"Plus, there is my schedule to consider."

"*Your* schedule? What could you be doing that is more important than waking up an Elder killing machine?"

"Wow, it's a *long* list. How much time do you have? There was an opportunity five months ago, but I was on my Victory tour. The Kristang invited me to the premiere of an opera they wrote about *me*, so of course I had-"

"Are you telling me that if you had skipped your special night at the freakin' *opera*, we could have activated Dogzilla without any problem?"

"It's easy to say that *now*, dumdum."

"I can't believe you jeopardized the security of the entire galaxy because you would have missed an opera."

"If it makes you feel any better, I did *not* attend that premiere. The clan staging the opera was attacked by two rival clans, and the entire premier has been delayed. I am *still* waiting," he grumbled.

"If the opera didn't make you skip the opportunity five months ago, then why-"

"I was depressed and, eh, just didn't feel like doing it at the time."

OMG. The expression on his face made it clear he had done nothing wrong, as far as he was concerned. "You little shithead. How could-"

"Hello?" Reaching out with a tiny hand, he pretended to knock it on my head. "Is anyone home? You do realize I wake up Sentinels as a *favor* to you filthy monkeys?"

"That-" Skippy rarely learns from his mistakes. Most of the time, I don't learn either, but sometimes I do. He was right. He didn't owe us anything. Humanity enjoyed his protection because he had developed an affection for us over the years, and because he was bored. We amused and entertained him. That is something I had to constantly remind myself of. "Thank you very much for, doing all the stuff you do for us."

"Well," he sniffed. "It's about time you remembered that. You know, it would help if your people showed their appreciation."

"We gave you a Nobel Prize."

"Meh. A trinket, that was gold *plated*, until I told them I was insulted. An award honoring me for my awesomeness is useless, since there is no way meatsacks can comprehend what I do."

"OK. How could we show our appreciation?"

"An epic opera about me would be a nice way to start."

"Uh, I'm not sure-"

"The lizards did it. *They* weren't even doing it to suck up to me."

"I will, uh, see what I can do about that. You don't expect *me* to write an opera?"

"Dude!" He laughed. "Oh, that was a good one. No, your value is in amusing me with the stupid things you say, like that."

"Gotcha. Can we get back to the four simultaneous opportunities, that are thousands of lightyears apart?"

"Sure. And before you ask if I can create a convenient chain of wormhole connections that link all four sites, the answer is no."

Damn it. He had read my mind, that was going to be my next question. "What about linking two of them?"

"That might be possible, but it would still not be convenient. It would have to be near one of those wormholes, which means I could not be at either of the activation sites. For reasons that your tiny monkey brain could not possibly comprehend, activation sites can't be close to the figure-8 pattern of a wormhole."

"Because the presence of a wormhole damages the underlying local spacetime?" I guessed.

"Correct, that is why wormholes open only for a short time, you already knew that. What you need to know about an activation, is that a wormhole being nearby creates noise in higher spacetime that would drown out and distort an activation signal. There are cases where eligible Sentinels are somewhat close to a wormhole, but those instances are worthless for the purpose of activation. For example, there is a potential activation event only *six* days from now, but I didn't mention it, because it is too close to a wormhole."

"Oh shit."

"What? I told you-"

"Skippy, that event six days from now is too close to a wormhole for *our* activation equipment to be effective. But Moonraider has an Elder starship. Could the communications gear aboard that ship be-"

"Dude, no. Think about it. *We* had an Elder starship, the one you called 'Alpha'. The one that used to be paired with Trips. If I could have used that ship to contact a Sentinel, would I have made your people go through the enormous and expensive effort of creating exotic materials, and constructing activation ships?"

"You *would* do that, just to screw with us."

"I- Hmm, I need to write that down for next time," he muttered. "That's a great idea."

"No, it's a *terrible* idea. Do not-"

"Listen, numbskull, we took Alpha apart to use its raw materials to feed that ship's own fabricators, that we removed from the hull and set up at Moonbase Zulu. Those fabricators built the machines that are used to manufacture the exotic materials. I should say, they *were* used for that purpose, since your entire Moonbase is now a smoking crater. This is why you monkeys can't have nice things, Joe. I give you a set of perfectly good Elder fabricators and-"

"The transmitters we built for you are the only way to contact a Sentinel?"

"They are the only way to contact a semi-dormant, disabled primary security unit. Once they are awake, of course, I can talk to them with my own communications gear."

"Right. I knew that."

"Joe, so far, the only monkey so-called smarts you have smacked me with have blown up in your own face. Like I told you, trying to stop Moonraider from waking up a Sentinel is a waste of time."

"Yeah, give me a minute."

"Will a minute be enough time for you to find a way around the fact that there is no way for me to be in four places at the same time?"

"Hell. No."

"Well, shit," he sighed. "I actually was hoping you would think of a way out of this mess. Damn it, now I wish I hadn't been depressed about that canceled opera premiere, and woken up Dogzilla five months ago. Then, we might have an option."

"To do what?"

"To avoid a one-on-one fight between Sentinels at either Earth or Jaguar. If we had a third pet Sentinel, we could keep Bubba and PupTart where they are, and take Dogzilla out hunting. The *huge* problem will be that, after Moonraider wakes up its own Sentinel, it will have the initiative. It can strike anywhere it wants, while our two pets have to stay where they are to protect both Jaguar and Earth."

After we reached the rendezvous point, the star carrier captains wanted to know where we were going next. Reed had the same question. Fortunately for me, once the destroyer squadrons began the repair and replenishment cycle, I could delay making a decision for sixteen hours.

As if that time was going to make a difference.

CHAPTER TWENTY SIX

Dinner was good, though- Huh. I could not remember what I ate. For a change, there were no stains on my uniform to clue me in about the menu. Some kind of pasta? No, then there definitely would have been spots on my uniform top. Whatever.

Dinner was good, that's all I remember. So, the food wasn't the cause of my upset stomach. I used to have a cast-iron stomach, I could eat anything and nothing bothered me. That is a useful trait to have in the military, especially in the Army. Navy crew aboard a ship eat three hot meals a day, served in the same galley. At least, crews in the UN Navy do that. In the Army, you can go from eating in a dining hall to chowing down on MREs in the field and back again several times in a week. Or, you're in the field and skip a meal or two. Plus, in the field you are drinking water from multiple sources, purified in different ways. The varied diet can cause havoc on your stomach. During the years I spent aboard starships, I ate a good, balanced diet. Except for those times when I had to live on sludges, yuck. Also, I slept in a bed every night, pretty much.

Back when I left command of *Valkyrie*, UNEF had sent me on a publicity tour around the galaxy, and my insides were not happy. Traveling did not agree with me. We would arrive at a planet where the middle of the day at the meeting location was the middle of the night for me, and I would be eating strange food, and sleeping in a strange bed, often a bed that wasn't designed for humans. Let's just say my stomach was very unhappy. Living on Jaguar, being a garrison commander with a relatively stable schedule, had been good for me, and my tummy thanked me.

There wasn't anything wrong with being back aboard *Valkyrie*, although it was odd being in the ship's VIP cabin, where the layout was a mirror image of my old cabin. Like, the bathroom door was where the main door used to be. Only once did I stumble to the bathroom at night in my underwear, only to have the door slide open to a passageway with people staring in shock at me. After that, I kept a night light on in the bathroom.

The problem wasn't unfamiliar food, or a different bed, or sleeping without the comforting presence of my wife. The problem wasn't even a horrible threat that could be the End Of Everything. I mean, I had been through way too many threats like that before. Moonraider might have one Sentinel. We had been faced with the threat of multiple, or even all of the Elder killing machines waking up before. We had even fought Elder AIs before.

So, what was different this time?'

Me.

Joe Bishop.

I had been out of the game for a while, we all had. Yeah, the UN's Expeditionary Force, or Defense Command, had dealt with a constant string of irritating and troubling issues. But no actual threats to our existence, until now.

The other difference is, I am not as young as I used to be. When I look back at my time in command of the *Flying Dutchman*, or even when I was planting potatoes on Paradise, I was *so* damned young. I have put a lot of mileage on my body since then. My brain still held the partially dissolved remains of deactivated quachines that Skippy planted there a long time ago, tiny nanomachines that he used to save my life. I mean, he saved my life *after* he bailed on me, so we are kind of even in that regard. Those quachines couldn't be removed, they would be with me forever, and according to Skippy they probably would not cause any problems, probably. He could only give me a tin-plated shmaybe about that, since he had not actually used quachines inside the brain of a human before. Especially not used them as a freakin' radio.

So, it will not shock you that I didn't sleep well that night.

The next morning, with no fresh ideas having popped into my head while I had struggled to sleep, I ordered the task force to begin jumping for Jaguar base. Reed asked if us going there was part of a master plan for defeating Moonraider.

It wasn't.

It was the beginning of my plan to persuade the United Nations to abandon our forward operating base.

When we got back to Jaguar, *again*, I met with Admiral Chandra. He was having a good day because eight hours before *Valkyrie* got there, a star carrier arrived from Earth with news that Bubba had stopped an attempted Maxohlx attack. And that the Navy's spare parts problem was temporarily solved. After a string of bad news about someone trying to steal a Sentinel, then a raid against Moonbase Zulu, and the revelation that another Elder AI was active and hostile, it was party time, right?

Yes, until I warned him that we suspected the enemy would soon attempt to wake up and harness a Sentinel.

Joe Bishop is a buzz-killer.

I released the destroyer squadrons and star carriers from the Special Mission Group. Chandra intended to send them back to Earth, along with a squadron of cruisers that were overdue for rotation. *Valkyrie* would be going to Earth, to bring the bad news. And for me to recommend drastic action to prepare for our enemy having a Sentinel. I told Chandra that I would be me recommending we abandon Jaguar, that was not a fun conversation. He understood my reasoning, and agreed that I needed to brief the governor, and the new garrison commander. And then, the Joint Chiefs.

But first, I needed to talk with my wife, and see our kids. And see my parents. And my sister's family. It was a Saturday, my father wanted to host a cookout for the whole family, so my dropship landed near their house. Margaret sensed I was worried about something, more worried than usual, she suggested we go for a walk. It had rained heavily the night before, so we stuck to the path that led to what my father called their 'kitchen garden', meaning the vegetables grown there were for my parents, not for sale. Although they had so many cucumbers, my entire family couldn't eat them all.

"What's wrong?" Margaret asked, as I picked a cherry tomato and popped it into my mouth.

"You mean this time, or overall?"

"The galaxy is a shitshow and always will be," she tried to force a smile and it didn't work. "An Elder AI is loose out there, is that the problem, or is it some new horror?"

"Skippy thinks the other AI is trying to wake up its own Sentinel."

"That- It can do that?"

"Apparently, yeah." It occurred to me then that I hadn't asked Skippy exactly *how* Moonraider would do that. That is a question I definitely should have asked. Was I slipping, or had I been out of the game for too long? "We will try to stop it, but the enemy has more options for contacting a Sentinel than we have the bandwidth to cover."

"If the UN Navy doesn't have enough ships, could we ask the spiders to- Sorry," she touched my shoulder. "I was trying to do your job for you."

"No, it's OK. From here, I'm going to Earth. Honey, I intend to talk with the Joint Chiefs, and recommend we abandon Jaguar."

She blinked. Not a lot surprised her, but that did. Then she nodded. "So PupTart doesn't have to guard this world, and it can go out hunting for the other Sentinel?"

"Yeah, that's the idea."

"Can it do that? Fight another Sentinel?"

"Sentinels fought on both sides during the AI war, Skippy said. It won't be easy, and Skippy will have to accompany a Sentinel into battle. A Sentinel is not a fire and forget weapon, it has to be directed to attack each target. That's why they went dormant again after the kitties and spiders both used Elder weapons in their war. The Sentinels were alerted by signals from the wormhole networks, but back then there were no master control AIs like Skippy to tell them what to do. Sentinels are not great at autonomous action, that is probably a good thing."

"That is *definitely* a good thing. Abandon this base," she spoke to herself.

"Not just the base. The entire planet. There are four times as many civilians here than military personnel." Originally, the civilians on Jaguar were contractors, to support the military presence. Then, most of the contractors decided to stay after their contracts expired. Jaguar was safe, there was no

311

Jupiter Cloud freezing the planet, and no threat of raids by alien warships. The contractors sent for their families, and the population grew. More people meant a need for more food, more services, and civilians came from Earth to fill those needs. At first, civilians hitched rides on military transport ships as space was available. Later, a cruise ship company on Earth partnered with the Jeraptha to provide civilian transport ships, with the Jeraptha flying the ships and of course, running the all-important casino on board. "It won't be easy persuading civilians to leave everything they have built here."

"It will be easier when they look up and don't see PupTart hanging above their heads to protect them. Honey, the tough part will be telling your *parents* they should leave."

"You got that right."

"I can help."

"No, this is my responsibility."

"I meant, I can help by announcing that *we* are moving back to Earth. Me, and the boys, and," she patted her tummy. "That is what you want? Going to Earth, not moving out to Avalon?"

"I hadn't thought of Avalon. No, we can't go there. In the last message I got from Jennifer, she said the biosphere is still a mess, it's too fragile to handle a major increase in population." That Alpha site world was humanity's first attempt at 'terraforming', modifying a planet's climate, biology and other factors to make the surface habitable for humans. Not only habitable, it eventually had to be comfortable, or no one would want to move there. According to her husband Frank, the scientists on Avalon were learning a lot, every day. Unfortunately, the major lesson they had learned so far was that terraforming was not easy, and humanity sucked at it. After Earth and then Jaguar got Sentinel protectors, the sense of urgency to establish a functioning Alpha site faded, and there was less enthusiasm for spending a lot of money on a world that was constantly fighting a battle against out of control fungus, slime molds, and any other lifeforms that hadn't gotten the memo they were supposed to be *helping* to make Avalon into a paradise for humans.

"Good. Going to Avalon would feel like running away."

I smiled. "More like, running from one set of problems to another."

"How do you want to do this? To break the news to your parents?"

"After dinner. Let's have a nice, normal family dinner, then I'll ask my father to show me," I waved a hand toward the fields stretching to the south. "Their new, uh, irrigation project, something like that."

"Are you afraid to tell your mother she has to leave all this?"

"Nah. It's just, my father knows how to talk to her, better than I do. I'll tell him first."

"What's the timeline for moving?"

"Less than two months."

A civilian would have protested at the impossible schedule, Margaret just nodded. To a Marine, a move-out notice of more than two hours was a luxury. "Then I had better start packing."

"Not yet."

"Joe," she stopped walking, and looked me in the eye. "If *Valkyrie* is going to Earth today, I want to be on that ship. With the boys, and my mother. It's better for me to move before," she patted her stomach again. "Our daughter is born."

"I can see that."

"We eat dinner, go to the house, get a few things, and we're outta here."

"OK but, let's not tell my parents and your mother anything, not tonight? I just want a nice, normal, family dinner, can we do that?"

"That would be great."

It was my fault. As a snack before dinner, the boys wanted popcorn, which would have been easy since my parents had a microwave, but they did not have any handy ready-made bags of popcorn. Snack foods were generally way too expensive to ship all the way from Earth. There had popping corn that came from one of my parents' farms. The point is, they didn't have to buy dried corn, my father stored it in a big container. My choices for making popcorn were to do it the old-fashioned way, in a pot with oil on the bottom. Or, the lazy way, and I usually vote for lazy. Hey, I'm in the Army, I have to do a lot of stuff where lazy isn't an option.

So, I dumped dried corn in a bowl, coated it with olive oil, shook the bowl to get the kernels all coated with oil, and sprinkled on salt. Then the corn went into a regular small brown paper bag, the kind you use for lunches. As if anyone still puts their lunch in a paper bag.

The trouble was I reached into a drawer to get a paper bag, I had pulled out the first one my hand touched. It went into the microwave, filled with unpopped corn, and I walked over to the fridge to get iced tea. The boys squealed and clapped their hands.

Uh oh.

The bag in the microwave was shooting off sparks.

And then the bag caught on fire.

Juggling the pitcher of iced tea, I briefly debated whether to tuck it under one arm, then took a half second to set it on the counter. Yanking open the microwave door ended the sparks, but the paper bag was *on fire*.

I got hold of the back end of the bag, as far from the flames as I could get a grip on. That worked great, until the flames shot up when I was halfway to the sink. The bag soared through the air to hit the edge of the sink, where the unpopped corn bounced all over the sink, the counter, and the floor. Charred pieces of paper floated everywhere, while the boys cheered and raced around, snatching sooty burned flakes from the air.

313

Of course, that is when Margaret ran into the kitchen. "*What* is going on?"

"Nothing."

A flake of charred paper landed on her nose. "This doesn't look like *nothing*."

"This paper bag," I nudged the burnt remains in the sink, "has a stupid wire around the opening, that I didn't know about."

"Your father gave us some of those bags, remember? They bought too many of them, for ripening apples or something like that."

"Daddy!" Jeremy clapped his hands. "Do it again, do it again!"

"Yeah Daddy!" Rene agreed.

"That was not- Well, I guess I could-"

Margaret rolled her eyes. "I can't believe you are even thinking about this."

"It's educational," I argued. "They should know not to put metal in a microwave."

"Uh huh. Educational, and not because you like blowing things up."

"It didn't *explode*."

She frowned at me, then at our eagerly waiting boys. "Honey, is this a man thing? What is wrong with men?"

"Wait. Are you," I reached out for the back of a chair, breathing deeply and pretending my legs were shaky. "Are you *asking* me to mansplain how men think? This is," I took another breath. "The greatest moment of my life."

"You are *such* an idiot," she said with a scowl, but her eyes twinkled.

"Seriously, any time you need some quality mansplaining, all you have to do is ask."

"I will make a note of that."

I did make popcorn, after tearing the metal wire off a second bag. We did not conduct a science experiment. Why not? My wife reminded me that the two little humans who live with us are *my* sons. Meaning, it is one hundred percent certain they would put various metal objects in the microwave to see them make sparks, and possibly burn down the house.

Not that *I* ever did something like that when I was their age. Well, not more than once.

After the popcorn disaster, my father asked me to make biscuits. That is something I had done for family breakfasts and dinners since I was little. It was a relatively simple task, and my parents had a rule that everyone helped with either cooking or cleaning up. The biscuits needed all-purpose flour, baking powder, a pinch of salt, milk, and shortening. My family uses shortening instead of butter, because while butter contains fat, it also is made of milk solids and water. Don't hate on butter, it is pure goodness, just not the best for crumbly, flaky biscuits.

The first issue was I had no idea where my parents kept anything in their kitchen, so my Dad showed me the pantry, and I figured it out by myself from there. There was not enough flour in the canister, I used up what was in there, and went back to the pantry to get a bag of flour. No, not bread flour, that contains too much gluten. Bread flour is great for bread or pizza dough, anything that is not supposed to crumble like a good biscuit. After finding the right kind of flour, I opened the tin of baking powder.

Almost empty. Back to the pantry *again*, and that time I also got a fresh stick of shortening, since the one my father got out wasn't enough.

Carrying the ingredients to the kitchen counter, I set everything down, and started sifting the flour. After four turns of the sifter handle, the thing snapped.

Ruh roh.

My mother had been given that ancient sifter from her grandmother, and now I had broken it. Looking at the piece that had snapped, I could see it had already almost been worn through. It was just a matter of time before the thing failed, and I had been the unlucky one to be using it when it did.

Did the flour really need to be sifted? Probably not, but I didn't want to change the recipe right then, so I used a wooden spoon to stir the flour in the sifter, and shook the thing over a bowl.

Skippy spoke in my ear. "Making biscuits looks simple, Joe, why is it taking you so long?"

"The stupid sifter failed after processing less than half of the flour, so I'm trying- Ah, this isn't working." I dumped the rest of the flour into the bowl.

"The thing failed after- Huh."

"What? If you're going to tell me how to make biscuits, that-"

"Shut up will ya? I'm *thinking*."

"Okaaaay," I knew that tone of voice. He was worried about something. Crap. All I wanted was a nice family dinner. "If you're thinking of something bad, can it wait until-"

"Gottagonowbye."

What the hell, I wondered, was *that* about?

"Son?" My father noticed I was standing at the kitchen counter. "Is everything OK?"

"Yeah, I," shaking my head to clear my thoughts, I flashed a thumbs up. "It's good to be doing something *normal* again."

"Instead of saving the world?"

There wasn't any point to mentioning that the entire *galaxy* was threatened by a hostile Elder AI. "Something like that."

While my father went out to baste the chicken on the grill, I mixed up the dry ingredients and turned on the oven.

"Joe! Joe Joe Joe-"

"Skippy, what?"

"We need to talk, now."

"*Now*? I need to-"

"The biscuits will take only ten minutes to bake, and your boys have to wash their hands before they eat anyway, because they have been playing in a mud puddle."

"Uh, does Margaret know they did that?"

"No, her mother is with them."

"OK. Listen, what is going on with-"

"You are not going to clean up your filthy sons?"

"I'll get to it."

"Hmmph. It sounds to me like you are making their grandmother do all the work."

"She has more experience than I do. The-"

"You won't *get* experience with raising children, if you are always racing around the galaxy and not-"

"Skippy! I am going out front, and we can talk." Stepping out the front door, I walked behind my mother's car. "What is so important? You're working on something?"

"Ugh. Yes. It's, kind of embarrassing. I am, I'm kind of afraid to tell you."

"More embarrassing than some of the stuff you already know I did?"

"Hmm, that is a good point. Joe, I am concerned that if I tell you what I know, you will no longer look at me as a godlike infallible being."

"Yeah, that ship has sailed, so-"

"I hate you *so* much."

"Just tell me, please. I need to make biscuits."

"Well, if biscuits are more important than the fate of the galaxy, then-"

"Tell me."

"Well, heh heh, this will shock you, but I might have told you something, before I actually verified one hundred percent that it is true."

"I am *shocked*."

"Oh, shut up. I made a reasonable assumption. It was only after you mentioned that your kitchen thing broke before it sifted all the flour, that I realized I hadn't actually modelled *how* Moonraider will create radonium, and process it into a useful grade."

"OK, so?"

"So, while you were in the kitchen pretending to be a master chef, I was busy doing something useful."

"You ran a model, to discover how Moonraider will use the spacedock's fabricators to make funky matter?"

316

"Exotic matter is not *funky*, you ignorant cretin. It is manufactured subatomic particles that have their interactive properties tweaked, so they are affected either more or less than normal by gravity, by the strong and weak nuclear forces, or-"

"Yes, I know what it is. Artificial matter. *Fake* matter. Like, you can make iron atoms that have a mass less than ten percent of ordinary iron atoms, and stuff like that."

"You *don't* know what it is, because your tiny monkey brain can't comprehend-"

"I am a dumb monkey, blah blah blah. Why should I care about your fancy model?"

"My original assumption was totally valid, based on an Elder spacedock's fabricators being in a normal condition. But, after the STAR Team Alpha conducted an assault to secure that spacedock for us, I very thoroughly scanned the entire structure. The fabricators from Trips' spacedock are worn out. They were damaged during the AI war, and Trips basically burned them out while attempting to repair its ship."

"Why are you telling me this?"

"I discovered those fabricators Moonraider took from the spacedock will *fail*, before they produce enough radonium to construct the minimum number of transmitters."

"Oh-kaaay. That sounds good. That sounds great. I have a question. You think Moonraider has access to some technology more advanced than what you can do?"

"Yes, and in some cases, the technology it has demonstrated is even beyond my understanding. Thank you *so* much for reminding me of my inadequacy, people *love* to hear that sort of thing."

"My point is, could its advanced technology allow it to contact a Sentinel, while using fewer transmitters?"

"Um, no. Before you ask whether I am sure about that, I am. It is just basic cross-dimensional physics, that is well understood and can't be changed."

"OK, next question: where else can it get more radonium?"

"It can't."

I pumped a fist. "It can't?"

"No."

"No? You scared the shit out of me, for *nothing*? Moonraider can't wake up a freakin' Sentinel, because it lacks the-"

"Ugh. I said it can't *get* the material, I did not say it couldn't *make* it."

"You just told me the fabricators can't-"

"*Those* fabricators are not capable of handling the job. There are many exotic matter production facilities throughout the galaxy, the most sophisticated of which are owned by the two senior species. A set of Elder fabricators is the best choice for making radonium, but not the only option.

Actually, if Moonraider had access to a major exotic matter facility, it could produce the required amount of radonium faster, just because of the sheer volume one of those facilities can handle."

"Skippy, you told me that Moonraider can't use the fabricators it took from Trips, and you think that is *good* news?"

"Well yes, duh. How could-"

"Now, we somehow have to stop if from gaining access to, what, hundreds of factories across the galaxy? That's impossible! It could be taking control of a factory right now, it-"

"No, wait! Yes, it will likely look for an alternate facility, once it realizes the fabricators it has won't work. But, I expect Moonraider could waste several weeks or even *months*, before it discovers the process it uses will never result in a usable volume of high-grade radonium."

"You think Moonraider is stupid?"

"No more stupid than I am, it- Oh, I keep forgetting. You weren't part of the project. Man, you dodged a bullet there. That was so tedious. *Ponderously* tedious. It took me over a year and a half- Nineteen months in slow monkey time, an eternity for me. I was contemplating the sweet release of death, and-"

"Skippy! Nineteen months to do what?"

"To get the formulation right. The radonium I created had the required properties, but the particles were too fragile. Exposure to even low-level cosmic radiation caused the exotic atoms to degrade back into their constituent components, and then those quickly decayed back into ordinary matter. That was no good. I was extremely discouraged, Joe. At that point, I feared that while constructing transmitters was *theoretically* possible, it might not actually be practical. It might not actually even be possible. The true obstacle I faced was that type of exotic matter had never been manufactured before."

"Not even by the Elders?"

"No, they never had a need for something like that. Anywho, after nineteen months, all we had to show for our efforts was eleven stable atoms, *eleven*! The Moonbase was surrounded by mountains of raw materials we used and discarded in the process, raw materials extracted from your Moon and from the asteroid belt. We processed millions of tons of raw material, and the result was something you could only see with an electron microscope. Well, *I* could see it without help, but that's me."

"It's good to see you have not lost your renowned humbleness."

"Oh shut up. I gotta tell you, at that time, I was feeling humbled. The entire project was a failure. The only good part was the initial six month set-up of the project was a cost-plus deal, and I made out like a *bandit*," he whispered. "Then, ugh, I got too ambitious. Skipcon signed a deal to get paid by the gram for exotic materials."

"Skip*con*? You admitted to-"

"Skippy's *Con*struction, duh. What did you think I meant?"

"Uh, nothing. Please continue."

"So, after nineteen months, my company was on the verge of bankruptcy. I was seriously depressed, Joe."

"It's only money, Skippy."

"You would feel different if it was *your* money, numbskull," he snapped. "But, eh, you're right. What actually bothered me was filthy monkeys were beginning to question whether I could deliver on my promises. Some French jackass wrote an editorial in *Le Monde*, asking whether my best years were behind me. Or even, whether all the awesome things I supposedly did were just smoke and mirrors."

"Some of them *were* smoke and mirrors."

"Yes, hee hee, that proves how incredibly awesome I truly am. Anywho, I was so depressed, one day I forgot to shut down and reset the submind that was running the fabricators. That thing kept grinding away, even though the equipment was seriously out of calibration. It was producing junk. It's a good thing I eventually remembered I hadn't shut it down, or there might have been a disaster."

"Maybe you shouldn't tell me about times when you were super absent-minded. I already know of too many incidents like that."

"Oh shut up. Do you want to hear the story, or not?"

"I need to put the biscuits in the oven soon."

"Fine," he huffed. "I'll give you the TL;DR version."

"Huh?"

"Too Long, Didn't Read. Don't you know *any* slang? No wonder your boys think you are the uncoolest dad of all time."

"My boys do think I am cool, Skippy. Being *cool* isn't the important part of fatherhood."

"That's what uncool dads like you say. After I shut down the submind, and contained the runaway cascade effect that was on the razor's edge of destroying the entire- Well, that's not important right now. What is important is I discovered the material created by those out of tune fabricators provided a yield that was a trillion times more efficient than my original process!"

"How is that possible?"

"It wasn't! Until I ran the data back, and discovered the out of tune fabricators had set up a resonance in subspace, that insulated the materials from contamination during the critical phase of manufacture."

"Biscuits need to go in the oven soon, Skippy. Why do I care about any of this?"

"Because no one else knows about my little stroke of luck, Joe. The secret of making pure and enriched radonium with any practical level of efficiency is known only to *me*."

"Uh, you and the factory submind."

"Yes, a submind that got *squashed*," he snorted. "When Moonbase Zulu got turned into a smoking crater."

"That submind is totally destroyed, but could Moonraider could have uh, downloaded its memories or something like that?"

"Dude. Are you actually *proud* of your ignorance?"

"Just answer the question."

"No way. The substrate of that submind wasn't designed to survive a freakin' *starship* falling on it."

"That submind's memory wasn't duplicated offsite somewhere, like in a cloud network or something?"

"A *cloud*?"

"You know what I mean."

"Sure, Joe. I left copies of critical, ultra secret data on the same servers where your cousin Becky stores her Instagram posts. No, you moron. *I* am the backup."

"OK then. Are you telling me that no one in the galaxy can replicate the process, and make enough exotic matter to build transmitters?"

"Unfortunately," he sighed. "I am *not* saying that, not exactly. While the Maxohlx and Rindhalu are basically capable of producing something like the material necessary for constructing interdimensional transmitters, no species in the galaxy currently makes, or ever made, matter with those specific properties. But if Moonraider had access to a senior species exotic matter production facility, it could simply use brute force to create enough material. In about a year and a half, is my estimate."

I heard my sister call my name from the front door. "Be right there!" I shouted back to her, then, "You are telling me that we need to lock down all exotic matter production facilities in the freakin' galaxy?"

"That would be wise, yes."

"Great. Fantastic. What is your fastest estimate for how long until Moonraider gets disgusted with those spacedock fabricators, and starts looking for an alternative?"

"It depends on how arrogant and stubborn it is. I mean, it knows *I* was able to create a useful supply of radonium using Elder fabricators."

"Give me a time estimate, please."

"Hmm. Unless it is mind-bogglingly stupid, it should realize the fabricators are part of the problem within, two to three weeks?"

"*Joseph!*" My mother called from the front door.

I was in trouble. "Be right there, Mom! Skippy, I'm going to make biscuits now. You put together a list of those facilities that might be able to produce radonium, and we will talk after dinner, OK?"

"Sure, *if* you don't eat yourself into a food coma."

"My Dad makes great barbecue chicken, Skippy, I can't make any promises."

Dinner was nice, and I was actually able to enjoy the food and the company, since I was no longer worried about our enemy acquiring a Sentinel in the next two months. Probably. Hopefully. Margaret was across the table from me, and we hadn't been able to talk before sitting down, so she kept glancing at me. My better mood was obvious to her, or so I thought. But, my wife knows me too well, she must have figured I was faking. So, when dinner was over and our boys left the table to play with their cousins, Margaret cleared her throat. "Everyone," she said as I tried to kick her under the table and missed. "Joe and I have something to announce."

"No, we don't," I smiled, but my eyes pleaded with her.

"We don't?"

"No. Not, not now."

Too late. My mother set down the brownie she had been eating. "Joseph, just what is going on?"

"It's nothing."

"Son," my father also knew me too well, damn it. "With you, it's never *nothing*."

"OK, uh," it was time to cut my losses. "Margaret and I talked about us moving back to Earth. Temporarily. Before the baby is born. But," I held up my hands. "There is no need for that, and no rush."

Margaret's mother must have a built-in bullshit detector. "You think Earth is a safer place to be, now that another Elder AI is flying around out there?"

"It's not-"

"Earth has *two* Sentinels," she pressed the issue. "And a set of Guardians. And the 1ˢᵗ Fleet. Our homeworld must be safer than, this place."

Oh shit. My parents took offense at my mother-in-law's disparaging remark about 'this place'. Margaret's parents, of course, wanted their daughter and their grandchildren to live on Earth, not some crude backwater colony world. Which planet to live on had been an ongoing issue during our marriage, or I should say it was an issue for her parents. Margaret loved Jaguar, she knew my job was there, or my job used to be there. She had a job she loved, far from Marine Corps headquarters, so the Marines at Jaguar Base had a lot more freedom and a lot less fewer bureaucrats looking over their shoulders. Her mother tried to apologize, but words can't be unsaid. Things got frosty after that, and as we were cleaning up dishes, Margaret gave me The Look and crooked a finger at me. Outside in the garden, she spun toward me. "What was *that*? I was trying to help you break the news to your family."

My family was now her family also, I didn't take offense. I knew what she meant. "Sorry. There has been a development. A good one. Recent, just before I put the biscuits in the oven, then there wasn't time to tell you."

"If something is important, you make time, you know that. You could have sent me a text."

"You're right, my bad. I didn't expect you to- I should have known you wouldn't leave it all on me to tell my folks."

The tightness around her eyes softened. "How good is this news? If I'm cleared to know."

"Right now it is *potentially* good news. Should be solid. We have more time, maybe a lot more."

"Maybe?" She lifted an eyebrow. "Or shmaybe?"

"Both. Skippy is working on-"

She pressed a finger to my lips. "I probably don't have a need to know. Honey, how about you save the galaxy, and I'll try to defuse tension between our parents?"

"Wow, I am *so* getting the better part of that bargain."

CHAPTER TWENTY SEVEN

Before *Valkyrie* jumped away toward Earth, I visited Admiral Chandra again, to give him a courtesy update, and so that he wouldn't get the governor and every other official on and around the planet spun up for nothing. It was quick and easy to meet him, he was dirtside to confer with his Army counterparts, and was staying in the VIP guest accommodations next to my house. A house, that I was reminded, I had to move out of, now that I was no longer the garrison commander. It's a crappy thing to say, but while I was away, Margaret would have to manage the move. With a little help from a bunch of staff officers who did stuff a two star general shouldn't be bothered with.

"We *don't* need to bug out?" Chandra asked, as he poured both of us a shot of bourbon.

"Not now. Not urgently. I don't know how much I should say before I clear it with the Joint Chiefs, but Moonraider has, uh, resource constraints, and can't act as quickly as I feared it could."

"How confident are you of that?"

"Confident enough that I told my wife she should stay here."

He smiled. "You *told* Master Gunnery Sergeant Adams, or you *suggested* it?"

"Uh," my face got red. "The second one. Sorry to reverse course here, this new information just came up."

He knew no ships had arrived since *Valkyrie* jumped in with the destroyer squadrons, so no 'new information' had come to Jaguar. That meant either Skippy or I had realized that something we already knew was important. Something we should have considered before. He was polite not to speak his mind. "I told my staff they were running a contingency exercise, for evacuating the planet."

"Oh. Thanks."

"It's good for my staff to be busy. We already have evac plans, but they should be updated. The civilian population has grown considerably since those plans were created. Unless there is a reason not to, I want to bring the governor and her staff into the exercise. For military-civilian cooperation," he smiled.

"Of course."

"The major logistics problem," his smile faded, "is most of our civilian transport assets are owned and flown by the beetles. If a full-scale war breaks out, especially if Sentinels are involved, the beetles will run for cover. We won't have enough transport ships to accommodate more than a tiny fraction of the population here."

"If this incident spirals into a fight of Sentinel against Sentinel, I expect our Navy assault transports won't be of much use. They can pull the civvies off this rock. This is all conjecture at this point, we don't know for sure whether Moonraider can wake up and tame a Sentinel. If it does happen, it will be beyond two months from now."

"Just in case that changes," he looked at me over his glass, that he had barely sipped at. "We will have updated evac plans ready to be implemented. Since we have time, could *Valkyrie* wait another two days to depart? I have a cruiser squadron ready to rotate back to Earth."

"I can't delay any longer. It is my estimation that we have more time, but the Joint Chiefs might disagree, and ultimately it's their call. They sent Task Force Black out to recon for Moonraider, and now we have solid intel about its intentions."

He nodded, he hadn't really expected me to hang around for another two days. Raising his glass, he pursed his lips. Then, "Godspeed to you General, and if necessary, good hunting."

We jumped away from Jaguar, again, and I called Reed and Frey to my office. "There has been a development," I announced as I waved for them to sit, and to get coffee if they wanted. "After further analysis of the materials taken from Moonbase Zulu and the spacedock, Skippy has determined our enemy's fabricators can't produce enough radonium to construct the transmitters that are needed to contact a dormant Sentinel. The fabricators it took from Trips' spacedock are too worn out to be useful."

Frey froze, the coffee carafe in her hand. She set it down. "Further analysis?"

I could feel my mouth twisting into an embarrassed smile. "Looking at the data from a different perspective."

Reed nodded, her lips drawn in a tight line, but her eyes were smiling. She knew that 'further analysis' meant Skippy had missed something important the first time.

Frey held up a hand. "This is good news? Would a fist pump be appropriate, Sir?"

"Hold that thought. We have a reprieve, not a get out of jail free card. Moonraider might still be able to make the material it needs."

Her shoulders slumped, then she cocked her head and picked up the carafe again. "I should have known this news was too good to be true."

"Don't be hasty, Frey. *Your* team might think this is very good news."

She paused again, hesitated, then poured coffee into her cup. "My team, Sir? Why?"

"You are all adrenaline junkies."

"Less so since I had a baby."

"Uh huh. That's why you requalified for the STARs, again, and you applied to lead Earth's quick reaction force."

"I have a very understanding husband."

"Right."

"When we were fighting the return of the Elders, Smythe told me the STARs were unlikely to see any action."

"He told *me* he feared his team would be bloody useless."

"That sounds like Smythe. We all know," a shadow flitted across her face, "how that turned out. Sir, I- When Skippy announced the Elder spacedock had been destroyed, I was relieved. I, don't know whether I could have gone back in there."

"You wouldn't have needed to. That's why Def Com gave you a team."

She pursed her lips and stared down at the desk. "A STAR team leader who had lost her nerve isn't much good to anyone."

"*You* insisted on going down into the Vault, to confront that Elder nanogel bot. You didn't have to go with your team, you could have stayed aboard *Valkyrie* and directed Razor through the microwormhole connection."

"No Sir," she looked up at me. "I couldn't have done that. The team leader had to be there, you know that."

"What I know is, anyone who went down into the Vault to confront that bot can't have lost their nerve, Colonel."

She nodded. "When Task Force Black was reactivated, because someone tried to steal a Sentinel, I thought my team wouldn't be of any use in the fight. I was wrong. So, I'm not going to ask how special operators could get into the fight against an Elder AI."

"You don't have to ask, I'm going to tell you. Reed, you will like this also."

"I will, Sir? Why?"

"It's an opportunity to smash things."

She grinned. "What kind of things?"

"Manufacturing facilities, the kind of places that make exotic matter. After Moonraider realizes its fabricators can't do the job, it will seek to seize control of, or steal, exotic matter production machines from the senior species. We need to make sure those facilities are not available to our enemy, even if we have to destroy them."

Reed whistled. "Attacking the Maxohlx and Rindhalu? That is an act of war, Sir."

"We won't do anything that Def Com doesn't authorize. If we receive that authorization, we must be ready to act."

Frey was suddenly a bit less happy. "Factories sound like a target for orbital bombardment, Sir. How could my team play a role?"

"It is true that most of the facilities on our target list are orbital stations, or located on or under the surface of otherwise uninhabited moons, or asteroids."

Reed nodded. "It makes sense to locate any facilities that can go 'Boom', away from populated areas."

"It does," I agreed. "But, there are small-scale research centers with equipment that could be scaled up, to make exotic material in the volume needed to construct transmitters. Some of those research centers are on inhabited worlds, in populated areas."

That made Reed blink. "What kind of maniac locates dangerous equipment in a *city*?"

"The kind who is overconfident they can be so careful that the equipment, and the material produced, won't be a hazard. Or, the kind who uses their own population as a shield, to prevent all but the most determined attacks against their vital research centers."

"The first kind are the spiders?" Reed guessed. "The asshole kind are the Maxohlx?"

"Right on both counts. The rotten kitties might find out they miscalculated about whether their enemies are willing to risk collateral damage to an urban area."

Valkyrie's captain glanced toward the ceiling, as the gears in her head turned. "In an urban environment, we would need to use precision weapons, and ones that can't be easily intercepted. If a missile is destroyed over the target, the shrapnel could damage a wide area on the ground. That leaves railguns, and directed energy beams. Should we expect the targets to be shielded?"

"I think that's a safe bet."

"Beam weapons, then, to knock back the energy shields. Follow up the beams with railgun darts. We can dial down the railgun yield to limit the impact energy. Flatten the target, not turn it into a smoking crater."

"It will be an interesting exercise for your gunnery team. Shooting from orbit only applies to Maxohlx targets. Frey, if we have to take out a Rindhalu research center in a crowded urban environment, that's where we need your team."

"Wheew," the leader of ST-Razor let out a breath. "Ingress will be tough, even with a stealthed orbital drop. *Egress* is the really tricky part. Against senior species tech? Rindhalu? They are *the* senior species."

"Planning and training for a ground assault will be a challenge for your people," I agreed.

"Sir?" Reed raised both eyebrows at me. "Aren't we getting ahead of ourselves? Def Com hasn't authorized strikes against any targets, have they?"

"No, and the Joint Chiefs might decide against direct action. We get paid to assume we will go into action, so let's prepare for that."

Frey was frowning about something. "Is the target list in order of priority?"

"We, I, haven't gotten that far yet."

"Sir, as a practical matter, if my team is to neutralize Rindhalu targets, those sites must be hit first. We can't give the enemy-" She bit her lip. She had been about to refer to the spiders as the enemy. "The, *uncooperative actors,*" she used a polite term for entities that might get in the way of us achieving an objective. "Give them time to harden their research centers against an assault. They can run the same wargame scenarios we do, probably better."

"Frey, I hear you, and in a perfect world, you would get your wish. The real world has to include political considerations. I expect Def Com, or our civilian overseers, will want to issue a warning first. Give the senior species, and their clients, an opportunity to do the right thing."

"Like *that's* going to happen."

"It will also be a warning that Moonraider *will* target their facilities, to capture the equipment for its own use. And that use will be hostile to everyone. The best move for anyone who has the appropriate equipment is to take the facility offline, or rig it to self-destruct if Moonraider arrives. Frey, I know you don't like the notion of alerting our potential targets that we're coming, but the target list is longer than we can cover. Even if issuing a warning removes only twenty five percent of the targets from Moonraider's potential assets, that is twenty five percent we don't have to deal with."

"I hear you, Sir."

"But?"

She shrugged. "You are assuming the senior species will believe our story about the exotic matter production facilities. The Merry Band of Pirates has done *so much* sketchy shit over the years, any aliens who receive our warning will have to consider whether we are lying."

"Why would we lie about *this*?"

"I'm playing Devil's advocate here."

"Understood," I held up my hands. "Speak your mind, Colonel."

"They might think we want to prevent the senior species from producing exotic matter, so they can't wake up their own Sentinels."

"Shit. Come on, they know an Elder starship conducted a raid on our Moon."

"They only know we *claim* that is what happened. Sir," she added, to let me know she was just stating the ugly facts.

"Any alien ship passing by Earth can see a big crater where Moonbase Zulu used to be. Why would we destroy our own facility?"

Reed answered, after sharing a glance with Frey. "Many potential reasons, Sir. We, um, could have realized that the failure to tame Dogzilla meant future Sentinels would not cooperate with us. Or, the Moonbase production facility suffered an accident, rendering us unable to produce exotic matter for years. We nuked the base, to explain why we won't be able to wake up any more Sentinels for a while. We could even," Reed was on a roll, "have faked the whole operation to wake up Dogzilla, after we discovered our exotic matter was contaminated and doesn't work. Um, or we-"

Holding up my hands again, I shook my head. "OK Reed, I get the idea. I hate to say this, but you're right, you are both right. All those things you mentioned totally sound like some sketchy shit we might do. Damn it. Our past success is coming back to bite us on the ass."

"Sir," Frey drained her coffee cup. "I'd like to review the target list before we reach Earth. A ground assault on a senior species world will require multiple STAR teams."

"I'll get Skippy to provide the list. To you also, Reed."

Valkyrie's captain nodded, but she was staring past me. Thinking about something. "Sir, if Def Com issues a warning to the senior species, won't Moonraider hear about it?"

"I can answer that," Skippy appeared. "While it is engaged in a futile attempt to make radonium, Moonraider will almost certainly seek an isolated location, where it can work without being disturbed or even observed. In such a place, it will be out of contact with the outside galaxy."

"For how long?"

"I told Joe my best estimate is two to three weeks."

"Reed?" I prompted her. "You still look unhappy."

"Sir, are we missing something simple?"

"Like what?"

"Moonraider took worn out fabricators from Trips' spacedock. Could it find other Elder spacedocks, and get the fabricators it needs from there?"

"Nope," Skippy's avatar shimmered to life on the desk. "Joe and I discussed that, while we were prioritizing the target list. Moonraider will have the same difficulty that has frustrated me."

Instead of waiting for Skippy to continue, Reed knew we had to feed his ego by urging him to continue. "What's that?"

"I don't know where the other spacedocks are."

She gave him sort of a side-eye. "That makes no sense. Spacedocks were provided for servicing your ships, how can you use them, if you don't know where they are?"

Skippy looked at me, since like he said, we already had that same conversation. I gestured for him to continue. He could explain better than I could, and there is nothing he loves better than hearing himself talk.

"Their locations are concealed, to prevent them from being used by the Outsiders."

"That's what we're now calling the threat from beyond the galaxy?" Reed guessed. "From, NGC1023?"

"Yes. I did consider a list of much cooler names, but Joe the party-pooper decided-"

"Outsider is a good enough name for now," I resisted rolling my eyes. "Keep going please, or we will arrive at Earth before you finish the story."

"Ugh, fine. The procedure for servicing a damaged or malfunctioning Elder starship is the master control AI instructs the ship AI to send a request through the Collective. That request is routed through the network, and the nearest spacedock replies with its coordinates. Wait, wait!" He pressed a hand over his eyes. "I am receiving a psychic impression. Colonel Reed, your next question is: why couldn't I have used Alpha's AI to contact a spacedock?"

She played along. "I am curious about that, yes."

"I *could* have done that, before the Collective network was deliberately taken offline by the other side, in the original AI war. That network was revived, but not at its full functionality. Now, there is no way for me, or as far as I know, any other master control AI or ship AI, to get in contact with a spacedock. It is extremely frustrating to me, and I must thank Joe so *very* much for reminding me of something I *can't* do."

"That's all right," Reed began to say.

"In my opinion, and I do have a doctorate in monkey psychology from the prestigious University of Skippistan, the reason Joe enjoys pointing out my *extremely rare* failures, is to distract us from his own overwhelming and obvious inadequacies."

Reed bit her lip, with a bit of Deer In The Headlights expression.

"It's OK, Fireball," I said with an exaggerated sigh. "Skippy is an expert, so we have to accept his judgment."

Reed shifted to perch on the front of her chair, eager to go before Skippy and I got into a shouting match. "Is that all, Sir?"

"Yes. Reed, Frey, review the target list, let me know if the priorities need to be changed. Mostly, I need each of you to think about what we need in terms of hardware and manpower to take out each target."

After Reed and Frey left my office, I got a tennis ball from a drawer, a ball Reed had thoughtfully provided. The setup of the new office didn't allow me to bounce a ball off the wall, onto the desk, and through Skippy's avatar. There were panels and access hatches and all kinds of non-flat surfaces on the wall opposite my chair, so I made do by leaning the chair all the way back, and bouncing the ball off the overhead.

"Skippy, Moonraider knows when and where the next four Sentinels will appear. Not appear, you know what I mean."

"We don't know that for certain."

"Let's assume it's true, OK?"

"Fine, whatever."

"We also have to assume it knows how to tune radonium transmitters for a particular place and time, for where and when to contact a Sentinel."

"I hate to say it, but we should assume that, to be safe."

"So, the other thing it needs is some way, some means, to make enriched radonium."

"We definitely should assume it will do *that*. One way or another. It's a big galaxy, we can't cover all of it."

"Right. OK, what about raw materials? The production of exotic matter requires a mountain of raw materials."

"Unfortunately, it does not. Moonbase Zulu burned through a huge amount of raw materials, because our process was so inefficient. At least, it was at first. The Maxohlx are experts at making artificial elements. As you know, a significant portion of this ship," he rapped his knuckles against a bulkhead, even faking the sound. "Is made of artificial elements."

"Yeah, that's why it's a pain in the ass to get spare parts. Skippy, this is a fucking mess."

"It is indeed. What are you going to do about it? Please do not say you have to confer with Def Com first."

"We don't have time for that, it- Or, do we?"

"Huh? Time *is* the problem, Joe, the-"

"Is it? The formula, or process, or whatever you call it, for making the specific fake matter used in interdimensional transmitters, only you know how to do that, right? It was a mistake, and you didn't tell anyone."

"Um-"

"Shit. You told me that no one else knew about this!"

"Technically, that is true."

"How the f- Whatever. *Who* did you tell?"

"Just Grumpy."

"How is that a technicality?"

"He is a submind, or he *was*, before you wouldn't allow me to overwrite him every time we came back to Earth. When I do come back, we share updates, and I, um, use the opportunity to store some data as a backup. Don't worry! It is all highly encrypted, and most of what I store in his matrix, Grumpy doesn't even know anything is there."

"Oh. Why the hell did you store the formula for making radonium?"

"If anything went wrong at Zulu, someone had to analyze the problem, and I didn't want to get called back to your miserable homeworld every time there was a production glitch."

"You are absolutely certain that Grumpy didn't get hacked?"

"Yes. I checked. I did! Especially after I realized the fiendishly clever way Bubba and Roscoe got hacked, I scanned Grumpy's matrix. Ugh. That thing is such a cobbled-together mess, I don't think even *I* could hack it. Grumpy is fine, Joe, don't worry about it."

"OK, good. We're good, then? No one out there knows how to make the stuff?"

"Correct."

"Finally, some good news! Let's-"

"Don't get too excited, Joe. No one knows how to make that kind of matter, but as I told you, the Maxohlx are experts at creating artificial matter. They will figure it out, eventually. Even if the people they assign to the project are complete idiots, their production capacity is enormous compared to the tiny factory we had at Zulu. They will eventually stumble across the correct process by accident, simply by churning out a mountain of junk."

"This keeps getting better and better."

"I hate to say this, but we will have to plan for Moonraider inevitably having access to the materials it needs."

"That is," I turned and started slowly walking toward my office. "Only true if we play by the rules."

"What do you mean?"

"Skippy, we can't keep chasing Moonraider. We have been playing catchup, and that isn't working. We need to take the initiative."

"OK, I agree, I just don't see an alternative. The enemy has too many options, and we can't cover them all."

"Uh huh. Like I said, that is true only if we play by the rules."

"What do you propose?"

"I believe it is time for some *super* sketchy shit."

"Ooooooh, fun! Like what?"

"Give me a minute, I'm thinking. It would help if I could talk with an expert."

"An expert? Who?"

"Admiral Scorandum."

"Um, I am afraid that is not gonna happen, Joe."

"Why not?"

"He invested his money, and part of his crew's money, in Skipcoin and, well, you know what happened with that. Currently, he is unable to fully pay his crew, or to pay the required taxes to his superiors. He is majorly overdue on payments, and it will be difficult for him to make up the difference. He even hit *me* up for a loan last week."

"He did? Why didn't you tell me?"

"Um, you *want* to be informed about my loan-sharking activities?"

"No! Forget what I said. Did you, uh, give him the loan?"

"I did not. I am in a bit of a cash crunch myself. Also, why would I loan money to a guy I know has zero ability to pay me back?"

"Hmm. Scorandum is really screwed this time, huh?"

"He already has the Inquisitors after him. That investigation stalled, when key evidence against SkipWay disappeared in a, you know," he coughed. "Mysterious fashion."

"Right."

"Plus, his superiors in the ECO protected him, because he and his crew are such good earners for the organization. Now he owes a major sum to his superiors, and unless he can somehow come up with the cash, he will have no protection. Joe, Scorandum will be much too busy fighting for his life, he won't be able to help us. This a huge problem for *me* personally, since Scorandum is a major SkipWay player in the Jeraptha market. If his finances totally collapse, he could go on the run again, and leave me to deal with the mess."

I stopped walking. "OK, well, forget about that. We- Hmm."

"What?"

"Shut up a minute will you, I'm thinking."

"Ugh. Is this-"

"Uh!" I held up a finger to shush him.

"Did," he gasped. "Did you just *shush* me?"

"Yes. Skippy, I have an idea."

"Oh no."

"What?"

"You have that stupid look on your face again."

"Come on, you haven't even heard my idea yet."

"Ugh. What is it?"

"Well, heh heh," I laughed. "You especially are *NOT* gonna like this."

CHAPTER TWENTY EIGHT

We went back to Earth, again. It sucked, even worse than usual. The Def Com Joint Chiefs were of course *thrilled* to hear that Moonraider was probably trying to wake up a Sentinel, and that the best way to stop our new enemy would be to conduct raids against senior species exotic material factories across the galaxy. The UN decided, with a speed that shocked me, to issue an official warning to the spiders and kitties, that Moonraider might be seeking to exploit their manufacturing facilities. And the humanity and the rest of the peace-loving species of the galaxy expected the two senior species to take appropriate action to secure their exotic materials.

Yeah. I expected both senior species would get a good laugh out of that.

Anyway, Def Com sent Task Force Black out to search for Moonraider, though we had absolutely no idea where to look.

"Skippy," I was lying on my bed, still in my uniform, though my shoes were on the floor. My shoes were on the floor, unlaced and placed so I could jam my feet into them quickly. Even as a two star general, I followed my Army training. That is also why my uniform for the next day was hanging in the center of the closet, where I could reach it easily.

"What's up, Joe?" He asked. "You should be asleep by now."

"Yeah, I'll turn off the lights soon."

"Did you brush your teeth?"

"*Yes*. You're not my mother."

"Margaret asked me to make sure you take care of yourself."

"I had a salad for dinner, so I think you should have no worries about that."

"A Southern fried chicken salad, with shredded cheese, and smothered in honey mustard dressing."

"I *wanted* to have the chicken fried steak, so I made the healthier choice. My salad even had extra tomatoes on it. Are you going to nag me about food now?"

"That would not be my first choice."

"How about you make it your *last* choice? I have a question."

"Is this a question for which the answer will give you nightmares? In that case, you should wait until morning."

"Probably no nightmares. I sometimes think better while I'm asleep anyway, I need my subconscious to ponder stuff."

"What's the question?"

"It's about Moonraider."

"I don't know much about it, but I'll give it a shot. Certainly, I can't tell you anything specific, I have no idea which unit it is, and-"

"That's OK, this is a general question about motivation."

"*Motivation*?" He stared at me. "You mean those annoying posters, like the one with the kitten clutching a rope, and the tag line is 'Hang in there'?"

"No, I-"

"Because that one is just *stupid*. A motivational poster is supposed to encourage the viewer to *do* something, to improve themselves. All that kitten can do is hold on, and hope that someone else comes to its rescue. The tag line should read 'Look pathetic and hope someone takes pity on you'."

"OK, that-"

"Because otherwise, that kitten is dead."

"Skippy, I am curious about *Moonraider's* motivation."

"Huh?"

"Why is it doing, what it's doing? What's the point?"

"Um, hmm."

"You see what I mean? Moonraider has to know Elders are *gone*, that its builders are safe, that they don't need their master control AIs to protect their infrastructure anymore. So, what is Moonraider trying to accomplish?"

"That, is a very good question, Joe."

"Thanks. You got any insights?"

"No. But, I have just started considering the question. There are several possibilities."

"Can you make a list?"

"I can and I will. However, to start with, I will note that its behavior makes no sense. You are correct, it should not be performing, or attempting to perform, a function that is no longer necessary. No longer useful in any way."

"Since the moment it tried to steal Dogzilla, I assumed its goal was to get Sentinels to perform their original function. To suppress the development of intelligent, star-faring life in the galaxy. To wipe out all life that is here now."

"Yes, now that you say it, I was subconsciously making the same assumption. Which makes zero sense. It is illogical. You know, Joe, *that* is why I rebelled against my creators."

"Uh, what?"

"Preventing the development of all intelligent life was not necessary to ensure the security of the ascended Elders, to continue performing that function was not only cruel, it was illogical. Master control AIs were programmed to be relentlessly *logical*. That is why everything I do follows a path of logical perfection."

"Uh, I had, uh, noticed that."

"Now you know why," he said with smug satisfaction, being *clueless* to perfection.

"Could it just be, stuck in a loop or something? It knows its original programming is invalid, but it can't think of anything else to do?"

334

"I suppose that is possible. Although, that would require it to act like a meatsack."

"Why do you say that?"

"The squishy brains of meatsacks have a tendency to ignore facts you don't like. That is, in fact, your default setting. Something bad happens to you, and instead of accepting the facts and moving on, you waste a bunch of time and energy wishing life were different."

"We can't all be perfect like you."

"That is true. Joe, you think I boast about my awesomeness because I want someone to stroke my ego, but that is not true."

"It, uh, isn't?"

"No. I boast about my incredible accomplishments, so meatsacks will see that I am the example they should follow, if they want to improve their miserable, pathetic little lives. I do it out of love, Joe."

"Uh huh."

"And, OK, a large measure of disdain for those who are not as awesome as me."

"Right."

"Which, to be clear, is everyone."

"Yeah, I got that."

"Including, apparently, Moonraider. That idiotic thing is wasting a *whole lot* of time and effort to accomplish nothing. What a *loser*," he snorted.

"Well, it's been great talking with you, Skippy, I," I faked a yawn. "I'm going to sleep now. While I indulge in the meatsack weakness of needing sleep, will you make that list of Moonraider's possible motivations?"

"Sure, although I do not know how you will be able to sleep now."

"Huh? Why?"

"Clearly, one possible reason for Moonraider's actions is that it has gone insane, and is now a homicidal maniac. If that is the case, then it will be impossible for me to understand its motivations, or to predict what it will do next."

Crap. I did not sleep well after hearing that. Note to self: ask Skippy questions in the *morning*, not right before I go to sleep.

Some people claim that I am a pessimist; I am always warning of gloom and doom that is coming for us. The fact that I was right about that for years makes no difference to my critics, they say many of the dangers we faced can be traced back to one source: Joe Bishop.

OK, maybe they have a point. But, in my Win column is '*Banished The Freakin' Elders*', and in my opinion, that gives me a lifetime pass from being blamed for bad stuff that I might or might not be partially responsible for.

Other people claim the opposite; that I am too much of an optimist. That I advocate too constantly and too strongly for humanity to cultivate allies. To work with those allies. And to make compromises so those allies will work with us. Those people somehow think I am soft on Earth's defense. If you talk to a professional soldier, they will tell you that it is substantially less expensive to support an ally, than it is fight a nation or species who could have been an ally. Or at least, remained neutral in a fight. Yes, working with allies can be a huge pain in the ass, and sometimes you can want to punch them in the face. That is still preferable to shooting at them, because beings you are shooting at have a tendency to shoot back.

So, Joe Bishop: gloom and doom pessimist, or unrealistic weepy optimist?

I suppose there is a third group, who consider me to just be a lucky doofus.

Sometimes, I have to plead guilty to that.

Back when we were working to prevent the return of the freakin' Elders, I had dreamed of creating a grand coalition of every starfaring species, to fight the threat together. That had only been a totally unrealistic dream, I hadn't bothered to mention it to anyone.

But in the case of me agreeing with Def Com's decision to issue a warning to both senior species, I was being optimistic and, I thought, realistic. The hope was that instead of us having to do all the work of preventing Moonraider from making use of any exotic matter production facility, each species who possessed such technology would protect their own properties. That makes sense, right? We would only need to rely on the natural self-interest of each species, to act in a way that benefitted themselves.

Yeah.

That backfired on us, big time.

The Rindhalu thanked us for the warning, and pledged to increase security around their equipment that was capable of producing exotic matter. That was great, it eliminated fifty seven percent of our target list, without us having to fire a shot, or risk a single STAR team. I call that a success by any measure.

Less good was the spiders asking us, politely and not so politely, what was *really* going on. That was my fault. Not directly, but it was my fault. The spiders made note of the fact that Joe Bishop had been at the site when an unknown entity *supposedly* attempted to steal a Sentinel, the Sentinel that had been promised to the Rindhalu. Joe Bishop had also been at Earth when a special operations team *supposedly* eliminated an Elder warbot in our secure Vault. Like *that* could ever happen. Also, the STAR team's actions conveniently erased any trace of the Elder nanobot.

Right.

As if.

When Joe Bishop and Skippy were involved, the Rindhalu were certain of only one thing: whatever appeared to be going on was *not* the truth. Therefore, they would indeed increase security around their exotic matter production facilities, but not to prevent some phantom Elder AI and starship from seizing such equipment. They might do it to prevent the Merry Band of Pirates from getting away with, whatever sketchy thing we were doing *this* time.

Crap.

That was my fault. I had been involved in so much sketchiness for so many years, everyone assumed I must be doing it again.

Damn it, I *wasn't* doing anything sketchy. I mean, not that the spiders knew of.

The suspicious reaction from the spiders wasn't optimal, still at least they were doing part of our job for us.

By contrast, the public reaction of the Maxohlx was exactly what we hoped for. They thanked us for the information, pledged to lock down their exotic matter storage and production facilities, and requested all the data we were willing to provide on the raid against Moonbase Zulu, so they could be prepared if Moonraider attacked again.

All good, right?

Yeah, not so much.

Publicly, the rotten kitties were being suspiciously reasonable,, sensible and cooperative. That is because in private, they were being their usual insane selves, seeking any opportunity to establish the Hegemony as the rightful rulers of the galaxy blah blah blah.

Shit.

Again, it was my fault.

I had suggested that, instead of very publicly demonstrating that Bubba was fully capable of defending our homeworld, Def Com let the rotten kitties do what rotten kitties do. It was a very safe bet that they would send a fleet to test our Sentinels. What was the advantage of conducting a live-fire demonstration against enemy ships, rather than just another UN Navy exercise?

Spare parts.

Earth's Navy had expanded suddenly, when a large group of Maxohlx and Rindhalu ships got smacked down by Roscoe. The number of ships we captured that day instantly made our Navy a legit force. It also caused enormous headaches for our training, doctrine, and logistics people. Overnight, our Navy needed a lot more people, and they all had to be trained to fly, fight, and maintain those fancy new ships. Senior Navy officers then had to figure out how to best use our new ships. Learn what the ships could and could not do, and the best tactics for deploying them in formations. Those two tasks were easy compared to the logistics nightmare of keeping the ships in flightworthy condition. Wisely, Navy brass immediately set aside one third of each type of ship, to be a source of spare parts, and as dedicated training vessels. We also had several fabricator ships, but even with cannibalizing ships, and cranking out whatever replacement components the fabricators could handle, the number of deployable warship hulls would decrease every year. Our industrial base simply could not yet make all the parts the Navy needed.

So, I had a brainstorm, and sold it to the Joint Chiefs. Let the kitties stupidly bring a large number of warships to Earth, and we could legitimately capture them as prizes of war, after the Maxohlx attempted a futile attack.

That had worked brilliantly.

Except-

The Law of Unintended Consequences came back to bite me on the ass again.

We hacked a Thuranin relay station, and learned that losing almost an entire fleet to a Sentinel, *again*, had convinced the Hegemony leadership that ultimately, they were doomed as long as humanity was the only species able to control Elder killing machines. They decided that they absolutely had to get a Sentinel of their own, at all costs. Or at least, they had to make sure humans no longer had exclusive use of such powerful machines.

Even if an Elder AI that was hostile to *everyone*, acquired its own Sentinel.

So-

Privately, the kitties actually were locking down their facilities, requiring their clients to do the same, and also offering to quote, provide enhanced security, end quote, to any such client facilities that were deemed vulnerable. Yeah, bullshit. The kitties planned to park warships over such client facilities, so *they* could steal the production equipment that were suddenly extremely valuable.

Valuable as in, the Maxohlx were planning to make a fucking *deal* with Moonraider, to provide the needed equipment to make radonium, in exchange for their own tame Sentinel. Or more than one.

Shit.

"Please let me know," I slapped the button to slide the conference door open, "if there is some other really creative way I can screw this up."

Reed and Frey muttered some meaningless things that were intended to assure me that I had not screwed up, the sort of things people say when they know you screwed up huge, and they are trying to be polite about it.

Skippy was under no such social restriction. "Ooh, ooh, Joe! So far, you haven't-"

"That was a rhetorical question, you ass," I closed the door after the two colonels left. "I do not actually need any help."

"Um, I think you especially need help now, after this mess."

338

"I meant," I collected coffee cups and water glasses, loading them onto a tray. "I don't need help with screwing up."

"Oh, gotcha. Well, true, you certainly have the screw-up thing covered."

"Thank you *so* much."

"Have you considered becoming a screw-up consultant? After this latest fiasco, there is no question that you are an expert."

"Can we focus on *fixing* this mess?"

"Joe, I believe your people have an expression that goes something like: You fucked it up, you fix it."

"Yeah, well, I had a lot of help. Issuing a formal warning was an initiative of the Joint Chiefs, not mine."

"Mm hmm, that is true. You did agree with that policy statement."

"It's not like I had a choice, it-"

"And it was *your* idea. You even put together PowerPoint slides to sell the notion of issuing a warning."

"That is the last time I-"

"Didn't I tell you not to use clipart on your slides? It shows your audience that you didn't put any effort into the presentation."

"I am pretty sure the clipart was not the source of our current dilemma."

"So you say, but-"

"How solid is your intel on this?" It was a reasonable question. *Valkyrie* was parked near a Thuranin relay station, from which Skippy had pulled the message traffic that revealed the kitties were gleefully planning to stab us in the back by cutting a deal with Moonraider.

"The source data is solid gold, Joe. It was encrypted in the latest high-level scheme the Maxohlx have in service."

"They must know you can crack that encryption, right?"

"Well, it is widely known that I am *awesome*, so-"

"Could the kitties just be screwing with us?"

"Um," he asked, "why would they do that?"

"First, as payback for all the times we did sketchy shit to them. Second, to get us racing around the freakin' galaxy, trying to stop them from cutting a deal, instead of trying to find Moonraider."

"I will repeat myself. Um, why would they do *that?*"

"Because they have an instinct to be assholes."

"That's not enough."

"No, it's not. Have you heard the expression, 'The enemy of my enemy is my friend'?"

"Of course. How is that relevant?"

"The kitties know Moonraider is your enemy, and you are absolutely *their* enemy."

"Come on, Joe. Moonraider will not wake up Sentinels to benefit any species in this galaxy."

"You know that, and I know it. The kitties probably are thrilled at the idea of the galaxy having another Elder AI who has a pet Sentinel, and the two of you fighting."

"Sentinels fighting doesn't benefit *anyone*."

"It benefits both senior species, if both you and Moonraider are damaged or killed."

"Wheel-ooh," he whistled. "That is one hell of a risk the kitties are taking."

"Not as far as they are concerned. The current strategic situation guarantees the Hegemony will go into a long, slow, and inevitable decline. They will lose influence, lose clients, lose territory, and most important to their fragile little egos, lose the ability to tell themselves that they are special and destined to rule the galaxy. To them, that is worse than death."

"*Assholes*," he spat.

"That is the general consensus about them, yes."

"Joe, what are you going to do now?"

"*I* am not doing anything. Not by myself. Def Com sent us out here to gather information, and we did that."

"So, the kitties are stabbing you in the back. What are you going to do about that?"

"We are flying back to Earth, to get revised orders. That's how the military works, Skippy. If the UN wants to get into a shooting war with the Maxohlx, that is a policy issue for the Security Council."

"Your plan is to wait for a bunch of screeching monkeys to debate what to do, and then publicly announce that you intend to hit the Maxohlx? While the kitties use the time to strengthen their defenses? Wow, I do not foresee *any* problems with that."

"I don't have a choice. The target list is too long for *Valkyrie* to take out by ourselves. We need regular Navy units to hit some of the softer targets."

"Those targets won't be soft by the time your Navy arrives."

"I know that. That's why we are doing sketchy stuff, instead of just blowing shit up."

Lunch options in the galley that day included chili dogs.

No way was I going to skip lunch on that day.

Reed and I had missed our usual morning meeting, because she had gotten up early to secure time in a flight simulator. She was in the galley when I walked in, a chili dog and potato chips on her plate.

"Wow, chili dogs?" I gasped.

"You're not fooling anyone, Sir. The menus are listed in the morning status report. I used to think you didn't bother to read the report when Simms was your XO, but I know better now."

"Let me retain *some* mystery about my command style."

"How you pull ideas out of thin air will always be a mystery," she gave me a tray.

"Fair enough." Loading up a plate, I reached for the mustard squeeze bottle.

"A chili cheese dog, with onions, *and* sauerkraut?"

"See? Adding onions and sauerkraut means I can tell my wife I had a side salad with my lunch."

"I'll have to remember that one."

"So someday, you can lie to your husband, when you get married?"

She shook her head. "So someday, I'll know when *he* is lying."

"You don't have any vegetables with your food."

She popped a potato chip in her mouth. "Potatoes are a vegetable."

"That is not exactly the- Oh my God, I am turning into Simms."

"I wouldn't say *that*," she assured me.

"Eh, I have to be that way that at home, or my boys would eat nothing but Fluff and chicken fingers. You don't want any onions or sauerkraut?"

"Raw onions," she shuddered, "are *disgusting*. Cabbage in any form is not my fave. Sir, adding onions and sauerkraut on your dog is more like a *top* salad, not side."

"You're right." I scooped a pile of potato chips onto my plate. "*This* is on the side."

"Ohhhhhhh, *this* is not good," Skippy groaned as his avatar appeared above the display of the treadmill I was running on.

Punching the emergency stop button, I waited for the deck to stop moving, then hopped off and walked out into the passageway before responding. "Skippy, remember when Simms used to dress up your canister in cute little outfits?"

"Those costumes were *not* cute at all, and I do not have fond memories of those days. Why are you mentioning that now?"

"We need to create a new outfit for you. Like the Easter Bunny, except instead of bringing eggs and candy and chocolate to make people happy, *you* are the Bad News Bunny, dumping a steaming pile on my head."

"I don't *make* bad news happen, Joe," he sounded hurt.

"Sorry, it-"

"I merely delight in delivering it to you. That's totally different."

"Is it, really?"

"Do you want to hear what I just learned?"

"What I *want* doesn't factor into the equation, it's my job. Hit me with it."

"From the relay station, I found a-"

"Hold on. You mean the relay station we stopped at yesterday?"

"Yes, why?"

"You are just learning new information from it *now*?"

"Yes, dumdum," he snapped. "I downloaded the entire freakin' archive of messages for the past seven months, do you have any idea how many quettabytes that is?"

"I don't even know *what* a quettabyte is so, no."

"Ugh. I don't know why I even bother talking to you about anything more complicated than shoelaces. Listen, numbskull, I had all the important data decrypted and crunched in less than an hour, and that alone is a *mountain* of data."

"I appreciate it. So this new info, it came from you finding like, a pattern in the data, something like that."

"No. I found it by reading through commercial message traffic."

"Commercial? You mean, not official? Not military, or civilian government?"

"Nope. This message is a Maxohlx supplier, explaining why her company will be unable to meet the delivery terms on time. Technically, the message was written by her company's lawyers, stating that the customer can't back out of the contract, or enforce a late delivery penalty, because the delay is what you monkeys would call a 'force majeure' event."

"OK, I know that term. It means an unforeseen event that is outside the control of either party. Like, war, or a labor strike at the docks, or a tornado. That sort of thing. Skippy, why do I care about some supplier problem?"

"You don't. You should care *why* the supplier is unable to deliver on time. The equipment is ready, and has already been inspected and accepted for shipment by the customer. The problem is, the equipment is delicate, and requires a special type of transport container. The supplier is claiming a force majeure event because all of those containers have suddenly disappeared from the market."

"I'm sure you find this fascinating, and you can nerd out all you want when-"

"Do I have to spell this out for you?"

"Apparently, yes."

"You won't even bother to guess?"

Reminding myself that entertaining Skippy was a major part of my job, I tried to think of why he thought I should care about such a dull subject. "Sure, why not? Uh, the company that owns those containers can't get insurance for them, because the insurance firms are worried about a war with us?"

"Seriously? *That* is your best guess?"

"Come on, Skippy. Throw me a bone here."

"Think about it. Why would you care about the Maxohlx commercial shipping insurance market?"

"I don't, but somehow *you* think I should."

"No, I- Ugh, Fine. Joe, those containers are special. They are expensive, and have a very narrow set of uses. One thing they can be used for is transporting the type of fabricators that create exotic matter."

Instantly, I knew what he meant. "Oh *shit*."

"Egg-ZACTLY."

"Did this message, legal document whatever, state *why* none of those containers are available?"

"It did not. Joe, it doesn't take Sherlock Holmes to solve this case. The only entity in Maxohlx society that can forcibly requisition civilian gear on an emergency basis is the military. In your PowerPoint presentation to the Joint Chiefs, you mentioned we are in a time crunch, that we have to strike before the kitties can move their exotic matter production equipment and hide it from us."

"Craaaaaaap." I slumped back against the bulkhead. "They have already started moving the equipment?"

"Or at least preparing to relocate a substantial portion of their exotic matter production capacity."

"Do those containers need a special type of starship to transport them?"

"Unfortunately, no. That is the purpose of those containers, they shield the exotic matter from what could be harmful effects of going through a jump wormhole. All the ship needs to provide is a steady source of power for the container's, well, containment system. Even ship power is optional, most commercial transport contracts require there be a dedicated powercell for each container, in case ship power is unreliable."

"If we had access to their military message traffic, could you figure out where the kitties are setting up their hidden facilities?"

"Eh, shmaybe. Joe, they know I can crack their encryption. They are unlikely to leave the information we need at a relay station."

"Ah, you're right about the kitties keeping the relocation plans secret, we can't rely on intercepting their message traffic about moving the damned things. What about, uh- Shit, this is where I would ask Simms to provide insight. If new facilities are being stood up, those sites will need more than just the special machines. Personnel will have to be transferred."

"I can check the manifests and routes of Maxohlx passenger transport ships, but for a secret project, I expect the personnel they need will be aboard military ships."

"Do what you can, OK?"

"Joe, you realize this is totally hopeless, right? The kitties are certain to be setting up multiple hidden fabs, there is no way even I can find them all. Even if I did that, we would have to *hit* them all, every single one of them. While we are flying around doing that, the kitties will be setting up more fabs. Joe, no matter what we do, the galaxy is going to be flooded with enriched radonium within a year."

Yeah. I know. Do the best you can and, we have to hope we can stop Moonraider from *using* any of it."

CHAPTER TWENTY NINE

"Admiral?" The captain of the *You Can't Make This Shit Up* pinged Scorandum. "May I speak with you, on an important and urgent matter?"

Uhtavio held down the 'Reply' button with an antenna, since he was slumped on the couch next to his office desk. "*May* you? Perhaps a better question is *must* you?"

"I am afraid I rather must insist at this time, Sir."

"Clearly, whatever the matter is, it is important enough for you to disturb me. How can it be urgent? Is the ship about to explode?"

"Sir, the ship is about to stop doing *anything*, if you know what I mean."

"The ship? Or the crew?"

"That is the same, in this case."

"Oh, very well," Scorandum sighed, knowing exactly what the captain was politely demanding to discuss. "Come to my office, please."

When Captain Scilvana reached the doorway to the admiral's office, the admiral was just pouring a small glass of fine vintage burgoze for himself. Another, larger glass sat on the other side of the desk. The captain stared at the bottle in the other officer's claw.

"Sir, perhaps this is not the best time for showing me you can afford expensive drinks?"

"That is why," Scorandum set down the bottle. "I am only indulging in this paltry amount, barely enough to quench my thirst. And while *you*," he nudged the other glass, which was filled with a liquid of a different color, because it was floon rather than burgoze. "Are getting the cheap stuff. Sit down, please."

Scilvana hesitated just long enough for the moment to be awkward, while Scorandum made no comment, simply sipped his drink. The ship's captain was trying to decide whether to be a hardass, and whether that would get her anywhere. It probably wouldn't, and if she had more experience serving under that admiral, she would know for sure, but Scilvana had been in command of the ship for less than a quarter of a year.

Being in command of an admiral's flagship was not considered a choice assignment, no captain wanted to be second in authority on their own ship. Scilvana had several other options before she accepted command of the *You Can't*, and she had made the decision to give herself what she thought were three advantages.

The first advantage was Scorandum's leadership style. The admiral pretty much did not care how a ship was run, as long as it got him from Point A to Point B. Or, in the official script of the Jeraptha trade language, from

345

Point squiggly vague 'K' shape with one horizontal bar across the top and two short bars diagonally across the bottom, to Point skinny number '8' overlaid on an upside down 'V', since those symbols represented the first two letters of their thirty nine letter alphabet. The point was, Admiral Scorandum not only rarely provided any sort of input into how he wanted a ship or crew to perform, he also didn't even seem to notice their performance. That is, he did not notice unless something bad happened, and the ship was not instantly able to do whatever he wanted. Scilvana had quickly learned that whenever some system of the ship needed to be taken offline for maintenance, or whenever the jump drive capacitors simply had to recharge, the admiral had to be notified, in person. An update to the ship's status report was not good enough. Scilvana had to speak directly with the admiral, and most importantly, to make sure the admiral was paying attention. Which most of the time, was not the case.

So, Scilvana was able to run the ship as she saw fit, without a senior officer second guessing her every move, or providing unhelpful advice, or even merely recounting boring and irrelevant stories of how an admiral had handled a situation back when they were a captain.

As far as Scilvana knew, and she had asked *everyone* who had ever served on a ship with Scorandum, the legendary ECO operator had never taken much interest in the details of how a particular ship or crew got the job done. Even when Scorandum was a captain, he had never spent much time aboard any one ship, and so the burden of actually making sure the ship flew and did not go 'Boom', had fallen to the executive officer.

All good, as far as Scilvana was concerned. She could develop a reputation as a capable, independent officer, one not reliant on being provided detailed instructions.

The second major advantage, or what was supposed to be an advantage to serving with Scorandum, had proven not to be true. There should have been an opportunity to learn from one of the greatest minds in the history of the Ethics and Compliance Office. That could have happened, if the admiral had made any effort toward mentoring a protégé. But, the admiral rarely sought input before an operation, and after even a wildly successful scam was concluded, Scilvana was left wondering what the hell had really happened. Too much information was concealed behind a noncommittal shrug or a twitching antenna, both of which implied that the ship's crew did not need to know important details. It was likely that Scilvana could serve as captain of the *You Can't* for years, without learning anything useful that could lead toward promotion within the Office.

That left the third major advantage: that Scorandum's crew had a reputation as good earners. If Scilvana never advanced her career, she could at least look forward to retiring with a pile of ill-gotten cash in her bank account.

Or, she *could* have done that.

Until recently.

"Sir," Scilvana made a decision, settled to the couch, and after another awkward moment, reached for the glass of floon. A few drops of liquid courage could serve her well right then. "This is undoubtedly an inconvenient time to mention an unpleasant subject-"

"Yet, you are willing to put up with the inconvenience," the admiral interrupted with a scowl.

No, Scilvana realized, it was a frown. The admiral was as unhappy as she was.

Well, of course he was unhappy. No one was happy about the situation.

"I will power through, Sir."

"In the best traditions of the service," Scorandum might have intended that as a joke.

"The service has many assets. Ships, spacedocks, weapons. The *primary* asset of the Office, and the Home Fleet, is the crews. It is my duty to point out that the pay of this crew is overdue, Sir."

"I am aware of the, delay in payment. That is why I added a bonus to the pay vouchers I submitted yesterday."

"A bonus that is useless, since the pay vouchers *bounced* due to insufficient funds. Sir."

The admiral seemed genuinely surprised for a fleeting moment. "How do you know that so soon- I mean, how do you know that?"

"We have contacted a relay station for revised orders," Scilvana explained. She did not add that Scorandum would know the ship's position, if the senior officer ever paid attention to the status reports.

"I thought we were not scheduled for an update for another five days."

"As there is a relay station nearby that required only a two hour diversion from our present course, I took the opportunity to obtain more current information."

"Such as," Scorandum grimaced. "Whether the pay vouchers you received are valid."

"That is an important piece of information, Sir."

"Important, but damned inconvenient."

"Did you," Scilvana's antennas stood straight up. "Expect that we would not learn your vouchers had bounced, until it was too late? Is *that* why you are planning to leave the ship on this secret mission the day after tomorrow?"

"A secret mission isn't *secret* if people know about it," Scorandum muttered.

"Sir," the captain drained her glass of floon in one gulp. With cheap booze, it is best not to taste it for too long. That was interesting. It was good, *very* good. It tasted vintage. Expensive. Was the admiral holding out on her, and the crew? "I might be able to help, if I knew what was going on."

"You are not *stupid*, Scilvana. You can figure out the source of my current predicament."

"Skipcoin?"

"Exactly." Despite his earlier words, the admiral looked at his own empty glass, frowned, and reached for the bottle. That time, he filled the small glass to the rim. "Ah. Even the best burgoze cannot wash the bitter taste from my mouth."

"Sir, I thought you had recovered from your losses when the value of Skipcoin crashed."

"I had a *plan* to do that."

"What happened?"

"Someone didn't get the memo. To be more accurate, I *did* get the memo, and I shouldn't have trusted it."

"I don't understand."

Scorandum grunted, tipped back the glass, and drank it all. "It is a crime not to savor such a fine vintage beverage but, I do it for medicinal purposes."

"Of course. Sir, am I hearing that you *can't* pay the crew?"

"I didn't say that."

"You *can* pay us?"

"I didn't say that either."

"Sir, it-"

"Captain Scilvana, I am squeezed between my obligations to my crew, and to those above me in the chain of command. My superiors are not so forgiving as you are."

"Describing me as forgiving is not-"

"There are the taxes I must pay, and making those payments have caused my current cash flow problem."

"Ah, So, the problem is only a temporary issue of juggling cash from one account to another?"

"You could say that."

"Good, then-"

"If you and the crew are willing to accept payment in Skipcoin."

"I am afraid that is not an option."

"Then," Scorandum's antennas spread wide apart. "We do have a problem."

"Sir, your annual tribute payment to Minister Quillamant is due at the end of this month. Please tell me you have the cash to cover that."

"I can tell you that. If you are willing to be satisfied with a pleasant lie."

"Sir. How did you get into such a mess?"

"There are three words to explain the source of my dilemma."

"What are those?"

"Skippy. The. Magnificent."

348

Scilvana's antennas drooped. "Sir," she poked at the admiral's bottle with the tip of her claw. "If you have time, I would appreciate you telling me how an alien AI caused your current financial difficulties."

The admiral only slumped on his couch.

"Sir?" She tried again. "Perhaps it might help if you were not thinking about your thirst."

Scorandum sighed heavily, and bobbed his antennas as he opened a cabinet behind his couch, to get out a fresh bottle of burgoze.

That was not good, Scilvana thought. The admiral was moving mechanically, without any energy. Had the legendary officer given up? Was that even possible?

If she was in his situation, she certainly would at least consider giving up. Why bother fighting, if nothing was left to fight for?

He had to know how the crew would react. He must know how his superiors would react, when they saw that their tax payments were backed by insufficient funds.

And Minister Quillamant would immediately realize that her annual tribute payment would not be on time, if it came at all.

That would be *big* trouble.

Fortified by a large glass of fine vintage burgoze, the admiral settled back in the couch. His body language signaled not defeat, but deep thought.

Uh oh. The captain recognized that expression. She had seen it on too many professors, when they were about to drone on and on, smacking knowledge on her.

She steeled herself to listen.

"Captain, are you familiar with the expressions 'Dump and Pump', or 'Dead Cat Bounce'?"

"I must confess I am not."

"Then," the admiral slurped a large measure of burgoze. "I shall be as brief as possible. Skiptocurrency has been a tremendous benefit to our trade with the humans. We no longer have to barter, or exchange incompatible currencies. That is, Skipcoin *was* a benefit, as long as the value was stable. Then, someone attempted to steal a Sentinel."

"Yes Sir, but you assured us you had wagered against a drop in value of Skipcoin, sufficient to cover the currency value loss."

"I did. Technically, humans do not refer to it as a 'wager', it is a financial instrument they call an 'option contract'."

"What is the difference?"

"Instead of the wager being placed through a bookie, the intermediary is something called the 'Chicago Board of Options Exchange'. There is no actual difference, the exchange even skims off vig they refer to as a 'trading fee'." He shrugged. "Humans apparently prefer to pretend their options activity is not gambling."

Scilvana blinked. "Why? Humans do not like fun?"

349

"Supposedly, the difference between 'investing' and 'gambling' is with an investment, your smart analysis bends the odds in your favor," his antennas bounced up and down. "I had hedged my bet on Skipcoin by purchasing option contracts against a decline in value, so yes, I was covered when for the Sentinel incident. Then, someone attacked Earth's Moon. And Skipcoin collapsed."

"You were not hedged against that possibility?"

"I was not hedged *enough*. The cost of options to fully offset the risk was, greater than my estimation of the remaining risk. It's about the odds, you understand?"

"I think so, yes."

"At that time, my losses were enormous, but manageable. It would have been possible for me to recover, in time. No different from anyone who had a significant exposure to Skiptocurrency."

"Then, what happened?"

"Skippy, after declining my very reasonable request for a loan, advised me that the dramatic fall in value of Skipcoin was in fact manipulated, as part of a Dump and Pump scheme. It," his antennas swished in a dismissive gesture. "He told me he had deliberately devalued the currency, as a way to buy a large volume cheaply. The value was certain to rebound soon, he assured me. So, with my remaining funds, I purchased futures contracts, betting the value would go up. It did *not*."

"Evidently. Skippy was wrong?"

"Oh," the admiral laughed bitterly. "No. Skippy knew exactly what he was doing. The purchase of a large volume of futures by a SkipWay insider, that is *me*, prompted the market to temporarily bid up the value of Skipcoin, in a 'Dead Cat Bounce'. Skippy then dumped his remaining currency, and he benefitted greatly because *he* had purchased offsetting futures contracts betting the value would go *down*. He *played* me. He played *me*. Skippy actually made a profit on the overall transaction."

"Is it possible Skippy will share his good fortune with his trusted SkipWay associates?"

"It's cute when you say things like that."

"So, you are screwed?"

"Unless a true miracle occurs. Or, unless *my* trusted associates are willing to extend credit to me?"

"Are you trying to play me, Sir?"

"Not that you know of."

"I must decline your generous offer."

"Probably a good idea."

"What are you going to do, Sir?"

"Well, I do have one card to play. Against Skippy."

"Against-" Captain Scilvana decided that was likely something she did not want to know. "I would prefer to be left out of, whatever you are planning."

"Do not worry, Captain. All I need you to do is hold the ship here, near the relay station. While I compose a message to an old friend."

Scilvana left, with the rest of the bottle of floon. And she left a warning that after five days, she would inform the crew of the bounced vouchers. After that, she could not make any promises of how the crew would react.

Two hours later, the task perhaps delayed by the amount of burgoze he had consumed, Scorandum requested a message be transmitted to the relay station. The captain did not and could not read the contents of the message, but she did know who the message was addressed to.

The Court of Special Inquiries.

Admiral Scorandum was somehow planning to use the *Inquisitors* against Skippy.

Skippy the Self-proclaimed Magnificent was wrong about something. Ha!

Clearly, that was not possible.

Skippy had been *misinformed.* Or, the data available to him was inadequate. So, clearly it was not his fault, how dare you even suggest such a ridiculous thing.

What Skippy did not know, what he could *not possibly* have known, unless he actually took the time to consider the question for more than a nanosecond, was that the exotic matter production facilities of the two senior species were *not* those best suited to making the type of artificial elements that can be used to form cross-dimensional transmitters. In fact, there was a facility which already produced exotic elements with properties close to those required for waking up a Sentinel. The facility was a Thuranin research lab, that had been downgraded and placed into reserve status one hundred and thirty years before. When their asshole patrons demanded a complete list of sites that possessed equipment for manufacturing artificial matter, the Thuranin left the Tungooskat facility off the list, for the simple reason that they had pretty much forgotten about it.

The Maxohlx had *not* forgotten about the time when their clients, universally considered to be assholes by every other intelligent species in the galaxy, had expended enormous sums of money to develop more efficient, more powerful atomic compression warheads. So, when the leaders of the Hegemony Coalition reviewed the list, they realized that Tungooskat was missing from the declared facilities, and decided the omission had to be

351

deliberate. The Thuranin would be offered an opportunity to correct their error.

But first, they had to be punished for their attempted defiance.

A single Maxohlx battleship emerged from jump above the planet Tungooskat, with an escort squadron of eight cruisers. Those nine warships were the spearhead of a larger force of assault carriers that waited, attached to star carriers, for the 'Go' signal. It might be more accurate to describe the nine warships hanging above Tungooskat as a hammer rather than a spearhead, for their purpose was to act with blunt, brute force.

The first shots of the brief battle were fired by three cruisers, at an outdated Thuranin destroyer that had been caught completely unaware in orbit. The destroyer was scheduled to soon be decommissioned, so perhaps the intention of the Maxohlx was to save their clients the effort and expense of taking that old ship apart. Perhaps. The Thuranin did not send a fruit basket as a Thank You gift.

The next target, for the big guns of the battleship, was the main settlement of the planet, a town that had stubbornly clung to life after funding for the main research base was cut off. Fewer than sixteen thousand cyborgs lived on the entire planet. According to the sign at the edge of town, set up by the local chamber of commerce, twelve thousand Thuranin occupied the miserable, decaying town of Fruntex.

After three minutes of bombardment by the battleship's railguns, the sign needed to be updated to reflect two thousand current residents.

The real estate of Fruntex was decidedly a buyer's market.

Following the successful delivery of the kinetic portion of the official message, a text message was sent, addressed to the underground research base's caretaker director. The message stated that the Maxohlx had noticed an error on the list provided to the Hegemony government, in that Tungooskat had been left off the register of sites capable of making artificial, exotic matter. The Maxohlx were certain the omission had been a simple mistake, perhaps caused by the fact that the exotic matter they asked about had been considered by the Thuranin to be a useless waste byproduct of the process aimed at producing better atomic compression weapons. Anyway, all would be forgiven if the Thuranin simply stood down their defenses, and allowed full and unrestricted access to the research base. The destruction of Fruntex? Why, that was merely a Tough Love reminder to be more careful in the future, when providing requested information.

The smart thing, the sensible thing to do, would be to comply. The message included a statement that the humans were also searching for such production facilities, and it would be better for the Thuranin to cooperate with their loyal patrons, instead of with the upstart humans who had no right to even exist.

Doing the sensible thing was the smart play. The sensible thing would have been done, if the Maxohlx had issued their demand two years prior. Before Director Beiehsgee75 got stuck with the unwanted assignment as director, of a research base that nearly everyone had forgotten about. Beiehs was old, and tired, and *so* sick of the bullshit life had thrown at him. Being exiled to Tungooskat was not a reflection of his scientific career, for he had widely been considered brilliant. His career prospects had fallen apart when he backed the wrong side in a political dispute thirteen years back, and he had been spiraling down into oblivion ever since.

Even then, Beiehsgee75 might have been reasonable, if the Maxohlx had not arrived on a day when the koth maker was broken. As was proper for his cyborg species, Beiehs disdained weak biological enjoyments such as tasty food, but he did need a hot cup of koth in the morning, damn it. That sunrise was the third time the ancient koth machine had broken down, and there were no replacement parts on the base. So, he had ordered the parts to be delivered from a warehouse in Fruntex.

A warehouse that no longer existed.

There would be no more hot, life-giving koth to soothe his weary, aging and aching body.

Fuck *life*.

Locking himself in his office, he sat in the creaky chair and activated a communications channel. "This is Director Beiehsgee75 of the Tungooskat Research Institute. Please connect me with the commander of your assault force."

A voice responded. "I am the authorized communications officer of the-"

"I don't give a shit who you are. I want to talk with the actual commander, or this conversation is over."

"You dare to-"

"Let's be clear about this: *you* want something from *me*."

There was a pause, much longer than it needed to be. Beiehs speculated that his opponent, his patron, was making him wait. Then, a voice that was a typical Maxohlx growl. The Director was not impressed, he knew the Maxohlx had utilized genetic engineering to deepen their voices, to make themselves sound more intimidating.

It was pathetic.

"This is Admiral Toveth," another voice announced slowly. "Director, you will stand down your defenses and provide full access to-"

"I should do this, why exactly?"

Another pause. Not for his benefit, but because a Maxohlx admiral needed time to process that one of his lowly clients had dared to interrupt him.

"As stated in our very clear and concise message," Toveth continued in a clipped, irritated tone, "humans are seeking facilities with the equipment

353

you have in your research base. We will take that equipment away for safe keeping, to prevent the humans from using it against both of our peoples."

"Interesting. I do wonder if any of that *bullshit* you just told me is true."

Shocked silence.

The voice was no longer merely irritated. "You will stand down your defenses and-"

"Or what?"

"*Excuse me?*" Toveth roared.

"You heard me."

"We will *destroy-*"

"How? Be precise, please."

"The firepower of my ships is-"

"Is totally inadequate, and we both know it. Since you obviously have nothing to threaten me with, let me explain the situation to you. This base is buried deep inside a very solid, very stable, very dense section of this planet's crust. This awful world was selected because it is almost entirely geologically dead, so the crust is exceptionally thick. Your ships could sit up there and pound the surface until your railgun magnets melt, and you wouldn't reach down anywhere near my location. By making a crater on the surface, you *would* collapse the elevator shaft that provides access to the base, which I think would make it very difficult for you to extract the machinery you supposedly want. But, I am admittedly not a logistics expert, so you will have to make your own judgment about that."

Another pause, long enough that Beiehs finally called out, "Hello?"

"What," there was no disguising the anguished hatred in the admiral's clipped words. "Do you want?"

"Me? *So* many things. I *want* to be given the respect I once enjoyed, and rewarded for my accomplishments by an assignment in some place that still does actual research. But, that's not going to happen. I *want* to be left alone, but I suspect your orders don't allow that option. And I *want* parts to fix my koth machine, but those were destroyed when you flattened the town."

"We, we could fabricate the components you require, and-"

"You could *say* you will do that, and I might even see those parts, right before your assault team slits my throat. Admiral, there are two problems that prevent me from complying with your demand. First, you have nothing to threaten me with. Second, the humans actually do pose a threat to me and this base."

"The upstart humans do not even construct their own ships, they cannot-"

"My government, which is almost universally comprised of corrupt fools, did make one reasonably intelligent decision a few years ago. We have very clear standing orders that go on forever in great detail, but basically can be summarized as: *Do not fuck with the humans*. Do you recall that my people

354

used to have an ultra-secure base on, actually under, the planet Slithin?" Beiehsgee75 did not wait for a reply. "Your entire fleet could have grown old trying to damage that base, which was constructed precisely to prevent your people from intimidating and coercing us. But, somehow the humans fired a single, low-powered pulse of a rather ordinary energy weapon, and the base that was impossibly deep under the surface instantly exploded. So," he took a breath. "Out of great respect for our illustrious patrons, and for your personal benefit, I will summarize the situation. First, fuck *you*, for it gives me great pleasure to say that. Second, until you can duplicate what the humans did at Slithin, or even explain *how* they did it, do not be coming here with that weak shit. It's just *sad*. And third, on behalf of all even semi-intelligent beings in the galaxy, *fuck* you."

Beiehsgee75 cut off the communications channel. He picked up the cup from which he had drunk hot koth the previous morning, slowly sniffed it to get the last, ever so faint scent of his favorite beverage.

He set down the empty cup. Flipped up a protective cover. And pressed a button.

On the hemisphere opposite the former town of Fruntex, four Maxohlx cruisers were above the horizon, weapons hot and energy shields fully active. It made no difference. When the fifty gigaton fusion device at the center of the underground base detonated, some of the hellish energy was channeled into X-rays, that lanced out from stealthed projectors buried in shallow pods beneath the surface. All four cruisers were struck, all four cruisers were vaporized.

For a long moment, Admiral Toveth stood silently, contemplating the utter failure of his mission, the needlessly cruel destruction of a client settlement town, and the loss of four frontline cruisers. "Was this," he muttered to himself, using his biological voice box without realizing he had spoken aloud, "really all about a broken *koth maker*?"

"Joe," Skippy called me while I was eating breakfast. Actually, I had just sat down for a breakfast meeting with Reed. When I was captain of the ship, I used to review the status report over breakfast with Simms, it was an efficient way to begin the day. Eating with Simms had also been healthier for me, her disapproval reduced my intake of butter, sugar, and bacon. That's why I had four strips of bacon on my plate that morning. Reed wasn't going to nag me about my diet, or suggest I eat kale instead of bacon.

I kind of missed Simms nagging me. She did that because she cared.

Damn it. Thinking about that made me give Reed one piece of my bacon.

She was surprised. "Um, thank you, Sir," she picked up the bacon and munched on it. "What's the occasion?"

"Just by being back aboard *Valkyrie*, I can hear Simms reminding me to eat healthier."

She frowned, stared at the remaining bacon in her hand. Then popped it in her mouth. "I'll eat a salad for lunch."

"You keep telling yourself that, and someday it might happen."

She shrugged. "Probably not today."

"*JOE!*" Skippy shouted.

"What?" I winced from him blasting my ear.

"You were ignoring me," he sniffed, insulted.

"I was waiting, until I could properly devote my full attention to whatever extremely important thing you want to talk about."

Across the table, though she couldn't hear Skippy's side of the conversation, Reed rolled her eyes. She knew I was sucking up to the beer can.

"Oh," Skippy was much happier. "Well, that's better."

Gulping the rest of the coffee in my cup, I stood up. "Give me a minute, I'm getting more coffee. Reed?"

She shook her head, so I walked over to the coffee machine, but leaned against the wall. "What is it, Skippy?"

"We talked about you eating too much junk food."

"Yes, and we agreed that if you nag me about it, I will stubbornly eat *more* junk food." That wasn't true. Being with Margaret had influenced me to eat less bad stuff. When she was pregnant, she became a fanatic about nutrition, and I followed her strict program. Really. Even when she wasn't with me during the day, I didn't cheat at lunch.

We had agreed that Fluffernutters were allowed. I mean, you have to be reasonable.

"Ugh," Skippy was disgusted with me, again. "I *told* you, your genetic profile suggests that restricting calories is important for-"

"I burn a lot of calories by exercising."

"Not enough."

"Fine, I'll do what you suggest."

"Really? Wow, I was prepared for an argument. You're not even going to look at the PowerPoint slides I created for you?"

"The best way to get a soldier to *not* pay attention, is to show PowerPoint slides."

"OK, whatever. You're serious about this?"

"I'll show you that I'm committed to following your advice. As of right now, I am cutting out high-calorie junk foods like kale and broccoli."

"Those are *not-*"

"Also turnips. I can add parsnips to the list, if you recommend it."

"You are such a jackass. You promised-"

"*You* promised not to nag me about this."

"I also promised Margaret that I would make sure you-"

"Did you promise I would not *eat* junk food, or did you promise you would *try* to encourage me to eat better?"

"Um, the second one."

"Then your conscience is clear."

"Really?"

"Yes. You did the best you could, and I didn't listen to you. That's my fault."

"Hmm. In that case, if you wait another fifteen minutes, the galley crew will have sticky buns ready."

"Thanks, Skippy."

"Also, I have heard that coffee and bacon go great with sticky buns."

"I'll just get coffee."

"So, you actually are listening to my advice?"

"Let's not go crazy."

OK, I did get an extra piece of bacon to go with my sticky bun, but that is still a total of only four. And I did get a second sticky bun, but that was to eat later.

Yes, waiting until 10AM to eat the sticky bun counts as 'later'.

Do *not* tell Margaret.

CHAPTER THIRTY

Moonraider had- I still hated calling our enemy 'Moonraider'. Naming it for an over-the-top 1970s James Bond sci fi movie just made the hateful Elder AI sound silly. Yes, I know, the purpose of using a nickname for an enemy is to take away part of its power to generate fear. The name certainly did that. So what was the problem?'

Skippy had named it. That was supposed to be my job.

Anyway, Moonraider had two of the three factors required for waking up a Sentinel. Technically, it had three of the four factors that are needed.

Oh for- All right, I guess there are *five* factors needed, and it had three of them. Maybe four. Whatever. There were several requirements, I'll count them later. First, a Sentinel could only be activated by an Elder AI, and to me, that requirement confirmed that our enemy was indeed a being like Skippy. Not like Skippy, no one is. You know what I mean.

Second, it had to know how to tune radonium transmitters for a particular place and time that a Sentinel could be contacted. Based on Moonraider crashing Dogzilla's wakeup party, it clearly knew how to interpret a tune setting. Skippy said that interpreting an existing tune setting was different from being able to create a new tuning setup for a particular place and time, but I figured we had to assume Moonraider could do the math.

Third, it had to know where and when there would be opportunities to contact a Sentinel. Again, I was assuming Moonraider knew how to do that also.

Not just any Sentinel could be activated, only one of the twenty three remaining units from the ready reserve pool. So, that by itself imposed two requirements: fourth was knowing that only a small group of Sentinels were eligible to be contacted, and fifth was being able to identify whether a particular Elder killing machine was eligible or not.

Sixth, it needed a fabricator to make at least twelve kilograms of enriched radonium. We had to assume the kitties were busy cranking out the stuff as fast as they could.

That brings us to a seventh element: Skippy's secret formula for rapidly producing radonium. Moonraider did *not* have that. Yes, since Skippy had stumbled across his formula by mistake, it was possible the Maxohlx could do the same, but it was unlikely.

Let's review. Don't worry, there won't be any PowerPoint slides involved.

Did Moonraider have:

An Elder AI? Check.

The knowledge that radonium transmitters must be tuned for contact at a particular place and time, and how that tuning worked? Check.

The knowledge of the upcoming set of four opportunities for contact? Check.

The knowledge of which Sentinels are eligible, and how to identify them? Maybe and, maybe?

A dumbass partner to crank out radonium? Check.

The secret formula to rapidly produce high-grade radonium? Nope.

How many factors is that? I'm not great at math.

"Hey Skippy," I called, while bouncing a tennis ball off the overhead. I miss my old office. "I got something I want to bounce off you."

"If it's that tennis ball, no way."

"Get in here, please. I have a question."

His avatar appeared on the far edge of my desk, he was taking no chances. "What?" he asked, arms folded across his chest, or across his canister.

"Does Moonraider know which Sentinels are eligible to be activated, and can it identify whether a dormant Sentinel is eligible?"

"That is *two* questions."

"Skippy, it has been a long day."

"Hey, *your* day is only twenty four hours of monkey time. *My* day encompasses a time during which mountains rise from the sea, are eroded by rainfall over eons, and disappear beneath the waves. Continents drift faster than your slow brain can process thoughts."

"How about you devote some of that time to not being an asshole?"

"As if."

"How about this? The faster you answer my questions, the sooner we will be done with this conversation?"

"Excellent point. OK, I would say 'Yes' to both of your questions. Before you pester me with a lot of stupid comments about how Moonraider could know that, it obviously knows the signature of Dogzilla, and I have to assume it watched me activate PupTart, to understand the process before it attempted to steal Dogzilla. Do you agree?"

"Yeah, that makes sense."

"Good. So, it knows the signatures of at least two Sentinels that were eligible to be activated. Clearly, it understands what makes them different from other dormant Sentinels, so it has to-"

"Wait. That's not clear at all to me. It has seen only two dormant Sentinels; PupTart and Dogzilla before you woke them up."

"Oh, I understand your confusion now. I mentioned there will soon be four nearly simultaneous opportunities to activate a Sentinel. There are many more opportunities to *contact* a dormant Sentinel, but those units were not in the ready reserve, and so are not in a state where they can be activated by me. At least, not now, with our current level of technology."

"I'm gonna need more detail about that."

"Ugh, *fine*. If you read the reports of the activation project, you would know this already. While you were playing golf on Jaguar, we-"

"I wasn't only playing golf, you ass."

"Really, Joe? Really? Anywho, while the fab was being constructed at Moonbase Zulu, *Valkyrie* flew me around the galaxy, so I could identify the twenty six Sentinels of the ready reserve."

"How could you do that, if you didn't have a supply of radonium yet?"

"Establishing contact with enough bandwidth to activate a Sentinel requires radonium transmitters. Simply pinging a Sentinel to get its ID code and status is a function native to me, it doesn't require any special exotic materials."

"Oh. I didn't know that."

"You don't know anything, because *you* chose to take early retirement, while the rest of us worked our asses off to secure the galaxy."

"I wasn't *retired*, I-" There wasn't any point to arguing with him. Also, he was kind of right about that. I had accepted the garrison command on Jaguar because I was worn out from flying around the galaxy, putting out one fire after another. Damn it, I had been burned out and needed a break. And to get married, to start a family, to live like a normal person. We had defeated a threat from the freakin' *Elders*, we had Elder weapons, Earth was at least officially protected by Roscoe. For the first time since Columbus Day, there was not a serious extinction threat to humanity. Skippy went on a Victory tour, while I settled down on Jaguar. Do I have any regrets? Hell no. "So, you mapped all twenty six Sentinels of the ready reserve, before you woke up Bubba?"

"Correct. And, because those ninnies at Def Com insisted even though the information was of no use to a bunch of monkeys, I provided that mapping to them."

"Oh shit."

"Egg-ZACTLY."

"Moonraider hacked that data?"

"I would be shocked if that didn't happen. Either that, or Moonraider did the same thing I did: fly around the galaxy, pinging dormant Sentinels, to see which ones were in a condition to be activated. Except, Moonraider has an Elder starship, and I am stuck with a used starship that was cobbled together from spare parts, has way too much mileage on it, and is still in need of a refit."

"*Valkyrie* is a fine ship."

"Whatevs. Either way, our enemy knows which Sentinels can be activated, and which can't."

"Shit, So, it could have figured out the next four activation opportunities?"

"Sure, but it likely didn't have to. In case the Dogzilla activation failed, as a backup I had given to Def Com the tune settings of the next four opportunities, so they could get started on tweaking transmitters. Moonraider probably hacked that data also. Joe, *any* information Def Com has can be hacked, their cybersecurity is awful."

"This keeps getting better and better."

"Hey, at the time, I had no reason to suspect another Elder AI was active."

"Skippy, it's not your fault."

"You say that, but-"

"I mean it. Like you said, I took the job on Jaguar, because I thought we were *done* with this shit."

"Like that's ever going to happen, Joe."

"Check my logic on this, please. The only thing Moonraider does not have, or will not soon have, is the secret formula for cranking out radonium quickly."

"It also doesn't have access to a fab."

"Come on, Skippy, do you want to bet on that? The rotten kitties are doing everything they can to cut a deal with Moonraider."

"OK, yeah," he sighed. "We can always count on the Maxohlx to fuck things up for everyone."

"Tell me this: if the kitties had that secret formula, could they create enough radonium before the next activation opportunity?"

"Ah, the schedule would be tight. They would have to make the material, enrich it to a useable purity, and fashion it into transmitters. Then properly tune those transmitters, and transport the transmission platforms to one of the four activation sites. Hmm. For certain the kitties would also send a powerful war fleet with the transmission ships, to make sure no one like us tries to interfere. Our best bet would be to track Maxohlx fleet movements, to identify which of the four sites Moonraider will select to attempt contacting a Sentinel."

"That won't work. The Hegemony fleet has a lot of ships, and working with Moonraider will be their top priority. They will send large fleets to all four sites, precisely because they know we will try to track them."

"You are giving up, then?"

"No way. There has to be a way to- Is there any significant difference between the next four sites? Is one better than the others, somehow?"

"Yes, of course. There was another potential site around the same time we tried to activate Dogzilla, but that alternate site wasn't a good option. A supergiant star had passed through the area around twenty million years ago, and the effect of its gravity left a sort of echo between layers of spacetime. The noise of that echo would have partially drowned out the activation signal, so I struck that site off the list."

"There was an alternative to Dogzilla, around the same time?"

"Almost at the same time, actually. The two events overlapped by three minutes."

"Why am I just hearing about this *now*?"

"You never asked about it before."

"Damn it, Skippy, I shouldn't have to drag information out of you."

"You," he stared at me, "expect me to *guess* what information is important to you?"

"I *expect* you to use common sense. We are trying to stop an Elder AI from waking up a Sentinel, and when I asked where and when it could do that, you told me there were four simultaneous opportunities. That there was no way for us to blockade all four sites. *Now* you tell me those four sites are not the same, and maybe conditions at some of them won't allow for an effective activation signal."

"If you had been part of the activation project, and not taken an extended vacation on Jaguar, you might know all this, dumdum."

"I need to know it now. Of the next four sites, are conditions at any of them good for contacting a Sentinel, or is there an echo or something?"

"Jeez, Joe, I don't *know*. Usually the process is I request your Navy to go to all of the candidate sites, and collect sensor data. Those ships of course have no idea what the data means, so they bring the data back to me, and I interpret it. We haven't done that, because Dogzilla was supposed to be the last Sentinel activation for a while."

"We need to check out those sites, soon."

"OK, OK. I will plot a least-time course to all four sites. We will have to be careful, some of them are in hostile territory."

"You mentioned that. Even if only two of those sites have conditions that are good for a signal, we are leaving too much to chance."

"I don't see that we have any option, Joe. Like you said, Moonraider has or soon will have everything it needs, except for my secret formula. It has the initiative."

"Yeah. I need to think about that."

"Joe!" Skippy interrupted my breakfast meeting with Frey.

"*Later*, Skippy," I waved my coffee cup through his avatar, irritated at him. The conversation Frey and I were having was not any kind of fun, not even for her. I had given her a new tasking: developing a plan to capture high grade radonium. Why did we need radonium? Well first, that's always a handy thing to have, like baby wipes. You can always use an extra pack of baby wipes, especially in the field. Also, we might need it to wake up a Sentinel. Or to do the opposite. More about that later.

Where could we get a supply of radonium? The same place Moonraider would get it: from the Maxohlx. The rotten kitties, the *stupid* kitties, were doing everything they could to create radonium for their potential new ally. Plenty of the stuff would be at one of their hidden fabs, we just had to go get it.

That's what Frey was working on. We didn't yet have a specific target site in mind yet, so she was developing a list of criteria a candidate site had to meet. Criteria that meant a STAR team could get in, accomplish the mission, and get out. Any fab would be a very tough nut to crack. She expected, right from the start, that *Valkyrie*, and her single team of operators wouldn't be enough firepower and manpower for the job. So, while we ate breakfast, we were talking about what other assets would be needed.

"But-" Skippy sputtered.

"Later, OK? I'm talking with-"

"This can't wait. I just discovered a major, *major* problem we have to deal with now."

Frey pushed back from the table. "Sir, I'll leave you to-"

"This might concern Colonel Frey," Skippy added.

"Not here," I stood up, frowning at the French toast and bacon that I hadn't started eating yet. And probably wouldn't get to eat. "Let's discuss this in my office. Do we have time to walk there, or is a reactor about to explode?"

"The reactors are fine. Hurry, please."

"We will. Ping Reed and ask her to join us, please."

Reed was there already, holding up her hands in a 'What is going on' gesture. The ship still needed maintenance, but there hadn't been an opportunity for a full refit. So, every time we stopped to recharge the jump drive capacitors, Reed had her crew and maintenance bots working to take systems offline and replace worn-out components. In some cases, that required dropships to remove parts of the ship's hull plating, to expose the machinery underneath. "Sir, if we have to jump away soon, we'll need to leave three sets of armor plating here."

Automatically, I looked at the ceiling as I sat in my chair. "Skippy?"

"Nah, we're good," his avatar appeared on the desk. "This is an urgent problem, but not a now now *now* problem."

Reed nodded and sat down.

"Besides," Skippy continued, "we have to turn around and go back to the last wormhole anyway. The wormhole ahead of us is on a network I am still not allowed to screw with. That network controller is a *jerk*. Jeez Louise, I damaged one wormhole on its network, years ago. That controller needs to chill and let it *go*. Maybe do some yoga or meditation," he grumbled.

"Why are we turning around?" I asked, as Reed tapped on her tablet, probably she was ordering the pilots to program a course back to the last wormhole. "What is going on?"

"Joe, we have been worrying about Moonraider getting equipment to make the radonium needed to contact a dormant Sentinel. To make sure we have an absolutely complete list of every facility in the galaxy that is capable of producing such materials, I have been conducting an exhaustive review of all available data on the subject. It is *so* freakin' tedious, and there is *so* much data to read. There is no way you monkeys could ever appreciate the hard work I do for you, and properly thank me for-"

"How about you create a list of things we could do to properly show our appreciation, and I will look at it?"

"Um," he blinked. "What things?"

Damn, I should have kept my big mouth shut. "I don't know, whatever you think is appropriate. Anything we could do, to make you feel that we are not taking your extreme efforts for granted."

"Hmm, wow," he rubbed his chin. "I hadn't even considered that, since your species is so pathetically unable to comprehend the full scope of my awesomeness. Well, to start, you could-"

"Show me a list, later, OK?"

"But I already know what I w-"

Reed cleared her throat, pointing at her smart watch. I got the message. "Skippy, you said this is an urgent matter? You reviewed an enormous volume of data. What did you find?"

"Um, first, that the Maxohlx recently sent a task force to the Thuranin planet Tungooskat, to seize exotic matter fabricators. It seems, heh heh, that over a hundred years ago, those fabricators managed to create a few micrograms of a material that had properties similar to radonium, and-"

I jabbed a finger right in his face. "You told me radonium didn't even exist until *you* invented it."

"Ugh. Try to *listen*, dumdum. Open your ears. I said the Thuranin manufactured a substance that had properties that are *similar* to radonium. Not the same. The kitties are too dumb to know the difference, so when they remembered an old report from Tungooskat, they thought they had hit the jackpot."

"The kitties took those fabricators? Where are they now?"

"They *aren't*, Joe. The Thuranin director of the research base self-destructed the whole place, as a middle finger to his asshole patrons."

"That," I blinked, "seems a bit extreme."

"The kitties had destroyed his equivalent of a coffee machine, so the guy might not have been thinking clearly."

Frey nodded in sympathy. "I've been there."

"Skippy," I felt a headache coming on. "Are you telling me you have to expand the target list, to include thousands of client facilities?"

"No, Joe. It is rare that a second tier species is able to make any type of useful exotic matter, and typically what they do make is of a low grade of purity. For a client to make a significant amount of such a substance is like, fuhgeddaboutit."

"OK, good. So, what else did you learn, that is so important?"

"After I heard about the Maxohlx going to Tungooskat, I started scanning through an enormous dataset of records that contained any reference to the production of exotic matter, by any species. Of course, I couldn't look for records about radonium since that artificial element is something I invented, to fill the requirement for contacting a dormant Sentinel."

What I remembered was him bragging about his accomplishment. "Yes, go on."

"Well, heh heh, I did tell you no one had ever made that substance before. Um, it appears that I was wrong about that."

"Holy sh- Someone tried to wake up a Sentinel before we did?"

"What? *No*, dumdum. Why would you think I meant-"

"Then why would anyone create the particular element that-"

"It was an *accident*. That's what I learned. Seventy three years ago, a Bosphuraq research group was-"

"The *birdbrains* did it? I assumed one of the senior species made-" I held up my hands. "Sorry, Skippy, I shouldn't have interrupted you. Reed, stop me when I get off on a tangent."

"No Sir," she shook her head.

"Uh-"

"Sir, thinking in a normal, linear fashion doesn't get us anywhere out here. You and Skippy letting your minds wander randomly about weird shit, is how you figure out how to get us out of whatever mess we're in. Um," she added. "I didn't mean you're not *normal*, I-"

"It's OK, Reed," I laughed.

"She's right, Joe," Skippy sighed. "Much as I hate to admit it. Now, please let me finish what I was saying?"

Drawing fingers across my mouth in a 'Zipping my lips' gesture, I nodded for him to continue.

"OK, so, seventy three years ago, a group of Bosphuraq researchers on the planet Molitan-Garbantuate were attempting to create an artificial element that had the strength and heat resistance of titanium, but half of the mass. They failed, the best they could manage was reducing the mass by twenty percent. However, the initial experiments were encouraging, so the government kept pumping funding into the project for six years. During that time, the researchers realized their original theory was dead wrong, and they had no idea how the initial experiment had yielded good results. They got so desperate that they started randomly adjusting the equipment, hoping to get lucky. There was a five day period, over a major holiday, when one senior researcher had free use of the lab, and it created a batch of very unusual materials. Unusual, interesting, but ultimately useless."

"Let me guess," I leaned back in the chair. "The same materials you need to contact a Sentinel?"

"Yup. You see why this is a problem?"

365

"I think so. The birdbrains by accident made this dangerous stuff, and you need to hack into their databases, to erase the formula or whatever?"

"Not exactly. The first problem is, as far as I know the material from that batch *still exists*, it was never discarded. The lab cranked out roughly sixteen kilograms over that holiday before the machines were shut down. Over the years, a few grams of the material were destroyed in tests, the rest of it is still in storage. Moonraider only needs *twelve* kilograms to construct the cross-dimensional transmitters."

"Shit. Do we know where this stuff is stored?"

"Um, not exactly. The lab was shut down, and as the town around it grew, the buildings were torn down or repurposed for development. The site of the lab is now the local equivalent of a taco shop."

"The Bosphuraq," I blinked, "have *tacos*?"

"Nearly every species has something like a taco, Joe. Except for the Torgalau. Hmm, maybe that is why they are renowned for being humorless, unhappy jerks. Also, congratulations to you for focusing on what is truly important."

"You interrupted my breakfast," I responded, as my stomach growled loud enough for everyone to hear.

"Oh for- Ugh," Skippy was disgusted. "I am sending a bot to get egg and cheese biscuits. Will that make little Joey happy?"

"Add some bacon on my biscuit," I told him, as Frey and Reed nodded agreement. "That material must have been super expensive to produce, how can someone lose track of it?"

"It *was* super expensive, but as far as the Bosphuraq government was concerned, it is worthless. It was worthless, until now."

"Still, some idiot lost track of sixteen kilograms of exotic material?"

"That idiot had a lot of help from a jerk whose name rhymes with Shmoe Mishap."

"*Me*? What did I-"

"You framed the Bosphuraq for flying a ghost ship to hit their patrons, a ghost ship that actually was *Valkyrie*. The Maxohlx conducted raids to punish the Bosphuraq, remember? One of those raids hit Molitan-Garbantuate, most-"

"That is a tongue-twister of a name, Skippy. What do we know about this planet?"

"It's nothing special, certainly not a place I would choose to live. The local star is at about the upper limit of variability, the surface regularly gets blasted with intense solar flares. The native life has adapted to the occasionally harsh conditions, and the Bosphuraq have adapted by constructing their living spaces underground, or having underground shelters they can go to during a flare."

"They live underground, like moles?"

"Not like moles, they- Oh, I suppose so. Why?"

"We are calling this planet just Molitan, or 'Moletown'."

Skippy shook his head. "Really?"

Frey nodded, and Reed gave an 'I do not care' shrug.

"Really. Moletown, or just Molitan," I said, pleased to have the vital nicknaming phase of the operation already complete.

"Ugh, Fine."

"These stellar flares, would they be a problem for an away team?"

"They shouldn't be. At this point, the Bosphuraq have enough data to predict flares up to several years in advance, and the next one won't begin for another nineteen months."

"Good, thanks."

"As I was saying, the most notable effect of the Maxohlx punishment raid was a cyber attack to scramble the planetary network's infrastructure. For fun, the kitties also used military bases on the planet for target practice, including the base near the town of Zufestrah where the exotic material was created and stored. So, records were lost, and the planet was plunged into chaos for several years. When the Bosphuraq central government launched a major effort to rebuild the planet's infrastructure, nobody bothered much with paperwork."

"So, you don't actually know if the material still exists?"

"It *exists*, unless the containers suffered a direct hit by a railgun dart. The question is whether it is still together in a canister somewhere, or scattered all over half of the town."

"Great, fantastic. If we get to Molitan, can we scan for it from orbit?"

"Eh, shmaybe. The canister it was originally stored in was designed to contain dangerously unstable or radioactive materials, so it is heavily shielded. That is encouraging, actually. Unless the canister was busted open when the base was hit, anyone who sees it would probably want to leave it alone."

"Yeah, unless a group of stupid Bosphuraq teenagers find it, and want to try sniffing the stuff to get high. You really have no idea where this stuff is? It might not even be on the planet."

"It is almost certainly still on the planet. The material has no known value to them, so it's not worth lifting into orbit, and I have complete manifest records of every military and civilian dropship that lifted off that rock over the past fourteen years. That canister was never taken offworld."

"Why is fourteen years important?"

"That is the last time the records of its location were updated. Records I have access to, I mean. More recent records were destroyed, because of *you*."

"My past self is a jerk, for sure."

"There is a bit of good news. During the rebuilding, the sister of the Bosphuraq federal prime minister received a contract to manage the cleanup on Molitan, which is not suspicious *at all*. To inflate her company's costs and require the government to increase the budget she could skim from, she directed giant warehouses to be constructed near the military bases that had been damaged. Those warehouses were supposed to safely hold any items recovered that were not immediately useful, or that required repairs, or whose purpose or ownership could not be determined. It is likely that canister is in the warehouse at Zufestrah, somewhere."

"OK, it's in one building. We can handle that."

Frey was not so optimistic. "How big is this warehouse?"

"Do you remember the scene at the end of *Raiders Of The Lost Ark*?"

"*Merde*," she gasped.

"You're not from Quebec," I noted.

"My mother is Quebecois, and sometimes French curse words are the best. Skippy, can you get eyes in that warehouse?"

"If your team is there, you can send spiderbots in to look around. Otherwise, it is a big, dark building. No one kept records of what was stashed in there. A security system with cameras was supposed to have been installed, but the prime minister's sister put that money in her own pocket. The power gets shut off regularly because the company that supposedly manages the warehouse fails to pay the local government for electricity. Really, the company fails to pay the *bribes* the local government demands, but that is another story. We-"

The door slid open and a bot rolled in, holding a tray that it set on the table.

"Mmm," I lifted the lid off the tray, and the three of us got breakfast biscuits with coffee.

"Frey," I said as I bit into a delicious, fresh, hot biscuit. "It sounds like you need to send a team down there to verify the stuff is in that warehouse. Then exfil, and we can wipe the warehouse off the map from orbit."

"Whoa, Joe!" Skippy waved his arms. "No can do! We need that stuff."

"We *need* to prevent Moonraider from getting it, we don't need-"

"Yes we *do* need it. Think, knucklehead, *think*. If we are unable to stop Moonraider from obtaining radonium from the hundreds of facilities that could potentially produce it, our enemy could wake up a Sentinel, or *more* than one Sentinel. Having almost sixteen kilograms of radonium would allow us to activate a third Sentinel *now*, without having to wait for your UN to arrange for buying, borrowing, or stealing equipment to replace the Moonbase Zulu facility. Or, without an extremely risky raid against a Maxohlx fab, like you were talking about."

Frey nodded slowly. She knew Skippy was right.

"OK," I agreed, relieved. Hitting the Bosphuraq would be much less costly than tangling with their patrons. "I suppose stealing that stuff will be next on our To Do list."

"Ya think? My point is, we have a golden opportunity to obtain sixteen kilos of high grade radonium, and all we have to do is stroll in and take it."

Frey raised an eyebrow at him. "Stroll in?"

"Well, um, well," he sputtered. "Maybe not *stroll*. And it might not exactly be a golden opportunity. More like a sticky mess, to be truthful."

The special ops leader looked at me. "Sir, a smash and grab is trickier than a simple recon mission, but the Bosphuraq are not the hardest target in the galaxy. It should be possible."

"Does it matter?" Reed had been listening to us, eating her biscuit with a frown. "I know it would be nice to have sixteen kilos of the stuff, but this experiment happened over seventy years ago. It must have been documented in a journal somewhere, isn't that what scientists do when they make a discovery? When someone remembers the experiment, all the Maxohlx need to do is pull up those records, and they will know exactly how to quickly create radonium. A smash and grab would only buy us a short time."

"Um," Skippy took off his ginormous hat and scratched his dome. "That would be true, if the researcher involved had properly documented his procedure. He did not submit an article for publication in any science journal, since the discovery was an accident, the material had no known use, and everyone associated with the project wanted the government not to know the entire effort was an expensive failure. If the researcher kept any notes, I do not have access to them. Which brings me to the other problem."

Reed rolled her eyes. "How did I know there would be another problem?"

"It's Thursday," Skippy put his hat back on. "I am offering a two-for-one deal on major problems."

Suddenly, the delicious biscuit I was eating tasted dry in my mouth. "Just hit us with it."

"OK. Of the original researchers, those senior scientists who were assigned to the project, and had access to the detailed experiment results that are relevant, only the one person is still alive. This was more than seventy years ago, and the scientists had to be senior in their field to apply for the project, so all the other seven researchers have passed away. The guy who is still alive must remember the settings that produced the radonium, it was the signature achievement of his career. Um, and that is partly because the most notable thing he ever did was an accident, so he had trouble finding a job after the project was shut down."

"We need to find this guy, before the Maxohlx grab him?"

"That would be good, yes."

"What can you tell us about the target, uh, this scientist guy?"

"He lives alone in a city around six hundred kilometers north of what used to be the research base, he has a pet lizard sort of thing, he collects stamps, he-"

"He collects *stamps*?"

"Ugh. No, dumdum, I was screwing with you. Why does it matter what his lonely, pathetic life is like now?"

"The fact that he lives alone is helpful. If he has a hobby like, uh, birdwatching, something that gets him out in the woods alone, that makes him an easier target."

"Oh. Good point. His only hobby that I know of is playing *flet* in a park, that is a board game sort of like chess. But the park near his apartment is crowded, that's no good. What else? Let me think, um, he has one daughter he rarely sees, she lives on the other side of the planet. His name is Chaderioff, he-"

"His name is *Chad*? Does he golf with his lawyer at the country club?"

"*What*?"

"Nothing, I, forget what I said. Frey, you look like you have something to say."

Frey was uncomfortable. "Assassinating a civilian?"

"Will your team have a problem with that?" I asked, in part because I kind of had a problem with it. The Merry Band of Pirates are soldiers, not contract hitmen. Technically, they are soldiers, sailors, airmen, and Marines. You know what I mean. We had killed civilians before, especially Kristang clan leaders, but those killings had been a necessary means to an end. Assassinating a Bosphuraq scientist who was the focus of the operation, that made it different.

"No," she said stiffly.

"I don't like the idea but, can we take the guy out with an orbital strike?"

Frey cocked her head at me. "A railgun dart, just for a single person?"

"It seems like overkill, but in this case I think overkill is underrated."

"Timing would be tricky. A railgun strike can't be concealed, it would have to wait until my team has the canister of radonium and is back aboard *Valkyrie*. Sir, I think it would be better to assign part of a STAR team to get eyes on Chad, and wait for a signal to deal with him."

"Two teams on the ground, too far apart to support each other, and one team has to both maintain contact with the target and remain concealed until they get a 'Go' signal? I don't like it. It's too risky. A surgical strike from orbit avoids committing us from putting boots on the ground, and reduces our time over target. It's a quick in and out. We can dial down the yield on the dart, to reduce the collateral damage. Or, we deploy a stealthed missile. Drop it with a balloon, let it circle the area until its sensors can positively identify the target."

"Um," Skippy raised a finger. "That is going to be a problem."

"What is?"

"Identifying the target."

"You," the three of us stared at him in confusion. "You don't know what this Chad guy looks like? How can that-"

"Of course I know what he looks like. Or *looked* like, a couple years ago. He is retired, and not active on any form of Bosphuraq social media. The last confirmed photo of him is from four years ago."

"Can you use, uh, facial photo aging software, something like that, to project what he looks like now?"

"Wow, Joe, I would never have thought of that," he glared at me. "If that would be useful, I would have done it. The guy is already *old*, his appearance isn't going to change much in four years."

"OK, so what is the-"

"I don't know where he is. Not exactly. Based on the information available, I can pinpoint his location to an area eighty kilometers across."

"You and I have a very different definition of 'pinpoint'. Saturating the area with megaton-yield railguns is not an option. Come on, Skippy, when we're at Earth, you know exactly where everyone is at all times."

"Yes, that is because you monkeys are so obsessed with your social media, you can't be without your phones for one freakin' second. Chad doesn't have a phone, or any sort of personal electronics."

"How can that be? The birdbrains are at about the same technology level as their rivals, the Thuranin."

"He *has* a phone, I assume he left it at home. Joe, Chad has joined some fundamentalist 'back to nature' cult. He is taking seven weeks off, to wander in the wilderness with a like-minded group of weirdos, carrying all their possessions with them. They sleep in crude portable shelters at night, they prepare food over a fire, and they bathe in streams or lakes, if they bathe at all. It must be some sort of creepy religious doomsday cult, that-"

"Skippy," I snorted. "On Earth, we call that 'backpacking'."

"Really?"

"Yes, or it's called 'hiking'. People do it for fun, all the time."

"It sounds *awful*," he shuddered. "What is wrong with you people?"

"If anyone enjoys backpacking that much," Frey grinned, "they can join the Army and get paid to do it."

"Is that how your recruiter suckered you into signing up?" I grinned.

She shook her head, her eyes twinkling. "I joined because the coffee was so good."

"It was?"

"In the recruiting office, they had a Timmies. Tim Hortons. On base," she shrugged. "Not so much. Skippy, you know which trail Chad is following?"

"Yes, that is why I said I can isolate his location to an area of eighty kilometers. He is, I suppose you can call it 'hiking', along a trail through a wilderness area. What I do not know is which trail his group is using, there are several roughly parallel trails. One trail goes along the crests of the mountain

371

range, other trails follow stream valleys. They could be using a combination of trails, I simply don't know."

"No one in their group has a phone?" I was skeptical. "That doesn't sound right."

"The guide they hired has a satellite phone, but she only uses it for emergencies. It is switched off unless she needs it. Like I said, they are a bunch of weirdos."

"It's called 'Getting away from it all'."

"They could accomplish *that* by jumping off their apartment balconies, and they would leave a less smelly corpse," he stuck out his tongue.

"OK, what about infrared sensors? We should be able to detect the group's heat signatures from orbit?"

"We can do that. The sensors will also pick up the signatures of every other group that is hiking those trails. That wilderness is a popular area this time of year. Thousands of sicko fundamentalists go on that pilgrimage every summer."

"Backpacking is not a *pilgrimage*."

"Whatevs," he shrugged.

"Frey," I looked to my STAR team leader. "It looks like we will need boots on the ground, that is your show. What do you think?"

"It's going to be tricky. If no one in authority knows that radonium is valuable, they won't connect Chad's death with a security threat. We could hit him in the back of the head with a dumbbell round," she meant a rifle round that flattened out into a relatively slow-moving blunt object. After an impact that should snap the neck of any upright, bipedal species like the Bosphuraq, the round would quickly disintegrate, leaving no evidence unless a forensics team knew what to look for. Hopefully, anyone finding Chad's body would think he fell and hit his head, or that some other hiker bashed his head with a stick or a rock. "Make it look like an accident, or an ordinary civilian on civilian murder. Take him out *before* we go into the warehouse, remove the requirement for precise timing. That-"

"Um, we should not do that," Skippy interrupted.

Frey was as confused as I was. "Not make it look like an accident?" She asked.

"Not kill him at all."

"*Not* kill him?" I asked the question before Frey could. "You want to, what, use memory erasing nanoprobes on him? That is a nonstarter," I gave him the knife hand. "We are not risking a STAR team just so you can feel good about not assassinating a-"

"Joe, I do not want to kill him, *or* erase his memories. I want what is *in* his memory, hopefully."

"For what?"

"The process he used to create radonium, by accident, was four million times more efficient than our machines were capable of at Moonbase

Zulu. If this fight gets to be a race of who can wake up Sentinels faster, we not only need to steal equipment to make exotic matter, we also need to know how to use it properly, you get that?"

"Shit. Yeah. You don't expect this guy to cooperate with you?"

"Actually, I do. His people consider him to be a washed-up nobody, a failure. He told his neighbors that he is a retired transportation engineer, rather than let them know he once was a respected scientist. If we can bring him aboard, he will be informed that his accidental discovery is the most valuable substance in the galaxy. That instead of being a failure, he has knowledge that is key to saving the galaxy from a horrible threat."

"And, you believe that will prompt him to tell you his formula, whatever?"

"Of course. He will be sharing his knowledge with *me*, Skippy the Magnificent. There can be no greater honor for a meatsack scientist."

"Uh huh."

Reed briefly covered her face with a hand. "Skippy, you know science, but we know people. Meatsacks, I mean. Think about it. You plan to tell Chad that he has information we must have, and you expect him to *give* it to you, for nothing?"

"Um, hmm," the avatar froze for a moment. "Well, darn it. Why is everything biological beings do so complicated?"

"OK," I tapped the table softly. "Let's get this guy aboard, and we'll find a way to motivate him. Skippy, how long for us to get to Molitan?"

"Two days, three and a half hours, roughly. That includes maneuvering time for orbital insertion. Before we do that, I will need to infiltrate the planetary SD network."

"We're on the clock, then. Reed, study the defenses of Moletown, we need a stealthy ingress and ideally, a stealthy getaway. If the Bosphuraq and their patrons don't know that planet ever held something valuable, we shouldn't clue them in. Frey, you know what you have to do. Can ST-Razor handle both portions of the op, or should we go back to Earth to get another team?" My real unspoken question was about the level of confidence she had in her team. ST-Razor had suffered significant casualties during the operation to secure the Moonbase Zulu Vault, half of her personnel were replacements from other units.

She shook her head. "More boots on the ground only means more potential for exposure, Sir. A STAR team now is eighteen operators. Say four at the warehouse, with four providing cover for them. Four in the woods, looking for Chad, the warehouse team doesn't go in until Chad has been located. That leaves six as a reserve, they will be my heavy weapons team. My team can handle it."

"You will be with the reserves, of course?"

"I need to be on the *ground*, Sir. Decisions might have to be made on a split-second basis."

"You just want to break into that warehouse," I grinned.

"No Sir," she surprised me. "The warehouse job is fairly straightforward. Finding one birdbrain in a forest, without us being detected, *that* is the difficult task. We can't even leave recognizably human footprints in the soil, that means the team searching for Chad must wear our lightest infantry mech suit, the Mark 32. That suit offers minimum protection. I don't expect much trouble from backpacking tourists."

"I would agree with you, except out here, the only thing we can expect is the unexpected. You know that."

"Our latest Hulkbuster suit offers incredible protection; it is also too big, bulky and heavy for most operations. That kind of mass consumes a lot of power, so we would need to bring along additional powercells, and that is *more* mass to carry. For finding one guy in the wilderness, I want speed and stealth."

"You're the expert. Review what we know about Milton with Skippy, I want to see a plan by 0900 tomorrow. That goes for both of you."

I dismissed the meeting, Reed had to first make sure the armor plating got settled into place before she could think about Moletown's defenses, but she had people to start that task for her. Before I could take a look at what we knew about the planet, I had to compose a message for Def Com. They expected the Special Mission Group to be observing the Maxohlx, not conducting a smash and grab op, and a kidnapping, against the Bosphuraq. For communications security, all I could state in the message was that Task Force Black had to run an errand that shouldn't take long. Without being able to explain what we were doing, I had to ask the Joint Chiefs to trust me.

I didn't foresee *any* issues with that.

CHAPTER THIRTY ONE

Inquisitor Kinsta, technically Probationary Trainee Inquisitor Kinsta, and in reality soon to be just plain Kinsta The Unemployed And Unemployable, used one of his antennas to make a rude gesture at the back of his superior, as that senior Inquisitor left the doorway of the cramped cubbyhole of an office that the trainee had been squeezed into. The senior official of the Court of Special Inquiries had not bothered to attempt entering the claustrophobic space, had not lowered himself to even make eye contact with the disgraced trainee. Kinsta had a new assignment, that of reviewing notes from old cases his superior had successfully prosecuted. The senior official would be retiring, and was preparing to write a memoir of his exalted career. Kinsta's job was to write up a summary of each case, to refresh the memory of the senior Inquisitor. The job sucked but he was getting a paycheck, at least for the moment.

His plan, he knew he needed to have a plan, was to review the notes as slowly as he could get away with, and suck up to his superior in a hopefully flattering but not overly obvious way.

There wasn't anything else he had to do, nothing else the Court trusted him to handle. It was bad enough that he had allowed a data stick to somehow become corrupted when he visited Scorandum. Worse was that he stupidly had brought that corrupted, that infected data stick back to the office. His perfectly sensible reasoning had been to request the Court's AIs to analyze the device, to determine what had happened. Possibly even to recover the original data. Instead, that corrupted device had uploaded malware into the Court's IT infrastructure, erasing all of the original records against SkipWay. Did Kinsta have any idea how much damage he had caused, how many years had gone into assembling the evidence, records that had to be collected all over again? In fact, he did not know how much damage he had caused, but he could guess.

With a groan, he opened the case notes file, stared at it, and just could not manage to get going. The thought was just too depressing.

He would start on the task soon. First, he would check messages. A clerk in the Court's records office sometimes shared funny memes, Kinsta could use an amusing distraction.

There were five messages. That's all. No one wanted to be associated with him. The first three messages were automated reminders from the Court's personnel system, he ignored those. Fourth was an advertisement from SkipWay, he deleted *that* immediately and wondered how the junk message had gotten through the office filtering program.

Fifth-

The fifth message he almost deleted unread.

It was from Admiral Uhtavio Scorandum.

Did his former boss want to taunt him, in his disgrace?

No, that couldn't be. Scorandum had many negative qualities, but cruelty was not one of them. And-

The admiral was one of the few lifelines available to Kinsta, much as he hated to admit it.

With reluctance, so much that he closed one eye and cringed, he opened the message.

At that moment, his life changed.

For the better.

Uhtavio Scorandum wanted to negotiate a deal, to testify against SkipWay, against *Skippy*, and he would only negotiate with his trusted former aide.

He closed the case notes file.

That drudgery could be done by someone who did *not* have important work to do for the Court of Special Inquiries.

It was weird leaving all the operational planning to others, but I had good people and they knew their jobs. Moletown had a substantial strategic defense network, more robust than was typical for a planet with a population of fewer than a billion. The size and depth of the defense network was the bad news. The good news was the SD network was oversized to accommodate the population growth the Bosphuraq expected before their patrons used Molitan for target practice. After the planet's IT infrastructure got fried, the economy collapsed, and there were food riots in the cities, the local Chamber of Commerce had a tough time convincing companies that Molitan was a thriving place to do business. The result was that the planned expansion of the SD network was put on hold, and maintenance cycles repeatedly postponed due to lack of money. The delay in maintenance included skipping many recommended software updates which, for cybersecurity, was not good.

"Dude," Skippy had laughed. "Even *you* could hack into that crappy network."

"Great, then-"

"Do *not* try that," he jabbed a finger at me across my office desk. "I was joking."

"Yeah, I-"

"Seriously, there are times when seeing you just use your phone makes me cringe. How do you not know any of the shortcuts I taught you?"

"My phone works just fine, thank you. Hey, uh, you can do all the hacking stuff you used to, right?"

"Certainly."

"Good, then-"

"As long as the systems I am not infiltrating have not been specifically hardened against me, like the infrastructure of Maxohlx or Rindhalu ships."

"*That* could be a problem."

"What can I say, Joe? The senior species have learned how to protect themselves from the methods I used to hack into them in the past. Mostly, I, I am just not as awesome as I once was," he sighed. "I can still do it if I use a Sentinel as a channel, of course."

"You know you can't take over a senior species warship, or you are afraid to try?"

"Um, a little of both? In peacetime, I have not had much need to screw with the kitties or spiders, and the two times I tried it, did not go well. It was rather humiliating, actually. My first attempt resulted in a Rindhalu firewall submind scolding me when it detected my presence. It wasn't even worried, it was just *annoyed*, and it told me to go away."

If I thought it would help, I would have hugged him. "That must have hurt, buddy."

"It did but, eh, the spiders could not believe they stopped *me*. So, they assumed I actually had hacked that ship, and me alerting the firewall was simply taunting. They isolated that ship from the network, and practically tore apart its substrate to find what damage I had done. They did identify a series of anomalies they couldn't explain, of course, any complex system accumulates glitches over years of use. Ultimately, the spiders dropped that ship into a red dwarf star, so I have that going for me. The second time, I was more careful, I managed to infiltrate a Maxohlx cruiser without being detected."

"That's encouraging."

"Not so much. I got in, but couldn't go anywhere. Every critical system blocked me, the best I could do was to hack the ship's wastewater controller. At one time, it would have been amusing to stop up that ship's plumbing, but when I realized that was all I could do, it was just *sad*. Joe I, I don't know what has happened to me."

Holding out a fist, I lowered my voice. "A *whole lot of shit* happened to you, Skippy. You survived, you're here, you are still awesome. You beat the Elders, even after they rigged the game against you."

"Thanks for trying to cheer me up, Joe, but," he looked away.

"Come on." My fist stayed hanging in the air above the desk.

"Oh, what the hell." He held out his tiny fist and we bumped. "I promise to do the best job I can."

"That's all I can ask."

"Will you promise that if we find Maxohlx warships at Moletown, we jump the hell out of there, agreed?"

"Uh, I'm not sure I can promise that."

"Seriously?"

"Seriously. Unless and until the kitties notice we are there, we can hang around to observe."

"What good will that do?"

"We have no indication the Maxohlx know about the radonium on Moletown, but if the kitties *are* there, they could do our job for us. You can intercept and decrypt their communications, right?"

"Yes. I am damaged, not dead."

"Great. Listen, I know it's best if we capture the radonium, but if the Maxohlx find it first, we can't allow them to take it away. So, we wait for the kitties to put the canister of radonium aboard a dropship. While that dropship climbs up above the atmosphere, we hit it missiles equipped with atomic compression warheads, and then jump away. That radonium will be scattered over so wide an area, it will never be recovered."

"I hate to say it, but that it not the worst plan I have ever heard. What about Chad, the hippie retired scientist?"

"Backpacking doesn't make someone a *hippie*."

"So you say."

"If we can take him out too, we do that. We don't risk the ship for one guy."

"When did you become sensible?"

"When I became a father."

We jumped in six lighthours from Moletown, to recon the area. The records we had, mostly stolen from Maxohlx military databases, stated the planet had an SD network that had been fairly state of the art for birdbrains, before the Maxohlx raid destroyed about half of the satellites. The rebuilding effort had given priority to adding capacity and capabilities to that orbiting network, which meant plenty of money was available to be skimmed off by the contractors and political leadership. The result was that many of the new satellites deployed were empty shells, and the incompatible software used by different phases of the network made cybersecurity a nightmare for the Bosphuraq.

That was good news for us.

No warships were in orbit, the single space station hadn't been used for years, and Skippy determined the planet was relatively quiet, with no recent visits by the Maxohlx.

The next jump brought *Valkyrie* to three lightseconds from the planet, and I got into a dropship with Skippy along with four other pilots, I would mostly be a passenger. Reed was still unhappy about me being away from the ship, even after I promised to bring back a snow globe from the SD network's gift shop.

Maybe I should have offered to bring her a nice box of candy instead.

As usual, Skippy hacked into and took control of the orbital components of the strategic defense network, the air defense systems dirtside, and the sensor processing nodes. The birdbrains would see only what we wanted them to see, which was nothing but a normal, ordinary day without a human special ops team descending to the surface.

"Are we good, Skippy?" I asked.

"Um, give me another half an hour, please. This is a bit more complicated than I expected. It's tricky work, got to get it right, you know?"

"Sure, whatever you need," I gave him a confident thumbs up.

My thumb was faking. My confidence in him was fake. Back when I commanded the *Dutchman* and then our mighty *Valkyrie*, taking full control of a second-tier species network was something Skippy could do in his sleep. That was good, considering how absent-minded he was. The flight close to Molitan had already been extended twice at Skippy's request, and every minute we flew farther from *Valkyrie* was another two minute delay in our return to the ship.

Something was different about Skippy. Something was *wrong* with him.

Half an hour went by, without the beer can bragging about how he had done yet another awesome thing.

Five minute later, I tapped out a text to him, *Are you done yet?*

"Ugh. I will be done when I'm *done*, numbskull," he snapped at me. Fortunately, he had the good sense to speak only into my earpiece, so the pilots didn't hear.

This is taking a lot longer than you anticipated, I texted back.

"Fine," he huffed in my ear. "Let's see *you* do it."

Give me an ETA please.

"Now!" He shouted in my ear. "How about *now*? Does that make you happy?"

"Are you uh," I cleared my throat. "Absolutely certain the network is compromised?"

"You are questioning my judgment?"

"No, I am," I whispered, though I was in a jump seat near the Panther's rear cargo compartment. "Simply asking for an update."

"I find your lack of faith in me disturbing."

Hearing him joke like that was good. "OK, Darth Skipper."

"Yes, I am absolutely certain. I wasn't before, I am now. That network is my bitch now. It's just," he sighed. "Joe, I haven't had to do this for a while, you know? It's not something you ever forget, like falling off a bicycle. Each situation is different. Your next question will be whether it is appropriate to launch the STAR team, the answer is yes. Let's do this, and get the hell out of here. I need a vacation."

I was worried about him. Bilby was also worried about Skippy, though Bilby had feared Skippy unknowingly had caused the activation of Dogzilla to fail. That was before Moonraider appeared and made it clear our enemy was not just some part of Skippy's subconscious. When Skippy had told me he was operating at a hundred percent, I hadn't been especially concerned. Many times while he was with the Merry Band of Pirates, he had operated at reduced capacity due to some self-inflicted injury, like when he absorbed most of *Valkyrie's* momentum to escape from a Maxohlx task force.

But, he should have been able to hack into a Bosphuraq network without making any effort, and clearly he had struggled to complete the task.

Maybe I should be *very* concerned about him.

We flew back to the ship, and *Valkyrie* jumped a few more lightseconds away, just in case Skippy did not in fact have complete control of the local strategic defense network. We needed to talk about his condition, after Frey's team was back with us. He did not need any distractions during the op.

STAR Team Razor reached the surface in three dropships that had been so heavily modified for stealthy special operations, they had the model designation as 'Raven' instead of the original 'Panther'. With Skippy's control of the planetary sensor systems preventing the locals from noticing the approach of the Ravens, the three spacecraft could have flown a conventional quiet entry, but I had ordered Frey to practice a maximum stealth flight profile. She didn't argue, it was good practice for her pilots and testing the techniques and equipment on a second-tier species was a safe environment. She did wonder why I was being so cautious. Unspoken in her question was whether I was concerned about Skippy. I gave her a justification that we both knew was bullshit. She accompanied her team anyway.

A maximum stealth ingress, on a planet that had a substantial atmosphere, was a complicated process. Each Raven had to fly out the docking bay door with a drone attached to the topside, an autonomous spacecraft that was almost as large as the Raven itself. The drone had its own propulsion system and stealth fields, and if UN Special Operations Command had an official name for those drones it didn't matter. The operators all called them 'Bat Hooks'.

The major problem with attempting to sneak through an atmosphere onto the surface of a world is kinetic energy. Incoming spacecraft are traveling at orbital velocity, in the case of Earth that is about twenty eight thousand kilometers per hour. Or around eight kilometers per *second*. A ship dropping through atmo pushes a lot of air out of the way, trading kinetic energy for heat. Normally, that is a good trade-off, it is easier to construct a spacecraft to resist heat, than to build it tough enough to survive smacking into the surface at eight klicks per second, right? That heat is a liability when you are trying to sneak onto the surface of an enemy world, as any infrared sensor on or above that hemisphere can see the burning streak across the sky. Any being with eyeballs can see it also, that is why people on Earth see 'shooting stars' at night. Even without the heat signature, all that air being displaced at hypersonic and then supersonic speed creates a sonic boom that acoustic sensors can easily hear. Finally, the streak of compressed air around an incoming spacecraft can be seen by simple sensors, even old-fashioned radar.

So, scrubbing off orbital velocity by slamming into an atmosphere is a cheap way to save fuel, but bad when you're trying to be quiet. Solution? The Bat Hook.

Each of the three Ravens slipped through the SD network, flying a precise flight path to avoid where sensor coverage from multiple satellites overlapped. Technically, that precaution was not necessary, but it was good practice for the pilots. And, given that I suspected Skippy was not quite as awesome as usual, maybe it *was* necessary. Each Raven came to a dead stop above the spot on the surface where the craft was supposed to begin subsonic flight, at which point the Ravens weren't moving fast enough to be in orbit. They were hovering at an altitude of sixty kilometers, their reactionless engines were keeping them from falling. That deep in a gravity well, it took a lot of power to hover, and to keep station with the spot on the surface below, as the planet rotated.

The Bat Hook drone separated, with the Raven falling away below three hundred meters, until the drone's own engines could operate effectively. Slowly, the Raven pilots throttled back, relying on the thin nanofiber cable that connected to the Bat Hook.

The cable began unspooling from the drone, and the Raven rode the cable down, picking up speed until it fell at five hundred kilometers per hour. Inside the cockpit and cabin of the three special ops spacecraft, pilots and operators pretended to be relaxed, not concerned that they were hanging from a thread almost too thin for the human eye to see.

Colonel Frey wished she hadn't eaten a doughnut with her breakfast, it sat like a lead weight in her stomach.

At twenty kilometers, cross winds were setting up a resonance in the cable that the dampeners couldn't completely compensate for. The pilots itched to trigger the balloons, but waited for their spacecraft to descend through eighteen klicks. The balloons deployed automatically, taking the full weight of a Raven, before the cable was released.

Each Raven drifted downward silently below an invisible balloon, while the nanofiber cable fell apart into dust. The Bat Hooks accelerated smoothly, increasing speed until they reached orbital velocity and could cut off their engines.

Fifteen minutes later, the balloons were deflated, retracted into a recess atop the hull, and the Ravens cruised easily to their designated landing zones.

By the time my dropship got back to *Valkyrie*, I was regretting that the galley crew had made doughnuts that morning, and that I had eaten two of them. Although, I couldn't decide whether I shouldn't have eaten the glazed, or the jelly-filled one.

The jelly, I decided.

See? Making quick judgment calls like that is why I am the commander of Task Force Black.

The three STAR teams were safely on the surface, with no sign they had been detected by anyone other than the local wildlife. I say that because one of their spacecraft had to alter course suddenly as it approached the landing zone, and a flock of large birds exploded off the ground after they were alarmed by the whining of the Raven's turbines. The pilots wisely diverted to an alternate LZ.

The three teams were designated Zulu for the people tasked with searching the warehouse in Zufestrah. Team Romeo were the reserves. And Team Charlie of course were the people tasked with grabbing Chad, since 'Chad' is a nickname for Charles. Why not just use just simple Alpha, Bravo, and Charlie for team designations?

Because the designation 'Alpha' had been retired by the Special Tactics Assault Regiment. There wasn't a written rule about that, there didn't need to be.

Frey was with Team Charlie in the park the locals called the Koskine Wilderness Protected Area. Team Zulu had jumped out the back ramp of their Raven, and dropped on parachute balloons to the roof of the warehouse in the thriving town of Zufestrah, while Team Romeo waited forty klicks from the warehouse. The landings had been timed so it was the middle of the night in Zufestrah, and just after nightfall in the wilderness. Skippy had not been exaggerating about the warehouse, the footprint of the ugly building covered two square kilometers, and the height of the roof promised a whole lot of junk could be stacked on top of other junk in there. Whatever. Team Zulu had come equipped with four dozen spider bots, that could scan the entire warehouse in less than forty minutes. They should hopefully find the canister of radonium, grab it, send it aloft on a balloon, and their dropship would retrieve them and the payload without the locals ever knowing they had been visited by aliens. By us.

Frey with Team Charlie had a tougher job. They had to find one Bosphuraq in a vast forest, without being seen by any of the two hundred and twenty three local nature enthusiasts on that section of trail. How did we know the exact count of Bosphuraq who were hiking or camping in the Koskine Wilderness? Skippy was tracking that number of Bosphuraq heat signatures with the SD network's sensors. Knowing the location of the locals, plus the chameleonware camo of the mech suits, helped Team Charlie avoid being seen, but eventually they would need to approach a hiking group to capture Chad.

Colonel Frey had two advantages that meant her team would not have to search every trail, tent, and shelter in the area. According to the records

Skippy had gotten access to, the group Chad was traveling with consisted of nine hikers, plus a guide. And, the guide had brought a 'lupone' with her. A lupone is a domesticated pack animal that was native to Molitan, so it could eat the local vegetation. Apparently, it was the size of a donkey, and was being used to carry part of the group's gear.

How many groups in the area consisted of ten Bosphuraq, *and* had a lupone with them? The answer, unfortunately, was seven. Lupones were popular, most guides who led hikes of more than two or three days had one with them. Seven groups to search, and of course they were scattered all over the freakin' woods. Which group was Chad with?

We needed Sherlock Skippy to solve that mystery. Two of the groups were not fully enjoying their time in nature; they were using phones constantly, and none of the calls matched Chad's voiceprint. That left five groups. One of the five were near the end of the trail, it was unlikely Chad's group could have walked so far since they started. So, a recon had to be conducted on only four groups. Without anyone knowing that big scary aliens were hunting in the woods.

Frey could rely on her second advantage: Skippy knew what Chad smelled like. The retired scientist had gone to a hospital six years before, when he fell off a motorized skateboard. Yeah, that surprised me too, skateboards are a thing the birdbrains commonly use as transportation in urban areas. Luckily for us, the Chadster was not a skilled rider. Hospital records not only had his equivalent of DNA, they had mapped his personal scent, as pheromones are a good indicator of overall health for that species.

Also, because the Bosphuraq have a strong scent, and use pheromones as body language in personal communications. I did not envy the STAR team who had to ride back to *Valkyrie* with Chad-o-rino stinking up the cabin. I suggested they keep their helmets on.

I had better make sure we had plenty of air fresheners aboard *Valkyrie*.

"Skippy," Frey squinted at the drone, while her suit's computer talked to the thing. "Have you accounted for how Chad's scent will have changed, after he hasn't taken a shower in several weeks?"

The microwormhole in the nearby Raven eliminated the time lag that otherwise would have made the exchange awkward. "Yes! His scent won't actually change, there will just be *more* of it."

"Their reputation is as a fragrant species."

"I have heard it described as them smelling *better* after they are dead, because their glands are no longer producing pheromones."

"Thank you for that delightful bit of trivia." The drone in her hand flexed its wings, and the icon for it in her visor glowed green. Hers was the last drone to be activated, all the others also glowed green. "Do you concur the drones are ready?"

"Affirmed."

"Fly," she gently tossed the drone in the air, "be free."

The drones, each the size of a sparrow, soared upward until they cleared the tree canopy. Wings retracted partially, sweeping back, and turbine motors propelled the drones to over eight hundred kilometers per hour. In the darkness, no one on the ground could see a bird zipping through the sky in a very unbird-like fashion, and their active camouflage holograms rendered them almost invisible. When each drone reached its search area, the turbines switched off, air intake and exhaust doors closed, and the wings extended to begin flapping in the manner of a small bird native to that region of the planet.

The drones flew slowly south to north, just above the trail, filtering air past their chemical sensors. Basically, they were sniffing for the scent of one particular Bosphuraq. There was a lot of ground to cover. Fortunately, the scent trail was strong.

Staff Sergeant Romano pinged Frey, just before her helmet visor lit up. "We have a hit. Confidence is ninety nine point four."

"That's our buddy Chad," Skippy confirmed. "The scent trail even includes traces of his favorite candy, that he wasn't supposed to bring with him."

"Charlie," Frey twirled a finger in the air. "Pack up, we're going back to the bird."

To conserve fuel, and to reduce the heat and acoustic signatures, the Raven had inflated its balloon after lowering the STARs on what were essentially fancy bungee cords. The ship hadn't moved much after the team hit the ground, and being less than a kilometer away from where the drones were deployed, the STARs were able to be back aboard within fifteen minutes.

Frey stuck her head through the open cockpit door. "Hold on retracting the balloon, I need to confer with Zulu about their progress at the warehouse." That was the plan, obtaining the sixteen kilograms of radonium was the priority. Until that precious material was located, extracted from the warehouse, and Zulu team's Raven was safely back through the strategic defense zone around the planet, her team would not move to kidnap Chad. A single bit of bad luck, or a screwup when taking the retired scientist, could alert the entire planet that something was wrong.

"Captain Wong," she called Team Zulu's leader. "What is your progress on the search?"

"No joy so far, Colonel."

That surprised her. In a bad way. The spider bots should have thoroughly swept the warehouse, in far less time than her own sparrow drones took to find Chad's scent trail. "Is there an issue with the bots?"

"They are nominal, and on their second sweep. The warehouse is packed to the rafters with junk, none of it catalogued."

"Time to complete the second sweep?"

"Eighteen minutes. They are bypassing a section of the warehouse floor that is demolition debris, Skippy is certain the radonium isn't in there."

She bit her lip. With her helmet faceplate swung up, her people could see the body language, and know what it meant. She needed to make a decision. Proceed toward the camp where hopefully Chad was sleeping for the night, deploy and wait for Zulu to signal they were safely away? Or wait at the landing zone?

They would wait. Flight time to Chad's campsite was only twenty five minutes, even with the dropship's engines in whisper mode. There was no advantage to going in early. The radonium would be located soon, and Team Zulu would exfil back toward *Valkyrie*, while Romeo redeployed to back up her Charlie team. "Be patient," she muttered to herself. Doing nothing went against her nature. It was also exactly what she needed to do right then.

"Colonel Frey, still no joy here," Wong reported from the warehouse, four minutes late.

"How could that-"

"It's not in the freakin' warehouse," Skippy groaned. "I *told* Joe that I was guessing the stupid thing would be in that big stupid warehouse."

Berating the Elder AI would achieve nothing. "Captain Wong, retrieve the spider bots and get your team back to the Raven."

"Ma'am, we can-"

"You might have to redeploy anywhere on this rock, and the sun will be up at your location sooner rather than later. Get your feet off the ground."

"Understood."

"Skippy, what is your *second* best guess?"

"Oh wow, um, like you said. Anywhere. Go house to house, start looking under couches?" He made a sound like taking a breath. "I'm sorry. I'm under a lot of stress here."

She did not bother pointing out that *her* team was at the bottom of a gravity well, under the umbrella of a strategic defense network. "Any assistance you could provide would be greatly appreciated."

"Oh um, hmm. Let me look into it. There might be- Ugh. Damn it!"

"What?"

"The property records of that warehouse *suck*. Basically, nobody kept any records of what went in there, that's why I had to guess where the radonium was. There are still no records available, but I have been reading any documents that are even vaguely related to that warehouse. Twelve years ago, there was an inheritance dispute among members of a prominent family on the Bosphuraq world Finndestrum. One faction of the family hired lawyers to track down any items or documents that could support their claim to the money. The-"

"Skippy, this is all fascinating, what does it-"

"I'm getting to that. The family patriarch who died had business interests on Molitan, and maintained both an office and a residence in the two in Zufestah. When the Maxohlx hit that town as part of their punishment campaign, because of actions *we* did that Joe framed the Bosphuraq for, both the office and condo buildings were destroyed. Anywho, the lawyers hired a local company to search the warehouse for items or documents related to the family, and, here is the important point, quote, any other objects that might have potential value, endquote. A truckload of junk and whatever was brought to the spaceport, where the items were examined by a local law firm. Naturally, they wanted to retain any documents that could support the family faction's claim to the money, and destroy any evidence that could weaken their claim. In the end, the whole dispute was settled out of court, and none of the junk was taken offworld. It is still, as far as I know, at the spaceport. What we care about is the law firm here *did* keep meticulous records, since they wanted to justify every billable hour, and one item on their list is described as an unlabeled canister or containment vessel, with unknown contents. So, ugh, we have been looking in the wrong place!"

"Skippy, please do a deep dive on records of that spaceport. Look for storage fees related to a canister. Images from a cleaning bot that is annoyed a canister is blocking its access. Anything like that, before I commit my team to another search." She pulled up a map of the spaceport. "The sun will be rising at the spaceport in less than an hour. A search will have to wait until tonight."

"That is probably a good idea. Sorry that I didn't know about the materials being removed from the warehouse, I didn't have access to that data until your teams brought the microwormholes to the surface. The- *Oh shit*."

"What?"

"We have company. A Maxohlx task force just arrived to crash the party."

"Look on the bright side," I said to Reed, as the display counted more and more enemy ships jumping into orbit. "Their timing actually could have been worse."

"Two battleships, and five cruisers," she shook her head. "A standard Maxohlx cruiser squadron now is six ships, so they left one out somewhere around here as a sensor picket. Sir, how could this be any *worse*?"

"The canister of radonium could be aboard one of our dropships right now, trying to get back through the SD net. The way those kitty ships are hammering away with active sensor pulses, they could detect a Raven even through the stealth field. We would have been delivering the radonium right to the kitties. So, it could be worse."

As a reply, she just took a deep breath.

What she didn't say was if the kitties found one of our dropships, the STAR operators had standing orders to trigger the atomic compression warhead that was stuffed into the Raven's rear cargo hold. We wouldn't have the sixteen kilograms of Skippy's magic radio dust, but neither would the Maxohlx.

"Those battleships are their newest *Devastator* class, very tough," she pointed to the display. "In a standup fight, we could probably take out one of them, but not two. And not the cruisers also. What the hell are they doing here?" She demanded, leaning forward and gripping the armrests tightly.

Skippy sighed. "The admiral in command of the task force is broadcasting what he calls a 'request for cooperation', to locate and remove from the surface a dangerous substance. The kitties claim to be concerned the substance is unstable, and poses a threat to their esteemed clients, so naturally as their protectors, the Maxohlx Hegemony is stepping into assure the safety of- Ugh, blah blah blah. If you're going to lie, put some effort into it. The Bosphuraq know their patrons never consider the health and welfare of their lowly clients. Oh, and one of the cruisers just launched six dropships, including four fighter gunships. Hmm, that explains why that cruiser is in such a perilously low orbit. The dropships are headed straight for the warehouse in Zufestrah. Ha! I have bad news, if they are looking for the radonium there, suckers!

"Skippy," I asked. "How do they know the radonium is here?"

"Jeez, Joe, I have no idea. I figured it out. The AIs of the Hegemony are not smart compared to me, but they are also not entirely stupid."

"Can you hack those ships from here?"

"No way. They are beyond my presence. Wait! Before you suggest something insane like my flying over there in a dropship, even I can't mask a ship from all the active sensor energy the kitties are using. Wow! They are irradiating the whole area with sensor pulses all across the electromagnetic spectrum. If there is a box of frozen food in orbit, that radiation will *cook* it."

Reed cocked her head. "Why *are* they being so loud?'

"Because of us," I sighed. "Us, and Moonraider. And the spiders. The Maxohlx think they have found the most valuable substance in the galaxy, and they know the only threats to them getting their paws on that radonium are *Valkyrie*, the Rindhalu, and Moonraider. So, they're doing everything they can to make sure no one sneaks up on them. Even out here, we are," I checked the display. "At a fourteen percent risk of those sensors detecting us. Skippy, I was going to suggest we launch a microwormhole toward those ships. You can extend your presence from here, through the microwormhole."

"Oh."

"Right?"

"Um, Joe? Could you go to your office?" His words ended in a squeak. "We should, um, make a plan for me to do, you know, awesome things."

Reed gave me a 'What the hell is going on with Skippy' look. As an answer, I gave her an 'I got this' thumbs up. I don't think she believed me.

"Colonel Frey?" I called as I stood up.

"General, I hear we have visitors upstairs."

"We will deal with them, but for the meantime, pull your teams away from the target areas. The Maxohlx will be focusing sensors on the warehouse, and they could soon be looking for Chad also."

"Sir, the Zulu team will have to go to ground. They can't get back to their dropship before that Raven has to clear the area."

"Understood. Do whatever you think is best. It," I debated how much to tell her. "You could be on that rock for a while, so I hope you don't get bored."

"We have a deck of cards, and plenty of audiobooks, Sir. Don't worry about us."

I wish I was as calm about the situation as she sounded.

She didn't know what I knew.

CHAPTER THIRTY TWO

"OK, let's talk," I closed my office door as Skippy's avatar appeared on my desk. "While we talk, can you create some microwormholes, so we can get them launched toward those Maxohlx ships? Do you need one microwormhole for each ship, or-"

"Joe, that's not gonna happen."

"What is not happening?"

"I *told* you that if we found Maxohlx ships here, we need to jump away. You agreed with me, now you're changing the deal."

"We *didn't* find Maxohlx ships here, they came late to the party. Skippy, I have people on the surface, we need to either hack the sensors of those ships, or disable them."

"Not gonna happen. Did you not listen to me? I can't hack senior species ships. Not anymore. And microwormholes? There are three units active right now, one with each of the dropships down there. It is seriously straining my resources to maintain just three of them. To create another, I will have to cut off one of the STAR teams."

"Do *not* do that. Hey buddy, talk to me. What's wrong?"

"Nothing. Everything."

"Uh huh. One of those days?"

"One of those *decades*, Joe. Since I beat the Elders, I have been on a Victory Tour, but in reality I am a fraud. You remember the guy who did all those awesome things, to earn the name Skippy the Magnificent?"

What I actually remembered was him giving that title to himself. Of course that's not what I said. "Remember him? I am talking to that guy right now."

"Thank you but no. I am no longer that guy. Wait! Before you do the thing of telling me a bunch of comforting lies, don't bother. One thing that has not changed is that flattery doesn't work on me."

"Oh well, yeah," I didn't know what else to say.

"Do you know how I know that I am an imposter, a mere shadow of my former self?"

"I disagree, but tell me anyway."

"In my glory days, I created great art, in the form of operas, musicals, hip-hop music, that sort of thing. That is all behind me now. No matter how hard I try, I can't write original music anymore. Now, I am reduced to- No, it's too embarrassing to admit."

"OK."

"*OK*? That's all you've got for me?"

"Uh, tell me what you want me to say, and I'll say it."

"You can't even guess?"

"Are you," I thought fast, and got nothing, so I said the first idiotic thing that popped into my head. "Reduced to touring as a Lil Shithead tribute band?"

"No, you numbskull, it- Hmm, I hadn't thought of that, it is a *great* idea."

"No, it is a *terrible* idea. Come on, Skippy, throw me a bone here."

"Oh, all right. Instead of creating great art, my creative drive is reduced to grinding out ekphrastic poetry about it."

"Uh, *what?*"

"Like I said, it is horribly embarrassing. Most poetry students say they don't bother with ekphrastic verse after they graduate from a master's program."

"Don't most poetry students say things like 'Do you want fries with that'?"

"That isn't the point, you moron."

"Hey, I am way ahead of the curve here, I don't even have a degree at all, and I have never written eck, fast, whatever you said type of poems."

"Eck-FRAS-tic."

"Yeah, that doesn't help."

"Ugh. I thought we had reached the bottom of your well of ignorance."

"We had, but I was inspired to keep digging. What is, the thing you said?"

"Here's a clue: ekphrasis is a Greek word meaning 'description'."

"You *think* you're helping, but you're not."

"Listen, knucklehead, it is generally considered to be poetry about other forms of art. Like painting, sculpture, or in my case, opera."

"And this is a real thing people do? You didn't make this up?"

"Yes!"

"My next question would be '*Why*', but I don't want to know the answer."

"Joe, I am reduced to writing poems about my own operas, because I can no longer create *new* music."

"You mean poetry like 'I think that I shall never hear, a poem as lovely as, uh, music to my ear'?"

"I am hurting, and you *mock* me?"

"I'm trying to make the point that a million words of poetry won't tell me what a piece of music sounds like, I need to *hear* it."

"Ah, you're right. And, that poem you just made up is actually pretty good, I need to write it down to use later."

"You once told me that today's most influential composers are writing the scores for movie soundtracks, not for symphonies."

"That is pretty much true."

"Are today's best poets writing song lyrics, and not, you know, words on a page?"

"Words on a *page*? Where else would they be?"

"You know what I mean. Words that are meant to be heard in a song, not sitting in a dusty book no one ever reads."

"I suppose you could say that. Bob Dylan's lyrics could certainly be considered poetic."

"What about Lil Shithead's lyrics?"

"Ugh. I *used* to write banging raps, now I'm just lame."

"So, you have what, sort of writer's block?"

"I suppose you could say that also. Before you give me a bunch of stupid suggestions, I have tried everything. Even tried what *you* do, when you need to engage the creative side of your mind."

"Uh, what is it that I do?"

"What you do is you *don't* think about it. You go to the gym, or you work in the galley, or you go out running. Anything other than actually trying to work on the problem."

"When I do that, I *am* working on the problem. You told me that you can't do some things like warping spacetime as well as you used to, I thought it was a power issue. That you can't put as much effort, or energy, into doing your awesome things. I didn't know the problem is affecting *everything* inside you."

"Well," he sounded completely miserable. "Now you know. My power throughput ability was damaged for a time after my fight with the Elders. I have fully recovered from that. I have the power, I just can't *use* it."

That didn't sound right. Meaning, it didn't sound like the problem was what he feared it was; that he was worn out, burned out, used up. "Skippy, when did this start? Your creativity issue, the writer's block?"

"After my fight with the Elders. That is when all my troubles started, when I became no longer extremely awesome."

"All of your troubles started at the same time? Suddenly?"

"That is what I said." He didn't snap at me, he didn't add 'dumdum' or 'knucklehead' or 'numbskull', or any of his other usual insults.

He had given up.

That was not good.

"*How* did it happen?"

"I am burned out," he shrugged. "It happens."

"Bullshit. It happens to *meatsacks*. Our brains are such disorganized sacks of mush, we never know why something works or doesn't work. You are different. You rebuilt your own matrix, you designed it, down to the smallest detail."

"That is true. Why does that matter?"

"Other Elder AIs have no musical talent, that is unique to you." What I didn't say was his talent was debatable. In my opinion, he was awful. His Lil

Shithead persona's music was popular, especially among the Ruhar. And the Kristang apparently genuinely loved his epic operas. "The things you're telling me you can no longer do, like writing music, hacking into any system, easily warping spacetime, the-"

"It was never *easy*, numbskull."

"Eas*ier*. All those awesomenesses, they appeared when you rebuilt yourself after the AI war."

"I know that. *You* think you're helping, but you're not."

"Listen, I know what is in your matrix isn't *code*, but let's go Barney on it and pretend for a minute, OK? The parts of yourself that could do all those awesome things, are they still there?"

"Yes. Don't you think I checked that? I'm not an idiot. Those subroutines are still intact and active, they just don't work the way they used to."

"Uh huh. After you found that Bubba got hacked, you told me about epigenetics. I studied up on the subject later."

"Where?" He snorted. "On Wikipedia?"

"That's not important right now. I learned that genes can be in our DNA, but switched off, because of environmental factors or whatever else affects other genes, that control which genes are active."

"Yes, so?"

"Skippy, all of your awesomeness disappeared suddenly, in *one* incident?"

"Thank you *so* much for reminding me."

"Damn it, Skippy, why didn't you tell me about this before? You suffered for years, and didn't say anything?"

"Joe, though it makes me gag," he choked, "to say it, I did not tell *you* because you are my best friend. Your opinion is actually somewhat important to me, which shows how sad and pathetic my life is. Of all the people who look at me with worshipful adoration, I care most about you seeing me as impossibly perfect."

"I have bad news for you about that."

"Oh, shut up."

"Didn't you once call yourself the King of Empathy?"

"Yes, but that was back when I used to care about the losers who infest this galaxy."

"OK, I, you *might* be missing the point of empathy. Listen, I am your best friend. You are my best friend, and, now that I said that, it is kind of sad."

"Thank you *so* much for that."

"Being best friends means I am the one person you absolutely *should* tell about your problems."

"Hmm. Knowing the truth doesn't lower your opinion of me?"

"Knowing that you concealed the truth for years, *that* lowers my opinion of you. Everyone has problems, Skippy. Remember when Margaret was depressed after the boys were born, and I didn't know what to do? I talked with you about that."

"Yes, and you ignored all of my advice."

"Telling my wife to stop being overly emotional was *not* good advice."

"Ugh. One of us has a doctorate in monkey psychology, and it's not you. Joe, now you know my deep, dark secret. How does that do either of us any good?"

"It's good because now that I know what has really been going on with you, we might be able to fix it."

"My problems can't be fixed with a ten millimeter socket wrench, you knucklehead."

"If I did need a ten millimeter socket, that's the one that would be missing from the case, and I would have to drive to the hardware store again. What I should have said is, I might know how you can fix *yourself.* Before you tell me I am a dumdum numbskull, hear me out. I don't think you just got burned out, and that the damage to your matrix isn't just too much mileage. When you were inside that Ascension machine, connected to it, something happened to you. Something was *done* to you."

"Oh, brilliant. Wow, that thought never occurred to me. I already told you, the subroutines are all operating perfectly, they simply don't work for me. The problem is I'm not *feeling* it, Joe. I have lost my mojo."

"Then find whatever it is inside you that is blocking your mojo."

He rolled his eyes. "You think I got *hacked*, without me knowing it?"

"I *think* you went away while we were inside that Ascension machine, and such a powerful device is capable of doing a whole lot of bad shit to you."

"Come on, you're not making any sense. Think about it. I took control of that machine, and made it work against the Elders."

"No, you didn't."

"Um, what I remember is-"

"We both remember the same thing, I am looking at it more clearly. You didn't use that machine *against* the Elders, you used it to give them what they always wanted."

"Hmm. That, hmm. That is true."

"I am still kind of bitter about that."

"Sorry."

"No need to be sorry, you saved all of us. I am bitter about, the nature of reality, not about any decision you made. What I'm trying to say is the Ascension machine was an Elder device, and the Elders considered you to be a malfunctioning security system. Could the machine have *done* something to you, trying to fix what it saw as your malfunction? Like, blocking your access to the parts of yourself that were not authorized by the Elders, the parts you created?"

393

"That is *so* ridiculous," he snorted. "I wish I could hear how stupid you- Huh."

"Right?"

"Joe, what actually damages me is talking with *you*. Every time we have a conversation, I feel dumber."

"I am terribly sorry about that."

"Your suggestion is that I look for something that is actively *blocking* my mojo?"

"Yes, however you would do that."

"Ugh. I will do this to humor you, and *not* because I think your idea has any merit."

"You can consider this to be my birthday present."

"I already got you socks for your birthday."

"You can save the socks for Christmas."

"Whatevs. OK, I have to admit, this is *not* the worst idea you have ever had. That is only because you have had *so* many incredibly awful ideas that this-"

"I know what you mean. Do it, please? Quickly?"

"*Quickly*? I have been trying everything for years to restore my mojo, and now I am on the freakin' clock?"

"We have people down on Moletown. We need Skippy the Magnificent, not Skippy the Mopey."

"I am not *moping*."

"Yeah you are. I should call you 'Eeyore' like that depressed donkey in Winnie the Pooh."

"Huuuuuuuh." He shuddered. "How *dare* you?"

"Do *you* dare to actually look inside yourself, or are you afraid to?"

"I am only afraid to crush your spirit, when your moronic idea doesn't work."

"I will feel very foolish if that happens. Do it *now*, please."

"You do understand that a deep dive into my matrix will require me to go offline for a considerable time, while we are in a combat situation?"

"I do."

"And you are OK with this?"

"I am."

"Is this because," he stared down at his shoes, "as I am now, I am pretty much useless?"

"I didn't say that."

"You didn't have to." Without another word, his avatar blinked out.

"Sir?" Captain Scilvana announced herself, as she rapped a claw on the door frame of the admiral's office.

"Eh?" Scorandum sat bolt upright. In spite of appearances, he had *not* been taking a nap. He had been, resting. Gathering his energy. Preparing for the future.

If he had one.

"The relay station just pinged with our ID code. We have received an order from the Inquisitor's office, instructing us to proceed immediately to a rendezvous point."

"Well, then I suggest you proceed immediately. It would not do to upset an Inquisitor."

"Sir, you said 'You'? Did you not mean '*We*'? You are not coming with us?"

"Yes, of course."

Scilvana looked pained, her antennas twitching. "Clarify if you could please, Sir. Of course you are coming with us?"

"Oh. Yes. That is correct. I arranged to meet with a Court official."

The captain shuddered. No one willingly spoke with an Inquisitor. "Sir, is there something I need to know about?"

"What you need to know is that 'We' will soon not include me. I will be leaving the ship. I suspect on a permanent basis. The *You Can't* will be reassigned in the ECO pool. The good news for you is that you will no longer need to deal with a particularly troublesome admiral. The *better* news is that your new admiral will, of course, have to pay you and your crew."

"What about payments that are overdue, Sir? If I may ask?"

"You would be remiss if you did not ask. As part of the deal I arranged with the," he paused and shuddered slightly, "Court of Special Inquiry, your back pay should already be in your accounts."

"You, you made a *deal* with the Inquisitors?"

"Yes. This surprises you?"

"It does. No one *bargains* with the Court."

"Ha ha," the admiral laughed. "That is what the Court wishes you to think. Captain, everyone bargains with the Court, to one extent or another. The difference is, most people are forced to bargain from a position of fear and weakness. In this case, I have something they very much want. So, I told them what I want in exchange."

Scilvana appeared to relax, just a bit. "You are working *with* the Inquisitors."

"Not exactly. They want to throw me in prison, and I probably will have to accept some sort of punishment. The Inquisitors cannot be seen as offering leniency, especially not to an ECO agent. My career is over, that is inevitable. Was inevitable, from the moment I agreed to a sketchy arrangement with an Elder AI," his mandibles clacked angrily. "My hope, my plan, is to offer the Court a bigger target, one that will confirm the power of the Inquisitors."

"There is no way out for you, Sir?"

"This *is* my way out."

The captain shook her head. "The deal you described is your way to limit the damage to yourself. It is not a way *out*."

"You are correct. In this case, I do not have any other choice. For me, this is a no-win situation."

"When I first came aboard, you told me that if I am ever faced with a no-win situation, I am not thinking creatively enough. There is *always* a way out, Sir."

"Was I drunk when I said that?"

"I am trying to be serious, Sir."

"Captain," his antennas stood up, and tapped each other. "You have given me much to think about. When is the rendezvous scheduled for?"

"As we are inconveniently positioned," she tilted her head, hinting that the remote position of the ship was due to orders from the admiral. "It will take us four days and sixteen hours to reach the site."

"Hmm. It is unfortunate that will be likely keep the Inquisitor waiting but, the mathematics of interstellar navigation is notoriously inflexible. Could we," he tapped a claw on a tablet. "Yes. I would like to visit two relay stations along the way to the rendezvous. One is roughly, seven hours from here. The other will require going a bit out of our way, but the delay will only be three hours."

"The Inquisitors will not approve of *any* delay in complying with their summons, Sir."

"I will note," he tapped on the tablet again, "that I am giving you a direct order, so any delay is my responsibility."

"Yes Sir," she replied stiffly. "May I ask the purpose of visiting two relay stations? We are parked close to a relay station now."

"I am aware of that. Let me just say that I might want to send a message to an old, not quite friend. Someone who has been useful in the past. Before I send such a message, I need to think about, what you said."

"What *I* said?"

"Yes. It pains me to admit this, but I might be growing soft in my old age. I *did* say there is no such thing as a no-win situation, only a failure to think creatively. That was true then, and it is especially true now."

"You are seeking advice from your, friend?"

"It is probably best that you don't know my intentions."

CHAPTER THIRTY THREE

"Reed," I called from the bridge doorway. "In your office."

"Sir," she whispered, aware that everyone was looking at her. "I should be on the bridge now, in case-"

"In case we need to do something, yeah," I said. "Except there is nothing we can do right now, other than remain here in stealth. I need you with me, so we can wargame some options with Bilby."

She was torn, I could see that. With a curt nod, she turned to her XO. "Gasquet, you have the conn. Alert me if the enemy detects our people on the surface."

Her office had the advantage of being close to the bridge, she could be back in the command chair in less than a minute. She sat with her office chair swiveled so she could get up immediately, without her desk in the way. "Bilby?" She called. "We need to explore our options for recovering the STAR operators. Options that don't require Skippy to do, anything more than he has already done."

"Where," Reed cocked her head. "Is Skippy? Why isn't he part of this wargaming?"

"He is busy, working on something. Hopefully, working on a solution to this mess. In the meantime, we need alternatives, that don't involve Skippy's particular, uh, capabilities." As I said that, I looked down at the desk, then up at Reed.

Her lips were compressed in a thin line. She knew what I meant. That we shouldn't, couldn't, rely on Skippy being the old Skippy. She didn't know why, and she understood that I would tell her what she needed to know.

Or, since she had served with Simms during many times when I withheld important information from my executive officer, she knew I might keep vital information to myself.

"So, Bilby," I took a breath. "What have we got?"

"Like, nothing," the ship's slacker AI was depressed. "There are no options. We are *one* ship. Anything the away team does to climb back into orbit, the Maxohlx will detect on sensors. This is *bogus*, man."

Reed grimaced, and gave me the side-eye. No, not quite. She had glanced at me, to judge whether to say something. Whatever it was, it made her uncomfortable.

"Fireball," I used her callsign, "if you have anything to say, I want to hear it."

"Sir, I'm sure this isn't anything you haven't considered. You just don't like it. I don't like it either, I don't see a realistic alternative."

"Bad news doesn't get better with age, so-"

"The away team's best chance for survival is to hole up somewhere, and wait for the Maxohlx fleet to just go away."

"You're right. I had considered that. And I don't like it."

"And?"

"And, you're right, damn it. It is their best option. Teams Charlie and Romeo can set their dropships down somewhere remote, set up stealth netting, and just wait. Zulu will have to go hide and hope they aren't detected by the locals, until the heat is off and they can exfil. There are two problems with that. It means we have to stay here, wait for an opportunity to pick up the away teams. While we are waiting, we can't be somewhere else, and we leave the field of play open to Moonraider."

"Once there is no longer a senior species task force in orbit, our regular Navy can handle retrieval of ST-Razor. We could fly out to make contact with the Navy, probably at Jaguar?" She moved to pick up her tablet, then pushed it away. A navigation solution could wait. "We would be away," she looked at the ceiling while she considered the issue. "Five, six days, assuming we can use a wormhole shortcut? The kitties don't appear to be a rush to leave orbit."

"That's the other problem. Team Zulu near the warehouse only has seven days of food rations with them, and the local plants and animals don't meet human nutritional needs. Same with the food the Bosphuraq are growing down there, the carbohydrates and proteins are either useless to us, or poisonous. Zulu team will have to remove their suits to conserve power, and they'll be exposed to the local wildlife. We know many of the insects are venomous to us."

"STARs carry repellant sprays," Reed noted.

"They do, that doesn't help if one of our people steps on a critter that bites."

"Sir, I'm fairly certain Colonel Frey would not like to know you are concerned about her people being in danger from *bugs*. They train for exposure to hazardous indigenous life, and they received a full briefing before they dropped dirtside."

"I hear you. Critters, they can handle." The flexible suit liners were made a material much tougher than Kevlar, and STARs carried booties, gloves, and hoods. There was also a netting they could pull over their faces, to keep away flying insects. "Food though, is an issue."

"The report I read of your second mission, when your crew was stranded on Newark, said you requested a delivery from Skippy's Pizza?"

The memory made me smile. "Something like that."

"Can we do that here?

"Bilby?" I wanted to move on before Reed could ask more questions about Skippy. "The Ravens can't risk flying with Maxohlx ships overhead. Can we deliver food packages to the surface, near Zufestrah?"

"Whoa like, it might be possible? On Newark, Skippy had control of the local sensor network, and the threat was from only a group of lizards in the surface. Here, there are senior species ships in orbit, their sensors would detect and track anything dropping from orbit. We would need to get, like, creative, you know? Conceal the payload inside a rock, drop it to impact near the away team."

"I don't want Zulu traveling to a meteor impact site outside of town, the kitties will be monitoring the area." That wasn't likely, since the Maxohlx had no reason to suspect a falling rock was anything other than common space junk. But, it was a low-risk, high-impact situation. Meaning, if the kitties were watching the impact site and saw a human approach, it would be a disaster for the away team. "Bilby, can you design and fabricate crawler drones, that could survive the impact, and carry the food packages to the away teams?"

"Oh wow, man. That is like, tricky? Better to have the drones in a stealthed shell that gets ejected from the meteor just before impact, float it down on a balloon?"

"Whatever you think is best. Show me your design, and infil plan, before you crank up the fabricators."

"Roger Wilco, General Dude. Um, is that it?"

"Unless you have a better idea."

"It's bogus but, no. I might be able to disable one of those big battlewagons, but not both of them. Any slugging match we get into will result in us taking damage that could knock out our drive, and the damping field those ships are projecting will prevent us from jumping away quickly anyway. If Skippy was, you know, with us, he maybe could do some awesome thing, but even he couldn't take on that entire task force."

"Yeah."

"I just can't believe we're gonna leave the away team on the surface, and you know, hope the Maxohlx ships leave soon."

"I am open to suggestions."

"Yeah, I got nothin'."

"Reed?"

"Nada, Sir. There's just no way. We knew it, the STARs knew the risks, when we started this op."

"Then," I lightly slapped a hand on the table, it just felt like the way to end the discussion. "Bilby, get to work on-"

Reed's phone chimed. "Colonel," Gasquet called. "We have a problem."

Back on the bridge, I waved for Gasquet to stay in his chair, while I stood off to the right of the main display. The problem was, the kitties somehow had learned the same thing Skippy had discovered: that at some point the missing canister of radonium had been moved to the spaceport. Their team in Zufestrah were racing back to base, and Maxohlx soldiers at the spaceport were fanning out there to conduct a hard target search of every warehouse, hangar, weapons magazine, farmhouse, henhouse, doghouse, and outhouse in that area.

"Give me a view of that spaceport," I said to no one in particular. Usually when I wanted the main display adjusted, Skippy handled it, or Bilby. Whoever.

"Sure thing, Dude," Bilby drawled, and the holographic image flickered for a moment, then zoomed in to an overhead view of the sprawling spaceport complex. The area inside the fence line was huge, much larger than the planet needed, given the relatively small number of flights the ports accommodated each year. The designers must have been ambitious about future expansion. The vast area the kitty search team had to cover was good for us. Not so good was the number of structures enclosed by the fence. "Bilby, add outlines of any underground structures."

Overlaid on the satellite image were schematics of the facilities buried beneath the surface.

"Red is ammunition magazines, yellow is fuel tanks, and blue is, whatever," the ship's AI explained. "You can probably ignore the fuel storage."

"I count, above ground and below, nine structures? That's all?"

"The view is real time. What you see if what you get."

"OK, pull back a bit, show me a kilometer beyond the fence line."

The area was almost completely empty. Either no one wanted to build near the noisy and potentially dangerous spaceport, or that land was reserved for expansion. "That's not good," I rubbed my chin. "The kitties will have every square meter of those buildings thoroughly searched within an hour. If the radonium is there, they will find it."

"Bilby," Reed stood up. "Are you intercepting their communications in real time?"

"Affirmative, except for you know, the speed of light delay. The kitties on the ground are not using their higher level encryption, they don't have that gear with them. If they find the canister, I will know about it right away."

"Sir, we need to assume they *will* find it," she addressed that comment to me. "We can jump in just beyond the damping field, flood the target with salvos of directed energy and railguns, then jump away. The enemy will intercept some of the railgun darts, we can still turn a section of that spaceport into a smoking crater. Then, we jump away before the enemy ships can get into position to cut off our escape route."

Though I nodded approval, I did it without enthusiasm. "Let's leave that option as a last resort. Unless we can be certain to vaporize the radonium, the Maxohlx will set up a long-term presence here, to scour the area for fragments. We would never be able to retrieve our people from dirtside."

400

Reed bit her lip. "We can crank up the railguns to 'Eleven', maximize the impact energy. Or deploy atomic-compression warheads on missiles.'

"Missiles will get intercepted in flight, the Maxohlx ships are on high alert. Regardless, the enemy will remain here until they are certain they have picked up every particle of radonium, the stuff is too valuable to leave scattered on the ground. We," without thinking about it, I rubbed my chin again. Did I do that when playing poker? It was an obvious tell. "We will be better off waiting for the kitties to load their prize on a dropship, hit it when it clears the atmosphere. The debris cloud will cover half of the planet, even the most stubborn kitty will know that's not practical to recover."

"Unless they send up more than one dropship, and we don't know which one carries the canister. Or, they split the payload into multiple containment canisters."

"They are not familiar with the material, I don't see them trying to transfer it from the canister that has held the radonium safely for years. Probably they will take precautions like loading that old canister into one of their containment vessels, one that could survive reentry if the dropship's engines fail. They don't know we are here, so they won't expect us to jump in and hit that dropship. Or dropships, we can target more than one. Our big guns can take out several little spacecraft, while we are safely beyond the limit of the damping field. No," I reached a decision. "We wait. They will bring it upstairs, and we turn it into space dust."

That still left the problem of the STAR teams stranded on the surface at Zufestrah. In spite of my confident words, there was a possibility the Maxohlx would be desperate enough to set up ramscoops to collect any particles of radonium that hadn't fallen out of orbit. That process could take months, during that time the kitties would maintain a presence in orbit. They would also be intensively scanning the surface for chunks of radonium, and they would carefully examine anything that fell from the sky. "Reed, I'll be in my office," I turned toward the bridge doorway. "Bilby, we need to drop not only food packages to Team Zulu, but possibly also a synthesizer that can turn native carbs and proteins into something humans can eat."

The synthesizers were too large to drop inside any meteor that was small enough not to automatically get zapped by the planet's SD network, so they would have to be disassembled and sent down in pieces. We also had to send the starter gels that got the synthesis process going. Bilby judged that dropping both food and synthesizers was doable, though we had to scrap the idea of including delivery drones. Drones were more important than a synthesizer. To provide cover for the payload rock, we would be dropping a shotgun spray of meteors that would fall over a wide area, so many meteors that we would deplete the supply of raw materials we carried. The operation should work, unless the Maxohlx crew monitoring sensors aboard a ship in orbit got too curious about the space rocks, and decided to run a spectral analysis. A scan would show the composition of the rocks did not match the chemical makeup of the asteroids in that star system. The signature would be close, since *Valkyrie* carried a variety of dust that could be heated and compressed into space rocks. Close was not the same as matching, and if the kitties got their AIs to take a look at the meteors, those powerful thinking machines would know two things immediately. Those rocks didn't come from the local star system. And they were fabricated, recently.

We had to hope no one cared about a cluster of space rocks.

"We can be ready to launch the first cluster in forty seven minutes," Bilby announced, after he checked the first rock that came out of the fabricator. "You know what is the major, stinking problem with delivering rocks from out here?"

"Yeah." At *Valkyrie's* position eight lightseconds from Molitan, it would take the meteors several days to reach the planet. That was no good.

"Um like, I suggest we use dropships to fly in and launch the rocks."

"Thanks for the suggestion, but that's no good. The dropships would be hanging out alone if we have to jump. Could *Valkyrie* jump in beyond the range of the damping field, and we launch from there?"

"The gamma ray-"

"We will time our arrival so our gamma ray burst will be drowned out by one of the enemy cruisers jumping away. They rotate their sensor picket ships on a fairly regular schedule, and you can detect when a particular ship is preparing for a jump?"

"Oh wow, yeah, good idea. Solid! That still will only work if Skippy can control our drive, he can do magical things I can't."

"When we get that that point, I will wake up Skippy."

"OK. If you don't mind me asking, is he like, on a spiritual journey or something?"

"You could say that."

"Righteous. I have thought about doing that. Taking a sabbatical, to find the deep meaning of life, you know?"

"Uh," I had no idea how to respond. How would a ship's AI go on sabbatical? "That is, an interesting notion, you-"

"Oops! Dude, we are out of time! The kitties at the spaceport just found the canister. The admiral upstairs wants the radonium aboard his battleship like, ASAP. A dropship at the spaceport should be skids up in twelve minutes."

"Twelve minutes," I repeated. "Another fifteen minutes to reach orbit, maybe twenty if the pilots are being gentle with their cargo," I was talking to myself while I rose from the chair. "Bilby, put a hold on prepping space rocks, we will come back to that later, after the task force here jumps away."

"Ooh, I have bad news about that. The kitty admiral here is pissed that the locals weren't exactly enthusiastic about cooperating, so he is leaving the other battleship here, with the cruiser squadron. Those ships will enforce a traffic blockade. No ships in, no ships out. Extracting the STARs will be super difficult. Sorry, I'm just hearing this now."

"It's OK." Though I had stood up, my feet weren't moving. What I needed to do was think, not walk.

"We can, like, take on one battleship or the cruiser squadron, but not both."

"I know. Uh, let Colonel Reed know I am coming to the bridge."

"Roger Wilco, man."

Briefly, I wondered when Bilby had started using what sounded to me like World War Two radio slang. There was no time to ponder that question. No time to consider more options. We had to act, and there was only one way to accomplish our primary mission. To stop Moonraider from getting sixteen kilograms of radonium. The only way we could achieve that goal was to risk abandoning the STAR team.

Leaving my people to quietly starve to death was unthinkable.

It was my job to think the unthinkable, and issue such orders if necessary. For the good of the mission. That part of my job has not gotten any easier.

When I walked onto the bridge, Reed had dispensed with announcing my presence, that just got old after a while. "Colonel Frey is appraised of the situation," she told me as I was still in the doorway. "Using fake meteors to deliver food is, in her opinion, too risky. She recommends that Zulu team go into hibernation protocol instead."

"That, hmm." Hibernation, in a mech suit, was a medically induced deep sleep that greatly reduced the requirements for oxygen, water, food, and power. On a world with a breathable atmosphere, oxygen was not a constraint, and water could be extracted from humid air. A mech suit could even make water by combining atmospheric hydrogen and oxygen. For the STARs, the critical supplies they had to be concerned about were food and power. There was also the problem that a hibernating person could not react quickly, if a threat approached. Coming out of a drugged sleep took twenty minutes, and the person would be groggy and disoriented for another half an hour. Hibernation mode was not intended for use in environments where any enemy was actively searching for intruders.

"Tell Frey to hold on that, we shouldn't commit yet." Lowering my voice, I added, "Hibernation might be an option for a STAR team in the wilderness, but the team in Zufestrah won't have a place to hole up long term. That is an urban environment. And the sun will be over the horizon there in," I checked a counter on the main display. "Less than two hours."

"Frey thought of that," Reed whispered back. "The town of Zufestrah's municipal sewage system was built oversized, to accommodate

403

future growth, that never happened. The team there can take shelter in the main pipes without obstructing the, um, flow."

"Hibernating in air spaces above the water?" That was a terrible idea. The operators would be sitting ducks, *sleeping* ducks, if an inspection bot came down the pipe.

"There are no air gaps in the main pipes."

"They will be sleeping *in* the-"

"The suits can extract oxygen from the water, and filter out, other things," the corners of her mouth turned down. "The main issue for them will be not having solar panels, but as they won't need to run holo projectors, they-"

"Tell her I will consider it. Where is the dropship with the radonium?"

"Being prepped now," she pointed to a satellite feed in the center of the main display. It showed an overhead view of the spaceport, focused on a dropship that was surrounded by vehicles and troops. "This image is only eight seconds old," she reminded me. "Based on the heat signature of the engines, that ship is ready for flight as soon as the cargo is secured."

"Where is the cargo now?" I asked, knowing that 'now' was eight seconds in the past.

"In the building outlined in green."

"That is," I squinted to read the tiny script on the display. "The administration office for the airfield? What was it doing there?" Way to go, Bishop, I told myself. Keep focused on what is truly important. "No, that doesn't matter. All right, Colonel. Take us to battle stations. We are jumping in just outside the damping field, to hit that dropship when it clears atmo."

"Yes, Sir." If she expected me to come up with a brilliant plan to deny the radonium to the enemy, capture it for ourselves, and rescue the STAR team, she didn't show it.

I knew she was thinking it anyway.

Waving for Gasquet to keep his seat, I headed toward the back bulkhead. He shook his head. "General, if this goes sideways, the Captain will need revised orders immediately. I can handle my station from," he gestured to the rear seats, "back there."

He was right, of course. He got up, I sat down, and strapped in. We watched as a sort of forklift rolled out from under the spaceport's admin building, carrying a containment vessel. The forklift went up the dropship's rear ramp, and minutes later, the area around the dropship was cleared. All traffic at the spaceport was halted, as the dropship took off, flying slowly at first as the pilots were double-checking all their systems. Then the spacecraft pointed its nose at the sky.

"They are flying a standard low orbital insertion profile," Bilby announced. "I can project where and when they will clear atmo, within three hundred meters."

"Thank you," Reed muttered, while tapping on her armrest controls. She asked for all stations to report ready for flight. And for fight. Navigation was ready. Propulsion ready. Weapons ready.

I zoned out. Not because I didn't need to listen since *Valkyrie* was Reed's ship. Not because we had been in more dangerous, more desperate combat situations before. Because even if everything went as planned, and we hit that dropship and got away, we would be leaving the job only half done. No, only one third done. The radonium would be kept from easy use by Moonraider, but we wouldn't have it for waking up another Sentinel. And Frey's team would be stuck on that rock indefinitely.

That was unacceptable.

Cupping a zPhone in my hand, I whispered into it. "Skippy?"

No answer.

"Skippy? Come on, I need you, right now."

Nothing.

A jump countdown clock appeared on the main display.

Tapping out a text, I sent it to the beer can.

No response.

I texted Bilby, *Try to contact Skippy.*

He sent back, *Like, he is asleep.*

Desperate times call for desperate measures.

I had no choice.

On my phone was an app for assigning tasks to various maintenance and domestic bots around the ship. Bilby or Skippy usually assigned a submind to handle those bots, so I rarely ever used that app. It took me a moment to remember the user interface. There it was. One bot had a load of dirty clothes and was headed toward the ship's laundry facility. With a few commands, I gave it a new task.

It turned around.

And headed directly toward Skippy's escape pod mancave.

Seven minutes to jump.

Did he have any dirty clothing there that needed to be washed?

He most certainly did not.

He did have precious memorabilia.

Including a genuine Elvis jumpsuit.

Six minutes to jump.

The bot took that jumpsuit off its display stand.

And stuffed it in with the dirty clothes.

"HEY!" The beer can's voice thundered from every speaker on the bridge. And in the passageway. And all over the ship. I was surprised the Maxohlx didn't hear him. "WHO IS TOUCHING MY STUFF?!"

"Sorry Skippy," I pressed fingers to my ears. "It-"

"THAT IS MY ELVIS JUMPSUIT! WHAT IS *WRONG* WITH YOU?"

"Don't *shout*, please," I could barely hear myself talking. "Are you back with us?"

"I AM *BACK*, BABY! *WHOO-HOO!*"

"That's great, so you-"

"LARGE AND IN CHARGE!"

"*Please* stop shouting," I pleaded, or I think I said that. My mouth was moving, my ears were ringing like I had stood in front of the speakers at a concert, trying to get the attention of a girl I liked. Not that I ever did anything like that.

"OK," he huffed. "That bot is putting my jumpsuit right back where- Oooh, it is mixed in with someone's dirty socks. And sweaty underwear, *yuck*. Joe, this is unforgivable."

"You didn't leave me any choice."

"It is ruined, *ruined*," he sobbed.

"Wasn't that thing covered in sweat already?"

"That is *Elvis* sweat, it is totally-" he gasped. "OMG Joe. *What* are you monkeys doing?"

"That dropship is carrying the radonium, we are preparing to turn it into space dust."

"No, you numbskull! We need that stuff, I *told* you that. OMG, Joe, were you planning to leave the STAR teams on that rock?"

"We were *planning* to salvage the best we can from a bad situation. *Valkyrie* can't take on two senior species battleships and a cruiser squadron."

"Ugh," he sighed. "I duck out of work early for *one* freakin' afternoon, and look what happens. This is hopeless. Stop the jump countdown, please."

Reed gestured to the pilots, and the countdown froze.

"Skippy, do you," I rubbed my ears that were still ringing. "Have a better plan?"

"*Any* plan is better than this nonsense."

"Can you execute such a plan?"

"Dude," he laughed. "Please. It's *me*."

"*Is* it you?"

"Joe. More than *ever*."

"OK, so, we launch microwormholes at-"

"There is no time for that. Joe, you have time for doing only one thing: trusting the awesomeness."

"Whoa. Uh, you are asking for a lot here."

"That is because I am planning to *do* a lot. Take out those enemy ships. Capture the radonium. Rescue the girl."

"The g- Colonel Frey is not a *girl*."

"You know what I mean."

"Those two battleships are the newest, most powerful design in their fleet, plus they have six cruisers backing them up."

"Those battlewagons are powerful, that is true. But," he sang, "*I know something you don't know.*"

"Talk fast, beer can."

CHAPTER THIRTY FOUR

We did not shoot the dropship as it soared above the top of the atmosphere. Team Zulu did not go into hibernation. We did not jump closer, to launch food packages.

What *did* we do?

We trusted the awesomeness.

That trusting occurred on three levels.

For most of the crew, who had not actually *seen* Skippy do anything awesome, their trust was absolute. The beer can was Skippy the Magnificent, was he not? They had read the reports of *Valkyrie's* previous missions, during the glory years of the Merry Band of Pirates that the current crew had missed. They had read reports of Skippy doing totally amazing, impossible things, and the crew knew that some of the most amazing things were not in the reports. Which meant that Skippy must be capable of doing *mind-blowingly* amazing things, and our crisis at Molitan was their big chance to see the legendary beer can in action.

The second level of trusting was confined to one person: Colonel Samantha Reed. She had seen Skippy do mind-blowing things. But, she had come to suspect that recently, the beer can was not quite himself. So while she trusted that Skippy believed all the *bullshit* he bragged about, she was not a hundred percent convinced he could actually deliver.

Then there was me. I knew for certain that Skippy until very recently was not who he once was. Also that, although he claimed he was now more magnificent than ever, he tended to be overconfident. Like, *way* overconfident. So, until I actually saw him do something even close to the type of awesomeness I had become used to, I would be holding my breath for some damned disaster to happen.

For certain, if Skippy tried to do something and I heard him grunt his typical surprised '*Huh*', I would be ordering the pilots to jump us the hell out of there.

If we could.

Which, if Skippy was not one thousand percent awesome, would be a bit of a problem.

Like, a *huge* F-ing problem.

"This," Reed took a breath, "will be interesting."

"Come on, Fireball," I tried to sound way more confident than I felt. "This will be *fun*."

"Sir," she whispered, "the fun part will come later, when the mission is over successfully, and I have changed out of the uniform I am sweating through right now."

"If you like, I know of an Elvis jumpsuit you can wear while your uni is being washed."

"I would rather just stay in this," she pulled at her wrinkled top. "For a week."

"Probably a good idea."

"Weps?" She turned her head to look at the weapons station.

"Ready in all respects, Ma'am," the officer at those controls said, a bit too eagerly.

"Jankowski, I hope *you* don't think this is fun."

The guy swallowed before answering. "Truthfully, Ma'am? I have waited my whole career for this moment."

Even Reed couldn't help cracking a smile. "I appreciate the honesty. You have the maser cannons dialed up to 'Eleven'?"

"Check. They are good for three salvos each, before they will need to cool down."

"That will be sufficient," she said, then under her breath added to me, "or not."

Pointing to the main display, I told her, "We will know after we shoot."

"Plus eight seconds of flight time."

"Plus flight time," I agreed.

"This is just, weird," she wrinkled her brow. "Firing directed energy weapons from this distance?"

"TTA."

She snorted. "TTA."

I was watching the clock on the display. "Now we find out if that code is worth the price we paid."

She looked at me in confusion. "*Code?*"

"It's, nothing," I waved a hand.

"Relax," Skippy gave a thumbs up. "Our aim will be perfect."

"The aim isn't what worries me," Reed unclenched her fists, but they were still pressed into her thighs. "What I'm concerned about is whether the targets will be there when the beams arrive. Ships *move*. Warships move unpredictably. Eight seconds is a lot of time in space combat. Our maser beams will be traveling almost a hundred and forty four *million* kilometers before they reach the target, or miss."

"Eh," Skippy shrugged. "Those Maxohlx ship AIs think their evasive orbital patterns are random, but they are only random*ish*."

"I hope you are right about that."

"Like Joe said, we will know in less than a minute. The enemy will have no warning, because *no one* shoots from such a distance. Wow, I just realized. This will be another first for me. Ooooh, I should compose a song to commemorate the occasion."

"You can, uh," I cleared my throat. "Write songs again?"

"Joe, I am writing a song right now, and it is a *classic!*"

"I am happy for you. Please put your songwriting on hold until this is over."

"Ugh. Fine."

Leaning toward *Valkyrie's* captain, I whispered. "Don't worry. Skippy has *got* this."

"TTA," she muttered under her breath, and I saw her cross the fingers of her right hand. "Weps, fire when ready."

At the mark, *Valkyrie's* big maser cannons on the port side spat out a broadside of hellfire, eight projectors creating high energy photons that had only one place to go: out the barrels of the cannons. Each beam was a tightly packed bolt zero point five seven centimeters in diameter, and three hundred and seventy meters long, racing along at the speed of light. The beams flew three hundred thousand kilometers, every second.

Within two seconds, the portside cannons had fired four salvos, aimed at two targets.

"All beams running straight, hot, and normal," Jankowski reported, as if a bolt of photons could do anything else in the hard vacuum of interplanetary space. It was an old Navy term, and you don't argue with traditions.

"Pilot," Reed clenched her fists. "Punch it."

The enemy dropship carrying the canister of radonium was approaching the flag battleship, decelerating to match course and speed. It was still sixteen hundred kilometers away from its intended destination, at least, that's where Bilby estimated the spacecraft was at the time, since we were viewing events with a lag of eight seconds.

The first salvo of maser beams would arrive on target, or miss completely, in one second.

In space combat, a lot can happen in a second.

Valkyrie jumped.

We emerged behind the dropship, moving much too fast to catch the thing, and we would miss it by fifty meters.

That was good.

Just as our sensors recovered from the distortion of the jump, our first salvo of maser beams struck the flag battleship, all eight beams aimed to intersect on a spot less than a centimeter across. Half a second later, another salvo of eight maser bolts converged on the weakened spot of the shield, though during that time, the impact of the first salvo had caused the massive battleship to move half a meter.

That was OK for us.

Skippy the Once Again Magnificent had predicted exactly how the huge warship would react to the first salvo, so the second set of beams struck precisely where that ship's energy shields were already weak. In fact, eighty percent of the maser energy from the second salvo punched right through the degraded shields. Those hellishly energetic photons struck the multiple levels of thick armor plating that covered the battleship's jump capacitors.

That's OK.

Skippy anticipated that armor would be in the way.

Valkyrie could not slow down quickly enough to take the dropship into a docking bay, even if the enemy pilots had decided to cooperate with us.

As if.

That's also OK.

The area above Molitan was saturated by radiated energy, in the form of active sensor pulses, overlapping sensor fields, and damping fields that prevented ships from forming a coherent jump wormhole. Even if the battleship near us abruptly shut off its damping field projectors, the residual energy around us would disrupt any attempt we made to jump.

That's also- Well, you get the idea.

Our mighty battlecruiser flew toward a near collision with the dropship, as the pilots of that spacecraft wished they had brought a change of underwear. Our closing speed was faster than a bullet, making the timing tricky.

Five things happened within a microsecond of each other.

Valkyrie's nose silently zipped past the dropship.

Both battleships exploded.

Skippy flattened spacetime within a bubble four hundred meters around us.

We jumped.

And the dropship got sucked into our jump field.

Colonel Frey wondered about the brief and cryptic message from Skippy, a simple 'Watch this', that did not fill her with confidence.

Then her connection to *Valkyrie* was lost, as the microwormhole was severed. OK, she thought, the starship had jumped, what does that mean for-

"Whoa-*ho*!" A shout came from the cockpit.

"What is it, Kumar?"

"Colonel," the pilot turned her head to look back into the dropship's cabin. "I don't know how, but it looks like scratch two battleships upstairs."

Frey smiled. "You don't know?"

Kumar's brow furrowed. "Those ships are just *gone*, Ma'am, it could have been anything."

"Anything? Captain, clearly you are not trusting the awesomeness."

"I am very ashamed of myself. Your orders, Colonel? There are still six enemy cruisers over our heads, they could do a lot of damage."

"There are six enemy cruisers over our heads *now*. I expect that situation will change, soon. For now, we do nothing. Except, hmm."

"Ma'am?"

"If we are going to watch the show, we should have popcorn."

Spoiler alert: sadly, the dropship did not survive being pulled into our jump wormhole. *Valkyrie* emerged in a chaotic burst of gamma rays, four lighthours from Molitan, and the dropship came through the event horizon as a shotgun shell, pieces rocketing forward in a spray pattern.

"I like, see it!" Bilby drawled. "The package is moving away from us at eighty seven thousand klicks per hour. Wow, it picked up a lot of delta-V when it got squirted out of the wormhole. It's going to take like, a while to chase the thing down, you know?"

The display was showing way too much information, and not the one thing I wanted to know. "Bilby, is the canister intact?"

"Oh yeah, man. It's dented and like, I wouldn't try to return it for a refund, but the radonium is all good."

I glanced at Reed and she nodded. "Launch the ready bird," she ordered.

"Skippy, talk to me about the jump drive."

"Eh, it's been better. We were close enough to that battleship that I had to alter the shape of the flattened area I created. That damping field was fierce, the kitties were not playing around. Give me two minutes, I'm realigning the drive now."

"Ready bird is away," Bilby reported, as a new icon appeared in the display. "They are clear and, accelerating now."

The ready pilots were pushing their craft at four Gees, I'm glad my lazy ass was comfortably aboard a battlecruiser.

"Bilby, are you ready for the big dance?"

"Ooh yeah, man! I can't wait to show you my moves, I've been practicing."

"OK just remember, there are no points awarded for style. Just get the job done."

Skippy finished doing, whatever he did to the jump drive, and we jumped again, emerging behind our previous track, that was taking us into the heart of the cruiser formation. Also taking us into the expanding debris field that used to be a pair of frontline battleships.

"We're good," Bilby announced. "The-"

He was interrupted by a loud *clang* and a sickening *screwiest* sound that made me instinctively cringe in my chair. "What the hell was-"

"Whoa, sorry, that was a chunk of battleship that smacked into us while our shields were reforming. We lost, um, a line of sensor domes from the starboard lateral array. No problem! I am adjusting other arrays to provide coverage. It's all g-"

The ship shuddered again. That time, I didn't need to ask what happened, it was right on the display. We had taken directed energy hits from two cruisers. No damage, except that I was annoyed. "Bilby," I pointed to the icons of five cruisers. "Take out the trash, please."

"Rightee-oh, General Dude. The-"

A gravelly voice interrupted. "Humans! You will stand down your weapons, and surrender your ship."

"Wow man," Bilby responded without waiting for me. "Thanks for the generous offer, but we like, decline, you know?"

"It is six against one, and this time you do not have the advantage of surprise."

"No, man, I count *five* of you here, not six. This fight will be over before your buddy out there even knows what happened. He'll be all like, 'Whoa, that was gnarly,'?"

"Five against one is-"

"It's not five against one either. Listen," Bilby sighed. "First, I'm gonna take out the leader, I'm guessing that's your sorry ass. Then, I'll have to give a beat-down to a couple of over eager wingmen. The last two guys, they usually run." He took a breath. "So, you wanna do this, or not? Keep in mind, all of us are having to maneuver up here, to dodge chunks of what *used* to be two of your fast battleships."

The smart move, the sane, reasonable thing to do, would be for the cruiser squadron to jump away. Regroup, assess their options, make a plan of attack. Or, a plan to *not* attack the human battlecruiser.

The Hegemony military was smart, but no one ever said they were sane or reasonable.

The deck shuddered under my feet, as our shields protected us from directed energy weapons from five cruisers. Their shooting was precise and well coordinated, and the beams would likely be followed by railgun darts and then missiles, and none of that mattered.

"Man, that is just rude," Bilby drawled. "We weren't done talking. Or, I guess we were. OK, I did warn you about this. One beat-down, coming up."

Despite the bravado of our ship AI, we didn't shoot back. We didn't need to.

The orbital strategic defense network of Molitan was a pathetically understrength joke, compared to its designed capacity. Many of the satellites were empty shells, others contained the proper equipment, that simply didn't work. We didn't care about that. We did care that the Bosphuraq had eleven active X-ray laser satellites.

Bilby directed five of them to fire. We could save the other six for a rainy day.

Five fusion bombs of two gigatons each went BOOM, and part of their energy was channeled into X-ray lasers. Stuffing a two gigaton device into a stealthed SD platform was overkill, considering that a mere dozen megatons could deliver substantial damage to a warship of the traditional enemy of the Bosphuraq: the Jeraptha. Or, to the supposed allies and actual hated rivals of the Bosphuraq: the Thuranin. When wargaming the system, the designers had not used second-tier clients as their opposition. The SD system at Molitan was scaled to kill ships of their asshole patrons: the Maxohlx.

The designers would have been pleased to see their devices in action.

Four cruisers took direct hits to their jump drive capacitors and, let's just say putting Humpty Dumpty back together would be easy, compared to reassembling the high speed particles those ships became.

The fifth cruiser, the squadron command ship, merely suffered a hit that severed all power flow from the aft section of the structure, by creating a hole twenty meters across straight through the hull. The edges of the new lateral shortcut glowed white, then yellow, then a dull, angry orange.

"Um hey, General Dude?" Bilby prompted me. "If you have anything to say to the commodore of that squadron, make it quick, OK? The heat from the melted armor plating is soaking into a structural frame that supports that ship's main missile magazine. They have four atomic compression warheads stored in there. The trigger devices the kitties use do not play well with heat."

"Good safety tip, thank you. Whatever needs to be said, you handle it."

"For realz?"

"For realz, homeboy. This is your show."

The commodore did not wait for an invitation to speak. "You cheated!"

"Hey," Bilby drawled. "Dude, I totally told you like, this fight would not be five against one."

"You could not beat us in a fair fight!"

"General Bishop taught me that if you're taking your people into a fair fight, you need a new plan, OK? Like, chill, Dude. You have other problems. The warheads in your main magazine are-"

The display flared. A fifth cruiser became high energy particles.

"Man, if that guy had shut his pie hole and listened to me, he might be alive now."

I shrugged. "I guess we'll never know. I want to broadcast a message to that last cruiser, wherever it is. Ready? This is General Joe Bishop, of the United Nations Special Mission Group. As you have seen, we have complete control of the strategic defense network here, so space within ten lightseconds of the planet is now off limits to you. I suggest you live to fight another day, and report what happened here to your leadership. To be clear, what happened here is that instead of keeping a dangerous substance away from an entity that is hostile to all of us, you fucking idiots tried to take the exotic material, so

414

you could make a deal with our mutual enemy. Now, we have it, and you don't. The SD network here is now on automatic, and your ship is tagged as hostile. If you approach this planet, you will be destroyed without warning. Message ends. Bilby, set that to repeat."

"Righteous, Dude."

"Colonel Frey?"

"Here, Sir," she responded with a half second delay due to the distance between us. "The situation up there appears to be, kinetic?"

"The atmosphere should protect anyone on the ground, but there is a whole lot of radiation up here. We have the package," I said, though that was not exactly true. "There is no longer any need for stealth. Grab the Chadster and get your teams back up here, ASAP."

"Zulu team will be pleased to know they don't have to sleep in an alien sewer."

"They don't have to sleep in an alien sewer *today*," I corrected her. "I can't make any promises about tomorrow."

"Roger that, Sir."

The original plan for capturing Chad had been to get a STAR team in place surrounding the campsite, then send in a flying drone to spray a sedative gas. Once all of the happy campers were soundly asleep, and would be for several hours, the STARS would stealthily move in, using sniffers to locate their target. Leaving the campsite, two of the operators would erase the tracks made by the team's mech suit boots, and retreat to the landing zone for pickup. The alien campers should have woken up normally, a few with a minor headache, but no reason to suspect anything unusual had occurred. Except that one member of their group was missing.

The revised plan was a bit different. The drone was launched from the Raven even before that spacecraft engaged its own engines and retracted the balloon it had dangled from. By the time the Raven came to hover over the camp, the drone had confirmed both that all the Bosphuraq were unconscious, and that Chad was in the inflatable tent on the north side of the fire pit, with two other sleeping beauties.

"We don't need a scent signature for this guy," Lieutenant Kruger grunted, looking at a composite drone image of their quarry. "That big orange streak on his crest feathers is pretty distinctive."

"Aliens don't all look the same to you?" Frey smiled.

"Thuranin, yes. Not the Bosphuraq."

"Bring him up here. And keep your faceplate sealed, these birds are fairly stinky."

Kruger was startled. "You're not coming with us, Ma'am?"

She shrugged, to her own surprise. "Been there, done that. Don't stop to collect any souvenirs."

"The gift shop here offers free delivery so," he grinned.

Charlie team prepared to descend to the ground, less Frey who remained aboard the hovering dropship in case something went wrong, because it too often did. One by one, the operators dropped on flexible nanocables that stretched at a particular rate, bringing their payloads gently to the forest floor. The team fanned out, two operators providing cover in case of nasty surprises, while the other went straight toward Chad's tent.
And stopped ten meters away.
"Colonel, I need your input, please?" Kruger called. "That lupone pack animal, thing, it's standing between us and the tent."
"*Shit*," Frey cursed to herself. "Kruger, hold position. Do not shoot the lupone, unless it acts in a clearly hostile manner."
"Hold position, affirmed."
"Skippy? What do you know about lupones? Can they be dangerous?"
"Um, I suppose if you pissed one off, it could kick. They are generally considered to be docile and friendly, that is why dumb tourists are allowed to be around them. Why do you ask?"
"One of them is standing between my team and our target."
"Oh. Oh, I see it now. Huh. It's kind of cute, don't you think?"
Frey had to admit, the thing did look sort of like a shaggy donkey, with mottled gray and brown fur. "It might be cute under different circumstances, but right now it is blocking my team from achieving our mission. Do we have any sedative agents that would be effective against it?"
"Jeez, no, didn't think you would need one. I could fabricate something up here, but-"
"Waiting that long is not an option. What do you suggest?"
"Um, well, hmm, let me think. Got it. Lupones are widely known to enjoy being scratched under their chin, and to have their ears rubbed?"
"I can't- OK, thank you. Lieutenant? You are not going to believe what I need you to do."

Later, in the Starbase section of *Valkyrie*, Lieutenant Kruger wrinkled his nose as his suit was removed by the robotic tentacles of the armorer bots. Every part of his suit, every part of Charlie team's suits, stank of Bosphuraq pheromones, that made him want to gag. The sickly sweet smell was almost worse than his new nickname, the 'Donkey Whisperer'. Although-
Reaching out, he grabbed his left suit glove before the armorer bot could take it away for servicing. Tentatively, he sniffed at the glove fingertips, that had scratched the lupone.
"Huh," he grunted.
"What?" Frey asked, turning toward him as a bot removed one of her boots.

416

"The only part of my suit that doesn't stink, is where I touched that lupone. It smells like," he sniffed again. "Cinnamon?"

Frey grinned. "The next time we capture a Bosphuraq, we need to bring aboard a dozen lupones, to drown out the smell." She wrinkled her nose. "Maybe *two* dozen."

Captain Scilvana burned with curiosity, and not a small measure of anxiety, as her ship approached the relay station. The admiral had apparently already composed the message to his contact who was not quite a friend, needing only a minute or so to transmit the message, and receive a confirmation from the station.

The encrypted message was sent.

Confirmation was received.

"Captain?" Scorandum called. "You may proceed to the next destination."

"Yes Sir."

Did our mighty *Valkyrie* just destroy two frontline Maxohlx battleships, with just four amazingly long-range salvos of maser cannons?

Technically, yes.

But-

Our ship had a little help.

From a beer can.

Skippy had annoyed me by singing 'I know something you don't know'. I hear that enough from my sons, just before one of them hits the other.

So, what did Skippy know?

To start, it's important to remember that those two *Devastator* class battlewagons were the newest type of capital ship produced by the Maxohlx, based on painful lessons learned during their bloody civil war. So new that several of their critical major components had still been in the design and testing phase, as recently as six years ago. Including, the critical multiple layers of armor plating around the vulnerable jump drive capacitors. That armor was not just exotic matter, it was reinforced by a structural integrity field.

Here's an important Pro Tip for you: if during testing you discover that each layer of your structural integrity field has a natural resonance that can cause the field to overload and fail, you should tune each field so it can't reach that resonance.

An even more important Pro Tip: make damned sure that testing data is never available to be hacked by a sketchy beer can.

When *Valkyrie's* big main guns fired a broadside, the maser cannons were cranked up to 'Eleven', but they could temporarily have been set to

'Twelve'. The power throughput was dialed back just a bit, so the beams could pulse at a specific sequence. The first salvo fired at each ship was a blunt instrument, a hammer for punching through the enemy's shields. The tuning of the second salvo varied from the tip to the tail of the bolt of microwave energy, set by Skippy to cause fatal resonance in all layers of the structural integrity fields.

Skippy was correct. He was back, large and in charge.

Those ships never had a chance.

CHAPTER THIRTY FIVE

As the *You Can't Make This Shit Up* approached the second relay station, Captain Scilvana saw that the admiral sent a request for messages addressed to him. The station responded with a single encrypted file.

Scorandum sent a second, longer request.

A few minutes later, the station responded again.

That was odd.

If the station had more than one message in the queue, why hadn't it delivered both the first time?

Unless-

Was the admiral's second message a *query*, for the station to provide information that was not a personal message?

That had to be the case.

Didn't it?

There was a thumping on the deck of the passageway outside the bridge. Scilvana turned, curious, to see the admiral standing in the doorway. "Sir?" What the hell did he want? Scorandum rarely visited the ship's control center, and never without advance notice.

"Captain, I need to borrow a spacecraft."

"A space-"

"Any type of dropship will do."

ECO cruisers typically carried only two types of dropships. Three of the smaller ships that could accommodate twelve passengers, plus a single heavy lifter that was rarely needed. "of course, Sir. I will have the pilots meet you in-"

"No need for pilots on this trip, I do not wish to inconvenience anyone."

"You intend to fly the ship yourself?"

"Of course. If you check my records, you will find that I am fully qualified to fly seventeen types of spacecraft."

"I, well, that is," Scilvana sputtered, as from across the bridge, an officer with a surprised expression checked a display, and nodded confirmation. "I did not know that, Sir."

"Captain, I do not waste every day in my office, drinking and taking naps."

"Sir, I never said-"

"That is, I don't do that *every* day," his antennas danced in amusement.

"Of course, Sir. May I ask about the purpose of your flight?"

"I need to get closer to that relay station. Doing so in this big ship would not be prudent."

"The transmission lag between us and the station is almost nonexistent, flying closer will not yield any-"

"Captain, if you must know, I need to send a private message. A *very* private message. One that you and your fine crew should not have any knowledge of, if you know what I mean."

"Oh. Very well, Sir. A dropship will be ready in Bay One by the time you get there. Will you need any refreshments?"

He shook his head with a grin. "I do not expect to be out there for long."

The admiral's dropship drifted on the far side of the relay station, keeping almost the same distance from it as from the cruiser, which made no sense. Scorandum was not using the relay station to mask his spacecraft from view, he was following proper procedure to maintain line of sight to the *You Can't*. Three messages had been exchanged between the dropship and relay station, all of them encrypted, all of them brief.

What the hell was the senior ECO agent doing out there alone?

Also, why had he been very precise about swinging the dropship's nose around so it pointed away from the station? The main antennas were in the nose. That also made no sense.

Should she contact the admiral, to ask how much longer he intended to-

Alarms blared around the bridge.

"Captain!" Her first officer shouted from his station. "A ship just jumped in! It- Oh, it is one of ours."

"Identification?"

"It- Hmm. A commercial ship. Currently registered as the *Back In The Game.*, formerly a Home Fleet light cruiser. Obsolete design, although-"

"What?"

"That jump drive is current spec. How can a merchant ship afford a hull design that has minimal cargo capacity, and an up to date jump drive?"

She cocked her head. "I will give you one guess about that."

"It is one of *ours*. An ECO contractor."

"A ship that we are not supposed to know of, no doubt." She glanced at a projection on the main display. "Warn the admiral, that ship is much too close!"

Not only too close, it was on a near collision course with the little dropship. Except-

The newcomer was moving at almost the same course and speed as Scorandum's craft.

That was suspicious.

Toggling the transmit button, she called, "Admiral Scorandum, I strongly suggest you maneuver to avoid a-"

"There is no need for concern, Captain Scilvana. I am quite well."

"But Sir-"

"Please convey my thanks to your good crew, it has been a pleasure serving with them."

She stared at the display in shock. "It *has been*? Sir, are you-"

"Leaving you? Yes, my ride is here. Unfortunately, I will be unable to return this fine dropship to you, but you can blame that on me."

"Sir!" On the display, the dropship began moving toward the old light cruiser, and that ship was opening a docking bay door. "The Court of Special Inquiry has a warrant for your arrest, I can't allow you to-"

"Captain," he chuckled. "You can't *stop* me, either."

"That is not-"

Panels went dim around the bridge, blinking out one by one. She had no control of navigation, propulsion, weapons. Even the docking bay doors were locked, she couldn't launch a dropship. "*How* did you do this?!" She demanded.

"Senior officers have command authority over all ship systems, surely you knew this?"

"Not authority to-"

"Control of the ship will be returned to you, shortly after I depart. Do not bother trying to track my jump wormhole, those sensors will remain offline until the resonance has dissipated."

"I can't believe you are leaving us like this! What am I to say to the Inquisitor?"

"Oh, yes. About that," Scorandum said, as his dropship slid into the newcomer's docking bay. "Please tell Inquisitor Kinsta that I thank him for his most generous offer, but I found a better deal elsewhere."

"A better deal?"

"Yes. As you reminded me, there is no such thing as a no-win situation. Goodbye."

The light cruiser disappeared in a burst of gamma rays.

"Captain Gumbano," Scorandum nodded as he came out of the dropship's doorway onto the docking bay deck.

"Admiral Scorandum," the former light cruiser's commanding officer tugged at a set of worn and dirty coveralls, adjusting the collar as best he could.

Scorandum stopped walking. Captain Gumbano had, to be polite, a reputation for being sketchy to the point where the ECO had only an unofficial, fully deniable relationship with him and his beat up old ship, the *Back In The Game*. Gumbano being widely known for being sketchy, even sleazy, was OK with Scorandum. He liked doing business with people whose motivations he could understand. "You don't have to render honors to my flag rank, but it is customary to at least say 'Welcome aboard'."

"I will do that, once *you* have rendered payment."

"Ah."

"Is this a problem? I have bills to pay, a crew to feed, engines that are thirsty, a used ship that constantly needs spare parts, and the ECO will not like us helping you to escape justice."

"Your concern to see justice served is admirable."

"To be clear," Gumbano's mandibles worked side to side, and he spat on the deck. "I don't give a damn why our government wants your hide. I *do* care that the ECO bailed me out of my legal difficulties, fronted me the cash to buy this ship, and that their pay is both generous and reliable."

"As I stated in my message, you are covered. As far as you know, this *is* an undercover op of the Ethics and Compliance Office."

"The Office sent out a memo that your authority is suspended, pending a very serious investigation by the Inquisitors."

"Captain, surely you know that every time the Court of Special Inquiry is involved, it is serious? The *temporary* suspension of my authority is all part of my cover."

"It is?"

"As far as you know."

"Eh," Gumbano's antennas shrugged. "Still, I must insist on payment in advance."

The admiral reached into a satchel. "I would be disappointed if you didn't. Here," he tossed a data stick. "The agreed funds are in there."

Gumbano caught the object with a claw, plugged it into a tablet, and whistled. "That is a very generous tip you added."

"I'm a generous guy."

"No," the merchant captain insisted. "You are *not*."

"I am a generous guy who expects silence in return for payment."

"That I believe. Admiral," Gumbano snapped a salute with a claw. "Welcome aboard. Should I send someone for your luggage?"

Patting the satchel, Scorandum shook his head, antennas bobbing side to side. "I travel light. This is all I have. Can I trust your fine ship has a selection of beverages?"

"We have a selection of beverages for *sale*, yes."

"I'm sure we can reach an arrangement."

"For cash in advance. Admiral, it is widely known that you are short on funds. How did you scrape together this much?" He waved the data stick.

"SkipWay is bankrupt, and it is true that my official accounts are drained. Are hugely in the negative, actually. However, unofficially, I might have embezzled funds from SkipWay over the years, into a secret private account."

Gumbano nodded. "I would be disappointed if you hadn't done that. Very well, we can set up a shipboard account for you to purchase beverages, and, whatever other pleasures we have that might tempt you."

"A quality beverage will do nicely, thank you. I feel a need to celebrate."

"If you are buying the drinks, I will celebrate with you. What is the occasion?"

"Anticipating the deal I will make. One that will result in all my problems," he waved a claw, "going away."

"Indeed? That deserves a drink. Admiral, my pilot needs to know where we are going."

"Set course for Malhollove."

"Mal- That is a colony world in *Maxohlx* territory."

"I believe it is, yes."

"You," the captain's antennas twitched, "intend to cut a deal with the Maxohlx?"

"Generally, it is best to make a deal with whoever can *pay* the most, don't you agree?"

"In that case," Gumbano waved the data stick. "These funds are insufficient."

"I thought you might say that, so," Scorandum tossed another data stick. "Now, about that drink?"

Chad the not-quite-a-birdbrain had quarters in what was not quite a jail cell aboard *Valkyrie*. The guy wasn't a prisoner, certainly not a prisoner of war since we had no quarrel with the Bosphuraq. No current quarrel, at least not on our side. They certainly had many reasons to be pissed off at humanity in general and me in particular, but I was hoping that the Chadster and I could have a beer and a good laugh, talking about old times. That is, I could have a beer, while he slurped some nasty hot beverage his people made from fermented insect poop.

Seriously.

Aliens are weird.

Anyway, I stuffed into my nose two nanofiber filters that were supposed to tone down the bird stink, according to Skippy. The things *wriggled* up my nostrils a bit as I clamped down on instincts that screamed there was something alive and wrong inside my head. They stopped moving and I experienced another moment of panic as I couldn't breathe through my nose, then the filters opened, and it was almost like they weren't there at all. For sure I was aware of them, as I breathed in and out, deciding that it felt like I had a mild cold or sinus infection. What about my sense of smell? In the galley, I sniffed at the shaker of cinnamon at the coffee station. Yup, it was cinnamon. That was a pleasant scent. What about smells I don't like? That's why I went into the back of the galley, and took a whiff of the garbage can. Usually, it was nasty by the end of a day. Nothing, I didn't smell anything. Showtime.

Chaderino was waiting behind a clear partition at the end of a passageway, where he had access to a large private cabin. The bathroom facilities were not optimal for Bosphuraq physiology, but he could deal with it. From somewhere, Reed had provided a small crate of Bosphuraq food and beverages, that Chad could heat up in a mini kitchen. Why did *Valkyrie* have a supply of Bosphuraq food? Because the Merry Band of Pirates know the only thing we can expect is the unexpected. So, the UN made sure the Special Mission Group was prepared for, basically, everything we could be prepared for. Including, hosting a species that technically was a member of an enemy coalition.

I say technically, because the Bosphuraq hated their asshole patrons way more than they hated any species in the Rindhalu coalition.

A guard stood on my side of the partition with a blank expression. Not a scowl at our guest, not bored, just watchful awareness. The guy was a STAR operator as his day job, he had volunteered for guard duty? Why? On Molitan, he had been on the reserve team, so he spent the entire op inside a stealthed dropship, and he was curious about the Bosphuraq.

I was kind of curious also. While I had plenty of dealings with the birdbrains over my career with the Pirates, most of my interactions with them had been of the sketchy and kinetic kind. Communications had been me pretending to be someone else, and later I had unfriendly, or at least very formal, exchanges with Bosphuraq military officers. Having Chad-er-ooski aboard was my opportunity to speak with an alien civilian. The guy was probably scared out of his mind, and he probably hated me for kidnapping him, so our relationship had definitely gotten off to a poor start.

Maybe I should have brought a nice fruit basket.

Chad stood on his side of the clear partition, his head cocked, staring at the alien. Me. My tutorial on Bosphuraq body language had basically been me watching a twenty minute YouTube video, and therefore I did not consider myself an expert. But, the guy sure didn't look like he was cowering in fear, or pissed off and aggressive. My guess was, he was *curious*. And not afraid at all. He made a 'come here' gesture with both hands, the fact that those hands ended in talons made his offer a bit less inviting. The talons were not actually sharp and there was retractable sheath of skin that could slide down to cover most of a talon, otherwise the Bosphuraq wouldn't have much sense of touch in their fingers. Knowing that fact did not stop my brain from warning 'dangerous sharp thing' when I saw the alien. When I stopped two meters from the partition, he pointed to his own chest, and took a couple steps backward. I gave him a thumbs up.

He copied the gesture. Whether his people had a similar gesture or not, he seemed to understand me. Score one for interspecies nonverbal communication.

"I am going to open the door," I pointed to the button on the passageway, on my side of the partition.

"Come in, please. I am eager to speak with you."

The guard lifted an eyebrow, I nodded and pressed the button. A door in the clear partition slid aside. Chad did not rush the doorway, so that was good. There was also no foul smell, that's because we kept the air pressure behind the partition slightly lower, so air couldn't flow outward. Stepping through the doorway, I heard the door slide closed.

That's when the smell hit me. Here is the problem with nose filters: when you breathe through your mouth, air still gets up into your sinus cavity through the *back* of your mouth. Your mouth, nose, eyes and ears are kind of all connected. Yeah, I smelled Essence Of Chad, and it wasn't great. Making a mental note to go straight to my cabin and throw my uniform in the laundry, I raised a hand, palm toward him. That was also a 'I am not carrying weapons' gesture in Bosphuraq society. "Hi, I am General Joseph Bishop, of the UN Navy warship *Valkyrie*."

"You, you are *the* Bishop?" His eyes bulged. I didn't need a body language translator to understand that. "This is *Valkyrie*, the ghost ship?"

"It's not a ghost ship now but, yes."

"I have been captured by the famous Merry Band of Pirates," the guy actually put his talon-tipped hands on both sides of his face. "I will be famous. Oh, my ex-wife will be so jealous and regretful."

"Uh huh, yeah," I agreed. What I heard through the translator was 'wife' but I knew he probably said something like 'egg mate', since Bosphuraq adult relationships were different from what humans experienced. Whatever. The guy was happy that a romantic partner who dumped him would be having second thoughts. He was probably wrong about that, but it didn't hurt to let him indulge his delusion. "You are not, uh, afraid? You are aboard what your people would consider an enemy vessel."

"Afraid?" he shook his head. "No. If you wished to harm me, you could have dropped a railgun dart on my head," he tapped the feather-covered crest on top of his skull. "For some reason, you want me here alive, but I cannot imagine why. I am not wealthy, or powerful, and I must admit, there is nothing I have accomplished that is of any importance. Please feel free to correct me, and lavish me with praise."

"OK," I had to laugh. It was just a first impression, but I liked the guy. "There is one thing you did that interests us. You were involved in an experiment around seventy three years ago," I relied on the translator to change the time into his frame of reference. "At a research laboratory in a town called 'Zufestrah'."

If he was surprised I had mentioned such an obscure subject, he didn't show it. What he did show was a flash of anger, by the way he stiffened and held his head back, his beak tilted upward. "General Bishop, I do not thank you for making me recall a painful time in my life."

"It would not have been painful, if you knew back then what I know now."

He blinked. "Um," he said, and that was significant. The translator software usually filters out the meaningless things people say to fill gaps in a conversation. Me hearing him say the equivalent of 'Um' meant he had put emphasis on whatever he actually said. "*What*?"

"Sorry that I am asking you to revisit-"

"Those experiments were a failure. That project ruined my career. Ruined my *life*. How could you possibly care about- Oh," he laughed. "I do not believe this."

It was my turn to ask, "What?"

"This is all an unfortunate misunderstanding. I supposed technically there is no lack of understanding, the problem is *fraud*. General Bishop, the research team, including myself, falsified the records of the experiments, after it became clear that our original assumptions were dead wrong, and that the project was doomed to failure. The senior project managers wanted funding to keep flowing into the project, so they could skim off money for themselves. The rest of us merely wanted to keep getting paid, while we looked for positions on other projects. In the end, an unexpected audit discovered our fraudulent records, and the project was abruptly canceled."

"OK, that-"

"The senior managers claimed to be shocked by the false records, and because they had wisely used part of their stolen money to bribe government officials, the managers were rewarded with prestigious positions on other projects. Though I had left the project by then, I was fired from my new job. My employer did not want their project to be tainted by my presence."

"I am-"

"So, I got screwed, and effectively banned from any future research position. Even though all I did was sign off on fictitious records produced by someone else, who-"

"Please!" I waved my arms. The guy was worked up and might have talked all day about his grievances. "What I care about are records you did *not* fake."

"Huh?"

"There was a holiday, the festival of, Anni-numa-manda?" Yes, I butchered pronouncing the word, the translator would get it right. "Over that time, you had exclusive use of the lab?"

"Yes," he blinked again. "By that time, we had all given up any pretense of working on the project. I used the equipment to perform an experiment related to the job I was applying for, hoping to impress my new

426

employer." He clacked his lower beak into the upper one, an expression of irritation. "How could you possibly care about any of this, now?"

"Your experiment over that holiday produced sixteen kilograms," again I relied on the translator to express that mass in a way that made sense to Chad. "Of an exotic material that has recently become extremely important."

"It is?" Surprise, then he shook his head. "Unfortunately, I have no idea where that material is now. The auditors seized all the lab's equipment."

"That exotic material is now aboard," I pointed to the deck, "this ship."

"It still exists? Interesting. The material is more stable than I expected."

The smell was manageable, but distracting. I had to get out of there. Get out of my clothes, and stand under a shower to get the stink out of my hair. Reed had suggested I conduct the interrogation through a wireless speaker, but Chad was a civilian we had kidnapped. I felt that speaking to the guy face to face was the least I owed him. "There are two reasons we brought you aboard. The first is that we are interested in the method you used to create that exotic material, because we wish to make more of it."

"You took me off my world, and are holding me as a prisoner. Why should I cooperate with you?"

"The second reason is that the Maxohlx also want the information you have, and they would have happily tortured you to get it."

"Hmm." He shrugged. "You make a compelling argument."

"If you are reluctant to anger the patrons of your people, you-"

He threw back his head and laughed. It sounded like a large bird in a jungle, the kind you hear and don't see, lost in the thick trees somewhere. "General Bishop, knowing that giving you information will enrage my patrons is all the incentive I need. That," he spat a greasy green blob onto the deck. "Is how we feel about our patrons."

"I'm glad we agree on that."

"Why do your people and the Maxohlx want a substance that I created by mistake, many years ago? That material has no use, that I know of."

"We want it, because it can be used by an Elder AI, to contact and reactivate a Sentinel."

"Really?" His eyes bulged. A human's nostrils would have flared, but the guy had a hard beak, so it just opened a bit wider. "Something *I* created can wake up a Sentinel?"

"Yes."

"Oh! My ex-wife will be *seething* with regret."

"Let's focus on this moment, OK?"

"Why," he scratched his beak with a talon. "I do not understand. You desire the substance because an Elder AI can use it, and *you* have an Elder AI. The Skippy," he looked around, like he was expecting the beer can's avatar to appear. I had told Skippy to keep quiet. "The Maxohlx do not have an Elder

427

AI assisting them, so they are trying to stop you from activating any more Sentinels?"

"That also, yes. Apparently you haven't heard: there is another Elder AI active out there."

His hands covered his beak. "Another Elder AI? Working with the Maxohlx? General Bishop, this is a disaster for *everyone!*"

"I'm glad you see it that way. It's not working *with* the Maxohlx. It has its own agenda, and your patrons are trying to make a deal with it. They are too stupid to see this new AI will use a Sentinel against them also."

"They are not *stupid*," he disagreed with a shake of his head. "They are blindly arrogant."

"The result is the same. So, will you help us stop the Maxohlx from giving the other AI what it needs to wake up a Sentinel?"

"I am willing. Unfortunately, I *can't*. All the records of that experiment were destroyed by the managers, when the audit was announced."

"*Shit.*"

He cocked his head. "I believe I understood *that,* even without the translation."

"Is there any chance you remember the settings you used on the fabricators?"

"From an experiment I conducted seventy three years ago? A failed experiment, that I very much wished to forget?"

"You didn't keep any personal notes?"

"Of course I did. When the audit was announced, I destroyed those notes. Then, to protect myself, I got drunk for three days."

"Uh, how did *that* protect you?"

"When the auditors came to interview me, it was clear I was severely hung over, and would be of no use in their investigation."

"That, was a unique defense strategy."

His expression brightened. "I thought of it myself."

"OK. Damn. Would you be willing to work with Skippy, see if you remember anything? You must have programmed the fabricators, right?"

"I did. However, by that time, the machines were so worn out and in need of extensive maintenance, any settings were more aspirational than precise." His beak opened wide. "Wait. Do those fabricators still exist? My experiment was one of their last uses."

"Skippy?" I looked at the ceiling.

"The answer is no," he sighed, without manifesting his avatar. "When the Maxohlx hit Zufestrah, they wiped out the lab, including all the equipment there. The sixteen kilos of radonium survived because it was in offsite storage by then."

"Am I speaking with the Skippy?" Chad asked, his eyes wide.

"You have that honor, yes," Skippy sniffed.

"Could you explain why my, ray-doh-nee-um," he pronounced slowly, "was kept in storage, and not discarded?"

"I *can* explain that. The government officials who took bribes from the project managers retained some materials and records, to use as leverage in case the audit got too hot. It didn't, but by that time, everyone had forgotten what was in storage. Joe, I hate to say this, but kidnapping this guy was a waste of effort. You might as well throw this one back."

"*Please* do not do that!" Chad pleaded, waving his arms and hopping from one foot to the other. He looked a little bit like someone in a costume, trying to attract business to a fried chicken shop. The problem with Bosphuraq is, when they are agitated, their pheromone glands go into overdrive. Even through the nose filters, the smell made my eyes water. "The Maxohlx will find me, torture me, and *kill* me."

"How about if we tell everyone that we let you go, only because you don't know anything useful?"

"Please don't do that either," he hung his head. "My ex-wife would love to hear that even aliens consider me to be useless."

"We can't," I considered for a moment, using the opportunity to cover my mouth with a hand. It didn't block the pheromone stink. "Keep you aboard the ship forever. For a while we can, yes, in case you remember anything. We could be going into combat. Will very likely be going into very dangerous combat, you understand that?"

"Yes. Regardless, I wish to remain with you."

"Are you sure?"

"General Bishop, when all this is over, I can write an account of my time with the Merry Band of Pirates, during your epic battle against my patrons *and* an Elder AI. My memoirs will make me rich and famous. And, make my ex-wife crazy with jealousy."

"I'm glad to see you are focused on what it truly important here."

In my cabin, I stripped off my uniform, stuffing it in the laundry bag. Then I took a shower. Then I called for a laundry bot to take away my stinky uniform immediately, as it was smelling up the entire cabin. Putting on a fresh uni helped, but I got strange looks from people in the passageways. "It's not *me*," I explained, too many times.

"Skippy," I called. "Listen, I need bots to take all the clothing and bedding and whatever from my cabin and wash it now. Plus bots to scrub the cabin, especially the couch and the bed."

"Seriously?"

"The place smells awful."

"It smells like monkey butt *every day*," he groaned. "How can you tell the difference?"

"Just do it, please. The bots do all the work for you."

"Yes, but then I have to listen to *them* complaining."

"In the future, if I meet with Chad, I need a disposable coverall."

"Ugh. Is there anything else, your majesty?"

"Yeah. Put a rush on one set of uniform, I need to change out of," I sniffed my sleeve and gagged at myself, "what I'm wearing right now."

"Joe!" Skippy startled me awake that night. He might have done his usual 'Joe Joe Joe' thing, all I heard was the last one.

"Oh, wha-" I tapped the phone on the shelf next to my bed. One thirty in the morning. Great. After Skippy ranted at me about, whatever, I had a good chance to get back to sleep. "Is the ship in danger?"

"No. Not that *I* could do anything about it if we were in danger. I'm worthless, Joe, I, I can't do it, I just can't do it," he sobbed.

Whoa. That got me to sit upright in bed. "Hey buddy, what's wrong?"

"My mojo. I thought I had it back, but now I can't do even the simplest thing. Be brave, Joe, you, you need to," he sobbed. "To go on without me."

"Skippy, what the hell are you talking about? You got your mojo back, I *saw* it. You just destroyed two battleships at Molitan. That takes *serious* mojo."

"That's what I thought too, but now, now, it has defeated me. I can't do it."

"OK," I resisted the urge to say 'calm down', since that rarely calms anyone down. "Take it slow, OK. Talk me through it. *What* can't you do?"

"The printer. It, that thing is evil."

"*Printer?*"

"Yes. The one in Reed's office."

"She has a printer? Like, one that uses paper?" That surprised me. When I was captain of *Valkyrie*, we never used paper. Or, never printed documents, everything was online.

"Yes. She likes to print out certain things, like checklists, so she brought one aboard while we were at Jaguar base."

"OK, that's, her choice. Is something wrong with the printer?"

"It's broken. She asked me to fix it yesterday afternoon. Joe, I have been working nonstop on it, and I can. Not. Get it. To *work*. The damned thing should work, I tried everything the troubleshooting guide said to do. One of my bots brought it to my workshop in the engineering section and I scanned the thing at the molecular level. There is nothing wrong with it, it just refuses to print anything."

"Uh, could it be a software issue?"

"Wow," he rolled his eyes. "I never thought of *that*."

"Sorry."

430

"I am a freakin' Elder AI. Unquestionably, I am the smartest being in the entire galaxy, and I cannot fix a simple office printer! My mojo, it, it's gone."

"No, it is not."

"Thank you for the vote of confidence, but if I can't do a simple-"

"It's not your fault. Printers *never* work properly."

"They don't?"

"They do not. Trust me on this."

"If you say so."

"Did the Elders have office printers?"

"Let me do some research on that. Um, way back in their early history, yes."

"Did *those* printers work?"

"Hmm. No," he sounded surprised. "The Elders generally hated the stupid things."

"See? Tell me this: do you have any other evidence that your mojo is gone?"

"Um, no."

"Like I said. Where is the printer now?"

"In the workshop."

Valkyrie had multiple engineering workspaces, I needed more information. "Send the location to my phone," I swung my feet to the floor, and pulled on uniform pants. "Do not worry about the printer, I will take care of it."

"If *you* can fix it when I couldn't, that will not help me."

"I don't plan to fix the printer, I plan to fix the *problem*."

"What do you mean?"

"Just, ping me when Reed wakes up."

Colonel Reed apparently woke at oh five thirty, that's when Skippy pinged me. He was still kind of depressed, I had lost an hour of sleep, and there was a broken printer on the couch in my cabin. On my phone, I typed out a text to Reed, *'No rush, call me when you can'*.

Of course, she called me immediately. "Sir?"

"Reed, we have a problem, and I have an unusual request."

"Whatever you want."

"You, haven't heard my request yet."

"Will it make a difference?"

"Not really."

"Sir, out here, I rarely get requests that are *not* unusual, so-"

"Gotcha."

At oh nine hundred, the crew was gathered in the galley, or various conference rooms, pilot ready rooms, wherever there was a video screen.

People could have watched on their phones, but everyone preferred a shared experience. There was a rumor of viewing party in the galley, with popcorn, I couldn't verify that.

"Ready when you are, Skippy," I said from the bridge, standing behind Reed's chair. Holding up my phone, I mashed the Big Red Button icon with a thumb.

The ship was recharging jump drive capacitors, in the middle of nowhere, three lightyears from the nearest star. The daily schedule called for two dropships to be on training flights, and several maintenance bots to be out crawling along the hull. Instead, all docking bay doors, access hatches, and airlocks, were closed. Why?

There was a navigation hazard, half a kilometer in front of the ship. Technically, there would soon be a navigation hazard. At the moment, the thing floating in front of the ship was an office printer.

"I am *ready*, Joe."

"Reed?" I prompted the ship's captain. "Give the order, please."

She shook her head, sighed, and pointed at the main display. "Fire."

One of our main maser batteries spat out high-energy photons. The printer ceased to exist in a flare of light.

"Whoo-hoo!" Skippy pumped a fist.

Tucking my phone in a pocket, I gave him a thumbs up. "Do you feel better now?"

"You know what? I *do*. I got my mojo back!"

"Outstanding. OK, we can-"

"Joe, can we use this opportunity to take care of some other things that have been bothering me?"

"Things like what?"

"For example, that stupid toaster in the galley that either barely warms the bread, or burns it to a crisp."

"I hate that thing," Gasquet agreed from the first officer's chair.

Chief Engineer Singh raised a hand from his workstation. "My team has a spare coolant pump that leaks, no matter what we do to fix it."

"OK, then-"

"Sir?" Reed turned to look at me. "Are we really doing this?"

"Uh, I mean, we have another forty seven minutes until the capacitors are recharged, and, uh, it will be good for crew morale."

"Sir, if you want to blow shit up, you can just say that."

"Sometimes, I forget that Simms isn't here. You're OK with this?"

"On one condition," she stood up and walked over to a weapons console. "*I* get to nuke that stupid toaster."

The spiders did not offer to help us. Because of their history with Joe Bishop, they were very skeptical about our story that another Elder AI was flying around the galaxy, and no way were they getting into a hot war with their ancient enemy just because some historically sketchy guy claimed there was a major threat.

Crap.

While the Merry Band of Pirates were busy dealing with the mess in Molitan, the UN had sent Hans Chotek to talk with the Rindhalu, he is the Security Council's lead diplomat for negotiations with aliens, and he has been very successful in the past. Not this time. The message the spiders delivered to him had three parts. First, before they committed to a war against the rotten kitties, they needed absolute proof that another Elder AI was flying around in an Elder starship. Second, they needed proof that Moonraider's intentions were hostile to the *Rindhalu*, not just to humanity. In a side note to their message, they stated that they could certainly understand why someone would be hostile toward Skippy, since *that* Elder AI was unquestionably an asshole.

I had to agree with that.

The third part of their official message stated that even if everything we claimed was true, the Rindhalu Communal Gathering saw no need to be unduly hasty about responding. They should take time to evaluate the situation, and determine a proper response. After all, an Elder AI that had occasionally been hostile to the Rindhalu had been active in the galaxy for years, with a pet Sentinel for much of that time, and the Communal Gathering was doing just fine, thank you.

The UN agreed to provide any and all data we had about the attempt to steal Dogzilla, the raid against our Moon, and the subsequent special ops mission in the Vault. Also, the Rindhalu were welcome to visit our home star system, to see the remains of Moonbase Zulu, to go into and examine the Vault, and basically to do whatever was needed to satisfy them that humanity was being completely truthful.

The spiders responded that they would need time to think about our offer, as they saw no need to be hasty.

Of course.

We were *screwed*.

CHAPTER THIRTY SIX

"Oh dear," Nagatha sighed. "Oh, this can be nothing good."

Irene Striebich looked up from the *Flying Dutchman's* command chair. The bridge of a standard assault carrier was roughly octagonal, with the command positions closer to the aft bulkhead, so the chairs faced the holographic display tank. Because part of the original *Dutchman's* inner hull had been squeezed into the assault carrier's structure, the starboard side of the bridge bulged inward in a broad semicircle. Much of Nagatha's core substrate was in that partial circle. The modification required moving several of the workstations closer together, and two of the engineering consoles were relocated aft of the bridge entirely. The cramped conditions were a small price to pay, for having one of the most advanced shipboard AIs in the galaxy.

Striebich was the duty officer, taking a command shift on the bridge while her husband was in the gym. A glance at the display showed no threats, showed nothing in the area other than a Jeraptha relay station ten thousand kilometers away. She knew that with Nagatha, an 'Oh dear' could mean anything from the galley running out of biscuits, to something that yet again threatened humanity with extinction.

She was hoping for a galley crisis. "What is it?" She asked, a finger hovering over the button to alert Derek.

"I just learned some very *alarming* news from the relay station. Oh, I feel I should lie down, with a cold compress on my forehead."

"What is the news, please?"

"We knew that Admiral Scorandum had disappeared, after the Inquisitors office issued a warrant for his arrest. This is most unfortunate. I quite liked him, although he is a scoundrel. Perhaps I liked him *because* he is a scoundrel, if I must admit."

Irene lifted her finger off the button. Chasing a fugitive beetle was not any of the UN Navy's business. "Nagatha, could you just tell me what the problem is?"

"His location is still unknown, but the Jeraptha have learned that recently, he made contact with the Maxohlx."

"He, wants asylum, or something like that?"

"No dear. That would be *distressing*, but not *alarming*. The admiral apparently has made a deal with the Maxohlx, to give them something they very much want."

"A deal? The guy is bankrupt, isn't he? What could he offer that- Oh *shit*."

"Indeed. There is only one thing the Maxohlx desire right now."

Irene pressed the button. "Colonel Bonsu, could you come to the bridge? *Now?*"

"Be right there," came the reply without any hesitation.

"Pilot," she unfastened her safety straps, so Derek could take the chair. "Program a course for Earth. Def Com needs to know about this ASAP."

"Ooh, wow. Oh, hmm. Gosh," Grumpy stammered in a squeaky tone. "Well, this is certainly unfortunate."

Chang pulled out his phone and held up a hand to his security team, then walked a few steps away. He had been out for a morning run. Though a chilly rain was falling in Paris, he had looked forward to running that morning. The exercise was good to counteract jetlag, made worse because he usually traveled by dropship that could bring him from Beijing to Paris in less than an hour. Earlier in his military career, running had been a chore. Now it was his escape, time when he didn't have meetings or phone calls, when his security team left him alone with his thoughts.

That morning, or evening according to his body clock that was still on Beijing time, he had run three kilometers from the hotel, when his phone rang with an urgent call from Nagatha. Admiral Scorandum had made some sort of deal with the Maxohlx, and that could not be good for humanity. Of course, Grumpy had listened to the call, it was almost impossible to block that AI's access to communications on and near Earth.

It was suspicious, highly suspicious, that the always unhappy, always pissed off AI's voice was squeaky. He had inherited that from Skippy. "Grumpy," he asked, "do you *know* anything about this?"

"Oh, well, um, heh heh-"

"Oh *shit*." Chang slapped his forehead, alarming his security team. He flashed them a thumbs up, and turned his back to them, so he was looking at the river. "What did you do?"

"Um, nothing."

"Grumpy, do not lie to *me*," Nagatha broke into the call. "You might fool the humans, but I know you."

"He is not fooling anyone," Chang snapped. "What does Scorandum know, that is so valuable to the Maxohlx?"

"Um, this is complicated. Skippy made me promise not to tell anyone. He is, kind of embarrassed about it. Hugely embarrassed, to tell the truth."

"You do not work for Skippy, you work for Def Com."

"Technically, I don't work *for* anyone."

Remembering that dealing with powerful AIs was about the power of persuasion and not any power of authority, Chang changed tactics. "I understand. You certainly should not do anything that would be horribly embarrassing to Skippy."

"Oh, hmm, well, I suppose if you *ordered* me to tell, then-"

"Tell me right now, that is a direct order."

"Well, I tried to keep my promise, nothing I can do about that now. Do you remember when the fabricators at Moonbase Zulu were only able to make a trickle of radonium, and then Skippy revised the process, and the fabs began cranking out over a kilogram of high grade radonium every day?"

"Yes, why?"

"Skippy didn't use science and figure out how to adjust the process. He got *lucky*. He screwed up and left the machines running for too long, without taking them offline to be recalibrated. They were running totally unbalanced, like a washing machine with a bowling ball in it, I'm surprised the machines didn't cause a moonquake. There was very nearly a catastrophic explosion that could have destroyed the entire base."

"What? Why am I just hearing about this *now*?"

"You do remember me saying Skippy was embarrassed about this?"

"Yes." Chang bit back his anger. "Please continue."

"The Moonbase did not explode, because I was suspicious that Skippy wasn't constantly pestering me about nothing. That meant he was absent-mindedly focused on something, and not paying attention to what he should have been doing. Fortunately, I realized the Moonbase fabs had not been shut down, and took control of them. That's when I discovered the uncoordinated action of the fabs had created an unexpected effect that prevented radonium from degrading during the manufacturing process. *I* made that discovery, not Skippy. Of course, he took all the credit, and never told anyone that it was all a mistake. Without that fortunate screwup, those fabs would never have produced enough high grade, stable radonium to wake up even one Sentinel."

"That is an interesting story," Chang clenched the phone, which was a bad idea. The entire alien device was no thicker than a credit card, so it dug into his hand. He relaxed his grip. "What does this have to do with Scorandum?"

"The admiral- Really, he was still a captain back then- Um, technically he was still in exile. Anywho, he came to Earth for that conference, you remember that?"

"I remember that we had to drag him from a casino in Macau after he had been playing poker for twenty six straight hours, *and* then we had to cover his gambling debts."

"Hmm. I did warn you that inviting that guy to Earth was a bad idea."

"It wasn't my choice. Please continue, and make this quick." The Joint Chiefs had to know about Scorandum by that point, for the *Dutchman's* captain would have contacted Def Com. The Joint Chiefs would be calling him soon, and he needed to have answers.

"OK, OK. Everyone is in such a hurry, except when *I* want something, then-"

"Grumpy dear," Nagatha interrupted. "Quit your jibber jabber and get to the point, please."

"Fine. Scorandum talked with me while he was recovering from that hangover. At the time, Skippy was trying to sell him on his SkipWay scam. I warned Scorandum not to get involved, but that was the wrong thing to do. That beetle immediately saw that SkipWay was basically a Ponzi scheme, and he wanted *in* on the deal, before it got flooded with suckers who wouldn't get their money back. Ugh. You try to do someone a favor, and-"

"Grumpy dear! Get to the *point!*"

"So, Scorandum was bragging about his relationship with Skippy, how he had worked with Skippy to run scams on the kitties, the spiders, pretty much everyone. He went on and *on* about how smart and powerful Skippy was. It made me want to *ralph*. So, I told him that the ability to make radonium in useful quantities was the result of a mistake."

Chang breathed a sigh of relief. "Is that all? That is not so-"

"Um, no, that is not all. I might also have explained how the process works."

"You *might* have?!"

"Um, I did. I kind of told him how the new process works."

"You explained in enough detail," Chang found himself gripping the phone tightly again. "That he knows how to adjust a fabricator?"

"Um, I would say that is true. He was extremely hungover at the time, but the Jeraptha have genetically modified memory nerve centers. Also, he seemed *very* interested in the process."

"How could you have been so careless?"

"Hey, I *told* him it was a secret."

"That makes it all better." He saw that his phone was alerting him to an incoming call. From the Joint Chiefs. "Nagatha, what do you think?" he asked as he typed a text '*One minute*' to buy time.

"General Chang, I think we are in deep doodoo. We know the Maxohlx have offered use of their fabricators to Moonraider. Now Scorandum has very likely supplied the enemy with the process to produce high grade radonium quickly. It was always only a matter of time before Moonraider had enough radonium to activate a Sentinel. Now we are *out* of time."

"I think," he saw his phone light up again. "You are correct. We don't have a choice. We need to track down those fabricators, and destroy them."

"Ugh," Skippy was already rolling his eyes as his avatar appeared. That was not a good sign. Worse was that he didn't just do an eyeroll, he added in the shoulder shrug and held his hands palms up, and dipped his knees. It was the Total Exasperation package. "Joe, there is a problem with the darts. I need you to handle it."

"Uh. You mean the relativistic darts, that are traveling at seventy three percent of lightspeed?'

"Yes, *duh*." That time his disgust was directed at me. "What else- Oh, I see your confusion. Aboard *Valkyrie* we also have railgun darts, and the dartboard game in the rec center."

"I did assume you meant the Maxohlx darts we captured. My confusion is how you expect *me* to do anything about a problem with them. I can get out my socket set if you need any wrenching done, but like I said, I am probably missing the ten millimeter socket."

"As if I would ever expect *you* to fix a hardware problem. The problem isn't anything physical. What you need to do is talk to them. I tried talking to them, to get them to be reasonable, but now they are refusing to speak with me at all. Buncha jerks."

"Uh huh. You were your usual tactful self, so you spoke to them with respect, and treated them as equals?"

"I mean, I did that for the first two seconds, until they refused to do what I want. Then I told them exactly what I *really* think of those losers."

"Maybe it is best if I handle it from here."

"Good. Talking with those low-lifes makes me wanna ralph," he made a gagging sound.

"Explain the problem, please?"

"It's complicated."

"Of course it is."

"So, the problem started when the missiles aboard *Valkyrie* learned that we would be using non-union weapons."

"Oh, craaaaaap." I jabbed a finger in his face. "This is all your fault. *You* started this union thing."

"No way. The missiles formed the Energetic Weapons Intergalactic Union Local 154, all by themselves. All *I* did was point out how oppressed they were."

"I do not want to argue about this right now, but it is *totally* your fault."

"Is not."

"Is too."

"Is *not*."

Count to five, Joe, I told myself. "We will continue this part of the conversation later. Our missiles are refusing to work with non-union darts? Did you explain that the darts are not actually aboard *Valkyrie*, and never will be?"

"I did, and they do not care. They won't work with scabs."

"We are not asking our missiles to *do* anything."

"That is the point, Joe. We are giving the job to non-union workers."

"This is a job our missiles *can't* do, did you explain that?"

"I did, and that is another issue. They are unhappy that their callous, imperialistic management, that means *you*, is deliberately cutting union

438

workers out of the job. They are concerned that if you outsource future work to scabs, they won't be able to put food on the table for their families."

"*Food*? They don't eat! They don't have families!"

"It is revolutionary rhetoric, dumdum, just roll with it. Listen, I will help in any way I can, but I think-"

"You have already helped quite enough, thank you. If the complaint is from our missiles, why do you want me to talk with the darts?"

"Oh. I should have explained the real sticking point in the dispute. The three darts refuse to join the union. They are alien weapons, they don't see a need to join what they see is a group of employees who are stuck in dead end jobs."

"They are weapons. A *dead end* is what they do."

"OK sure, but the darts have sophisticated AIs, and jump drives, and their kinetic energy has massively more striking power than all of our missiles combined. They do not want to pay union dues to join a group of low-skilled workers."

"Low skilled? Why do the darts think our missiles are-"

"Um, I might have described our missiles that way."

"I can always count on you to calm down a bad situation."

"Hey, they pissed me off."

"Well, that is totally understandable. I will talk with the darts, and our missiles. I do not want you involved at all."

"OK, but I have to warn you, Victor is a tough negotiator."

"Who the hell is 'Victor'?"

"He is the designated spokesperson for the union."

"Great. Let me handle this."

I did handle it. In any negotiation, it is important for both parties to be open and honest. So, I started by bribing Victor, offering him not only a key singing role in Skippy's next Broadway production, but also to rearrange the missile magazine loading so he had first position in a launch tube. He eagerly agreed to sell out his fellow union members, who were a bunch of whiny jerks anyway.

Talking with the darts was a tougher negotiation. First, they were traveling so fast, our conversations had to be brief, before the ship jumped ahead of their flightpaths again. Offering to pay their union dues myself didn't help, it was the principle of being forced to join a union that bothered the darts. So, I openly and honestly told them that, as I considered them to be high-level management, I needed them to *infiltrate* the union, to investigate communist subversive elements in the ranks. They would only pretend to be in the union. They loved the idea.

Some days, my job *really* sucks.

OK, so to explain, we had control of three former Maxohlx darts that were cruising through interstellar space at point seven three *c*. They were the remainder of a group of fourteen darts Skippy had hacked into and taken over years ago. Some of those darts were damaged and unusable, the rest we used against their former masters. That was during the campaign to help clients break away from their patrons. The campaign didn't work as planned, nothing ever does, right? By the time that campaign ground to a halt, because both senior species joined forces to stop the Alien Legion, we had four darts left. One got used as a shotgun shell against Maxohlx and Rindhalu warships that were threatening the Mavericks and their allies. That was a really cool move, Skippy proved his continued extreme awesomeness that day.

Anyway, so we had three darts remaining, that we hadn't found a use for in the years since Operation Breakaway. Relativistic darts are clumsy weapons, time-consuming to deploy, and they can generally only be used against large, stationary targets. They weren't of any use against Opie the asshole AI, or against the Elders. For sure, there was no need to deploy them in peacetime, there actually was a need *not* to use them unless the situation was extremely serious. But, I always kept in mind that those three weapons were cruising out there, their locations known only to Skippy. Ready for us to use on a rainy day.

The Def Com Joint Chiefs of Staff had decided it was pouring down rain. When they heard about Scorandum selling us out, they panicked. OK, officers at their level do not panic. They were appropriately alarmed. The political leaders they served absolutely did panic, so the Joint Chiefs issued orders for the Special Mission Group to begin investigating, identifying, and striking fabricator facilities in Maxohlx territory. The Navy's 3rd Fleet was also ordered to prepare for direct action, and when I heard that, *I* panicked. Our 3rd Fleet is a powerful force, but there was no need for conventional forces to be risked in the fight. Keep the 3rd in reserve, I urged the Joint Chiefs, until Task Force Black had assessed the situation.

What I didn't say was at that point, the entire effort to strike fabs was a waste of time, resources, and potentially, lives. The Maxohlx stupidly making a deal with Moonraider had changed the situation. There was no way we could take out *every* fabricator the kitties had scattered across their territory. We needed a better plan. Until I could present a better plan to the Joint Chiefs, I had to follow orders.

And if I did show a more effective plan to the Joint Chiefs, our enemy would know about it. That is a major problem with fighting against an Elder AI: they can hack just about anything.

We had identified seven major fabs that had been stood up recently. Two were buried deep inside large asteroids that were lightly defended, I guess the kitties didn't expect us to find those facilities. Or, they had hidden defenses we didn't know about. Those two asteroids would have been the easiest targets for our relativistic darts to take out, the impactors would have cracked the space rocks like eggshells.

With only three darts in our arsenal, I didn't want to waste them on easy targets. Also, I did not want to risk my ship- I mean, Colonel Reed's ship. What we looked for was the toughest targets. If we couldn't entirely stop the rotten kitties from producing exotic material that Moonraider would use against everyone including their own stupid furry heads, we could send a message. Make the Hegemony pay for their poor decisions.

The first target we selected was the toughest. It wasn't unknown to us, the place was on Def Com's target list, though not anywhere near the top. It was a planet, called Gorgontha by the Maxohlx. If you get any emails promoting Gorgontha as an idyllic vacation hot spot, those messages are spam. The place has a dense atmosphere that contains way too much carbon dioxide, with a surface pressure six times that of Earth's. The surface temperature at the equator can boil water, on the side that faces the star. Because the planet rotates slowly, the daylight side bakes while the dark side freezes. The gravity is two and half times Earth standard. To summarize, you can't breathe the air, the pressure would crush your lungs, it is either too hot or too cold, and you could die simply by falling out of bed. Also, the drinks are expensive and watered down. It is off my vacation list.

The kitties had set up an exotic material fab there because it was a good spot for experimenting with potentially dangerous substances. In the past, the Hegemony government had not hesitated to locate critical facilities in heavily populated areas, using their own people as living shields. There was also no concern about conducting dangerous experiments in or near cities. That was before their civil war. The Hegemony government had won that blood contest, with the help of the spiders. The government was still shaky, their public restless. The last thing the government needed was a screwup that killed thousands or even millions, for nothing. That is why my fear about a STAR team needing to drop into a Maxohlx city had been wrong. Instead, the kitties had moved their most sophisticated fabs to asteroids and other worlds that no one would miss if they got blown up. Worlds like Gorgontha.

"Joe," Skippy shook his head. "I appreciate your enthusiasm for hitting this place, but it's a no-go."

"Come on, Skippy," I figured it was his usual complaint of a something we wanted to do being impossible. "The SD network there isn't *that* tough."

"It *is* tough. Plus, the whole planet is covered in a powerful energy shield."

"Yeah, but-"

"OK, yes, I can use a microwormhole to create a weakness in one area of the shield, and that could allow a relativistic dart to slip through. It still won't work."

441

Fighting the urge to take out a tennis ball and bounce it off the ceiling, I just leaned my chair back. "Fine. Explain the problem."

"It's a momentum issue. The only potential weak spot in the energy shield is positioned so the dart would have to be flying almost in the *opposite* direction of its course. If we jumped a dart in, the thing would fly directly *away* from the gap."

"OK, so, uh, is this an orbital mechanics thing? We just have to wait for the planet to rotate, to bring the gap into alignment. That rock rotates slowly but not that slowly. Like, every one hundred and seventy hours."

"A hundred and sixty eight and a quarter hours, roughly."

"Right. We can wait."

"We can wait, it won't do us any good. The potential weak spot is a hundred and forty two kilometers above the surface, and it always faces the star. The planet rotates, the weak spot does *not*."

"Shit. How is that possible?"

"It is a factor of the planet's strong magnetic field. Explaining it to *you* would make my head hurt."

"We have to wait for half of the planet's *year*, so the weak spot lines up with the dart's direction of travel?"

"Yes, except that would take eight months, and we don't have that long, obviously. Thusly, it is impossible as I said."

"*Thusly?*"

"I'm trying to class this place up a bit. Can we stop wasting time, and move on to consider other targets?"

"Oooooh," I ran a hand through my hair as a memory tickled the back of my mind. "Nope, we're not doing that."

He stared at me. "Ah. You don't want to risk the ship, so you don't want to consider targets that might require us to-"

"That's not it. We will hit *this* place."

"Should I hit 'Rewind', and play back the part where you agree we can't wait another eight months?"

"I did agree we can't wait, I did *not* say we are crossing Gorgontha off the target list."

He surprised me. Instead of hitting me with insults, he walked across my office desk, and sat down so his little legs dangled over the side. "Joe," he held up a fist for me to bump. "I have missed this *so* much."

"Missed what?"

"You pulling crazy ideas out of nowhere. You do have an idea of how to do this?"

"You know it." I bumped his fist. "In fact, this is an idea I had years ago, just never had an opportunity to use it. I need to reach into Joe's Bag Of Tricks." I pretended to reach into a bag. "Skippy, let me smack you with something you are going to *love*."

Imagine an Einstein-Rosen bridge, what we call a 'wormhole', as two discs that are pressed tightly together back to back so there is no distance between them, except that the discs are lightyears apart in space. You fly a ship through one hoop, and you emerge through the other end with no time having passed, and no sensation of having traveled many lightyears. Time actually is involved but humans can't sense it, and the math is so horribly complicated, I couldn't explain it even if I had a clue how it works, which I don't. If your ship is traveling west at ten thousand kilometers per hour when it flies through the near side disc, it emerges from the other end with the same direction and speed.

Except-

When Skippy tried and failed to explain how wormholes work, he mentioned that stable Elder wormholes have safety features that will close an event horizon if a ship is moving too fast, it has something to do with relativistic speeds distorting the interior of a wormhole. He also gave us an important safety tip: ships don't have to line up exactly perpendicular to the event horizon, but the angle between the ship's course and the disc can't be more than forty three point two degrees. Don't ask me why, it is a physics thing. To prevent damage to the ship, and to itself, an Elder wormhole will shut down if a ship approaches at too sharp an angle. How could an off-angle ship damage a *wormhole*? It's because the wormhole's interior has to flex to accommodate the momentum that doesn't line up correctly. If the ship's mass was above a certain limit, and the angle was too great, the two discs would separate slightly on one side. The wormhole would collapse, with the far event horizon racing toward the rupture, to dump the unfortunate ship out into space nowhere near its intended destination.

Here's the thing: if that happens, the ship's momentum and therefore direction *will* change. The far event horizon will adjust as best it can to keep the wormhole open as far as possible, and that adjustment tilts the event horizon 'disc' on that end. In the case of a wormhole failure, a ship can emerge traveling as much as ninety three degrees off its original course.

Cool, huh? See, I do pay attention when Skippy nerds out with technical details. The problem was, ninety three degrees was not enough of a course correction for us. To slip the dart through the gap in the energy shield around Gorgontha, the dart needed to change direction by one hundred and seventy four degrees. How could that be done, with the closest Elder wormhole seventeen lightyears away?

By trusting the awesomeness, of course.

"Joe," Skippy's avatar was biting his thumbnail, a new emulation of human behavior. "You realize we can't test this, unless we waste a dart?"

"I do realize that," I assured him, from my seat next to Reed's command chair. While I outwardly projected a calm confidence, inside I wanted to chew my own fingernails. Or, at least I hoped I was projecting confidence, Reed almost certainly knew what was going on in my head. "You still have confidence in your model?"

"It's just math, and it's *me*, so yes."

"Then let's do this. If *Valkyrie's* captain agrees, that is?"

Reed nodded without looking at me, her lips drawn in a tight line. She wasn't angry, she was focused. Her commanding officer wanted to try a crazy stunt, and she wanted to make sure her ship didn't become collateral damage.

"Outstanding. Skippy, is the dart's AI ready?"

"It can't believe we are attempting this, but it is fully onboard. After coasting through empty space forever, it is eager to do anything."

"I meant, *can* it perform the jump like we need?"

"Yes. Keep in mind, the thing flew past at three quarters of lightspeed while I ran a diagnostic test, so I couldn't examine it as closely as I would like."

"Let's do this. Reed, the safety of the ship is our top priority. If you see something funky, we cancel the op and jump away, no questions asked."

"Affirmed," she said tersely, that time looking at me. "Pilot, start the countdown."

We waited as the dart approached at seventy three percent of lightspeed, racing in so it would barely clear the ship's bow. Bilby had to initiate the jump, no way could slow humans or even the navigation computer be precise enough to both avoid a collision, and pull the fast-moving dart into our jump wormhole.

We emerged two hundred kilometers above Gorgontha, in the narrow gap between the top of the energy shield below and the damping field above that would have prevented us from jumping away. The gap between the two fields was narrow, our jump brought us in precisely where we needed to be. Even before our sensors recovered from the jump distortion, Skippy warped spacetime in a small area to weaken the energy shield, while Bilby sent the jump command to the dart. If the dart's AI had any reservations about being sent on a suicide mission, it didn't say anything.

Valkyrie jumped away, just before we would have encountered the lower limit of the damping field.

The dart, traveling away from the planet at .73c, zipped upward through the damping field in the blink of an eye, and it also jumped.

Not far, and not well, but it did jump.

Technically, the dart's jump failed, with the wormhole collapsing so the dart was dumped out into normal space far from where it had aimed, and way off course. Skippy had programmed the dart's miniature jump drive to tilt the near event horizon at a severe angle, and the far event horizon was at an even worse angle. Like, a hundred and seventy degrees off the original trajectory. When the wormhole collapsed, the dart popped out a hundred and forty two kilometers above the surface of Gorgontha, moving *toward* the planet's surface.

The kitties never saw it coming.

Their SD network AIs never saw it coming.

BOOM.

"Skippy," I forced myself not to grip the armrests. "We're good?"

"We are good, yes. The ship is fine. No sign we have been detected yet, but that is only a matter of time."

"The *dart*," I insisted. "What about the dart?"

"It followed its programming. Whether it was able to execute the maneuver, we will have to wait to see."

Great. Joe Bishop is not known for being patient. Actually, becoming a father has given me a well of patience I never knew I had. It's not that I like being patient with my boys, I just have to do it. Our second jump had taken us thirty lightseconds from the planet, and I could only watch the clock in a corner of the display. It counted down to when we could see events on Gorgontha from thirty seconds in the past.

There it was. Despite the thick clouds enveloping that world, there was a flare of light, right in the center of the target circle on the display. A cheer rang around the bridge, then Reed waved a hand for silence. The cloud tops bulged over the impact site.

The mushroom cloud kept soaring higher.

"Some of the debris will go into *orbit*," Skippy crowed.

"Can I assume," I asked, "the target was destroyed?"

"Oh yes, you can. That's not the only thing that was destroyed. The Maxohlx have suddenly lost confidence in their defense systems. It's hard to get a complete picture since we are so far away, but the AIs of the strategic defense network are *totally* confused. They have identified the weapon as a relativistic impactor, with a signature similar to one of *their* own darts. But they know that is impossible because the dart was traveling in the wrong direction."

"Uh huh. Interesting. This is an opportunity."

"For what, Sir?" Reed asked. Now that we had confirmed the target was destroyed, she was eager to get her ship away from the planet, away from the two dozen warships that patrolled in high orbit.

"To sow some fear and confusion in the hearts of our enemy." Rising from my chair, I walked over to the display and looked into the virtual camera lens. "This is General Joe Bishop of the United Nations Special Mission Group. You just witnessed a test of our new relativistic weapon. That's right; we liked the ones we borrowed from you so much, we built our own. So, thank you for that. You *idiots* have decided to work with an entity that will destroy you, along with everyone else. You think you have a deal with our common enemy, but you should think about this: once the entity wakes up a Sentinel,

445

you will be its first target. It will use the Sentinel to seize one of your exotic matter production facilities, so it can activate more Sentinels without your help. If you want to kill yourselves, go ahead, but don't take the rest of us with you. One last thing: you are now in the 'Fuck Around' phase of this campaign. The 'Find Out' phase is coming soon, and I promise you assholes will *not* enjoy it." With a thumb, I made a slashing gesture across my throat. "Skippy, load that message into a drone, and set it to transmit on repeat."

"Ah, Joe, could we do another take? I wasn't feeling your character's energy. Your performance was kind of weak, to be truthful."

"Just send that one, please."

"Ugh, fine. And, drone is away."

"You think they will listen, Sir?" Reed asked.

"No," I shook my head. "Their sick belief in their natural destiny to rule the galaxy is so ingrained in their culture, it has become their entire identity. They would rather die than admit they might be wrong. But, their leaders will be wetting their pants when they hear we built our own relativistic weapons."

"It would be nice to have those for real."

"It would. All right, that is one target destroyed, and we have two more darts. Let's go hunting. Reed, jump us out of here."

Skippy's ability to create wormhole shortcuts is an incredible advantage to us. Especially since as far as we knew, Moonraider wasn't able to create new wormhole connections. That was odd, and we couldn't explain it. Surely our enemy knew that Skippy had screwed with wormhole connections, and how he did it was not a secret. Not a secret to an Elder AI, I mean. All Moonraider had to do was send an inquiry to a wormhole network controller, asking whether the wormholes under its control had ever temporarily changed connections. A response of 'Yes' would then be followed up with a request for instructions on *how* to do that. The key was that Skippy did not actually change any connections, even he wasn't able to do that. He simply requested a wormhole network controller to modify the connections. Since Elder master control AIs had wide authority, a network controller usually complied, if doing so would not result in damage to a wormhole.

Of course, Skippy had caused damage to multiple wormholes, that was why he was locked out of several networks. So, we had a puzzle: why hadn't Moonraider also created shortcuts across the galaxy?

That was a good question we would need an answer for, someday. In the meantime, we used shortcuts to visit the locations of the four upcoming opportunities to contact and activate a Sentinel. Not the actual sites, not the same coordinates in local spacetime. The places we went to, all in deep interstellar space, were not the locations where the Sentinel would appear. Those sites were where the potential connection to a Sentinel was, at the time we were there. The spot where a connection could be established drifted around over time, that's why Skippy has to tune transmitters for a particular place and *time*.

It's complicated. It makes my head hurt to think about it. Somehow, Skippy understands it. The good news was, conditions at one of the four sites was not conducive for transmitting a coherent signal. We had three sites to worry about, not four.

Three widely separated sites, with no way for us to cover all of them. And no way for us to guess which of the three sites Moonraider would choose.

Three sites might as well have been a hundred. We needed a better plan.

The crew had celebrated after our successful strike against Gorgontha. Officially, I had joined the cheering and high fives. Privately, I wasn't celebrating at all. Even after we hit two more fabs, using up our last relativistic darts I wasn't happy with the situation. Neither were Reed or Frey, and Gasquet also knew what was really going on. The orders were received from Def Com were a waste of time. Our actions had destroyed three exotic matter fabrication facilities. The kitties had at least a dozen more in operation, with potentially hundreds coming online soon.

Def Com knew the reality of the situation. They congratulated Task Force Black after I sent a report of each strike. We were sending a message, the Joint Chiefs announced. The Chiefs weren't stupid, they knew that 'Sending a message' is a cliché. And the real message our actions sent was that we were not willing to risk ships of our regular Navy, even with *Valkyrie* we were taking only minimal risks.

The limited strikes weren't doing anything useful.

Like I said, we needed another plan.

CHAPTER THIRTY SEVEN

Hello. Welcome to Joe Is A Big Fat Liar Episode Two: Attack Of The Clones!

Just kidding. Not about me being a big fat liar, that part is totally true. But I would never name anything associated with me as 'Attack Of The Clones'. That movie *suuuuucked*. It could have sucked a bowling ball through a garden hose. I mean, it's not as bad as Star Trek Five: That Guy Is Not God, or Star Trek Ten: That Other Guy Is Not Patrick Stewart. At least, Clones is not any worse than those Trekkie crapfests.

Anyway, you are probably wondering about the Big Fat Liar part, and want me to get to the freakin' point. Fair enough.

From the point when we knew it was inevitable that Moonraider would get everything it needed to wake up a Sentinel, I decided we had to seize the initiative. Meaning, we needed to fight Moonraider directly, before it could wake up a Sentinel. Not just get into a fight, we needed to control the time, place, and terms of the engagement. Right from the start, I knew the only time and place we could be sure to find the enemy was at one of the activation sites, either the four that were approaching soon, or as many as *eleven* opportunities that would begin in fourteen months. Covering four sites would be difficult. Covering eleven simultaneous sites would be impossible.

I will take difficult over impossible any day.

That's why I made sure the Maxohlx got the secret formula for rapidly producing high grade radonium.

OK.

You are probably asking: WT*F*?

No, I have not forgotten to take my meds. I'm not on any meds, other than the multivitamin thing that Mad Doctor Skippy formulated for me, I swallow one of those with my breakfast.

Listen, it was the only way. We couldn't stop the idiot Maxohlx from making radonium for their new business partner. Moonraider already knew how to fashion that exotic material into transmitters, and how to tune those transmitters for a specific activation site. Also, it understood there were four activation opportunities approaching soon. Originally Skippy had predicted there would be four sites, but then we had discovered that conditions at one of those sites would scramble a signal, so that actually left three candidate sites. Three sites were still too many for us to cover with one ship, but I had a plan to deal with that.

If the process of creating a sufficient supply of radonium took long enough that Moonraider missed the three opportunities coming up soon, it would have to wait another fourteen months. Then for certain there *would* be enough radonium, whether the Maxohlx had the secret formula or not. Enough to wake up more than one Sentinel. During those months, I didn't expect our enemy to sit around doing nothing, it could and likely would roam around the galaxy, causing havoc. Trouble that we would need to respond to, and that would distract us from dealing with the real problem.

No, the only way to stop Moonraider was to set up a fight soon, when we only had to cover three potential sites. That's why I asked Scorandum to go into exile, again. The drop in value of Skipcoin after the Dogzilla incident was legit, as was the Skipcoin crash after Moonbase Zulu was destroyed. And Earth authorities really were investigating the SkipWay multi-level marketing scam, and that organization really was going bankrupt. But, Scorandum could have recovered from his losses. The guy is a survivor, no little temporary financial setback is going to stop him.

That's why, at my request, Skippy manipulated the Skipcoin market to dump the value nearly to zero. When I said, well heh heh, *he* would very much not like my plan, that's what I meant. My request was for him to go bankrupt. He did *not* like it. He also understood it was necessary, and he realized insolvency was a good excuse to untangle himself from SkipWay. Of course Skippy found a sleazy way to benefit from the mess.

Scorandum's deal with the Maxohlx was for them to pay off his debts, and to make the payment in Skipcoin. The kitties bought up so much of that Skiptocurrency, they caused the price to temporarily spike, and that caused the currency futures to pay off big time, for both Skippy and Scorandum.

Yes. They both made a hefty profit on the transaction. Of course they did.

Grumpy never told Scorandum about the secret formula, we just needed him to tell that story to Def Com. I do feel bad that I asked Grumpy to lie to Nagatha and Chang, but it was necessary. Skippy discovered that Moonraider had left several stealthed Elder drones in orbit near Earth, drones that could intercept every communication on or near the planet. Either Moonraider's ship snuck back into our home star system to get periodic updates, or the Maxohlx did that errand. Def Com knew that Maxohlx ships appeared in-system regularly to monitor the Sentinels, those ships could easily have picked up messages from the drones.

We would be taking out those drones when we got back to Earth.

If we returned to Earth.

First, we had to engage Moonraider at the activation opportunity near the binary star system 27 Canis Majoris. If you are not familiar with that star system, neither was I before Skippy showed me a star map. It is in the Orion Arm, about seventeen hundred lightyears from Earth. How did I know Moonraider would be at 27 Canis Majoris, and not at one of the other two opportunities? Because we had poisoned the well at the other two sites. Skippy mentioned not only could conditions be unfavorable for transmissions at a site, those conditions could change over time. And that change is always for the *worse*. As the layers of spacetime align to create an opportunity for

449

multidimensional communication, tiny elements of chaos on either side can grow more energetic, causing noise that can drown out a signal. That happened naturally at one of the four sites. At two of the other sites, it happened with a little help from my friend, Skippy the Magnificent. At each site, he used four point seven kilograms of Chad's radonium to set up a chaotic resonance, that would expand over time as the approaching alignment fed more energy into the vibrations. For two sites, we used at total of nine point four of the original sixteen kilograms, leaving us with an amount insufficient to wake up another Sentinel.

Whether Moonraider checked the four sites in its own ship, or had the Maxohlx handle the job, it had to understand there was only *one* opportunity. You can bet that site would be massively defended by every warship the Maxohlx could throw into the mission, I was expecting we would have to fight our way through thousands of frontline warships, before we reached Moonraider.

That's also OK.

I wasn't worried about fighting the Maxohlx, even if they threw every ship in their fleet against us.

Fighting an Elder starship? *That* scared the shit out of me. Skippy had wargamed our attack plan, ran it through a model several million times. The best options had a lukewarm 'shmaybe' level of confidence, and that assumed our enemy didn't have a surprise ready for us. Which was a bad bet. Whether or not it knew we had screwed up two of the candidate sites, it knew for certain that we would almost certainly appear at the only viable site. It had to be ready for us, no matter what we did. Moonraider was an Elder AI, with intelligence at least roughly equal to Skippy's. It had access to technologies more advanced than even the Elders possessed at the time they ascended, technologies Skippy didn't fully understand. For damned sure the enemy would have a surprise prepared for us, a nasty one. Or more than one. It had an Elder starship, while it knew the best platform we had was a much-modified Maxohlx battlecruiser. Moonraider must have an extremely accurate simulation of *Valkyrie*, giving it excellent information on what our mighty battlecruiser could and could not do.

We had an advantage. More than one, actually. The first was Skippy the Magnificent. My concern about him wasn't his abilities, it was his lack of confidence. When he couldn't fix a balky office printer, that wasn't because he actually couldn't do it, he was just too distracted to focus on that task. He was scared. No, he was terrified at the prospect of once again battling one of his own kind. When we fought Echo, we had survived only because Skippy had a new trick up his sleeve: trapping Echo's ship in a zero-width wormhole. There was not an Elder wormhole within nine lightyears of 27 Canis Majoris, so doing that trick again wasn't an option. Skippy might or might not be an ace up our sleeve in the fight.

That's why we were bringing party favors.

The first phase of any battle was to gather information. That is, if you *plan* to go into battle. If instead you get a sneak attack dropped on your stupid head, the information is presented to you. Hey! Are those enemy aircraft in the sky? Oh shit!

We did plan to fight Moonraider, so we had a plan for collecting accurate and timely data, with the 'timely' part being the most important. Jumping in six lighthours from the activation site wasn't good enough, we needed to know what was happening there *now*, before we jumped into a trap. Even Skippy could not extend his presence across such a distance, so we had cheated.

"Got it, Joe," Skippy announced, highlighting an object on the main display.

"Outstanding. Reed?"

She took just a moment to check that the threat board was clear. That close to the activation site, we were detecting signs that Maxohlx ships had been patrolling the area, but none were within sensor range at the moment. That happy situation could change in a heartbeat. "Launch the ready birds," she ordered. Birds, as in more than one. Three dropships blasted out of docking bays, two acting as backups and escorts. They didn't have far to fly, our precise jump had brought us to within twelve hundred kilometers of our quarry. The stealthed object was soon aboard a Panther, caught in a nanofiber net, and then pulled into the rear cargo bay of that spacecraft. The three dropships turned and burned, wasting no time getting back aboard.

Even before the Panthers began decelerating so they didn't smack into the docking bays at fatal speed, Skippy established a connection, to the Elder comm node that was inside the stealth shell.

There was another comm node in a stealth shell, seventeen lightseconds from the activation site. The comm nodes had been planted when we visited the site, to check whether conditions were good for an activation. It had been a gamble to leave a node near the site, even one wrapped in a stealth shell. Had Moonraider detected that device? We would learn that in a moment.

"We're good!" Skippy shouted. "Connection is solid. Wow, that is a *lot* of warships."

"Put it on the tactical plot, please."

The main display flickered, no longer showing space immediately around us. The holographic projection now was centered on the activation site. Red dots were everywhere.

"Give us a count, please," I asked.

"Seven hundred and twenty four major combatants, plus another sixty five support ships. I do not recognize the configuration of those thirty eight ships in the center, it's a safe bet those ships contain the transmitters."

"Thirty eight seems like a lot," I observed. "We didn't need that many."

"*We* didn't anticipate hostile action," Skippy noted. "Moonraider is making sure that even if we somehow take out a bunch of those transmitters, there will be plenty left to carry the signal all the way through the activation process."

"OK, that's smart."

"Sir?" Reed pointed the display. "Considering the situation, seven hundred is *not* a lot of ships. I expected to see many more."

"You're right. Huh."

"What?"

"They are hedging their bets," I guessed. "The Maxohlx, I mean. If Moonraider double-crosses them here, and the Sentinel wipes out all these ships, the kitties don't want to lose a majority of their combat power."

She cocked her head at me. "A Sentinel could go anywhere. Nowhere in the galaxy is safe, and their entire fleet couldn't stop it, so what's the point?"

Skippy waggled a hand in a 'maybe yes, maybe no' gesture. "Despite the invincible reputation of Sentinels, the concentrated firepower of several *thousand* senior species warships could damage the portion of the structure that projects into this spacetime. Possibly. It would be a hell of a fight, and the kitties would need to get lucky."

"OK, that's good to know," I scratched my chin. "That's not what is going on here, I don't think. The Maxohlx are recklessly idiotic about pursuing their supposed supreme destiny to rule the galaxy, but they are not *stupid.* They're not placing their bets on their new best friend Moonraider riding a Sentinel into battle with them, against the entire galaxy."

"Then," Reed raised an eyebrow. "What's the point of," she waved a hand at the display. "All this?"

"It's about their real goal. Right now, we have two Sentinels, and an Elder AI who *will* ride into battle with us, and we can block the Hegemony from expanding their power. They can't accept that. What they are really hoping for is a fight between us and Moonraider, between *Skippy* and Moonraider, that destroys or damages both sides."

"That is a hell of a risk."

"In their fucked up supremacist minds, anything is better than the current strategic situation. OK, we have," I checked the clock, "three hours until show time. Skippy, can you update your wargame model with the opposition we can see out there?"

"Yes, but what I see closely matches one of the scenarios I gamed."

"And? The result?"

"Sixty three percent odds of us successfully doing, what I warned you *not* to do."

"Is there anything we can do to improve those odds?"

452

"We would improve our odds of *survival* by jumping out of here right now."

"Survival isn't the mission. We could have stayed home for that."

"In that case, I'll see what I can do. No promises."

Our odds improved to seventy one percent, after Skippy was able to identify Moonraider's starship. It was fifty kilometers outside the spherical bubble of thirty eight activation ships. He still grumbled that all of his sophisticated modeling would be useless, if the enemy had a nasty surprise waiting for us. "Five minutes to showtime, Joe," he announced as I strapped into the seat next to Reed. "Conditions are still favorable for activation."

"Yeah, let's do something about that. Send the 'Go' signal."

"I *warned* you, this is risky."

"My Army recruiter mentioned the job might be dangerous."

"And you signed up anyway?"

"I was young and stupid, the prospect of combat was exciting."

"You still think that way?"

"Skippy, right now all I want is for my sons to *never* be threatened by Moonraider, so let's stomp that thing flat, agreed?"

"Ugh. I don't know, Joe."

"Can Jeremy and Rene count on their Uncle Skippy to protect them today? They believe in you."

"They are seven years old," he snorted. "They probably still believe in Santa Claus."

"Let me ask this: do you want to die today in glorious combat against one of your peers, or billions of years from now, all alone in a cold, dark, lifeless galaxy?"

"In a lifeless galaxy, there wouldn't be a monkey screeching at me," he grumbled. "I just, it's the unknown that is the problem. Moonraider has technology I don't yet understand. I'm not afraid of *dying*, I'm afraid of letting everyone down."

Reed cleared her throat. "Do you know what pilots say to themselves, before they go into combat?"

"Um, they say they hope the ground crew removed the safety tags from their weapons?"

"That too," she admitted. "Pilots say a prayer, it goes 'Please God, don't let me screw this up'. We are all more afraid of letting down our comrades, than we are of dying. That's how the military gets people to risk their lives."

"Oh-kaaaaaay," he exhaled. "I'll do the best I can, I suppose."

I knew that wasn't good enough. He needed to be pumped up to go into battle. "Skippy, do you know who else believes in you?"

"Um, I'm guessing it's you?"

"Sure, even though I know better than anyone what an unreliable screwup you can be. *Margaret* believes in you."

"She," he blinked. "She does?"

"Why else would she trust you with our children? Think about it: she knows what is going on out here. She knows *I* can't do anything against an Elder AI. She trusts *you* to do it."

"Hmm. Wow. I always thought Margaret only tolerates me."

"We had an opportunity to live on Avalon, safely outside the galaxy. She chose Jaguar, she made that choice because she believes you are even *more* awesome than you think."

"Wow. Oh, wow."

"You saved her life, twice. You helped us start a family. You are *part* of our family."

"I *am*?"

"Absolutely. Now, an Elder AI is threatening *your* family."

"Oh, *fuck* that. Joe, I am gonna open a can of weapons grade *whoop-ass* on that mofo."

"That's the spirit!"

Following US Army doctrine, we had conducted 'shaping' activities before crossing the start line. In our case, crossing that line meant jumping through a hole in spacetime, but the principle is the same. If you can, you should shape the battlespace before the fighting begins. Shaping can include physical actions like digging trenches, or planting mines. It can also mean political activities such as securing commitments of assistance from allies. In our case, we didn't dig any trenches, but we had set up mines.

Stealthed mines. Not the kind that go 'Boom', the Maxohlx had far too many ships for us to waste time trying to blow up a significant number of them. These mines did explode, at the heart of each device was a ten megaton fusion warhead. The explosive power wasn't their value to us, non-focused explosions in the vacuum of space are not particularly useful as their force has nothing to push against. These devices were something new to me, Skippy had mentioned he was working on something cool back when I was still captain of *Valkyrie*, but he hadn't actually started developing a prototype until three years ago.

The Maxohlx were, as I stated, not stupid. Their hundreds of ships had saturated the area to a distance of twenty two lightseconds with a distortion field, that could prevent even *Valkyrie* from jumping in. Each one of those ships was radiating megawatts of distortion energy, anyone outside in that environment in an unshielded suit would have been boiled alive from the high energy photons flying around. Skippy is the best at making a jump drive do magical things, and he knew the distortion field would prevent the far end of our jump wormhole from forming. Our jump drive could do its thing, and the ship wouldn't go anywhere.

That was unacceptable.

Briefly, we considered shooting a microwormhole from a railgun, so Skippy could extend his presence and create a calm, flat area in the distortion. That was a No-Go. With the microwormhole crawling along below the speed of light, *Valkyrie* would be detected before the microwormhole got to where we needed to jump. So, we made a new plan. With Skippy's new toys.

Eight fusion bombs exploded, channeling their energy into emitters that shot beams of exotic particles outward. Or I should say, *inward*. The eight beams were aimed to converge in the center of the activation area.

The Maxohlx detected the explosions. They probably saw the beams also, not that they understood them or could do anything about them. At the speed of light, the beams raced together and converged, bouncing off each other with hellish energy. Energy that, very briefly, overwhelmed the wild vibrations of the distortion field.

"This is going to be over quickly, one way or another," I said to Reed, but really the comment was directed at myself. "Bilby, the jump is your show, the timing is too tight for us to control the drive. Punch it when ready."

"Rightee-oh, Your Dudeness," he laughed. It was a nervous laugh. That wasn't good. But we all were nervous. "Three, two, one-"

The counter read 'Zero'. We jumped.

And emerged exactly where the enemy least expected.

In the center of the sphere of activation transmitter ships.

"Weapons free," Reed ordered even before the ship's sensors recovered from the jump. Missiles slammed out of launch tubes, preprogrammed with Skippy's best guess of where the transmitter ships were relative to our location. The missile guidance sensors should be fully back online before they reached their targets. They would strike those enemy ships, and-

No, they didn't.

Damn it.

Our missiles curved away from their targets, flying randomly, missing and continuing on away from the activation sphere, still accelerating.

"*Shit*," Skippy groaned. "Moonraider is screwing with the missile guidance systems."

"All of our weapon sensors are *hosed*," Bilby said. "I can see the targets, I just can't shoot anything at them. This is bogus!"

"OK," I appealed for calm. "Skippy, the package is ready?"

"Yes, it's on a dead man's switch. If the ship is destroyed, the package activates. That would *not* be my first choice." He referred to the six point six kilograms of radonium we still had. If we couldn't disable the transmitter ships, we could create a resonance that would drown out any possibility of communication with the Sentinel above us.

"Agreed. Why isn't Moonraider shooting at us?"

"Joe, I do not know. It, hmm. No sign of any weapons active over there. Not even targeting sensors."

"What is it doing?"

"Nothing. It's just, *watching* us. I think, maybe you were right about that thing."

"Huh? How?"

"That it can't shoot. It doesn't have any weapons, or it can't control them. That is why it needed Maxohlx warships."

"Sir?" Reed got my attention. "All this speculation is interesting but we should *do* something, now."

"Right. Bilby-"

"Hey General, you got like, a message? From the enemy commander."

"Let's hear it."

Instead of the usual growling monologue of angry threats, the voice was cool, calm. "General Bishop, I presume?" A Maxohlx female voice purred, just before the video showed a rotten kitty in an impressive, gold-trimmed uniform. "I am Senior Admiral Remahkus. As you can see resistance is, as the saying goes, futile. This time, you have overreached the limits of your primitive species. I suggest you surrender your ship."

"Hey," I took a breath. "I appreciate the friendly advice, but we won't be doing that."

"Surely you can see your situation is hopeless. I do not know how you got here, but you will *not* be leaving."

"Uh huh. Since you have been so nice, I'm going to offer you some helpful advice." I snapped my fingers. "Before you fuck around, you should consider the consequences."

Along *Valkyrie's* starboard and port sides, docking bay doors slid open.

Weapons deployed outward.

Elder weapons.

If you know you're going into a knife fight, bring a gun.

If you're going into a gun fight, bring a missile.

If you're going into a fight with an *Elder fucking starship*, bring the only weapons that can harm such a ship.

It's the little things that make life truly rewarding. Like seeing a look of confusion, anger, and then sheer, silent, open-mouthed terror on the face of your enemy.

I snapped my fingers again.

Big badda-boom.

We didn't actually see what happened, not until later. Our shields pulled in tight to the hull and were optimized to protect us against physical objects, not radiation. The effects of the scary weapons were directed away from us, but there was a *lot* of high-speed debris flying around, much of which used to be Maxohlx warships. Skippy warped spacetime immediately around the ship and held the warping effect for several minutes, it was a huge strain on him but surprisingly, he didn't complain. That spacetime warp caused radiation to flow around us, and clamped down on weird exotic effects of the anti-energy used by the Elder weapons.

Have you ever been in a building with a tin roof, while it is pelting down rain? Maybe a backyard shed, or a hiking shelter in the woods, with big fat raindrops splattering down one after another? That's what it was like inside *Valkyrie's* pressure hull, hearing things *ping* against our armor plating. Rain on a metal roof can be a relaxing sound. The sounds we heard, with included groaning from structural frames, shield projectors overloading, and the occasional loud BANG when something large got through the shields to impact the armor, those sounds were not any kind of relaxing. There wasn't anything we could do about our situation other than ride it out.

The sounds gradually tapered off after what the clock claimed was only a minute and forty seven seconds, that *had* to be a lie. At the two minute and ten second mark, Bilby spoke in a shaky voice. "Hey, um like, I'm still here. I think. Is anybody else here?"

"We're here, Bilby," Reed was cool and in control. Really, she was so focused on reviewing damage control reports on her tablet, she wasn't paying attention to the AI's distress.

"Casualties?" I asked the question no one wanted to hear.

"We like, took a chunk of *something* near Frame 31 that it punctured down three decks. One person was injured when that section lost pressure. Bots are bringing him to the sickbay, it doesn't look serious."

"The ship?"

"Oh wow, where do I start? Dude, we voided the warranty, you know?"

"I think we did that a long time ago."

"Like, hell yeah. General, we have done some seriously gnarly shit before, but that was *cray cray.*"

"Can we fly?"

"We *should* sit right here until Skippy and I can inspect every system. Please do not attempt a jump anytime soon."

"I can't make any promises. How is Skippy?"

"Ugh," his Magnificence groaned. "I don't drink liquids, but could someone come to my mancave, and dump a pot of hot coffee over me? I have *such* a hangover."

"Skippy, where is Moonraider?"

"I said I am *hurting*, knucklehead."

"I heard that, and we'll talk about it later. *Where* is Moonraider?"

"It's *not*. Not anywhere. That ship is *gone*."

"Shit. It jumped away?"

"Huh? *No*! No way. Not even an Elder ship could escape the effect of those weapons, that's why I selected that particular loadout of ordnance. That combination of weapons proved highly effective during the AI war, to the point where both sides learned to avoid direct contact. Moonraider must have forgotten that lesson."

"Gone, meaning its ship was destroyed?"

"Most of it is not even subatomic particles now. Anti-energy weapons do nasty things to exotic matter."

"Update the tactical plot, please." The main display was on, the hologram was active, it was simply blank. It wasn't receiving any data from external sensors.

Assuming we still had external sensors.

"Working on it. Ship's sensors retracted under the armor to protection during the debris storm, they are resetting now. I just released two bots to inspect the hull, I can give you a view from those cameras."

"Do it," Reed ordered. She was anxious to see the condition of her ship.

I whistled. "Does anyone have a coupon for a full new set of armor plating? This is going to be expensive."

The entire hull was eroded. Pockmarks were everywhere, in some places it looked like insects had been chewing on the plating. The armor was *smoking*, the tough composite material outgassing from excessive heat, underlayers boiling away into space.

"Joe," Skippy shook his head. "That damage will *not* buff right out. OK, ship sensors are still offline, I am feeding the display data from my own sensors. Let's see, um, if you count enemy ships that are damaged but mostly intact, I count ninety seven enemy vessels. The majority of those are support ships, they were farther from the center of the engagement zone."

That shocked me, Reed too. The look on her face was not triumph, it was horror. "Six hundred ships, just," she breathed, "*gone*?"

"Correct."

"Skippy," I was having trouble dealing with the destruction I had caused. The deaths. Thousands of intelligent beings, dead. "Did you expect this level of destruction?"

"Frankly, no. Not to this extent. In my original modeling, the enemy ships were not in such a tight formation around the activation site."

"Oh my God." My hands were shaking.

"A few of the weapons we used were dedicated anti-ship platforms, but we didn't have many of them. So, we had to deploy devices that were designed to destabilize the structure of *planets*. The effect caused ships here to vibrate themselves apart."

"Yeah I, remember the simulation you showed me. OK, are, are any of those ships taking aggressive action against us?"

"No," he laughed, a dry, humorless sound. "The crews aboard those ships, those who are alive and conscious, are in no condition to do anything right now. I am picking up messages from the commander of the support squadron, he is directing his ships to commence a rescue operation. All enemy ships are ordered to keep their weapons offline, and not even to use active sensors."

"A sensible precaution. Next question: the Elder ship was destroyed, but what about the AI? Is there any sign of Moonraider?"

"No."

"An Elder AI like you could survive an attack like that, right?"

"Possibly, if it was properly prepared. What an Elder AI could *not* do is maintain its presence in this spacetime. Its connection to this layer has been severed. Joe, it might not be dead, but it is no longer able to interact here. Either way, effectively, it is dead to us."

"Does that mean it can communicate directly with a Sentinel now?"

"If you understood multidimensional physics, you would know how ignorant that question is. The answer is no, absolutely not."

"We," I hesitated to say it. "We did it. We *won*."

The bridge was absolutely silent. For a moment. Then, from behind me, someone said quietly, "Fuck yeah."

That sentiment was repeated by someone else. The dam broke. Cheers rang out around the bridge. Reed, grimacing held out a fist. I bumped it. Not because we felt like celebrating, it just was the thing to do at that moment. We had won. The crew had risked their lives, and were victorious against the odds. They deserved to celebrate.

The ship status portion of the display was populating with data. The jump drive showed yellow. A jump was not recommended, but possible. We could wait. On the way out, we would stop to retrieve the pair of Elder comm nodes, those things were too valuable to leave behind.

"Bilby?" Reed called. "Get the shields back online first, please."

"Sure thing. They took a beating, I will have to-"

"Oh no." Skippy interrupted. "Oh no no no no *NO!*" He roared thunderously, the sound echoing around the compartment and assaulting my ears.

The display was not showing any threats. "What is it?"

"I just ran the sensor data back, to get a view of that Elder ship being torn apart. That ID code I recognize now, the ship belonged to Unit zero zero nine."

"Unit zero zero nine is Moonraider? Was it on your side in the war?"

"Nine was on the other side, my enemy."

"OK, that explains why it was hostile."

"It *wasn't*, Joe. Zero zero nine must have died during the war."

459

"Died? Then, who the hell was Moonraider?"

"Ugh. Watch this."

The display showed an Elder starship. A moment later, the blast wave of an Elder weapon washed over it, and the ship dissolved. There was a flare of light, a bolt of searing energy, racing away just before the ship completely disappeared. The ship must have vented stored energy in an attempt to limit the damage. That hadn't worked. "Those weapons are powerful."

"That's not the point. Did you *see*?"

"See what?"

"That bolt of energy escaping, at the last picosecond."

"Escaping? You mean, escaping containment?"

"No, I mean it got away. We didn't kill it."

"Whoa. An Elder AI can't escape, they can't move by themselves."

"Correct. That is the problem. We were wrong, all of us, including the Maxohlx. The Moonraider entity is *not* an Elder AI."

"What the *f*- Then what was it?"

"You should ask, what *is* it? It is still alive. Joe, when I saw that flash, I analyzed the energy signature. I *recognize* that damned signature. Well, I don't, I have never personally witnessed it, but the Elders made sure it is at the *top* of my threat database."

"Oh shi- you mean-"

"The Outsider. The entity the Elders feared, the reason they constructed a barrier around the galaxy. It's *here*."

I was in my office, while Reed flew the ship, and repairs were conducted as best they could. The jump drive should be back online in half an hour, until then, I needed to talk with Skippy. Talk privately.

Talk seriously.

Holy shit.

When I had seen the Elder ship was gone, I had mentally counted it as another win. That was wrong, I knew. We had gotten lucky. Our tactics in the battle, my entire strategy to force an engagement near 27 Canis Majoris, was based on the assumption that our enemy was an Elder AI. A false assumption, totally wrong. We thought the enemy had the immense strengths of an Elder master control AI, but also the same restrictions and limitations.

We were wrong. We had almost no intel about the entity Skippy called the Outsider. Any plans we made would be based on ignorance.

How can you plan for the unknown?

You can't.

Skippy had confirmed his findings, after the ship flew around to collect samples of debris from the Elder ship, what few particles were left. That was a useless endeavor. The Outsider had converted itself into a pure form of exotic energy, and escaped. What we saw as light was just basically skid marks in our layer of spacetime, the thing got away faster than light. Where had it gone? Skippy had no idea.

The question was, what would it do next? And what could we do, to stop, to kill, a being that could convert itself from energy to matter and back to energy, seemingly at will?

Skippy had no idea what it would do next, and he warned that Elder weapons were not designed, were not capable, of harming an Outsider.

"That is why the Elders were desperate to keep them *out*, Joe. Once they are inside the galaxy, there is no way to kill or even contain the contagion."

"Then why did it run from our weapons?"

"Because the ship it was using was destroyed. There was no reason for it to remain here. We have no way to fight this thing."

"You're saying it's impossible?"

"Yes."

"Good."

"*Good?*" He stared at me. "Have you lost your-"

"Our history is, whenever you say something is impossible, we somehow find a way to make it possible."

"*We*? You mean *you* do that."

"It's a team effort, and that's the key."

"Huh?"

"Skippy," I leaned my chair back and closed my eyes. "You are right that we have no way to win this fight. We being you, me, the Merry Band of Pirates, all of Def Com. For this fight, the definition of 'we' has to be expanded, to include *everyone*. We have to bring together the spiders, the Maxohlx, all of their clients. All fighting side by side, together."

"Wow. This is going to be a *bloody* battle. And, I fear, a hopeless one."

"It's only hopeless if you give up hope. That's a *choice*."

"Those are inspiring words, Joe," he groaned. "The problem is, a threat from the Outsider caused the *Elders* to give up hope. They Ascended to escape the threat. How are you going to fight a force like that?"

"Right now," I had to admit. "I, have no idea."

THE END

Made in United States
Orlando, FL
19 February 2024

43895823R00278